Rebels All

A Novel

Mel R. Jones
Marian N. Jones

MEL & MARE™
Publications, LLC

Publishing management by Marian Jones
Assistant publishing management by Mark Jones
Editing by Marian Jones
Cover design by Timothy Flatt
Interior layout and formatting by Mark Jones
Author photography by Joseph Szebeni and Lifetouch

Library of Congress Control Number: 2020912088
ISBN-13: 978-0-9997651-5-9 (Paperback edition)
ISBN-13: 978-0-9997651-7-3 (eBook edition)

Mel & Mare Publications, LLC
Wales, WI

DEDICATION

To Mel R. Jones, my late husband, who first conceived the story and characters of *Rebels All* during his first tour of duty in Vietnam in 1962–1963. Several setbacks held up the entrancing tale from being finished, the final being the demise of the author. But his intentions were left in his notes, which guided his co-author to finish his vision filled with lively characters and an intriguing plot.

CONTENTS

ACKNOWLEDGMENTS

Rebels All was born out of the experiences of Mel R. Jones during his first tour of duty in Vietnam, 1962–1963. It was the first novel he began, but it remained unfinished by the time he passed. Instead, he had transferred his novel writing efforts to his other novel, *Pursued: Ten Knights on the Barroom Floor*, a World War II literary mystery novel. He had realized time was running short for many World War II veterans who might enjoy his story. Jones finished this novel not long before his passing, and his wife Marian and son Mark self-published it in 2018 through Mel & Mare Publications, LLC.

When going through Jones's outline, papers and notes for the yet to be finished portion of *Rebels All*, his wife Marian decided to complete the writing herself, aided by memories of long discussions with her husband about the Vietnam novel. Earlier, having done much research and secretarial work for her husband, Marian supplemented it with Internet research and non-fiction books about the additional places and events Jones had witnessed in Vietnam but had not yet incorporated into the novel.

Non-Fiction books such as *Mission in Torment* by John Mechlin, *Once Upon a Distant War* by William Prachnau, *Misalliance* by Edward Miller, *Diem's Final Failure* by Philip E. Catton and *Finding the Dragon Lady* by Monique Brinson Demery were some of the very helpful references in filling in the historical background of the time period.

Captivated by the already completed part of *Rebels All*, Marian felt the well-drawn characters placed in an authentic setting deserved to have their story in the 1962–1963 time period in South Vietnam told as their author had envisioned it. May the efforts of the co-authors afford the readers of *Rebels All* a worthwhile experience.

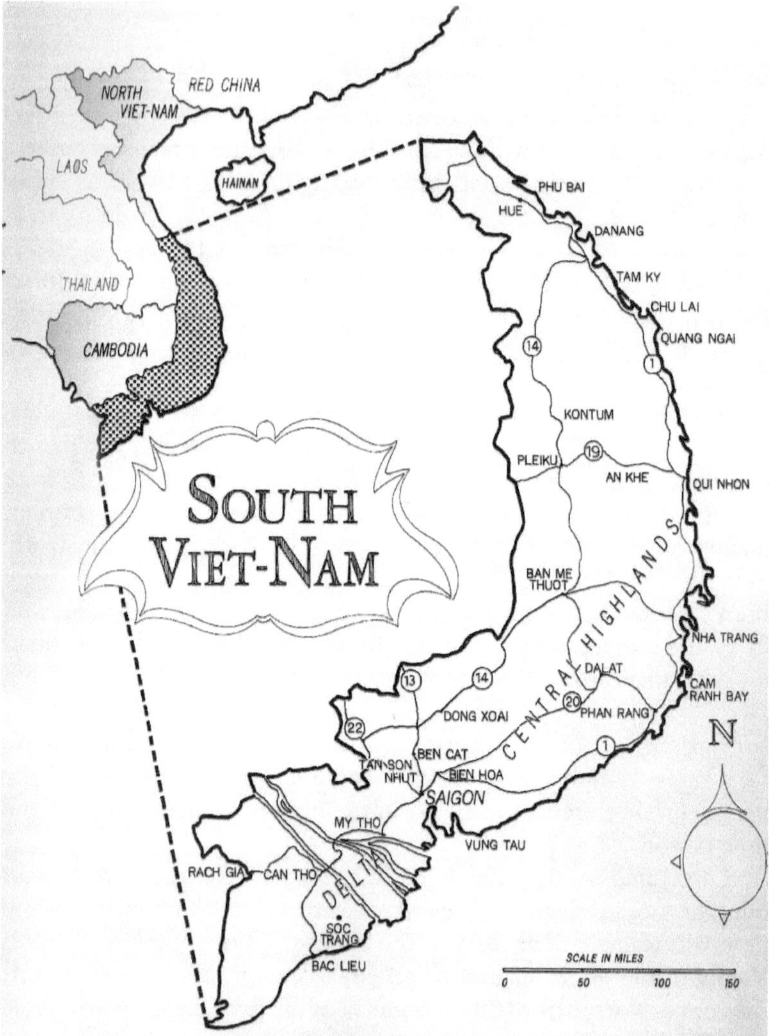
SOUTH VIET-NAM
NORTH VIET-NAM
RED CHINA
LAOS
HAINAN
THAILAND
CAMBODIA
PHU BAI
HUE
DANANG
TAM KY
CHU LAI
QUANG NGAI
14
1
KONTUM
19
PLEIKU
AN KHE
QUI NHON
CENTRAL HIGHLANDS
BAN ME THUOT
NHA TRANG
DALAT
CAM RANH BAY
13
14
20
PHAN RANG
22
DONG XOAI
BEN CAT
TAN SON NHUT
BIEN HOA
SAIGON
MY THO
VUNG TAU
RACH GIA
CAN THO
DELTA
SOC TRANG
BAC LIEU
N
SCALE IN MILES
0
50
100
150

REBELS ALL

Mel R. Jones
Marian N. Jones

PART 1:
A CORRESPONDENT'S ASSIGNMENT TO SOUTH VIETNAM, 1962

"Your breath first kindled the dead coal of war
And brought in matter that should feed this fire:
And now 'tis too huge to be blown out
With that same weak wind which enkindled it."
—William Shakespeare

1 TO FACE THE SUN

If you look too deeply into the abyss, the abyss will look into you.
—Friedrich Nietzsche

OH, YEAH. SO, YOU'RE a war correspondent. It's 1962. Where's the war?" the San Francisco cab driver asked the tall man seated in the rear with a newspaper spread across his knees.

"In Vietnam," came the terse reply. The passenger's penetrating brown eyes, framed by thick eyebrows, filled the rear view mirror with a gaze so intent the driver looked away.

"Never heard of the place. Is that in Africa?"

The New York Times reporter shook his head in disbelief, then impatiently swept stray, black strands of hair off his high forehead with his hand, repositioning his hat which had become dislodged.

The cab driver persisted. "Wait a minute. That's the place mentioned in Sunday's paper. I thought the guy was writing about Africa though."

The reporter's full lips broke into a sardonic scowl. "No, Vietnam's a Southeast Asian country. But by the time I get back, it'll be a household word. By the way, where do you get your information?"

"From the guy who writes the 'Branding Iron' column in the *Times.* I hardly miss one of his pieces. You know him?" the cab driver asked, turning to look over his shoulder.

A smile replaced the scowl. "Sure, and he'll be pleased to learn he's got a fan in the Bay area. What do you like about him?"

"His guts," said the driver.

"How's that?" the man asked setting the newspaper aside.

"Yeah, well, you know. He writes about the things ordinary people have on their minds. Really knocks heads with the power brokers. Speaks for the common guy and leaves little doubt you can't trust everything dished out by the high n' mighty. There's a word for this. On the tip of my tongue. Maybe you know what I mean?"

"Some people say Brand's a cynic or distrustful of human nature. Could that be it?"

"Yeah, cynic. For my money, all news hounds dig up and throw dirt on people. Following you guys is like standing behind a pack of starving dogs after a buried bone. Driving a cab is a whole lot cleaner."

"Then what makes Brand different?"

"At least your buddy at the *Times*, writes about how things ought to be better. Take your war for instance. He'd dig and dig 'til he finds out why people kill each other."

"And why do you suppose they do?" asked the reporter. He leaned forward in his seat to await the answer.

"Born mean, I suppose," the driver replied. "Here we are at the terminal. When you get back to New York, say hello to the 'Branding Iron' guy. I'd sure like to meet him someday."

"You just have," said Winston Spencer Brand. He handed the driver a five dollar tip and stepped out of the cab.

"For that kind of money, you can be anybody you wanna be, Mister. Good luck in Africa, or wherever the war is," the cabby shouted out the passenger side window at the retreating reporter.

Inside the Military Air Transport Service (MATS) terminal at Travis Air Force Base, in the San Francisco Bay Area, Winston Brand stood puzzled looking at the theater played out before him. People pushed and shoved each other more reminiscent of a stock market rally than an orderly military operation charged with ferrying troops to Vietnam in February 1962. A woman grabbed the reporter's trench coat, fixing her gaze on Brand's clear-cut, forceful face.

"Oh, sir, you look like an official. Please help me. My husband was on that plane!"

Before he could respond, the crowd swept the woman toward one of the ticket counters where groups huddled in a frenzied search for information. Brand seized the arm of a young soldier and asked, "What's happening here?"

"They just announced that the last flight to 'Nam never made it. Lost over the Pacific or something. I was supposed to be on that plane. Me and a buddy got bumped to this afternoon's flight. Talk about luck," the soldier replied in a high, thin voice.

A cold shiver shook the 38-year-old, Pulitzer Prize winner on this, his hard-won overseas assignment. Aircraft accidents of any kind brought bitter memories of his parent's death on final to Washington's National Airport and his own near miss in Vietnam at Dien Bien Phu in 1954. For a moment, he saw himself wet, cold and bleeding behind his right knee as he lay trapped between the French and Viet Minh forces, who searched the tarmac on the reserve field at Hong Cum for his downed aircraft. Brand commented, "Air travel in wartime carries certain risks," and probed for more information. But the excited soldier anticipated the reporter's question.

"Sabotage, if you ask me," the young man volunteered.

Another passing soldier grabbed his comrade, shaking the startled youth out of Brand's grasp. "Hey, man, where'd you hear this sabotage crap?"

Brand strained to hear a reply. But the crowd herded the two soldiers in the direction of the woman in the gray coat. Then came a voice over the public address system:

"At ease in the terminal. Settle down now. We're trying to get information as fast as possible. Please, do not start rumors. If you have any questions, form a line at one of the ticket counters. We'll get to you in turn."

Brand ignored the appeal, elbowing his way toward a public pay phone.

"Get me Louie Cohn on the foreign desk," he told the *Times* operator.

When his editor answered, the anxious Brand blurted out, "Louie, this is Winston in Oakland at the MATS terminal. You got anything on a downed aircraft out of here?"

"Yep, according to an AP bulletin just off the wire, a Flying Tiger military charter en route to Vietnam with Defense communications specialists on board is reported missing somewhere between Guam and the Philippines."

"Anything about sabotage?"

"No, but the Pentagon admitted this is the second military aircraft to disappear under similar circumstances since the beginning of this month. 'Coincidental' the brass calls it."

"Some coincidence."

"I thought so, too. And if I were you, Winston, I'd cancel your plans to fly military charter and go by good old Pan Am."

"Good advice. Either way, I'll get next week's 'Branding Iron' column to you from somewhere along the line."

"Speaking of your column, a certain titan in congress found last Sunday's piece indigestible and told the publisher you ruined his breakfast."

"That could only be Thomas 'Tank' Kearney, Sr., our friendly Senate Armed Services Committee Chairman," said Brand in a tone so sarcastic his normal voice assumed a deep growl.

"Right on. And this time he's got a couple of howitzers pointed at your stubborn hide. Do yourself a favor, Winston. Don't give the S.O.B. anything to chew on in your next column due here by Thursday midnight. Call it in on my home phone if you need to. You got the number?"

"Better give it to me again. Wait a minute 'til I get something to write on."

Brand found a crumpled piece of paper in his coat pocket, spread it out on the telephone stand and wrote Cohn's number in the margin. Then he noticed the bold block letters in the center of the yellow sheet: "DON'T GET ON THE PLANE."

"Where'd this come from?" he gasped into the receiver.

"Winston, you're mumbling. Are you on the sauce?"

"No, Louie, don't worry. You'll have my column before deadline."

"If it's not here, we'll rerun that piece you did on the North Vietnamese troika."

"You won't have to. I told you. It'll be there in time."

Brand hung-up. Then, with slow, deliberate steps, he inched through the crowd toward the nearest ticket counter, searching for the woman in the gray coat, the young soldier or the other G.I. Convinced one of the three had slipped the warning into his pocket, Brand wanted to know why he had been singled out, if indeed that were the case.

He saw that his flight to Vietnam showed a three-hour delay on the notice posted behind the ticket counter. "Observe how all things are borne of change," he quoted Thomas Aquinas to himself. To the philosopher's axiom, he added a personal addendum, "We should thank God for every day that we live long enough to change." Unsuccessful in his attempt to spot any of the persons he sought, Brand found a seat near one of the departure gates from which to observe the crowd from a secluded vantage point.

Besides, he needed time and a quiet place to sort out the disruption in his own schedule. "Plan the next move carefully," he reminded himself backing the fedora off his forehead until the crown crease reached the collar of his three-quarter length trench coat. With the shadow lifted from his high cheek bones, he again surveyed the situation.

Soldiers in their olive drab field jackets and green fatigues passed by, shooting a bewildered glance at the reporter whose intention was to view the war from their perspective. He could feel their eyes question his presence and purpose, his civilian attire and especially the old-fashioned felt hat setting him apart. He planned to use the stop-over in Hawaii to drape his six-foot frame in the more comfortable correspondent's mufti, a short gray tunic with matching slacks, and trade his fedora for a field cap. No doubt, he thought, the soldiers, too, would shed their heavy uniforms for a lighter set.

Across the corridor, Brand watched a solitary uniformed figure of nearly his same stature dispense what looked like candy to children who squirmed restlessly on the green benches lining the terminal wall. When the blond-haired man turned to retrieve a fresh supply from his coat pocket, Brand spotted the rank and insignia of a marine corps major. The major saw Brand at the same moment, but the reporter ignored his inquisitive stare.

***

Hours before dawn, 7,000 air miles from the California coastline, a World War II vintage teleprinter sprang to life. Brand's name flashed above the keyboard.

"Urgent. From: Hanoi. Subject: Concern: Winston Brand, American correspondent. Our file indicates subject dangerous to our efforts. Use all means to dissuade from returning to Vietnam, or eliminate him at first opportunity. Advise on plan to execute this directive."

The Viet Cong radio operator looked up at the darkly hooded figure whose face was concealed, but whose figure was barely illuminated by a candle-powered lantern.

"Will there be a reply?" he asked.

"Turn off the machine," R-3 commanded.

"But, sir, Hanoi will think the line has gone dead."

"Turn off the machine," R-3 repeated.

When the radio crackled its last breath, R-3 stepped out of the thatched hut into a light drizzle that fell upon his black hood. His Russian made-boots thumped against the swaying wooden planks. Each step along the darkened wharf produced a creaking sound. Across the lagoon, a pair of white cattle egrets rose against the waning moon, then settled nervously on the east bank of the delta formed by the mouths of the Saigon and Dong Nai Rivers, away from the man-made disturbance.

Hurry," said the boatman to his assistant. "Uncover the lantern to light the master's way, and remember to keep it low so that you do not see his face. To look upon the master is to die."

***

Although order returned in the terminal, Brand could feel the fear in himself grow. Suddenly, a familiar, sinister force emerged from the shadows of his own anxiety to grip his heart. Beads of sweat started to line his forehead that washed away the confidence that had shown in his countenance before entering the terminal. He needed a drink. Alcohol alone would plunge the demon of fear back into the recesses of his mind before he lost control, a fearful prospect for Winston Brand. More frightening than dying was an inability to set and keep his life in order.

Because his philosophy centered on orderly or logical thinking as the key to success in human endeavors, Brand hated to have someone else set the agenda for him, especially one whose motives remained unclear. It had happened in his youth, in his marriage, in his career and more recently with the decision to return to Vietnam. Here, too, his constant requests to return to the field did little to settle the matter. More likely, the desire of the *Times* hierarchy to distance themselves from a columnist known to relieve tension with alcohol had finally persuaded them to acquiesce to his requests. Not surprisingly, Brand had to admit that his attempts to use booze to subdue the demon of anxiety would backfire and rendered him even more out of control.

Aware the flask filled with bourbon in his breast pocket offered little more than an escape from reality, Brand nonetheless opted for these moments of suspended rationality. The first drink, innocuous enough at the outset, led to a series of follow-ups dictated by the chemical itself. Throughout it all, Brand denied any serious alcoholic tendencies.

He did admit to his ex-wife Eleanor that after the first drink he felt like a man who had swallowed a snake, only to have the snake turn the tables. He began to personify the whole matter, referring to his flask as "Willie," the snakebite kit. He had even gone so far as to have a silversmith place an inscription on one side of the flattened container that read, "My Willie, the flask, the only friend that lasts. W.B."

Now, as he walked through the terminal, he fingered the engraved words, deriving comfort from what had started as a joke, only to become a crutch. He was beginning to feel out of control again. News of the missing aircraft unsettled him, raising doubts about whether he should proceed as planned or not. He slipped outside the terminal in search of a darkened corner where he and Willie could sort things out.

***

From his position on the main deck of the 36-foot motorized sampan, R-3 surveyed the shoreline as the craft glided into the dark, murky waters of the Saigon River. A light from the far shore drove a path across the water, then died out in a flicker that sporadically illuminated the wake, churning the water into silver flakes.

"Comrade Leader, they are signaling us to return to the communications center," Capt. Nyugen Huu Bao, R-3's adjutant informed him.

"To what purpose?" the hooded figure asked.

"Sir, my reading of the signal is that Hanoi has another urgent message for you," said Bao adjusting an eye patch over his right eye.

"The fool disobeyed my instructions and resumed communications," snapped R-3. "Take the fast auxiliary craft and two men. Return to the center and deal with this problem while I continue on to the rally at Queen's Bishop en route to Saigon. You know the penalty for disobedience. After you have eliminated the radio operator, replace him with someone who can obey orders. Rejoin me at the meeting place. And, *Dai-uy* Bao?"

"Yes, *Ayr Ba*, our supreme leader."

"See to it that our communications center is relocated to Sector Queen Pawn Two. We must assume the Americans intercepted our message traffic with Hanoi because this fool's insolence gave them time, and they know how to zero in on the obsolete equipment we captured from the Japanese long ago."

***

The 42-degree temperature stiffened Brand's resolve for another drink as he crouched among the yellow flowers of the winter jasmine and raised the flask of bourbon to his lips. A rustling sound in the pyramid-shaped shrubs behind him momentarily caught his attention, but Brand ignored the noise, dismissing it as the wind blowing up from San Pablo Bay. He took a second gulp of bourbon, then rose to retrieve a pack of cigarettes from his breast pocket.

He started to move one hand to reach inside his coat when the collar was pulled down his back pinning his arms against his sides. As he whirled to confront his assailant, the area behind Brand's right ear imploded in pain, like a vise constricting his skull. When the grip on his coat collar was released, he tumbled forward and instinctively dropped the flask. With his hands now freed, he reached for the injured spot with one, while the other groped for something to break his fall. He clutched a long, soft fabric. Then he heard a woman's voice, "Get him off my coat! Hit him again! He mustn't get on the plane!" The second blow smashed through Brand's fingers almost at the exact spot the first had landed. Fighting against the plunge toward a dark abyss, he felt the pressure mount inside his head. But as his mind began to spin out of control, images of a much earlier painful confrontation flashed into his mind:

"Winston, why can't you face the sun? People don't think much of a man who lurks in the shadows. Look at me, boy," the voice demanded.

With trepidation, the younger Brand lifted his eyes from the floor of his father's imposing office on the E-ring of the Pentagon, and faced the vice admiral who sat erect before an open window like an American eagle basking in the sunlight. Sunbeams were everywhere, on the man's thinning gray hair, on his jutting chin, and on the three silver stars on each collar, which seemed to the boy like a constellation.

"Now I want you to listen to me, boy, and listen well. Your mother tells me you've been in trouble again at Dawes. How many times do I have to remind you I graduated first in military science at that prep school and again first in my class at Annapolis? Well, how many?

"I don't know, Father."

"Well then, let me enlighten you, boy. Until you get the word that you're embarrassing your old man with your attitude toward the military, we're going to remain on a collision course. And speaking of courses, your sister tells me you're now majoring in journalism and philosophy, following in your mother's footsteps. Is that just to provoke me even more? You needn't answer. That's not why I've called you here today."

The elder Brand leaned across his mahogany desk and pointed a saber-shaped letter opener at his son. "It's this business of drinking on campus. Not out of your teens and caught drunk four times in the past year according to the Dawes commandant. At the rate you're going, there isn't a navy on earth that'll have you. Instead of an officer, you'll end up in the gutter, a drunken bum. Well, what have you got to say for yourself?

"Father, will you please pull the blind down a little? It's so bright," said Winston in a manner so sluggish anyone but an outraged parent could see he still suffered from a hang-over.

"It's the curse of hell," roared the vice admiral. "My only boy. At 18 the sunlight is already too bright for him!"

"Please, Father, Colonel Pavler can hear in his office."

"Good. Let's get Geronimo in here to see a kid who can't face the sun!"

These images mercifully vanished as Brand began to lose consciousness, but not before an apparition of the cab driver hovered over the reporter sprawled among the jasmine bushes. "Born mean, I suppose," said the ghostly voice carried by the wind.

2 INVITATION TO A CHESS MATCH

The chess board is the world, the pieces are the phenomena of the universe, the rules of the game are what we call the laws of Nature. The player on the other side is hidden from us. We know that his play is always fair, just, and patient. But also we know, to our cost, that he never overlooks a mistake, or makes the smallest allowance for ignorance.

—Thomas Henry Huxley

WINSTON BRAND SLOWLY opened one eye at a time attempting to focus on the figure outlined by the dazzling white overhead light. Next to his bed in the base dispensary stood the marine major he had spotted earlier distributing candy to the children.

"Don't tell me, Major, you're either the resident chaplain, military intelligence or the local candy man."

"Oh, the lollipops," the officer said patting his pocket. "Just something for the kids and the young soldiers' wives in the terminal there to see their men off. Everybody's weary from the long hours of waiting. A lollipop goes a long way in placating youngsters. The name's Spear, Alex Spear."

"Winston Brand."

"You're lucky a security patrol came upon the scene before your assailants could do any more damage, Mr. Brand. As it was, the doctor says your head wound required twelve stitches."

"Do you know who roughed me up?"

"Unfortunately, the people responsible escaped."

"Well then, Major Spear, since I've received medical care and have no need of mollycoddling, what's your interest in me?"

The officer returned the direct gaze of Brand's piercing brown eyes.

"I came here to tell you our military charter has been rescheduled for takeoff tomorrow morning at 11:00. Until then, I intend to do whatever it takes to convince you to rebook on a commercial flight."

Brand glared at the major. "And if I say okay, you'll give me a sucker. But if I refuse, you'll send me a threatening note. Is that how it works?"

"What's that?"

"Nothing," said Brand brushing a forefinger across his long nose in his trademark gesture signifying subject closed for the moment. The reporter winced as the movement made him realize his hand and fingers were badly bruised. "Before I consider giving up a hard-earned seat, Major, fill me in on the missing aircraft. Have they been hijacked or sabotaged?"

"We've already had enough public speculation on this unfortunate incident."

"You mean incidents, don't you, sir?" Brand interrupted.

A slight smile, actually more of a smirk, cracked the corners of Brand's full, firm mouth, framed by his strong chin. The reporter decided to inject trivia to break the embarrassed silence that inevitably followed a "got cha" question needed to correct the facts. But first, he watched Spear remove a battered pipe from a coat pocket, then bend down to retrieve a small, paper tobacco pouch hidden in one sock. Shortly, an aroma of maple-scented tobacco filled the space between them.

"If you worked for one of the wire services, that pipe would get you fired. A lot of editors figure a pipe smoker doesn't fit the image of somebody on top of a fast-paced story since he's constantly fidgeting with all the paraphernalia he has to carry. Sure you won't have a cigarette instead? I must have a pack in my coat on that chair."

"No, thanks," said the major drawing on the pipe and sending a puff of smoke out the side of his well-formed lips. "You're right about the extra baggage though. Even the marine corps prefers fewer bulges in the uniform pockets."

Spear crossed the room, leaving a sweet-smelling trail. Brand could hear him confer with someone in the hallway. The major reentered the room and shut the door behind him.

"I've asked we not be disturbed. If you insist, I'll defend pipe smoking as part of the thoughtful, Sherlock Holmes, chess-playing image. Otherwise, I'm here to convince you to relinquish your place on the aircraft."

"Hey, I'm not all that enchanted with flying military air—the airline with time to spare. And since I'm certainly not going any place tonight, you've got a captive audience."

"First, let me apologize for the cramped conditions," he said, pulling up a chair next to Brand's bed.

"I've been in closer quarters. Usually, it's with the opposite sex though."

"Yes, I saw you earlier with a woman on your arm. Someone to see you off, I suppose?"

Brand could feel the major's anxious eyes searching his face, so he looked away as he replied. "If you're referring to the lady in the gray coat, she was probably someone's wife who thought I might have information on the missing aircraft. At least that's what she said."

"I see. Then she wasn't a friend of yours?" asked Spear.

"No, but that doesn't mean she couldn't have been one of yours," said Brand now staring back at the major.

"What do you mean?"

"Nothing." His sore finger flicked across his nose, and he winced again. "Surely, all this is not about a casual encounter."

The major started to relight his pipe, but instead laid it on the bed stand.

"It's too close in here to be filling the room with any kind of smoke, so let's both agree to clear the air as much as possible. You've guessed correctly, Mr. Brand. I'm assigned to naval intelligence, and know more about you than you'd ever agree I should."

Brand started to interrupt, but Spear held up his hand to indicate he wanted to complete the statement.

"The reason for our interest is simple, and indeed connected with the disappearance of the flights to Vietnam. But before I go on, you must promise to accept this information on a deep background basis."

"Oh, yeah, suddenly it's 'our' interest—meaning yours and that of some military cause you espouse. And if I can't publish it, why offer it to me in the first place?" Brand demanded.

"Because it involves your personal safety."

"How's that?"

"That I can't tell you until you agree on the background conditions."

Winston Brand looked at the major's fair, close-cropped hair and arched eyebrows. He saw the same long straight nose, poised confidently between direct, expressive eyes of the trusted Greek correspondent, who had comforted Brand on the tarmac after their aircraft had been shot down at Hong Cum. Throughout that cold, perilous night, Abraxas, (Brand could never remember the young Greek's first name) had continually inquired about the American's well-being. The Viet Minh scouts, who took Brand into custody, found him alone shivering under the coat his companion had placed over him. Brand never saw the Greek again.

Spear's pointed chin stretched toward the reporter, and he asked, "Well, do we have an agreement?"

"For the time being, I suppose so since we're on your turf."

"Well, then, Mr. Brand, we don't know for sure, but there's a good possibility the two flights unaccounted for were either hijacked or sabotaged. No warning, no Mayday, no sign of mechanical failure. Two aircraft disappeared in clear skies without a trace. We're concerned those responsible could strike again."

"Like on my scheduled flight, you mean?"

"Exactly. That's part of the reason we're asking you to surrender your seat."

"And the other part?"

"Everyone else on board World Airways Flight 740 is military and has been screened or selected because of special training, like expertise in dealing with explosive devices."

"So, if I read you correctly, Major, I'm the odd man out since I don't have a military specialty to fit the occasion. What about the civilian crew? They've got a job to do—flying the aircraft. I see myself in a similar role, only my job is to report on our troop movements to Vietnam."

"The crew was hand-picked for this mission. Background checks and everything. You're the only one left out of the calculations when we devised a contingency plan for handling this situation. Before we realized there was a problem, you were already coming our way. Of course, there's nothing in your background to suggest a security risk, seeing that you're the son of the late Vice Admiral Willoughby Brand. In short, we've no way of dealing with civilians in these matters."

"Why didn't you just cancel my confirmation?"

"Knowing the kind of reporter you are and the reputation of *The New York Times*, this would only cause speculation, and at this juncture, that's something we wish to avoid. First, because there's enough speculation already. Second, because we don't want to tip off the other side that we see their fingerprints all over these aircraft disappearances."

Brand closed his eyes. He had attended enough military briefings to know the marine major had a number of other points on his agenda.

"Third," continued Spear, "We already have a theory as to where the finger of responsibility points for sabotage of the U.S. war effort. However, again, I must warn you, we're talking deep background. If you ever repeat this information, we'd deny the conversation ever took place. Of course, you might be interested to know the 'we' in this case includes an old friend of yours, Maj. Gen. George 'Geronimo' Pavler."

Brand's eyes fluttered open at the mention of his father's former chief of staff. Pavler had served the elder Brand at the Pentagon and at NATO headquarters in Paris. But most of all, Brand considered the general a devoted family friend.

The truth is, Winston Brand arranged his friends into three neat categories—those who befriended him before he won the Pulitzer Prize for reporting in Vietnam in 1954 and those who claimed to be his friends after he had secured this prestigious award. In the middle category, Brand placed those he suspected more interested in his father's military power than in the son who had staked out his own career independent of Vice Admiral Willoughby Brand's influence. George Pavler, nicknamed 'Geronimo' for his exploits as an Army paratrooper in Korea, fit in a special category. During Winston's formative adolescent years, Pavler served as a surrogate father to the boy estranged from the elder Brand.

The major lowered his voice. "General Pavler and I are convinced a North Vietnamese operative has infiltrated the highest levels of the South Vietnamese government. I'm on special assignment to discover and expose this individual we believe operates under the code name R-3, for third in line in the resistance movement behind General Giap and Ho Chi Minh.

"Where does this put Le Duan? He's part of the troika I wrote about."

"We believe he's more of a political figurehead. As far as we've been able to determine, the real power is divided among the two leaders in the North and R-3 in the South. Anything else?"

"Sooner or later, I hope you're going to tie this history lesson into the missing military aircraft. For example, how does this Resistors-Three business fit in with my Vietnam flight plans?"

"I'll get to that in a moment," said Spear. "For now, a bit more history, or rather legend, might help set the stage, or at least indicate how seriously we regard the threat from R-3."

Brand waited as Spear picked up his pipe and started to light it. He was relieved to see the major set it down again on the stand next to the bed.

"Mr. Brand, have you ever heard of Vu Huyen and the chess game that saved the nation?"

"No, but I can see you're determined to enlighten me."

"But of course you play chess. General Pavler taught you the moves, I'm told."

"You sure have the book on me. I'm afraid to ask what else you know," remarked Brand.

"While a captive in North Vietnam following your evacuation from Dien Bien Phu, you played chess with Ho Chi Minh. Extraordinary rapport, wouldn't you say?"

Brand suddenly sat up and, forgetting his injured hand, struck the bed stand so hard with his fist, the major's pipe took flight and fell to the floor.

"I'm beginning to see where you're headed with this line of questioning," snapped the reporter, his eyes glowing like live coals. "You guys are doing Senator Tank Kearney's dirty work for him. You know the reference to Ho in my last column was to show that, unlike reports about the ideas of our political elite, right or wrong, the North Vietnamese political leader expressed a universal philosophy in his prison writings…"

"Mr. Brand, calm down," the major urged before Brand again interrupted.

"No, you listen to me for a change, Major. If Senator Kearney has convinced you guys I'm some kind of 'pinko' sympathizer because I quoted Ho Chi Minh, then you should at least hear me out."

"You've got it wrong and will feel silly once you understand where we're coming from, but go ahead. Get it off your chest," said Spear.

"You're damn right I will. And I'll start with Ho's quote, the one shared with me during one of our bedside sessions in Hanoi. For your information, the first line comes right out of Aristotle who said that goodness and badness are 'least manifest in sleep.'" Brand launched into a recitation:

Faces all have an honest look in sleep.
Only when they wake does good or evil show in them.
Good and evil are not qualities born in man:
More often than not, they arise from education.

He paused briefly, choosing his next words carefully. "I put Ho's verse in my column to make a point. If the North Vietnamese leader really believed good and evil are not inherent in man, at least we could begin a dialogue on rebellion. Only a politician like Kearney would fail to grasp the significance of a dedicated communist quoting one of the West's foremost philosophers. The senator gets his information from government sociologists. They consider the Vietnamese the most bellicose people on earth and, like Kearney, see aggression under every conical hat. I said so in my column. Now, if the senator's unfavorable paring of me with Ho is cause for you guys to harass me, then our own system is worse off than I thought."

"Can we get back to R-3, Vu Huyen and chess," asked Spear smiling.

"Only if you explain what it's got to do with Kearney and my column."

"That's easy," said the major still smiling. "There's no connection. I'm sorry if my mention of chess and your article in the same breath set you off in a most interesting tirade. The point is, we're more concerned about your reference to the matches played against Ho than the political ramifications outlined in your column. More specifically, we'd like to know who else was present at these bedside chess sessions, or whether another player filled in for Ho from time to time. If you'll let me finish my story about Vu Huyen,

I believe our interest in your Hanoi chess opponents will make more sense."

"Go ahead," Brand murmured sheepishly, lying down again as he nursed his throbbing hand.

"Vu Huyen was a chess master. Indeed, legend has it the survival of the Vietnamese nation rested on the outcome of one of his games. I'm sure the stakes were never so high in one of your matches, Mr. Brand."

"Maybe not in chess, but my column has checkmated many a false step by some of your political superiors," snapped Brand.

"Capitalizing on an opponent's arrogance and ignorance is the exact point of my story, if you ever let me get around to telling it."

"Do I have any choice?" asked Brand expecting his question to go unanswered.

The major began. "Each time before the Chinese invaded Vietnam, the emperor would first send in his ambassador to engage the Vietnamese king in a game of chess. The emperor's scheme was simple—use the chessboard to measure his opponent's probable military prowess. While no match for his Chinese adversaries, either militarily or in chess strategy, the king knew his nation was in peril if he failed to give a good account of himself in the match.

"Enter Vu Huyen, a mandarin who had recently been appointed an advisor to the royal court of 14th Century Emperor Tran Du Tong. 'Allow me to dress as a lackey during the chess match with the Chinese ambassador which you must insist be played outdoors at midday,' Vu Huyen advised his sovereign.

"'The umbrella I'll be holding to protect your majesty and the Chinese ambassador from the hot rays of the afternoon sun will have a hole pricked in the fabric to admit a single ray of sunlight. I shall focus the tiny light beam first on the chess piece you are to move, then to the spot on the board to which you are to position the piece. In this way, it is I, a chess master, equal in skill to the Chinese, who shall play this deadly game.'"

Spear paused. Brand looked up, letting his silence serve as assurance he had followed the account.

The major continued. "After losing three consecutive times to the hidden chess player Vu Huyen, the Chinese emissary returned home advising his emperor against an attack on Vietnam. Meanwhile, the grateful Vietnamese sovereign awarded Vu Huyen the title 'Savior of the Country.' Word of the chess victory spread, and the mandarin stood revered by his countrymen as a super patriot, if you will, Mr. Brand."

"Well, again, Major, this is all very interesting, but I'm finding it difficult to make the tie-in between some medieval chess genius and my current circumstance."

"Ask yourself, Mr. Brand, who else except a modern day Vu Huyen possesses the intelligence, dedication, cunning, and yes, nerve to tackle a superpower?" The major pressed on before Brand could reply. "In probing R-3's mind, General Pavler and I see him as we believe he sees himself, a kind of reincarnated hero like his long revered countryman, Vu Huyen. Only R-3 has gone beyond anything the gentle mandarin could've imagined. He operates under the umbrella of ruthless terror casting a darker and more widespread shadow than any of his predecessors."

"Okay. Are you suggesting this R-3 guy has tentacles stretching beyond his immediate area of operation and into the United States? Did his henchmen sabotage the aircraft or hijack it to China or North Vietnam? Is that what I'm supposed to get out of all this?"

"No, you'll have to draw your own conclusions on that score."

"Then what's this chess business got to do with my situation?"

Brand waited as the major bent down to retrieve his pipe from the floor.

"We're looking for someone who fits the profile of Vu Huyen, and thought you might have encountered such an individual during your two month recuperation in Hanoi."

Brand started to comment. The strange deductions of military intelligence types in search of a lead never failed to amaze him. Then recalling the number of times he had himself followed flimsy evidence while tracking down a story, he decided to play it straight with the major.

"No, I don't recall anybody like your R-3, or anyone else for that matter, getting in or offering advice during the chess sessions. Even Ho seemed more intent on venting his political spleen, or trying out his philosophy, rather than demonstrating his prowess on the chessboard. Sorry, but that's all I can offer."

The disappointment registered so intently in the major's face, Brand thought about the crumpled paper in his pocket. Should he share the "DON'T GET ON THE PLANE" warning with Spear, he wondered? Intelligence people thrived on intrigue of this sort.

Brand doubted the message had anything to do with the major's mission to ferret out a super-spy operating in South Vietnam.

Yet, make no mistake about it, he reasoned. Military intelligence had shown an unusual interest in his return to Vietnam. He wanted to tell the major in no way would he violate his objectivity by involving himself in an intelligence operation. Still the note in his pocket disturbed him. Should he surrender the evidence, risking the chance Spear might misinterpret his motives as a sign of cooperation? Then, again, if giving Spear the information meant saving American lives, the ethical considerations overshadowed his personal objections. A knock on the door postponed an immediate decision.

Spear got up and opened the door slightly. At that moment Brand caught a glimpse of a woman held between two military policemen.

"Sorry to bother you, Major," said one of the security guards. "We found this woman and two male companions in an unauthorized area near the flight line. The two men got away."

Brand saw the major place a forefinger to his lips and, inclining his head toward the bed, whispered to the guards, "I'll be with you in a minute. Take the woman to the detainment area for interrogation."

Before Spear closed the door on the two MPs, Brand spotted the woman's gray coat.

"Hold on, Major, there's something you should know," Brand said. "That's the woman who bumped into me when I first entered the terminal. She may have slipped me this note. I also talked to two soldiers, one of whom said he was booked on this afternoon's flight." Brand watched anxiously as Spear unfolded the paper and read the message.

"Well, we'll have to look into this. Thanks for sharing this information. In intelligence you never know how things are connected. Mind if I keep this long enough to have our people analyze it?"

"Sure, but I'll need the telephone number written in the corner. It's my editor's."

The major started to tear off the corner, then hesitated. Instead he copied the phone number onto a prescription pad and handed it to Brand.

"Here's your number. I'd better keep the original. There might be some fingerprints other than yours and mine. Let's see what the experts come up with. I'll let you know what I find out, on our deep background basis, of course."

"Of course," said Brand. "For what it's worth, I suspect that woman at the door might be one of the muggers. I heard a woman barking orders and caught sight of her gray coat before her accomplices knocked me out."

"We'll investigate that, too," said Spear turning to leave. He paused to face Brand.

"By the way, in light of your cooperation, I'll recommend you proceed on Flight 740 in the morning, if your physical condition allows. That's if you're still willing to take the risk. Please advise the chief flight attendant, Maria Monclova, of your decision. She'll be at the boarding gate and will have you on the manifest should General Pavler concur."

"Wait a minute, Major. A sudden change of heart like this demands an explanation. Before I make my decision, I want to know if you think that woman passed me the warning note, and whether or not you uncover evidence someone has a hit out on me."

"You're right. I'll get back to you. It may take some time, but I'll try to meet you at the boarding gate half an hour before departure. Okay?"

"I suppose it'll have to be," replied Brand.

Spear extended his hand, but Brand shielded his swollen fingers. Instead he said, "Since we're going to meet again, perhaps we should get on a first name basis. Call me Winston."

"Alex," said Spear.

"Alex, it is, but don't get the wrong impression. I remain an objective reporter, or observer, if you prefer."

"Yes, observer, Winston. Every war needs them, especially those who can remain neutral."

"One more question."

"Certainly."

"How does a marine major get involved in a matter better suited for army intelligence, or even the CIA?"

Alex smiled, then chuckled. "General Pavler actually heads up our operation, and wanted a marine officer on the team. He's convinced R-3, like myself, is an amphibian."

"Is that spook talk for an operative equally at home on land and sea?"

"Something like that," said Alex. "Before I leave, Winston, the MPs said they placed your personal items in a drawer of the doctor's desk. Can I get them for you?"

"No thanks. Rest is all I need at the moment."

Alex left, turning out the overhead light.

Listening to the major's footsteps retreat down the corridor, Brand thought about calling him back to search among the items in the desk for Willie. Then he remembered his promise to his ex-wife Eleanor to never mix booze and pain killers again, after his friends had smuggled bourbon to him past her nurse's night station at Walter Reed. "No wonder your head hurts so much. You've produced the chemical equivalent of dynamite in your brain," she had admonished him, her dark eyes flashing more concern than anger. To take his mind off his current injuries, he settled back in the darkness to harvest more pleasant memories of Eleanor.

These "love fest" recollections, a term he had coined following his divorce in 1960 after four years of marriage, almost always began with him and Eleanor on a secluded beach in Jamaica during their two-week honeymoon. He recalled their daily routine down to the smallest detail. By 9:00 a.m. the morning swim was over. They would lie back on the blanket to bask in the early sun. She would hand him the suntan lotion, and he would spread the white cream over her alabaster body beginning at the neckline. To make it easier for him, she loosened the strap to her two piece bathing suit, letting the garment come to rest on her jutting nipples aroused by his touch. His creamy fingers brushed back and forth, edging ever closer to these standing sentinels, exciting her even more. Soon her own slender fingers would glide across his muscular thighs with an enticing invitation. Brand remembered the several trysting places they had made love, especially during a shower taken together. Finally, after a moonlit walk along the beach, they'd return to the cabin recharged with love that found expression in another union of their bodies.

Dwelling on these memories in the silent room, Brand wished circumstances had turned out differently. He surmised that neither he nor Eleanor were to blame for their breakup, since he viewed their relationship in the cosmic sense of two meteors brilliantly converging on one another from different directions, yet heading along separate pathways. While joined, the brightness, although momentarily blinding in the sensual perspective, never lingered long enough to reach the soul. It was as if each knew neither had the capacity to change course.

"I certainly could use Eleanor's tender, loving nursing care right now," Brand said to himself, saddened by the melancholy tone of his inner voice. Then he heard footsteps converging from opposite directions of the corridor outside his door. At first he thought it was Alex returning with his assailants in custody. But if this were the case, the steps in the hallway would be coming from one direction. Alarmed, he half rose in the bed. At the same moment, someone tried the door knob while whispering in a low voice, "Are you sure this is the room?"

"Who's there?" Brand shouted.

"That's him all right," whispered the voice beyond the door.

Before he could respond, Brand saw the door fly open. An object struck the tile wall with a metallic sound a few inches from his head. There followed the scurrying of fast flying feet in the corridor, this time echoing from the same direction. For a split second, Brand lay stunned in his bed, expecting an explosion. Instinctively, he searched the bed for a grenade or bomb, hoping he would have time to throw it out the open door. His fingers closed over the metallic object. About to hurl it toward the lighted corridor, he felt the familiar inscription on his flask.

"Well, I'll be damned. It's Willie," he sighed. "Somebody's got a strange sense of humor, but whoever it was, he must have broken into a drawer in the doctor's office to get Willie." Despite his anxiety, he laughed to himself, thinking how the major would undoubtedly turn this incident into a chess move by R-3, or whoever it was trying to keep Brand from his mission in Vietnam. He put his flask on the nightstand next to his bed, but he was apprehensive about a return visit by the flask throwers.

The rest of the night, the slightest sound in the corridor sent Brand bolting upright in the bed, leery his attackers had returned to finish the job.

3 PAGODA RALLY

Let them obey that know not how to rule.
—*William Shakespeare*

R-3 AND FIVE HENCHMEN secured the sampan in a small tributary, then continued by lorry toward Cholon, the Chinese section east of Saigon. At 3 a.m. in the predawn rain, most of the city's 850,000 residents remained asleep. Others choked the road, hauling produce from outlying districts to the An Dong central market place. The communist leader's vehicle joined this convoy of merchants as far as Ap Tan Hoi, a small hamlet southwest of Cholon.

The vehicle braked in the walled courtyard of a three story Buddhist pagoda. Pulling his hood over his forehead, R-3 strode past the commercial stalls and lighted tapers placed in large tripod-pots at the temple's entrance. Inside, 150 of the party faithful, disguised as monks and supplicants in a variety of saffron and brown robes, greeted their supreme leader by bowing low and chanting "*Ayr-Ba*," the Vietnamese equivalent of R-3. Attendees were divided into two groups, separated by a corridor in the center of the hall. On the left side facing the stage sat the public delegates who lived full time in the jungle as revolutionaries. Rarely venturing outside the communist network, these cadre members had no need to conceal their identities from each other. On the other side, however, the secret delegates hid their faces behind a variety of scarves and handkerchiefs because they moved in two worlds—one in government controlled areas where they functioned as normal citizens, concealing their main activities as communist operatives.

Capt. Nguyen Huu Bao, emerged on the stage through a haze created by the burning joss sticks and heavy scent of jasmine, to direct R-3 to a chair situated parallel to the assembly, facing the lectern. R-3 coughed twice into a handkerchief he held in front of his unexposed features. Silence filled the hall. Adjutant Bao bowed to the hooded figure with whom he shared the platform, then addressed the audience:

> Until it's safe for the noble *Ayr-Ba* to come out of hiding, we must content ourselves with other heroic voices in our struggle. This morning we salute the words of our fallen comrade, Col. Nguyen Van Tam of Phu Bai, whose philosophy springs from *Ayr-Ba* himself. Listen well, comrades, and you will discover the real strength in our struggle:

Bao cleared his throat and began to read aloud:

> In August, 1945, we had no guns, not a rifle. Yet, we toppled the French colonialist and its feudalistic system. We had no powerful army. But we had 20 million people willing to die under the revolutionary flag. After nearly nine years of struggle, North Vietnam was recognized by the Geneva Agreement and the French left. But the Americans and their South Vietnamese puppets, who never signed the treaty, have succeeded the French. Unlike their fellow French imperialists, the Americans do not camp in military posts. Still, the U.S. lackeys hold power and influence government in every area of South Vietnam.
>
> Our revolt against the French had a twofold goal under Chairman Ho and the Communist party: first, independence, rice and clothing, and freedom for ourselves; second, to extend the power of our revolution and its dominion among others under the communist banner. To achieve these goals, our people have paid with their blood and bones.

> We have the people's respect, because we have earned their trust through steadfast devotion to three rules: One. To speak in a manner comprehensible to the people, and to do for them all things that do not prevent us from attaining our ends. Two. To enjoy only such pleasures as are necessary for the preservation of health. Three. To seek only enough money as is necessary for the maintenance of our life and health, and to comply with such customs as are not opposed to what we seek.
>
> This is the weakness of the enemy. The enemy cannot get along without the people, for who will be his army or who will support his army? If the people don't support the enemy, he is nothing.

Bao hesitated, letting the word "nothing" roll from his lips several times.

A young Viet Cong inductee at the rear of the hall on the public side seized the opportunity to whisper to his comrade crouched next to him, "Yes, nothing. Perhaps like this *Ayr-Ba*, who might be snot in a handkerchief for all we know."

Immediately, the companion summoned one of the cadre and repeated the blasphemy. Within minutes, the offending youth was dragged down the center aisle and taken backstage. Barely pausing at the peak of the disturbance, Bao droned on:

> Our support from the people also comes from the international field where the U.S.-Diem clique and the imperialist camp are cursed by people everywhere, especially among our comrades in the powerful socialist and communist camps.

Again the speaker paused, this time to acknowledge the exit of R-3. Backstage, the hooded figure conferred with the guards, then whirled to face the boy whose dark eyes revealed the terror his taped lips could not utter. "Remove the gag and leave us," R-3 directed the guards. "I'm interested in our young comrade's reason for disrupting the people's rally."

"Sir, I was only joking with a friend from my village," the boy stammered.

"And what village produced so bold a comic?" asked R-3 mumbling within the folds of his hood to further distort his voice.

"Like Nguyen Van Tam, the hero we have gathered to honor, I, Vo Duc Dai, come from Phu Bai"

"I see. You say that so proudly you must want me to know that Phu Bai produces one comedian for every revolutionary hero. Is that it, boy?"

"Oh no, sir. Nguyen Van Tam was my teacher and a very serious Marxist. After he was killed by the Americans, I joined the Viet Cong to honor his memory."

"Well, then, we are getting somewhere, my funny little comrade. Your desire to follow in the footsteps of the late Nguyen Van Tam is commendable. We shall make haste to put you on the road to correct thought, matched by words and actions, so that, like your teacher, you will exemplify the seriousness of the revolution."

"Oh thank you, sir. Just as you have honored me, I'll go back to my friend and tell him about you, and that he was right to tattle on me. At least my poor joke brought me face-to-face with the great *Ayr-Ba*."

"Little fool, you have only heard my voice. Would you really like to see that I am more than nasal mucus in a cloth?"

Before the boy could answer, R-3 carefully moved aside the folds of his hood and stared straight into the youngster's bewildered eyes, terrifying the boy.

"Now, that we have cleared up this matter, young comrade, let's return to the business of the revolution where each can make his contribution, whether Dai, the clown, or Tam, the hero," said R-3 repositioning the folds of his hood to re-cover his face.

He walked over to the nearest sentry, spoke in the man's ear, then handed him the white handkerchief. Meantime, at the lectern, Bao continued speaking, occasionally shooting a glance at R-3's empty chair on stage:

> People all over the world long for peace and are opposed to war. By making the U.S.-Diem clique look like the aggressors, while we use peaceful political and propaganda methods of struggle, we act in harmony with the aspirations of mankind…

For another hour, the speaker regaled the faithful with communist successes in the political struggle. Under the rubric of "relatively peaceful means," R-3's adjutant included mobilization of public opinion, strikes and protests, other political acts and sabotage at home and abroad. Finally, he turned to the subject they had long awaited:

> When the time comes for armed struggle against the aggressors, we will make the Americans pay dearly for their interference. But we must prepare the right time to strike, for revolution is a matter of timing. As for this puppet Diem, soon *Ayr-Ba* will show him all the Americans in the world cannot keep him safe in his own palace. After this tyrant is gone, his army will rebel, making it easier to defeat in the armed struggle that will follow. Then we shall turn our guns on the Americans who have no stomach for the battles to come.

When Bao finished, the crowd applauded enthusiastically. As they filed quietly out of the pagoda into the first rays of sunshine, some gave a quick glance and moved on. Others paused to look up at the body of a boy hanging from the central merchant stand. A lantern on the four-cornered stall illuminated his tear stained eyes and blood soaked cheeks. More blood around his chin and neck indicated that before death he had put up a fierce struggle to either free himself from the noose or remove the white handkerchief tied securely between his swollen lips. A placard with the single word "traitor" dangled from one ragged trouser leg of young Vo Duc Dai.

A few miles away in a three story house on Saigon's fashionable Rue d' Espagne, R-3, dressed in a western-style business suit, sat down to a continental breakfast. Outside, his chauffeur stood next to a government limousine smoking a cigarette and nervously checking his watch. As usual his distinguished passenger was running late, this time for an appointment at the Presidential Palace.

4 BLUEPRINT FOR REBELLION

Political activities were more important than military activities, and fighting less important than propaganda.

—*Vo Nguyen Giap*

ABOARD THE FOUR-ENGINE Lockheed Super Constellation parked at Gate Three, Major Alex Spear walked up the aisle toward the cockpit, occasionally stopping to jab his fingers or pipe stem into the seat cushion crevices. Aware the bomb squad had made an earlier sweep of the aircraft, Alex wanted to satisfy himself that the ordnance team had not missed anything.

"How long ago did you say Lieutenant Kearney made his check?" Alex asked the woman standing in the aisle behind him holding a clipboard.

"About an hour ago," said Maria Monclova, the only flight attendant assigned to Flight 740.

"Has anyone else been on board since then?"

"No, sir. Only the captain and his crew who are on the flight deck."

"I'll want to talk to them as soon as I'm finished here."

"Then I'll go forward and tell the captain to stand by for your meeting."

"Thank you, and Miss Monclova, please ask him to patch me into a secure line through the tower so I can establish contact with my headquarters in Vietnam."

"Yes, sir. Anything else, Major? Could I get you a cup of coffee from the galley?"

"No, thank you. But there is another matter I'd like you to handle while you're checking the passengers on board."

"Yes?"

"One of them will be a civilian named Winston Brand, who, judging by the shape he was in when last seen, might need that cup of coffee. But what I'd like you to do is stall him at the gate until I can get down there with further instructions."

"As it stands now, I don't have any civilians on the manifest. Will Mr. Brand be flying with us?"

"That'll be decided after I've made my call."

A few minutes later, Alex sat in the engineer's seat in the cockpit with a headset on, listening to the voice of Maj. Gen. George "Geronimo" Pavler.

"Straight Arrow, this is Checkmate Leader: We've got some distressing news regarding Winston Brand. Over," the gruff voice echoed in the earphones.

"Checkmate Leader, this is Straight Arrow: Go ahead with your message. Over," Alex replied.

"Checkmate Leader: Intercepted radio message from Hanoi to R-3. Subject—keeping Brand out of Vietnam. What do you suppose they're up to? Over."

"Straight Arrow copies: Threatening note planted on Brand here at the terminal. Later beaten by unknown assailants. Found unconscious by security police patrol. Injuries meant to brutally stun rather than kill according to attending physician. Over."

"Checkmate Leader: What's his condition? Over."

"Straight Arrow: Unsteady on his feet, but able to proceed if that's your decision. Over."

"Checkmate Leader: Hanoi's message clear on Brand posing danger to their mission. Want him stopped. Termination not ruled out. Your comments. Over."

"Straight Arrow: Puzzled by R-3's involvement. Unlike him to botch a hit. Maybe we can find out more once Brand is in country. Over."

"Checkmate Leader. Good thinking. Could be the break we've been looking for. Other side might tip hand as to what mission Brand poses threat to. Over."

"Straight Arrow: Then we're to proceed to your location? Over."

"Checkmate Leader: That's a 'roger.' And I expect to see you both here safely soon. Out."

In the terminal, a voice boomed over the public address system, "MATS Flight 740 final boarding at Gate Three." Brand thought about "Willie," and was about to take a shot, when he changed his mind, slipped the flask back into his pocket and unsteadily made his way toward the gate. As best he could, he had concealed what felt like two golf ball-sized lumps beneath the bandage over his right ear by gently easing his hat down over the injured spot. Every movement brought an audible wince as the dressing rubbed against his wound closed by the stitches. He wondered why the pain killers didn't do more to ease his suffering since the air force doctor had sewn him up yesterday.

"Like everything else in the government, this damn stuff is slow to work," he grumbled to himself, but within earshot of the woman who barred his way.

"Sir, you've obviously been drinking, and I'm not allowed to let you pass in your condition," said Maria Monclova, eyeing his tilted hat, torn clothing and disheveled appearance.

"Check with your boss. You'll find out it's approved for me to board," he growled.

Although he realized his anger should be directed at the people who had ambushed him, unfortunately, they were not in his pathway as was the flight attendant in her late twenties who stood her ground with elegant grace.

"But it's for your own good. You may get sick on the long flight," she protested.

"Miss," he said as his voice took on an unnatural softness. "Have you ever been to a football game?"

"Why, yes, of course, sir."

"Remember how there always seemed to be one obnoxious drunk seated in front of you making one helluva scene?"

"Sometimes."

"Well, for this flight, or this game, I'm that drunk. So resign yourself to your fate. Look, I've come too damn far to turn back now." He pushed past her and wobbled toward the aircraft.

"Don't worry, ma'am," piped up Lt. Thomas Kearney, Jr., from the sidelines. "I'll take care of that nasty punk for you."

As Brand reached the top of the gangway, Alex Spear appeared in the doorway of the four-engine super constellation.

"Winston, it's good to see you up and about. Welcome aboard. We've got clearance for you to make the flight with us if you're still of the frame of mind to do so."

"You're damn right I am, and you owe me some answers. Who struck those two blows to my head?"

"We'll talk about that inside, Winston, after we get airborne."

Brand hesitated long enough to see the flight attendant and an army lieutenant charging up the ramp behind him.

"I don't want any trouble from your minions, Alex."

Spear responded by motioning Maria and Kearney to back-off with one hand while directing Brand into the aircraft with the other.

Fifteen minutes later, 32 passengers breathed a sigh of relief as the Connie took off without incident. However, one sprawled in a window seat could care less, for the pain killers in Winston Brand produced the desired effect once he relaxed. Before more alert passengers spotted the Golden Gate Bridge, he was already asleep.

Lieutenant Kearney seated next to Brand poked a camera past the reporter's nose to attempt a high angle shot of the bridge below. But Brand's hat, pulled down over his eyes, blocked the view. The young officer slowly lifted the fedora, as if it were the lid on container of explosive ordnance, shot his picture and repositioned the hat. His movements were so adept Brand never stirred.

Standing in the aisle, having glimpsed Brand's bandaged head, Maria Monclova admonished the lieutenant, "Wouldn't it have been easier to take your picture from another seat?"

"Yeah, but I keep in training that way," replied the ruddy complexioned young man.

"In training for what?" She placed a steaming cup of coffee on his tray.

"Pass the sugar and cream, and I'll show you. Now what's coffee without sugar and cream, and what's a bomb without explosives and a fuse? I'm the guy who puts the powder in the bomb like this." He dropped two lumps of sugar in his cup.

"I have to put the fuse in place as carefully as I pour this cream. Spill the milk in my business, there's no time to cry. It's just curtains. You know. Boom! And old Kearney would go flying in eight different directions."

Kearney inadvertently illustrated the point by knocking the hat from Brand's head with one of his outstretched arms, bumping the reporter's wound in the process.

Brand's eyes took in the startled pair with a sleepy but angry gaze. "Just what in the hell's going on here?" he snapped.

Apologetically, the flight attendant reached across Lieutenant Kearney's chest to retrieve Brand's hat from between the seats. Her breasts brushed against the lieutenant's arm. Brand saw her tanned face take on a crimson glow at this unintentional contact as she handed him the fedora from this awkward position.

"I'm terribly sorry to have disturbed you, sir. The lieutenant just demonstrated a war technique," she said.

Brand bellowed, "I'm sure he did. But why don't you find some empty seats to play your little parlor games with him? I've got one helluva headache."

The girl bolted upright. To Brand it seemed as if her spine had suddenly been replaced with a steel bar.

"Sorry," she repeated backing into the aisle.

"Look, Buster," the lieutenant said. His face flushed redder than his close-cropped hair. "It wasn't the lady's fault. If you want to take your hangover out on somebody, try me for size!"

"Excuse me, Lieutenant," said a voice from the seat behind Kearney and Brand. "Would you change places with me? I need to speak to Mr. Brand."

All three turned to see Major Alex Spear step into the aisle. He quickly exchanged seats with Kearney, and inquired whether lighting his pipe would bother Brand.

"Go ahead, if that's your way of defusing the situation. One more word from your lieutenant, and he'd have found 180 pounds of lean muscle in his face. I'm tired of people messing with me. Someone threw a flask at my head back in the dispensary, and now this idiot's taking aim at me."

"Another attack?"

"All I know is two people used me for target practice. Probably the same ones who mugged me earlier."

"Perhaps," said Alex. "We had to release the woman in the gray coat. Not enough evidence to keep her in custody. Was she there, too?"

"No, the voices I heard outside my room were both male, and they weren't discussing chess either," said Brand flicking a finger across his nose.

For the next hour, Alex chatted amiably about the weather, air pockets, the long Pacific flight, journalism and politics, with no further mention of Brand's beating or the dispensary incident. Whether intended or not, this gave the reporter time to clear his head as he dozed off at intervals during the major's monologue.

From the seat behind them, Lieutenant Kearney snored. Forward, Maria Monclova chatted with a navy lieutenant commander, and those who weren't either asleep or reading had their eyes on her shapely figure. Alex gestured toward the unoccupied galley in the tail of the aircraft.

"Come on, Winston. Let's grab a cup of coffee."

Alex stood up and walked down the aisle. Winston followed close on the heels of the marine. Bending over the coffee urn and filling a paper cup, the officer passed it to Winston. He filled a second cup for himself and leaned back against the counter.

"I must confess, we're at a loss as to who's behind these incidents. If it's the same people who slipped you the warning note, their motive seems directed at frightening rather than incapacitating you, or worse."

"Thanks a lot, Alex. I'm supposed to be grateful I'm not dead, is that it?"

"No, I'm puzzled. We're used to dealing with types who play for keeps. You have my word we'll stay on top of it."

"Maybe I ought to run my own investigation from here on out. The word of guys like you, playing fast and loose with the truth, offers no comfort whatsoever."

"Too bad you feel that way, Winston. Your knowledge of the military and ability to travel freely throughout Vietnam as a civilian could help us bring R-3 to justice."

"I knew you'd tie this into R-3 and the game you've got underway. R-3's your problem."

"Considering the circumstances, that may not be true," said Alex.

Brand calculated the consequences of involvement with Spear and military intelligence. For whatever information he might offer, they would expect to see it played out according to their rules. And for what privileges or information he received as compensation, they still called the shots. That wasn't the Brand way.

"No dice. You're asking me to jettison freedom of the press and all those other things I support as a member of the fourth estate."

Brand hadn't noticed the briefcase until Alex plopped it open on the coffee counter and removed a manila envelope.

"To show good faith, you may borrow this study I did on the Viet Cong. It's part of Operation Checkmate, the code name for our group, which I'd like you to keep to yourself. The document is unclassified, so feel free to use any part of it you like. The American people need to know what the hell we're up against. Perhaps you're still the right guy to tell them."

"Thanks, I'll take a look at it, but I can't guarantee it will see the light of day in my newspaper."

"Good enough, Winston. Just remember we're dealing with undercover agents who know how to use the democratic values we're trying to instill in their country to their own advantage. Westerners don't understand the Oriental strategy for the defeat of a stronger opponent by a weaker adversary through finding a way to turn the foe's greater strength to his own benefit."

"Maybe, but the Asian mind doesn't have a lock on strength. Socrates reminded us long ago that weakness is found in the ignorant."

"Then we can agree, R-3 has the best of both worlds. He gets intelligence handed to him from newspapers like yours and reports of TV journalists who are just doing their jobs. One-sided reporting, however, makes someone's job even easier. Not mine though."

With that Alex excused himself to radio his position report to the States. Alone, but with mindful heed of the other passengers, Brand removed Willie from his coat pocket and poured a hefty shot into his coffee cup.

Only one drink he promised himself, a promise he never kept, for there was always another for those poor bastards in Korea sold down the drain by the politicians back home. Then one more for the French lads at Dien Bien Phu who had the carpet pulled out from under them in much the same manner. A fourth drink commemorated the miserable years on the desk. Finally there was that special double shot reserved for memories of Eleanor and the failed marriage. The bourbon helped him forget her parting words,

"Winston, if you insist on running off to every war in Asia like a chauvinistic school boy, don't expect me to share a bamboo bed with you in every dirty thatch hut along the way."

He raised the cup to his lips.

"Mr. Brand, this isn't a bar," said a scornful voice from behind him. Awkwardly, he lowered the hand holding the cup and turned to face his accuser.

"Well, if it isn't my friend, the pesky flight attendant. How come you turn up everywhere?"

"I'm the only flight attendant on board. And out of concern for the welfare of my passengers, you're advised it's against regulations to drink that poison on this military charter."

"Poison? I hadn't thought about that possibility. You may have something there," said Brand, realizing Willie could have been tampered with while in the hands of his attackers. Perhaps they were playing for keeps, regardless of what Alex had surmised. "I suppose we'd better get rid of this nasty stuff." He emptied the bourbon from both the flask and the coffee cup into the sink.

"Good, I see you've resigned yourself to your fate, Mr. Brand."

"Touché, pussycat. I've heard those words before," he said tossing the empty flask to the startled woman. "Keep that for me 'til you think I need it. My life is in your hands." Bowing slightly, Brand brushed past her and walked up the aisle to his seat.

The aircraft engines droned on marking the passing hours. After the evening meal had been served and cleared away, heads began to bob forward and back in the seats as weariness and the hypnotic effect of the engine noise combined to lull most of the passengers to sleep.

In the rear seat, Maria Monclova dozed with her head on her arms, her long, black hair tucked provocatively between cheek and forearm on one side and between arm and breasts on the other. Her legs were drawn up under her with her knees turned toward the passage way.

Several seats forward and across from her, Lieutenant Kearney feigned drowsiness as he contorted his body until his head was positioned on the rim of the arm-rest where he could watch the gap between Maria's knees. It pleased and excited him whenever the aircraft bounced through an air pocket, tussling Maria so that the gap widened. He wished there were some way he could turn the overhead light on above her seat for a clearer view. He even considered a bold stroke, like turning on her light on the way to the lavatory and returning to his own seat before she awakened. He dismissed it as too risky, since Brand sat reading under a lamp immediately to his front.

In the dim light, it was hard to tell, but Kearny thought he caught a glimpse of yellow briefs above Maria's stockings. The thought thrilled him, especially for the intelligence an experienced rogue like himself could obtain from the color, shape and texture of the clothes a woman allowed to touch her body. To Kearney, briefs the color of sunlight signified a love spirit which viewed chastity as the treasure stored for the beloved's reward. Women so clad were apt to be less permissive than their pink-bottomed sisters, but not as chaste and cold as the girls who wore panties as white and pure as the driven snow. The goldilocks (as he called them) could be wooed, bedded and won only after a fierce struggle involving heart and mind, as well as the body.

He cursed the darkness. For, with a little more light, he could determine whether Maria wore sharp Vs or lazy double Us, with or without lace. The Venus look, as Kearney called it, indicated a woman proud of her figure, while the double U usually concealed a roll of flesh or a surgical scar. Lace stood for ultimate femininity in the Kearny lexicon.

Meanwhile, Winston Brand sat curled under the glow of the overhead seat lamp, examining the manuscript lent him by Major Spear entitled, *Notes from a Revolutionary Hero.* Alex began the introduction:

> As an intelligence officer, I have herein merely translated this work from Vietnamese to English. Written in the late '50s, this document gives us some insight as to what rationale the enemy applies to the war. Of course, this information wasn't offered voluntarily. The manuscript was separated from a Viet Cong fighter when an American-led Army of the Republic of Vietnam (ARVN) patrol found the body following a Viet Cong ambush. Apparently the soldier was also a teacher of sorts, and had carried his 'lesson plan' with him into battle. I discovered it when I ordered his remains removed to Phu Bai for burial. Phu Bai is about 20

kilometers south of the former royal city of Hue in central Vietnam.

As luck would have it, our patrol encountered a group of students upon entering the village, and one of the students, a 16-year-old boy, named Vo Duc Dai, identified the trussed up pencil pusher as his revered teacher, Nguyen Van Tam, from Phu Bai. Convinced we had made a mistake, the youngster insisted we treat Tam's body with greater respect. But I pointed out his beloved teacher had been shot as he lay in ambush with a cocked Chinese rifle in his hands.

Dead Viet Cong are hardly ever identified, so I was grateful for this opportunity to trace the soldier's background. Young Dai told me Tam's parents still lived in Phu Bai. They would vouch for his teacher's innocence, the boy assured me.

I went to see Tam's father, a grizzled old mandarin, grief stricken at the news he had lost another son, yet answered my questions without hesitation because he vehemently disapproved of how the communists had torn his family apart. Yes, his son had fought with the Viet Minh against the French in 1953-54. So had Tam's older brother, Nguyen Van Dan. Dan and Tam had been two of the 25,000 South Vietnamese who had fought with the communist North against the French.

Yes, his sons had been ordered back to South Vietnam by Ho Chi Minh after the French defeat. They slipped back to the South after the war, took up residence in their former villages and carried on guerrilla war under the Viet Cong banner. The old man seemed most upset that Tam used his teaching position to entice village boys into the service of the local guerrillas. One such recruit was the mandarin's own grandson and Tam's nephew, Nguyen Van Thi, an apprentice technician at the Hue radio station who joined the communists after his own father's death. All told, the revolution had cost the old man of Phu Bai two sons and a missing grandson.

From the intelligence viewpoint, the manuscript has little value, as it reveals nothing we don't already know about the Viet Cong. However, it does provide us with the political blueprint for the communist take-over of Southeast Asia.

> It's a blueprint we've seen put into effect in other places. The document's real value relates to propaganda. It lays naked before the world the communist myth that the Viet Cong are merely rebels fighting for a just cause. For no one can read these words of a dedicated communist and still cling to that erroneous concept.
>
> Don't be fooled by the nationalistic rhetoric. It is plainly evident, like most communist actions, the strings to these puppets are manipulated by others miles away from the din of battle, not behind jungle foliage in South Vietnam, but behind brick walls in Hanoi, Peking and Moscow.

"A little hyperbolic, Alex, old boy," Brand thought as he began the translation. The communist manuscript read:

> In August, 1945, we had no guns, not a rifle. Yet, we toppled the French colonialist and its feudalistic system. We had no powerful army. But we had 20 million people willing to die under the revolutionary flag… Our revolt had a twofold goal under Chairman Ho and the Communist party: first, independence, rice and clothing, and freedom for ourselves; second, to extend the power of our revolution and its dominion among others under the communist banner. To achieve these goals, our people have paid with their blood and bones.

Brand took a note pad and pencil from his pocket and wrote, "*Notes from a Revolutionary Hero*, Ho's twofold goals, possibly from Bacon." Brand read on, then paused again when he came to the passage detailing the three rules by which the Communists expected to gain the people's support. After noting the passage, he excitedly wrote, "Unquestionably Spinoza." He resumed reading:

> So, unlike the people of the North, the people of the South aren't free. The imperialist Ngo Dinh Diem and his crew of American lackeys dominate South Vietnam where the people are not masters in their own land. Can we say that this is independence?

Brand scribbled on his note pad. "Get interview with Diem ASAP." Then he continued.

> In our revolution, we will use basic techniques which have been successful elsewhere, namely political and armed struggle. The essential difference between the two techniques is in the methods of resistance that are applied. Some argue that since many of us have no weapons, we cannot wage any struggle. This is not correct. Weapons are not the decisive factor. The will and strength of the people is what counts. We need three to six years to complete the switch to the armed struggle.

Brand wrote, "Armed struggle, 1965-68?" But then he thought he heard an odd sound from an engine on his side of the airplane. Nonetheless, he read the rest of the communist propaganda to the end of the manuscript.

As the reporter replaced the document in the manila envelope, he suddenly realized why everyone on flight 740 was headed for Vietnam, and why his government had started to build up troop strength. In 1962, the communists were dedicated to their goal of building readiness for the armed conflict.

When Brand heard one of the port engines give off a queer sound, like metal striking metal, he saw Lieutenant Kearney leave his perch on the arm-rest to move over to the window. The officer cupped his hands over his eyes and peered out into the darkness.

Alerted by Kearney's quick movements, Alex Spear excused himself from his chess game with Dr. Nick Jenicoso, a navy physician in the forward section, and made his way down the aisle. The major slipped quietly into the seat next to Kearney where the view of the wing was better.

"See anything?" the major whispered.

"Naw," said Kearney. "Some unknown object must have struck one of the propellers. The noise has stopped now."

"Keep an eye on it. I'll check with the aircraft commander."

"Sure, Major, but I don't think it's anything to worry about."

"Perhaps. Let's hope you're right."

Kearney felt the urge to shout at Spear's retreating form, "You're damn tootin' I'm right, Major. I'm the expert, remember?

If there's a bomb or explosive device on this aircraft, I'll find the goddamn thing and save your brassy butt."

There were three reasons why he failed to follow through on this urge. One, he had explicit instructions from his father not to buck authority. Two, if he shouted at Spear, it would surely awaken Maria and ring down the curtain on his private peep show, and three, the prospect of a hidden bomb had begun to frighten him.

He reached under his seat and removed a flashlight from his demolition kit. The beam of light reflected off the silver wing, danced momentarily on the whirling propeller of the number one engine, then came to rest on the inboard engine manifold.

"What is it?" Alex had returned with the flight engineer.

"Looks like a crack in the manifold," whispered Kearney.

"Let me have a look at that," said the engineer. As Kearney moved away from the window, he saw Maria stir, then sit up and rub her eyes.

"That's just normal oil seepage, not a crack. These engines look okay to me," said the engineer.

"Reassuring words," Alex said.

"Looks like you woke everyone up," announced Kearney as they were joined by Brand, the rotund doctor, who still grasped a chess piece, and Maria.

"Is there something I can do to help," she asked.

"No," the engineer said. "We're just checking…"

"Everything's under control," Alex interrupted. "Please, folks, just return to your seats."

They moved off silently, but Brand shot a glance back at Alex, who saw the questioning look and said, "I'll fill you in later, Winston."

"Better check the starboard engines, too," said the engineer.

"Good idea," said Alex.

"Don't forget, that's my flashlight you have there," called Kearney.

"Anybody care for coffee?" asked Maria.

"Yes, please, when you get a chance," said the plump doctor. The others shook their heads.

Back in his seat, Brand watched the flashlight beam probe the darkness on his side of the aircraft, heard the engineer say, "Nothing wrong," as he tossed the flashlight back to Kearney and moved up the aisle with Alex close on his heels.

Moments later, Alex Spear slid into the seat next to Brand.

"For a moment there, Winston, I thought we'd get a chance to check out the bombed or hi-jacked aircraft theories," he said fanning tobacco into his pipe.

"Flight's not over yet, Major," Brand reminded him.

"Yes, I know, and that's why we're so edgy."

"No doubt you can scratch the hi-jack theory until we get past Hawaii. There isn't an unfriendly island in the area for hi-jackers to take this aircraft to without being pursued by U.S. interceptors, and there isn't enough gas in this crate to fly to China non-stop."

The cheekbones in Alex's oval face were clearly outlined as he puffed on his pipe.

"You're right, Winston. A bomb is our big worry between here and Hawaii. The aircraft commander doesn't like the sound of the number one engine, nor do I." He looked at his watch. "Another hour to go. Then Kearney and I will give this aircraft a thorough shake down."

"What's the junior league officer got to do with all this?" Brand asked with a jerk of his head toward Kearney.

"He's our resident demolition's expert, just as Lieutenant Commander Jenicoso's our onboard physician. We also have a couple of survival experts, an aerodynamics engineer, an extra pilot and a spare navigator on board. As I told you, Winston, except for you, almost everyone on this plane has a mission in connection with its safe passage."

"I'd feel better with a more mature person in charge of bombs and their disposal."

Alex smiled. "I'm told Lieutenant Kearney, Jr., cut his teeth on a stick of dynamite in his old man's explosives factory. He'll produce if he has to."

"You mean that's Senator Tank Kearney's kid?"

"Right."

"Well, then, we've got an interesting situation here. Either the risk factor on this flight has been overblown, or the senator doesn't give a damn about the lives of American boys, even if one of them happens to be his son."

"That sounds a bit harsh, Winston. In one aspect, you're right though. If any military flight is to get through, I'd expect it to be flight 740, because we've taken every precaution."

Both men watched Maria glide past with a cup of coffee on a tray.

"How about her?" Brand asked. "What's her mission beyond building morale?"

Alex left his question unanswered. Instead, the major's eyes fell upon the document still held in Brand's hand.

"What did you think of the communist propaganda document?" asked Alex.

"I'd like to keep it a little longer to do more thorough research."

"Then you find it intriguing?"

"Actually, what interests me is the philosophy interspersed with the propaganda."

"How's that?"

"Well, the implication of your preface indicates the document is suspected of being the work of an Oriental writing in a backward country. I find this farfetched, because the author is too well steeped in Western philosophy."

"Perhaps he studied in the West?"

"Perhaps, Alex, but only if we're talking about Saigon intellectuals. Even then it's a far stretch."

"Maybe the author could've picked up Western ideas from the French colonialists," suggested Alex.

"That's unlikely. The document itself makes the point the French only gave these people a hard time during their 90 year occupation of Indochina."

"Then, you suspect the author's credentials?"

"Hey, you're the intelligence officer. All I'm saying is the source of this document has more than a casual acquaintance with philosophers, possibly Bacon and to a greater extent, Spinoza."

"Could you elaborate?"

Brand referred to his note pad, then turned to see Alex staring intently at his every move. "Well, then," said Brand with a smile that betrayed his delight in discussing philosophy with an interested participant. "I don't know how well versed you are in Sir Frances Bacon and Benedict Spinoza, but as I read the communist document I made these notes. First, there seems to be a very thin link between Chairman Ho's two goals for the communists and Bacon's three grades of ambition in mankind. The communists write of extending the power of their revolution to their own people and the dominion of others. Bacon added a third, much less covetous and more wholesome goal to these first two, by suggesting man's ambition would be better served by extending the power and dominion of the human race itself over the universe."

"So, you're suggesting the author used Bacon's description of the first two grades of man's ambition, but left out his third wholesome element, to describe communist goals," said Alex.

"Maybe," Brand replied. He reached into his back pocket to remove his wallet, and produced a well-worn card from his college days that he handed to the major. "As you can see, the lines to Spinoza are less tenuous than those to Bacon. On that card, word for word, are three rules Spinoza outlined for a philosopher to assimilate himself in society. These exactly match the communist document's rationale for gaining the acceptance of the populace."

Alex took the card and placed it next to the section of document pointed out by Brand:

1. To speak in a manner comprehensible to the people, and to do for them all things that do not prevent us from attaining our ends.
2. To enjoy only such pleasures as are necessary for the preservation of health.
3. To seek only enough money as is necessary for the maintenance of our life and health, and to comply with such customs as are not opposed to what we seek.

"Incredible," exclaimed Alex. "I've never looked at this document in that light before."

"Well, I'm glad to have been of service. And for what it's worth, the guy you're looking for seems to be interested in philosophy like me. However, it appears his interest is not so much in original philosophical ideas, but in their use for his own version of them to fit his specific goals. Now please return my card. It gives me a philosophical outlook to help me deal with a world deceived by illusion."

"Philosophy isn't your only interest, I take it. I'm told you're a poet, too."

"Surprise, surprise, you mean in all your background checking on me, you guys never came up with my out-of-print book, *Fire in the Soul*?

"I knew you'd written a book of poetry, of course. Admittedly, I've never read it."

"Well, we can remedy that," said Brand, reaching into his flight bag. "You can borrow this rare copy, so the file on me can be complete." He handed the slim volume to Alex.

"If it'll help relieve the anxiety of getting us to Hawaii safely, then it'll be worth the effort. By the way, Winston, I'm sure you've thought about keeping an eye out for the soldiers you encountered back in the terminal. Didn't you mention one of them said he was booked on this flight?"

"Yes, except I haven't felt much like moving around checking passengers."

"Then maybe we should position ourselves at the gang plank upon landing in Hawaii. That way you can signal me if you spot any characters linked to the threatening note or beating. For my part, I'd just as soon not stir up any in-flight trouble unless it's related to a possible bomb on board."

"Whatever you say, Major. It's your investigation."

Alex excused himself and walked to the front of the aircraft to confer with the engineer. Relieved there had been no further reports of engine trouble, Brand still found himself unable to shake the anxiety growing in his mind. Alex's reaction left little doubt military intelligence suspected R-3 as the real author of the captured communist document. If this assessment proved accurate, R-3 could be a Saigon intellectual—one of the many followers of Ho Chi Minh who had studied in Paris. If so, R-3 stood more formidable than Brand had imagined. He would have to be taken more seriously in regard to the success or failure of Brand's own mission, he thought. Equally disturbing, Brand had sensed Alex's own uneasiness at learning he faced a chess master/philosopher with all the cunning, knowledge and intelligence implied. Although left unsaid, Brand discerned that Spear's own confidence had been shaken.

Brand realized Alex's dogged determination in the pursuit of 'justice' might not be enough. The major had sounded a pessimistic note despite the banter about Brand's poetry book. Assuming a correct reading of the situation, Brand expected the Operation Checkmate group to redouble their efforts to enlist his services, or at least his cooperation, yet he remained determined to resist on both counts. Brand believed the 'truth' he was determined to uncover would be the actual weapon to unmask the disguised, subversive communist commander, who had infiltrated a high office in the South Vietnamese government.

5 HARBOR OF MISGIVINGS

You could not step into the same river even once.

—Cratylus

TWO RED SIGNS PREGNANT with alarm flashed on above the cockpit door. Awakened by the activity around him, Brand reluctantly pulled the seat belt tight over his muscular thighs to get ready for what he viewed as mind-game time between the crew and passengers. The pilot cried wolf with those lights, while the sheep in the rear blinked uncertainly as one man with his hands on yoke and throttle decided their destiny. With eyes fastened on the lights, Brand listened for the reassuring words of the flight attendant.

"The captain has just turned on the 'Fasten Your Seat Belt' and 'No Smoking' signs. We'll be landing at Hickam Air Force Base, Hawaii, in 15 minutes. Please remain seated until the aircraft comes to a full stop. Temperature in Honolulu is 78 degrees; local time is 1900. Our flight will resume after a 12 hour layover. Please be on board by 0630. Thank you."

Maria clicked off the intercom.

From his window seat, Brand spotted the island of Oahu. Reminded of his first visit to Hawaii in 1950, he tried to discern the shape of Mauna Loa. On the earlier occasion, the volcano's eruption had rocked the decks of the Korea-bound troop ship anchored in Pearl Harbor with reporter Brand on board feeling anxious about reporting in a combat zone that first time.

Brand had intended to emulate Pulitzer Prize winning journalist Ernie Pyle, who was honored by correspondents throughout World

War II. Pyle's dictum to never write or say anything that disparages the character of the American fighting man resonated with his young successor headed to Korea. Brand retained healthy skepticism toward the politicians who send them into battle, but he resolved to respect all uniformed personnel for their service.

Throughout Korea and again on his first assignment to Vietnam, Brand had followed Pyle's advice to the letter. His own 1954 Pulitzer Prize was inspired by Ernie Pyle, the brave, indefatigable 1944 recipient who had led the way in both word and deed. As the aircraft touched down, Brand found himself hoping he could repeat his earlier record and win a second Pulitzer Prize.

A group of impatient soldiers pushed by Brand's seat before the plane came to a stop. He could hear them exchange obscenities about the native girls as they gathered around the exit waiting for two ground attendants to maneuver a mobile staircase in place.

Listening to their banter, Brand surmised that levity and language among the troops hadn't changed since 1950 when another generation of soldiers had been equally anxious about tasting the island's forbidden fruit.

"Hey, Chuck," yelled one soldier to a comrade closer to the door. "Tell any grass skirts you see out there, that I brought my lawnmower."

Laughter.

"Hey, fellas, I hear these Hawaiian girls make terrific leis."

More laughter.

"The doctor says I'm suffering from an old Hawaiian disease, lack-a-nooky."

The high-pitched and strained voice of Lieutenant Kearney shattered the mirth-making. "Knock off the barracks talk, you goddamn grunts. There's a lady present."

Brand turned in his seat and watched as Kearney helped Maria Monclova down the stairway.

"Bastard lieutenant," murmured a soldier near Brand. "He's got his, but it pisses him off to think we're gonna get ours."

Brand stepped into the aisle to retrieve his hand carried luggage in the overhead rack. He heard Alex ordering the soldiers to return to their seats, and the marine major motioned Brand to move forward. Moments later, the two men stood outside watching the others disembark.

"Recognize anybody?" Alex asked.

"No. But I find myself pitying the wives and sweethearts of these men of war who see chastity as a spent cartridge ejected once separated from home and hearth. War or combat does that to a man," said the reporter. "My womanizer brother-in-law is a case in point, even though my sister certainly must suspect, but denies to herself, his infidelity. You should know him, Alex, Sean O'Boyle, Office of Naval Intelligence (O.N.I.), stationed here in Hawaii."

"I can't recall ever running into him in O.N.I."

"Consider yourself lucky. Sean's seduced more officers' wives than the Allies did with chocolate and silk stockings in World War II. Why Clementine looks the other way despite his many affairs still amazes me. The kids, pressure from the Catholic Church or my dad's influence probably sway her."

"Will you be staying with them during our stop-over?"

"Hell, no. It's been three years since I saw Clemie or my nephews. I'll steer clear as long as the hypocrite husband comes with the package."

"In that case, we'll find room for you in the crew's quarters at the hotel," said Alex.

That evening upstairs in her room in the Hawaiian Village Hotel, Maria Lindsay Monclova's nude body swayed in an impromptu hula dance. She paused in front of a full-length mirror long enough to give her 28-year-old, beauty-contest figure the once-over. Settling in a steaming tub, she vigorously rubbed the back of her neck where the strands of long black hair were now tied into a neat pony tail. Massaging that particular spot seemed to erase the strain of a ten hour flight from the mainland.

Playfully she raised a slender, smoothly tanned leg out of the water, then, letting it fall with a splash, she giggled to herself, too excited to be tired. Another flight attendant would pick up Flight 740 and its all-male cargo in the morning. After a three-day-layover vacation in Hawaii, it was home to the Philippines for Maria.

She waved a bar of soap in front of her imitating the motion of a band leader's baton. "Ladies and gentlemen, I give you the pride of Manila," she said, mimicking the master-of-ceremonies at her coronation four years ago. "East and West have finally come together, for the blood of three continents flows within Maria, and never was there a more beautiful river than our Miss Philippines, Maria Monclova!"

She giggled again. Then the phone rang in her room shattering her thoughts. With her full lips pursed in a pout at the interruption, she ignored the call. After six or seven rings, the phone stopped. A few minutes later, it rang again. This time she decided to answer and reluctantly stepped from the tub, grabbing a towel.

"Maria Monclova," she said nestling the phone against her cheek. Instinctively she pulled the towel more securely around her at the sound of a male voice.

"This is Major Spear," came the deep reply. "I'm terribly sorry to disturb you, Miss Monclova."

"It's all right, Major. What can I do for you?"

"Let me get right to the point. We've run into some trouble getting your replacement on Flight 740 cleared before flight time. Probably just a snag in the red tape. Follow me?"

"Yes, sir."

"I've checked with the airline. No objection on their part to your continuing on. The official I spoke to said it's your call."

"How far are we talking about, Major?"

"All the way—to Vietnam."

Her gasp was clearly audible. "Couldn't you get someone else to take the flight from Guam or the Philippines?" The plea in her voice was unmistakable yet did little to advance her cause.

"I'm afraid we'd run into clearance problems again, and there isn't that much time. You've no idea the difficulty of finding someone like you, Miss Monclova. I mean, if your mother hadn't been an American citizen, the security problem might've cropped up in your case, too."

"I just can't."

"We realize the strain you're under, and I'd be the last to minimize the danger involved, but if you don't go, there'll be no flight attendant on board when we depart in the morning."

"Major, put yourself in my shoes. After a short layover here, I'm looking forward to being home in the Philippines for a while after putting in my time as a flight attendant in the States for a year. I agreed to give you part of my vacation time to serve as a flight attendant on the military flight as far as Hawaii, but I've no intention of going to Vietnam first. Sorry."

"Miss Monclova, should you change your mind, I'll be in the hotel bar 'til ten and then in my room, number 215. I'm sorry to have disturbed you. Good night."

"Good night, Major."

As soon as the phone touched the receiver, it rang again.

"I've been trying to get you for the last five minutes. This is Tom Kearney. Tell me, who's the competition, so I can plant a charge of TNT under his derrière."

"It was Major Spear. He wants me to stay with the flight 'til Vietnam."

"And you told him no dice."

"Yes."

"For shame. Think of all us poor little soldiers off to war without your soft shoulder to nestle up against."

"Please, Tom. It's not funny. The major was so serious."

"He's always that way. It's part of the field grade image. The military likes its leaders to look mature, thoughtful, and serious while they manipulate the lives of others. But I'm the darndest black sheep you've ever seen, and I've got a date with a beautiful flight attendant, remember?"

"Just for one drink. I told you I'm tired."

"Agreed. Two drinks, then you can play the Cinderella bit. I'll be knocking at your door in ten seconds."

"No, I'm not quite dressed—er—ready. Let me meet you in the lobby."

"Compromise. Let's meet in the bar."

"All right. In about 20 minutes then."

Annoyed she had accepted the date with Lieutenant Kearney earlier, Maria now wished she had not given in to quiet his incessant chatter. She had Kearney pegged for the type of guy who, if he ever succeeded with a woman, would not let her forget it, nor any of his bachelor buddies. No matter how hard he tried, if getting her in bed was his intention, he'd find himself thwarted.

"Men," she thought as she fumbled through her flight bag looking for her lipstick. "Do they really think sex drives every relationship with a woman?"

As if in answer to the question, out of the bag and into her lap tumbled a thin, silver flask. She turned it over and spotted the inscription:

My Willie, the Flask,

The only friend that lasts.

W.B.

Staring at the object, she remembered the sad, brown eyes of the man who had tossed it to her on the aircraft. Beautiful but melancholy, his eyes reminded her of a river that had run its course too early. She recalled, too, how his lips seemed anchored in a constant snarl as he spoke his harsh, arrogant words.

He had insulted her. But there had been a smile, too, when he had called her "pussycat." She thought it strange now, alone in her room preparing for a date with another man, she should remember that smile. It had filled his face with lines shooting out from those magnificent eyes like sunbeams momentarily embracing her with warmth.

"The grouch," she said aloud as she banged the flask down on a dresser. Then to herself, "Kearney can take it to him in the morning. Straighten up, Maria, don't get sentimental. Under your new schedule, you'll be flying in and out of Vietnam often enough as it is."

Below in the crowded bar, Brand was the center of attention.

"Oh, suck it up, Alex, ole buddy." Brand slurred the words in his raised cocktail glass. "So the little suntanned beauty turned you down. Whadaya expect anyway? Didn't you say her mother's American and her father's half Spanish and Filipino? Eurasians are hard to figure out. But in Miss Monclova's case, I knew she couldn't be trusted when she stole Willie. What the hell do you think of a woman who'd steal a man's bottle?"

"Shhhh," Alex said, "everyone in this bar can hear you."

"Let 'em," Brand shouted banging his glass down on the table. "Let 'em, let 'em, let 'em! Let everybody in the world hear what I've got to say about a thieving flight attendant."

"If that's a reference to your flask, you told me you gave it to her for safe-keeping."

"I did?" Brand peered incredulously at Alex. "What a stupid, goddamn thing to do."

"Let me take you to your room, Winston," Alex pleaded. He stretched a hand toward Brand. It was brushed aside.

"I know this flight attendant thing is none of my business, but it's yours, and you're my buddy. So let's have another drink to an ole buddy's business of getting a plane load of scared farts to Vietnam. May you succeed without getting shit on."

Alex rose abruptly from the table. "That's enough, Winston. You're drunk, and you'd better let me take you to your room before someone calls the police."

Brand jumped up from the table. "I don't see anybody here big enough to rat on me." His eyes fell on Kearney's back at the bar.

"Hey, Alex," Brand whispered. "Guess who I just saw? Isn't that the loud-mouthed lieutenant over there? He looks like a flask-thrower if there ever was one. You oughta check him out."

"Winston, I'm warning you. Any more trouble and Flight 740 leaves without you in the morning. Now, what's it going to be? A nice, soft bed or have your press credentials pulled?"

"How much have I had to drink?"

"Six of these," Alex held up a cocktail tumbler. "Without any food. That's by your count. I counted eight."

"All right. Good night, Major." Winston gave Alex a mock salute, turned and walked unsteadily from the room.

The moon peeked through the fronds of a single, tall, green palm the wind had attacked so violently it looked like an inverted umbrella. There were other, straighter palms which stood in a line along the ocean front like sentinels ordered to hold the line between nature's water and sand and man's planted grass that circled the hotel like a carpet. The trunks of all the trees except the inverted palm angled and curved back in a concave manner, then disappeared in the grass. The palm that held the moon in its fronds stood five feet closer to the pounding surf, out of line and in the sand.

To this tree Winston clung tightly as his stomach emptied its poison on the sand. He sucked in huge gulps of ocean air like a man taking his last breath. His head spun, and the salt air and vomiting brought water to his eyes. He sought relief at the cement water fountain beside the tree. He washed his face with his handkerchief and pressing the cool cloth on the back of his neck where the veins seemed to be pounding a passageway through his skin, irritating his head wound. A bitter-sour taste, like a mixture of grapefruit juice and vinegar lingered in his mouth. He tried to wash it away with water.

A few minutes later, he stood confused on the second floor landing as he searched his pockets for his room key.

"Probably dropped the blasted thing," he shouted at someone coming down the stairs. "Don't see it anywhere here on the floor, do you? My eyes aren't too good. Too much salt air will do that, don't you know?"

A pair of dazzling blue eyes met his as he looked up. The woman bent over, and her blue scooped-neck dress gaped in front to inadvertently reveal her soft beauty.

"Is this what you're looking for, Mr. Brand?" asked Maria Monclova as she handed Winston a key.

He snatched it from her hand. "Damn, if you don't have a knack for turning up with things that don't belong to you."

"It was right here on the step," she said. "Just trying to help."

"You can help all right by returning Willie."

"Don't you think it would be better for you to have some hot coffee?"

"See here, Miss Holier-Than-Thou, don't pull that sanctimonious pity on me. Where was it when you decided to desert those war-destined troops in your care? Maybe you never heard the word 'patriotism.' But that figures; you're part Filipina, not all American, aren't you?"

It could have been his rude words, his sarcastic sneer, a stray strand of black hair bobbing jauntily across his forehead, his bourbon-saturated breath or the finger that jabbed the air uncomfortably close to her breasts. Whatever it was, it ignited Maria Monclova. The sound of her hand meeting his cheek echoed so sharply, a passerby might have mistaken it for a rifle shot.

Winston stumbled into his room rubbing a hand against his inflamed cheek. "Damn it," he muttered. "The whole world's trying to knock my brains out."

He started to pour a drink from a decanter left on the dresser by room service, thought better of it and collapsed on the bed. His eyes tried to focus on the ceiling light fixture, but the bright glare forced him to bury his face in the pillow, while his hands tried to calm the throbbing ache of the wound behind his ear. With thoughts of regret for losing control, Brand fell into a fitful sleep.

Later, across the hallway, Maj. Alex Spear sat propped up in his bed as he composed a letter in a small tablet. Frequently he halted his pen in mid-air and gazed thoughtfully at the ceiling where the smoke from his pipe gathered in a hazy cloud around the light. His steel gray eyes revealed a marine who had stared down the phantom of death on the battlefield. Yet, except for a scar on his left cheek, Alex Emerson Spear appeared for all the world like a clergy man of any faith.

"His methodical manner, honest face, warm smile and middle-age maturity are among this officer's main assets," wrote a superior in Alex's fitness report. "But don't think he's mamby-pamby, for I've seen him outsmart men who thought they had the upper hand on him, outfight the toughest enemy, and turn a bunch of scared recruits into marines almost overnight. Except for a streak of stubbornness, he's a leader in the finest sense of the word."

To Gwen Spear, Alex was the considerate and loving guy who shared as much of his sedulous life with her as he could. For the Spears, a nightcap was a letter to each other, posted almost every day of his non-accompanied tours of duty.

Alex wrote in his strong, meticulous stroke:

> You know, Gwen baby, I was just thinking tonight what a lucky guy I am. There's this correspondent who's traveling with us (he's my age) whose idea of coping with life seems to be tied up with alcohol. He's intelligent and likable, until he starts hitting the booze. He could've been an admiral like his father if he hadn't passed up an appointment to the Naval Academy in order to study journalism and philosophy. He certainly could have been a poet judging by the quality of the book of poems titled *Fire in the Soul* he lent me. Here's an example called "Kindred Spirits" that reminds me so much of our situation:
>
> *Somewhere out there sharing this sky,*
> *Under this moon flying so high,*
> *She walks alone just like I do,*
> *No, not alone, my heart's there too.*
> *Somewhere out there sharing this breeze,*
> *Sitting beneath falling leaves,*
> *She dreams alone just like I do,*
> *No, not alone, my heart's there too.*
> *Somewhere out there 'mid fields of clover*
> *When these parting days are over,*
> *She'll join with me eternally,*
> *She'll join with me eternally.*

His name is Winston Brand, and he writes a syndicated column called the 'Branding Iron.' I'm sure the Boston papers carry it. Brand is a mixed up divorcé, and every time I see him I say to myself, "There but for the grace of God and the love of Gwen go I."

This flight has everything—characters like Brand, suspense, and even a dash of romance. Our flight attendant seems to be interested in one of the lieutenants on board. Earlier this evening she was quite emphatic in her refusal to continue with the flight to Vietnam as I requested. Well, right out of the blue, she called me (no more than 20 minutes ago) to say she had changed her mind and would stay with the flight to Vietnam.

Shortly after supper, I saw her and the lieutenant enjoying a cozy drink together. I'm indebted to the young man for changing her mind and plan to tell him so when we check the aircraft over. That'll be at five, so I'd better turn in now to make it easier to turn out in the morning.

Kisses for Alesha and little Alex. Tell them Daddy misses them already. Go ahead and buy that new dress you wanted. I know it'll do wonders for your morale. Wish we men had a comparable system going for us. I'd buy a new suit or uniform every month if I thought it would help ease the loneliness. That you understand I must do my duty is comforting enough, though. I only regret it takes me so far from the ones I love.

Yours, Alex.

Before he could reread his letter, the phone rang again. It was General Pavler, this time on a non-secure telephone line from Vietnam.

"Thought I'd check in, Alex, to see how things are going with you and young Brand. What's his condition?"

"His wounds seem to be no problem, judging by the awful scene he made in the hotel bar little more than an hour ago."

"I'm sorry to hear that," said Pavler with a softness in his voice Alex had never noticed before. "Take it from me, this rowdiness is a temporary thing with Winston. Be patient with him. He'll dig himself out from under the sandbags he's piled upon himself."

"Sir, I hope you're right, since he knows more about our operations than someone with his problem probably should. After what I saw, I'm reluctant to confide in him further."

"Stay the course, Alex. You'll find Winston Brand honest to the core. He's disposed to doing the right thing, but has yet to make it a habit. As you must have surmised from his dossier, this latest binge like the others follows a pattern. They have increased in frequency since his divorce two years ago from a woman not unlike your gentle Gwen. The breakup couldn't have come at a worse time. Battling against the hierarchy at his newspaper to get out of a desk job he was never cut out for, Winston fell apart at the loss of Eleanor, his former wife.

"Neither she nor the *Times* people understood something I spotted in Brand's teenage years. He thrives on adventure in the sense of pursuing life's experiences seeking truth. Knowing him the way I do, he's more philosopher than anything else. And I don't know about you, but I've never heard of a lover of wisdom who found what he was looking for in a bottle. So my advice regarding your misgivings about Brand is to hang in there with him. You'll find him more than salvageable."

"Yes, sir, you know him better than I do."

"Exactly, and I want you to redirect your attention to your immediate mission. Get that aircraft with crew and passengers safely to Vietnam without incident. We're counting on you!"

At 5:00 a.m. the phone rang in Winston Brand's room. Half asleep, he nevertheless put the phone against his uninjured ear.

"What is it?" he growled.

"What's it going to take for you to get the message?" a deep voice retorted. "DON'T GET ON THE PLANE!"

Brand heard the caller's receiver click off, leaving him with an anxious feeling that this problem had followed him from California. A few moments later he heard footsteps in the hallway. Not wanting to wait for another ambush, he leapt from the bed toward the door grabbing a shoe along the way. Hearing the footsteps pause on the other side of the door, he lifted the shoe over his head ready to strike. He stood there for a moment with his good ear pressed against the wood until the footsteps retreated. Opening the door, slightly, he smelled the aroma of maple-scented tobacco. Then he caught sight of Alex Spear hurrying toward the exit.

6 PALACE INTRIGUE

Men are such dupes by choice that he who would impose upon others never need be at a loss to find other victims.

—Honoré de Balzac

IN THE BACK ROOM of a bar on Rue Catinat Street, R-3 sat in a darkened corner across from his adjutant Nguyen Huu Bao, who was dressed in a captain's uniform of the Army of the Republic of South Vietnam (ARVN).

R-3 spoke quietly so not to be overheard. "Bao, were you successful in convincing Diem's brother Nhu of your request for a more responsible position in the South Vietnamese government?"

Nguyen Huu Bao nervously adjusted his black eye patch and replied, "It was your ingenious plan for me to use the document of recommendation bearing the seal of the Roman Catholic Arch Bishop of Hue, their brother, Ngo Dinh Thuc, which brought me to their attention and enabled my interview. I must tell you that I spent much time pacing the floor holding the manila envelope containing the document in my hand while my empty scabbard brushed my leg repeatedly as I waited for my interview.

"Yes, go on," urged R-3.

"But I stood frozen as the door to the counselor's study abruptly opened and Ngo Dinh Nhu, President Diem's brother, appeared wearing a Western-style business suit. Surprised to see the chief counselor himself charging toward me bouncing on the balls of his feet, I took a few steps backward and bowed politely. The minister bobbed his prominent head as he spoke, and I was pleased to see that Nhu, like myself, bore the dark eyes and eyebrows, the pale complexion, the high cheek bones and thin lips of the Chams who look more Polynesian than Vietnamese."

R-3 impatiently leaned forward and encouraged Bao to get to the point saying, "You needn't have been concerned. Many things are in your favor and have long aided you in avoiding detection as a communist—your family's Catholic background, their anti-communist views and their being followers of Diem's brother, the arch bishop."

Bao replied, "Yes, I know. And I remember the many times I have made a show of renouncing communism, despite my early joining of the Viet Minh to fight the French colonists, and later my supposed defection. Since then I'd joined the Army of the Republic of Vietnam (ARVN) and have risen in rank, disguising my communist affiliation.

"But because of my early background with the Viet Minh, I felt an unease asking for a more responsible position in the South Vietnamese government. I was nervous, *Ayr Ba*, that, if asked, I couldn't describe an actual relationship with the arch bishop. But if so, I'd have had to say that regretfully I'd not seen him since my confirmation some years back. But then I could add that my father had been in touch with his holiness and together they discussed whether I could be of assistance to our president and the fatherland. I could say this truthfully, because this is what my father has hoped for at least."

R-3 reassured Bao that he needn't worry as the document verified his story, and he had seen to it that word of Bao's ambitions in the Diem regime had been spread widely both in Hue and Saigon, pleasing his family as well. But Bao was still leery of the chance of being discovered using half-truths, although his life as a double agent was a choice he had made long ago.

Bao hurried on with his narrative, "What, I thought, would I say if asked what those who knew me in Hue would say about my trust worthiness? I decided I would tell the truth and reply that they'd tell him that in my youth, despite my confirmation, I was wild, more interested in girls than my studies at the *lycee* in Saigon. I would go on to say that only during the August revolution of 1945 was I awakened politically and joined the fight against the French, losing an eye for my troubles. But I would conclude by saying that since then I had seen clearly why our fatherland needs patriots like

President Diem and his brothers if we're to remain free."

"Did he actually ask you these questions?" asked R-3.

"No, thankfully he did not. But the document did note my brother's connection with the communists. Duong had defected to the North and serves in the position of an ambassador for the Ho Chi Minh regime. It made me feel even more uneasy, especially because of our early service in the Viet Minh."

R-3 replied, "Don't worry, Bao, it's common knowledge that many did fight with the Viet Minh against the colonialists, believing their nationalist loyalties would rid Vietnam of the Bao Dai collaborationist government with the French. But when the Diem regime eventually displaced the French, many who fought with the Viet Minh became loyal supporters of the Republic of South Vietnam under Diem's presidency."

Bao replied, "That's true. The hatred we Vietnamese felt toward the French rose up again when they tried to reassert their control over our country at the end of the global war. It was the reason so many of us were caught up in the fight against them. At the time, brother Duong and I would've joined the devil himself to rid our homeland of the evils of French colonialism. Although untrue, I would've said that I regretted this association with the communists, and, like a repentant son, renounced the Viet Minh and returned to my Catholic upbringing and benefactors."

R-3 then asked how Bao would explain his brother's opposite choice."

Bao replied, "I would say that unfortunately, Duong renounced the church and substituted the Marxist lie as his salvation."

"Don't worry, Bao. I think the reason you weren't asked these questions that so concerned you is that they already knew the answers to them beforehand," remarked R-3.

"So the interview was perfunctory, even though I was told my credentials had to be checked according to regular security procedures. Perhaps I was summoned only to look me over."

R-3 observed, "That's what I surmise given such a short interview. And now we must wait to see what their next move will be!"

Bao responded, "But all was not lost, *Ayr Ba.* When I left the Counselor's office, as I stepped into the corridor, I saw three children. There were two boys about 14 and 10 in age, each holding the hand of a little girl between them. She was three at most.

"Then on my blind side I caught the fragrance of expensive French perfume before turning to see the petite woman who smiled at me from beneath dark, wispy bangs that touched equally dark eyebrows. She pointed a finger at me, and her long mandarin-type nails decorated with pink polish nearly came in contact with my eye patch."

"So, you met Madame Nhu and her children, too, except for her oldest daughter," responded R-3. "Perhaps that was the opening to your most crucial interview. What happened next?"

Bao continued, "It was indeed Madame Ngo Dinh Nhu. I must admit I was stricken with her beauty, and I found myself speechless."

Bao knew better than to extol Madame Nhu's charms to R-3, but he thought how wrong both the Americans and communists had been in their public descriptions of her. Instead of a 'dragon lady,' relying on cosmetics and a manicured appearance to hide an unrevealed shallowness, he saw only a fiercely proud women whose entire five-foot frame exuded a royal elegance. In that moment he decided the personal attacks on her sprang from jealousy. Never had he seen such finely chiseled features in so delicate a countenance. Her dark, almond-shaped eyes, high cheek bones, full lips, invited further exploration. He saw how her pink silk *ao dai* clung to her body all the way down to her high-heeled French shoes. Up until this moment, Bao had thought the women he had met in Paris had no peers. Yet Madame Nhu was more than a match for them, and the realization struck pride in his Vietnamese heart.

Bao could see R-3 was becoming inpatient, so he continued, "Madame Nhu's son asked about my eye-patch his mother had pointed to."

R-3 responded, "I trust you were very careful with Madame Nhu and her children. Undoubtedly, her impression of you is very significant."

"Indeed, I could see the calculation of her silent evaluation of me in her beautiful eyes, so I decided to avoid the truth of my injury as a Viet Minh and instead couch my answer in a story for her children. Should I repeat it for you, *Ayr Ba*?"

At that moment, they were interrupted by a waitress who replenished their drinks.

When she left, R-3 said, "We have been here quite a while, Bao, and I hesitate to prolong our conversation any longer and perhaps raise unwanted suspicions. But it's important that I gauge Madame Nhu's perception of you. Go on."

Bao said, "I kneeled to come to eye level with her children and started spinning my tale. I told them that when I was a boy of ten, I used to walk around with my head tilted toward the sky, my eyes looking at the clouds in the day, or the stars at night. I mentioned that my father had warned me to lower my sights or harm would befall me, but that I paid no attention, until one night when I fell into a deep ditch, striking my eye on a pointed stick placed there by the communists to injure boys like me. Then I paused to see if my tale was connecting with the children. I was encouraged by the interest shown in their eyes."

"What was Madame Nhu's reaction?" asked R-3.

"She didn't cut me off, but was clearly impatient to have me finish."

"As I am," commented R-3.

Bao continued, "So, I told them that in the hole with me were a lot of other young boys much worse off than me, because both their eyes had been struck with the poison-tipped sticks. I said I found myself trapped by the communists in the hole with all these blind kids whining and wailing about our fate, until one day a maiden with eyes bright enough to melt the snows of Dalat came to the pit and peered down at us. I remarked that I had wondered if she had been watching us all along.

"I sensed their mother was becoming quite impatient, so I hurried on with my story. When the children asked the maiden's name, I appeared as if I were trying to remember her name when the name suddenly came to me, and I said that if I was not mistaken, it was Tran Le Xuan. I said, 'Yes, 'beautiful spring.' That's it! How could I forget something so fitting?'

"Immediately her children commented that name used to be their mother's name. 'Well, imagine that,' I said."

"So I continued my imaginary story saying that Tran Le Xuan scolded us about looking up in the sky, so we couldn't even see our own feet, or where we walked. Then I told them that this goddess spoke directly to me and said, 'Bao, you foolish boy, stop whining. Though it be true that two eyes see more in a panoramic sense, yet a one-eyed advisor to those who are blind has all that's needed to aim at some mark for the common good. It was then that Madame

Nhu clapped her hands and instructed her sons to take their sister to play."

R-3 asked, "Did Madame Nhu see you only as 'Charmer of Children,' or did she also discern your true mission as an applicant seeking a position?"

"I'm sure she knew who I was and what I wanted, and she only indulged my imaginary tale for the sake of the children. But I hoped that she could see my light-hearted approach would be helpful to the Diem regime in dealing with the Vietnamese peasants. However, I left the Presidential Palace with the feeling that my request would at least be considered."

R-3 looked thoughtful, and then he said, "In South Vietnam, Counselor Nhu is the tough guy who does the unpleasant work and is vilified to spare his brother. But as the head of the new Strategic Hamlet program in which the Diem regime places great hope, Nhu's perceived persona could be a detriment to the endeavor.

"As we've planned, they can't miss seeing a great benefit from taking advantage of your engaging personality as their front man to interact with the public in administering the Strategic Hamlet program. The peasants are sure to resent being relocated into strategic hamlets. And they can't help but think your talents can also be put to good use in dealing with the Americans, themselves childish in understanding our ways. You have done well today, Bao, but we'll just have to patiently await the results of your interview," said R-3.

"I'm privileged, *Ayr Ba*, to be able to contribute to our great revolutionary cause in this way," remarked Captain Bao.

R-3 thought a minute and then said, "This chess move of ours has great strategic significance for our revolution. If you succeed in securing a position in the Diem government, you will be in a post of tremendous influence if chosen to help administer the Strategic Hamlet program, such as I am in my position. If so, together we shall set a true course toward reuniting our fatherland."

"Your trust in me will be fulfilled, *Ayr Ba*, and though the double life I have led up to this point will be increasingly fraught with danger, I take comfort that we would be traveling the same pathway."

"But yours could be the harder course, Bao, for I remain hidden from all sides, while you will be exposed at every turn."

"Yes, Supreme Leader, the brazenness of my being so open in

our cause with our comrades in the field has served to solidify my position as your adjutant. But even now my hidden double life often confuses those who do not know me outside our worthy revolution. They are apt to consider my humor and daring as mere naïve foolishness not to be taken seriously."

"True. But up to now, you have been able to move freely without disguise among our comrades, but should you gain a position in the Strategic Hamlet program, it will change everything and require your total attention. Regretfully, then your field service with our comrades must be terminated. Sometimes, we must give up one freedom to bolster another."

"There's only one freedom for me, to serve you in our noble cause."

"Commendable. But if you secure such an important new position with the enemy, it will severely test both freedom of movement and freedom of will. It is the latter that concerns me most."

"Sir, help me understand where I've ever failed you on either score."

"Maybe I should explain this differently. Consider a needle drawn to a high power magnet. Would you say the needle is free?"

"Most certainly not."

"Why?"

"It must obey the force of the magnet."

"Exactly. Now in the absence of this compulsion, that is, removal of the magnet, can we say the needle is free?"

"Yes, free in its function to any who have need of its use, but only if it is separated from the magnet."

"So if the needle were a person, rather than a metallic object, one's freedom, without the presence of a strong force, would depend on one's will to resist temptations offered by others."

"Yes, I begin to see, sir. To resist the enemy wherever we encounter him is our true freedom. For the greatest power lies in our own internal force that an enemy cannot control."

"To your clear thinking, I would add only the words of the ancients which mock us still—'freedom is only the dream of the falling sand.' You must remember this when tempted by the enemy."

"I can't help but regret the termination of my post as your adjutant, *Ayr Ba.* Isn't there a way to remain a secret delegate to the field rallies, even if I should be embedded in the heart of the enemy's plans? This would keep me closer to our subversive actions and your wise counsel, sustaining my resolve."

"No. It is already too late. Your double identity as ARVN Captain Bao and being known to our followers as Adjutant Bao as well is not compatible with a high profile position in the public eye. You must appear beyond reproach. Any slight slip up could only attract unwanted attention on both sides, cause confusion and provoke loyalty questions. Your former comrades would want to know what had happened to Adjutant Captain Bao, whom they have been aware is also an ARVN infiltrator, but, if all turns out well with your interview, your new position as a trusted administrator of the Diem government must be believed by all on both sides."

"And what will my comrades be told when I no longer show up beside you in their encampments?"

R-3 paused, sliding deeper into the shadows, his voice barely audible. He continued, "We shall tell them you have defected to try to secure a higher rank in ARVN and an important position offered by the enemy."

Bao wiped sweat from his forehead, took a gulp from his drink and then started coughing uncontrollably. Finally regaining his composure, he said, "But, this means my friends in the movement will revile and curse me, even try to kill me."

R-3 responded, "We must let them vent such anger. The greater the display of hatred directed at you as the former comrade captain, my adjutant, who has traded up for higher rank and position, makes you more credible in everyone's eyes as the ambitious Bao. All sides will believe they know your price. Trust me though, no bodily harm will come to you from our side as long as you continue to follow my instructions. Meantime, you must learn to delight in what you have and desire not what is closed to you. Only then is the commitment totally within your power to perform."

"Then, my interview at the Presidential Palace today with the outcome we desire will seal my fate!"

"Yes. But while you wait to get an answer from the Diem government, I want you to go to Loch Ninh and covertly contact the resistance forces there on your last mission as you have always done as my representative. You will be given documents shortly to deliver. But we must end this discussion before its length I fear has already raised suspicions. Have you other questions, Captain Bao?"

"Yes, sir."

"Well, go on."

"When will I see you again?"

"This is our last meeting. Until our forces prevail over the enemy, we must communicate by courier."

"And who will be my contact, *Ayr Ba*?"

"You know the curio shop on Tu Do Street?"

"The one specializing in chess sets from the Philippines?"

"Yes, that one. On the second Tuesday of each month, go there and ask for a portable chess set with your name on it. If I have any message for you, it will be inside the secret compartment on the bottom of the set. Otherwise, the proprietor will tell you she has no such item."

"What if I need to contact you, Wise Leader?"

"That you must not do except in an extreme emergency. But if a life or death matter arises, follow the same procedure. Madame Binh, the female proprietor, who brings you the chess set, will also show you how to conceal your message and will get it to me straight-away. What else is on your mind? I see puzzlement in that one good eye of yours."

"I was just reflecting on my visit to the palace this afternoon and wonder what will happen to Diem and the Nhu's when we come to power."

"That's nothing to be concerned about. Like the Russian Czar Nicholas and his family, they must perish to fertilize the revolution."

"All? Including Madame Nhu and the children?"

"Especially that devil woman, my dear Bao. Need I remind you, she helped thwart the 1960 coup by influencing her brother-in-law into resisting the military's demands? Don't tell me you have succumbed to her charms like the general who publicly boasted he would make her his concubine following the next coup d'état?"

"Oh no, *Ayr Ba.* No such thought entered my mind."

"Then why bring it up?"

"You've never asked me to kill women or children. Perhaps you'll find someone more suitable to the task."

Bao felt R-3's hand rest on his own. He grew uneasy at the icy touch, realizing that the face in the shadows remained as cold as this gesture.

"Relax, my young comrade," said R-3 now patting Bao's hand, "when the time comes, you'll have your hands full with the coup. Leave the others to me. What's this? That unsatisfied eye bespeaks further concerns. Be quick about it. I really must go."

Bao pulled his hand away pretending to stir his drink. He was glad to change the subject.

"If I secure this new assignment, I'll have to work with the news media—something foreign to me." Aware of his trembling fingers, he raised the glass to his lips.

"You need not fear this pack of untrained dogs," said R-3. "Keep your wits and sense of humor, remembering that journalists, especially those from the West, can be fooled by a subversive, but charming double agent like you, who can provide them with information they seek to fill their daily news deadlines. Except for one, they are like so many needles drawn to a magnet."

"And who is the one, sir?"

"The American, Winston Brand of the *Times*, who writes a weekly column as he searches for the truth in his interviews. He's on his way to Vietnam and will arrive soon. We're keeping an eye on him and will see if what he uncovers is useful to us. If not, he, too, will cease to be a problem."

7 NEAR MISS

But the bravest are surely those who have the clearest vision of what is before them, glory and danger alike, and yet notwithstanding go out to meet it.

—*Thucydides*

TOM KEARNEY FIDGETED UNCOMFORTABLY in his seat as Maria passed by with a tray of coffee. She hadn't spoken to him since the plane departed Hawaii more than two hours earlier. It disturbed him to see her now bend over the laps of two soldiers pouring coffee from a silver decanter. Seated on the aisle four seats back, he could see her tight fitting blue uniform slide a couple of inches above her knee. Her tapered buttocks protruded into the aisle and her thin ankles turned provocatively toward him like a golfer who has just teed off. He tantalized himself for a moment by imagining how splendid it would be to have his arms around her slim waist with his fingers interlaced and resting on her smooth, round cheeks with her ankles wrapped around his back.

He had carried this vision over from last night. Before their layover at the hotel ended, he had counted on seducing Maria. But something had gone wrong, and several things still puzzled him. She had arrived in the bar jittery, like a cat on a high wire, demanding to leave after one cocktail. He had insisted she stay for two. Still, she had sat there colder than the ice in his glass of Scotch.

Thomas Aloysius Nathaniel Kearney, Jr., refused to believe any woman could reject him, unless of course, she was in the middle of her period. That cranky time of the month seemed to be nature's way of getting even with Kearney for being born rich, moderately handsome, and endowed with an overload of hormones. Convinced he had accounted for Maria's coolness, nevertheless his thin lips turned into a downward arc with the thought of Maria's rejection, and he leaned his head into the aisle.

"Is your neck bothering you, Tom?" said a deep voice from behind him.

Kearney turned and came face-to-face with Alex Spear.

"Er, no, sir, Major. I'm just trying to order a cup of coffee."

Out of the corner of his eye, Kearney saw Brand seated beside Alex. When both men chuckled, Kearney felt his face turn crimson from neck to forehead. Their merriment at his expense, he thought, cleared up a piece of the puzzle for Kearney. Earlier during the inspection of the plane before take-off, Major Spear had been unusually cordial to him. The major had told Kearney:

"Tom, the Pentagon tells me you're the best man in this explosives business and that you've handled the big stuff since you were 16 in your old man's plant. Give this aircraft the same attention you gave that pretty little flight attendant last night, and we'll all get to Vietnam safely. For a while, it looked like Miss Monclova was going to get away from us, but I'm glad someone succeeded in changing her mind." The major then did a strange thing. He had winked at Kearney.

"That's it!" Kearney thought. Somehow Spear and the reporter knew he had failed to score with Maria during the layover. Now they were laughing at him. He remembered what his father, Tank, Sr., had told him all his life growing up in Massachusetts. "No matter how trivial the matter, a Kearney, once made the butt of a joke or held up to ridicule, retaliated until the offender and the offense were both obliterated from memory."

Tom Kearney, Jr., or Tank, Jr., to his classmates at Whitfield College, saw the family dictum applied in his senior year. During the telecast of a football game, a sideline camera caught Tank, Jr., seated on the team bench slyly trying to lift up a cheer leader's skirt. For days afterward, his teammates greeted him with "fumble fingers." Then one day Tank, Sr., turned up with six other wealthy alumni and persuaded the college administration to accept their support for soccer rather than football. The senator donated land for the new sport, contributed a trophy named the "Kearney Cup" in honor of his son being named the first soccer team captain, and funded scholarships for the younger Kearney's successors in that position. Kearney, Sr., and alumni sponsored the soccer program as well. In time, football faded. The new sport caught on and the Kearney name and reputation as its benefactor flourished beyond Tank, Sr.'s, expectations, except some of the old timers ridiculed the new sport as the old man's way of helping his son keep his hands to himself.

Whitfield owed its existence to the Kearney Munitions Plant, the town's largest single employer. The senator boasted to his colleagues in congress that three-fourths of Whitfield's population of 27,000 lived on Kearney money. In case any Whitfieldians had a short memory, Tank, Sr., returned every year from Washington to present the Kearney Cup and remind them in a thick, exaggerated-for-the-occasion Irish brogue, "Ya know well who 'tis butterin' your bread."

The only other time he set foot in his hometown or ventured into nearby Boston came during the week of campaigning for his senate seat every six years. Democrats from across the state held all night sing-alongs, testimonial speeches, and integrated clambakes with both Irish and Italians in attendance. Reading about it in their local newspaper, Whitfieldians took it all in stride, proud their community had sent a man of growing national stature to the senate for three terms. After Kennedy, there was even talk of a Kearney presidency, despite the political sentiment against choosing successive candidates from the same state.

Whatever his thoughts on this matter, Tank, Sr., kept them to himself, preoccupied as he was with America's headlong plunge into the French fiasco in Vietnam. He had supported Ike's military aid to the French in the early fifties, hoping that would be enough to turn the tide of communism sweeping across Southeast Asia. After the Viet Minh victory at Dien Bien Phu, he advised the president to cut America's losses and get the hell out of Asia. Kearney's lone opposition came from Vice Admiral Willoughby Brand, who wanted NATO to save the French from defeat. "Preposterous," stormed Kearney in a Senate speech. "We're not going to let some senior American advisor in Paris lead us into World War III. Get that guy's name. We'll want to remember it when he comes up for promotion."

Kearney also disagreed with the new, young president's policy of increasing American aid for the war in Vietnam, a policy at first kept out of the public eye as much as possible. But sometimes, when needed for political advantage, Kearney switched positions clamoring for whatever it takes to rid the area of the Red menace.

Tank, Sr., surprised his Washington colleagues and Whitfieldians as well, however, when he suddenly returned home in December 1961 with no election in sight and months before award of the next Kearney Cup. Attributing this change in schedule to urgent family matters, the senator secluded himself at the family estate.

"Urgent, indeed," claimed the gossip reporter who broke the story. Tank, Jr., had impregnated demure and naïve Carlotta Simoni, the mayor's daughter. Kearney, Sr., berated his son both privately and publicly for getting the 18-year-old girl pregnant. At a joint meeting of the Italian War Veterans Club and The Society of Transplanted Italian Ladies of Whitfield, the senator proclaimed his son would do the honorable thing and marry the woman who carried his grandchild.

"Tis a proud thing, no matter what the circumstances," he told the Society, looking straight at the weeping Mrs. Simoni as he spoke, "to join together Massachusetts' two great ethnic groups, the Italians and the Irish, and at the same time forge closer relations between your senator in Washington and your mayor here in Whitfield. After the wedding, it will be 'Erin go Bragh' and 'Viva l'Italia.'"

But privately he told his 26-year-old son, "If you'd used protection, that barely-old-enough senorita wouldn't be walking around Whitfield, getting everyone's sympathy and putting us in this helluva mess! Why'd you have to rob the cradle with the mayor's daughter? He's a good Democrat with a lot of voter appeal, and she's too young and thin to have caught your eye. We'll have to think of something to get you out of this, son."

In the end, just as the Whitfieldians expected, the senator found a way to extricate himself and his son.

"My boy's more patriotic than anybody here," he told Post 132, Whitfield American Legion. "Yesterday he withdrew his ROTC deferment, requesting an immediate assignment in Vietnam. In case you haven't heard, there's a little war going on there. Until it's settled, other things, like his planned marriage to the mayor's daughter in February, will have to take a back seat. War's a dangerous enterprise, and I give the boy credit for not wanting to leave a weeping wife behind, worrying about his safety every day. Mayor Simoni and I agree the wedding of these two fine youngsters will just have to wait 'til Uncle Sam is finished with the boy, and he comes home safely. Love for country is stronger than any other emotion to us Kearneys."

Both Kearney, Jr., and Carlotta Simoni left town the next morning. One went to a crash course at the Ordnance School in Aberdeen, Maryland. The other was packed off to a convent in Canada to discreetly await the one thing that couldn't wait—the birth of their child.

Lieutenant Kearney slumped back in his seat and closed his eyes. He would have the last laugh on Brand and Spear. His father would get the telegram he intended to send when he reached Guam, and in it would be a request to do something about these two men who dared cross a Kearney. The thought pleased him, and he looked up smiling at Maria Monclova as she passed by his seat, her hip bumping against his elbow he extended in the aisle.

After stops at both Wake Island and then Guam, Flight 740 waded into the dark sky like a silver night heron bent on putting space and distance between itself and the choppy waters of the Pacific below. As she had done at Wake Island and with every take off over the Pacific, Maria Monclova, concealed in the lavatory, clutched the wash basin so tightly her knuckles turned white. She glanced in the mirror, recoiling at the terror revealed in her face. Ashamed, she loosened her grip to cover her face with her hands, at the same time trying to blot out the sound of the struggling engines and the rushing wind as the plane fought to gain altitude. Crashing into the Pacific was the only real fear she had ever known.

The terror had begun at age 12. One evening her father came to her room and sat beside her on the bed, his hands trembling as he puffed nervously on a cigarette. She noticed his face was the same color as the burnt ash. She wanted to cry out, "Has anything happened to mother?" But instead she waited for him to speak. He took her in his arms and stroked her long, black hair.

"Precious," he said in a broken voice. "It happened over the Pacific on takeoff from Wake Island. The engines failed. Your mother was on that plane returning from her visit to the States. There are no survivors."

Later that evening she had tossed and turned in a tearful, nightmarish sleep. She dreamt that a pterodactyl had swooped down from a black sky, grabbed her budding young breasts and carried her off into the darkness with horrible shrieks of delight, only to drop her into the dark waters below into the flailing arms of her mother. She woke up screaming, and it was all her grief-stricken father could do to comfort her.

Together they tried to erase the traumatic vision of that night from memory, but for Maria, during flight attendant training, the nightmare returned. Despite her fears, she got through training, concealing the fact that take-offs over water left her gasping for breath and shaken.

Once she had quit flying for several months to clerk in a department store, but decided to return to the airways in order to meet the problem squarely. She had succeeded in reducing these fear attacks to two geographical areas, Wake Island and Guam, both in the vicinity of where her mother perished. Though she hated to be alone when these seizure-like attacks occurred, the airplane lavatory was a convenient place to hide her fear.

Maria reached for the wash basin again as an ear-splitting explosion, like the sound of an artillery piece fired at close range, shook Flight 740 from cockpit to stabilizers. The nose of the aircraft pitched sharply downward while the wings yawed to each side like the balance pole of a high wire walker. Maria's scream might have been lost in the sound of the explosion if Alex, who was already reacting, hadn't seen the lavatory door fly open and the woman tumble forward, striking her head on the galley counter.

"Winston, see to the flight attendant back there. Kearney, check those starboard engines. Everyone else keep your seat belts fastened," Alex shouted as he worked his way toward the cockpit.

Although the galley was only about ten feet from his seat, the aircraft was weaving so wildly, it took Brand nearly a minute to reach the unconscious woman. Another minute passed before he located her pulse. Satisfied she wasn't dead, he cradled her in his arms and maneuvered his way back to the nearest seat. She gave a barely audible moan as he gently brushed her hair back away from her face. His hand came away moist with blood. After a moment's search through the long black strands, he found the open cut just above her ear.

Because of her position on his lap, he couldn't reach his

handkerchief. To stop the bleeding, he pressed her head tightly against his chest and could feel the blood soaking through his shirt. When she opened her eyes, Brand saw the frightened stare that indicated the early stages of shock.

"It's all right, honey. You've just had a nasty bump. Try to lie still if you can."

"Have we crashed?"

"No."

"I've got to go to my passengers."

"They're big boys. They can take care of themselves. You just lie still."

"Are we on a boat?"

"No, the pilot must be trying to level off this crate."

"Then why is my hair wet?"

Brand pressed his lips against her forehead. "No more questions from you. Lie still."

A few minutes later, Brand felt a tap on his shoulder. He turned to see the queer-looking navy lieutenant commander Alex had identified as a doctor standing in the aisle.

In a cheerful voice, the officer said, "Jenicoso's the name; surgery's my game. Anything I can do?"

The commander's thin face, sagging jowls and protruding stomach all seemed to defy gravity as he moved deftly on pipe stem legs and pigeon-toed feet. Brand gave the officer an incredulous look. Up close, Nick Jenicoso had that effect on everyone. Like a scarecrow improperly stuffed with hay in a ludicrous way, the commander's thin head would have come to rest on his chest were it not anchored on one end by a double cowlick at forehead and crown and on the other by the pendulous jowls.

Stretching to his full five feet, eight inches, the doctor retrieved a blanket and pillow from the overhead bin. "Here, we'll cover her with this," he said to Brand, shaking his head from side to side so that the cowlicks formed what looked like to Brand a two handled water pitcher. "Believe me, I don't think we need worry about her going into deeper shock, since your body warmth and this blanket should alleviate that concern."

Brand blinked uncertainly. "Alex must have sent you back here, Doc."

"That's right, and I'd better make myself useful before he decides to lighten this plane by tossing excess baggage overboard."

He chuckled, then instantly turned serious. "Did you see what happened?"

"Struck her head, just above the left ear, I think. At least that's where all the blood seems to be coming from." Brand noticed how expertly Nick Jenicoso's fingers moved over Maria's head.

"Believe me, head injuries bleed profusely, but you probably know that from your own experience." The doctor eyed Brand's own bandaged head. "Don't think she's suffered a concussion though. The pupils in those beautiful blue eyes seem normal. We might put this pillow under her head to elevate it a little more."

"It's all right, sugar," Brand said as the commander maneuvered the pillow into place. "The doctor knows what he's doing."

"Believe me, that's right, young lady. Your job is to think of those palm-lined shores of Guam. That's where we're heading now, you know. Back to Guam with a tailwind. Heard the pilot say so to Major Spear. Also something about feathering an engine or two, or losing altitude. Believe me, everything seems to be under control now."

As he spoke, Jenicoso reached in his bag for supplies. He worked quickly to cleanse and bind the woman's head wound, chatting amiably with Brand all the while. "We'll get her some stitches at the hospital in Guam, and believe me, the two of you will sport matching bandages before this day is over." Brand chuckled at the doctor's cheerful humor. The shaking of his body caused Maria to stir.

"There, how's that, Miss?" The doctor applied the finishing touches to her wound.

"I feel better, doctor. Can I get up now?"

"No, that wouldn't do at all. We need you to stay warm and calm right where you are in this gentleman's arms until we get safely back to Guam."

"Oh, dear," she sighed.

"Believe me, your spirit sounds a little low. I think we can do something to patch that up as well."

Jenicoso moved with alacrity as he produced a ukulele from his black bag. "This is the best tranquilizer I can prescribe under the circumstances." He sang out huskily plucking at the ukulele, "Down among the sheltering palms, oh, honey, wait for me; oh, honey, wait for me." Soon he was joined by two soldiers. Then others on the plane began taking up the tune.

Brand watched as Jenicoso strutted up and down the aisle, a wandering minstrel, encouraging the frightened passengers to join in song. Maria raised her head slightly.

"What's he doing?" she asked.

"Our strange doctor friend is now leading a sing-a-long."

"He's wonderful," she sobbed. "He's doing what I should've done. He's calming everyone."

8 INTERLUDE

Read the things of the flesh with the eyes of the spirit and not the things of spirit with the eyes of flesh.

—*Zoroaster*

FROM OUTSIDE THE WINDOW of the military guest quarters, Brand heard the surf striking the rock levy below. There followed the swishing sound of sand tugged reluctantly back into the Pacific.

For the past three days, Brand marveled at how Guam survived against the merciless, incessant pounding of the waves. Gratified at his own turn of fortune, he realized how close the plane came to crashing, relegating all on board to the mercy of the sea. He totaled the other bits of serendipity that had buoyed his spirits since the near tragedy. He had used the time to complete his first column on the Vietnam war. Maria had thoughtfully returned Willie before the ambulance took her to the hospital, and although he had cleaned the flask for any possible poisonous residue and replenished it with bourbon, he had not had a drink since Hawaii. One problem remained unresolved.

He cursed the surf, blaming it for his call not getting through to New York. Two more hours delay and he could forget Sunday's column. He wanted a drink real bad. Yet he knew the slightest slur in his voice once the call came through would panic the Sanhedrin, a term he coined for the *Times* senior editors. This he couldn't afford. Not this early into the Vietnam assignment. In retaliation, the Sanhedrin would assign a younger reporter to dog his steps. He had seen it happen to other Pulitzers. They kept their by-lines for appearance's sake, but some young punk straight from journalism school wet-nursed them through the important assignments. The tip-off came when one of the editors suggested the seasoned reporter take along a younger man for on-the-job training.

Brand grabbed the phone the instant it rang.

"I have your party in New York," said the operator. "Go ahead, please."

"Louie, Winston Brand. Got my column ready. I'll shoot it to you over the phone."

"Where in the hell has it been?"

"I've been trying to get through to you since Thursday. We had an accident with the plane. Had to turn back to Guam. All the troops on board must've had the lines tied up calling home until this evening."

"What kind of accident?"

"An engine exploded."

"Was it sabotage?"

"The experts don't think so. They're going over it now. The aircraft won't be ready to fly for another day."

"Why didn't you cable your copy?"

"Same problem with the telephones."

"Bullshit."

"What do you mean by that?"

"You've been stoned for the past three days. That's why your copy's not here."

"Do I sound like I'm drunk?"

"No, but that doesn't mean a thing."

"It means I can give you this story if you'll cease and desist with your suspicious nature."

"Don't get tough with me, Brand."

"Okay, Louie, you're the boss. Look, do you want this story or not?"

After a pause, Louie Cohn replied, "Late as it is, I'm ready to take it down. Read slowly. Damn it!"

Brand read:

> Just how different the Vietnam conflict is compared to other wars America fought in this century surfaced in two ways en route to that war-torn country. One is the manner

in which we transport our troops into combat. The other is the type of enemy the troops are up against.

Our boys are no longer marched up long gangplanks and onto the decks of swaying ships while crowds cheer the way they did in World Wars I, II and Korea. Today, they are quietly whisked into chartered and vintage aircraft like air mail sacks on their way to an Asian country most know little about, nor really care about. So there's no military band present to whip up a spirit of patriotism by playing sentimental soldier songs.

"Go a little slower," Cohn yelled.

There are only the sounds of a few mothers, wives, and children weeping for these loved ones who seem to slip away like thieves with the dawn. I overheard one lad tell his mother in the terminal before we departed, "I don't mind going, Mom. The trouble is nobody else gives a damn."

The kid may be right where his countrymen are concerned. More than half the Americans probably could not place Vietnam in the right continent. But in Hanoi, Peking, Moscow and some unpronounceable jungle villages, lots of characters are interested in "Johnny's marching orders." They want to know whether or not America intends to interject itself in what they want us to believe is a civil war.

According to a captured communist document lent me by my traveling companion, an alert marine major on his way back to Vietnam, the Reds have pinned their hopes for victory on a thin but durable fabric called world opinion formed through propaganda. They are convinced this tactic will work against the Americans just like it did against the French, and that before long Johnny will be sent flying right back home again with world-wide denunciation as a tail-wind to hurry him along.

To nudge public opinion along the desired path, the enemy has turned to an old weapon. Propaganda gives an extra dimension to the Viet Cong soldier. He's a jungle fighter steeped in Marxist philosophy with the whole Communist party as his international press agent.

"So far, what do you think, Louie?"

"I'm sorry I said you're drunk. You're crazy."

"Why?"

"Who's going to believe you?"

"The guys fighting this war."

"Do they buy the *Times*?"

"No, it's probably too liberal for them."

"You're just a columnist, Brand. You don't set editorial policy for the syndicate. That stuff about the world-wide Communist party backing the Viet Cong gets cut."

"If you take it out, take my name out, too. I mean it. I've seen the evidence."

"Some major's word. Who the hell is he?"

"A dedicated officer as far as I can tell, but it's not his word. It's the Viet Cong's written word. So run it."

"How come you've got all the answers so fast? You aren't even in Vietnam yet."

"I work at it, Louie, I keep my eyes and ears open and my mouth shut. Try it. Besides, if I'm wrong, you get to do the hatchet job yourself."

"You won't be around long enough, Brand. Somebody else will get you first."

"Perhaps, Louie. Now if you're ready to copy, let's get on with it."

"Okay, but don't hang up when you finish. I've got some other matters to go over."

"It's your nickel. Here's the rest of my copy:"

The Viet Cong infrastructure, a shadow government, exerts influence down to the village level in South Vietnam. Elected officials, school teachers, doctors, lawyers, agricultural workers and others who are not sympathetic to the communist desire for conquest are the targets. The South Vietnamese government recognizes the need for anti-Viet Cong efforts, but so far has made little progress in thwarting the communists' systematic, selective program of murder. At least that's how the Viet Cong outlines it in their blueprint for rebellion. Innocent civilians subject to such terrorism are not willing to cooperate with or support the South Vietnamese government.

Jungle fighters with weapons that include guerrilla warfare, terrorism and propaganda pose a new kind of challenge for American military forces advising their South Vietnamese allies. We will see how well the U.S. adapts in the days ahead.

"Okay, Winston, I've got it. Now I need to bring up the other matters. Remember when you were in Oakland, I mentioned Senator Tank Kearney, Sr.?"

"Sure, the Senate Armed Services Committee Chairman."

"He's really after your ass this time. The chief got a copy of a telegram he sent to the Department of Defense to request your accreditation be pulled."

"What in the hell for?"

"Says you're a drunken slob and a poor example to our fighting men."

"Louie, give me a couple of days in Vietnam. I know General Pavler. He'll help me work this thing out. Pavler owes my dad a favor."

"Your father was a gentleman. What makes you so sure anybody in his right mind would buck a senator to help you?"

"You don't know General Pavler."

"Oh, yeah? I'll give you a week to make your miracle. But there are conditions attached even if you get to stay."

"Like what?"

"We're sending in a guy from the Caribbean as the new Saigon Bureau Chief."

"What happened to Paul Steffans?"

"Like you, Winston, he pisses people off. Gives everybody migraines. We'll have to pull him out of there soon as we can do it diplomatically."

"Who's the new guy, and what's his background?'

"His name is Sheenar Tillerstein."

"You're making that up, Louie. Nobody has a name like that. Next you'll tell me his friends call him 'Sheet' or worse."

"Go ahead with your jokes. If you'd read other parts of the paper besides your articles, you'd know this kid made a name for himself following Fidel Castro around after the Bay of Pigs fiasco last year."

"Well, remind the Sanhedrin that Vietnam's not Latin America, and I'm too senior and seasoned to take orders from a guy covering his first real war."

"For the time being, you'll report directly to me on your column. But any hard news you develop goes through Tillerstein."

"We'll see," said Brand.

"Yes, we will, won't we, Winston? But it seems to me as your options dwindle, you'd also want to shorten your enemy list. Being in Senator Kearney's sights ought to be enough, even for you."

"Good advice, Louie. With friends like you, why worry?"

"Go to hell."

"I'm already en route, but first it's beach time."

A wave broke over Brand's knees, drenching his rolled up trousers. He shivered. The cold ocean water made him glad he had brought the blanket draped over his shoulders forming a cape. He had hoped a walk along the beach would allay the disturbing news Cohn had given him about Senator Kearney and Sheenar Tillerstein, but it did not.

"Willie to the rescue," he said to himself, but then he hesitated. He was about to return to quarters when he spotted Alex illuminated in the light at the doorway. The major thumped his pipe against the door post, then pointed it in Brand's direction. As the marine officer walked back inside, Winston saw another silhouette move out of the shadows toward him at a quick pace.

"Who is it?" he called.

There was a pause in the footsteps.

"Maria Monclova. I'd like to speak with you. Major Spear said I'd find you down here."

"That guy's getting on my nerves. He keeps tabs on everyone. You've come to the wrong place looking for someone with spare time. Can't you see I'm busy as hell checking each little wave 'til I find one big enough to wash all this ugliness out to sea and me with it." He spread his blanket on the sand.

"Why, it's a beautiful spot," she said.

"Are you kidding? There aren't any beautiful spots left any more. Man has seen to that." He fussed with the corners of the blanket, trying to hold them down against the wind.

She put a sandaled foot on the corner in front of him. He looked up and saw Maria illuminated in the moonlight, her dark hair blowing in the wind that pressed her blouse and skirt against her so that breast and thigh were outlined.

"I came to thank you for all you did for me on the airplane."

"You've got me mixed up with that odd-looking doctor. He's the one who took care of you."

"Dr. Jenicoso told me this morning as I left the hospital you had done all the right things."

The girl jumped as Brand's laughter drowned out the sound of the waves.

"Oh, God, that's a good one. Winston Brand doing all the right things. Damn, if I wouldn't like to have you for my editor."

He stood up to face her. "You're cute, sweetie, but naïve as hell. Any red-blooded American male would leap at the chance to get you in his arms. I'd almost forgotten what it was like. Check the mirror sometime and tell me what you see. No, I'll tell you. A beauty, a real beauty with just the right mixture of everything laid out in perfect form. You must have been a helluva glimmer in your mother's eye. Don't thank me. I should thank you, or maybe even Plato for pointing out that there's such a thing as beauty in itself."

"I'd better go. Please know I'm grateful to you. Sorry you insist on treating people like objects. I came here hoping if I made the first step, we could be friends. That seems even more remote after you continue to embarrass me."

"Embarrass you? Damn it, I meant to compliment you. And didn't anybody ever tell you it's impossible for a man to be friends with a woman like you? Lovers, yes; enemies, yes; friends, never!"

"Then there's nothing more for me to say, except 'don't drown.'" She turned and began to leave.

Surprised at the urgency in his voice, Brand shouted after her, "No, please don't go, Maria. I'd like to talk to someone just now. If you leave, I will drown, you know. I'll drown myself in this." He held up the familiar silver flask.

"It wouldn't be the first time, would it, Mr. Brand?"

"No, Maria, it wouldn't. But you can't blame me for hoping the last time was really the last. I'm sorry. It's not your problem. Goodnight. Thanks for stopping by."

He gave her a mock salute with the silver flask, then tossed it at her feet. "Mind taking Willie with you again? I'll pick it up tomorrow."

"Why don't you just pitch it in the ocean?" she shouted.

"I've tried that, but I always go diving in after it."

"Then you're completely hooked on alcohol?"

"Oh, no, never even think of the stuff when there's a pretty girl around to write poems for. Come, sit for a while, and I'll tell you the poem I've created for you."

"A poem for me? You're putting me on, Mr. Brand."

"Maria, I do a lot of bad things. Lying about something as heartfelt as poetry isn't one of them. Besides, I read somewhere that 'insincere emotion is the ulcer of ugliness.' Entirely out of the question where you're concerned."

"When did you write this poem?"

"Just now as you were walking away in the moonlight."

He lay back on the blanket and looked up at the star-studded sky as if it alone held his attention, but his mind was counting the steps through the sand the woman was taking back toward him. With one graceful movement, she curled her tanned legs under her skirt and joined him on the blanket.

"I'd like to hear the poem, Mr. Brand," she murmured.

"It's not quite finished, Maria. Perhaps if we talk for a while, the ending will come to me. By the way, the name 'Mr. Brand' is so formal. People usually call me 'Winston.'"

"I know you write beautiful poetry, Mr.-er-Winston. I read your book at the hospital. Major Spear lent me his copy. He said you'd also authored a book on Vietnam about the French fighting there. But he thought a woman would be more interested in your poetry."

"He did, eh? And what did you think of it?"

"He was right. I truly found it delightful writing. *Fire in the Soul* is a beautiful book. I especially liked the title poem. In fact it's something that lingers with you well after the first reading."

She began to recite:

In love, in war, in all man hath,
Above all, there's this desire,
To turn the soul on its natural path,
Away from darkness toward inner fire.
A soul afire doth wisdom make,

Forged from laws in eternal spheres,
Soul fire, cosmic fire, the two relate
To dissipate rebellious fears.
Yet, though this truth so deductive
Guides us to that higher plain,
We alone turn self-destructive
Forever lowering the inner flame.
Why choose to be so tormented
Like a furnace starved of coal,
When unhappiness is easily prevented
By stirring the fire in the soul?

"Wow! I'm truly impressed. You didn't miss a word."

"It's easy when someone arranges words like nature does roses on a trellis with the same beautiful simplicity. It's a gift that should be shared, and I'm glad you shared these treasures with others. Your book of poetry made me want to read whatever else you've written. I've always thought of poets as sensitive people, and it must be the same with you, despite…"

"My appearance or attitude," he offered.

"No, I really wasn't going to say that. Despite the fact most people can't look past your words when they sting. I've felt the bite myself. Yet, there's an unmistakable cry in your poetry, Winston Brand. How did you happen on a title like *Fire in the Soul*?"

"I owe that to Plato's *Phaedrus* where he has Socrates declare that a writer's true value lies in his ability to inscribe justice, beauty and goodness upon a soul. Fire up the reader with thoughts beyond which he or she already knows, so to speak."

"Here's a test to measure your success. Tell me if I'm right," said Maria.

"Go ahead," he urged.

"It seems to me, in this book, you are begging others to understand and measure up to life, not as it is, but as you know it should be. Although this idealistic position is unattainable, you persist in constantly reminding yourself, and others, of these ideals in contrast to our weaknesses. I don't know how else to say it, Winston, except that your poetry, especially the love poems, has a message worth embracing. It's much better than the stuff we had to read in school."

"Something tells me you're a literary critic or aesthetic genius disguised as a flight attendant."

"I did write a column for the college lit magazine."

"Too bad you didn't review my stuff. If your fellow students shared your opinion, Maria, *Fire in the Soul* might've been a runaway best seller. I can see your review of *Fire* now. It goes like this: 'Mr. W. Brand has shown us that clarity is the hallmark of poetic perfection by pressing a rose to our lips so that we taste every scented petal. Unfortunately, we come away from this experience puzzled at how and why sober society denounced this man as a drunken, sentimental, one-book poet."

"There you go again showing a low opinion of yourself. Is yours the only monopoly on misfortune?"

"I've had more than my share of life's brick bats."

"Whose fault is that?"

"Half mine and half everyone else's."

"All of us make more trouble for ourselves than others do. My father said you spend more time with yourself than any other person, so you'd better learn to get along with yourself. It shocks me to see someone dislike himself so much. I'm sorry," she quickly added. "I shouldn't have said that."

"Why not? You believe it. So why not say it? Even if it's not the truth, I admire frankness."

"I've noticed your frankness, too."

"You're being polite, Maria. Call it what everyone else does—crudity. They don't know any more than you do that my gruffness is really a partial cover-up, keeping everyone at least one person away from my heart."

"Is your heart so fragile you have to erect a barrier to protect it?"

"I didn't build it by myself. Many people have contributed. Those who are too lazy to work hard enough to win success sometimes have taken it out on me in order to bring me down to their level. Then there are the uncaring people in my life, both male and female, who wish to keep me on the bottom rung of the ladder of success to suit their own purposes.

"You know what? My navy father measured success by the number of stars collected, as if life were a kindergarten game of pleasing authority and being rewarded. He got three stars for his effort, but died broken-hearted because politicians in Washington denied him the fourth. Although shrewd in war, the vice admiral was ignorant of the hazards in a political situation. That's not going to happen to me."

"Then you don't really have such a low opinion of yourself?"

Brand picked up a handful of sand and let it drain through his fingers. "On your own background, Maria, you're about as silent as sand passing through an hour glass. I'd like to hear more about you instead of all these questions about me."

"Please, Winston, I'm hanging on every word. You're the first writer I've ever known. It's wonderful just to listen. I had forgotten that people spoke so eloquently."

He smiled at the excitement in her voice. "So had I until now," he said softly.

"Please tell me what it's like to be a famous writer."

"If it's a lecture you want, Maria, then here goes. First, you're wrong about the self-esteem issue. Every writer has a high opinion of himself, or he could never believe others would be interested in what he has to say. For a book to be good, it need only strike a chord with something familiar in the depth of the reader's soul."

"Please, tell me more. I see a dozen more roses on the trellis."

He smiled again, and the warmth reflected in his dark, brown eyes laid his own soul bare before this enchanting creature, albeit momentarily. But he caught himself. The arrogance returned and with it a change of direction.

"As a writer with a background in philosophy, I've searched for the truth in order to write about life in ways ignored by scientists who presently hold sway over the minds of the people. Together with the militarist, they use scare tactics, such as holding up a test tube of some mysterious chemical claiming it can destroy all life, including that ocean out there and the writer and woman sitting here.

"But writers know better. We'll stack the well written word up against an army's weapons any day. Eventually the guns fall silent, and the rhetoric of politicians fades. But not words of truth. Their echoes are endless."

"My father would challenge your dismissal of politicians. He works for the Philippine diplomatic corps."

"Well, maybe he's more statesmen than what I've got in mind."

"And what is that?"

"The dishonest politico, who like the scientist, and some military types, feed the people a lot of untruth wrapped in jargon that nobody understands and with promises never intended to be kept."

"So are you on a quest or crusade to make yourself understood?"

"Never thought of it in those terms. Perhaps we all are. Except the writer's the only one people understand. That's why they pay no attention to us writing the simple truth. We aren't complex enough."

"Aren't you going to Vietnam as a writer? That sounds complex to me."

He picked up more sand before answering.

"Yes, but that's different. I'm going as a reporter. There's still a need for the chronicler of military deeds, so armchair flag officers back at the Pentagon can bleed along with the troops they've sent to fight for them. The lines are more clear-cut in reporting. As long as you uphold motherhood, the editorial policy of your paper, and preach against sin, you have lots of leeway. Almost everything else is fair game. Oh, yes, avoid poetic phrases. That's considered lousy reporting."

"Then, why do you write poetry?"

"I'm afraid, little hour glass, if I answered that question, I'd get slapped again, and you pack a hell of a wallop."

"I see, so it's just a line to pick up women. But that can't be all there is to it. What if I promise to sit on my hands?" She hunched forward, then dropped back on her hands in one quick sensual motion. "Now will you reveal your real inspiration?"

He raised himself up to both knees, kneeling to face her. "First let me tell you the poem written for you moments ago. If you still need an explanation when I am finished, then I'll tell you." He began in a soft, deep resonant voice.

The soft darkness of the night looks with envy upon her raven hair.
The gentle curve of her red lips is more than the prettiest rose can bear.
The brightest star in heaven is hard pressed to match the sparkling beauty in each beguiling eye,
And when Maria walks, she seems to change the moon and rearrange the sky.
Surely, then, all nature is cast beneath her spell,

And I rather suspect that man has fallen as well,
For I watched others die of yearning from a single smile she gave.
Whence, like Mona Lisa, comes such power to enslave?

Even before he had finished, he felt she awaited his kiss. As their lips met, she responded, not in surprise, but willingly. The same warmth he had experienced while holding her in his arms on the aircraft crept back again. This time the indescribable magnetism between them pulled them closer and closer.

Soon it was hard to determine which sound was the pounding surf and which his heart as he found her lips again and again, smothering any thought of doubt for either of them. When she murmured with undeniable pleasure, he was encouraged and unbuttoned her blouse, burying his face in the warm valley between her breasts. While his hands sought out the sentinels that had filled his dreams of Eleanor, he was about to softly whisper his former wife's name.

Catching himself, Winston whispered "Maria" instead. Feelings of pure ecstasy stole into the hearts of the two wrapped in each other's arms, drawn together by desire stronger than either had ever felt before and which neither had the strength to resist. Winston mumbled that Maria needed to speak to stop their encounter before it should take them to the stars.

"Oh, Winston," she responded breathlessly. He felt her respond to him again and again, and he and the cool ocean breeze together brushed against her thighs.

Soon their hearts beat in tune with the rhythm of the ocean ever inundating the shore. Physical flame merged with "fire in the soul," lifting two spirits as one.

9 PARIS OF THE ORIENT

Conscience is not innate, but is acquired and varies with geography.
—Benedict de Spinoza

BRAND PEERED THROUGH the grill-covered bus window at the hundreds of Vietnamese filing by on their way to nowhere and everywhere. Outwardly little had changed. As he remembered from 1954, these diminutive, twig-shaped, sun-baked people were constantly on the move by foot, bicycle, motor bike, pedicab, and cycle. Given a wheel, the Vietnamese discovered a way to mount a frame over it to transport something. Surprised the years of Western influence had had little effect on the dress of the Vietnamese, he watched young women pedal by in the morning sun in traditional *ao-dais* trailing the rear panels of this silk garment like a rooster tail. The pedaling motion combined with a gentle breeze exposed sheer pantaloons that barely masked the women's long limbs from ankle to panty-covered buttocks.

"Ah'll be damned! I can't believe it! You can see women's entire ass-sets through their flimsy dresses!" exclaimed a soldier from his monkey-like perch over the bus window.

"I'm gonna like this place. When the sun shines through their dresses, you can see everything, and they say the sun always shines here," screamed a soldier hysterically pounding his seat-mate on the shoulders.

While the GIs in the rear of the bus cheered their comrades, egging them on, the officers up front feigned disinterest by staring straight ahead.

"Believe me," observed Dr. Jenicoso. "Those characters will be out raising hell tonight. Bet the VD rate runs high here."

"If you say so, Doc," said Brand.

"You've been awfully silent since we left the airport. Anything wrong?"

"No, Doc, I've just been thinking back eight years ago. I used to drive a Jeep over this same Cong Ly Street on my way to the airport at Tan Son Nhut about twice a week to get my dispatches out. The mixed Asian and French influences in Saigon all look the same to me—the broad avenues and tamarind trees, walled-in French villas, red tiled roofs and bustling open air markets where peasants hawk their goods. Even the people are carbon copies."

"Believe me, the Vietnamese women look very attractive. Of course, I haven't seen one who compares to our Maria." Jenicoso bit down on his cigar, then continued. "I'm going to miss that beautiful young woman with the charming personality. Told her I'd visit her at the airport when she flies in from the Philippines, but I doubt they'll keep me in Saigon too long. Up-country's where they need a doctor. You two seemed to hit it off well at Guam. Maybe we'll all meet again at the airport on the days you're there to file your dispatches."

"That's all handled out of the bureau in Saigon now."

"Even so, I hope you're not indicating that you're brushing off Alex, Maria and me. We've already gone through a lot together, and I'd hope it'd meant something to you. At least come by the dispensary and let me remove those stitches before I ship out."

"Sure, Doc. I value friendship as much as the next guy. Only in a place like this, it's hard to cut through egos, intrigue, plots and schemes to expose the souls in hiding. Nothing personal. My mind needs sorting out before I can make any plans beyond this week."

"Believe me, I know it's good to be alone with your thoughts now and then. I'll just clam up and enjoy the scenery."

Brand decided against sharing his concern with the navy physician about being tossed out of Vietnam by Senator Kearney, just as he had withheld this information from Maria during their farewell at Tan Son Nhut Airport. She had wanted him to commit to a future rendezvous, but he had been careful to avoid any such discussion. He could feel the uncertainty she tried to hide by the way she trembled in his arms. Not since Eleanor had he experienced the sad longing that made him want to hold on even tighter to what seemed at the moment more warmth and softness than he felt he deserved.

Then, too, pangs of guilt for having gone all the way with this beautiful woman, a stranger no less, cascaded over his conscience like a waterfall, intermittently dousing the fire in his inner soul dealing with matters of the heart. Confused and puzzled by his own actions, he wondered if Maria had felt the same overwhelming desire to suspend that precious moment for all time.

Upon further reflection, he concluded he might be wrong. The whole matter came down to raging hormones, too long unattended and heightened by the tropical setting. He wondered if they would have clung together so passionately without the shared experience of an aircraft near miss and the subsequent joy of coming through it alive. Better for both of them to get on with life without romanticizing physical desire into something more meaningful, and under the circumstances unsustainable, he decided.

With this in mind, he had tried unsuccessfully to make their last kiss perfunctory. As his lips had met Maria's during their farewell embrace, doubts and fears evaporated, replaced by such seducing warmth stealing over him it caught him off guard as it had done on the beach. Once again the fire between them had rekindled, a sort of fateful magnetism almost impossible to resist.

Yet, in the end, with great effort, he had pulled away from the warmth of their embrace and bid her farewell, leaving no word as to whether they would meet again. Outwardly, Maria appeared calm, although Brand saw in her eyes the yearning of her heart for some signal that their time together in Guam meant something special. He remembered how her face had brightened as he had handed her the copy of *Fire in the Soul* in which he had inscribed: "To Maria Monclova, beauty in itself, whose goodness deserves the praise of more than one poem."

After this episode, Winston Brand tried to be objective as his own feelings threatened to overwhelm him. Hadn't he gained two pieces of knowledge to add to his philosophy? First, only humans held the capacity to divert their minds from disaster by directing their passions toward one another. Second, no matter how false the start, man possessed a divine gift that enabled him to try again. This last point he tied into one of his mother's often stated axioms. "The good Lord never closes one door without opening another." But this time he'd have to think long and hard before he walked through the open door, weighted down as he was with so much baggage.

A nearby explosion jolted Brand out of these thoughts toward his own safety. Suddenly, the bus heaved to one side as it lifted slightly on to two wheels, forcing Jenicoso's weight against Brand, pinning him along the window. In an instant, Alex appeared at the side of the seat and began pulling the doctor into the passage way.

"That was an aerial bomb," Spear shouted. "We need to get out of here and take cover."

Once the bus righted itself, it halted along the curb and soldiers poured from the exits, diving for the hedge row in front of the steel fence surrounding the Presidential Palace. Near the main gate of President Diem's residence, three Vietnamese cyclists lay twisted among the frames of their bicycles. Blood covered the white pantaloons in several places. As he darted from the bus with Lieutenant Commander Jenicoso on his heels, Brand heard a young woman scream. Both men started toward the wounded cyclists. Brand felt a tug on his shirt and turned to see Major Spear.

"Stay down," Alex commanded. "Whoever is doing this hasn't finished."

He had barely gotten the words out when a scout armored vehicle mounting a 50-caliber machine gun jumped over the curb and began firing at an aircraft pulling up from a dive. Circling the palace, another South Vietnamese Air Force A1 Skyraider passed overhead.

"Let's see what this guy's got under his wings," called the major, turning toward Brand.

"What about those injured kids out there in the street?" asked Brand.

"Believe me," urged Jenicoso. "We should be helping them."

"Too risky right now. It looks like the other Skyraider is making a bombing run. Let's hope those Vietnamese gunners can get a bead on him before he comes our way again."

"Some welcoming committee. Do you suppose they're after us?" Brand asked.

"We're not the target. Over there, see the dark smoke. That used to be the South Vietnamese president's living quarters in the Presidential Palace."

Brand could hardly hear Alex's words, for down the street came the wail of a fire engine and out of the main gate roared a medium sized tank followed by an armored personnel carrier and two jeeps. In a few moments, the South Vietnamese firemen and soldiers had cordoned off the area, ignoring the three civilian cyclists sprawled in the street.

"Let's go, Doc. We can't let those kids suffer," implored Brand.

"I'll help. Remember, though, we shouldn't be out in the open too long," cautioned Alex.

"Let's go," Brand repeated.

Dodging military vehicles that rapidly appeared on the scene, the three men dashed into the street. Each cradled one of the young girls in his arms setting them down behind a line of trees. Overhead, Brand heard the choking, coughing sound of an aircraft engine in distress. One of the tracers had found its mark, sending one of the renegade aircraft toward the Saigon River trailing smoke.

"That's one guy who won't do any more bombing," muttered Brand, loosening the high collar on the young girl whom he had placed on the grass. He could see a superficial neck injury no doubt caused by striking the handle bars. He moved his hands across the girl's body until he felt a massive soggy spot over her right hip. A gaping wound ran from her waist across her thigh in the pelvic area.

"Hold on, sweetheart. We're going to get you some help," he said, peering into her tear stained face. Alarmed at the final stages of shock reflected there, Brand called out. "Doc, this one's badly hurt." Jenicoso was already making his way toward him.

"Believe me. We have one dead, another slightly wounded. Then there's this poor girl. We might be able to save her if I can get my bag from the bus."

"Do you need help?" Brand asked.

"I'll get the bag for you, Doc. Nothing more to do for this one," said Alex.

A few moments later, Alex returned. He handed the medical kit to Jenicoso and said he had commandeered a jeep to take the physician to the hospital with the girls needing further medical attention. The bewildered jeep driver stood beside the major. Brand heard Alex command the soldier, "*Mau len! Kiem mot cai cang.*"

"What did you tell him?" asked the reporter, surprised to see the soldier bolt for his vehicle.

"To hurry and get a litter," the major replied.

After Jenicoso had left with the two surviving girls, Brand followed Alex and the other passengers to the bus resting against the palace fence. He saw Spear pause to look at his watch and heard him say. "Attack lasted about 15 minutes by my reckoning. General Pavler might find that information useful when we brief him."

Half hour later, the bus passed under an archway labeled HQ U.S. Military Assistance Advisory Group, Vietnam (MAAG).

"Never thought I'd be so happy to be on a military post," said Brand as Alex ushered him into the head of Operation Checkmate's office.

Maj. Gen. George "Geronimo" Pavler stood feet planted apart in the center of the room like a paratrooper about to plunge out of an aircraft door. This was his "angry stance" as he called it. Members of his personal staff gave their chief wide berth once he assumed a position they knew signified Pavler had yet to make up his mind on some disturbing matter.

"I understand you gentlemen got in some combat time on the way here. Glad to see you're in one piece." The general thrust his hand toward Brand, cocking his head toward Alex as he spoke. "Winston's colleagues have already figured out the bombing attack on the palace. Nobody has had time to conduct an official investigation, but the American media is jamming the telephone lines with stories saying how Diem's enemies in the armed forces are responsible. They're fingering Buddhist officers."

He then turned and fixed his squinting eyes on Brand. "Winston, you could've set this matter straight after the investigation, but damn if you didn't get yourself in a fix with the Chairman of the Senate Armed Services Committee who's calling for your immediate ouster."

"I've heard that from my editor. And, General, if you have any idea why Senator Kearney wants to keep me from this assignment, I'd appreciate straight answers." He spoke between teeth so tightly clenched, the dimple in Brand's chin deepened and the lines in his cheeks became more prominent.

The general lowered his head. Brand recognized the tactic. When Pavler was uncomfortable with a subject, he pretended to inspect the shine on his combat boots.

"You can see your reflection, the ceiling and everything else in those boots, but by looking there, can you tell me what Kearney's up to?" he demanded.

"Tank Kearney doesn't want you here. It's as simple as that. Who am I to second guess a powerful politician? You'll have to leave on the next available aircraft."

Brand sank into one of two upholstered chairs. He dropped his head into his hands, rubbing each side of his scalp separated by the black peak that gave his face a mask-like quality. "This can't be happening. I've just suffered another mugging only this time from an old friend of my father's," he murmured.

"Are you sober enough to take it like a man this time?" Pavler asked.

Brand's head bolted upright. "Your minions exaggerate. I haven't had a drink since Hawaii. So, let's get the facts straight."

Both men stared at each other with eyes as fiery red as ball bearings caught in hot lava. Pavler was the first to turn away. "Major, I'd appreciate it if you'd leave us alone for a moment."

"Certainly," Alex said heading for the door.

Pavler walked across the room, positioning himself in front of the reporter's chair, feet still planted apart. The general's short, dark hair streaked with gray hardly moved as he shook his head from side to side.

"Winston, Winston, tell me what to do with you?" he asked, shifting to the fatherly tone Brand remembered from his youth. "The admiral tried 'til his dying day to get you to tow-the-line. God rest his soul. Am I supposed to come up with solutions for your self-inflicted problems? Why not make peace with Senator Kearney, and we'll take it from there?"

"And compromise principle? You know better than that."

"Go ahead. Let your damn principles, whatever they are, continue to alienate everybody in your life, except for your sister, that darling, sweet woman. Sure wish some of her charm had rubbed off on you."

Brand smiled, relieved that the conversation had taken a civil turn with the mention of Clementine. "You old rascal. Caught in the act. The two of you have kept in touch through the years."

"Well, she's been a damn sight more thoughtful than you."

Brand read the nostalgia in the older man's eyes. He could almost see a reflected vision of a youthful Clementine tossing her pigtails in defiance at her younger brother's attempts to tease her off the lap of GG. For a while, he too, had adopted his sister's pet name for the man the adults called George, or Geronimo. Pavler and his wife Norma visited the Brand home in Annapolis regularly when the children were young. In one of the oldest traditions of the services, Vice Admiral Willoughby Brand dispatched his trusted friend to check on the wife and kids left behind at the family estate while he trotted around the globe answering the call to duty.

Winston's mother, Candace Spencer Brand, accepted this arrangement like any fine Maryland socialite of the time. The children, however, never concealed their delight in having the Pavler's as weekend guests.

"We were all close-knit once out of necessity," said the general. Brand felt the old man had read his mind. "Maybe there's an opportunity here to bring us together again," Pavler continued. "Clemie would like that and so would I. You could've called her while in Hawaii."

"How do you know I didn't?"

From behind his back, Pavler produced a paper that he offered Brand. "Here, read this. It says it better than I can."

Brand unfolded the single page and began to read:

> Dear GG,
>
> Hope you are well in that terrible place and that "Aunt" Norma is adjusting to life in the Philippines without you, although I don't know how that could be possible. I know the separation is hard, but you must admit, it is thoughtful of the army to allow dependents to set up a household close enough to the war zone, so you can get together occasionally. For these kinds of perks, the navy remains in the Dark Age, and the marine's unaccompanied tours are even worse. At least, so I'm told. When will they learn a family too long apart causes morale problems all around?
>
> Oh, well, the point of all this is to enlist your support in tracking down wayward Winston. I called the *Times,* and they said he was en route to Vietnam and should be there by now. I thought he'd call us from the stop-over in Hawaii. They still pass here, don't they? We'd all love to see him. He needs family more than ever at this stage

in his life—you know, after the divorce from Eleanor and all. Please, dear GG, if you see Winston before I do, give him our love and take care of him as you always have. I don't like it. The two favorite men in my life, after Sean and the boys, are again in harm's way.

Sean arranged for me to send this letter by diplomatic courier to Vietnam. (Vietnamese here tell me it should be "Viet Nam." Is it one word or two?) Have you ever known Americans to get anything right regarding Orientals? Anyway slipping this in the diplomatic pouch shows the kind of priority you two guys have in our lives. Take care, and as Dad used to say, "Keep your head down."

Love, Clemie

Brand rose awkwardly from the chair. He returned the letter to Pavler then walked over to the only window in the general's office. He stood there in silence watching the military people stride confidently from one Quonset hut to another in the crowded MAAG compound. "Everything's neat and orderly in yours and Clemie's world," he said to Pavler who had joined him at the ground-level window. "You guys know how to take orders. In my business, it's not so simple. The person issuing the orders is often the problem when the truth comes out. And getting at the truth requires more trust in oneself than most of us have."

"I don't see the connection between your shabby treatment of Clemie and this quest, whatever it is, that you've embarked on."

"Well, I don't want you, nor my sister to pressure me. I'll never embrace your route-step world. I'll face my uncertainties alone, thank you." Brand flicked a finger across his nose.

"If you're going to flick your finger, I'll check my boots again."

"Touché, GG."

"Fine. Since you don't want anybody controlling you, tell me when we can expect to see you get control of yourself?"

"I'm working on it."

"Not hard enough."

"From your standpoint perhaps."

Pavler laughed. "Yes, Winston, my standpoint. That's it. Don't tell me you've forgotten the lesson I taught you so many years ago about treating life like a parachute jump. Let me repeat it for you: Stand up and be counted. Hook up with someone or something going in the same direction. Shuffle toward the door of opportunity. Jump when it's your turn to do so, and finally land on your feet safely as close to the target as possible. What could be simpler?"

Winston smiled, recalling a younger Pavler directing him off the top of the parachute jump at the state fair. The other teenagers marveled at Brand's professional landings.

"Okay, I'm trying to follow your advice. If I don't hook up with you, how else can we get around Senator Kearney's interference? Aren't we headed in the same direction on this one, General?"

"Yes, about duty, honor, country and truth, but I'll not support you on the road to self-destruction."

"I told you the drinking thing is overblown, so let's not use that as an excuse to turn your back on me."

Pavler walked to his desk. Brand heard him click on the intercom and ask his secretary to send in Major Spear. "Before Alex gets in here, I want you to pledge two things. One, you'll refrain from drinking any type of booze for at least the next 30 days, and hopefully thereafter. Two, at some time during that period, you'll write or call your sister."

"Thirty days? According to my editor and your own words, I'm to leave Vietnam immediately, *persona non grata*."

"Regardless, I want you to shake on our deal. If you have to go, you'll at least go sober. Here's Alex," said Pavler returning to his desk.

"By the way, major, thanks for getting that airplane here safely. And, Winston, before you go, I want to say again how terrible I felt when I heard about old Willoughby—I mean going through the war, and then being snuffed out like a match in an airline crash. Your mother, too. It shocked us all. Take care, son. Now get out of here so we can get some route-step business accomplished."

"Can someone drop me off at the Caravelle Hotel?" asked Brand.

"I'll take you soon as I'm finished here," said Alex.

After Brand had departed, Spear and Pavler sat across from each other in the upholstered chairs. The general listened intently as his subordinate described all that had taken place since he had last spoken to him. Only when Alex reached the point in his report dealing with the palace bombing did the general interrupt by handing the major a preliminary serious incident report that stated:

At approximately 10:20 a.m., Tuesday, February 27, 1962, two AD1 Skyraiders assigned to the lst Squadron Vietnamese Air Force (VNAF) took off at Tan Son Nhut Airport heading south toward the central part of the city. Both aircraft were armed with rockets and incendiary bombs.

At 10:40 a.m. they converged on the Presidential Palace from the southeast and southwest violating air restrictions of the capitol city. Radar at Tan Son Nhut and at the U.S. MAAG Headquarters picked up the two aircraft, but since they were immediately identified as 'friendly,' no scramble was authorized.

One of the aircraft made a low level bombing run over the palace, severely damaging the president's living quarters in the area housing his brother, Ngo Dinh Nhu and his wife, Madame Nhu and their four children.

Soon after, this aircraft was immediately engaged by elements of the Palace Guard who scored a direct hit as one aircraft pulled up from its dive. At this point, the pilot did not eject, but rather jettisoned his remaining bombs and rockets onto the street in front of the palace injuring several civilians.

Meantime, the second aircraft began its descent toward the palace when it too was struck by anti-aircraft fire. This aircraft veered away from its target, trailing smoke, rapidly losing altitude as the aircraft plunged toward the Saigon River where it and the dead pilot were recovered by the South Vietnamese Navy.

By this time, other elements of the 1st Squadron were ordered airborne and pursued the first damaged aircraft as far as the Cambodian border when they were directed to break off contact. Preliminary investigation leads us to believe that this pilot escaped by displaying extraordinary flying skills in an aircraft so severely damaged.

President Diem escaped unharmed, although his sister-in-law was slightly injured when she fell down a flight of stairs. Three members of the Palace Guard were killed as were eight civilians in the vicinity of the attack. Twenty-six other Vietnamese nationals, mostly members of the palace

> household staff were injured. No U.S. casualties were reported.
>
> Since there was no coordinated ground attack on the Palace, or at any other government facilities, South Vietnamese and American intelligence believe this attack was an isolated incident perpetrated by two disgruntled officers. The investigation continues as to why they took this action.

After he had finished reading the document, Alex handed it to the general. "You might like to know I timed the first explosion to the moment the two aircraft broke off the attack, which lasted about 15 minutes."

"That's interesting because the whole damn South Vietnamese Council of Ministers was meeting at the palace and had just recessed before the attack began. If our man, R-3, had anything to do with this, he certainly would have had time to get out of there before all hell broke loose. What I want you to do, Alex, is to try to get a list of the ministers who left the palace during the recess, and let's match this against any who were absent from the meeting with the president," said Pavler obviously delighted with the prospect the two had stumbled across a promising lead.

"Yes, sir. I'll get on it right away. But before I do, let me put in a plug for Winston Brand. He showed willingness to cooperate by providing new insight into R-3's thinking."

Pavler asked Alex to elaborate, and the major recited Brand's uncovering of R-3's possible interest in Western philosophy indicated in the documents the two had shared en route to Vietnam. Pavler clapped his hands together, then pointed them at Spear with both index fingers extended. "It'll be good for Winston to dangle in the wind on his static line for a while before we help him get his chute open."

"But, sir," the major interjected, "Have you considered the danger Brand is in if R-3 has him marked for destruction?"

"Certainly, Alex, and that's the second part of your assignment. I want you to keep your eye on Winston 'til we can figure out what R-3's got up his sleeve as we discussed earlier. That reminds me. On your way out, stop by the arms room and pick up an ankle holster and Derringer for Winston. He'll probably refuse the weapon, but leave it with him anyway. Meantime, we'll have to stall this damn senator who's gumming up the whole operation."

In his suburban villa, R-3 sat at a writing desk. The short, wide sleeve of his embroidered kimono made a swishing sound as his hand moved up and down, leaving bold strokes upon the parchment-like paper. As usual, he worked under a single lamp with his back toward the door of the study. This was to conceal his identity and actions from anyone who might be eavesdropping as he addressed the letter in front of him to the highly secretive Cuc Nghien-Cuu Trung-Uong (C.R.A.). The Hanoi-based Central Research Agency, so called by Western intelligence, operated a world-wide network whose primary focus was to support clandestine operations in South Vietnam.

R-3 began his letter:

> Comrades R-1 and R-2, by the time this message arrives, you will have heard the news of the palace bombing. Regretfully, the devil Diem and his family escaped. Yet, he must know his days are numbered, and we must remember the propaganda our side derives from this incident is enormous. Therefore, we must continue to capitalize (such an ugly word to spring from the mind of a revolutionary, nevertheless to the point) on the growing rift between Diem and his U.S. partners who will now see him as a liability in their imperialistic scheme.
>
> Speaking of liabilities, I know you will contact our comrades in Phnom Penh who are giving sanctuary to the heroic pilot responsible for bombing the palace, advising them that after a five day celebration, I recommend he be obliterated, so that no fragment of his existence can ever be traced to us. I'll have his Buddhist leader venerate him as a martyr of their cause of religious equality, stirring more hatred for Diem.
>
> Next, we shall humiliate Diem's army on the battlefield, exposing his weaknesses while our own strengths are exaggerated through the enemy's own propaganda machine. Buddhist complaints will be helpful here as well. Trust me, contrary to the reports you will see in the American press, these minor skirmishes will not be the beginning of the "Armed Struggle," only a way of sowing further confusion

in the ranks of our foes. Taken together, the assassination attempt, terrorist attacks and Buddhist unrest will serve to drive the final wedge between the puppets here and their puppeteers in Washington.

Please also trust my decisions with regard to American correspondent, Winston S. Brand. I know you are concerned he might be able to identify me based on the time he spent in Hanoi in 1954 as our "guest" recovering from his wounds. Be assured that at no time did we meet face-to-face. I was careful to observe him in secret and am convinced Brand's stubborn devotion to truth as a pseudo philosopher could prove useful in molding world opinion.

Brand is like his co-worker here, a bitter Pulitzer Prize winner apt to sew mistrust in those foolish enough to listen to him. Neither he, nor this Paul Steffans, have a head for the task and are easily discouraged. Steffans' frustration in dealing with the Diem clique has set him on a collision course, but Brand, even more of a loner than Steffans, will fall harder, for his drinking binges indicate he lacks heart for a protracted struggle. Should he prove more obdurate than anticipated, we can eliminate him at any time we deem necessary.

Please, no more messages by antique radio regarding this matter, or others of equal sensitivity. The Americans have little trouble reading our message traffic, just like they did that of the Germans and Japanese who used the same equipment during World War II. Congratulations for the first step in improving this situation. My plan to obtain American radios is on schedule. As soon as we can secure the radios needed, I shall send comrades up the pipeline to be trained by the U.S. communications specialists now in your custody. Greetings to my family.

Your comrade, *Ayr-Ba.*

When he had finished, R-3 picked up a small, wooden chessboard sitting on the desk, and opened a secret compartment into which he placed his letter. With the compartment once again concealed, the chessboard returned to its original shape as a portable travel set like those frequently used by air travelers.

Summoning his new adjutant, R-3 handed the captain the small box. He instructed the officer to deliver it to Maj. Oskar Wajonowski, Polish representative on the International Control Commission team overseeing the Geneva Peace Accords for the United Nations. "Advise Maj. Wajonowski this chess set will keep him occupied on his next flight to Hanoi. His Indian and Canadian counterparts could use a lesson in chess from the side that produces masters of the game," said R-3, inwardly pleased the diplomatic immunity afforded the ICC team member insured safe passage of his message. "My dispatch will get to Hanoi right under the nose of one of America's staunchest allies," he added.

Before retiring, R-3 composed a second message to the commander of the field headquarters in sector Queen's Bishop at the pagoda in Cholon. The directive ordered Viet Cong agents to refrain from harming or harassing U.S. and foreign media personnel until further notice. As he dispatched the order to another courier, he knew speed of execution would countermand any instructions to the contrary Hanoi might have issued through separate contacts in the Viet Cong infrastructure, especially regarding Winston Brand.

After Alex left him, Brand checked in at the Caravelle Hotel on Rue Catinat Street in downtown Saigon. In the evening he met four colleagues in the bar of the hotel. One was an over-aged reporter, who complained of stomach discomfort, and two others who were wire service correspondents with youthful faces, each with a curvy Vietnamese woman clinging to his arm. The fourth man, a weekly magazine type, sloshed down a martini, and bombarded the ash tray with an olive pit. Not one of the reporters looked as though he'd seen the sun in weeks.

"Don't you fellows ever leave the incestuous gloom of this bar? There's a war going on out there that requires first-hand reporting," Brand challenged them.

"Oh, yeah. If you come across any action, or find a Viet Cong guerilla fighter who is willing to be interviewed, let us know," replied the journalist who bombarded the ash tray with another olive pit.

"If I come across any VC needing target practice with olive pits, I'll send them to find you," retorted Brand.

His comment failed to move his colleagues, who brushed it aside, along with Brand himself. He sensed that their main interest was political and pertained to rumors of Washington's growing dissatisfaction with Diem. In that moment Brand decided the Caravelle could never be his headquarters, located as it was in the center of Vietnamese political intrigue and about as close to the war as walled off Vatican City. Tomorrow morning, he decided to move to more suitable quarters.

Alienated by the confrontation, Brand left the hotel and turned in at the first bar on Tu Do Street—a run-down cabaret called *Slice of Paris.* A slim, buck-toothed Vietnamese girl dressed in a khaki uniform stepped from the shadows and draped herself seductively along a strand of bamboo curtain that separated the filthy bar room from the filthier kitchen or back room.

"What you like drink, numbah one 'Melican?" she asked swaying toward his table.

"Got any bourbon?"

"No got birbon."

"Scotch whiskey?"

"No sootch viskey."

"Then give me a beer."

"Beer whokay," she said heading for the bar.

He was the only customer in the place, but the parade started anyway. First came a little girl about nine-years-old selling peanuts in a soiled paper napkin. He tried to shoo her away, but she remained headstrong.

"Why you no buy my pee-nots, 'Melican?" she asked with a flutter of angry dark eyelashes.

"Because you should be home in bed, young lady."

"Goddamn, sonofabitch," she screamed on her way out of the door.

"Charming young lady," Brand said to the waitress who placed a bottle on the table.

"She make beaucoup dollah from 'Melican soldier. All call her little sister. Tiche her Engleesh."

"They're doing a fine job."

He began to sip the warm beer recalling the formaldehyde flavor that came in each bottle, and who knew what else. Then he recalled his promise to General Pavler to refrain from drinking and prepared to leave with the beer almost untouched. Blocking his way stood a toothless old hag with a flower basket tucked under her only arm. She had crept through the open doorway unnoticed.

"Flowah, mistuh? Pritty flowah for pritty girl," she said as she turned her wrinkled face toward the buck-toothed bar girl.

"Not interested."

The bar girl hurried over to Brand's table to confront him. "Why you no buy me flowah? You no rike me or sumpin'? Maybe you no rike me 'cause Madame Nhu make me wear ugly suit, or other Gee Eyes speak I sick. I no sick. You look see. I no sick." She raised her short skirt and tried to grab his hand to thrust inside her panties, but Brand pulled his hand back.

He heard the old hag cackle with delight as he stormed out leaving a pile of piasters on the table. As he stepped into the dark street, a heavy object whizzed by his ear. Instinctively he hit the pavement. There was an ear-deafening explosion, followed by what sounded like a motor scooter racing its engine.

Smoke poured from the bar as he made his way back inside. Blown against a table in the far corner lay the old woman with the head of the bar girl cradled in her lap. They looked at him with deathless eyes opened wide, as if they had stared in the face of death before it struck. Coughing from the smoke, Brand stumbled outside where a crowd of Vietnamese had gathered.

"Did any one see who threw the bomb?" he asked.

There was a murmur, but no intelligible answer came from the crowd.

Brand gave his account of the story to the American and Vietnamese military policemen who arrived 15 minutes later.

They listened. Then the American told Brand, "This one's got VC written all over it. They use plastic bombs. Sorry, sir, you'll have to come along with me and answer any additional questions Major Spear might have. He's honcho in all terrorist attacks."

"Alex, the ubiquitous one," Brand muttered starting to flick a finger across his nose.

"What's that, sir?" the MP inquired.

"Nothing. I was just wondering whether your Vietnamese counterpart found out anything from any of these people as to who threw the grenade."

"The fellow who runs the flower stand across the street said he saw a young girl jump on the back of a motor scooter driven by an older man immediately after the explosion occurred."

"Incredible," Brand whispered as he mounted the jeep and spotted the peanuts strewn along the curbside.

10 FIVE OCEANS

Our minds thus grow in spots; and like grease spots, the spots spread. But we let them spread as little as possible: we keep unaltered as much of our old knowledge, as many of our old prejudices and beliefs as we can. We patch and tinker more than we review. The novelty soaks in; it stains the ancient mass, but it is also tinged by what absorbs it.

—*William James*

AT THE FIVE OCEANS Bachelor Officer's Quarters (BOQ) in the center of Cholon, three miles southwest of Saigon, Alex Spear, with a pipe protruding from the side of his lips, poured orange juice into a large glass. He handed it to Brand who sat quietly in an arm chair. Alex, dressed for bed, seated himself on the couch opposite Brand after placing a pin with a red flag attached on one of the many maps that lined the apartment walls.

"Winston, I had the MPs bring you here, because it's relatively safe and well-stocked with cool refreshment." He raised his glass. "To your health," he said and then continued. "You were nearly killed tonight, and I feel responsible for not adequately impressing upon you the seriousness of your situation. And I'm surprised you went to a bar after your talk with General Pavler."

"Alex, you're not my keeper. But don't worry, I didn't break my promise to the general. However, this clandestine horseshit is beginning to irritate me. So a maniacal little kid tossed a bomb at me for old times sake, or some other reason. Don't make an international incident out of it."

Spear clutched his bathrobe with one hand while he shook the pipe stem at Brand with the other.

"Be arrogant, Winston. Be independent. Be a loner. Be an objective correspondent, or whatever. But for God's sake, man, don't be naïve in this country. You'll never make it. Everything in the Orient happens according to somebody's plan. You were nearly killed tonight because someone wanted you dead. Why we don't know. But we do know that bomb wasn't thrown by a nine-year-old kid because you wouldn't purchase her peanuts. No, this kid has been a party member since she was seven. Little kids can throw plastic bombs, but they don't make them or plan terrorist attacks."

Alex paused, sipped from his glass, then pointed to the maps. "Each one of those red flags represents a terrorist attack conducted by military men, but espousing totally different ideologies than mine, who make the bombs in rooms like this for little kids to throw. Call it counter-espionage, counter-intelligence, counter-spying, or terrorism. It's the same dirty business, and I'm sorry you refuse to see how it involves you. For whatever reason, you're in it as far as the other side is concerned, and you'll need our protection. If you wish to stay alive, you're going to have to cooperate."

The major placed his pipe and glass on the coffee table next to a small pistol that he removed from its holster and held up for Brand's inspection.

"For starters, General Pavler wants you to carry this Derringer concealed in an ankle holster." The major demonstrated by fastening the leather strap around the calf on his own right leg.

Brand eyed the major suspiciously. "There's no way I'm going to walk around like a cowboy inviting a shootout. I told you. I'm a non-combatant and neutral in this war."

"Does that include your own safety? After all, we're talking about a guy who's been threatened, mugged and now bombed."

Despite himself, Brand laughed at the sheer number of incidents Spear had cataloged. "You've got a point, there," he conceded.

"Since it's a concealed weapon, and a small one at that, look at it as a fire extinguisher to be used only in an emergency."

"Well, you can leave it with me, but I'm not promising I'll use it."

"Good," said Alex. "Now that we've got that settled, let's turn to a more pressing matter."

"And that is?"

"How we're going to keep you safe until we find out who's behind these attacks. General Pavler recommends you stay here with me in my extra room, which will be your base of operations, as we'll have to know your whereabouts at all times."

"Are you saying I am your prisoner, Alex?" Brand was surprised at the soft, plaintive tone in his own voice.

"God, no, Winston," Alex replied.

Brand looked around him at the room adorned with multi-colored maps and the network of incidents they represented. This was not a place conducive to the creativity or contemplation he needed to do his job. Yet, he felt simpatico with this super patriot who had no doubt lived his life in a shadowy world until it came time to lay it on the line for his country. Did this war really produce men like Alex Spear, or did men like Alex Spear produce the war? Brand thought this too intriguing a question to be left unanswered, especially by a Pulitzer Prize-winning war correspondent. So, in the end, Brand acquiesced to the temporary arrangement.

There were two other reasons why Brand decided to move in adjacent to Major Spear, neither of which he wanted to state publicly. First, he felt he and Spear shared a camaraderie that comes infrequently in the life of a man. Women may count their friends on both hands, but men like Spear and Brand might have one true friend of the same sex in a lifetime, one who is never an adversary, only a person with whom adventure must be shared to make it adventurous. Brand felt it and surmised that the marine officer did as well.

The second point was more practical. The close proximity to someone like Alex Spear with his fingers on the pulse of every activity of significance could prove an invaluable news source. Brand reasoned he would pick up enough unclassified material to fill his weekly column, as well as fast-breaking news he could feed to the *Times*, providing he got to stay.

The next morning after breakfast Alex and Winston were back in General Pavler's office. Brand, dressed in his correspondent's mufti noticed the military personnel wore either khakis or fatigues in the MAAG compound or when on official duty. Otherwise, their short sleeves and slacks blended in with the civilian population which was what they had hoped to accomplish to keep their adversaries guessing as to their strength in numbers. However, the service men and women's close-cropped hair styles and youthful complexions distinguished them from their civilian counterparts among the American embassy staff and the press corps, who represented the bulk of U.S. presence especially in Saigon in 1962.

General Pavler motioned to the two men to be seated. "Glad to see you're in one piece, Winston. Nasty business, these bomb throwers. Well, gentlemen, Senator Kearney refuses to budge, leading me to believe he has a personal vendetta against Winston. The question is, what's our next step?"

"Sir, I have an alternative you might consider."

"You know, General," said Winston glaring at Alex, "this guy has a knack for butting into things that don't concern him."

"Damn lucky for you he does," admonished the general. "If you think it's none of Alex's business, you're wrong. He's also singled out in the letter I received from Senator Kearney. His crime? Consorting with 'undesirable' elements of the press. So carry on, Major," prompted the general. "Winston, try to listen. Maybe you'll learn something."

"Well, sir, as I mentioned earlier, I think I know who's fanning the flames of the senator's ire—his son, Lieutenant Kearney, Jr., who was on our flight."

"What did you two do to the boy?"

"Not a damn thing," interrupted Brand.

Alex continued as if he were thinking aloud, "Whatever young Kearney's motive is for stirring up trouble, I don't think it's anything serious. His father, however, as we're all aware, is prone to play politics with our commitment in Vietnam."

"Serious! I consider being called 'undesirable' serious. I resent that kind of slander," protested Brand.

"Simple, let's get Lieutenant Kearney up here, and get to the bottom of this," Pavler demanded.

"General, are you sure you want to do that? If it's something political between Winston and Senator Kearney, the lieutenant may not have the answers. I suspect that young Kearney's problem is more a clash of personalities. To interrogate the senator's son at this juncture may infuriate the chairman even more. We need all the congressional support we can muster, so if we let Brand stay, we'd want to do it in a manner that mollifies the senator without his knowing he's been thwarted."

Pavler jabbed a thumb toward Brand. "Alex, you're as bad as he is. Now you want me to risk the senator's ire, too."

Brand leapt from the chair and came face-to-face with Pavler. In his haste, he had missed the sly smile crossing the general's face, but was not lost on Alex. "General, you know I'm not going to accept this shabby treatment from you or Kearney. You're not talking to one of your web-waisted, ground-thumping airborne idiots. I'm a member of the press. If you won't help, my next stop is the U.S. Embassy, then CINC PAC Fleet, and my paper will take this up with the State Department. There's going to be one helluva mess before we're through."

"Lower your voice, Winston. My entire staff can hear. Do you want to pass your insubordinate ideas on to them? I'm supposed to be a mean-ass bear, and I intend to keep it that way. Major, I nicknamed this fellow 'Spunky' when he was only ten, and he hasn't outgrown it yet."

"I've seen the same trait, sir, but if we designate Brand a member of Operation Checkmate, we can avoid any further confrontation with the senator who won't ever know he's been bucked."

General Pavler pushed his chair back, roared with delight and beat both fists against his thighs. Brand could feel the wooden floor shake beneath him. "With clever staff officers like Spear at my side," Pavler proclaimed, "this war's going to be won, and I'll probably be Chief of Staff of the Army someday."

"I'm happy for you two," said Brand sarcastically. "I've already told Alex no dice on compromising my position as a reporter."

"Winston, perhaps you're unaware Operation Checkmate is a top secret intelligence gathering group that functions outside normal intelligence channels," said Alex. "If General Pavler cables Senator Kearney that you and I are members of Operation Checkmate, that's the end of it as far as Congress is concerned. Our activities and personnel are exempt from Congressional oversight. We operate much like the CIA, except we're controlled by one man instead of a committee. Operation Checkmate personnel are accountable to a senior White House official making us untouchable with immunity from other political pressures."

"Alex, how many times must I remind you? Military intelligence work and news reporting are incompatible. So, let's bury this wild scheme," said Brand.

"If that's your choice, Winston, then General Pavler has no alternative than to send you back home. We're not asking you to spy, only to do what comes natural in the course of your job—keeping your eyes open."

"And report what I see to you?"

"Winston," said General Pavler whose voice took on a softer tone. "Look at it this way. If you're on a routine reporting assignment, and you came across the Viet Cong laying in ambush on a roadside where an American convoy was making its way, would you warn the Americans, or would you wait to get a massacre story?"

"You know damn well what I'd do, General," replied Brand.

"That's all we're asking you to do now, son."

"I can't do it. Sooner or later, you'd want me to take sides in this war, which conflicts with my pledge to report the truth as I find it. From my earlier writing, you can see I was not wholeheartedly behind the French in '54, because of the arrogant way they ran roughshod over the Vietnamese in order to regain control, but I did balance this against the horrible way the Vietnamese treated their own people, especially the Montagnards."

"Fair enough. We're convinced in time you'll see the Viet Cong as we see them, not the genuine rebels they pretend to be, but cutthroats who've got even less regard for the South Vietnamese way of life than the French," said Pavler. "Until then, we'll carry you temporarily as a member of Operation Checkmate without requiring any information from you in return."

"Why are you doing this?" asked Brand.

"Maybe it's because I know your father was a wonderful patriot and some of him is bound to have rubbed off on you. I'm certain Alex would never have vouched for you if you weren't a good security risk, despite your occasional bouts with the bottle. Major Spear agrees if you do nothing more than tell the truth in the columns of your newspaper, you'll have helped the cause of the Americans who have come so far to do what they can to help. You're still a rebel in search of a cause, Winston. My troops have found it. Now, please, let me get some work done. Let's hope, unlike most of your colleagues, you'll do your reporting from someplace other than the Saigon bars."

Alex suggested Winston go out of town for a few days until this thing with Kearney ran out of steam, and he emphasized that a trip up-country to an advisory detachment might be safer for him than staying in an urban area like Saigon. Brand protested saying that he planned to use the next few days to interview President Diem, other Vietnamese officials and their American counterparts to get an overview. Pavler settled the matter.

"Alex is right, Winston. You'd better put the politics aside until you get your feet planted firmly. Besides, it takes quite a while to be granted an interview with Diem. Until then, maybe we can help you hook up with other people you need to talk to when you get back. I'll leave the details to you two to work out."

As they stepped into the corridor, Alex filled his pipe with the maple-scented tobacco. "I'm glad that's over. You seem to have real rapport with the old man."

"General Pavler's been my pal for a long time, Alex. As a kid, I spent lots of time playing in his office when my father was too busy to see me," said Brand wistfully.

Lieutenant Kearney rejected the calendar over the bar. "That thing can't be right!" he exclaimed to the officer seated next to him.

"Yep, sure is. Tomorrow's Thursday, and ah'm headin' up-country."

It astonished Kearney to learn he had spent two days cooped up like a trapped fox in the Five Oceans. When he had first heard the name Five Oceans, he had anticipated a plush, exotic, oriental hotel with Japanese gardens and permissive geisha girls that ran hot and cold with the water.

Instead, the Five Oceans, a former Chinese hotel which must have seen better days in the Ching dynasty, barely accommodated the 36 U.S. officers that called the place home. Kearney, as a junior officer, was assigned a room on the second floor, south side, the one next to the An Dong open-air market. The rectangular building had only a single staircase dissecting the north side, which faced the Vietnam Police Academy training ground. The north side was called the "clear-air" side by its occupants who were captains and above in rank. The long south side of the building was referred to as "other-air" by officers who were fortunate enough not to live there. This part of the structure got its name from the stench which permeated the market place on that side of the building. The market formed each midnight as the farmers and fishermen from distant provinces set up their stalls, loaded with fish-heads, ducks, goats, rice and fresh vegetables. Each morning at six, except

Sunday, thousands of Chinese and Vietnamese from Cholon and Saigon flocked to the market place to shop and bargain until noon.

On his first day at the Five Oceans, Kearney had noticed the birds never ventured on the "other-air" side of the building until after the people had left for their afternoon siestas. And who could blame the birds, he wondered? The noise of the two ethnic groups bargaining in two different languages over screeching pigs, wild fowl and clanging rice bowls had kept him confined to his quarters. There was no respite from the putrid smell of decayed matter or the eerie sounds of the market place. Finally, when the farmers and fishermen slept, rats as long as a man's arm patrolled the market place in packs of 20 or more. Then the sounds that drifted up to the Five Oceans' windows changed to those of rats screeching along the pavement below like motorcycle tires gripping cement.

Two officers in the room next to Kearney's considered it great sport to sit up in the window at night and blast the rats with .22 caliber rifles they had shipped from home for that purpose. Naturally, they were called the "Rat Patrol" by the other occupants and subsequent officers billeted at the Five Oceans, some of whom assumed vector control duties themselves.

It exhausted Kearney to think of the sleepless night ahead of him. He was very hungry as well, but he could hardly bring himself to eat. His head sagged over his arms on the bar as he sought to erase thoughts of the awful situation Carlotta Simoni, his father and the U.S. Army had thrust upon him.

The harder he tried the more irksome a rascal his mind became, refusing to rest on command. Weary in body, Kearney relented to a parade of painful pictures painted before him. He was tormented with the sight of Maria Monclova as she had brushed past him at the airport into the arms of Winston Brand. In that moment, everyone knew Brand had succeeded where he had failed. His own plan to seduce Maria, and then reject her had been carried out superbly by another. Kearney would never forgive Brand's interference, taking the prize away from him for all to see.

Kearney's father had taught him to understand human life by comparing it with animal life. In this respect, he saw himself and Winston Brand as two stags locking horns for the prime doe. Brand had cheated. He had won with the help of another male, Maj. Alex Spear. But only wounded, Kearney decided to prepare himself for the next encounter.

Kearney lifted his head from the bar, turned and snapped at the black Army captain standing in front of the juke box, "That's the tenth time we've heard 'Moon River.' Knock it off, will ya!" The lieutenant cupped his hands over his ears in an attempt to shut out the voice of Andy Williams as it started on its eleventh turn.

"You sick, sir?" asked Ling Ty, the Vietnamese bar boy.

"No, get lost," said Kearney.

"I fix 'nother drink. You better, chop, chop."

Kearney looked down at the mahogany bar where his head had lain. "Dandruff," he murmured.

"Danluff?" asked the bar boy. No got danluff. Got Scotch, viskey, bor-bon, yin-tonic, vodka, rum and beer. No danluff here. Solly. Next time you come, have danluff, whokay?" He rattled whiskey bottles on a shelf in front of him as he spoke.

"You're crazy. I'm talking about my hair. I've got dandruff. Never had it before I came to this rat-trap."

"You tell me how to make danluff. I fix good for you. You see. Make you forget 'lat-tap' Five Oceans."

Kearney patted his head. "My hair. I'm talking about my hair!"

"Ah, me understand. You need go *cat toc*. Tomorrow *cat toc*. No tonight."

"The boy just wants to tell you where to go to get a haircut," came the southern drawl of the officer still seated next to him.

The 215 pound, six-foot-two-inch frame of Rafe "Bonecrusher" Hewlett loomed over the smaller Kearney like a giant shadow that plunged the area into darkness.

"Ah believe you arrived on Flight 740," said the southerner resting a heavy arm on Kearney's weary shoulders. Mah name's Rafe Hewlett.

"Tom Kearney."

"Well, Kearney, it's nice to meetcha. Ling Ty here just wanted to be helpful. You're probably the first red-headed American he's ever seen. And the way he's been staring at your freckles, ah know he's never seen so many before. Neither have the rest of us."

"Well, tell him to get lost. I don't like him leering at me."

"Better get used to it, Kearney. There's a lot more of them to stare at us than there is us to stare at them."

Kearney pursed his thin lips and spat in Ling Ty's face. "I told you to get lost," he screamed.

"Hey, fella, you're too edgy. C'mon over here. Ah wanna talk to you." Hewlett half lifted Kearney out of the chair as he guided him to a table. "You shouldn't have done that to Ling Ty. He's a good ole boy. Always trying to cheer somebody up. You gotta handkerchief on you, fella?"

"Yeah, so what?"

"Take it out of your pocket and give it to Ling Ty to wipe his face with."

"I'll be damned if I will," said Kearney.

"You'll be worse off than that if you don't, fella," said Hewlett.

"What does he mean to you?"

"He's my buddy, same as you, Kearney. Ah just want to see my two buddies patch up a little misunderstanding. Now get on over there and give him your handkerchief."

Kearney did some quick, silent calculating. He was no match for Hewlett in the brawn department. To further anger the giant would spell disaster for his pretty-boy features. He had no doubt he was smarter, so why not team up with this mass of muscle that could be manipulated later.

Kearney got up, took his handkerchief from his pocket, walked over to Ling Ty, and wiped his face with a showmanship flourish.

"Good, fella," said Hewlett as Kearney returned to his seat. "That was a fine thing to do, and ah know by Ling Ty's grin that you and he are gonna be good friends from now on."

"You know, Hewlett, you look familiar for some reason or other. Ever play football?" asked Kearney guiding the conversation away from one unpleasant topic to another.

"Sure did, back at 'Bama. Class of '57."

"Hell, yes. I should have recognized you before. 'Bonecrusher' Hewlett, All-American fullback. You were terrific. One of my idols, as a matter of fact. I remember when you and Sammy Dantner knocked heads in the Orange Bowl. That Oklahoman was a good halfback, but you made him look sick in total yardage, as I recall."

"Fella, your memory is 'bout as good as your manners. Sammy Dantner outgained me on the ground by 25 yards in that game. All we got to do to verify it is call him over here. That's him playing the juke."

"It can't be possible," stammered Kearney.

"Hey, Sammy, 'Moon River' isn't going anywhere. C'mon over here. Ah want you to meet a buddy of mine."

Sammy Dantner strode across the room toward them, swung a chair around backwards, sat down and leaned his arms across its straight back. "Scuse me, gents, for sitting this way. It's a handy li'l trick I learned from some infantry types up-country." Kearney observed one of the most powerful runners the game of college football had ever produced. Now a captain, the athlete's powerful legs bulged with muscles that resembled thigh pads, even in baggy fatigues. With slim hips that nobody could hang on to, it was easy to believe his strong legs capable of carrying five heavy tacklers across the goal line.

"This boy knows nothing about infantry types up-country. He's only been here a day or two and is not hip to our jive," said Hewlett. "Me and Kearney have been reliving old football memories."

"Ever play football, Kearney?" asked Dantner.

Kearney didn't want to bring up his own experience on the grid-iron, lest they had heard of the infamous "bench-warming" incident with a cheerleader. "Some," he answered. "Mostly soccer," he quickly added. "But that's not important. What I want to know is what there is to do in this hell-hole. Where do you guys go for excitement?"

"Mah excitement is coming tomorrow," said Hewlett. "A month here is enough. By this time tomorrow, ah'll be an advisor up-country."

"Yeah, I envy you," said Dantner. "You'll have your own room, a maid who will also cook for you, a lot of Vietnamese soldiers at your beck and call and good family women following you around. On top of that you're getting promoted to captain next month."

"Yeah, tell me about the women," said Kearney. "How are these Vietnamese women in bed?"

Hewlett looked at his black friend. "Do you wanna educate him or should ah do the honors?"

"Please, be my guest," said Dantner.

"Here, in Saigon, and other major cities, there're two types of women, the good family girls and whores. Up-country, there're mostly good family girls, 'cause those who would be whores have gone to the big city where horny guys like yaw'l are a dime a dozen, although it'll cost ya quite a bit more."

"What's your point?" asked Kearney.

"If you just wanna get laid, Saigon's the place. If it's more than sex ya want, or sex with more meaning, then a good family girl up-country is an unspoiled prize."

"I see," said Kearney rubbing his hands together. "Up-country a man can get his hands on a virgin more easily. I've never had to pay for it yet, and don't intend to start."

"You missed 'Bonecrusher's' point, man," said Dantner. "Good family girls are the marrying kind, and that's what they expect."

"Oh, yeah, just wait and see me bed a good family girl without marriage."

The other two officers looked at each other and simultaneously threw their own hands up in a gesture of hopelessness.

"Kearney's gotta lot to learn about this place. Let's start by teaching him the Five Oceans theme song, otherwise known as 'The Smell of An Dong,'" said Hewlett.

"Yeah, man. It's the same tune as 'Workin' on the Railroad.' Rafe and I'll sing a few bars, then you join us in the chorus," said Dantner draping his arm around Kearney's shoulder. Soon the trio drowned out the strains of "Moon River" by singing out lustily:

The smell of An Dong is upon us
It will not fade away.
The smell of An Dong is upon us
It always blows our way.
Can't you always tell the difference
When you go downtown?
We'd like to move into the Brink, but
They always turn us down.
Wind won't you blow
Wind won't you blow
Wind won't you blow
The smell away?
Wind won't you blow,
Wind won't you blow,
Wind won't you blow
It away?

Downstairs in his room, Alex fumbled in the pocket of his fatigue shirt.

"Winston, I almost forgot. Here's the name of an advisor who's going up-country tomorrow to replace another officer in Binh Long Province." He passed Winston the slip of paper, then quickly added, "I guarantee you this guy has no connection with military intelligence."

"First Lt. Rafe Hewlett," Brand read aloud. "Could it be 'Bonecrusher' Hewlett of grid iron fame?"

Alex nodded. "That's the one. I can have you booked on the same aircraft he'll be taking. Is there anything I can do to help you get ready?"

"No, except here's a list of people I'd like to interview on my return."

"I'll get right on it," said Alex. "Meantime, I thought I spotted Lieutenant Hewlett upstairs in the bar. Maybe he's still there. If so, I could make the introductions."

Across town, the Council of Ministers, some in uniform, others in civilian clothes, sifted through the debris of the bombed out palace. They had been summoned to the grounds to claim personal items lost, misplaced or damaged when the two renegade VNAF pilots struck. The officer in charge at the site expressed relief that none of the ministers had been harmed. The young Vietnamese captain then read a message to the assembled officials:

> The Council of Ministers must put this incident behind us, and carry on with the people's work. The discussions underway when this cowardly act disrupted deliberations will resume. As you can see, the bombed palace has been opened to you and to members of the foreign press so you can reclaim any personal items. Those who would attack us can see that business is being conducted as usual, although moved to the alternate Gia Long Palace. In our struggle, appearances are important. Our people have a long tradition of supporting the strongest dragon. Our republic must be that dragon. If assistance is needed, please advise one of the adjutants here to help you. Until further notice, all meetings of the Council will be held in secret with only 24-hours-notice prior to the time and place. You all can understand why this is necessary.

Unnoticed by the others present, one of the ministers tightened his fist into a hard ball upon hearing the conditions set forth. R-3 would have to plan his forays to his field headquarters even more carefully under the new restrictions. Twenty-four hours meant he would have to rely on others to rally the far-flung outposts of the Viet Cong infrastructure. This would give his superiors in Hanoi more control than they already had, making it easy to bypass him in the name of expediency and the desire to keep his identity concealed. Unless of course, he could retain a degree of independence for the Viet Cong under his command by obtaining better communications equipment. However, R-3 realized that more efficient communication could prove to be a two-edged sword in that he would be tied closer to the policies originating from the North.

Even so, he decided the situation had become critical. The ideal place to find the equipment he sought was the U.S. supplied ARVN detachment at Loc Ninh in Binh Long Province, a few kilometers from the Cambodian border. To this sanctuary his troops could flee after they seized the radios. Tonight he would send a message to his general in Binh Long ordering the attack. Nguyen Huu Bao would deliver the plans under cover on his last mission as his adjutant. If his interview was successful, Captain Bao could also meet with the French plantation owners in the area regarding the enemy's Strategic Hamlet program.

R-3 bent down and retrieved a broken chess piece out of the charred ruins. It was a porcelain figure of a decapitated king. "Next time," he swore to himself, raising the clenched hand with the chess piece in it toward the president's damaged living quarters. "Next time."

11 THE STRONGEST DRAGON

Were half the power that fills the world with terror,
Were half the wealth bestowed on camps and courts,
Given to redeem the human mind from error,
There were no need of arsenals or forts.
—Henry Wadsworth Longfellow

AT MIDDAY, the single engine Army Beaver banked in position to land at Loc Ninh. Rain pelted the aircraft from all sides, making it necessary for Brand and Lieutenant Hewlett to shout at each other over the engine noise and steady drum of water striking the rear windows.

"Looks awful messy down there," shouted Brand leaning across the narrow aisle. "Sure we can get in safely?"

"No sweat," Hewlett shouted back, patting the top of the pilot's seat. "This thing's built for such conditions, and we've got an old bush pilot at the controls."

As if he had heard his two passengers, the pilot pushed the throttle forward, sending the aircraft up into the gray sky. Sensing the aborted landing, Brand instinctively looked down at the makeshift runway. He spotted a thin, short man standing in a jeep waving his arms in a circular motion.

"We've been directed to go around again," the pilot announced.

In his anxiety, Brand fingered the inscription on the flask in his breast pocket. "Well, Willie, old chum, if this is it, we'll at least go together," he told himself. Then he smiled, thinking of Pavler's reaction and everybody else's if they discovered his body in the wreckage clinging to a flask of bourbon. No doubt the general would be disappointed, thinking Brand had broken his promise to stay sober. Others would take the "I knew it would happen that way" attitude, since they had predicted his failure. All but Clementine, that is, and perhaps Maria Monclova. His sister's grief would be compounded with the thought she alone survived a family that once held so much promise. He wanted to believe Maria would be disappointed as well. Reminded that part of the conditions set by Pavler for his being allowed to remain in Vietnam included a call to Clementine, he vowed to comply at the first opportunity.

"That guy down there is waving us off again," said the pilot interrupting Brand's thoughts.

Brand looked at Hewlett, shrugged his shoulders and held his palms upward.

"There's one consolation," he yelled. "Whatever's wrong, it's not with the airplane but on the ground. Good thing, too. I've used up my allotted airplane mishaps."

"Ah think we'll get in on the next approach," replied Hewlett.

But they did not. Instead they were waved away from the runway a third time.

"It's your call, Lieutenant. Do you want me to try again, or head back to Saigon?" asked the pilot, turning in his seat.

"What do ya think the problem is?" asked Hewlett.

"I don't know. Can't raise them by radio. Somebody's jamming the frequency. Sounds like open mike static."

"Let's give it one more try," said Hewlett. "All right with you, Winston?"

"Sure, only I think you should know, the last time this happened I had a beautiful flight attendant in my arms."

"Sorry, no authorization for one for this flight. You're stuck with me. But ah'll be damned if ah want to end up in your arms, dead or alive."

Both men laughed nervously. On the fourth pass, the officer in the jeep signaled the aircraft to land, and it slid to a stop about 20 feet from the parked vehicle. Brand stepped out, unexpectedly sinking into mud up to his ankles.

"Sorry for making you go around so many times," the advisor explained to the disembarking passengers. "But if anybody had a bead on you from that jungle out there," he swept his Australian bush hat in a wide arc, "he'd have gotten trigger happy and tipped his hand by the Beaver's second pass over the field. No sense giving Victor Charlie a clear shot at a sitting duck. Keep 'em guessing is the name of the game. It's survival of the survivors out here."

The officer then turned to the pilot, telling him he would get some heavy trucks out on the runway to make a path through the mud so the Beaver could take off. Brand heard the pilot explain that in a couple days he would send a helicopter in to pick up passengers returning to Saigon. Citing security and weather conditions, the three officers, without consulting Brand, agreed a helicopter was the preferred mode of transportation in Viet Cong territory.

As Brand, Hewlett and Capt. Erik Fletcher drove toward the buildings nestled in the fringes of the jungle, the reporter noted the advisor directed his Vietnamese jeep driver to follow a zig-zag pattern across the cleared area. Brand used the time to size up his new host. Fletcher's long blond hair, non-regulation, walrus-style mustache and baggy fatigues put Brand in mind of a frontier cavalry officer rather than a spit-and-polish modern soldier. The officer's twangy voice identified him as a Texan.

"Here's the plan," said Fletcher. "We'll make a courtesy call to my Vietnamese counterpart, *Thieu-ta* Tien Si. Let me tell you, Vietnamese names are a mouthful for a southern boy. Hope you do a better job of pronouncing the major's name than I do, Rafe. These people are very sensitive about that."

"Wish ah'd taken the Vietnamese language course. Guess my college French will have to do."

"Hold on, boy, don't go spoutin' off any French around here unless you're talking to plantation owners. The South Vietnamese want to block out the French experience and don't cotton to anybody who reminds them of their colonial days."

Brand made a mental note that outlawing the French language among Vietnamese in the South was a drastic departure from his 1954 experience when every schoolboy spoke French as a way of moving up in society. Fletcher advised 'Bonecrusher' Hewlett his French could be put to good use the next day when they visited the nearby Devereau plantation.

"You're welcome to come along on our courtesy call to the Devereau's, Mr. Brand, but be warned. It's a dangerous half hour's drive from here. Besides the night, Charlie owns all the roads in and out of this compound and everything else along the way, except air space and the land ruled by the rubber barons."

"Count me in. French is my second tongue. I'd like to see what they have to say about the war," said Winston.

"Good, maybe you two '*parlez-vousers*' can find out how much in taxes they're paying to the VC to let them continue to operate. Like Major Si, my counterpart, the French pretend not to understand me whenever I ask tough questions. Perhaps they'll be more open with a civilian, but I wouldn't count on it, especially once they discover you're a reporter," said Fletcher.

"Ah heard the plantation owners are a snobbish clan," said Hewlett.

"You've got that right. All but one, the daughter. She's as down to earth as any Frenchie ever gets. You may be fortunate to taste pastries for your breakfast that will have come from her kitchen. She's always sending us goodies. A good looker, too, Rafe."

"Hey, things are looking up," said Hewlett as the jeep arrived at the compound. The rain had stopped, leaving everything saturated with water. Brand got out and bent over to squeeze mud and water from his trousers just below the knee cap.

"I know you guys would like to dry out, but right now we'd better beat a path to Si's headquarters before they shut down. Nothing happens in Vietnam between one and four, as the whole population takes a siesta."

The three men walked across a quadrangle at the center of which stood a flagpole flying three horizontal red stripes on a saffron field, the national colors of the Republic of Vietnam. Brand made a mental note of the layout. An assemblage of bamboo or wooden buildings arranged around three sides of the flagpole marked the ARVN camp. The fourth side was sealed by concertina wire with a break at one point to allow military vehicles and soldiers to come and go past two sentries, who controlled passage by raising and lowering a wooden barrier.

Major Si, a wiry officer in his middle 30s, greeted his visitors at the door of a wooden frame house with a tiled roof. Floors and walls were constructed of brick long since covered with mold. Divided into three rooms, Si's house also served as a briefing room, his living quarters and a small office. The Vietnamese major directed his guests to a wooden couch. Nearby, an orderly placed briefing charts on an easel.

The major picked up a pointer, tapped it against his broad forehead, his chest, then across each shoulder in the unmistakable sign of the cross. He tapped the easel, signaling the soldier to unveil the first chart, an organizational diagram. After completing this ritual, Major Si cupped a hand behind one of his large protruding ears to call for their silence.

"You see," Si began in a wavering voice, "we are organized like your signal battalions, but for two things. Major in command here, not lieutenant colonel. Also, we have three American advisors—one officer, two enlisted. Advisory detachment shown here," he said, pointing to a line and block drawn to the right of the commanding officer's slot. "We have many problems in this relationship," he continued, "but lots of time to work them out."

"Could ya give us an example of the types of command and control problems you're talking about, suh?" asked Hewlett.

"Sure. Good question. I try to answer, but please excuse my bad English. Big problem is security of U.S. detachment. They look to us for protection. We not always have soldier for body guard. Better if Americans arm themselves and make fight with Viet Cong."

"What's U.S. policy now?" asked Brand turning toward Fletcher.

"President Kennedy says we're non-combatants. That means we don't shoot unless shot at, giving the edge to the enemy, who can pick the time and place for the next fight."

After this exchange, the Vietnamese officer steered the conversation back to his charts. "Here we have battalion mission statement written in English," he said walking over to the easel which was about his height. He began to read, growing bolder in voice with every word:

"To establish a communications network north from Tay Ninh Province through Binh Long Province to Phuoc Long Province along the Cambodian border, then south to Gia Dinh Province, linking up all central provinces in between with ARVN Headquarters in Saigon."

"This very big job," commented Si when he finished reading. "Communication very important. Even hated enemy Vo Nguyen

Giap made big reputation maintaining contact with his forces in jungle against French."

"By the way, *Thieu-ta*," said Fletcher, "the pilot who brought *Trung-uy* Hewlett and Mr. Brand here tells me he couldn't establish contact with your ground control. Can you shed any light on this?"

The Vietnamese officer shifted uneasily on his feet and stared down at the brick floor so as to avoid direct eye contact with the Americans. His words slipped out between his fingers as he gripped his narrow chin. "These things happen. Sometimes our English-speaking soldier need break. Turn over radio duty to friend who no speak your language. Friend not know what to say when hear pilot, so only hold button down. No big deal."

"Damned if that's so," said Fletcher as he leapt to his feet suspending protocol and dressing down a superior. "These Americans could've been killed."

"Okay, maybe you make big problem before you leave. You want me to? I find radio man. Shoot him. Show everybody life of Vietnamese soldier not same-same American."

"That's not the point, and you know it. What the hell," said Fletcher, slapping Hewlett on the back. "After tomorrow, that's your problem."

"Yeah, well, ah think we'd best leave it there," said Rafe.

Obviously emboldened by the concession of the senior advisor, Major Si addressed his comments to Hewlett. "I'm sure new *Trung-uy* and me fix problem. Maybe he take time to learn Vietnamese and teach to all U.S. advisors who come here. That way no need every Vietnamese common soldier speak English. More easy to teach few than many."

"This is not about language. We're talking responsibility," said Fletcher determined to get in the last word.

The meeting with Si had gone so badly, Brand was not surprised to hear Fletcher excuse himself saying he had to pack. Displaying his own displeasure, Major Si assigned a subordinate to guide Hewlett and Brand on a tour of the facilities. The trio stopped first at a training room no larger than Si's quarters, except the interior walls had been torn down to make room for long workbenches. Each bench supported three to five AN/GRC-19 radio sets of 30 total, which could also be operated on the move, providing transmission over distances up to 50 miles.

"Imagine what General Giap could do with these," Brand observed.

"You can see American allies give us latest radio equipment. We train here to make relay station all the way to Saigon," said the Vietnamese escort officer.

"How are these radios tied in to your field units?" asked Brand.

"Very good question. Our armor, artillery and infantry units already use AN/VRC FM radio sets which have short range operation of 10-15 miles. They call relay station. We use this radio to get message to headquarters. All time know what Viet Cong up to."

"What about jamming? Is that a problem for you?" asked Brand jotting in his notebook.

A broad smile filled the face of the young officer who tried desperately to keep from laughing aloud. "Ho, ho, no worry about jamming. VC no have same-same equipment. No way for him to jam American radio."

"Can ya talk on the significance of jammin' though?" asked Hewlett.

"Sure."

"Well, go ahead."

"Bad operator no tell difference. Think jamming, faulty receiver, local interference all same."

'That's very good," said Hewlett. "Now can ya tell me how the enemy benefits from jammin'?"

"No understand."

Brand rescued the Vietnamese officer who obviously had exhausted his knowledge on the subject. "I asked the question," said the reporter, "recalling how my father had lost a ship in the Pacific because the enemy had interfered with its signal. The Mayday message never got through to other ships in the area, and he was convinced that if the inexperienced radio operators had not panicked, lives could have been saved."

"Mistuh Brand makes a good point, *Trung-uy*. How much time do yaw'l spend on anti-jammin' procedures?"

"Spend no time yet. Wait for American communications specialists to come teach our soldiers. Two times now, Americans no show."

"Could he be referring to the missing aircraft with U.S. Army and Navy signal personnel on board?" Brand whispered to Hewlett.

"Ah don't know anything about that," the Alabaman replied. "All ah know is we're supposed to have ten or more enlisted communication specialists and two officers assigned to this detachment, but they never came through the pipeline."

Brand flicked his finger across his nose. "Perhaps this is not the time or place to discuss that."

Hewlett addressed his next remarks to the Vietnamese officer.

"Jammin' is something ah'll have to take up with Major Si. It's a nasty business that in skillful hands can deny radio use to our forces, create confusion and delay, cause security violations and set the stage for deception."

"I'm impressed," said Brand looking at Hewlett.

Thirty minutes later, the Vietnamese officer, anxious to join his colleagues in the afternoon siesta, took leave of the two Americans. Brand and Hewlett splashed their way across the compound to the senior advisor's quarters.

Fletcher stood under the overhanging straw and palm covered roof of his small bamboo hut. "Come on in," he said. "It's slightly drier in here."

To accommodate his guests in the single room, he slid his half-packed duffel bag off the bed. Motioning Brand to the only chair, and Rafe to join him on the edge of the bed, Fletcher reached in his hip pocket and pulled out a wallet wrapped in a plastic bag. "Here's a field expedient for you, Rafe. Always carry enough of these little bags to keep your money dry."

Hewlett smiled as he shifted his huge hulk on the bed. A wet circle spread out from his damp fatigues.

"Man, if you let a wet ass bother you, you're in the wrong place. Now don't take offense, you big son-of-a-bitch," Fletcher added quickly. "Here the rainy season runs from May to October, and the rest of the year the ground's always so damn wet in this monsoon climate, you'd swear the moisture not only pours down to beat you on the head, but flows up to soak your butt, rotting everything in between. If I could stand the heat, my wallet isn't the only thing I'd wrap in plastic."

All three men laughed. Fletcher continued, "Here's the plan for the rest of the day. After a quick lunch, Rafe, you and I need to coordinate a smooth transition. Mr. Brand, you're welcome to sit in, but I promise you it'll be boring to a civilian. If you'd prefer, we can get you set up in your quarters, or you can wander on your own around the compound."

"Please call me Winston, and don't worry about me. I'll just nose around a bit."

"Good. Then why don't we all meet back here to go to chow at six—that is, if the Beaver you guys came in on brought our rations up from Saigon intact. If the black market's ripped off part of the damn order, there'll be no steaks. It's happened before. Afterwards, we'll get down to some jungle-style drinking to celebrate your arrival and my departure."

"Sounds good," replied Rafe.

"One more thing. Is there a telephone nearby where I could call Saigon, Hawaii and possibly the U.S. mainland?" asked Brand.

"Are you kidding? This is a signal battalion. But if I were you, I'd save the calls to Hawaii and home until we get to the Devereau plantation. Better international connections there. Hell, I wouldn't be surprised if they couldn't plug you in to Hanoi, Peking and Moscow," Fletcher said sarcastically.

"Saigon will do fine," said Brand.

Nguyen Huu Bao rose from the hammock and rubbed his good left eye, pleased to see a cook bearing down on him with a tray of tea and sweet cakes. He looked at his watch, noting the siesta had ended, and it was time to get down to business after his long arduous journey from Saigon to this jungle outpost near Loc Ninh. From his knapsack next to a packet sealed by R-3, he retrieved a black eye patch, placing it firmly over the empty socket of his right eye and sat down in a chair. He had hardly taken a bite of the cake when he heard his host calling to him from the bamboo pathway.

"Greetings, Comrade Adjutant. We trust you rested well and bring good news from our great leader, *Ayr-Ba*."

Bao rose from the wooden chair massaging his buttocks.

"Thank you for your hospitality, Comrade General. I apologize for my inattentiveness on arrival this morning, but I tell you, hours of travel by bus, motor scooter and finally a shared bicycle seat has produced more pain than the loss of an eye from the point of a French bayonet."

The leader of the camp laughed with his guest. Pleased that his unusual reputation for light heartedness had spread in revolutionary circles, Bao took a few gingerly steps toward the hammock, then stopped.

"Please, Comrade General, could you hand me that packet next to the knapsack? I feel as though I'm still one with the bicycle seat. And the thought of my return journey brings tears to my one good eye."

This time the host did not laugh. He picked up the packet, but instead of handing it to Bao, the senior communist general in South Vietnam broke the seal on the packet with stony silence, bordering on reverence.

"You look as if someone has ordered your execution, General Chien," joked Bao resuming his place in the hammock, knees dangling over the side. "Perhaps it is not the news you were hoping for?"

"It's better than expected, but I cannot share it with you because the document is clearly labeled for my eyes only," Gen. Tran Van Chien explained.

"Then, since I only have one eye, perhaps you can share half of it with me," mocked Bao. Seeing his witticism went unappreciated, he added quickly, "Of course, I'm only kidding, Comrade General. These instructions are to be followed to the letter. *Ayr-Ba* probably kept me in the dark for my own protection, knowing if I were captured after destroying the document, there is no way they could torture the information out of me."

"Surely, that explains the secrecy," said the jungle commandant.

For a long time after General Chien had left to brief his troops, Bao swayed gently back and forth in the hammock gazing at the afternoon sun filtering through the tops of the tall trees. To curb his growing anger, Bao did what R-3 had forbidden all of his subordinates to do without permission—commit thoughts or actions upon the written page. Bao took a small notebook and pencil from the pocket of his black pajamas and began to write:

February 29, 1962

More humiliation. Something big is planned, and I am relegated to a mere messenger/observer. As a Saigon intellectual, I find these assignments repugnant. I, who have met Ho Chi Minh during my studies in Paris, know that the great leader has more important things in store for me in the revolutionary cause. Someday, *Ayr-Ba* must let me lead men in battle. As is, no fame, honor nor glory has befallen me in six years as a double agent. What will my children, if they are to come, say of me if these deeds are not recorded? At the moment, they could only speak of Bao, the one eyed courier, lackey and assassin. But we must all trust that *Ayr-Ba* will recognize my potential to become like him—a true hero of the revolution. Patience.

Perhaps my possible new assignment in the Diem government shall bear less bitter fruit. At least this shows *Ayr-Ba* trusts me enough to allow me to move freely within the enemy's camp, knowing, if discovered, that even under torture, I would not betray him. I wonder whom he'll select to replace me as his closest confident? No doubt, one of these mindless workers from the dark, damp underworld who has fewer qualms about murdering women and children.

Bao replaced the notebook and lay back in the hammock gazing at the gray sky beyond the tops of the trees. He tried to focus his thoughts on the imminent battle, hearing Viet Cong comrades around him prepare their weapons. A woman soldier placed a cup of jasmine tea on the table next to him. The rich aroma filled his mind with visions of Madame Nhu which he desperately attempted to drive away.

Later that evening, Brand, Hewlett and Fletcher gathered in the latter's room as planned.

"Now for that drink," Fletcher suggested.

"Make it Scotch, Fletch," said Rafe.

"What about you, Winston?"

"No, thanks. Not while I'm on the job." He held up his reporter's notebook.

Fletcher busied himself at the makeshift bar on his dresser.

"Wish we had more time to get acquainted," he said handing Hewlett a water glass half filled with Scotch, but without ice.

"Sure you won't change your mind and join us, Winston?"

"No thanks," repeated Winston.

"Let's just relax, buddy," said Rafe. "Tomorrow's a big day. Winston and ah'll be making the rounds with ya."

"You've got that right," said Fletcher. "And then after one more wake-up call, it's home to Susan and the kids, unless my chopper ride to Saigon is late. How are things in the big city? Would you believe in 14 months, I've only been there twice?"

"Saigon nevah changes. Winston told me on the flight up how it looks the same as when he was there in '54," said Hewlett.

"No kidding. Ever been to Pleiku?"

"Not that I recall," Brand replied.

"There's a real garden spot for you." Fletcher dug an elbow in Hewlett's ribs.

Brand remembered Pleiku as one of the most isolated villages in the Central Highlands, a place of exile for French soldiers and legionnaires who failed to toe the line. Nevertheless, he allowed the two officers to continue their joke.

"Yeah, ya can't imagine the disappointment when mah orders read Loch Ninh instead of Pleiku," said Hewlett raising his glass.

"I'll drink to that," said Fletcher, "and while we're at it, let's sing a few choruses of 'Saigon' for our guest. If you care to chime in, the tune is the same as 'How Ya Gonna Keep 'Em Down on the Farm?'"

On Fletcher's cue, the two officers burst into song:

How ya gonna keep 'em down in SAIGON
After they've seen PLEIKU?
How ya gonna get 'em back to CHOLON
After they've seen BAN ME THUOT?
Fightin' the war from the desk to the floor,
MAAG's the word of the day!
We've been to HUE, BINH LONG, and back to BIEN HOA
And spent our money in a Catinat bar.
How ya gonna keep 'em down in SAIGON
After they've seen PLEIKU?

Following three more increasingly ribald verses of the song, Brand excused himself. But before he got out the door, Fletcher fired a verbal parting shot.

"Better get used to it, Winston. You'll soon learn we do more singing than fighting these days. Never trust an off duty soldier without home in his heart, a drink in his hand and a song on his lips, I always say."

"Ah'll drink to that," said Hewlett.

Retiring to his own quarters, the one room hut serving as the detachment's VIP facility, Brand lay in bed listening to a persistent mosquito as it tried to penetrate the protective netting. Outside he heard the Vietnamese guard slosh by his window. The rain had stopped earlier, and a breeze generated from a ceiling fan fought a battle with the jungle heat for control of the temperature of his naked body.

Beyond the open window next to his bed, lights flickered in the jungle on the far side of the airfield. His first thought was that soldiers from the South Vietnamese battalion were patrolling the perimeter around the camp. But then, realizing a signal battalion with all of its sophisticated communications equipment would hardly resort to such primitive tactics as flashing lights, he got up from the bed. Pulling on his slacks, he moved toward the open window and waited for the sentry to pass by again.

"You there," he called to the South Vietnamese soldier. "Do you speak English?"

"You *Bao-chi*?" the soldier asked as he rested his weapon on the window sill.

"Yes, press," Brand replied.

"Good. No want trouble for speak on duty. You got cigarette?"

"Sure," said Brand passing a cigarette out the window. "Those lights over there. Are those your people?"

The soldier laughed as he exhaled a puff of smoke. "No, *Bao-chi*, that Viet Cong. Charlie all time talk all night with light. Try to make us 'fraid to walk out there. We keep this place. They keep that place. No problem."

"Do they ever shoot at you?"

"No nighttime shoot. Only daytime when airplane come. They no like 'Melican airplane. Sometime one, maybe two, come in camp, steal food, take cigarette or flashlight. But you no worry. I guard you good. Gotta go now. No good for me if *Dai-uy* Fletcher see me speak and smoke on duty."

Returning to his bed, Brand wished he had brought along the Derringer Alex had given him at the Five Oceans. The thought someone could creep into his room from the rear of the hut nestled against the edge of the jungle made him edgy. The South Vietnamese guard had not been that reassuring, since Brand had not seen him once venture into the area behind the visitor's quarters exposed to the jungle overgrowth. For all he knew, people across the circular compound could see flickering lights behind him, as he could behind them, in which case, the camp was surrounded. How could two regular army officers like Fletcher and Hewlett tolerate a situation a civilian like himself spotted as dangerous? He shuttered to think the Americans were repeating the arrogant mistakes he had seen the French fall into during the siege at Dien Bien Phu and other similar *beau geste*-type outposts. All were eventually surrounded by a superior force and overrun.

When the pesky mosquito resumed its attack on the netting, Brand decided to forgo sleep for the time being and enter these reflections in his journal. Rather than turn on the overhead light, making his hut too inviting a target, he sat at the small desk and wrote with one hand while holding a flashlight in the other:

> Things are turned upside down in this kind of war. Darkness relates to tranquility and with the daylight comes danger. Soldiers on both sides spend a great deal of time either singing, smoking, signaling or stealing as if they're stuck on the letter "s" in the alphabet. So far, there's very little fighting. But this is the way the VC want it until they are strong enough to commence the armed struggle. What this means is that they control the agenda, and one must puzzle at how a great power like the U.S. can allow itself to have others dictate the terms of the conflict.
>
> There's an axiom in chess. He who rules the center of the board determines the outcome of the game. As things stand, there is no doubt Americans lack the initiative in this situation. Add to this the problems of leadership in the South Vietnamese government where three out of five ministers and military officers were repatriated from the North, then one begins to ask how it is in America's interest to stay the present course. This is a question to be answered up and down the line. Meantime, I'm struck with the pattern developing here in Binh Long province, my own experiences so far, and the bombing of the President's Palace. In all of these instances, the message to Americans seems clear. "Come here, or try to thwart us, only to find out how vulnerable you are." Intimidation is indeed a powerful weapon.

Under this passage, Brand scribbled a personal note:

> Sure, I could turn back. No one would ever blame me after all I've been through just to get this far. But that would be admitting I'm washed up and failure is my destiny. This runs counter to my belief. Man was put here to serve a more noble purpose than mere existence. As I write this, a mosquito tries to suck the blood from me it needs to sustain its own existence. Aren't we better than this unthinking creature? And if man has these same tendencies, then all the philosophers, except for the nihilists, are wrong. Once convinced there is no distinction between life and death, then we are already dead, because each is robbed of its purpose.
>
> My purpose in coming here is to follow truth wherever it may lead. To do otherwise is to forfeit happiness and to die within. Once your spirit has been broken, there are but two choices, give up and live as though dead, that is, existing only, or press on, hoping Socrates was right when he declared divine grace would make him whole. If so, an upright and virtuous path would follow.

Over coffee and French pastries the next morning, Brand, bleary-eyed for lack of sleep, brought up his concerns about camp security. Captain Fletcher said he looked at the enemy position around his outpost as ant hills best left undisturbed. Lieutenant Hewlett said he saw the situation in a similar light and reminded Brand advisors lacked authority to change the policy, even if they wanted to.

"Everything we do here is run outta Washington."

"Rafe's got that right. If my Vietnamese counterpart can't protect us, we're in deep shit," said Fletcher. "You heard him say yesterday he's having a problem. Doesn't have the manpower he needs for adequate protection of Americans."

"What about protection of the compound itself? Have you ever asked Major Si why he lets the enemy roam so freely in and around this facility?" Brand asked.

Fletcher brushed crumbs from the corners of his thick, blond mustache. "Hell, no. It's treated the same as the dumb ass soldier with his finger on the switch of a live mike. If I complained about security, Si would smile right in my face, pretending not to understand me. That's the Vietnamese equivalent of the Yankee bird. (He held up an extended middle finger.) My counterpart would follow this with a long speech on how laying wire, putting in radio nets, and establishing security were Vietnamese problems. Mine, and now Rafe's mission, he would politely remind us, is to stay out of his way, give technical advice when he asks for it and stay alive 'til our tour of duty is up. I told you, survival, survival, survival is all that matters out here. So far, I'm batting 100 percent on all counts."

"What happens if the enemy, or Si, changes the rules back to survival of the fittest?" asked Brand.

"Then it's time to call in the U.S. Calvary. But that's Rafe's problem, not mine after tomorrow." Fletcher adjusted a holstered Colt 45-caliber into position under his left armpit and started to place the strap of a Leica camera over his right shoulder.

"Here, since your hands are free, Winston, may be you can handle the photography. The information types in Saigon like nothing better than pictures of us winning the hearts and minds of these people." The senior advisor handed the camera to Brand then turned to face Hewlett.

"Get your weapon, and let's mount up, Lieutenant. Only fools and newsmen venture into Charlie's territory in broad daylight unarmed.

12 UP-COUNTRY DÉMARCHE

There are three kinds of friendship equal in number to the things that are lovable; for those that love each other wish well to each other in that respect in which they love one another. Those who love each other for their usefulness do not love each other for themselves but for some benefit that they get from each other. So, too, with those who love for the sake of pleasure.

—*Aristotle*

MAJ. ALEX SPEAR RUBBED his hand through his thick, blond hair, studying the note cards on the conference table in front of him. He looked up as General Pavler introduced a new member to the Operation Checkmate Executive Committee of Six. The major started to light his pipe when Pavler seated on his right motioned him to address the committee, but then the general had a second thought.

"Before we get into all this spook stuff, tell me what you've heard from our young firebrand up-country?" Pavler asked Alex who had taken up a position near the blackboard.

"Brand called yesterday afternoon. He asked about his accreditation status."

"Did he sound sober?"

"Yes, sir, far as I could tell."

"Who's Brand?" One of the field grade officers asked.

"I'll fill you in later," said Pavler turning toward Alex. "That reminds me. We need a code name for Winston. Any suggestions?"

The major barely hesitated. "'Live Coal' springs to mind."

"Excellent," said Pavler pounding the table for emphasis. "'Live Coal' it is." The general turned to face the other four officers seated around the conference table. "Gentlemen, strike the reference to Winston or Brand. Hereafter, in these circles, refer to him as 'Live Coal.' Let's hope this code name affords him some protection."

"Speaking of protection," said Alex, "'Live Coal' refused the weapon you offered him. It was still on his dresser when I left the BOQ this morning."

"Damn stubborn fool," said Pavler rubbing his forehead. "He'll learn one day that combat often erases the line between the brave and the foolish. What else did he have to say?"

"He asked about Senator Kearney's vendetta against him."

"And you told him?"

"Check with you when he gets back."

"Good. Anything else?"

"He wanted a progress report on our investigation into the threats to his life."

"Yes, go on."

"I told Winston, ah, 'Live Coal,' we did find a set of prints other than his on the warning note passed to him at Travis. He agreed to wait for the FBI analysis." Alex retrieved his note cards from the conference table and started back toward the blackboard.

"Hold on a minute," said Pavler rustling through a pile of papers. "Somewhere in this clutter are—ah, here they are— orders for Gwen and your youngsters to relocate to the Philippines."

"I can't believe it. The marine corps never makes exceptions."

"Well, they damn well did in this case. I told the commandant we need you for the duration. Until we catch this bastard R-3, we're stuck here, so we might as well make the best of it. I know you're not the kind of officer to abuse the privilege by flying off to Manila every weekend to bed your wife. Don't think Norma and I haven't given it some thought."

"Sir, I can't tell you how happy this makes me," said Alex.

"Thank 'Live Coal's' sister. She gave me the idea."

"I'll do that next time I'm in Hawaii. Better yet I'll have Gwen stop in on her way to the Philippines."

"You do that, and you'll be a helluva of a lot more thoughtful than her brother."

"In 'Live Coal's' defense, General, he had his hands full with the mugging and an incident with a young woman," said Alex relieved to shift the subject back to Brand.

"Really. Who's that?"

"A Spanish-American flight attendant based in Manila. Winston—strike that—'Live Coal' had a rocky start with her that turned romantic after our near miss at Guam."

"Really? What's her name?"

"Maria Monclova."

"I'll have Norma check her out. She might be helpful in getting your family settled and calming 'Live Coal' down as well. Enough chatter. I'm sorry to keep you waiting, gentlemen, but we had these loose ends dangling like a frayed boot strap. Now it's on to our update on R-3. Alex, what's the latest on the palace bombing?"

On the blackboard the marine major had previously listed the names and offices of 12 council ministers who had left a meeting with Diem before the bomb attack on the president. Across from the names in another column Alex listed reported excuses for their absences. As he checked off each column, Alex saw surprise register in Pavler's face. No doubt the number of high ranking uniformed officers on the list raised eyebrows among other members of the committee as well, because the heart of the South Vietnamese General Staff had managed to be out of the palace when the bombs struck.

"Note," said Alex turning to face the other five members of the committee, "we're unable to pin down locations on either the secret police or the national police since we wanted to avoid a spy versus spy situation."

"In other words," said Pavler, "the security officials were uncooperative."

"No, sir, we just thought it more prudent not to press the matter too vigorously, too soon, arousing suspicion among our intelligence or security counterparts."

"Then, following up on the general's question, how do we get them to furnish this information to rule them out as a suspect?" asked one of the two full colonels present.

Alex walked over to the table and took his seat beside Pavler. He lit his pipe, exhaling a thick puff of smoke with his reply. "Colonel, I didn't mean to leave the impression the palace bombing incident in any way cuts down on our list of suspects. As far as I'm concerned, anyone in the Vietnamese government could be our suspected R-3." He turned to face Pavler. "With your permission, general, this might be a good point to review our earlier findings."

"Go ahead," said Pavler.

"I'll make this brief," said the major, setting his pipe aside. "Either R-3 came south or was already here and stayed after the North Vietnamese signed the Geneva Accords with the French in 1954. The communists agreed to pull their troops back above the 17th parallel. But, of course, we know now that as many as 30,000 Viet Minh troops either stayed in the south or infiltrated the refugee movement headed south. "

"Alex, you're going back too far in history," said Pavler. "Take a breather. Let me summarize the point you're driving toward."

Alex picked up his pipe and tapped it gently against the side of an ash tray as he waited for the general to speak.

"Here's the point. Nobody puts that many troops anywhere without the command and control structure to direct them. We believe Hanoi decided to position someone who could move in both worlds—infiltrate the highest levels of the South Vietnamese government while retaining control over a Communist fifth column. In short, one slick cookie." Pavler paused, sweeping his hand toward the blackboard. "Nearly everyone on Alex's list needs to be covertly investigated as a possible suspect if our suspicions about R-3 are correct. However, we must be careful in our intelligence gathering operations not to interfere with national sovereignty rights or issues where we have no jurisdiction, unlike R-3, until we have proof. But any one of those occupying important positions or their staff members could be either former Viet Minh sympathizers or officials, as well as Catholic refugees from the north who generally support Diem. It's well known that communist infiltration in South Vietnamese society is rampant, not to mention the government. It's as simple as that." Pavler paused again to recognize the navy captain who had raised his hand.

"General, you said earlier we've intercepted message traffic between R-1 and R-2 in Hanoi and R-3 operating in the south, proving this infiltration by R-3. But my question to Major Spear is, has the palace bombing brought us any closer to identifying R-3 as a member of the ruling government?"

"Well, Alex?" said Pavler.

Spear rubbed both eyes with his knuckles as if to clear his vision before he responded. He further stalled by refilling his pipe and standing up behind his chair.

"That's hard to say, Captain. In the strictest sense, we can't make the connection. Yet, we'd be foolish to rule any suspect out at this point. We have to proceed on the theory that one of R-3's primary objectives is the fall of the Diem government, particularly in this bombing incident attempt to assassinate the ruling family. Someone ordered the palace bombing. My hunch is that it was an inside job orchestrated by R-3, which by definition places him in the highest government circles."

"And you'd ruin these men's reputations based on speculation?" asked the Captain.

"No sir, the investigations will be secret, but necessary for intelligence purposes, because I'd be the first to recognize that the laws of logic go out the window under wartime conditions. The job of intelligence is needed because of the paradoxes involved between beasts and patriots. In war they share a tremendous sense of comradeship similar to General Pavler's earlier point regarding the indistinguishable lines between the brave and foolish."

"We're not here to discuss philosophy, Major," said the senior naval officer.

"If it's my philosophy, it's damned well acceptable anywhere," said Pavler laughing to ease the tension. Please finish your point and sit down, Alex."

Spear continued, "All these men on the lists were hand-picked by President Diem. Logic says he would select only loyal patriots. Yet, we've all seen men change after facing death on the battlefield, and then again in the wake of a glorious victory. But in R-3's case, we're dealing with an unchangeable beast, disguised as a patriot and patient enough to wait us out. Our job? Find the slightest chink in his armor and expose the monster inside. If patriots are investigated in the process, the sincere ones will be revealed to us in time."

"I agree," said Pavler. "We've got to double our efforts to get into the minds of these suspects. Granted, not an easy task where fellow spooks or civilians are concerned. Got any ideas along these lines? Please be brief, Alex."

"Yes sir, regarding civilians, we've got moles inside the ministry of transportation, the national police and other agencies. But regarding the Western press, quite frankly, none of the American or foreign correspondents working in the South, using questionable sources and filing continuous negative reports, have won its trust, or ours. This might be an assignment for 'Live Coal' if he ever decides to cooperate."

"Forget that for the moment. What about the security agencies?" asked General Pavler.

"That's going to take some time. I believe they're less likely suspects though, because of security clearance procedures the government has in place."

"Hold it, Alex. That runs counter to the beast within theory you so eloquently defended a moment ago."

"You're right, General. Everybody stays on the hook at this juncture. But to make our list more manageable, I've narrowed it down to five prime suspects who might have been exposed to Western philosophy—the new lead we discussed earlier."

"And who are we talking about?" asked Pavler.

"At the top of the list, as unlikely as it appears, I've got Minister Nhu, the president's own brother. He has studied in Paris, undoubtedly exposed to philosophy, and he has intimated that if the U.S. balks at its commitment, he might consider doing business with neutrals, or even negotiate with the other side."

"What's all this philosophy stuff?" the navy captain interjected.

"Something Alex picked up from 'Live Coal.' I'll brief you later," said Pavler. Then turning back to Spear, Pavler admonished, "Go ahead, Alex."

"Next in order are four generals. Each is identified with one of three groups aligned with special interests—the pro-Buddhist wing, the rigid anti-communist hardliners and the pro-French faction. These three pro-groups whose loyalties are split might be eyed as possible fertile fields for communist infiltration, although, granted, they might be more inclined to participate in a coup."

"What about Madame Nhu? Or are you ruling out the possibility that R-3 could be a woman?" the air force colonel asked.

"Two excellent questions, sir," said Alex. "First, Madame Nhu is more fervently anti-communist than her brother-in-law, although both she and the president were Ho Chi Minh's prisoners. She was captured by Viet Minh guerrillas in December 1946, and imprisoned near Hue. During her captivity, she helped others survive, including her baby daughter and mother-in-law. This wealthy-born, intelligent woman was reduced to living in rags. Just before the French closed in on the camp where she was held, she used the confusion to escape to a convent where she plotted her revenge against the communists. She certainly has the cunning of R-3. But there's no way this woman would forge an alliance with Ho. I'm sorry, Colonel, I forgot the second part of your question."

"I wanted to know whether you thought R-3 could be a woman, seeing that you have no females on your lists of suspects."

"Oh, yes, thank you, now I remember. In light of the philosophical matter touched on earlier, General Pavler and I reviewed Ho's personal history searching for any one of his close associates who might share his interest in Western philosophy. The best we we're able to come up with was that he had several geographical wives, one each in Paris, Moscow and Hong Kong. One of these women bore him a daughter who turned up in Hong Kong. That was in 1932, the same year Ho feigned his death to escape from British authorities. She would've had no contact with her father and today would just be turning 30. No one on our suspect list is that young, and we're fairly certain that a female R-3 would have to be at least eight years older to match his exploits. That's where things stand at the moment."

Pavler stood up, planted his feet apart paratrooper style and addressed the committee. "Gentlemen, for the moment, we'll proceed as follows: One by one, we'll eliminate a name from the list of five as information becomes available to clear them as suspects. Once we've exhausted the initial list, we'll move down to the next five. Meantime, we'll keep all suspects under some minimum surveillance and investigation, then remove or move up any promising leads accordingly. This will conserve our own resources. Alex, you should continue your efforts to get some of our people into the civilian-headed ministries and in the security agencies."

Later, as Major Alex Spear waited for his driver to bring the jeep around, he still had the Committee of Six meeting on his mind. Left unsaid, yet lingering below the surface, he knew the question General Pavler and the rest of the committee wanted answered most was, "When are we going to stop reacting to R-3 and began anticipating his actions?" He chided himself for not having the answers after ten years' experience in military intelligence. He and Winston Brand were alike in this respect, he reminded himself. Both were experienced professionals on a make-or-break assignment that could turn out to be a career-changer.

When the jeep got underway, a red-headed officer without a cap waved him to a stop under the MAAG archway, Spear was pleased with the diversion. He directed his driver to pull over to the curbside.

"Lieutenant Kearney, what can I do for you?" he asked.

"Give me and my new friend a ride to the Five Oceans," Tank, Jr., replied.

"Sure, hop in." Alex dismounted from the passenger side and held the seat forward so the two men could climb in the back with Kearny leading the way.

"Meet Sheenar Tillerstein, Major. He's with *The New York Times* and just arrived in the war zone."

Alex could hear the reporter breathing heavily under the burden of settling his bulk into the narrow seat.

"My pleasure, Major," the civilian said. Alex watched him wipe sweat from his brow, dark mustache and beard with one hand and was relieved to see him extend the other one.

The man's pudgy fingers collapsed like wet plaster of Paris under Alex's firm grip. From the corner of the reporter's mouth, gum protruded, held in place by crooked teeth.

As Alex directed his driver to proceed, he asked Tillerstein, "What's your business at the Five Oceans?"

The reporter shifted the gum wad to the other side of his thick lips, exposing more yellow, uneven teeth.

"I'm looking for Winston Brand. He works for me. Kearney said he was staying in one of your extra rooms. You'd think he'd be on hand to meet his boss at the airport," said Tillerstein.

Alex stared at the man in disbelief. The reporter was closer to Kearney's age than Brand's, 27 at the most. He tried to imagine Winston in the company of this unkempt youngster, much less looking to him for guidance. *The New York Times* has a weird sense of humor, he thought. To Tillerstein, he replied: "Brand is up-country on assignment."

"That's where I'm going, too," Kearney said.

"I thought you were posted here at the headquarters," said the major.

"That's been changed. Up-country's where the action is. Maybe Sheenar will come and do a story on me."

"Better yet, I'll assign Brand the job as punishment for his negligence," chuckled Tillerstein, nearly dislodging the gum.

Spear tried to tune them out as the two traded inanities about Winston Brand. He was about to ask them to knock it off when Tillerstein tapped him on the shoulder.

"If Brand's not at the Five Oceans, I might as well grab a cab back to the Caravelle. Let me out at the next intersection, Major."

"Certainly," said Alex wishing Kearney would join Tillerstein.

"I'll give you a call when I get settled at Song Be," said Kearney.

"Yeah, do that, man. And, Major, the next time you're in contact with Brand, tell 'em his boss is pissed, and if he wants to get back in my good graces, he should show up at my welcoming party at Pierre Girard's pad, a week from this Saturday night."

"I'll give Winston your message. Will he know how to find this place?"

"Are you kidding? I'm told everybody in Saigon is acquainted with Girard's digs. You can come, too, if you want."

"Sorry, but I've got other plans," said Alex.

"Suit yourself, but it'll be a blast with hot and cold running geishas, if we don't get raided by Nhu's secret police," sneered Tillerstein.

"Damn, Sheenar, it sounds like my kind of party. Wish I were going to be around for it," said Kearney.

"There'll be others," promised Tillerstein. "We'll never let the war interfere with a good time."

"Where'd you meet that guy?" Spear asked when Tillerstein had gotten out of earshot.

"My dad told me Sheenar was going to be Brand's replacement, and he asked the guy to look me up. Nice fellow, wouldn't you say?"

Alex allowed silence to speak for him.

Brand watched Erik Fletcher signal Lt. Rafe Hewlett to slow down as the dust swirled around the rear of the captain's vehicle ahead of them on a bend in the road.

"Why is he stopping here? Don't tell me it's another photo op," Brand said eyeing the jungle foliage on either side of the jeep.

"Ah dunno. Suppose he's got his reasons." Hewlett reached past Brand to pick up a carbine from the rear seat.

Through the dust Brand saw Fletcher dismount. Was this another candy stop for the kids, the reporter wondered? Every five kilometers or so, the senior American advisor had conducted the same strange ritual. He would poke his automatic into the underbrush for several minutes, then wait for a group of Vietnamese youngsters to emerge laughing and removing their conical hats out of respect for the American. Each time Brand had snapped a number of photos while Fletcher passed lollipops out to the children surrounding his jeep. Brand heard the senior advisor remind his replacement, "Where there're no kids, start worrying." On the last stop Fletcher had announced they were 15 minutes out from the Devereau plantation.

Reminded of Alex Spear's lollipop escapade in the air terminal at Travis, Brand commented on the strange fetish the American military had for dispensing candy.

"You wanta heah somethin' more weird than that?" Hewlett had asked, not waiting for an answer. "Fletch slipped me what he called his last letter home and said that if anything happens, one of us should see that Susan gets it." He had held up a white envelope for Brand's inspection.

With this incident fresh in his mind and seeing no children in the road, Brand decided to leave the Leica in the vehicle this time. He followed close behind Hewlett as the two walked up to Fletcher standing behind his jeep.

"Look down there," the captain said pointing his Colt .45 at a stream bed that crisscrossed the highway with low hills rising on both sides less than 20 meters above the dust covered road. "Perfect spot for an ambush, or either I'm too much of a short-timer to think straight," the Texan added.

"What'll we do?" Rafe asked.

"Well, up the road a bit, it doesn't get much better. On one side, there's an abandoned rubber plantation all grown over now, and on the other a banana grove where we should be able to see some youngsters milling about. Don't see any kids there or even in this spot, do you guys?"

Almost in unison Hewlett and Brand shook their heads as they squinted against the morning sun.

"Probably just a case of jitters on my part," said Fletcher. "Charlie's never attacked at daylight on this stretch in all the months I've been traveling it. What in the hell would he want with two company grade officers and a lowly civilian scribe anyway?"

Brand shifted from side to side stirring up a cloud of dust. He wiped his forehead with the back of his hand, feeling the sweat run through his fingers.

"Maybe you guys should know, bad luck or worse has dogged me since I started out for Vietnam."

Fletcher re-holstered his weapon and twirled the corners of his mustache as he spoke. "Yeah, we'd like to hear about that sometime, Winston, but right now we should press on. Tell you what, though. With one jinxed guy and the other green, I'll take the lead. You two hold back until my driver and I get past the plantation and the banana grove out yonder. From there, it's gently rolling plateau all the way to the Frenchie's place. Just in case, Rafe, you should get on the radio and call base camp with our position. If push comes to shove, get that asshole *Thieu-ta* Si to send in the cavalry."

The authority in Fletcher's tone was unmistakable. Hewlett and Brand retreated toward their own vehicle. They had gone about 20 yards when behind them a deafening sound sent both men sprawling in the dust. Brand felt the weight of Hewlett's massive body trap his ankles. In a flash the lieutenant regained his feet, dashed back toward his parked vehicle, zigzagging and firing the carbine indiscriminately into the tall grass on either side of the road.

Still on the ground, Brand turned to see black and gray smoke encompassing Fletcher's vehicle on the knoll at the bend in the road where only moments ago the three men stood chatting. He checked himself for injuries and found none. He did discover, lying next to him in the road, the white envelope Hewlett had shown him earlier. Without thought, he slipped it into the pocket of his mufti and decided to work his way toward Fletcher's burning jeep. He had two objectives in mind—help Fletcher, or if beyond help, get the captain's weapon to fend-off any follow-up attacks.

Approaching the passenger side of the vehicle in a crouch, Brand came face-to-thigh with Fletcher's mangled right leg that twitched uncontrollably over the vehicle's twisted frame. Pulling himself up to eye level with the advisor, the picture turned grimmer—so much so that Brand gasped for breath and covered his mouth to keep from vomiting. He recoiled in horror taking a few steps toward Hewlett's vehicle waving his arms in an attempt to summon help. But the lieutenant was busy on the radio. Brand forced himself to look at the wounded advisor who lay back in the seat eyes fixed unblinkingly on the sun. Three wire springs from the vehicle's back cushion protruded from the officer's body. One coil on each side of his sternum pinned him to the seat. The third extended from his stomach spurting blood. Brand tried to free the impaled man who groaned louder with every attempt.

"Hold on, Fletch, old boy. I'll get Rafe to help," said Brand searching the captain's eyes for a sign of acknowledgment. None came. He started to leave, then remembered the weapon. An odor of burnt leather and skin assaulted his nostrils as he dislodged a smoldering Vietnamese Army boot with a bloody ankle still attached from under Fletcher's arm pit. Gingerly, he unfastened the .45 from the advisor's shoulder holster entangled with the Vietnamese driver's lifeless body. The slightest pull on the straps around Fletcher's upper torso brought forth more mournful groans. With the weapon in hand, the reporter searched the distant plantation and banana grove areas expecting to see a column of Viet Cong charging toward him up the road. Nothing moved and the stillness scared him into action.

Brand ran upright this time in a straight path toward Hewlett's jeep.

"Come quick! Fletcher's in a bad way. He's gotten the whole damn back of the seat embedded in his chest. I couldn't help him."

"Heah, get on the radio an' give 'em these coordinates. Then drive the jeep to the other vehicle and pick up Fletch and me." Hewlett tossed Brand a marked map and headed for the wreckage, carbine at the port position.

The officer called over his shoulder, "Any Cong headed our way?"

"Didn't see any," Brand shouted.

The radio mounted on the rear seat suddenly crackled to life. Brand scrambled for the transmitter and read the coordinates into the hand-held mike.

"Say again, your transmission, more slowly, over," said the Vietnamese operator on the other end.

Brand repeated the message and added: "Send help. American badly wounded."

"Whokay, help come soon, you see. Stay on this frequency. Over."

As he lifted the mike to his lips, pressing down the button to transmit, the reporter saw off in the distance two columns of armed men trotting toward him up the road. There was no way the South Vietnamese signal battalion had responded that fast. Brand knew the VC were bearing down on Hewlett and him. He tossed the mike into the back seat, jumped behind the wheel and gunned the engine, heading the vehicle in Hewlett's general direction.

He pulled alongside Fletcher's smoldering jeep and shouted to Hewlett, "VC coming fast on foot from our rear."

"Hold on. We can't leave Fletch here to die," the lieutenant shouted back.

Brand watched the giant give a final pull and twist at the seat. It broke loose from its weakened moorings, and before Winston could react, Hewlett had deposited Fletcher, with seat still attached, into the back of the vehicle.

"Let me drive. You take this carbine and ride shotgun. Try to keep Fletcher as still as possible," the officer directed.

"Where in the hell are we going? We're sandwiched between ambush sites," said Brand.

"We've got to take our chances on getting through to the plantation. If anything moves in that banana grove, don't ask questions. Shoot first."

But Brand tuned-out the lieutenant. He fumbled in his jacket pocket pushing the envelope aside to get at Willie. "With any luck at all," he told himself, "I'll be oblivious to the bullet that crashes into my skull." Then his eyes met those of the wounded officer, and he heard the man's labored breathing. The combination shamed him into returning the flask to his pocket.

"You're right, Captain Fletcher. We'll get the job done, then drink to your recovery." Brand picked up the rifle and tried to steady his shaking hands against its stock.

REBELS ALL

Mel R. Jones
Marian N. Jones

PART 2:
THE LAY OF A FOREIGN LAND
SOUTH VIETNAM, 1962

"We must all hang together or assuredly we shall all hang separately."
—Benjamin Franklin

13 THE KILLING ZONE

If you are not winning, you are losing, because the enemy can always sit out a stalemate without making any concessions.
—Sir Robert Thompson

CAPTAIN BAO PRESSED one side of the binoculars against his eye patch. With his good eye he tried to focus the instrument on the Viet Cong troops positioned along the road. He fumbled with the eye piece for a full minute and only gave up when General Tran Van Chien asked to have the binoculars returned.

"Never could get the hang of those things," said Bao in a cheerful manner as he wiped sweat from around his eye with the back of his hand. "Got anything less complicated?"

The VC general called one of his sharpshooters over to the knoll above the road on which he and Bao stood concealed in the elephant grass. He removed the sniper scope from the soldier's rifle and handed it to Bao.

"Perhaps this will fit you better," said General Chien.

"Thanks, Comrade General. But I sense we're close enough to the action to get a full view of our leader's plan which was my honor to deliver to you."

The general made no reply, so Bao again directed himself to activity along the road where more than 100 Viet Cong soldiers, camouflaged and ready to fire automatic weapons point-blank onto the highway quietly awaited Chien's signal. At intervals the general lowered his arm and the men on the road split-off into groups of five and disappeared into the dense foliage that covered the ground on both sides of the dirt road. The grass was high enough to conceal a standing man.

"Comrade General, is the enemy always so predictable that you know precisely where to ambush him?" Bao asked in a soft voice.

"Always. Watch when the shooting starts. He'll try to run his thin-skinned vehicles out of the killing zone and bring up his armor, if he has any, fast from the rear. But before he reacts, we will have slipped back into the jungle and vanished."

"Run away when you have him trapped? I don't understand," said Bao.

"That's because, like the enemy, you see but one phase of a two-part diversionary tactic."

Bao sensed that the field commander expected R-3's personal adjutant to report on how the secret plan was implemented, so he grew bolder with his questions.

"If this ambush is a second diversion, then, where was the first, and what is the main objective?" Bao searched the general's face for a reaction. He was relieved when a benign smile greeted his impertinence.

"The plan is simple," replied Chien. "Earlier, we ambushed a small convoy comprised of two American military advisors and a foreign journalist on their way to the Devereau plantation. That was diversion one. Here we intend to pin down those sent to rescue the Americans."

"The second diversion?"

"Exactly, and we will remain here only long enough for our comrades to ransack the enemy's compound at Loc Ninh while he plays cavalry-to-the-rescue taught to him by the Americans. Radios, not killing, are what we're after."

"Brilliant, sir."

"But there's an added bonus to this operation."

"Tell me. It'll add spice to my report to *Ayr-Ba*," Bao lied.

"At the first ambush site, one of the Americans was badly wounded. I'm hoping it's the journalist, Winston Brand."

The mention of Brand's name caused Bao to fidget with his eye-patch and a low whistle escaped from his pursed lips. He decided to bluff his way toward more information.

"Of course, Brand's the guy *Ayr-Ba* called shrewd and dangerous. What's your interest in him, Comrade General?"

"Didn't *Ayr-Ba* tell you Hanoi has marked the reporter for elimination? Or is this another matter our leader has kept from you for your own safety?"

The tone in the general's voice had turned hostile. Bao knew he had to lie his way out of this predicament or face the prospect that the field commander would discover he was no more than a messenger who had misrepresented himself. Besides, he thought, *Ayr-Ba* might restore his role as adjutant if he showed initiative, even if he secured a position in the Diem regime as well.

"Of course, I know this Brand." Bao lied, "As a matter of fact, my next stop is the Devereau plantation. Part of my mission there is to kill the reporter. If you must know, I was standing next to *Ayr-Ba* when the word came down from Hanoi."

"Good. Then perhaps my men have saved us all a great deal of trouble," said Chien.

Bao knew he had turned the matter to his advantage, so he pressed the point. This time he wore a benign smile.

"Be assured, Comrade General, if the American reporter lives, I'll finish the job and report to *Ayr-Ba* that we worked together. All I need from you is a contact at the plantation eager and willing to carry out the wishes of our superiors."

"I have just the man. He's the leader of our cell at the Devereau's. After this skirmish is over, I'll give you the code-words for contacting him," said Chien.

Bao raised the sniper scope to his eye and surveyed the ambush site. At one end of the road, he spotted a heavy weapons crew servicing what appeared to be a 75 mm recoilless rifle. He followed the road from this bend along the jungle foliage until he came to another curve west of the first gun position. A second 75 mm dominated the road at this point positioned about 15 feet into the jungle. These two formidable weapons marked each boundary of the killing zone, he surmised.

Suddenly an ARVN truck appeared in the scope, and Bao heard the engine strain as the vehicle geared down to negotiate the sharp curve in front of the VC gun position. Six other vehicles mounting machine guns atop their cabs followed in succession. Bao estimated the interval between vehicles in the ARVN convoy at three to four truck lengths. In this space, several jeeps crisscrossed in front of the larger vehicles darting from one side of the road to the other. Bao swung the glass to his left attracted by one of the jeeps which pulled ahead of the first truck as it approached the eastern boundary of the killing zone. He saw a South Vietnamese officer dismount the jeep and wave the lead truck to a stop. The major then pointed to an area near where Bao knew the hidden 75 mm waited.

On signal from the officer, the ARVN machine-gunner, standing in the bed of the halted truck, with elbows resting on the cab for support, fired a burst into the edge of the jungle. At the same instance, 10 to 15 ARVN soldiers leapt from the tailgate and fanned out along the road. When the Viet Cong soldiers answered only with small arms and automatic weapons from both sides of the road, Bao first thought that one of Chien's big weapons had been neutralized. He expected the general to show some sign of frustration that the ARVN major had denied Chien benefit of total surprise. Instead the seasoned jungle warrior merely cupped his hands over his ears and waited. Bao followed suit just in time to blunt the deafening roar of a 75 mm recoilless rifle round exploding on impact with the lead truck's gas tank. The flaming vehicle with its towed trailer still attached rolled to its side and blocked the eastern stretch of the highway.

Without the aid of the sniper scope, Bao was close enough to see the reaction of the drivers in the following trucks whose first warning of an ambush came with the explosion. Some halted in place. Others tried unsuccessfully to turn around in the narrow strip of dusty roadway. At the western end of the ambush site, the second recoilless rifle round slammed into the cargo area of the last truck in the convoy. The explosion hurled bodies and debris in four directions, although the vehicle itself seemed anchored to the center of the road. The trap was sealed at both ends. Bao asked General Chien to let him help mop up the confused and vulnerable ARVN forces.

"I told you, killing is not our mission. Not this day," shouted Chien over the sporadic small arms fire. "In five minutes, we'll stop shooting. The enemy will follow our lead, satisfied with a stalemate. Ten minutes after that, we'll both depart the field. One to celebrate victory. The other to discover his real losses."

"At least lend me a rifle to kill that bastard who almost spoiled your plans," pleaded Bao. He pointed the sniper scope at the Vietnamese major who had remounted the lead jeep.

"Again, comrade, I must say no. Every adjutant wants combat experience, but to kill poor *Thieu-ta* Si serves no purpose. You would only do him a favor. The loss of an American under his protection, plus the confiscated radios, by now in our possession, are disgrace enough upon his head."

"But he lives to lead the puppet troops against our brothers on another day," Bao protested.

"Not for long. *Ayr-Ba* himself reminds us that a disgraced foe is twice beaten—once by us and more severely by those he serves. Who knows? Si's bitterness may force him to our side one day."

"You are right to upbraid me, Comrade General. I know little about such matters."

"Well, if you finish this matter with Winston Brand as agreed, perhaps you'll find that killing zone better suited to an adjutant."

That same afternoon, Alex Spear and Nick Jenicoso paced around the helipad at Tan Son Nhut airport. Each time the two men passed each other, Alex saw the doctor brush back his cowlick and heard him mutter under his breath. Off in the distance a World Airways Connie taxied toward the terminal, and the noise was too great for Alex to make out Jenicoso's words. Finally, the marine major grabbed the short, squat man by the elbow and turned him around in his tracks.

"Doc, I haven't heard a word you've said, and the chopper is due any minute. What's bothering you?"

"Believe me, I'd feel better if you were going along."

"We went over that on the drive out here. There's room for you and two medevac litters. As it is, we don't know how many casualties there are. We do know of two ambushes at two locations less than an hour apart."

"Believe me, won't that be too much for one doctor?"

"ARVN has its own medics at the camp hospital at Loc Ninh. We want you to check on the three Americans headed to a French plantation along the Cambodian border. The chopper pilot has the coordinates. I know you'll do what you can." Alex paused, then added almost in a whisper. "Fixed wing, spotter aircraft reported one burning vehicle with a body inside. No sign of the second jeep."

"Believe me, you should've told me this before. How horrible. We can't let our lads go unattended."

"There's more bad news," said the major.

"I'm not ready for this."

"Winston may be one of the casualties."

"Believe me. My day is ruined unless there's somebody left to help."

"Well, Winston's like a cat with nine lives, so we shouldn't count him out yet," said Spear.

"How do we know which number he's on by now?"

"Good question, Doc. Let's hope you get the chance to ask him. Here comes the chopper. Please be careful yourself. Even a French plantation is not a safe area."

"Believe me. I intend to stay in touch."

"Yes, by radio, then by telephone once you've reached the Devereau place," said Spear.

Alex watched the helicopter until it was little more than a blip on the horizon. He filled his pipe and leaned up against the terminal building. Positioned out of sight of the troops who passed from the Connie into the terminal, his thoughts centered on Brand. He wondered if he had moved too fast in urging the correspondent to go up-country so soon after his arrival. Most of the news people preferred to hang around the Saigon bars for a week or more before they ventured into the field. Others never left Saigon, or if they did, were always back at the Caravelle or some other plush surroundings prior to nightfall. This guy Tillerstein should have gone in Winston's place, Alex told himself. After all, he's the *Times* head man. Then he remembered that civilians followed a different code. They led by pushing from behind, rather than out in front of the action. It cheered him to think Brand was like a marine in this respect.

Spear stepped from the shadows and gently tapped his pipe against the wall of the building. He crushed the smoldering tobacco embers underfoot. Again, this set his mind on thoughts of the man he had named "Live Coal." "Better for Winston to never know that designation," Alex told himself. "At least, if captured, Brand could look the enemy right in the eye and deny any involvement with military intelligence." He tried to imagine a scenario in which Winston would break or acquiesce to an interrogator's probe and came up with none as long as the reporter remained sober. If they got him drunk, ignorance of his 'Live Coal' status might prove Brand's best ally, Spear concluded.

About to enter the building, Alex heard someone call him by rank. He turned to see Maria Monclova. The women waved with one hand while she balanced a flight bag in the other.

"I could smell your maple-scented tobacco before I actually saw you." The cheerfulness in her voice served as a balm for his own anxiety. He held the door open for her.

"Let's add the aroma of coffee to the setting. My treat," he said.

"I've only got a few minutes before we takeoff for Bangkok. They don't allow us to dally too long in the war zone, you know."

"I can see why. That big Connie's too inviting a target. The pilots tell me they've had a few sniper rounds hit their aircraft on approach."

"I don't even like to think about it." She placed a hand against her temple.

"Then we'll put it out of our minds. By the way, you just missed Doctor Jenicoso."

"How is he?"

"Believe me, he hasn't changed." Pleased that his imitation of the physician's speech pattern erased the look of concern in her deep blue eyes, Alex saw that her whole face now radiated a fond remembrance.

Over coffee, he tried to keep the conversation upbeat and steer it away from Brand as long as possible. But as she got up to leave, she placed both hands palms down, leaned across the table and looked him straight in the eye.

"Something's happened to Winston, hasn't it?"

"How did you know?" He was caught off guard and so surprised, he abandoned any feeble attempts to stall the matter further.

She pulled back, and he saw tears glisten in her eyes. He searched his pocket for a handkerchief, but she had already retrieved one from her flight bag.

"I'm sorry, Maria. I should've told you straight out. Winston ran into some trouble up-country. We know someone in his party is wounded but have no other details. Nor do we know where any of them are at the moment."

He paused, then added: "Commander Jenicoso's on his way to the area. We'll know more when he reports in."

"Major, promise you'll call me in Bangkok with any news."

"Certainly."

"And will you tell Winston the next time you see him that I'm here every Thursday afternoon for about 30 minutes."

"Yes, of course."

"Then next week, I'll wait for him at this same table."

"Good. We should all hope for the best."

"And pray," she said.

"Yes, that too."

"God's not finished with him," she said.

"Nor with any of the rest of us," he replied.

Alex escorted her to the parked aircraft and waited at the ramp while she went aboard to write a note to Brand. He used the time to jot down Norma Pavler's address and telephone number in the Philippines. Maria was out of breath but smiled again on her return.

"Thanks for your support. If there's anything I can do for you in Bangkok or Manila, I'm at your service."

"Yes, Maria, here's someone I'd like you to look up." He gave her the slip of paper, and she handed him a sealed envelope marked personal for Winston Brand.

"Is there a message?" she asked.

"Not really. Just someone you should get to know, and who will introduce you to my wife Gwen, who's relocating to Manila. The Pavler's are like family to Winston."

"It'll be my pleasure to meet them all."

"And I'm sure they'll feel the same." He embraced her, and she kissed his cheek.

On the drive back from the airport Maj. Alex Spear whistled the Marine's Hymn over and over again. It buoyed his spirits to realize that whether Brand knew it or not, like him, he had someone to come home to.

14 ACROSS TWO CULTURES

The true way to be deceived is to think oneself more clever than others.
—François de La Rochefoucauld

BRAND STOOD ON THE second floor gallery and looked down upon the square in front of the Devereau Plantation. The litter used to remove Captain Fletcher's lifeless body lay next to Hewlett's jeep still parked on the cobblestones. A young Vietnamese servant appeared with a hose and brush. The boy washed the advisor's blood from the canvas stretcher, then looked up at Winston on the high balcony and pointed to the pool of blood in the back seat of the vehicle. Brand nodded and turned away as blood and water ran between the stones. The reporter found his cigarettes in the pocket of the borrowed robe. He inhaled deeply, then expelled the smoke in one breath between clenched teeth. He was saddened over the death of Erik Fletcher and with the way Rafe Hewlett had taken the news. He recalled how the lieutenant had talked of nothing else since their arrival. The young officer blamed himself: He had "driven too slowly." He should have "headed back to the ARVN compound where there was a doctor." He should have "taken time to stop Fletch's bleeding on the roadside instead of worrying about his and Brand's safety."

Winston thought the Devereau's daughter had offered the best arguments when she countered Hewlett: "Monsieur Brand said you drove at the right speed for the conditions. You were closer to our home than the ARVN encampment. You had people chasing you and there was no way you could've known that the plantation medical officer was away on his rounds."

Brand then assured Hewlett that, had the roles been reversed, Fletcher would have no doubt acted in the same manner. This comment seemed to take the edge off the lieutenant's guilt, and he retired to his quarters next to Brand's in the 28 room mansion.

As Brand started back to his own room, he heard the servant calling from below and walked over to the edge of the railing. The boy held aloft Fletcher's holstered Colt .45 Brand had retrieved during the ambush, but had left in the Jeep when arriving at the Devereau plantation.

"Monsieur, what you want me do with this?"

Brand shrugged, then changed his mind. "Stay there. I'll be down in a moment," he responded.

Since there was no external egress from the gallery, he retraced his steps through the French doors of his bedroom to the interior hallway. Just outside his door, a spiral staircase cut through the floor in a heart-shaped opening. He followed the red carpet to the first floor landing, recognizing the marble statue of Aphrodite that stood off to the side in the oak foyer. He bowed to the goddess in mock reverence. "Please excuse the informal look, your grace," he said tugging at the lapels of his robe.

"Sans clothes whatsoever, Monsieur, how can she object?" asked Lucette Devereau who stood in the center hallway.

"Mademoiselle, you must think I'm an idiot talking to inanimate objects," he said mindful of "Willie" upstairs on his dresser.

"*Au contraire*, Monsieur, in the jungle my most attentive companions are the trees. And as for the goddess, she is the best listener of all. At times like this, when mama visits Paris, and papa is out in the field, Aphrodite accepts my chatter without judging. Except, I see she now scolds me for being a poor hostess and urges me to ask how I can be of service?"

His embarrassment vanished, replaced by an eagerness to understand how so comely a woman survived in such splendid isolation. He sensed a desperate need for small talk on her part, and he decided to deliver.

"I'm on my way out to pick up Captain Fletcher's retrieved gun your man found in our jeep. Perhaps you could go with me and tell me about this place. That is, if you don't mind my attire," he said pointing to his sandaled feet.

"My pleasure, Monsieur, I like nothing better than to show-off our beautiful plantation. Come, we shall escape together. Be careful of the cobblestones. The laundress promised to have your clothes and shoes cleaned and polished before supper."

He held the door open for her, and as she passed under his chin, he caught the scent of jasmine. In that brief moment, he thought of Maria Monclova, and he closed his eyes to complete the illusion. When opened again, they fell on Lucette's shimmering gold hair to which the sun rendered a soft radiance. He wanted to reach out and touch the pony-tail that teased his eyes.

She turned and called, "Aren't you coming?" Her own eyes, Brand saw, were clear, bright and a wonderful blue like Maria's.

The man cleaning the jeep handed Brand Fletcher's weapon, and he shouldered it as he followed Lucette through the close cropped grass of the front lawn to the end of the clearing. There a line of magnificent trees formed a cavernous aisle extending from the mansion.

"This is our oak alley modeled after a similar setting in Mississippi," she said pointing to the trees. "At *Bon Sejour*, they are my closest companions." Brand followed her hand again as she turned back and pointed to two asymmetrical chimneys jutting out from the high-peaked West Indies-style roof of the home Lucette referred to as "Good Stay."

"We have borrowed many features from your part of the world," she said. "There, those eight great white pillars, covered with brick and plaster came from a Canadian forest. And inside, you might have noticed that the hand-hewn beams are carved from American cypress. Most everything is wooden. We must be careful of fire."

Brand released his hand from around the half-empty cigarette pack in the pocket of his robe. He decided to ration his smokes to make them last until he got back to Saigon.

"When was *Bon Sejour* built?" he asked.

"I'm sorry. Papa can give you the exact date. Out here, women do not discuss history and politics unless it's feminine gossip. I know that the materials arrived by ship to Siam, then overland by elephant during our colonial period. Upstairs, near your room, is a large marble bathtub that once belonged to Marie Antoinette."

"Must have taken an army to haul that load through the jungle."

"*Oui*, Monsieur, I do know that in my grandparent's time, we had 15,000 workers here. Today, there are only 3,000."

"How many are Frenchmen?"

"Six overseers here and 20 at our headquarters in Mimot across the border in Cambodia."

"Do you all live in the big house?"

"Oh, no. That is for the Director General, my father, and his family. The other overseers are in smaller houses throughout the plantation."

"Then, who lives in those two hexagonal-shaped, detached buildings on each side of the main house?"

"Those are *garçonnières*. You know this word, Monsieur?"

"The only *garcon* that comes to mind is a French waiter.

"Close. But unmarried man in English and French, are they not the same?"

"You mean bachelor?"

"*Oui*, those two dwellings we call the houses for a bachelor. Unfortunately, we have no permanent single man here, so they remain empty. Would you like to see inside one?"

"No thanks. You might save that part of the tour for Lieutenant Hewlett when he's up to it."

"Your friend, is he a bachelor?"

"Indeed he is. But I think he's too big for your little *garçonnière*."

Fifteen minutes passed before either of them felt comfortable enough to address each other by their first names. Brand saw how the young woman dotted her conversation about the house with references to Rafe whenever she could fit it in, like comparing the Greek Revival-style architecture of the Devereau home to "Bonecrusher's" massive physique.

"Like the lieutenant, this is a sturdy structure," she said. "I believe he will bounce back from Captain Fletcher's death. Were they friends long?"

"No. As far as I could tell, we all met just yesterday. But that doesn't make any difference to soldiers. They have a special bond forged from Valkyrian steel."

"I don't know this term," she admitted.

"The Valkyries were mythological Norse maidens who conducted the souls of heroes slain in battle to their last resting place. Scrappy in their own right, they represented the sensitive side of war," he explained.

"Is there such a thing as a special bond where killing is the goal?"

"Indeed, according to my father, a warrior all his life, death in battle strengthens the buddy-link and creates a chain of brothers," said Brand.

"And do you feel that same loyalty?" she asked.

He started to brush a finger across his nose. Instead, he replied with a note of finality. "As you can see, I'm not a military man."

"But you do carry Captain Fletcher's gun."

On the way back to the house, she explained that her father detested weapons of any kind, although he, too, had been a soldier and fought against the Viet Minh. It would be better Lucette suggested if she kept Fletcher's gun with Hewlett's rifle in a safe place, out of sight, until the Americans left. He agreed and told her that he was more interested in getting to a telephone.

"How could I forget," she said, tapping her hand against her forehead. "I called our embassy in Saigon, and they put me through to a Major Spear. He was sad to hear about Captain Fletcher, but said an American doctor was already on his way here, and that you should return with him tomorrow to Saigon. Is the major whom you wanted to call?"

"Not really."

"But he asked for you to call him."

"Spear's not my top priority at the moment." This time he did flick his finger across his nose.

"I'll have the telephone Lieutenant Hewlett used to call the South Vietnamese Army base in Loch Ninh brought around to your room."

"Thanks," he said.

Back in his room, Brand sat in a straight back chair and spread his notes out on the lower section of the four-poster bed left uncovered by a golden canopy that stretched to the oaken floor. While he waited for the telephone, he decided to consolidate his impressions thus far. He had long since formed the habit of writing down sensations and emotions impressed upon the mind. Like Aristotle's famous signet pressed against the wax, these indelible marks constituted memory for Brand. Not all sensations or emotions reached this status, of course.

His refusal to entertain a call to Alex was a case in point. He did not want to provide the major an opportunity to talk him out of reporting the death of Fletcher before the advisor's next of kin had been notified. Brand had seen top-breaking stories fall into a competitor's lap while the reporter on the scene waited for the bureaucracy to untangle itself from regulations.

Since he had no intention of talking to Alex before he filed his story through the *Times* Saigon bureau, it served no purpose to commit this thought process to memory or paper. Intention was the key. He sought another Pulitzer Prize. Anything that deterred him from that goal bore no semblance of immediate importance. While others might consider this approach callous, Brand marked it a sign of progress that sentimentality never stood between him and a good story.

He began to sort the scraps of paper for later transfer of the notes to his journal when the sound of a vehicle braking on the cobblestones caught his attention. He scurried to the edge of the balcony in time to see two men dismount from a Land Rover. One had thin, gray hair, and his face was the color of a killer whale's underbelly. He walked with shoulders slumped forward, drawn so by age and his own girth. Despite all this, Brand thought he had the air of a gentlemen and decided this must be Monsieur Devereau. The other man, although Vietnamese, was slightly taller than his host and carried himself erect like a military man. His dress was very simple—a jacket and trousers of the same black cloth. He raised his head toward the balcony, and Brand saw a black patch positioned jauntily over his right eye under a red beret. The one-eyed man raised a hand in greeting before Brand turned away embarrassed at being caught eavesdropping.

Back inside his room, Brand was pleased to see that the telephone had been installed in his brief absence. He sat down on the bed among his papers and began to compose a news story on Fletcher's death to call into the *Times* Saigon Bureau. As he picked up his note book, a crumpled white envelope fell on the bedspread. He recognized it as the one he had retrieved from the road during the ambush. The grime and sweat from the day's ordeal had already broken the seal, so Brand convinced himself that reading Fletcher's letter to his wife was not in the strictest sense a violation of the officer's privacy:

My Dearest Susie Q,

If this letter ever gets to you, it means I'm dead. Otherwise, we'd be sitting next to each other laughing over the silly things that go through a man's mind when he's escaped death and his next stop is no longer St. Peter's Gate. By now, you've survived the horror of the military vehicle pulling up to your door, and the two pasty-faced officers expressing the government's regret at your loss. But forgive them, these guys, like me, know little about losses—either as a father or husband until it reaches up and bites you in the ass. Unfortunately and unexpectedly, I've become an expert.

Let's begin with the birth of Erik, Jr., which I had to endure without anesthetic, and again when Erika blessed our home. I didn't show it, but those kids frightened me. I feared one day they would not find me entirely worthy of the worship I have seen in their eyes. God knows I've never been the hero my daughter thinks I am, or quite the man my son believes me to be. And it worries me that now they'll never know me firsthand at a more mature age in peace time. But I'm counting on you to set the record straight about this soldiering business that has kept us apart. Going away to war is like swearing and spitting through your teeth, not pleasant to God nor man, but sometimes necessary if others threaten what belongs to you.

Soldier fathers, and fathers of soldiers, grow old faster than other people. You know why? Because they have to hop on airplanes and fly off to faraway places where there's a whole lot of shooting going on. Or, like Grandpa, they have to stand at the railway station and wave goodbye to the uniformed son that climbs aboard. Don't get me wrong. Mothers and grandmas have it rough, too. But the difference is, women folk can cry where it shows, and all the guys can do is beam outside and die inside. Of course, when little Erik goes to war, now you'll have to play both roles, and it isn't fair. Just like it isn't fair that I won't be there to give Erika away to a man who isn't nearly good enough for her, but together they will have grandchildren prettier and smarter than any yet to be born.

> Even if you marry again (remember our talks about this), all I ask is that you tell our kids that their father fought dragons every day of his adult life. Some of these beasts had one fire-breathing head, others had three heads that I came to know as Weariness, Work and Monotony. Weariness almost got me that time we had 30 cents to our name, and I had to supplement my soldier's pay by distributing newspapers on the weekend. Work nearly did me in at the officer candidate school and later in signal school where I had to burn twice as many hours to keep up with my better educated buddies. Monotony never came close, because, as you know, I've always felt like a knight in shining armor when it comes to serving our country and being your husband. Love and country—on these two pillars, my immortality rests. Our love is the foundation for everything. It has kept me on an upward path that leads to God, and I'm truly thankful for a mate like you who has taken my hand every step of the way.
>
> Now, off I go to a new mission, not knowing whether there's a special place for soldier husbands and fathers. But I've got a good idea that after a long rest, there'll be some soldiering to do. I can't see myself sitting around on a cloud waiting for my best girl and children to join me. It seems to me military advisors would make good guardian angels, improving communications and smoothing the way for other freedom-loving people. But for you and the kids, count on a loving personal hero 'in the Fletch.'

Fletcher's testament was on Brand's mind while he finished writing his news story and as he waited for the operator to connect him to The *New York Times,* Saigon Bureau. Brand tried to dismiss the letter as so much romanticizing on Fletcher's part. He had seen the syndrome repeated in Korea and again with the French forces at Dien Bien Phu. The warrior immersed in battle tends to fantasize about the life he has left behind, creating an unwarranted reality in his mind no different in purpose than Brand's reflections on Eleanor.

His thoughts were interrupted when a voice came on the line and asked, "*AP/UPI/TIMES*, how can we help you?"

Brand recognized the voice of one of the wire service reporters he had met upon his arrival in Vietnam at the Caravelle Hotel.

"I must have the wrong number," he said. "I'm calling for the new *Times* Bureau Chief."

"You mean Sheenar Tillerstein. You've got the right office, but he's out for the moment. Can I take a message?"

"Hell, no!" snapped Brand. "You guys are the competition." Brand could hear the man whispering to someone else.

"You must be Brand, the new guy," he said. "We operate in a spirit of cooperation these days. It helps us beat our military and the South Vietnamese propaganda machine."

"This has got to be a trick. I've had too many stories swiped by the opposition to fall for this deal. The last time I had a story stolen with such a lame ruse, I was a cub reporter. Tell what's-his-name, Tillerstein, if he wants what I've got, he'll have to call me personally." Brand gave the wire service reporter the number of the Devereau plantation.

"See here, Brand, you'd better learn who your friends are if you want to survive out here."

"Seems to me you've got your friends, friendly competition and enemies all mixed up."

"Tillerstein won't like this."

"Well, that's just tough for 'Sheet.'"

Brand hung up in disgust. He could not believe that in his eight years away from the field, journalistic practices had deteriorated so badly that correspondents were pooling their efforts. The inevitable consequence of this method would be news coming out of a particular area slanted one way. And if he could believe the reporter, this slant amounted to a violation their own countrymen's trust, and of his own code to follow the truth wherever it might lead. The more he thought about the idea of Americans back home getting their information from what amounted to a consolidated news source with a bias, the angrier he got.

The stakes are too high, he told himself, to allow the independent observer to drown in a sea of complacency, intrigue and agenda setting. News reporters who formed their own clique, betray their calling and country, he decided. At least with Alex and his henchmen, objectivity is neither feigned, nor pronounced.

The phone call to his sister Clementine went much smoother until he sought to enlist her in his scheme to circumvent the Saigon news bureau with the article on Fletcher's death.

"I don't mind relaying this information to your editor, Winston, but as a navy wife, I'd like to know that Captain Fletcher's next of kin have been notified before it's published in the *Times*. Could I have Sean run it by the military first?"

"No, I'd prefer you didn't. Somebody might leak it to my competition, and with the time difference between here, you, and New York, I don't see where this is such a big deal."

"Well, on my calculation, that's putting the information on fast forward as far as publishing it is concerned."

"Look, Clemie, if you don't want to do it, just say so."

"How about a compromise? I'll call your story in to your editor, Louis Cohen, and ask him to check with the Pentagon before he releases it."

"Fine. Do what you're going to do anyway."

"That's settled then. Now, back to our relationship, Winnie. You forget how hard it is on those who love you when you seem to drop off the face of the earth. If GG hadn't kept me informed about you all these years, I'd have gone nuts with worry, especially since you've already had some close calls. As you know, family is very important to me."

"Yeah, well, Pavler likes to control things, just like dad. It comes with the uniform."

"I prefer to think of it as love," she replied. "For example, GG has already put me in touch with a woman named Gwen Spear."

"Did you say Spear?"

"Yes, she's coming through Hawaii with her children on the way to the Philippines to be closer to her husband. He's in Vietnam, too. I'll ask her to have her husband look you up. Maybe the Spears can help me keep tabs on you, too."

"Save the effort. I'm rooming next to the guy in Saigon."

"Great, great!" she exclaimed.

"Are you sure you aren't part of a plot to get me to cooperate with military intelligence? Who else is in on this?"

"I don't know what you are talking about, Winston, but just before you called, I got a call from Gwen Spear who's all excited about meeting Aunt Norma and someone else when she gets to the Philippines. Wait a minute. I wrote the name down. Let me get it."

Brand cursed the delay. This business was getting out of control and too close to his personal life.

"Oh, here it is—Maria Monclova."

Brand nearly dropped the telephone.

"Good God! Where does she fit in?"

"You tell me. From your reaction, you must know her. All I was going to say is Gwen's husband arranged the meeting just before she called me. Isn't it marvelous to live in an era of instant communications? Too bad more of us don't take advantage of it."

"Yeah. Well, intelligence types seem to move faster than the rest of us in this small world."

"On the subject of little things, sure you don't have time to say hello to the boys?"

"No, but tell them I promise to stop in and see them next time through Hawaii."

"That would be wonderful, you know. You're the only uncle they've got. We all send our love. And by the way, dear brother, I'll keep Fletcher, his family and you in my prayers."

"It's been nice talking to you, Sis."

He remained next to the phone for several minutes engaged in a low conversation with himself. Why hadn't he acknowledged his acquaintance with Maria to his sister? Clemie of all people would have been pleased that he had found a female who interested him after Eleanor. He should have been more forthright with the one true ally left to him in this world. But then again, Pavler and Spear were obviously pulling out all the stops to get to him, and perhaps Clemie and Maria were part of their plan.

Impossible, he assured himself. His sister could never betray those she loved. Otherwise, she would have bounced her husband long ago. Maria though, was a different story and would bear watching. He smiled at the pleasant thought of keeping her under observation, no matter what the circumstances. But then, he almost wished she would turn out to be an adversary, since he had lots of practice in dealing with those who wished him harm.

This sort of introspection roused the old demons inside him. He walked over to the dresser and picked up Willie. Even Pavler wouldn't begrudge a man one drink under these circumstances, he told himself. But then, his inner voice checked the thought by mocking him, "Since when have you stopped at one?" To gird himself against temptation, he retreated to the gallery for the third time in as many hours.

A cool breeze rustled through the mighty oaks, and he could see the sun starting to drop below their swaying branches. Except for a strip of light along the entire length of the front banister, the gray planked gallery stood in dark contrast. Wrestling with his conscience and his anger, he paced back and forth with one hand on the railing as if to steady himself from falling into the shadows. Someone joined him on the opposite end of the gallery, although he could not immediately see who it was since the sun blinded him, and the figure stood partially in the shadows.

Brand imagined the figure to be Maria in an ante-bellum gown, and so he closed his eyes and his mind to any other possibility. In his brief fantasy, she called his name like she had done on the beach at Guam. As before, that same bright wave of warmth swept over him. He remembered their embrace on the beach when he had kissed her neck and her breasts above the bodice, feeling the beating of her heart as his fingers slipped to the fullness and warmth inside. He had felt Maria open to him like an unfolding blossom. But then he shook his head and the spell was broken. The figure had moved to the gallery's edge, and he saw Lucette Devereau dressed in a long gown illuminated by the setting sun.

"I'm watching for Papa and Captain Bao. They just went out to meet the helicopter. Did you hear it land? No matter. We shall all gather at dinner," she said.

In the Pagoda at Queen's Bishop, R-3 waited by the telephone. Two body guards paced nervously inside the small room, but the supreme communist leader in the South sat silently in a darkened corner with fingers tightened around the hand piece. On the first ring he picked up the receiver and at the same moment waved the guards out of the room with his other hand.

"Yes," he said guiding the ear piece under his dark hood.

"Supreme Leader, I need your counsel," said General Tran Van Chien.

"Yes, General, go on."

"I am the possessor of 30 voices and know not which bears the 'Brand' of truth."

"Let us hear but three, since by a sample the whole cloth is known."

"The voice of the north wind bids me strike hard and fast at the heart of my enemy's foreign friend. Then, just now from the south, your voice directs me instead to spare him who bears the devil's 'Brand.'"

"And the third voice?"

"The third voice is that of the servant of the south wind, but who has aligned himself with the policy of the north wind and would exact vengeance."

"And in what order have these voices come to you?"

"First from the north, then from the south's servant, and finally from the south wind itself."

"There, you have solved your own problem, General."

"How so, Esteemed Leader?"

"Do not two of the three voices belong to the winds themselves?"

"Indeed."

"And is not the middle voice that of a usurper?"

"Yes, a mere lackey."

"Or in this case, a fool unaware that the brother winds are reconciled, and that the last to blow carries the day."

"But even as we speak, the servant of the south proceeds with my help to follow the northern-most voice," confessed General Chien.

"As Buddha has said, 'Suffer no companionship with a fool.' And again, that 'If a fool be associated with a wise man, even all his life, he will perceive the truth as little as a spoon perceives the taste of soup.'"

"Then what would you, wise Revered Leader, have me do?"

After a short pause, R-3 replied, "First, you must turn a pure and spotless eye to the doctrine of undoing what has been decided blindly. That means thwarting the plans of the one off the true path without explaining your own actions. Finally, you must allow the fool to return to the south, since it is left to another to explain to him his error."

"Thank you, Noble Leader. I'll do my best."

"I know you will."

R-3 called his two henchman back into the room and directed them to return with three messengers. He addressed separate correspondence to Hanoi, General Chien's headquarters at Sector

Queen's Knight and to Captain Bao through the drop box at the chess shop on Tu Do Street.

"Comrades R-1 and R-2," he wrote to his colleagues in the Cuc Nghien Cuu Trung-Uong, the Central Research Agency, (C.R.A.).

> I'm honored to report the capture of 30 American radios to match the U.S. communications specialists hijacked under your bold direction. Permit me a bold proposal of my own. Rather than send the radios and our troops to Hanoi to be trained by the captive Americans, we can save time and the risk of detection by meeting in a neutral location, such as Sector Queen's Rook in Cambodia. Our allies there will cooperate through silence.
>
> In anticipation of your approval, to get started I am immediately sending half the equipment and half the trainees from 'the great frontline in the South', as R-2 refers to our heroic struggle, to be secured and trained by forces led by the commander of 'the great rear area.'
>
> The graduates then can serve as cadre to instruct other comrades here on the stored radios. Or I can send 15 more trainees to Queen's Rook to replace the initial graduates. The returned trained comrades then could be deployed, each with one of the stored radios to a designated position in the enemy's midst so we can begin creating confusion for the allies at once.
>
> If we decide to train a second group of comrades at Queens Rook, we then can evaluate whether to continue the plan, or bring the training radios back to South Vietnam with the second group for instruction of comrades here, or deploy them to other designated locations.
>
> Once our troops are trained, if we decide we have no further use for the Americans, we can eliminate them and dispose of their bodies so that they will never be found.

To General Chien, R-3 extended congratulations on a successful mission, then added:

> To begin with, select 15 of your brightest soldiers and send them to Queen's Rook along with 15 of the captured radios. All of the other communications equipment will be

> stored at Queen's Bishop until further distribution in South Vietnam for use with our newly trained comrades. The first 15 graduates of the communications course will be initially assigned to Queen's Bishop once their training is completed to await further orders.

R-3's most terse message went to Nguyen Huu Bao as he admonished his former adjutant:

> Concentrate on your main mission. Leave Brand and all other matters to me.

15 DIEN BIEN PHU LEGACY

Our country will have the single honor of being a small nation which, through a heroic struggle, has defeated two big imperialisms—the French and the Americans—and made a worthy contribution to the national liberation movement.

—*Ho Chi Minh*

THAT EVENING CAPTAIN BAO was the first of the Devereau guests to appear in the dining room. He stood with one arm leaning on the black onyx mantle over which hung a portrait of Marie Antoinette. Feigning interest in the art, Bao kept his uncovered eye on Lucette Devereau as she swept around a large rectangular oak table, directing the servants on seating and serving protocol. The woman hesitated in front of him, trying to figure out military officer ranking. She asked if Navy Lieutenant Commander Jenicoso was the ranking military officer who should be seated at the end of the table opposite her father.

"Are you open to a suggestion, Mademoiselle?" Bao offered.

"Certainly, Captain."

"Perhaps, in view of the circumstances, we should put protocol aside for the evening and leave the senior gentleman's guest chair empty in honor of the fallen American captain."

"What a wonderful gesture! Then I should seat Dr. Jenicoso at my father's right and you, Captain, at my father's left. Where do I place Mr. Brand who has no military rank?"

"Actually, Mademoiselle, the Americans assign their correspondents the honorary military rank of major according to protocol. So, it would be appropriate to put him on your father's left instead of me, directly across from Dr. Jenicoso."

"You are very up on your protocol, Captain, I must say. Help me now. See if I have this straight. You would be seated next to Dr. Jenicoso on the right with Lieutenant Hewlett next to Mr. Brand on the left. As hostess, I would be seated next to you on the right."

"Yes, and this would place your foreman, Mr. Ly, across from you on the left and next to Lieutenant Hewlett, which will mix an American, Vietnamese and French on the right, and two Americans and a Vietnamese on the left, with your father at the head of the table and Captain Fletcher's honorary empty seat at the foot."

"How can I thank you, Captain Bao? With mother away, I'm always worried about getting balance at the table."

"Mademoiselle, between you and this lovely portrait of Marie Antoinette, I cannot see how this room can bear any more balance or beauty."

He saw her face grow radiant with a shy pleasure, but as she was about to speak, the three American guests were ushered into the room by Monsieur Devereau.

During the early part of the meal, Bao felt as if Brand had been ignoring him by addressing most of his comments to Dr. Jenicoso who seemed to be more than a casual acquaintance to the American reporter. Actually, Bao was pleased with this turn of events since it gave him the opportunity to size up his quarry across the table. Even in those few moments when he turned his head toward the left to respond to Dr. Jenicoso, Bao kept Brand in his line of sight. He was both disturbed and pleased to see that he would be jousting with someone not unlike himself, who had a quick grasp of his surroundings at all times. Occasionally, his eye met Brand's and more than once, he was tempted to turn away to escape their dark, brown brilliance and depth of intelligence. At various points, Bao found Brand's gaze piercing, caressing, naïve and yet cunning, far off and yet intent.

Bao also observed Brand reach for the wine, then reluctantly set the glass back upon the table untouched. He sensed an inner struggle made obvious by the way Brand's eyes darted from guest to guest around the table to see who had noticed his hesitation. Monsieur Devereau was the first to comment on his guest's behavior.

"Mr. Brand, perhaps we can get another wine that will suit your taste?"

"No, thanks, I'm on some medication and can't consume alcohol for a while."

Brand's eyes told Bao that he had lied, and Bao followed this opportunity to gain his adversary's attention.

"My roommate in Paris shattered his brains by mixing spirits and pain killers," said Bao. "Served him right though. The fellow was a Methodist who preached against strong drink, warning that if one never takes the first drink, there is no chance he'll become an alcoholic. Never had I seen such a hypocrite."

Brand took the bait. "Come now, Captain, Paris has always crawled with charlatans. As a newspaper man, I prefer Saigon. At least the debauchery there has a charming innocence, especially among the intellectuals who've never gone abroad."

"You, have been misinformed, Mr. Brand, if you think Vietnamese measure themselves only against Western virtues or vices. Some of us, educated or not, wherever we are, retain our heritage and remain true to the revolution."

"And what revolution would that be, Captain?" Brand asked.

"Why, the Diem coup against Bao Dai, of course."

Bao had hoped to keep the playful dialog with Brand going a little longer. But Monsieur Devereau interjected, "If you ask me, this country was much better off during the Emperor Bao Dai's reign. At least my government supported him."

Brand encompassed both Devereau and Bao in the arc made by his fork. "I remember 'Belly High.' The legionaries gave him the name, but he built his own reputation as an absentee playboy head-of-state who spent more time in Paris than at home. Talk about your fakers. Bao's own ministers, like Diem, never knew whose side the emperor was on. I'm surprised he so easily convinced the French government of his loyalty. As I wrote in my book, Americans had no such luck with the French."

"Ah, but your country and mine were working at cross-purposes, and you couldn't get your British allies on board," protested Devereau.

"In hindsight, the Brits were right, and so were our other SEATO partners. The Brits knew better than to place themselves in a no-win situation in which our side thought it necessary to keep France in the war long enough to avoid a communist triumph at the conference table in 1954. France's purpose was to negotiate its way out of the military quagmire, yet keep your holdings in Vietnam," said Brand.

"And why couldn't America at least go along with such a proposition?" asked Monsieur Devereau.

"It wouldn't be long until the communist-controlled Viet Minh would be victorious over the French in the South. Captain Bao would be wearing a different uniform tonight if America had allowed that to happen in order to support French colonialism to continue," replied Brand.

Monsieur Devereau replied, "I don't see how America's failure to give France adequate help at Dien Bien Phu by providing crucial American military air strikes was a wise decision. It certainly didn't help the situation we find ourselves in today in the face of communist infiltrator's guerilla warfare in South Vietnam."

Brand retorted, "At least we backed the right horse by supporting President Diem, who trusts the French about as much as the communists."

"My American guest astounds me," Devereau protested. "You have waded into waters over your head, Mr. Brand. Certainly the French are more trustworthy, even to Diem, than the communists in this part of the world, and don't forget the alliance of the French with the Americans in World War II." The old man turned toward Dr. Jenicoso and Bao's side of the table. "Doctor, I trust you know better."

"Believe me, medicine's my game. I leave politics to others to work it out," said Jenicoso scratching the cowlick on the back of his head.

"Let me try to explain," Bao offered, anxious to regain control of the conversation.

"Believe me, If someone has to, it might as well be you."

"Your Mr. Brand has wandered into a sensitive area marked off like a triangle." To illustrate his point Bao formed the figure with his thumbs and forefingers. "At the upper point where my fingers are touching, we have the American position once occupied by French imperialists. The French are now at the base line opposite the Vietnamese, whom Americans are helping to reach the top. Until the Americans join the French at the baseline, relinquishing the pinnacle to the Vietnamese, there can be no peace."

Brand's outburst of laughter caught Bao by surprise. But he was even more shocked when the reporter extended two middle fingers across the table in his direction.

"Don't forget about these two guys. Each is Vietnamese, one communist and the other pro Diem. They represent what the Vietnamese side of the triangle hopes to do to its adversary as both stretch toward the top to replace the Americans. The questions are: Who's supporting whom? And will Ho's or Diem's guys get to the top first?"

"Very good, Mr. Brand. The next time I use the analogy, I'll be sure to include your addendum. But let's give our host the last word on this."

Bao pushed himself back in his chair and waited for Devereau to dangle more bait in front of the reporter so that he could observe the reaction.

Before the old man could utter another word, his daughter broke off her conversation with Lieutenant Hewlett and addressed her father. "If Mother were here, she would never allow heated political topics to dominate our table. Can't we turn to something more pleasant?"

"In a moment, dear, but first our guest has thrown down a gauntlet that demands a reply."

Bao saw that the young woman's intervention had served to calm the director general's demeanor as he addressed Brand directly.

"I'm aware, Mr. Brand, that you won a literary prize for covering our forces at the fall of Dien Bien Phu. What you could not have known is that long before this defeat, the French command was a beaten power. Although we had a knack for hiding unfavorable developments while emphasizing positive ones throughout the struggle, the crushing defeat at Dien Bien Phu revealed our policy for what it was, *mentir et dementir.* Do you know this term?"

"No, my French isn't that good," said Brand.

"It means to lie and deny," explained Bao smiling.

"Yes, that's it," continued Devereau. "And to be perfectly candid, *mentir et dementir* rules today among French and American officials."

"And I suppose the communists never lie and deny anything," retorted Brand. "I'll bet at this moment some communist official spokesman is protesting any involvement in the death of Captain Fletcher. If you guys want to look the other way, that's your business."

Monsieur Devereau replied, "This is neither the time, nor the forum to delve into your opinions, Mr. Brand. At least, as a minimum, maybe you, Captain Bao and I can agree with Joubert who said, 'It is better to debate a question without settling it than to settle a question without debating it.'"

Before anyone else could respond, Lucette tapped her fork against her water glass. "Really, Father, this end of the table suffers your neglect. Captain Bao, won't you help me lighten the conversation? Have you ever met Madame Nhu? From what I've heard, she's beautiful like Marie Antoinette."

"That's a wonderful comparison, Mademoiselle. Somewhat like our comments tonight, these two great ladies are open to misinterpretation. Only a few days ago, I saw our first lady at the palace, and she seemed to be taking the American criticism of herself in stride. We shared some poetry, and I've been trying to think of the last line."

"Oh, do tell us. Perhaps Mr. Ly, or one of the servants, can help you," said Lucette.

"I'm ashamed for my poor memory, because it is a legendary phrase in the Vietnamese language, and our young people today use it as a pick-up line."

"Then surely we must put our heads together and help you recall such a romantic thing," she said beaming at Hewlett.

"Well, the poem is set in Hue where the young man says to the young woman, 'There are many boats on the Perfumed River.' She responds in some fashion, and then he utters the memorable line which escapes me."

Bao searched the faces of the Vietnamese servants, but they all seemed perplexed at his attention. Then, Mr. Ly spoke up for the first time.

"I'm from the imperial city and know the verse well. The line you are seeking has the young man respond, 'So come with me, my darling. Do not cross alone.'"

Captain Bao responded, "That's it. How could anyone forget? Let's speak more about Vietnamese poetry after dinner, Mr. Ly."

"No fair," protested Lucette, "leaving the rest of us out."

"Maybe we can get Winston to read some of his poems," said Dr. Jenicoso. "Believe me, I hear they're a hit with the ladies."

"I don't know about you, Nick, but like Lieutenant Hewlett, I've kind of run out of things to say after a long, sad day. I plan to retire early," said Brand.

After dinner, it was with a heart full of trepidation that Bao escorted Mr. Ly to the front entrance of the plantation. He could see that the Vietnamese overseer now allowed himself a look of surprise that an ARVN captain was the bearer of the secret phrase from General Chien.

"I must compliment you, Comrade Ly, on maintaining a poker face in the presence of the others, especially when you furnished the last line of the Hue poem. Up until then, I had no idea who my contact might be and assumed that I would now be discussing this matter with a member of the household staff."

"There are other comrades among the servants," said Ly, "but only I am trusted with the code. Fortunately, for all of us, I was an invited guest tonight, although I am usually here when we are entertaining a Vietnamese military officer. None before has turned out to be a comrade. So, tell me how can I help you? If it's about Monsieur Devereau's taxes paid to our side, please assure General Chien that they will be delivered within the week."

"Oh, no," Bao chuckled. "I'm not here to extort money for either side. My cover mission as an ARVN officer is to inquire about support for Diem's Strategic Hamlet program amongst the plantation owners," lied Bao, who had not yet received word of the result of his interview with Nhu. "The regime in Saigon is concerned with the way we communists carry this war to the most remote and isolated villages. They want to get in on the act by herding men, women and children into a strategic village. Through such means, they hope to save lives and buy time, but without French support, especially in this region, they can only succeed in isolated areas."

"Do you want me to raise this matter with Monsieur Devereau?"

"No. This is my task, and I will speak to him before my departure. We are in the delicate stages of the beginning program. I need to be careful how I approach Monsieur Devereau, and how I frame my report to the Diem government. But enough about that.

Let me ask you. Of the three Americans at dinner this evening, whom would you say exhibited the greatest Yankee arrogance?"

"Why, Mr. Brand wins the prize in that category hands down. At times, I felt like punching him for his rude remarks directed at Monsieur Devereau and yourself, especially after I discovered you were one of us."

"Very good. You'll have the opportunity to follow through on your feelings toward Mr. Brand, which are shared by me and General Chien, as well as our leaders in Hanoi, who have marked him for assassination."

"It'll be our pleasure, Captain Bao, but I'll need to have people outside the household carry out the deed. Otherwise, suspicion would fall on me and others in positions of trust."

"Of course. You must remove him from the premises and do the killing in the jungle. Better that I leave it up to you how to proceed." Bao paused, allowing his co-conspirator to collect his thoughts.

After a few moments, the overseer spoke and Bao noted that the man was now full of enthusiasm.

"I'll have one of our household comrades get some chloroform from the infirmary, and later tonight, he'll enter Brand's room and incapacitate him while he sleeps."

"But I thought we didn't want to involve the household staff?"

"In the murder itself, no. Who but a servant has the excuse for entering a guest's room? After the American is knocked out, the servant will open the doors to the gallery and signal for his comrades, who will climb a ladder, enter the room and carry Mr. Brand off to be murdered."

"Yes, that will do nicely," said Bao, surprised that, for some reason, he did not express as much enthusiasm for this assumed deed as had Mr. Ly.

Lucette Devereau had a heavy heart as she tried to sleep that night. Her mind carried the weight of an unsuccessful dinner party, and she blamed herself for not foreseeing that with a dead officer in the house, the Americans had every right to cut the evening short. Yet, she wanted the moment to linger since rarely did the Devereaus entertain such interesting guests. In and out of her thoughts darted the memory of her cumbersome attempts to befriend the young lieutenant. He had rebuffed every overture and had, it seemed to her, created a moat of sadness around himself that she could not navigate. Only once during the evening did he offer her any hope for more favorable contact. That was when he had asked her if the family had a chapel to which he could retire the body of Captain Fletcher.

"Mah plan is to sit with him through the night," he confided to her. And if I happen to fall asleep, at least he's that much closer to God, Who will watch over both of us."

She remembered that his words had filled her eyes with tears, and even now, her pillow grew moist with the thought that this gentle giant had to be alone with his grief. Before they had said goodnight, Hewlett had put his arm around her and thanked her for helping him. Never had she felt so secure, so petite and so protected as she did at that moment. It brought back memories of her school days in Paris when her chums used to tease her about her small stature. "Little Lucette looks up to everyone," they taunted her. And in her diplomatic manner, she would remind them that it is every woman's dream to feel like a princess in the embrace of her beloved, and that she felt sorry for those gangly schoolmates who would never know the pleasures of the petite in the arms of one who made them feel even more so.

It was then she heard light footfalls a short distance from her door. Although she couldn't identify the owner, she ruled out the possibility that it was Rafe Hewlett. She next suspected Winston Brand, but then recalled on the way back from the chapel she had seen his door tightly closed against the world. Perhaps the night walker was Dr. Jenicoso whose light she had observed earlier. However, she assumed he had finished his medical report on the preparation of Captain Fletcher's body and had since retired. A fourth consideration came to mind. Captain Bao or her father had summoned one of the servants. If this were the case, then she should expect to hear the footsteps retrace themselves past her room. She fluffed her pillow and waited.

Twenty minutes later, she heard only her own breathing, and it began to occur to her that Lieutenant Hewlett might have pulled the servant cord from the chapel downstairs. Convinced she might be of assistance, she switched on the light, donned her robe, took a flashlight from the closet shelf and slipped out her doorway. At the top of the spiral staircase, she glanced across to Brand's room and saw that the door was open. For some strange reason the doors to the other side of his apartment were flung wide as well, and a sliver of moonlight shown on an empty bed.

Spurred on by concern and fear that one of her guests might be wandering around in the dark, she hurried down the steps, hoping to find Mr. Brand with Lieutenant Hewlett in the chapel. As she passed the statue of Aphrodite in the grand hallway, she thought she heard footsteps striking against the cobblestones outside the foyer, moving away from the house. She turned off the flashlight, pulled back the curtain and peered out into the darkness. The moon illuminated a strange form that cast a lattice-type shadow on the stones. She could recall no such structure that would cause such a phenomenon. She hurried on to the chapel.

Except for a single candle on the altar of the chapel, the room itself was dark, and she hesitated at the open doorway, afraid to trespass against the dead and not knowing whether she would find Hewlett slumped in the chair beside Fletcher's bier. She took in a deep breath and whispered into the room, "Lieutenant, please come quickly."

There was no immediate response. Turning on the flashlight, she followed the beam along the floor and then paused on a combat boot. Before moving it up past the knee, in the periphery of the light, she could see Rafe rubbing his eyes.

"Mah goodness. Ah hope it's an angel behind that bright light. At least your voice sounded like one, or was ah dreaming?"

"It's Lucette, and you might think I am a silly girl, but there are some strange things happening in the house tonight. Please, could you come with me to see if Mr. Brand is all right? He's not in his room, and the whole house is dark."

"Ah'll be with you in a minute. First, ah'll want to check under the sheets to make sure nobody's been messin' with old Fletch. Ah heard of people taking belt buckles and such off the dead for souvenirs."

She was relieved moments later when he slipped a strong arm around her small waist and asked her to lead the way while he held the flashlight. She told him that she didn't want to disturb her father and the other guests for what might turn out to be nothing at all. Yet, he should know that she had heard footsteps outside and had seen the shadow of something stationary outside the house directly under Brand's room.

'Don't worry, M'am. If this turns out to be a spooky dream, ah'll keep your secret."

Upstairs outside Brand's door, he told her to wait in the hallway while he checked out the reporter's room. She saw the light sweep back and forth from one side of the room and to the other. In a low voice, she heard him call, "Winston, where are you, man?" He kept calling as his body filled the doorway that opened on the gallery deck. Suddenly, she saw him whirl and retrace his steps back into the room. In another moment, he was at her side.

"Something's goofy," he said. "The bed is all messed up, and there's a ladder resting against the balcony railing. That must've been the shadow you saw downstairs out the door on the cobblestones. Before we go out there to look, you'd better fetch mah rifle in case there's more at hand than ah can handle. But, first, maybe you'd better come take a look outside. Again, she felt the strength of his body as he guided her across the room.

"Oh, dear," she gasped as they stood on the balcony looking down at the ladder, then along each side of the house. "Over there, the window upstairs, there's a light coming from the *garçonnière.* There should be no light!" she exclaimed.

"Let's get the rifle," he said.

A few minutes later, he told her to stay in the house while he investigated. She refused, arguing that she knew how to get into the bachelor quarters, and that it would save time if he took her along.

"Okay," he relented. "But you must promise me that if any shooting or rough stuff starts, you'll high-tail it back here to the main house and get some help."

"I promise, but I really am not frightened anymore," she said, and slipped her hand inside his.

In his other hand, he carried the rifle as if it weighed no more than a joss stick. He had given her the flashlight with instructions to turn it on only on his signal. Together they crept toward the two story building, careful to avoid the stones by walking on the edge of the grass. When they reached the first floor open air patio of the *garçonnière,* he stopped at the bottom stairway and released her hand. "This is as far as you go, missy. When ah bust through that door up there, ah don't know what we're going to run into on the other side."

"What if Mr. Brand's in there, reading a book or something? I did point this place out to him earlier, and he seemed very interested," she whispered. "Couldn't I just go knock on the door?"

"Yeah, but you're forgetting two things. Brand didn't bring any ladder with him to go snooping around your place in the middle of the night. And, two, he told Fletch and me up the road that somebody was out to get him. No, a guy like Winston has more sense than to cavort in uncharted territory by himself."

"*Oui.* But you've got to promise you'll call me up once things are under control."

"You've got a deal."

She could hear his boots strike against the concrete steps as he ascended the dark stairway. She said a prayer to herself asking the angels to watch over him and keep him safe. Then she remembered that it would have been easier if he had taken the flashlight, or better yet, her, since she knew every stone, hedge, bush and tree that surrounded what had been her playhouse when she was a little girl. Suddenly, she heard the upstairs door crash in followed by a stumbling sound, as if someone had fallen and was trying to get back on his feet. At the same time, from the front hedge at the patio entrance on her level, two dark clad figures scrambled into the underbrush now overgrown that surrounded her childhood playground.

"Rafe!" she screamed. "They're down here!"

He was at her side it seemed before her voice had died down. "Turn the light on so ah can get a shot."

She pointed the beam out the rear portal toward a clump of trees where an old rubber tire swing disturbed by the fleeing fugitives swung back and forth against a tall tree. He fired three rapid shots in that direction.

"Even if ah didn't hit anything, it'll sure scare the bejeevees out of 'em."

"*Oui,*" Her body trembled, yet she remained poised enough to smile at the humor in his speech and in the situation. "Looks like you stirred things up over at the big house as well," she said. They both stood for a moment watching lights flicker on, one by one across the upper deck, from the guest rooms of Captain Bao and Lieutenant Commander Jenicoso down to the master bedroom.

"What did you find upstairs here?" she asked.

"Brand's there all right, trussed up like a turkey on its way to the state fair, except I don't think he's hurt, just looked at me a little woozy-eyed above his gag. Shocked us both when that old door gave way so easily. Ah tumbled into the room and darn near landed in his lap. Suppose we'd better get up there, get him loose and have Doc Jenicoso check him over."

"This time I'm going with you."

"Sure, that's our deal, unless you want to get on back to the house and settle them other folks down."

'I'd rather stay with you."

Bao and Devereau reached the balcony at almost the same instant. The two men had already determined that the disturbance had come from the *garçonnière* by the time Nick Jenicoso pigeon-toed his way toward them.

"Believe me, it sounds like somebody's shooting up the place. Are we under attack?"

"No," said Bao. "It's probably one of the servants shooting at a poacher."

"*Oui*, please return to bed, doctor. Mr. Ly's house is right across the way, and I'm sure he'll fill us in at daylight," said Devereau.

Since Bao had no time to put on his eye patch, he cupped his hand over the empty socket as he searched the area around the outbuildings. He saw Lieutenant Hewlett and Mademoiselle Devereau with Brand walking unsteadily between them emerge from the hedgerow in front of the *garçonnière*. He quickly grabbed Devereau and Jenicoso each by the arm and turned them away from the scene below. "Please, why don't both of you gentlemen return to your rooms. Shooting is a military matter. I will get with Mr. Ly and together we'll get to the bottom of this."

"*Merci*, Captain. It's very kind of you," said Devereau. "But I'm surprised my curious little girl hasn't shown up."

"Perhaps she's too frightened. Anyway, I'll check in on her and the other Americans as well. Just leave it all to me and Mr. Ly."

After he had returned to his room and dressed, Bao did not have to go far to find his comrade. The overseer was waiting near the foyer by the time Bao reached the cobblestone driveway.

"Quickly," Ly said, pushing Bao into the shadows. The Americans and the daughter have just gone into the house through the kitchen, I believe, to revive this man Brand."

"Why isn't he dead?" demanded Bao.

"Change in orders."

"By whom?"

"By General Chien himself."

"Why?"

"I do not know, comrade, but just as my men were lowering the unconscious American to the ground, word came to abort this mission. I hurried to the main house to tell them. On my way, the light in the daughter's room came on, and rather than get caught taking him back up the ladder or through the front door, we placed him in the nearest guest house. We made sure that the family would find him there."

"Why such precaution?"

"Because General Chien was very clear that he would have our heads if this man were harmed, or if our organization here were compromised."

"Very well, comrade. We must all do as we're told. In the morning, I'll tell Monsieur Devereau his guest was attacked by robbers. I'm sure your men had sense enough to take the American's money as an extra bonus."

"Yes, they did, and other things of his as well."

"Good," said Bao and bid goodnight to the overseer.

Since Brand was not at breakfast the next morning, Captain Bao sought out Dr. Jenicoso. He passed a tray of hard rolls to the physician, removing one for himself. "I'll be escorting Lieutenant Hewlett back to the ARVN camp, shortly after you leave. The Devereaus and Mr. Ly are going along, so we've arranged for one of the other overseers to take your party to the helicopter when it arrives from Loc Ninh."

"Believe me, I understand," said Jenicoso, buttering the roll.

"And would you give a message to Mr. Brand?"

"Certainly."

"Please tell him that I apologize on behalf of the Vietnamese people and his French host for his mistreatment last night."

"Believe me, I'll be glad to have something to talk about on the way back to Saigon. Don't worry about us. But are you sure you guys will be all right on the road?"

Bao fidgeted with his eye patch before responding. "With the French along, we're safer than you are, doctor. Nobody shoots at them these days."

"Believe me, I'll remember that. If we get shot down and taken prisoner, I'll tell Winston, who can speak the language, to pretend he's a French correspondent. Fat chance of that succeeding, though. You've seen how difficult it is to tell Brand anything."

Bao handed Jenicoso a piece of paper. "I can be reached here in Saigon. Tell Mr. Brand I'm at his service. He need only call on me."

"Believe me, it'll be a while before he's up to socializing. He told me this morning he wants to stay out of the public eye for a few days. Strange for a newsman to go into seclusion, wouldn't you say?"

"Yet, understandable for one whose destiny is as undetermined as a grasshopper. Your Mr. Brand hops around never knowing where to move next, and depending on luck to get him to the next leaf."

"You people all talk in riddles. Believe me, I suppose that's one of the charms of this country."

16 WASHINGTON DEBACLE

Irrational opinions have a great deal to do with war and other forms of violent strife.

—Bertrand Russell

SAIGON AND WASHINGTON D.C. had more in common in the spring of 1962 than most people realized. To insure that this point registered in the minds of his fellow movers and shakers, Senator Thomas Aloysius Nathaniel Kearney, Sr., read into the Congressional Record his compilation of the similarities and differences between the two capitals. Under the column marked "similar," he had listed the following: Each is the seat of government for a fledgling democracy. Both Saigon and D.C. were designed by a Frenchman who made ample use of blossoms and tree lined boulevards to follow the contours of a major river. At the head of each government stood a young, energetic president whose intelligent younger brother served as his chief counselor, helping him retain control over factional elements in their respective societies. Finally, both capitals were graced by beautiful and regal first ladies.

In cloak room gossip, Tank, Sr.'s, colleagues used the last item on this list to joke about the Senate Armed Services Committee Chairman's frequent visits to a Georgetown brothel, or, when on an overseas junket, about the time spent comforted by a "first lady" of his choice. The mysterious woman seemed to always appear in the background photograph of his entourage. This gave rise to a favorite game played by both his political friends and opponents. Who could identify Tank, Sr.'s, latest conquest from the photos displayed prominently in his Senate offices?

At the top of his dissimilarities list, there was only one entry. The senator had delivered an undiplomatic blow to the South Vietnamese military, whom he had labeled as cowardly fighters in battle when compared to the American fighting men. One of Kearney's aides inadvertently disclosed to the *Washington Post* that Tank, Sr., had really wanted to insert in the Congressional Record that their cowardly fighting in battle amounted to nothing more than "chicken shit," but deleted the vulgarity at the last minute when the Senate chaplain, an Irish priest from Kearney's home town, talked him out of describing the performance of Vietnamese soldiers in such a manner.

So, it was no surprise to most people inside the beltway that this latest speech represented still another flip-flop by a politician whose positions on Vietnam rose and fell like a barometer, depending on where the greater pressure at the moment was exerted. Sometimes, as part of the Democratic Party leadership, he bowed to the president or majority leader's position. On other occasions, he used his constituents, or some news event, to score political points. Capt. Erik Fletcher's death fell right into his shifty hands.

Early in his first term, Kearney had boasted he would only mount the Senate well "when it's time to raise hell." The assassination of an American advisor certainly qualified, so Kearney confidently marched to the front of the presiding officer's podium, set his notes on the lectern, cleared his throat and leaned his 250 pound bulk back on his heels. He paused, running his thumbs up and down the underside of the lapels of his white Panama suit coat.

"Mr. President," he said as he took a step forward, then reeled back again, tossing his mane of dyed red hair toward the gallery. He removed a pair of half-moon, dark rimmed glasses from their perch beneath his thick gray eyebrows. As he waited for recognition, he pretended to clean the glasses with a blue handkerchief and then repositioned them at the tip of his prominent nose.

"The chair recognizes the distinguished senator from Massachusetts."

"Thank you, Mr. President," Kearney acknowledged. He gripped the edges of the lectern and pushed himself up to his full height of six foot three inches. "I'll try to be brief, because I want to yield part of my time to the senator from Texas. We've agreed that he'll give the eulogy for his fallen native son from that great state.

"As most of you have heard, one of our brave fighting men was ambushed and killed in Vietnam. Upon hearing this news, I made five telephone calls on behalf of the Senate Armed Services Committee. My first call went to the Secretary of Defense, and to be frank about it, this so-called whiz kid knew no more than I did."

At this point, the senator from Michigan rose and asked Kearney to yield. Kearney knew that the little man from the Midwest wanted to protest his characterization of Secretary Robert McNamara.

"I'd be glad to yield to our diminutive friend from the great state of Michigan, but as we all know, except for his stature, he is not known for his brevity." The Kearney supporters burst into laughter, and the senator from Michigan retreated to his seat. "After the Secretary of Defense, my next call went to our ambassador in Saigon," Kearney continued after the laughter died down. "I asked him whether the U.S. was at war in Vietnam. He hemmed and hawed, so I asked it a different way—were Americans killing and being killed? Far as he knew, one U.S. field advisor had been killed, but as of now, he said, U.S. advisors were not engaged in combat."

Kearney paused, assessed the gallery, pleased to see a number of reporters taking notes. "Now, Mr. President, I can't speak for you or my senate colleagues, but in my hometown of Whitfield, folks know a soldier on duty in a hostile zone, gunned down by the enemy, is damn sure engaged in combat.

"Wait, there's more. My staff checked with other sources in Saigon and the State Department here in Washington and learned that the dead advisor did not travel along that dusty road alone. With him was another American junior officer and an American correspondent. I personally called the publisher of the *New York Times* to see if the reporter was one of their people. He confirmed that the reporter was Winston Brand, who has since filed his story from the luxury of a French rubber plantation through Hawaii to New York. The *Times* people were damn displeased their correspondent had leap-frogged over his own news bureau chief in Saigon to get his story out ahead of official channels in order to beat his competitors.

"Again, Mr. President, I don't presume to speak for every senator, or every American for that matter, but where I come from, we don't put a news story, or ambition, ahead of common decency or compassion. I left no doubt with the *Times* editor that if he didn't hold up the story until I could ascertain from the Pentagon that Captain Fletcher's wife in Texas had been notified, they would hear from one irate senator at least. So, my next call went to the senator from Texas, being a courtesy to our colleague."

Kearney stepped back from the lectern, removed his glasses and smiled toward the senator from Texas. As if on cue from Kearney, the Texan leaped from his seat. "Mr. President, will the senator yield for a brief remark?"

Kearney stepped back to the lectern and leaned over the microphone. "I'm pleased to yield to my great friend from Texas."

"Mr. President, on behalf of all the citizens from the Lone Star State of Texas, I want to express our appreciation to Chairman Kearney for his diligent pursuit of the truth in this matter. Our boys need wise and seasoned heads like Senator Kearney's to watch over them in this difficult, undeclared war. We take our Stetsons off to you, sir."

"Mr. President, I thank the senator from Texas for his kind remarks, but if you'll bear with me, I'm just about to wrap up my own. My final phone call went to the White House. I advised the president we had a soldier victimized twice by cowardly behavior—first by the South Vietnamese Army which failed to protect him, and then by a fellow American reporter, who let our fallen hero, and the rest of us Americans, down in word and deed. President Kennedy agreed to an urgent meeting scheduled first thing tomorrow to discuss this matter. He also gave tentative approval to my suggestion that I lead a fact-finding mission to Vietnam as soon as practicable. Many of you know my son, Tank, Jr., serves in Vietnam as I speak. I would hate for him to fall victim to such treatment at the hands of the South Vietnamese and a renegade amongst the press. These are some of the matters I'll want to look into in the days ahead. And, of course, when appropriate, I'll be back here on the floor to report to you. With that I again yield to the gentleman from Texas."

En route to the White House by limousine down Pennsylvania Avenue the next morning, Kearney discussed strategy with his administrative assistant. Dressed in a conservative navy blue pinstriped suit, instead of his white suit, red tie and blue handkerchief ensemble reserved for special occasions like patriotic functions, social gatherings and addresses to the Senate, Kearney knew better than to upstage the president on his turf.

"After we make our pitch, mark my words, the first thing Jack is going to ask is whom we are going to take along as our military advisor," said Kearney. "Who have we got on tap?"

"I think it should be a Washington outsider. Someone we can easily mold to your point of view, Senator."

"That's what makes you a good AA. You practically read my mind. I'll tell you whom we'll put forth to the president. His name's Sean O'Boyle, a navy captain in intelligence in Hawaii."

"You mean Brand's brother-in-law?"

"Course I do. Remember, he's done a few favors for us recently, and like his father-in-law, he's itching for those admiral stars. I don't have to tell you that he and Brand are engaged in a pissing contest."

"Good choice, Senator, but the president's sure to want to add his own military expert to our entourage."

"Let him. Then JFK's guy will cancel out our guy, and that leaves me to break the tie over whether a great nation like ours should stay in that God-forsaken country, or turn heel and stop pissing against the wind. I want us out of there, my son along with us and Winston Brand first."

From the White House, Kearney's limousine headed for Foggy Bottom. His meeting with President Kennedy had gone as expected. Kearney knew the president was concerned with the conduct of the war by the Diem regime, whose popularity in Vietnam had plummeted, and that the conflicting reports from his advisory staff about South Vietnam's leadership had him worried. What's more, Diem's brother Nhu and his wife posed an especially nettlesome problem for the president. So, Kearney was more than happy to offer to look into the matter in Vietnam. He determined to pay particular attention to whether the Vietnamese were willing or capable of instituting the necessary political reforms. To assist Kearney in assessing the military situation there, the senator knew, as predicted, he would be assigned a two-star general to accompany his fact-finding group to Vietnam. The meeting had gone exceptionally well as far as Kearney was concerned, but unexpected was the request that the senator avail himself of the State Department's Vietnam situational briefing.

Seated in a VIP lounge chair, Kearney waited for the foreign-service officer to begin. "You fellows sure have it cushy down here in Foggy Bottom," he said nudging the Assistant Secretary of State of Far Eastern Affairs seated next to him. "I'll have to talk to my colleagues on the appropriations committee and see if we can't funnel some of this splendor over to the Pentagon."

Kearney noticed a nervous laughter ring the room. "You guys don't know whether I'm joking or not. Let's put it this way. After I hear what you've got to say, and after I've gone to Vietnam for a first-hand inspection, maybe we'll need to make some changes in our priorities. When the dust clears, who knows who'll be carrying the ball on our Vietnam policy? Anyway, I'll give you 20 minutes to tell me everything you know about the situation."

The Foreign Service Officer (FSO) began the briefing, but his hand quivered so noticeably that he dropped three or four of his briefing papers. As he started to retrieve them from the carpet, Kearney boomed, "That's all right. Leave 'em lay and give me what you've got left in your hand."

The young diplomat looked to his superior for guidance. "Do as the chairman says," said the assistant secretary. "Start your briefing from what will probably be the middle of your remarks."

"I've sat through enough of these sessions to know that the middle is where the meat is anyway," snapped Kearney.

"On the matter of deploying U.S. forces in greater numbers to Vietnam, we have conflicting positions," the FSO began to read. "On one side, there is the Commander-in-Chief Pacific, who recommends against deploying U.S. forces in Vietnam until we have exhausted other means for helping Diem."

Kearney interrupted. "Good advice, even though I've always taken everything an admiral says with a grain of salt. Do you know that Vice Admiral Willoughby Brand once advocated the use of NATO forces to bail the French out? I damn sure crimped his sails. But go on."

"CINCPAC's concern is that the use of U.S. forces would raise the colonialist issue and would spur the communists into greater action, making it necessary then to counter them with U.S. combat troops. He sees SEATO forces, not NATO, as a possible buttress to prevent infiltration of South Vietnam along the Ho Chi Minh

Trail." The state department officer waited while Kearney lit a cigar.

"And who's opposed to the commander's sensible position?" Kearney asked.

"The bleakest assessment came from the military group that left for Vietnam October 17, 1961. Do you want me to read the report, senator?"

"Certainly, if you think it's important. Lord knows when I'd ever find the time to read it on my own."

The report follows:

> Vietcong strength had increased from an estimated 10,000 in January 1961 to 17,000 in October. They were clearly on the move in the Mekong Delta, in the Central Highlands, and along the plain on the north central coast. The South Vietnamese were watching with dismay the situation in Laos and the negotiations in Geneva, which convinced them that there would soon be a Communist dominated government in Vientiane. The worst flood in decades was ravaging the Mekong delta, destroying crops and livestock and rendering hundreds of thousands homeless.... In the wake of this series of profoundly depressing events, it was no exaggeration to say that the entire country was suffering from a collapse of national morale—an obvious fact which made a strong impression on the members of the mission. In subsequent weeks as we meditated on what the United States could or should do in South Vietnam, the thought was always with us that we needed something visible which could be done quickly to offset the oppressive feeling of hopelessness which seemed to permeate all ranks of Vietnamese society.

With the fingers holding the cigar, Kearney pinned a strand of red-dyed hair against his forehead. "I suppose you fellows see red in every color, such as expressed in the report. Since when are any of you military and pin-stripers qualified to pass judgment on such sweeping and cultural aspects of a country that you know so little about? My fact-finding mission is interested in what the South Vietnamese are doing to help themselves, or, as it appears, sabotage their own efforts. Give me some facts on Diem and how he treats his people. Then maybe we'll find out why morale is so bad in Vietnamese society."

"With your permission, Senator, could I close out the report with that group's recommendations?"

"Go ahead, but make it quick."

"They want to shift our effort in Vietnam from advice to limited partnership, which means bringing in more Americans to work side by side with the Vietnamese on the key problems. In other words, we're to go from military advisors to something akin to governmental advisors."

"Hell, Diem can't protect a few U.S. military advisors. How in the hell does he expect to nursemaid a bunch of pasty-faced political, psychological and economic specialists running all over his country?"

"Yes, Senator, you've touched on a sensitive area in our relations with Vietnam. How do we turn a typical petty despot into a democrat? If you'll permit me to go on with this last segment, there is a counterpoint to this report advanced by our department."

"Go ahead, read me some more. It'll probably cure my insomnia if nothing else."

"We argue that pressures for political and administrative change in South Vietnam have reached the point of explosion. Without needed reforms, no program of assistance to that country can be fully effective, and we believe that if change does not come in an orderly way, it will almost certainly come through forceful means by Diem's opponents. But here's how our department has capsulized it:

> The situation provides an opportunity for the United States to stand once again for change in this part of the world, to press for measures that are both efficient and more democratic. We must identify ourselves with the people of Vietnam and with their aspirations, not with a man or an administration. We must do what we can to help release the tremendous energy, ability and idealism that exist in Vietnam. We must suggest, not demand; we must advise not dictate; but we must not hesitate to stand for the things that we and the Vietnamese know to be worthwhile and just in the conduct of political affairs.

"That sounds like a bunch of State Department gobble-di-gook to me. What kind of reforms do you have in mind? Can't you fellows ever be specific?"

"Mr. Nhu's suppression of dissent is one example, Senator. He's jailed most of the regime's political opponents. Then there's Madame Nhu's morality laws restricting individual freedoms down to the point of forcing bar girls to wear distasteful uniforms. And of course Diem's Catholic faith inclines him to favor the Catholics over the Buddhist majority."

"Now we're getting somewhere. These are the kinds of things I can sink my Irish teeth into to see who howls the loudest. Anything else I should know?"

"Yes, sir. The State Department is on record for separating the Nhus from President Diem. Vietnamese hatred seems directed at these two, who exert too much influence over the president. The question, and, perhaps this is where the Kearney Commission can help us, revolves around how to achieve this separation without endangering U.S. prospects in Vietnam?"

"Tell the Secretary of State that he, like the president, can count on me to do the right thing. Now, is that it?"

"Unless you have further questions, Senator."

"Indeed I do. Have you fellows ever heard of an U.S. outfit called 'Operation Checkmate' inside Vietnam?"

Again, the foreign- service officer deferred to the assistant secretary.

"Vaguely," the senior official replied. "It's some kind of hush-hush military activity, isn't it? I'd think your committee would have a better handle on it, Senator."

"Well, that's not the case. They've got a direct line to somebody in the White House. You tell the Secretary of State he and I need to get together and do something about that. We can't let the Defense Department 'screw up' the nation's foreign service policy without input from Congress, the CIA or your department." Kearney caught his slip immediately and backtracked. "I mean 'screw up' in the sense of being a lone ranger. Otherwise, the president only hears one voice on foreign policy."

"Are you making a suggestion, Senator?"

"I suppose I am in a way. I just want you to know I intend to look into this Checkmate shit while in Vietnam. I assure you that if it's run as slipshod as I think it is, you'll have my strong support to either close it down or add a State Department representative and a CIA man with proper congressional oversight to this group of planners and plotters. Checkmate, my Irish ass. There's at least one known renegade bastard on their payroll. And I aim to get Winston Brand out of Vietnam!"

17 IN THE EYE OF THE STORM

The most distrustful persons are often the biggest dupes.
—Jean François Paul de Gondi, cardinal de Retz

ON THE AFTERNOON of their return to Saigon, Doc Jenicoso went off with Alex Spear to attend to Fletcher's body, leaving Brand alone with his thoughts. The reporter made his way to the coffee shop in the terminal building at Tan Son Nhut airport where Maria would meet him in a half hour, according to the major's instructions. The two men had exchanged letters in the rain on the tarmac. Alex had handed Brand Maria's letter, while the reporter surrendered Fletcher's last testament to the major's custody. At this point, neither had spoken about Brand's up-country trip.

Brand forced himself to eat a hard roll, his first solid food since the chloroform incident. He was determined to fortify himself against the onslaught of questions the intelligence officer would raise once they returned to their adjacent quarters at the Five Oceans. Alex was bound to press him on the advisor's death and Brand's own narrow escape, twisting the two incidents so that they fit his and General Pavler's portfolio on R-3. Annoyed to feel himself grow flush in the face at the thought of some super spy tracking his every move, Brand resolved to counter with the weapons at his disposal and go on the offensive.

First, with whatever information gleaned from the marine's investigation, he would find this R-3 and expose him in the columns of the *New York Times*. But then he realized that he would have to get Alex's consent to use the information, since it had been given to him on a deep background basis. Even Pavler must be kept in the dark relative to his intentions. Brand flushed again, realizing he was already entangled in a situation controlled by others. Finally, he decided his best bet was to keep a lower profile and let this R-3 business play itself out in military channels, while his own personal investigation proceeded independently until cleared to publish the results.

"Of course, it's risky," he told himself, "but to just stand by while others take potshots at me is a whole lot more dangerous." This sounded close to his father's advice he called into the makeshift ring as young Brand boxed the chump of the week. "Jab and move, Winston. Make it hard for him to hit a moving target," the vice admiral had shouted, not the least bit concerned about how unfair it was to favor his son while the neighborhood boy had no coach in his corner.

As he sat at the table waiting for Maria, Brand felt abandoned in the same way, and now there was no Willie to lean on in these melancholy moments that stripped his mind of positive thought. Even his escape from the so-called robbers at the Devereau plantation had its negative side as he counted his losses—wallet, press credentials, cigarette lighter, a birthstone ring that his sister Clementine had given him, his silver flask and who knows what else. So far, he had salvaged the items placed in his dresser the night of the attack—his notes, Capt. Erik Fletcher's letter and a Leica camera. Considered government property, both the advisor's letter and the Leica were relinquished to Alex Spear from whom Brand also borrowed money.

"Bad move number one," he told himself. "You should've kept the camera long enough to remove the film and get it developed. Now you'll have to take Spear's word for what happened on the road. Some independent investigator you turned out to be, obligated to everybody and his brother!"

To drive these thoughts away, Brand turned to Maria's letter that lay unopened on the table. He closed his eyes and allowed his inner vision to recreate the scene on the gallery deck at *Bon Sejeur* plantation where, in his illusion, she appeared dressed in the antebellum gown. In another moment, his mind's eye, like the carousel on a projector, reversed the order of the slides, and he saw the two of them lying next to each other on the beach at Guam.

The rain pelted against the terminal window and the sound brought him back to reality. He began to read Maria's words:

Dearest Winston,

As I write, there is great concern for your safety, and I would join your friends in their anguish were it not for my faith. God could never be so cruel as to bring us together in such a romantic encounter only to dash all hopes of future happiness. Although I am young, love is a very old story to me, passed down from my grandmother and mother. I learned it is wrong to leave a piece of yourself on every doorstep here and there, for then there is little left to give when true love comes knocking. Count our rendezvous as the boldest thing I have ever done. Is it love that has come knocking for you and me? For myself, I have never met anyone like you before, and you have never left my thoughts since we joined together in such a sense of 'mountaintop' oneness.

My grandfather and father taught me that, though often maligned, men have as great a capacity for love as women, once they make themselves equally vulnerable. I can only hope that the ecstasy we experienced when we reached the point of complete surrender one to the other on that beach in Guam that it meant as much to you as it did to me.

I have always loved God, my family and in my dreams the one man who would make my life complete. Call me a foolish, hopeless romantic if it pleases your macho side, but when you're hanging your words on your poet's trellis, feel again the inspiration that springs only between the loved and beloved. Like stars in separate galaxies spread across the sky, alone and incomplete, there may never be enough time nor the right place for us to be together. But I'm willing to wait until the end of your quest if need be.

Do you imagine for a moment any one of us can play the great role we have set for ourselves in this life without divine guidance? Why not let this old-fashioned girl ease your journey along the road of life? No sense going alone, Winston, if you don't have to. I wait for your answer with 'fire in my soul.'

Love, Maria

He smiled to himself out of admiration for the poetic way Maria had fashioned her words. Brand thought Captain Bao's Hue maiden crossing the Perfume River could not have turned a more eloquent phrase. Yet, as he returned the letter to its envelope, he had already decided what he must do given his situation. He drew a line through his name on the face and wrote, "Maria Monclova, another time, another place."

When the waiter came for payment, Brand described Maria to him and placed her letter on the table next to the man's tip.

"I've doubled your gratuity. See that the young lady gets this envelope."

"No worry, I set her at same table. She no can miss. You see."

Outside, Brand huddled against the terminal building without much shelter and listened to the rain beat down upon his cap. Occasionally, he tipped the leather visor to allow some of the water to escape and wrung out his sleeves to the same purpose. It made little difference. After a few minutes, the wind-driven rain had soaked through his garments, pressing them against his skin. He checked his left wrist, but then recalled that his watch had been stolen. He wanted to go back inside to get dry and warm, but sensed that Maria's flight was approaching. Off in the distance through the fog, aircraft landing lights caught his attention as they pierced the rain from the east. He fished into his mufti pocket for the Vietnamese cigarettes he had purchased in the cafe. The package was soggy and the moment he pulled out a cigarette, it disintegrated in his hand.

"El cheapos," he murmured to himself and longed for his own pack of cigarettes he imagined were keeping Willie company somewhere in the rotten jungle. For a minute or two, he pictured some half-naked Viet Cong soldier sitting cross-legged under a bamboo tree sipping his bourbon and enjoying a good smoke. Of course, he mused, something as valuable as a full silver flask might make its way up the communist hierarchy, perhaps to R-3 himself, if such a person existed.

This headed his mind on a different course, and he tried to fathom why the communists wanted to kill him. He knew the kidnapping at Devereau's was well planned, and since none of the other guests were targeted, he wondered if the explosion that killed Fletcher hadn't been intended for him. These failed attempts by someone Alex had pegged as an expert assassin puzzled him most. Either he was extremely lucky, or Spear's master spy had lost his touch. In due time, he would have to discuss these matters with the major without letting the marine intelligence officer know he had decided to strike out on his own.

The voices of soldiers entering the building interrupted his thoughts. Behind a group of 15 to 20 American GIs came two female flight attendants scurrying across the tarmac beneath a single umbrella. He saw Maria toss her long, black hair over her shoulder to keep it from the rain. Her face radiated excitement and before reaching the canopy that stretched a few feet from the entrance, she broke away from her companion and dashed for the doorway. He barely had time to slip back against the wall out of sight.

It seemed she was only out of view for a couple of minutes before she reappeared under the awning and then stepped out into the rain. This time she was alone. When she turned to the right, he saw her beautiful face, and his heart pounded as he watched the rain mingle with her tears. She searched back and forth for some sign of him. In her hand, she clutched the envelope, and when she looked up as if to implore the heavens to treat her with greater kindness, he almost ran to her side to shield her from the storm and his rejection. But he knew why he was hiding in the first place. As hard as this moment was on her, at least she was safe from physical harm, which would not be the case if they were in a relationship. So he had decided against exposing her to the dangers he faced. Whoever it was that wanted him out of the way would show no mercy to such an innocent woman, he reasoned.

Brand had no idea how long she stood there in her anguish. All he knew was that he felt his own torment settle a bit when she gave up her search and walked slowly toward the parked aircraft. Again, he started after her, unwilling to see her vision of loveliness depart, but he checked himself and leaned back against the wall. He surprised himself by reciting the poem he had written to Eleanor on the occasion of a long assignment away from her. "Somewhere out there, sharing this sky, she walks alone, just like I do. No, not alone, my heart's there, too..." He couldn't finish. The next moment, he turned away as Maria disappeared into the waiting aircraft. He placed his hands against the wall with his head held down, the rain still pelting his dejected form until he heard Alex's jeep pull up to the front canopy.

En route to their BOQ, despite his damp clothing, Winston asked Alex to break away from the swirling traffic and swing by the Navy Exchange. He told the major he wanted to cash a check and replenish his personal items. The Headquarters Support Activity, Saigon (HSAS), occupied a two-story building on one of the city's side streets. There, the Navy operated an exchange, a small commissary, and nearby a 12 lane bowling alley was under construction. After buying a cartoon of cigarettes, a cheap watch and a vinyl wallet, Brand asked Alex if he had time to spare for him to go to the commissary where he wanted to purchase his favorite snack— orange juice and Fig Newtons.

"Sorry to impose on you again, old man," said Brand. "With no identification I'm lucky to get this far. Thanks for vouching for me."

"Maybe it would save another hassle if I went ahead alone and got the items for you," Spear suggested.

"Yeah, but look at the mob in the checkout line. Those soldiers are pushing three or four carts each. How can they eat all that stuff?"

"Awful timing on our part. That's probably field support service buying rations for the troops serving up-country. They have priority over all other customers."

"Yeah, I remember. Captain Fletcher mentioned them. C'mon, these quartermaster types look like they'll have the cashiers tied up 'til Christmas. I'll survive until I can get my accreditation card renewed and get down here on my own."

"Are you sure?" Alex asked.

"Sure. And these damp clothes are beginning to feel like burlap. Let's go."

Three blocks from the Five Oceans, Brand returned to the subject of the field support unit. He told the major he wanted to take a few days off from war and politics and do a column on how the Americans at far-flung outposts in Vietnam got their supplies. Since he had made no mention of black market involvement, Spear's response stunned him.

"Winston, that subject's been on my mind, too, especially when you brought back the Leica. Out of 400 issued, Fletcher's is the only camera returned, thanks to you. General Pavler believes there's a black market ring operating, and that the cameras are sold for as much as $500 each and reported as combat losses."

"No doubt, your R-3's behind this scheme as well."

"No, we can't lay this one at his feet. But he certainly benefits whenever Americans rip-off their own country."

"And countrymen."

"True. I can tell you here and now, the general and I will cooperate on any story that exposes the blatant betrayal of our country."

"Would these cameras go through the same field support pipeline as the food?"

"There's no other way to get them up-country and in the hands of the advisors."

"While I'm waiting for my interview with Diem, maybe you could arrange for me to spend a day with field support service. By the way, how's my Diem interview request coming along anyway?"

"We've run into a snag. Diem won't meet with you until you pass muster by going through Gen. 'Big' Minh on the military side and But Hieu, the civilian Minister of Information. These things take time unless you've got friends in the royal court. On the field support matter, no sweat. There's a lieutenant in our BOQ who's one of the team leaders."

"Alex, the last time you introduced me to a lieutenant from the Five Oceans, the two of us damn near got killed."

"Yes, but this time, you'll be operating well behind friendly lines in the company of support elements. I'd hate to tell you what the troops out in the field have nicknamed this type of soldier."

"Go ahead. You've piqued my interest."

"There're called REMFs."

"I know this acronym. GI's also used it in Korea to describe rear echelon personnel who participated in incestuous activities."

"Right on target. Never heard them described so eloquently though. If these guys are involved in illegal activity, they're not going to take kindly to outside snooping. You might want to keep your guard up."

"Are you kidding? After what I've been through, I've learned to walk on egg shells," said Brand. He heard Alex chuckle and decided to close the subject with a flick of his finger across his nose.

In his estate on Rue d' Espagne, R-3 leaned over a map spread on a table. Over the map, he placed a colored template configured like a chess board. He took a grease pencil and drew a circle around the lower point where the black space of the queen bishop intersects with the white space of the queen knight, indicating the French plantation of *Bon Sejour.* On another piece of paper, he jotted down the location 50 miles southwest of Saigon in the vicinity of the hamlet of Bac. He described the order of a proposed engagement to trap ARVN forces as follows:

> Throughout December of 1962, from the hamlet of Than Thoi, we will transmit signals from one of the radios captured at Loch Ninh. Once it is determined the puppet state radio research unit at Tan Son Nhut has intercepted our signal, we will move the radio transmitter to Bac. There we shall lure ARVN and their imperialist advisors into a trap. By jamming the American frequencies with their own captured equipment, we shall sow confusion in their ranks. After the initial skirmish, they will try to reinforce ARVN by flying in reserve forces aboard the American helicopters. By disguising our transmissions, we will cause the Americans to believe we are ARVN forces on the ground, guiding them to the battle. Actually, we will be scattering the enemy across the skies like mad geese not knowing where to set down. One by one, we'll lure the gunships into our cross fire, while making them believe ARVN has abandoned the field. The Americans can't tell one Vietnamese voice from another over the radio. They will eventually blame their allies for their defeat.

R-3 carefully re-read the instructions and committed them to memory. He sealed the document, then addressed it to the Peoples War Archives. He pulled the bell cord next to his chair, and in a few minutes his new adjutant stood behind him. R-3 kept his back to the officer as he waved the document in one hand and the template in the other.

"Get this on the next available International Control Commission (ICC) flight to Hanoi," R-3 ordered. "I also want you to deliver this coded template and map to Queen's Bishop for further distribution on a need-to-know basis. You are to advise our loyal comrades that they have nine months to prepare for the next operation. Do you think you can remember all that?"

"Yes, sir. I'll repeat it to you if you wish."

"That won't be necessary. We shall have to trust you, even though betrayed by our former adjutant, the traitor Captain Bao, who now serves our enemies hoping for higher rank and position."

"I could never betray the revolution like Bao did. The mention of his name makes me sick," said R-3's new adjutant.

"Ah, yes," said R-3, "but he had a flair for convincing our comrades in the field that they had more information than the skimpy, disjointed evidence he presented to them. Bao made them feel part of the big picture, instead of just pawns."

"I'll remember that, too, sir."

"See that you do, and one more thing."

"Yes, sir."

"Follow my instructions to the letter without improvising or deviating, and you will have proved yourself superior to Bao in every respect."

Two days after Brand had watched Maria walk off into the rain, Alex burst into his room, obviously excited. It was early morning and Brand had just finished his wake-up cigarette.

"Come quick, out here on the balcony," Alex shouted. "Diem and his whole retinue are over on the Police Academy grounds conducting some kind of ceremony."

"What's that got to do with me?" asked Brand, rubbing his eyes.

"The President's got the Nhus, 'Big' Minh, But Hieu and everyone else of importance in the Saigon regime there. Seems like a good time to look for an opening to plead your case for an interview. Extremely unusual for all of them to gather in one spot. Not their usual practice for security reasons. I wonder why we didn't get any advance notice. Perhaps it's meant to be a press photo op."

Moments later, Brand and Spear stood on their small balcony on the side opposite the An Dong market and examined the proceedings underway on the parade field. Below them, files of uniformed Vietnamese policemen, dressed in tunics bleached by excessive washings and exposure to the tropical sun, scurried about like white mice. The police officers linked hands and formed a human security fence around a flatbed trailer festooned with red and saffron banners. President Diem knelt in the center of the trailer, and on each side of him stood his cabinet and family members. Brand commented to Alex that the elaborate security arrangements seemed inappropriate for the occasion since he counted fewer than 100 Vietnamese citizens standing silent and sullen outside the human shield.

"All those cops are probably for show," Alex replied. "Diem wants to look like the strongest dragon."

"Then what's he doing on his knees, Alex?"

"Praying."

"For what?"

"For his country and his own soul. The man's practically a monk, you know."

"I've heard he's a devout Catholic."

"Yes, and a friend of Cardinal Spellman who introduced him to Senator John Kennedy when the two of them happened to be in New York City at the same time."

"So, Diem's got a foothold in the White House."

"One would think so."

"Then why does he need prayers or such an elaborate ceremony to impress the Vietnamese, Americans, or maybe just the press corps?"

"Good questions. Maybe you should ask him if you're granted an interview."

"I'll put it at the top of my list if I ever get him one-on-one," said Brand.

"Well, don't expect it to happen today. I've seen him pray for an hour followed by a two hour speech. Our best bet is to go down there and see if any of his advisors will speak to us."

"Where do we start?"

"From the way he's clinging to Madame Nhu's side, that Vietnamese captain with the eye patch is the best prospect, I'd say."

"That's Captain Bao," Brand exclaimed. He then told Alex how he had met Bao at dinner at *Bon Sejour* before he was later kidnapped. The next morning before Brand and Doc Jenicoso left for Saigon by helicopter, Captain Bao, at breakfast with the good doctor, had asked him to pass to Brand his offer of assistance once back in Saigon.

"Then, he's our man. Perhaps your meeting with him at the Devereau's can be used to your advantage in gaining an interview with Diem. Seeing that he just turned up at court recently, his clout has increased, since he's being considered as an administrator of the Strategic Hamlet program."

"I didn't know he was close to the Nhus. The question is, can we trust that guy, especially if he's merely a new guy on the scene?" asked Brand. "For all I know, he could've been in on the ambush on the road to *Bon Sejour*, or my subsequent abduction from the plantation."

"Hardly."

"What makes you so sure?"

"Well, if he's a Saigon intellectual, he'd never soil his hands with such dirty work. Besides, Bao has no motive for attacking a reporter. Indeed, your press colleagues initially report that he might be easier to work with than others at the palace."

"Who told you that?"

"Tillerstein, for one."

"Oh, Sheet, I'd almost forgotten him."

"Well, you're very much on his mind."

"Now what are you talking about?"

"Tillerstein wants you to meet him at Pierre Girard's party a week from Saturday. Of course, since you've been away, you haven't heard the latest. Diem, or Nhu, is on the verge of tossing the Frenchman out of the country."

"That's no skin off my backside."

"Well, if I were in your shoes, Winston, I'd go to the party. Bao might be there, and if we don't connect with him today on the Diem interview, you could corner him at Girard's place."

"Alex, you sure do have a lot of answers about trivial matters, but when it comes to the crucial questions, you're awfully mum."

"Well, what do you want to know?"

Brand laughed aloud. "You've got to be kidding," he said. "You owe me more answers than there's time for in this lifespan."

"Well, go ahead, fire away with your questions."

Brand held up five fingers on his left hand and began to tick them off. "Let's start in reverse order," he said pointing to his little finger. "Who was behind my abduction at the Devereau's? Who was the target at the road ambush? Who was behind the bombing at The Slice of Paris? Who called my room in a threatening manner in Hawaii, and who mugged me at Travis?"

"I can only give you theories at this point," Alex said.

Brand relaxed his hand. "I'll take anything you've got."

"Very well. Let's take it in your order. Viet Cong agents no doubt kidnapped you at the rubber plantation. For what purpose, we don't know…"

"Or if you do, you won't tell me," Brand interrupted. He shrugged his shoulders as Alex moved to the next question.

"As for the ambush on the road from Loc Ninh, your own photographs indicate that Captain Fletcher was the target. In several slides, there is a young boy who approaches the advisor's jeep with his hands held inside his conical hat. Upon leaving the vehicle, he has his hat on, but no lollipop in either his hands or mouth like the other children."

"Yeah, I get the picture. This kid planted an explosive device under the Captain's seat."

"Yes, I'll show you the slides if you want to see for yourself."

"No, I'll take your word for it. I'd prefer to put that incident behind me."

"That may not be so easy, Winston."

"Now, what are you driving at?"

"Today's English-language *Saigon Times* has a front page article, dateline Washington, in which Senator Kearney denounces your part in reporting the road incident."

"He can go look somewhere else to get press attention."

"Well, he's coming here instead, at taxpayer's expense no less."

"When?"

"Very soon in April, as an advance party for the Secretary of Defense's visit in early May."

"Oh yeah? I'll see to it I'm on opposite sides of the country from these politicians."

"Good idea, Winston."

"Wait a minute, Alex. Tell me who mugged me back in the states and started all this intrigue?"

"Well, there we do have some slim progress to report. The FBI checked the warning note planted on you at Travis, and after immersion in ephedrine, the fingerprint in question turned purple."

"What in the hell does that mean?"

"It means we've isolated a print with what looks like feminine characteristics, so it isn't yours or mine."

"That woman in the gray coat. I told you so."

"Not so fast, Winston. We've found no match in the criminal file, so the FBI's next step is to run the print through the national security data bank. If seven or eight characteristics match there, we'll know our woman applied for a security clearance, a federal job or a special passport at some point in her life. But this could be a long shot, so don't expect positive identification any time soon."

"Why did I think you were going to say that? I'd better get down there with Diem's group. Maybe I'll have better luck with the Vietnamese. Of course, I'll need your help since I don't have any identification of my own."

"Okay, but promise me you won't wear the ankle holster and gun General Pavler gave you. That could make the Vietnamese police jittery."

Brand laughed. "Alex, you know damn well I haven't worn that thing and don't plan to."

"Suit yourself, but if I were you, Winston, I wouldn't go around in the dark alone without some protection, especially with your shaky case history."

By the time the two Americans reached the outer limit of the police cordon, news correspondents of various nationalities had arrived, disrupting the ceremony on the academy grounds. Only President Diem, who continued in prayer atop the flatbed trailer, seemed oblivious to the clamor of 30 or more news people jockeying for the best vantage point. Pushed and shoved by eager photographers, Brand and Spear worked their way to the front of the pack where a young Vietnamese army officer endeavored to sort things out.

"Frontline here," he said drawing an imaginary line through a stretch of greensward passing in front of his toes. "Only photographer come this far. You two move back."

Alex hesitated but Winston pressed forward. "Get Captain Bao over here. He'll tell you it is okay," he said.

The officer studied Brand from head to toe. "Who you? Where *Bao Chi* pass? Where camera?"

Brand shouted over his shoulder to the major. "Seems we should have brought the Leica with us. You'd better help me straighten this thing out."

Spear rejoined his companion, but to both their surprise, the ARVN officer had turned heel and was headed toward the VIP trailer.

"Probably going to get someone with more authority," Alex predicated.

"Yeah, let's hope he comes back with Captain Bao," said Brand.

The reporter watched the officer proceed to where Captain Bao and Madame Nhu stood. Brand thought he had seen Bao turn his head in their direction to allow his good eye to take in the disturbance he had made. But if the captain recognized Brand, he gave no sign and instead bent his head toward Nhu's wife, the nominal 'First Lady,' to engage her in conversation.

Whatever transpired piqued her interest, for in the next moment she peered around Bao's angular body and looked straight at Brand with exquisite brown eyes that might have belonged to Maria except for their color and shape. Brand returned her gaze, and she turned away to speak to an official who stood near her at the back edge of the trailer. She and the gentlemen in question spoke briefly, and then, followed by the ARVN officer, the Vietnamese gentleman beat a path toward Winston and Alex.

Encouraged by the official's upraised hand summoning them, the two Americans stepped across the imaginary line. Dressed in a light weight blue suit and red tie, the Vietnamese civilian of somewhat more than average size and supple figure strode toward them with the authority of a mandarin, except that he kept his head down and chin tucked in against his throat like an athlete battling wind resistance. He suddenly stopped and raised his head at the approach of Brand and Spear. He had calm, noble features and his face was framed by wispy black hair that trailed off from his forehead, bent around the back of his ears and rested on a starched white collar. He extended his hand to Major Spear.

"Alex, long time no see," he said in a voice so soft Brand could barely hear him. "Is there a problem? And who do we have here?" He turned to face Brand, but it was Spear who responded.

"Winston Brand, it is my pleasure to introduce you to the Minister of Information," the major said.

"Propaganda and Information, But Hieu," the minister repeated and kept a tight grip on Brand's hand as he added. "Why haven't you been by to see me, Mr. Brand? Didn't they tell you in Hawaii that the in-country press accreditation process begins with me?"

"I'm sure they did, Minister Hieu, but protocol got side-stepped when I went up-country."

"'Otherwise occupied' as you Americans say. Yes, I heard you were with the advisor killed near Loc Ninh." Hieu finally released Brand's hand as he turned back to Spear.

"Alex, tell your superiors they have the condolences of the Vietnamese Government and people. I want you to know that Major Si, the officer in charge when this happened, is undergoing interrogation."

"We want to talk to him later as part of our own investigation," said Alex.

"Si won't have contact with American intelligence until we've concluded our assessment. But of course, none of these are matters that bring you to our humble ceremony. What can I do for you and your friend, Alex?"

"Winston wants to interview President Diem."

"His timing is bad. Our government is about to order the expulsion of Paul Steffans of the *New York Times*. Two more of Mr. Brand's press colleagues are bound to be thrown out by the end of the year unless they stop lying about the president and his family. We like Americans, but they must follow Vietnamese rules."

"That's got nothing to do with me," Brand protested.

"Rules apply to everyone. South Vietnamese officials most of all. Now, they can only take written questions from foreign journalists that are approved in advance. If you give me your questions by Monday, I'll try to arrange an interview with President Diem. As you Americans say, 'Sorry about that.' Without submitting questions beforehand, no interview. I've got to go now. The President is almost finished with prayer."

"Can't we meet at another time to discuss this matter and have you fill me in on the ground rules?" Brand inquired as the minister turned to head back to the trailer. Alex winked at Brand, then played his own trump card.

"Minister Hieu, if you need another to vouch for Winston's objectivity in reporting, you need only check with Captain Bao. The two of them were dinner partners a few nights ago and struck it off well I'm told," said the major.

"Indeed, no more than a few minutes ago Madame Nhu made a similar observation," said the minister addressing Alex, but looking at Brand, whom he had turned to face directly. "Tell you what, the

American ambassador and your bureau chief, Mr. Tillerstein, are coming to my office at 9 a.m. Monday to plead Paul Steffan's case. Why don't you join them? We'll 'kill two birds with one stone,' as you Americans say."

"I'll be there, Minister Hieu. Thanks," said Brand.

"My pleasure, Mr. Brand. Let's just hope, as you Americans say, 'one or two bad apples haven't spoiled the whole barrel.'"

On the way back to the Five Oceans, buoyed by his turn of good fortune, Brand thanked Spear for his part. "We sure landed one out of three big fish in that pond out yonder owing to your first name basis with this Butt Hill character."

"Better learn to pronounce it correctly, Winston. It's 'Boot,' like the kick in the pants his government feels some of your colleagues deserve. And, 'Hew' as in toe the line or you'll be tossed out next."

"Don't worry. I have no intention of crossing the minister. Where'd he learn to speak English so well?"

"Obviously from a teacher who knew every American colloquialism in the book, or as we might say, every hackneyed expression to come down the pike."

"Well put," chuckled Brand.

"Yes, but a word of caution. Don't call him by his first name unless he specifically requests you to. Notice he remains Minister Hieu to me although he has called me Alex for the past eighteen months. Not once has he ever asked me to reciprocate. Just one of those strange Vietnamese customs he follows despite being a Yankeephile."

"Yeah, well he can call me whatever he likes as longs as he comes through with the Diem interview. That might take some time, so here's what's next on my agenda." The major listened attentively as Brand outlined his plan.

"Tomorrow morning, I'd like to go with your lieutenant on an actual pick-up and delivery of supplies. Then, Sunday, I'll head over to the MAAG compound and interview the people who administer the program," Winston explained.

"Sounds good. But Lt. Ledger Smith and his crew start out awfully early on weekends. Those are their meat pickup and delivery days."

"How early?"

"0430. Or O' Dark Thirty civilian time."

"I'll manage. What about the administrators?"

"Like you press guys, they're pencil pushers. So, I wouldn't get to their desks any sooner than noon Sunday."

Despite his more relaxed mood, Brand found it hard to sleep that night. Images of the chubby little man in the white suit, kneeling in prayer disturbed him. He wondered how Diem could hold the country together with so many factions nibbling at his heels. There were the communists, the Buddhists, his own military advisors and the brigands he had driven underground since assuming office. Brand knew what it was like to have so many enemies one could never determine who his friends were. In this respect, Diem had his sympathy, for like himself, the South Vietnamese president depended on the fairness of certain U.S. officials for his own survival.

For an independent spirit, this amounted to enslavement of part of the soul. Although he sought to keep himself master of his own destiny, he, like Diem, had already compromised with alien forces. Of necessity, Diem's regime had to cozy up to a foreign culture and to please both his old and new owners, like a slave on the block, he had to prove himself valuable. Brand realized as he lay in his dark room that he was in a similar predicament. He wondered if General Pavler and Alex Spear would jettison their support for him if he didn't at least appear valuable. That's why it was crucial he follow the leads on this black market business. Here was a bone, like Diem's religious pretensions, for everyone to gnaw on. This thought had a calming effect and he drifted to sleep until awakened by gunshots fired across the hall from his room a half hour before he was to get up anyway.

18 TO SMELL OF THE LAMP

Once, Pytheas, taunting Demosthenes, told him his reasons smelled of the lamp. "Yes," Demosthenes sharply replied, "but there is a great difference, Pytheas, between your labor by lamplight and mine."

—Plutarch

DOWN TOWARD THE Ca Mau Peninsula where the Mekong lives up to its reputation as the "river of nine dragons," Lt. Thomas "Tank" Kearney, Jr., was having difficulty sleeping. The water in the canal below his room lapped against the stilts every time a boat passed. He cursed his poor luck. By rights, instead of living like a musk rat in the Mekong Delta, he should still be in Song Be high and dry atop his good family girl. The thought of the wide-eyed virgin naked and trembling on the bed stirred his blood. He recalled how the Vietnamese maiden seemed fascinated by his red, private hair. He couldn't wait for his next trip to Saigon to tell those "smart asses" at the Five Oceans how easily he carried out the conquest. Less than 24 hours after his arrival in the small village, Tank, Jr., had convinced the girl's father to invoke the provisions of the long discredited Gia Long Code first promulgated in 1815. By this decree, the emperor had given the head of the family absolute power over his household, including his wife and children. Kearney had discovered this form of slavery from a history book and applied the knowledge the moment the young girl presented him with flowers as a newcomer to Song Be. "What a sweetheart," he said to the girl's father standing proudly next to her. "With your permission, I'll make her my wife."

That same night the father had dutifully delivered his daughter to Kearney's apartments, unaware that the junior American at the detachment had been reassigned to Phuoc Xuyen in the southern most region of Vietnam.

An ugly departure scene had ensued the following morning, as what seemed like half the population of Song Be, led by the girl's father, turned out to hurl insults at the retreating officer. "Old bastard. Thought he was betrayed when I didn't hang around to poke his daughter more than once. What about me? Some sonofabitch gets dysentery, and I get diverted to this sink hole," Tank, Jr., complained to himself, angered that this remembrance shattered his earlier thoughts of the seduction.

Tired of trying to sleep, Kearney raised the mosquito net and carefully eased himself to the edge of the bed. Except for a narrow catwalk that led to ledges anchoring his bunk and a small table, the rest of the room was floorless. Twice in two days he had already miss-stepped and plunged into the water below. He climbed out on the floating deck and peered into the small fiberglass outboard moored there.

"Hey you," he shouted pulling a ragged piece of netting off the hammock strewn between the two raised seats in the craft. "Get your ass up and go out and get me a hamburger."

"Name Nguyen, not 'Hey You,'" Kearney's houseboy protested.

"Look, you little smart ass. If I yell shit, I expect you to come running. Now get out of here and get me a sandwich."

"'Melican meat maybe come two, three days. No have in village. No have at Third Battalion Tenth Vietnamese Regiment either. I fix you local chicken like I do for other senior advisor."

"That's probably what damned near killed the guy. Boil me an egg. It's hard to screw that up. But wash your hands first."

Before the youth could get out of the boat, Tank, Jr., climbed in the bow.

"Never mind," he said, "let's feed a different kind of hunger. Take me to your sister."

"No sister. Only two brothers away in army. You wanta meet my father? He leader of ho."

"Ho Chi Minh, that communist bastard?"

"No bad communist here. Only happy people. Soldier and Viet Cong respect my father all the same. 'Ho' mean 'head of community.' All village men elect him."

"You dummy. I'm talking about women or girls old enough to bed." Kearney made a circle with one hand and jabbed his forefinger from the other in it.

"Ah, you want prostoot. No have in small village. Better you go big city."

Kearney's irritation was nearing the boiling point, but he then remembered how finesse had gotten him his way in Song Be. Perhaps, he reasoned, the same tactic might work in Phuoc Xuyen, which by all appearances was even more backward.

"Tell you what, 'Hey You,'" Kearney said stepping back on the dock. "Tomorrow you take me to meet your father, and I want you to tell the headman I'm looking for a Vietnamese wife. If you have no sisters or cousins, he can introduce me to a neighbor's daughter."

"I see. You want girl who make food for tonight, do laundry. I get for you there." Nguyen pointed to the house closest to Kearney's on the banks of the Mekong River.

The lieutenant started to call the boy back and inform him that he had more than food on his mind. But he decided to check out the prospect first.

As he waited in the moonlight, he wondered what his fraternity brothers back at Whitfield College would say if they could see him standing here in his underwear beneath a bamboo roof covered with palm leaves and wet straw. He could almost hear the jokes and comments as they flashed around the campus.

"Did you hear the one about the senator's son who has gone native, or, more likely, 'bananas?'"

Angered by unpleasant past memories of ridicule, he slapped at a mosquito gorging itself in the middle of his forehead where his full, red eyebrows almost came together. The force was so great, the palm of his hand came away moist with blood, and he retreated into his room, groping in the dark for the repellent container. He knew better than to light a lamp. This would only attract a hoard of insects to feast on his pale, beefy flesh which already reeked of spilled kerosene. Giving up on the repellent, he snatched the netting from his bed and wrapped it around his head and shoulders like a woman's shawl. By the time he reached the narrow porch, gingerly stepping barefoot over planks of bamboo fastened together with rattan, Nguyen appeared on the swaying suspension bridge linking the two houses. The houseboy held a flashlight in his hand.

"This Miss Dieu Minh. She cook for advisor same as before," the youth said turning to shine the beam in the face of the girl who trailed him.

"Don't come any closer with that damn light," Kearney shouted, "but keep it on her so I can get a good look."

"All you see is cook and laundress. No can tell good or bad from face," the girl said brushing the light aside.

"How much do you charge?" Kearney asked.

"Twelve hundred piasters a week—50 cents a day American—and good seats at American movie for me and friends."

"'Hey You,' what in the hell is she talking about?"

"Girl like Hollywood flick that come every month with supply from Saigon. Old advisor before speak she hooked. Village people say she clay-zee dreamer."

"Give me the flashlight. I want to see what I'm buying."

The boy obliged. This time the girl stared straight ahead, then turned for Kearney to examine her profile. From the front view, her face formed a perfect oval with dark eyes and a slim, regal nose set above the most sensuous lips Kearney had ever seen. But as she turned her dark head and slender body to one side, he saw a child, perhaps 13 at the most.

"Throw her back. She's under the limit," he told Nguyen.

"Clay-zee girl, good cook. Speak better English than me. Wash clothes. I run boat, take you everywhere. She keep inside house clean. Same before. Old advisor like her velly much."

"Yeah, but something damn near ate his guts out. Maybe it was her cooking."

"Bull shit!" the girl said as Kearney took a step back startled by her directness, yet amused she showed more spunk than any Vietnamese he had encountered so far.

"Go ahead, Miss, whatever your name. Plead your case."

"Miss Minh, my name, but other advisor call me Lucas for Rifleman on televishun. You know this show?"

"Sure, Lucas McCain played by Chuck Connors."

"That's me. Advisor say mouth shoot like rifle when mad. So careful how you speak to me."

"See, I tell you, she clay-zee," said Nguyen.

"Crazy, maybe, but not chicken shit like some village people," she said sticking her tongue out at the boy.

"Let her finish," Kearney said chuckling to himself, delighted to find someone who spoke in his vernacular.

"Simple, like one, two, three," she said. "One, I no cook for you. Two, you no eat, so you starve. Three, only make Viet Cong happy. You better sleep on it. Everyone in this village afraid to work for American. Don't want communists to know."

"What about 'Hey You' here? He works for me."

"Nguyen's father say okay, his son learn English in advisor's house. My mother and father go away. Nobody here tell Lucas what to do."

"A real independent bitch."

"You got that right, Pilgrim." The girl turned and sauntered away hands on her swaying hips like a cowboy leaving his opponent in the dust.

Kearney buckled over with laughter. "Did she say her name was Lucas McCain or John Wayne? We're in for one hell of a shoot-out in the next twelve months," he told Nguyen between guffaws.

After he had regained his composure, he called to the girl who had already reached the other side of the bamboo bridge, "Hey, kid, you're hired, but only if you call me Lieutenant Tank."

With the moon as a backdrop and the flashlight beam on her face, she acknowledged by rendering a snappy salute in his direction.

It took Kearney awhile to settle down in his bunk. He couldn't remember when he had laughed so hard. Anxiety about his predicament finally subsided and he drifted off to sleep, looking out the open window toward the girl's dwelling. Tomorrow he planned to get Lucas McCain to procure older women for him.

19 THE PENCIL PUSHERS

It is better for you to be free of fear lying upon a pallet, than to have a golden couch and a rich table and be full of trouble.

—Epicurus

WINSTON BRAND STOOD outside the front door of the Five Oceans smoking a cigarette. In the predawn light, he watched the smoke encase itself in the beam of the nearest overhead security lamp. Across the parade field stood the flatbed trailer Diem had used the previous morning. In the dim light, he watched the colored banners dancing in a stiff morning breeze.

"A great day for Five Ocean dwellers. The wind is against An Dong," a youthful voice called from behind the reporter.

"Lt. Ledger Smith," said Brand turning to face an officer of average height and trim figure.

"At your service," the young man answered sweeping his baseball style fatigue cap from brown crew cut hair and bowing like a medieval cavalier.

"Do you prefer Ledger or Lieutenant?"

"Please, Ledger. In field service support, we're all hired hands except for the three field grade officers who run the show. How am I to address you, sir?"

"Winston's good enough."

"Fine, between us, that is. As for the enlisted men on my team, they call me L-T., and I'll insist that out of respect for your status, they call you *Bao Chi*."

"Whatever works for you," said Brand.

The lieutenant replaced his own cap, then examined Brand from the crown of the reporter's tan worker's hat to the tips of his leather loafers.

"Let me ask you what may seem silly now," the lieutenant said engaging Brand's brown eyes with his green ones.

"Are you packing any heat?"

"No, I'm unarmed. Why? Do you think I shot-up the BOQ earlier? I have a small pistol upstairs if you think I need to take it along," said Brand.

"Lord, no. The shots this morning belong to the rat patrol. In field support, our motto is, 'You call, we haul. You shoot, we scoot.'"

"Cute," said Brand adding finality to the lieutenant's rhyme.

"Major Spear said your words came wrapped in wit. But I already knew it. We studied your columns in Information School back at Fort Slocum."

"I've been there. Took the ferry across from New Rochelle once."

I know. I was one of your escort officers. You told me at the time Ledger was a great name for a newsman."

"Then, how did you end up in this job?" Brand deliberately turned the spotlight away from himself. He recalled that his speech to the Army Information School came just before the later height of one of his binges. His lecture on Ernie Pyle drew a standing ovation. But after a lengthy happy hour at the officers' club, his return to the mainland met resistance. He had tried to commandeer the Army-run ferry and pilot it to Manhattan. Disinvited the next year, Louie Cohn, the *Times* foreign editor, replaced him as guest speaker. Certain the young officer had heard about this incident, Brand noted the lad at least showed enough civility not to bring it up. Admirable qualities in one so young, he thought, but to Lieutenant Smith he repeated his question.

"How did you end up in this field support racket?"

"Beats me. With my training, background and military occupational specialty, you'd think I'd land an assignment in the MAAG Information Office. But the closest I've come to that MOS is escort duty for visiting dignitaries. Must be because I'm a reserve officer. The Army sticks us anywhere they damn well please."

"Yeah, in the military, the class system seems always to take precedence over logic, son."

"Major Spear says if I cooperate fully with you, he'll try to get me transferred out of this quartermaster business."

"Speaking of which, when do we get started?"

"While we wait for my driver, why don't I go over our schedule?"

"Yeah, do that," said Brand.

Following a brief stop at the USIS office in downtown Saigon to pick up three film canisters and an assorted number of television kinescopes, Ledger Smith directed his driver to the French-run cold storage warehouse near the waterfront. When Brand and Smith pulled up alongside an army two and a half ton truck backed into one of the loading stalls, Brand spotted three soldiers on the platform. The lieutenant greeted the two U.S. sergeants and a corporal. The enlisted men nodded at the introduction of Brand as they carried frozen meat packages toward the truck.

"Hey, L-T, what movies did you get?" a soldier called.

"The Apartment, The Misfits and Psycho," Smith replied.

"Them guys up-country won't sleep good after Anthony Perkins slashes-up that gorgeous Janet Leigh in the shower," the soldier added as he pulled aside the tarpaulin and rested his armload of meat against the tailgate.

"Yeah, and you haven't been near water ever since you saw the movie," a sergeant wisecracked.

Brand saw a Vietnamese woman grab the meat packages and disappear inside the truck. And when another soldier approached, a different woman from within the vehicle assisted him.

"I see you've enlisted the local populace," Brand remarked to Smith who had mounted the loading dock.

"The girls? They're bar flies supported by my men. They practically live in the back of the deuce and a half unless we have a full load. They don't bother anybody, so I let them hang around."

"Do you pay them?"

"Naw, the guys give 'em money and hair spray in exchange for a roll in the sack now and then."

"Aren't you afraid they'll steal you blind?" Brand asked in a haughty tone.

"They're not the problem." The lieutenant bent over the loading dock to whisper in Brand's ear. "Here it comes now."

Out of the darkness, stepped six to eight Vietnamese men who quickly surrounded the two vehicles and Brand caught standing between the jeep and truck. The uniform red bandannas covering their foreheads marked them as VC, brigands, or both.

The Vietnamese drew weapons and pointed them at the Americans. Brand heard the girls scream as they scrambled toward the cab of the truck, but the gang leader, a tall man naked from the waist up, sporting a large gold tooth protruding from the upper part of his mouth, ordered the women back out on to the platform. He waved an old French revolver in one hand while directing his antique musket toting comrades into a circle around Brand with the other.

"Who this?" Gold Tooth demanded now pointing the heavy pistol at Brand's head.

"He's American *Bao Chi.* Doing story on meat shipment," said Lieutenant Smith.

"No rike. Better we tie him up. You, me, talk business."

"Winston, play along with these guys for all our sakes," pleaded Ledger.

"What else can I do? They've got the guns."

"You, *Bao Chi*, have gun?"

"No, I left it home this trip. Want me to go get it?"

The robber shoved the barrel of his gun into Brand's neck. "*Bao Chi* make smart talk," he said motioning to his comrades. Four men got out ropes and a bandanna. They began to bind and gag Brand, then hoisted him to the loading platform where he landed at the feet of Lieutenant Smith.

"Now we talk," said the leader mounting the dock himself and straddling the trussed up reporter. "What got? Cigarette for us?"

"Eighteen cartons on board," Smith replied.

"Viskey?"

"Maybe one case."

"Camrah?"

"No more cameras."

"Hair splay?"

"A few cans for the girls."

"You take from. Give me. Sell big, black market."

"You're the boss," Smith said calmly. He then ordered his troops to collect the items demanded.

"No finish. You pay me two hundred dollah for *Bao Chi.* Him big man, use much rope." The man threw back his head and laughed exposing a rotted black gum line around the single gold tooth.

Brand squirmed upon hearing the extortionist's demands, but the leader placed a grimy sandaled foot on his back. From this position, the reporter lay helpless and watched the transaction go down. He saw Smith reach into his money belt, count out the currency and hand it to the renegade. At the same time, the GIs off-loaded the requested items and handed them down to the brigands who placed them in the passenger seat of a pedicab. Before departing, the man with the gold tooth examined Brand's watch and obviously rejected it as too cheap to bother with, since he said something in Vietnamese that made all of his comrades laugh again. A moment later, they vanished into the darkness as silently as they had arrived. Lieutenant Smith hurried to Brand's side and untied the reporter. The other Americans appeared preoccupied with comforting their frightened girlfriends who had retreated into the truck.

"That was a close one, Winston. If you'd had a weapon on you, the ransom would've gone outta sight. Anybody armed is considered an undercover agent who brings a higher price. Until somebody came forth with the cash you'd remain their hostage."

"Such humiliating crap from a bunch of thugs. How do you guys stomach it?" Brand demanded, rubbing his wrists to restart the circulation.

Smith looked around as if to make sure none of the GIs stood within earshot. As an added precaution, he whispered to Brand, "At my level, nothing can be done. And when I report it to my superiors, they tell me to go with the flow, asking me how much shakedown money I'll need the next time."

"Doesn't sound if it's on the up and up."

"What can I do about it at my level?"

"There's one way to uncover what's going on," said Brand whispering in return.

"How's that?"

"Follow the money trail."

"It's pretty obvious where it ends."

"Where? Give me names, Ledger."

"I can't at this point."

"I hear you, son. It's too risky in your present job. But let's make a pact. If I smoke them out on my own after your transfer, you'll confirm to me that I've got the right bastards. Nobody else needs to know about your cooperation, except Major Spear, of course."

"You got a deal, Winston."

On Sunday morning, a warrant officer from the MAAG compound telephoned Brand at the Five Oceans and canceled the reporter's appointment with the field support administration office. Speaking for the captain in charge, the warrant officer "declined to entertain the press at this time because of a heavy backload of work." But Brand saw this as an alibi. Those responsible higher up the chain needed time to consider how to deal with him, and their worst suspicions might cloud their judgment. Like so many past queries littering his investigative trails, the tendency was to assume Brand knew more about their activities than he did. Many a felon had panicked upon learning *The New York Times* was close in on his heels. A particular adage unscrupulous businessmen fondly quoted described their concern: "How's this going to look if it appears on the front page of tomorrow's *Times*," they asked themselves.

Brand was aware that military personnel were even more sensitive or schizophrenic to unfavorable coverage, since it often resulted in an unwanted career change. Why else did high ranking officers tolerate otherwise loathed public information specialists on their staffs? Brand's father had once offered to find a post for him working for a flag officer as a navy public information officer (PIO). "Keep the old man out of trouble. Point out the rocks, shoals and hard places of so-called public opinion, and you can write your own ticket," Willoughby Brand advised his son. But Winston so harshly dismissed the suggestion, the rift between them became a gorge. "Any true journalist who sells his skills in such a non-objective manner deals in 'prostitution,'" he had retorted.

In this black market matter, Winston considered asking General Pavler to intervene by directing the field support administrators to grant him an interview. But he rejected this idea as well on the basis that Geronimo represented the type of "heavy artillery" that might drive the matter farther underground. Undoubtedly the general had the smuggling operation under surveillance and wouldn't appreciate his unasked for interference in an ongoing investigation.

Better that he stick with someone like Lieutenant Smith for information. His rank and status appeared less intimidating. Yet, here he had to practice caution as well. Pushing too hard and too fast before Smith's transfer came through might place the young officer in jeopardy. So Brand decided on a more prudent course. Put the matter on the back-burner, he resolved, at least until he could question Alex Spear about it. But he'd have to wait until Alex returned from a week-long fact-finding trip to the ARVN signal battalion at Loc Ninh and the nearby Devereau plantation where he hoped to retrace the steps of the murdered Capt. Erik Fletcher.

Getting Smith safely ensconced in an information role first should pose no difficulty with Alex's help. The major had already moved mountains of red tape to help Brand stay in Vietnam. From his observations thus far, Brand considered Ledger an excellent prospect to serve as PIO on some general staff.

With this matter settled, in his mind at least, Brand spent a good part of Sunday afternoon updating his personnel journal. He expressed his disquieting thoughts in his log:

> At this crossroad, my enemies are more indefatigable than my friends are devoted. And with little effort I've managed to attract a new foe. He's a nasty little savage with a gold tooth. This protuberance no doubt signifies his status as leader of the mob. I encountered a similar thug in Korea. For the remainder of my sojourn in Vietnam, let's hope I never again cross paths with him.
>
> Credit the brigand on one score, though. His modus operandi is more direct yet less sophisticated than foes like Senator Kearney, members of the *Times* Sanhedrin, or R-3, for that matter. These insidious enemies seem bent on hurling my very soul into the nether world. Starting with my reputation and then proceeding by duplicity and treachery, they hope to strip away my dignity before leaving me to die. Only dreams of a second Pulitzer keep me going. My whole heart and soul longs for this recognition, which once won, can scatter these knaves before me like dust trampled under the hooves of a mounted knight. Enemies beware! After years predicting my decline, you'll have to contend with my success as measured by award of a second Pulitzer Prize for journalism. That is, if you even notice.
>
> Because they are fewer in number, friends are more easily dispatched. Like Maria, and Eleanor before her,

they flit in and out of my life—a sunset and a sunrise—each a bit of light and warmth with neither will nor power to linger. Even Maria's self-proclaimed devotion manifests itself in reality as little more than a romantic idealist who sees a shining knight instead of a dark avenger of my dashed hopes and dreams. If only such blind vision were true, or that I had the courage to test her devotion instead of trembling in fear at the thought of a second time cast down by love. Was it Socrates who said, "Fear is an expectation of evil?" In my present quest, there seems much evil to fear, except for Maria, of course.

As he closed his personal notebook, he turned his thoughts to preparation for his important Monday morning meeting with Minister Hieu.

Brand arrived late for the appointment with But Hieu on the following morning and assumed that the American engaged in conversation with the minister's secretary was Sheenar Tilllerstein. Brand extended his hand, but the obese young *Times* bureau chief ignored the gesture.

"You're late," Tillerstein announced through his crooked and yellowed teeth that reminded Brand of Gold Tooth.

"I'd say your comment was a BFO," said Brand.

"BFO?"

"Yeah, 'Blind Flash of the Obvious.'"

"I've heard you like to play word games, Brand. Is there one in your lexicon to explain keeping Minister Hieu and me waiting for 20 minutes?"

The secretary giggled, and Brand realized Tillerstein had his own game underway, playing or posturing to an audience of one.

"There's you, me and this comely young woman. But no minister, so what's the rush, Sheet?" he asked.

"Is that any way to speak to your bureau chief? That's not my name, and you know it. Besides, no gentleman uses vulgar terms in front of a lady. You're just trying to change the subject. Miss Lan can tell you. Minister Hieu has been out here three or four times asking for you."

At that the women nodded her head, once with a frown toward Brand and a second time smiling directly at Tillerstein. Like most Vietnamese of her age, Miss Lan presented finely chiseled features framed by black shoulder length hair. Her teeth were white and even, her cheeks and chin formed a rice bowl. To heighten the effect of breasts, small even by Oriental standards, Miss Lan sat erect, shoulders flattened against her chair, and was dressed in an *ao dai* that had been gathered in at the collar and bodice. Except for the round lower part of her face, the rest of her body was rapier thin. Notwithstanding that Brand knew her countrymen placed a high premium on oval faces mounted on thin frames, he was astonished to see the way Tillerstein devoured the young women with his pig-like eyes.

"I see you've profited from my tardiness," Brand quipped jerking his head toward the woman.

Tillerstein responded sarcastically, "So what? But you'd better find an excuse to offer Minister Hieu for being late."

"I'll tell the minister the truth," said Brand. "When I left the Five Oceans, there wasn't a taxi in sight, so I settled on a pedicab. Foot-power takes longer than a reciprocating engine. He knows that."

"I damn sure wouldn't tell him any such thing," Tillerstein said almost shrieking.

"Now what's your problem, Sheet?"

"If you'd read the minister's own guidelines, you'd know that bicycle taxis are off limits to correspondents," said Tillerstein turning to face the secretary. "Miss Lan, do you have the reference?"

"Certainly," she replied offering Tillerstein a thin pamphlet.

"No you read it to him. Maybe it'll sink in coming from you," said Tillerstein.

"Allow me to do the honors," said But Hieu, who had slipped into the room unnoticed. "As you Americans say, 'you can lead a horse to water but to make him drink is another matter.' Winston, I refer you to article 34 in my safety guidelines." The minister retrieved the pamphlet from his secretary and began to read:

> Four types of commercial road transportation exist in Vietnam— buses, taxis, rickshas and pedicabs. The first three pose no hazard for the traveler since the passenger has the driver in front of him and in full view at all times. Not so in the pedicab where passengers sit in the front carriage while the driver pedals the vehicle from a raised

> seat in the rear. From this position, the driver, if so inclined, can strike the passenger from behind and rob him before he knows what hit him.
>
> For their safety, we advise foreign correspondents to avoid the pedicab, especially at night. In this respect Vietnamese and Americans, as Americans might say, are in the 'same boat,' equally vulnerable to pedicab assaults. If you are the victim of such an attack, please report it to the police. In the case of foreign journalists, police must notify my office immediately.

Several sarcastic remarks ran through Brand's mind all centered on what he considered a greater waste of time than his own tardiness, yet for the sake of salvaging his interview with Diem, he followed a diplomatic course.

"Minister, why not give me a copy of your instructions to read later. I'm sure Mr. Tillerstein can go over them with me, saving your valuable time."

"Agreed, we'll proceed accordingly," said Hieu. "But one of our matters is already settled—'overcome by events' you Americans might say. Your office in New York conferred with your government, then telegrammed the ambassador here. They are recalling Mr. Steffans. Following this sensible solution, the Vietnamese government dropped its expulsion order, of course, so I advised the American ambassador he need not join us this morning."

"All's well that ends well," said Brand.

"Nice phrase," said Hieu.

Titlerstein just stared in disbelief. "You mean, I came all the way down here for nothing?" he asked.

"Hold on, Sheet. Let's be a little more tactful toward our host. Your business with the minister has been inadvertently concluded through Steffans' recall, but you've had a chance to visit with Miss Lan, so you didn't lose 20 minutes after all. In fact, why don't you stay here while I speak with Minister Hieu and continue your conversation with Miss Lan? If you ask her nicely, she's bound to accept an invitation to Pierre Girard's press party. If you don't, I will," he bluffed.

"I'm on to you, Brand. You intend to slip behind my back again like you did on the Fletcher story."

"Maybe so, but it'll take a while."

"Winston, I don't understand. Are you referring to another American expression?" Hieu interjected.

"No minister. Just a little in-house joke."

"Very well, but you referred to Miss Lan as a social partner. I encourage such fraternization. As you Americans say, it builds friendship across the sea."

"Thanks, Butt," said Tillerstein. "I'll chalk up my own birds."

Brand saw the minister wince. Either Tillerstein's mispronunciation of Hieu's first name brought the change in facial expression, or the minister disliked the familiar tone the bureau chief had sounded so early in the relationship. A third possibility was that Hieu failed to associate chalk and birds with dating procedures. Brand rescued his tongue-tied colleague by alluding to the latter alternative.

"Minister Hieu, Mr. Tillerstein says thanks 'but' for your good offices he'd have never encountered or thought such a lovely creature with bird-like qualities existed."

"Of course. He means Lan. I, too, call her little bird. And after she has served coffee to Mr. Tillerstein, we'll invite her to fly into my office with some for you and me as well, Winston."

For his status, But Hieu had a modest office that Brand discovered, like the minister himself, blended Vietnamese and American tastes. In the center of the spacious room stood a large black grand piano that Hieu had converted into a desk by removing the key board and pedals. Shortened legs lowered the top, making the writing surface ideal for someone of Vietnamese stature. Rattan and leather chairs with the wooden parts stained to match the color of the piano surrounded the desk.

On one wall in neat rows, the minister had hung framed pictures of himself with various Vietnamese dignitaries. On the opposite side, framed pictures featured Hieu as he gripped and grinned his way through an assortment of U.S. Senators, cabinet officials and ambassadors.

Minister Hieu noticed Winston pausing to peruse a photo of the U.S. vice president. "This picture was taken in May last year, a month after President Diem began his second five-year term," said Hieu pointing proudly to himself standing in the group with the U.S. vice-president. "Lyndon is the tall one," he added chuckling aloud.

"Yeah, but not as healthy, Minister Hieu, as I recall."

"Very good, Winston. You have an elephantine memory—oh dear that's not how you Americans say it. Correct me, please."

"We'd say that's 'close enough for government work.'"

"Another good one. Give me a moment to write that down," said Hieu scribbling in a note pad.

"Let's see, where were we? Yes, the matter of the vice president's health. We saw LBJ's stroke coming. In fact, President Diem was so alarmed at Lydnon's appearance, he dispatched me to his personal herbalist in Cholon to obtain Chinese heart medicine. The signed photograph arrived later. Would you like to know my interpretation of how they viewed their Vietnam fact-finding visit?" asked Hieu.

Brand nodded as the minister directed him to a chair closest to the piano-shaped desk.

"Allow me to paraphrase, interpret and recreate an imaginary meeting for you between the vice president, the ambassador, the Secretary of Defense and a White House assistant in which they discuss their impressions of the Vietnam situation," said Hieu. Not waiting for a response, he paused, leaned back in his chair, looked up at the ceiling and then startled Brand by closing his eyes and continuing as though reciting a scene from a play complete with voice inflections.

> "WHITE HOUSE MAN: 'Our venture in Vietnam is doomed. We can't trust Diem to make reforms. Not a dime's worth of difference separate Diem and Ho. Both are petty tyrants.'"
>
> "SECRETARY OF DEFENSE: 'Where is your data? Give me something I can put in the computer. Don't give me your opinions.'"
>
> "AMBASSADOR: 'Some of the reforms proposed by Washington policy makers have me worried. It would be difficult, if not impossible, to put a Ford engine into a Vietnamese ox-cart.'"
>
> "SECRETARY OF DEFENSE: 'Difficult or not, we can do it.'"
>
> "VICE PRESIDENT: 'We damned sight better. President Diem has to continue to kick the hell out of them commie bastards!'"

Brand gently applauded. "Don't tell me, Minister Hieu. I can guess by your emphasis in certain parts that the ambassador's and Johnson's comments are on target for you. "

"Indeed, they are. And do you know why?

"I'd rather hear it from you."

"As you Americans might say, they 'cut through the BS' and go to the heart of the matter. An admirable quality for people of the East to emulate. But I'm sure you wonder why I don't do so now regarding your concern. Very well, let us get to your problem straightway Winston, so that you can see I practice what I preach."

"Tell me what to do to land an interview with President Diem."

"You have the written questions?"

"Yeah, here in this portfolio." Brand slid the document across the smooth desk top to the minister who kept his hand on the folder but did not open it.

"How many questions are there?

"Three."

"So few?"

"With someone as verbose as I'm told your president is, even three may be too many."

"Who tells you these things?"

"A fellow reporter, who interviewed President Diem for three hours and got to ask only three questions."

Hieu threw his head back and laughed. He collected himself by running his fingers through his dark wispy hair.

"So you're already acquainted with the protocol," the minister replied.

"If I didn't, I'd be joining the number of reporters rumored to be in trouble with your government and on the way out."

Hieu laid the pad aside and stared straight across the desk at Brand. "We demand fairness above all, Winston, and if I may speak frankly, many of your colleagues fail to extend us a courtesy they give our enemies at every turn."

"I know a major who agrees with you."

"You speak of Alex Spear, of course. Too bad he's not in the information field. But whatever the major does, I'm sure he does it well. An upright American like Major Spear in your corner certainly bodes well for you at the palace. Meantime, you can improve your chances with some good, honest reporting."

"That's all I know how to do, Minister Hieu."

"Very well. I'll get back to you with a date. But I'd better 'bite the bullet' here and now, as you Americans say. Don't expect an interview at the palace until a congressional delegation headed by Senator Thomas Kearney, Sr., visits and the Secretary of Defense has come and gone."

"Let's hope I'm still here, or in one piece," said Winston letting his sad tone speak for his bitter disappointment. This set-back plunged Brand into a state of depression which he tried in vain to conceal.

"In the next week or so, I could arrange an interview with General Minh, 'Big' Minh, as you Americans call him," Hieu offered.

Brand's eyes brightened and the lines in his forehead receded.

"This General 'Big' Minh, does he know anything about black market operations?" Brand asked.

"Oh yes, he helped President Diem crush three powerful sects who operated as governments within a government. Two were religious organizations and the third was a bandit and racketeering group called the Binh Xuyen. From Cholon, they controlled gambling and prostitution as well. What is your interest in these brigands who were smashed years ago?"

"Yeah, well, one of them is alive, well and kicking right here in Saigon. I've got the rope burns to prove it." Brand extended his wrists toward Hieu.

"You mean the Binh Xuyen did this?"

"They didn't wear billboards across their filthy chests, but I counted a half dozen of them down at the docks Saturday morning. Led by an ugly creature with a gold tooth, they jumped me and the field support soldiers with me."

"'Big' Minh can tell you more, but I've heard about this bandit you describe. He's just a local petty thief called Rang, or in English, 'Tooth.' Rang hires himself out to the highest bidder. We can't apprehend him, because his alleged victims are all Americans who refuse to lodge a complaint with the police authorities because they fear later reprisals from his gang of bandits. Are you prepared to press charges, Winston?"

"No, sir, all I want is a story."

"All I can offer is speculation."

"That's always the first step in solving a puzzle of many pieces."

"First, you must promise not to attribute any of this to me, General Minh or any other Vietnamese government source. I wouldn't want westerners to think we tell tales 'out of school,' as you Americans say."

"You have my word, sir."

"Before President Diem initiated his crackdown, brigands had a safe and almost respectable South Vietnamese industry. In recent times, however, we have noticed a possible linkage between the plunderers on one hand and their so-called victims on the other." Hieu hesitated, and Brand saw that this subject made the minister uncomfortable. The reporter correctly surmised that Hieu's mind wrestled with a delicate way to describe the situation.

"It's as if Rang and his bunch have reached an understanding of sorts in which everyone looks the other way as long as no one gets injured," said Hieu.

"Or, as we might say in my country, 'don't upset the apple cart,'" said Brand.

"Yes, that's it exactly. You've expressed the situation with another interesting American idiom. But perhaps it's better for you to wait and ask General Pavler about the matter. I'm sure he has an investigation underway."

"On the Vietnamese side, could you give me some hint of whether Rang works alone with his gang, or is someone else running this mob?"

Hieu fell silent for about 15 seconds.

"I choose to say no more on this matter. Get what you can from 'Big' Minh about that."

That night alone in the BOQ suite in Alex's extra room, Brand reflected on the day's events and entered the following in his journal:

> Diem interview delayed. Must meet with 'Big' Minh first, as I get the idea from But Hieu that the Vietnamese military wants to look me over before I set foot in the palace. Hieu is my kind of bureaucrat—laid back with a "whatever it is, it's there" attitude, unusual among the uptight Vietnamese gentry. He did express misgivings about U.S. staying power in Vietnam. He demonstrated same by dramatically pointing out Diem regime's belief that it occupies shaky ground vis a vis U.S. policy

makers. Officials in the Kennedy administration regard Vietnam and its people as needing democratic reforms. Hieu gave me something quotable for a future article as I left his office. "Men long accustomed to deceiving others end-up deceiving themselves most of all," he'd said. I wanted to press him on whether he applied this to his government's relationship with ours, or to black market activities, the topic upon which he closed our meeting.

Hell, for all I know, the conversation with Sheenar Tillerstein and Minister Hieu about Miss Lan may have been what he was referring to. Sheet's pissed at me for my remarks, and I've some repair work ahead of me at Girard's bash, unless I want the Sanhedrin breathing down my neck. Louie Cohn had it right. I ought to cultivate more friends and pare down the enemies list. Willie, where are you when I need you?

As Brand returned the journal to his top dresser drawer, the Derringer and ankle holster slung over the mirror caught his eye. He removed the small pistol, opened the housing and with his forefinger and thumbnail gently lifted out a bullet seated in each of the two barrels. He placed the bullets on the dresser top, closed the weapon, cocked and fired it twice. He reversed the procedure and this time strapped the loaded weapon onto his right lower calf just above the angle.

After entering the courtyard of Fuji's Japanese Restaurant across from the Five Oceans, Brand followed the major-domo to the table he and Alex usually occupied.

"Meester Brand, I notice you have strange walk. Like leg too heavy. Maybe I get 'nother chair for you to prop up leg," said the waiter.

"No thanks. I'll use Spear's chair."

"Your friend. No show tonight?"

"He's outta town."

"So solly major no here. Him say you need good friend."

"What makes you think I don't have one besides him?" asked Brand patting his right leg.

"Solly, only make small talk. You order food now."

"Wait a minute. You're supposed to ask me what I want to drink first."

"Other time you come here no drink. Your friend say bad for you. Better you wait him come back."

"Like hell I will. Forget it. I'll go to some place where they've never heard of Alex Spear."

20 INTELLIGENCE BREAKTHROUGH

The highest reward for a person's toil is not what they get for it, but what they become by it.

—*John Ruskin*

MAJ. ALEX SPEAR WENT DOWN THE STEPS of the *garçonnière* into the yard where Lucette Devereau knelt among the flowers. She rose at his approach, and the morning sun seemed balanced on the tip of her golden hair tied in a neat pony-tail.

"Have you seen Lieutenant Hewlett this morning?" Spear asked.

"*Oui*, over there, beyond the children's play area near the old barn," the woman answered pointing a trowel.

He walked across the yard, past a rubber tire hanging from the branch of a full-grown oak tree and stopped outside the barn's dilapidated doors. Long since partially separated from their upper hickory hinges, the large doors leaned together, one overlapping the other forming a small inverted V opening just above the ground. Alex bent down and probed the dark crevice with his flashlight. Unlike the dust and cobweb-covered rest of the barn, the outer surface of the hole was clean, as was the narrow passageway that extended inward about 30 feet until blocked by debris that looked like part of the fallen loft. Spear tilted the light up inside and saw silvery gray siding warped by the weather positioned about three feet above the sandy floor of the barn. Since these overhead materials did not match those at the far end of the passageway, he decided to go in for a closer look.

"Find anything, Major?" asked Lt. Rafe Hewlett who, despite his height and girth, had slipped unnoticed from the tall grass around the barn.

Alex stood, tapped his pipe against the side of his boot. Then he crushed the embers in the grass. "Nothing in the little house where you and the girl found Brand that night. How about you?"

"Ah've searched the woods and brush within a 25 yard radius of the barn and, like you, came up as empty as a city slicker on a snipe hunt," the advisor replied.

"You didn't happen to go in the barn through this hole, did you?"

"No, suh. Even if ah'd thought about it, ah'd never fit through there. That's barely big enough for a coon dog to crawl through on his belly."

"Well, something has. Otherwise, we'd see a cobweb wall and dust on the edges of the wood." Alex outlined a circle around the entrance with the flashlight beam, then continued, "And when's the last time you've seen weather-worn timbers used to shore up the inside of a barn?"

"Can't say ah have. Not in 'Bama at least. Unless somebody dragged 'em in there, or the barn had no roof."

Alex handed his empty pipe and shoulder holster to Hewlett, but kept his Colt .45. "I don't want to go inside, but I suppose I must," he said solemnly.

"Major, ah hope you're not gonna try to fit in that teeny, bitty hole. Lord knows who's waiting on the other side. Let me just rip the door off for you. Won't take much, and it'll damn sure surprise anybody who might be waiting to get the drop on ya."

"No, the whole structure might come tumbling down burying any available evidence. I'd prefer you stand watch here in case I flush somebody out. My guess is they'd come from those loft doors just below the eve," said Alex pointing his gun at the spot.

"What if ah go get a ladder, and we both go in through the loft?"

"The ladder is a good idea for later once we're sure the structure will hold our weight."

"Then maybe we should forget 'bout crawlin' around in such a shaky place, or at least let me ask Lucette to send for her petite houseboy. He's less apt to cause a cave-in."

"'Bonecrusher,' I appreciate your concern, but we may be on the verge of an intelligence breakthrough. I can't risk disturbing this scene by any of the approaches you've suggested. What's more, whatever we discover must stay in my custody and not even discussed outside intelligence circles. As for my safety, if any part of this building comes crashing down on me, then you can bust through the doors and dig me out. Otherwise, please wait until I call for help."

"Ah don't want to lose another American on my watch, suh."

"Well, take my word for it, if the reward versus risk ratio proves as high as my estimate, many lives like Fletcher's hang in the balance."

In the next moment, the marine major lay on his back in the grass. He fastened the pocket-sized flashlight to his fatigue cap visor with a bootlace and inched backwards toward the entrance like a limbo dancer squirming head-first under a three-foot bar.

Once Alex's head cleared the opening, he felt like he had entered an oven set at 120 degrees in which a pot of *nuoc mam* simmered. The odor from this fermented fish sauce assaulted his nostrils with such ferocity, it alone nearly drove him back out into the air to catch his breath. Instead, he tightened his lips and pressed on. To propel his large frame deeper into the cavern, he relied on his one free-hand, the butt of the automatic in his other hand and the heels of his boots as "oars." But this made progress slow because the back of his head, shoulders and buttocks kept digging into the sandy floor. He tried raising himself on his elbows. This only reduced his head clearance from a foot and a half to a half foot.

On his first attempt at this new technique, he became claustrophobic when his makeshift miner's lamp brushed against the rotting timbers that served as a ceiling. Moldy pieces of siding broke loose and fell into eyes already stinging with sweat. With eyes closed, he started to call to Hewlett to pull him out by his feet, but realized at present this was no longer an option. The heat, the stench, the energy expended had left him exhausted where he lay, little more than six feet inside what he had begun to think of as a crypt. It also crossed his mind that any movement, even the sound of a panicky voice, might bring the whole structure down, burying him underneath before Hewlett could reach him. Worse still, he reopened his eyes on complete darkness. He surmised that when his head bumped a board in the ceiling, it struck the on/off switch on his light. His breathing came more rapidly, and he knew he had to do something to keep from hyper-ventilating. He summoned up every bit of marine corps training he had ever received on anxiety, but could think of nothing to fit the occasion.

Then he remembered Gwen's solution to stress. "Change the subject to something more pleasant," his wife would admonish him and the children whenever control began to wane in the Spear household. He tried to think of the thousands of times he had played "peep-eye" with little Alex and Alesha by placing a paper bag over his head and lifting one corner to expose an eye while yelling "peep-eye" to their squeals of delight. He played the game in his mind four or five times before his respiratory rate returned to near normal.

Shortly thereafter, he slid his free hand across his chest and face and switched on the flashlight. As he returned the hand to his side, his fingers brushed lightly over what seemed like glass buried in the sand. Fearing that this man-made object might be the trigger for a booby trap or the release mechanism for a punji stick poised ready to deliver its poison into his neck or chest, he rolled as far over on his side as possible. This maneuver brought his cheek in direct contact with another of the glass items. Since there was no place else to turn, he lay quietly on his side and counted off the seconds until a bomb blast or a sharp, poison-tipped stake ended his life.

After five seconds passed, he decided his chance for survival increased the closer he was to the burrow opening. He tried to backtrack lying on his side but his shoulder caught on the overhead boards sending large chunks of debris down the neck of his fatigue shirt. Alex again rolled onto his back and tried to propel himself feet first out of the tunnel. But the sand and dirt that he had used to push himself 15 feet inside, now blocked his retreat as it piled up against the soles of his boots. Exiting the way he had entered seemed impossible. The thought that he had entrapped himself wore heavy upon his extrication efforts, and he crumpled upon the sand in a pool of sweat contemplating what had gone wrong.

Hindsight told him he should have tied a rope around his ankles which Lieutenant Hewlett could have used to pull him out. Better yet, he realized how foolish he had acted in pursuit of a hunch at best. Where was that methodical manner and middle-age maturity his superiors had once rated him so high on, he asked himself. So far, these positive traits had taken a back seat to the streak of stubbornness that others, especially Gwen, feared might bring him or others harm. Alex recalled his wife's admonishment the evening he took the children on a roller coaster ride despite her protest that they were too young.

"Alex, your own mother compared you to an elephant when it comes to altering your course of action once your mind's made up. Mother Spear told me about the soap box derby race. After the wheels fell off your car, you hoisted it on your 12-year-old shoulders and carried it 50 yards across the finish line knowing full well that you'd been disqualified anyway. There's a time and place for super human efforts. Why waste them on lost causes just to prove you're a tough guy?" Gwen had demanded.

By way of reply, he had reminded her that it took such persistence to win her hand against a pack of weak-kneed suitors allied with her parents, who objected to her dating a marine. Now in the tomb-like darkness, he begged Gwen's forgiveness. Although the bobby-trap/punji stick fear subsided with every passing second, he still faced the possibility of a cave-in triggered by his call to Hewlett for help or a bungled rescue attempt. He shoved the hand gun into his belt freeing both hands which he cupped around his mouth.

About to shout for Rafe, he noticed that the *nuoc mam* smell permeated the fingers of his left hand that had earlier touched the glass object buried in the sand. He sniffed the right hand fingers as well. They bore no odor except his own sweat and a faint trace of gun oil. He extended the experiment by swiping these same fingers across the part of his right cheek that had also made contact with glass. This time the *nuoc mam* smell on his fingers overwhelmed the sweat and oil. He almost gagged. Yet, his heart pounded in excitement as the discovery fueled his imagination. He pictured himself a Viet Cong agent who operated so close to the Devereau plantation that extraordinary measures of concealment prevailed.

For example, no light must ever escape from the Viet Cong hiding place. This would mean moving quickly in and out of the tunnel in total darkness relying on senses other than sight—like smell and touch. Unlike him, the smaller Viet Cong could glide through the tunnel on elbows and knees, heads up slightly, sniffing the stale air while their hands remained free to grasp the necks of *nuoc mam* bottles marking the pathway borders. "Ingenious," he said digging his fingers into the sand along his body. He uncovered four more homemade beacons which he used to push himself deeper into the tunnel.

After about another body's length of progress, a new problem arose. Alex began gasping for air again, this time not from anxiety, but because of the distance away from his only air supply, the tunnel opening. He stopped and took shallow breaths. He tried to imagine how the occupants of this hidden place coped with this problem. They must have a fresh air supply somewhere along the route, he assured himself. He turned his head from side to side and to the left of his body he saw that another tunnel veered off in that direction. He wondered if he should change headings and explore this new route. Perhaps he had wasted time following a false trail all along, he reasoned. Then again, what if the left fork in the road led to a dead-end or a honeycomb riddled with holes designed to lure unwelcome visitors to more airless cavities?

In search of an answer, Alex dug into the sand around the entrance to this alternate route. He failed to uncover a single *nuoc mam* bottle nor did his nose pick up a stronger scent. As he slid his head back onto the main trail, his light fell on two hollowed out bamboo stalks hanging from the ceiling. He gripped the closest stalk in one hand, steadying it, while he placed the palm of his other hand over the opening. Satisfied that air passed through this makeshift ventilator, he brought the bamboo to his lips and drew in a deep breath, followed by several others. With his lungs replenished, he tackled the tunnel with renewed vigor, halting only when his head dipped into a dark basin about two feet short of the piled debris. He tried to bend his neck back like he had seen wrestlers do during warm-up exercises, but he could not get the light at the proper angle to probe the depth of the hole. He did spot, however, a rope, no doubt used to facilitate travel from the opposite direction. While his head lay on a declining plane, he gained enough headroom to attempt to turnover on his stomach. He also noted that fresh air circulated around the circumference of the hole, indicating a wider opening somewhere on the other side of the stacked debris.

He removed his .45 from his belt, estimated the declination at 15 percent and nose-dived into the trench. Now able to crawl on hands and knees, he rapidly struck bottom about six to eight feet below the debris. Before ascending the upward slope, he unfastened the flashlight from his cap and surveyed the path before him. He wanted assurance that no VC waited at the top exit, machete poised, ready to lop off his head. As far as he could determine, the incline resembled the downward slope on the other side of the debris, including another rope ladder which he eschewed figuring his size now became an advantage.

The dim natural light of an opening appeared less than three feet from his outstretched frame. He kept the flashlight and pistol at the ready position as he dug his toes into the bank to push himself upward. At that moment his right boot struck a soft object burying it deeper into the sand. Alex reached down with his gun hand, retrieved what felt like a cloth bag, shoved it into his belt and resumed his accent. Cautiously, he peered out the opening like an anxious gopher turning its head 180 degrees in one direction, pausing, then shifting its body to cover the rest of the measure.

The flashlight beam lacked power enough to extend to the far reaches of the barn, but his quick initial survey showed no hostile signs in his immediate vicinity. Against the possibility that someone had him in their gun sights from a dark corner of the barn, Alex turned-off the flashlight and, for the first time in over a half hour, stood up. He waited in the partial darkness surprised that so little natural light filtered in from the sides of the crumbling structure.

After a few moments, he switched the light back on and discovered the reason for this phenomenon. The VC inhabitants had painstakingly covered the major cracks in the barn with black material similar to that used in the manufacture of their pajama-like garments. Reminded of the cloth bag stuck in his belt, Alex pulled the draw string apart, stooped down and emptied the contents on the sand. Out of the ditty bag tumbled some papers, a photograph, a man's wallet, a watch, masculine ring with an aquamarine stone, silver cigarette lighter, and silver flask. Could they be Winston's stolen items? He picked up the wallet in his gun hand and leafed through it with his thumb, using his other hand to shine light on the documents. The major let out a low whistle for joy as he spied Winston Brand's press credentials. Quickly and with enthusiasm that drove away all fatigue, he scooped up the items, replaced them in the bag and returned it to his belt.

The discovery buoyed his zeal for the rest of the mission. His mind trained in intelligence took over, reverberating with one scenario after another until he finally settled on the most plausible.

In their haste to get away and avoid capture the night Winston had been abducted, at least one of the VC agents had crawled part way into their hideout where he had ditched the incriminating evidence taken from Brand before he scattered into the jungle. Hewlett's quick response that night and the shots fired must have knocked the VC off their stride.

"'Bonecrusher!' Poor, patient fellow. Time to signal him," thought Alex. But first he decided to check the loft. He pointed his light up toward the top of the barn and was relieved to see a bamboo ladder attached to a box like structure not much larger than one of the wooden shipping containers used by the Army Transportation Corps.

"Thank God, no more mole holes," he said testing his weight against the ladder. As he looked above him, he saw that his praise was premature. The top rungs of the ladder disappeared into a darkened trap-door from which hung the same black drapes used throughout the barn's interior. Spear shuddered. The thought of sticking his head into still another dark crevice gave him pause. His plan was to pass through the hole into the loft before anyone waiting inside had a chance to react. But since he needed one hand to balance himself on the ladder, he would have to surrender either the flashlight or the gun. He switched off the light and anchored it in his belt next to the bag carrying Brand's stolen items. He thrust the .45 caliber service pistol into the trapdoor opening and waved it in an arc.

At that moment something leaped from the black serge bunched around the hole, engulfed his bare wrist and hung on. The pain of sharp teeth tearing away flesh almost made him drop the pistol. Instead he twirled the gun in his hand, got his thumb on the trigger and fired. The recoil ripped the .45 from his injured wrist. Alex heard the weapon strike the ladder's lowest rung then drop to the sand in what sounded like a double thud.

Outside he heard Rafe Hewlett shout, "Ah'm coming."

Spear yelled, "Hold on a minute, Rafe. Stay at your post," as he jumped to the ground. If there was anyone in the loft above him, they would have surely shown themselves during the commotion. The beam of his penlight fell on the carcass at his feet. It was a gray rat larger than a man's arm measured from finger tips to elbow.

Alex leaned against the ladder and checked his injury. Fortunately, the nickel size chunk of missing flesh came from an anterior section of his wrist between two large veins. Working rapidly to stem the bleeding, he scrambled out of his dirty fatigue shirt, pulled up the bottom of his white undershirt and with his pipe cleaning knife cut away a large segment to bandage his wound. He then knelt down in the sand placing a knee on the dead rodent and began sawing through the animal's neck behind its gray pointed ears with the knife. Using one hand the marine officer transferred the items from the ditty bag to his pants pockets. Then he cut away a remaining segment of his undershirt and wrapped the rat's severed head in it. He placed this macabre bundle in the cloth bag which he hung around his neck. He stuck his gun in the deep side pocket of his utility shirt and wrapped the garment around his wound making sure the weapon was within easy reach of the hand also needed to steady himself on the ladder.

He remounted the ladder, momentarily hesitating at the spot of the attack, fearful some other demon lay behind the folds of black cloth. But shouting, "Semper Fi", he catapulted himself up off the ladder and breached the dark crevice.

"Are you calling me?" Alex heard Hewlett shout from outside as the major rolled across the bamboo floor grabbing the pistol from his shirt. He waited in the silence then answered in a conversational tone.

"I seem to be alone. Better stay put 'til I open the loft doors."

"You're not going to be alone in a minute. Lucette's here with me already, and who ever fired that shot a moment ago stirred up a hornet's nest. Half the population of *Bon Sejour* is headed down the hill toward us," said Hewlett.

"Ask Lucette to send them back, and if she could get me some iodine and bandages, I'd be obliged."

The walls were so thin Alex heard the woman's skirts rustling as she rose to answer his request.

"Monsieur, are you terribly injured?" she inquired. "No one ever goes inside such a dangerous place." "Please, Mademoiselle. *Je vous en prie*—I beg of you—don't let those people near here. This is a crime scene. I'll explain later," Spear responded.

When he heard her depart, he addressed the lieutenant again. "In a moment, I'm going to work my way to the loft doors and open them to get some light in this place, and some fresh air. This is a VC lair all right, although the two-legged rats seemed to have abandoned ship, leaving these cozy quarters to their four-footed brothers."

He then asked Hewlett to see if he could spot the flashlight beam as he turned it on. As expected, he received a negative reply. He could see that he was in the center of what looked like four boxes or crates fastened together by bamboo strips forming separate rooms. On one wall he spotted what looked like a latch and made his way toward it on his hands and knees. He loosened the bolt and the double doors draped in black material parted without so much as a squeak. He squinted against the sun, and before he could focus, Hewlett called up to him.

"Man are you a sight for sore eyes, Major."

"And never have I been so glad to see the army. Thanks for your patience, Lieutenant. We've stumbled onto something big. Just a little bit longer, and I'll be down to brief you. These birds seemed to have left in a hurry, abandoning Brand's stuff in their wake. Until I check the rest of the layout, please keep everyone away from here."

"Does that include Lucette?"

"Yes, I'm afraid so. At least for the time being."

"Ah understand. You really aren't hurt. You just sent her away on a ruse."

"Not exactly. I did encounter a nasty, hungry rat who thought my wrist was a chicken leg. I had to shoot the bastard, but he got his licks in anyway." Alex held up his bandaged hand, then pulled the draw strings of the ditty bag over his head. He tossed the bag down to Hewlett.

"Here's the varmint's head. When the girl comes back with the first aid kit, send her away with this little trophy and ask her to keep it on ice for me."

"Ah've heard you marines don't take prisoners, but this beats all. Don't tell me you're going to have it stuffed and mounted."

"No, just examined for rabies at the first opportunity."

"Ah'm sorry, Major, that's nothing to joke about."

Spear flashed the A-OK sign to his young companion before turning back into the main room. The light from the open loft doors penetrated three of the four rooms arranged in a stubby cross or plus mark. From his position at one vertical end he could see all the way to the back wall and part way into the box or container positioned horizontally to his right. Because of the angle of sunlight passing through, the room to his left remained in dark shadows. With flashlight and pistol poised, he began there. Inside was a wooden chair and three wooden beds, only one of which still had a straw mat laid on top of the boards used for springs. Exhausted and in pain, Alex wanted desperately to lie down and renew his energy level, if only for a moment, in the enemy's bedroom. He started to succumb when he spotted the nylon knapsack hanging from the back of the chair by a piece of rope attached to a loop of webbing. As he picked up the knapsack by its two shoulder straps and swung it over the chair, he got an adrenaline rush. The bag weighed at least 30 pounds. He practically sprinted out of the room to find a spot on the sunlit bamboo floor where he emptied the knapsack's contents item by item. He removed a mosquito net, a khaki uniform, an extra set of black pajamas and underwear—all clean and neatly folded. Beneath these items, Alex discovered a pouch of tobacco with cigarette papers attached, a small plastic bag containing matches, a tobasco-sized bottle of *nuoc mam* and smaller packets of salt and pepper.

Inside a green plastic sheet cutout as a ground cloth or tent fly, the VC had hidden his personal treasures—papers, photographs and a school notebook. Mustering the same interest he would have devoted to his own family heirlooms, the marine officer examined the three black and white photographs from the knapsack first. Photo number one, as he labeled it in his mind, showed a VNAF officer in his flight suit kneeling in front of a damaged Skyraider aircraft surrounded by dark-skinned Cambodians. Slightly above the pilot's head stenciled neatly on the aircraft's fuselage, appeared the name of the pilot. Spear repeated the name several times before moving on.

In the second photo, a solitary VC soldier stood against the jungle dressed in the traditional khaki-colored pith helmet, khaki pants and shirt, and black and white rubber flip-flops. Two Leica cameras dangled from straps on each of the man's shoulders, and he seemed pleased enough with his booty to flash an idiotic grin, made more so, thought Alex, by a single tooth that for some reason sparkled in the sunlight. Picture number three had the VNAF pilot, again with a garland of ceremonial flowers around his neck. Next to him stood a young boy attired in black pajamas.

Growing more weary and in greater pain, it took several minutes for Alex to register the significance of this last picture or to place in his mind the stenciled name he had been repeating. Seeing the boy and the pilot together did serve to connect two elements that would not have been linked under ordinary circumstances. Again, from some reserve, he summoned enough energy to crawl over to his fatigue jacket, lying in the doorway. From his shirt pocket he withdrew the photograph found earlier among Brand's personal items in the ditty bag.

"Bingo," he said loud enough for Hewlett to have heard him at his post below the doorway. But when he peered over the ledge, the lieutenant's huge frame was nowhere in sight. Spear shifted his gaze to the grassy knoll above the barn and saw Rafe in an animated conversation with Lucette Devereau, who seemed to balk at the bloody bag Hewlett was trying to thrust upon her. Behind the couple, Alex could see a large group of plantation workers slowly moving toward the house. Out of their midst sprang Mr. Ly, who started down the hill toward the barn only to abruptly reverse course and head for the plantation main house on the heels of the retreating pack. Certain the Vietnamese overseer had seem him kneeling in the loft, the major worked with greater urgency, sensing that Mr. Devereau himself would appear on the scene any moment.

"Bingo," he said again as he laid the photograph of the young man with the pilot next to the ditty bag photo found earlier in the tunnel. The same pajama-clad youth was depicted, this time surrounded by a bevy of young female plantation workers, four of whom posed behind him on the back steps of *Bon Sejour*. The handsome young man knelt like a peacock in the foreground beside two Vietnamese girls. One of the young ladies held onto a laundry basket, the other, the most attractive of the group, had one of her arms around his shoulders and the other provocatively resting on his knee.

To Alex this tender scene brought back to mind the name on the fuselage and he began to jog his memory. And then he had it! It was the name of the pilot who had bombed Diem's palace and then fled to Cambodia according to General Pavler's serious incident report.

Hurriedly he placed all four of the photos on the bamboo floor in front of him as he sat cross-legged, his wounded side toward the sun. His wrist throbbed with pain like it had grown an abscessed tooth all of a sudden, but he was too excited to tend his wound at the moment. Instead he made his way back to the center of the room where he had left the knapsack. He repacked the uniforms, mosquito net and other items, but placed the photos and notebook in the breast pocket of his shirt. This meager effort left him completely exhausted, and he realized that the loss of blood combined with the heat in the tunnel had taken its toll in the form of dehydration. Using his flashlight, he searched for a canteen or water jug. None turned up. He tried to raise himself by pulling on a leg of the small table in the center of the room but the cramps in his own legs forced him back upon the bamboo floor. Alex groaned aloud as he maneuvered the knapsack under his head in a vain attempt to relieve the wave of nausea that swept up from his throat dispatching a yellow-greenish fluid out through his nostrils. He wiped the foul smelling substance against his bandaged wrist and when he pulled the hand away from his face Alex saw the radio antenna strung up under the rafters.

In what seemed like a far-away dream, he could hear Lieutenant Hewlett and Miss Devereau chatting and calling out to him as they propped a ladder against the barn. Only then did he close his eyes, and, as he had often done as little boy on his father's spread in Wisconsin, tired from doing a man's work all day, fell asleep in the loft, this time with the knapsack instead of a swatch of hay for a pillow.

That night, Spear awakened several times and saw either Lucette or Rafe watching by his sick bed in the room that Brand had occupied on his visit to *Bon Sejour*. At one point, sometime after midnight, he remembered asking Hewlett, what had happened.

"Ah'm not sure you wanta know, Major. You were pretty much out of it when we found you. And no offense, suh, but you smelled like a coon dog who attacked the wrong end of a polecat."

"That bad huh?"

"Well, as mah pappy used to say, if you go in the barn after skunks, youse damn sure gonna come out smelling like 'em. But we pitched in and got you patched up. You even had a bath in Marie Antionette's tub, courtesy of the laundry staff."

"Where's my uniform and the knapsack?" Alex demanded surprised that he had cried out in panic.

"Mr. Ly took the knapsack to show Mr. Devereau. The overseer was also put in charge of icing down your rat's head that Lucette refused to mess with."

"My shirt, damn it. Where's my shirt?"

"By now, ah'd say in the laundry with your pants."

Spear fell back against the soft pillow and started to feel sorry for himself at how he had botched things up at the last minute. But in the very next moment, he swung his legs over the side of the bed and announced to Hewlett, "Let's go find the laundry."

The big man coaxed Alex back into bed and said gently, "Give me a moment. Ah think ah've got what you're after."

Alex watched Hewlett walk over to the dresser and return with all of Brand's items, the four photos and the lined notebook. He smiled as the army lieutenant laid them on his sick bed.

"How?" Spear asked.

"As I was haulin' you up to the big house, and you dragging along like a quarterback who had his bell rung, you whispered to me to remove and safe guard everything in your pockets."

"I don't remember any of that. You'd better keep the items 'til I get on my feet. And 'Bonecrusher.'"

"Yes, suh."

"Thanks, you're one helluva soldier."

"And if ah may add mah two cents to this mutual admiration society, let me say marines don't come any better or tougher than you."

Hewlett talked on about how *Bon Sejour* with all its beauty and grace had nearly cost him two new friends—Brand and now the major—in addition to Fletcher who couldn't have been saved. But he might have saved his breath for Alex, despite his intentions, had fallen asleep.

Alex awoke next just before dawn. Again, he heard the voices of Rafe and Lucette. This time they came from a verandah on the gallery outside his room. Although he had turned his back to the open door to avoid even the appearance of eavesdropping, he could hear them talking in French, their whispered tones competing with the sounds of crickets, frogs and other night creatures returning to nests carved under the whitewashed fence posts that marked the boundaries of *Bon Sejour*. Hewlett spoke to the women next to him, and Alex was astonished to learn that the Southerner dropped all trace of accent as the French words rolled off his tongue clear and soft like a child addressing a buttercup with lips pressed to the petals.

"I've been so happy to see you again," said Rafe.

"Yes, but don't forget, I've been to your camp twice at Loc Ninh since we met that horrible night Winston Brand was abducted from this very spot," said Lucette.

"I don't like your traveling alone. After Brand's experience and the major's close call yesterday, there's no denying the VC are prowling these woods. You must wait for me to come to you, little Lucette."

"Not if it means months. I couldn't stand to wait so long. Even now I cry thinking of the time when you return to America."

"I could come back as a civilian. You know, play a few years of professional football, earn a fortune and make *Bon Sejour* my first stop on a world tour."

"Oh, Rafe, would you?"

"Yes, and you could show me Paris."

Alex heard the woman squeal with delight, and he used this opportunity to make his presence known by calling her name. They both came into the room apologizing for waking him. The lieutenant wore fatigues and carried an old battered Australian bush hat that he shifted nervously about in his huge hands. She was in a floor length pink night gown over which a royal blue robe heightened the color in her long blonde hair that cascaded along each lapel of the garment. They appeared radiantly happy, and, under other circumstances, Alex would have shared their joy. But on a day when the usual letter to Gwen had already been forfeited to conserve his waking energy for a first reading of the captured school notebook found in the loft, he got right down to business.

"Mademoiselle, how many are on your laundry staff?"

"Why, six girls, Monsieur."

"No males?"

"No, Major." Alex saw her shoot a puzzled look at Rafe, and before the lieutenant could respond, he was asked to retrieve the photographs from the dresser drawer. Spear turned all but one of them face down on his bed spread.

"Please, Lucette, come closer. In this photo there is a young man. Is he a member of your household staff?"

"I've never seen him before. Perhaps you should talk to Mr. Ly. He would know better."

"What about the girl with her arms around the lad?"

"That's Le Thi Xuyen. She helped me clean your wound and apply iodine to it. She also washed your clothes."

"Would it be possible for me to talk to Miss Xuyen later this morning?"

"She does not speak English, I'm afraid."

"What about French?"

"*Oui*, I have been teaching all the girls on the laundry staff. But how is your French, Major?"

"Not as good as Hewlett's whom I hope will give me a hand."

"Mah pleasure, suh."

"Good. Then why don't we have Le Thi Xuyen here about eight o'clock?"

"Could you make that nine? Eight is when we have our lesson," said Lucette.

Rafe replied, "Sorry, Lucette. Transportation will be here by 0900 to take Major Spear to our station hospital in Nha Trang. We've heard from Doctor Jeniscoso, who is emphatic the major must undergo a lengthy vaccination procedure to prevent a possible fatal rabies infection from his rat bite."

"Oh, my," said Lucette. "I'm so sorry about your injury, Major Spear." You've also had a life-threatening experience at *Bon Sejour*, as Mr. Brand has had with his kidnapping. Thank goodness you have both survived. We're so thankful you can be treated at the hospital to prevent a serious infection from the rat bite you suffered in our barn.

"Thank you for your kind thoughts, Lucette. I'd hoped Rafe and I could go back to Loc Ninh in the morning. But now Rafe will have to run an investigation without me while I'm being treated at the hospital in Nha Trang. But please be advised I don't want this incident broadcast about."

"*Oui*, we will do our best, Major Spear. Then Lucette took Rafe's hand and offered, "I'll go to Loc Ninh with you tomorrow after the major has spoken to Le Thi Xuyen, if you like, Rafe."

"Alex said, "You two can work out your plans later. Right now please excuse us, Lucette, while I talk to Lieutenant Hewlett."

After extracting a promise from Hewlett to meet her shortly in front of the statue of Aphrodite, Lucette closed the door behind her. Spear wasted no time in getting to the point.

"While in Loc Ninh, I'd like you to pay particular attention to whether or not the Viet Cong absconded with manuals for the AN/GRC-19 radios they stole. What we seem to have uncovered here in the barn is an enemy radio relay listening post operated by a three man crew right under the noses of the Devereaus. Judging by the antenna set-up in the loft, they rigged a simple AM receiver from which they received coded broadcasts from Radio Hanoi."

"May I ask how the stolen Angry Nineteen radios tie in with Fletcher's murder?"

"I take it that's Fletcher's hat you're holding?"

"Yep. How'd you know?"

"You haven't been here long enough to batter a bush hat that badly. The same goes for our Viet Cong friends. Between the ambush in the road and now, they didn't have time to transfer pages of technical data on the AN/GRC 19 radio to a dog-eared school notebook that somebody started in Cambodia months ago. That's why it's critical we find out when, where and under what circumstances they came by this information. Get me an inventory of everything taken from the ARVN signal battalion at Loc Ninh."

"Ah'll do my best."

"And I know you'll do it on the q.t. We're talking SECRET classification as a minimum. That means trust no one unless I determine they have a need to know. Once checked out by the medics in Nha Trang, I'll fly back to Loc Ninh to resume the investigation from your end. Meantime, it might prove prudent to sever all foreign entangling relations until, to borrow a football metaphor, we know for sure who's on our side of the ball."

As she descended the staircase, Lucette saw Lieutenant Hewlett. He still clung to the battered hat that his lean, dark face looked down upon with a sorrow in his eyes that wasn't there earlier.

Her own eyes shone a brilliant blue reflecting the happy course of action that sprang to mind.

"I'm going for a little walk in the garden to watch the flowers I planted yesterday greet the new sun," she explained in French, immediately pleased that he remonstrated with her to not go alone.

Hand in hand they strolled over the familiar path of shared experience past Brand's *garçonnière*, indelibly etched as such in their minds by the events that transpired there. They paused at the spot where she had first surrendered to his tender, protective care.

"All that shooting frightened me to death, but I'm glad you let me stay with you to rescue Monsieur Brand that night. I felt terrible when you asked me to run home to father," she confessed.

"My concern was for your safety," he answered in her language, and she was not put off by his matter of fact tone.

"Only that, Rafe?" she asked moving closer and reaching out to twist her fingers inside the lapels of his fatigue shirt.

"The war brought me here and the war will take me away," he said. He pulled back from her.

"But not this moment, dear Rafe. And I promised to go with you to Loc Ninh. Have you changed your mind after talking with the major? Is this the reason for your melancholy?"

"There is a snag," he said switching to English. And when he fell silent, she realized the change was wrought by more than his inability to select the proper French word.

"I suppose this problem cannot be discussed in either of our tongues. So how are we to handle it? Surely not by silence," she said.

"Ah can't take you with me this mornin', and ah won't be seeing you for land knows how long. We'd best leave it there."

"No, that's unsatisfactory, Rafe. If I learned anything about you in our brief time together, it is that you are a man who would not hurt anything if he could help it. Papa even said he cannot imagine you playing a violent sport."

"So ah'm pegged as a 'mamby pamby' by your kinfolk. They should know that playin' by the rules doesn't make a man soft."

"No, it takes a strong, honest man to shoot over the head of a small, unarmed boy fleeing in the dark."

"You knew that all this time."

"*Oui,* and I confided it to no one but Aphrodite."

"Yeah ah'll tell you somethin', Missy. If ah'd run into that kid out on the road after Fletcher got hit, or found him later with a knife at Winston's throat, he'd damn sure need all the sympathy you and your folks could muster."

She was bewildered for a moment at how he had turned strange and stony. Part of her wanted to flee into her emotional self, but she decided to save her tears until he was gone.

"We are not sympathizers, Rafe. Like you, this war has found us. My father has ordered the old barn burned later this morning so that everyone at *Bon Sejour* can see we will not provide a haven for those who oppose our friends. Before turning our home into an arsenal for either side in this civil war, we'd burn the whole place to the ground."

"Ah'd like to believe that."

"Believe in more—believe in us." She lifted her imploring eyes to Hewlett's face and saw that the muscles in his cheeks alternately tensed and softened. She stood on her toes and kissed these twitching spots in the manner of a mother comforting an injured child. His arm went around her tiny waist, and as he gently lifted and pulled her close to him, she could feel her breasts press against his massive chest. He kissed her, and with the hand not holding her, he stroked her yellow-gold hair.

As soon as they broke to catch their breath, she shook with excitement. The softest contours of their bodies snuggled one against the other led to even more kisses. For her, the passion erased a lifetime of loneliness. When he reached inside her robe, it seemed as though her pear-shaped breasts swelled to the size of melons as they expanded to fill the huge soft hands that held her bare skin in a tender embrace.

Lucette shook her head, and her half-closed eyes pleaded for him not to go on, but at the same time she wished he would. She murmured almost inaudibly over the dawn's last chirping of the crickets and the croaking of the frogs, "I have waited all my life for you, Rafe. Days, months, even years are perfumed with a love that is patient still."

She felt the battle that raged within him, but at last he pulled away, turned and said 'goodnight' to her, his eyes reflecting the desire for her he had denied at great cost.

On entering the study later that morning, Maj. Alex Spear found Lieutenant Hewlett and Vietnamese laundress Le Thi Xuyen already seated at a small conference table. The marine officer apologized for his tardiness, explaining that he had stopped after breakfast to enjoy his pipe and that while on the back porch had seen the barn ablaze. He asked Hewlett if he knew anything about this and did not make a fuss when the army officer said it had been done at the direction of Monsieur Devereau.

"I wish he would have waited for us to get one long, last look inside that rat's nest. But then, it's his barn," said Alex speaking in English. He then switched to the language of *Bon Sejour* as he turned to face the Vietnamese maiden.

"Mademoiselle, no one is going to hurt you. We have just a few questions, and then you can go back to your duties."

The girl nodded, and Alex saw her chin trembling above her white jacket collar. She twisted a cloth of the same color around her fingers pressing it close to her black trousers that hung loose at the thighs.

"Can you tell us the name of the boy seated next to you in this picture?" asked Spear handing her the photograph. He watched as she laid aside the handkerchief and studied the picture keeping it in her lap. She puffed out her chubby cheeks and replied keeping her head low.

"*Oui*, Monsieur."

"Well, who is he?"

"*Mon ami*, Anh Hai."

"Does your friend live around here?"

"Sometime in Hue. Sometime Cambodia, sometime small hamlet near *Bon Sejour*."

"This Anh Hai travels a lot. Did he tell you he was an important person?"

"Before coming here, he say he run radio station in Hue."

"Do you believe him?"

"I think he had little job there, and I told him they not let boy run everything."

"And what about Cambodia?"

"Anh Hai go there for big radio school."

"Did he say where?"

"No, talk mostly about how he come here from Hue to take care of sick mother."

"Did you ever meet his family?"

"No, he come here all the time on bicycle."

"Who took this picture of Anh Hai, you and the other girls?"

"Anh Hai's friend, an older man who come here with him one day."

"Just a few more questions, and we'll be through," said Alex pausing to look at the writing tablet in which Hewlett had made notes for him.

"Did the older man tell you his name?"

"If he did, I forget it now."

"When was the picture taken?"

"A little time before Monsieur Brand and much trouble come to *Bon Sejour*."

"Was your friend interested in the Americans?"

"No, he never come here when Americans here."

"Was he a Viet Cong soldier?"

"I never hear that."

"But you know he lied to you."

"I don't understand," she protested.

"You told me he passed himself off as an important radio man from Hue, right?"

"*Oui*, but he too young for big job."

"And weren't you suspicious when he gave you a false name."

"Sorry, I don't understand again."

"What does 'Anh Hai' mean in Vietnamese?"

"Second eldest brother."

"Do you believe any mother would call her child by such a name?"

"No, and I mocked Anh Hai by asking who was his first eldest brother."

"And what did he tell you?"

"He laugh and say his first brother named 'Vo' something, I forget rest. Please tell Mademoiselle Lucette I truly forget, not try make for you trouble."

"You have been a very cooperative young lady, and I'm sure Lieutenant Hewlett will tell your mistress as much. Thank you. You are excused."

Both officers stood. The girl bowed and left the study. As Hewlett also turned to leave, Spear stopped him and asked, "Could you stay another few minutes? I'd like to dictate a message to my superior. When you get to the ARVN base at Loc Ninh, I'd appreciate it if you sent this over the U.S. net, only by the highest secure means, at top level priority to CHECKMATE LEADER from STRAIGHT ARROW."

"Certainly, suh. Ah'm ready when you are. But do you want me to get you a drink of water or sumptin'? You're looking awfully white around the gills if you don't mind mah saying so."

"No thanks. I'm in a hurry. I'll fill up on my flight to Nha Trang. But I would like to take an ice bag with me if you could arrange that with Lucette when we're finished here. The damn swelling around my writing hand won't seem to subside."

When the major took out his pipe and tobacco, Hewlett packed and tamped it down for him. After a few puffs, Spear began his message to General Pavler:

INVESTIGATIONS REVEAL VC RADIO LISTENING STATION OPERATING AT PLANTATION PERIOD NO DOUBT LIVE COAL INTERESTS TIED TO ENEMY PLANS HERE PERIOD FOUND PHOTO TAKEN IN CAMBODIA WHERE VNAF RENEGADE PILOT SHOWN ALIVE AND WELL AFTER PALACE ATTACK PERIOD ALSO EVIDENCE OF CONTACT WITH SMUGGLERS PERIOD RAT BITE DELAY PERIOD CAN REACH ME THRU SIXTH REPEAT SIXTH STATION HOSP NHA TRANG PERIOD MUST POSTPONE INVESTIGATION OF STOLEN RADIOS PERIOD NEED SMALL CHESS BOARD ASAP PERIOD ENDIT

21 THE IDEOLOGUES

The truth must be repeated again and again because error is constantly being preached around us.

—Johann Wolfgang von Goethe

IT WAS WELL PAST the dinner hour, and while other wealthy or well-placed residents of Rue d' Espagne settled in their drawing rooms to listen to shortwave or regular AM broadcasts from BBC, Voice of America or Radio Hanoi, R-3 stood behind drapes at his second story window and peered down at his front gate. He appeared fixed on a particular sound. The Western music carried on a cool, spring breeze wafting along Saigon's most fashionable boulevard made it difficult for him to concentrate. He had a different kind of music in mind from that emanating far down the street where Pierre Girard and other foreign correspondents shared a rented villa. He knew the newsmen had engaged a band for one of their many parties, and that, according to the flyer distributed as a courtesy to "fellow residents," the musicians were only rehearsing this particular evening. Either the cool air flowing in from the open window or the anticipated voice now heard above the music uncharacteristically shook him with excitement so that he nearly flung the drapes wide open for a better look.

"Sup," cried the voice from the street. It drew closer. The tone was melodious and that of a woman vendor. "Sup," she repeated, and by the fifth chant she had halted her push cart in front of R-3's whitewashed gate.

"Yes, noodle soup up here," R-3 called from the window.

"Right away, Excellency."

"Old woman, you'll have to bring it to the door. My servants are gone for the evening. Just pull your cart around back, and I'll meet you there."

After a short hesitation to unlatch the gate, she put her shoulder to the cart, and R-3 watched the woman disappear around the side of his house. He gathered his kimono off the bed and pulling it tightly round his neck, did not bother to put his arms inside the sleeves. On the way down the steps to the back entrance, he stopped long enough to adjust a white silk scarf tied about his neck, so that it covered his mouth from chin to nose. The street lamps were already on full power casting pockets of light from the front of the house to each side, but leaving the back in total darkness. R-3 did not turn on the porch light as the bedraggled figure limped toward his open door. Before closing the door behind her, he heard the band from the far end of the elm covered boulevard strike up the French National Anthem.

The soup vendor lifted her head, letting the faded gray shawl fall back on her shoulders, looked at him and said, "Fools. They still play the music of the oppressor."

He took her by the hand and lowered the scarf from his mouth. R-3 kissed her forehead just below the part in her silky black hair, coiffured man's style, and closely cropped over each ear. "Come upstairs with me, Madame Binh. We shall make our own music undisturbed by comrade or foe."

"First, I have an urgent message for you," she whispered.

"Then, let's have it," he said curtly, obviously annoyed.

"I have committed it to memory, since I did not want to take the chance of having it found on me if I were caught by our enemies."

"Out with it, woman, and shed those awful rags."

"The message came today to the curio shop from General Chien. He says the Americans have discovered the radio cell at Pawn, Queen's Knight Two."

R-3 reeled back against the banister and spoke between clenched teeth.

"Did they capture any of our people?"

"No. Comrade General said they had already left for Queen's Rook to train on the captured radios."

"Anything else?"

"According to General Chien, an American marine major found the cache, as well as reporter Brand's stolen personal items, while investigating Captain Bao's blunder. Those were his words, and he wanted to make sure you knew who to blame."

"Forget the finger pointing. That is not important to me," R-3 lied. "Did Comrade General Chien tell you what the Americans found at *Bon Sejour*?"

"Only that the American named Spear has been interrogating members of the household staff seeking information about a young boy caught fraternizing with a laundress. Mr. Ly reports the boy was one of our radio specialists."

"And because of this fool Bao, who ordered Brand's demise trying to please Hanoi, and a boy's testosterone, we could very well be compromised in an important outpost. What's more, that Brand's personal items were discovered by military intelligence in the cache links us to his aborted kidnapping. I cannot tolerate free-wheeling comrades who do not follow my instructions and sabotage our carefully laid plans with their blundering. If we hadn't already positioned Captain Bao with the Diem regime, he would be eliminated for his rebellion!"

R-3 saw the puzzled look in the woman's finely chiseled face, so he kissed her again on the forehead. "Later, in the afterglow of passion spent, we shall devise a strategy for dealing with these nettlesome problems you have brought with you tonight," he said.

By the time they reached his chambers at the top of the steps, she had transformed herself from a bent-over, baggy, black-dressed beggar to a stunning middle-age woman wearing a floral pattern high-neck silk *ao dai*.

Although the only light in the apartment shone through his window from the street lamp, R-3 studied her attentively as if she stood bathed in a spotlight. He lay naked propped against a pillow having discarded the kimono from around his own shoulders.

"How long has it been?" he asked watching her bend down to step out of her dark pantaloons.

"A month since I brought your last bowl of special soup, Comrade Leader."

Her face and upper body were close enough to the edge of the bed for him to see her dark smiling eyes drive away the masculine hardness that ten years as a revolutionary, five in widow status, had etched in her features. He spoke softly.

"Your breasts are like those of a 25-year-old. After Saigon is liberated you must share your secret with all our comrades over 30. Perhaps the soup has a special ingredient…"

"More likely my suppleness comes from pushing the heavy cart up so many driveways when you send for me. Forgive me, sir, I did not mean to complain."

"I like your spirited loyalty. Your sisters in the revolution should emulate that as well. Tonight is the last time you will push a cart."

He made several rough, clumsy attempts to penetrate her submissive body, but after sweating and groaning he failed to reach the excitement level he had felt in anticipation of their meeting. Finally he rolled over on his back, and she used her hand to complete the act.

As he knew she would, she blamed herself for his impotence, and he let her rant on about how she should have cleansed and perfumed her body before offering it to so great a leader. She even begged him to beat her, as her husband had often done before he was killed fighting against the French.

"The damn French," she stammered. Then she told him that hearing their anthem played so close to his home had upset her.

R-3 said nothing. Hands behind his head, he kept his eyes focused on Madame Binh, who dressed as she went on speaking, "Comrade Leader, please do not send me away. Let me come to you next week. It will be better. I promise. Oh, I am so ashamed to have displeased you."

When he had heard enough, he spoke to her in an emotionless tone.

"Perhaps some time apart will do us both good. You have so little to worry about, and I carry the revolution on my back. It's time others shared part of the burden."

"Tell me what can I do?"

"We must keep a closer eye on Captain Bao, my former adjutant."

"Yes, comrade leader, the one-eyed pig who now struts around in the uniform of a puppet captain, hoping to be promoted to colonel by the hated Diem regime."

"I want you to become his mistress."

R-3 waited while the woman fidgeted uncomfortably in the chair beside his bed. Even in the dim light, he guessed that the hardness had returned to her face. But he was wrong for when she turned to answer him, her eyes had filled with tears that rolled down her high cheekbones.

"Whatever my leader commands I will do," she said wistfully, then added, "But what if Nguyen Huu Bao will not have me?"

"He will. I'll take care of that."

"And what are my duties, sir?"

"Sleep with him, gain his confidence, be a wife in all but name, and report to me on his activities, paying particular interest to two, his relationship with the devil women Madame Nhu and any contacts Bao has with an American correspondent named Winston Brand."

"What about my duties at the curio shop on Tu Do Street?"

"You can carry on your normal responsibilities for our message drop. In the next few days Captain Bao is due there to pick up my directives, I shall add a note regarding your concubine status."

22 THE CURIO SHOP

Man is born free, and yet is everywhere in chains.
—Jean-Jacques Rousseau

ON THE AFTERNOON of the Pierre Girard press party, Winston Brand left Five Oceans and walked the two blocks past the barricade that marked the military restricted area. By the time he reached the curb, the heat and humidity had turned the inner rim of his denim cap into a sweat-soaked sponge. He waved the soggy item at a passing taxi but the little Renault was jammed with crew-cut Americans, no doubt on their way to a big Saturday night in Saigon. As Brand started to flag a pedicab, a long black Citroen sedan pulled up next to him.

"Can I offer you a lift?"

Brand bent over and looked into the rear seat. General Pavler had opened the door and was sliding over to make room for him.

"General, what makes you think I'm going your way?"

"Get in out of the heat, and we'll find out."

Brand hesitated.

"Now what's wrong, son?"

"Smacks of cronyism. My press colleagues already think I'm too cozy with the military."

Pavler chuckled. "I'm in civvies for gripe sake. Jump in before we get unwanted attention."

Brand replied, "Okay, but only to avoid creating a scene, General."

Brand settled in beside Pavler who asked, "Where to?"

"Anywhere downtown."

"Tu Do Street good enough?"

"Sure. Tu Do, a name changed from the old French name, Rue Catinat, I was formerly used to."

As the car threaded its way through heavy traffic, Brand stuck his bare head out the open window to cool himself. He could hear the sounds of young people engaged in conversation across a sea of bicycles that seemed to form a mounted escort on each side of the big sedan.

"All that exertion, and you never see them sweat," Brand observed.

But Geronimo Pavler maintained an uncharacteristic silence until his driver pulled the vehicle alongside a curio shop. The driver got out and opened the door for the general.

Pavler waved his driver away from the door. "Wok, go get yourself a cup of tea. Report back here in 15 minutes."

Then he turned to Brand. "C'mon, Winston. Let's take a slow stroll. I've got to talk to you."

"What's the subject?"

"Alex."

"So?"

"Spear's been injured and is in the hospital."

"Where?"

"Nha Trang."

"What for?"

"Rat bite fever, I think."

"That's bad stuff."

"Yeah. We need your help, Winston."

"What can I do?"

"Go up there and spread some cheer. Take along the chessboard he asked for. You're the perfect guy to deliver it."

"Wait a minute. Who said I'd go? This smells like a scheme to drag me into intelligence matters."

"Not on my part. I thought with Senator Kearney, Sr., coming to town, you'd jump at the chance to put some miles between you and him."

"Now I know this is Spear's idea," said Brand.

"Wrong again, my boy. It only popped into my head when I saw you on the corner near the Five Oceans. By the way, do you know you're being observed?"

Pavler pointed to an open doorway in which a Vietnamese man stood with his back toward them. "That guy has been dodging us since we got out of the car."

"Maybe he's one of your agents."

"Not with a black eyepatch. Too conspicuous."

"Just like your big, black sedan?" To feign disinterest, Brand brushed a finger across his nose.

Pavler chuckled. "If you're not worried, then neither am I. Now what about the deal with Alex?"

Brand was convinced General Pavler recognized Captain Bao and for some reason preferred to act otherwise. As part of his own investigation, the reporter decided to play out the charade and get a *quid pro quo.*

"Suppose I agree to go to Nha Trang to see Alex. Will you do me a couple of favors in return?"

"As long as they're not illegal, immoral or fattening."

"Glad you didn't say 'buck channels.'"

"Oh, oh. What is it?"

"I want you to get a Lt. Ledger Smith transferred from field support to the MAAG Information Office."

"May I ask why?"

"For his own safety. He's been very helpful on a story I've been working on."

"I assume you're talking about the black market ring," said Pavler.

"Why aren't I surprised? Smith does work for you."

Pavler assumed his paratrooper stance. "Testy, testy, testy. Nobody's attempting to compromise your reporter's position. Like I told you in my office. When it's mutually beneficial, we need to work together. Rooting out black marketers qualifies in my book. But we're not ready yet in our investigation process for public disclosure. But when we are, you'll have the information you need for your column. Even you know information spreading and intelligence gathering are incompatible. And that's our problem in Vietnam—too much of one and not enough of the other. As for Lieutenant Smith, if he's a qualified information officer, I'll consider his request."

"Don't wait, General. Ledger needs to be transferred."

"That's easy, Winston. I'll get on it right away. Maybe you'll have at least one friendly face to greet you at the Girard party tonight. The Frenchman has invited the MAAG Information staff, I'm told, whether or not they choose to attend."

"You military men amaze me, General. You've got enough time to look into press affairs, but you can't even help me get an interview with Diem. That's the other part of the deal. Alex seems to have gotten nowhere, so if you can help me, it's in your lap."

"Find out how far Alex has gotten with your request when you get to Nha Trang, Winston. Meantime, I'll put in a word with Gen. 'Big' Minh. It's the best I can do from my position."

"Okay. Where's the damn chess set you want delivered?"

"Back in the curio shop where the car's parked. I thought you'd like to pick one out for Alex. Need any money?"

"Hell, no! I don't want anybody getting any pictures of me taking money from you, especially photos taken by any press who might be in town today."

"I don't blame you," said General Pavler.

Brand shook his head as they retraced their steps to the curio shop. This time, Captain Bao was nowhere in sight.

Capt. Nguyen Huu Bao, out of breath and bathed in sweat, slammed the door of the curio shop behind him. "Quick, hide me in your back room," he demanded of the woman at the small counter.

"State your business here or get out," Madame Binh retorted.

Bao saw the woman had picked up a long, sharp letter opener, which she pointed at the open collar of his sport shirt. He fumbled for the right words in his mind. Then he remembered R-3's instructions.

"You have a portable chess set for Captain Bao," he said.

"Which 'Bao'? It's a common enough name. Show me some identification."

Bao pretended to reach inside his hip pocket. Instead, he grabbed the woman by the wrist and wrenched the weapon from her hand. In the next instant, he laid the sharp point of the letter opener against her throat above her high-necked *ao dai*.

"No more games," he said. "We'll go together to find my item."

"Pig!" she screamed, but offered no other resistance as he pushed her past the threshold into the back room.

They had barely cleared the bamboo-covered doorway when he felt hard steel pressed against his ribcage. She pushed the snub nose of the revolver deeper into his flesh. He winced as she ordered him to drop the makeshift knife.

"The only reason I didn't shoot you on the spot is that you're here on the right day, and you've got a patch over your eye, comrade."

"You knew who I was all the time?" he stammered.

"Certainly. But it would've been better for both of us had you followed correct procedures. Now who is it you're running from? If you've led the security police here, I'll shoot you and tell them I caught you stealing."

"No, it's not the police. Just a…"

Before he could explain, the bell over the front door tinkled twice.

"I've got a customer." She parted a small section of the bamboo and indicated he should peer into the shop. "Is that who's after you?" she asked in a whisper.

Bao recoiled as his eye met Brand's on the other side of the curtain.

"You, there. Can I get some service?" Brand called out.

"Get rid of him," Bao whispered to Madame Binh.

She held up the pistol. "With this?"

"No. Put that away. Find out what he wants. I think he's a spy."

Bao watched her return the small gun to a hidden pocket in the split of her *ao dai*, then step confidently into the shop proper. Concealed behind the door jam, he strained to hear every word of their conversation.

"How may I serve you, sir?" she asked.

"I'm looking for a chess set. Something for the traveler."

Bao gasped.

"Any particular material in mind?" asked Madame Binh.

"Nothing too expensive," Brand replied.

"Here's one carved out of monkey pod from the Philippines."

"Great. I'll take it."

In another few minutes, the transaction was completed and Brand left the shop with the package under his arm. In silence the woman returned to the back room, walked past Bao, over to a shelf, retrieved a chess set similar to the one sold to Brand and handed it to R-3's former adjutant.

Bao removed the false bottom and two notes fluttered to the table next to which he had seated himself. "I'll read them in private," he said.

"My instructions are not to let them out of my sight," said Madame Binh. Bao saw her hand glide under the folds of her *ao dai* as she spoke.

"Sure. It's your operation, comrade," he said.

Bao showed no outward emotion as he read R-3's short message that ordered him to cease-and-desist operations against Winston Brand. But within, Bao felt torn between his leader's instructions and those he knew came from Hanoi. To clear up this matter, he decided to write to his brother Duong at the earliest opportunity. Surely, the ambassador at an important post would have Hanoi's latest official position relative to Brand. With that out of the way, he turned to R-3's second directive that covered two small pages stapled together.

My dear Bao:

In my earlier message to you, I was much too terse and did not elaborate on why Winston Brand is more useful to us alive rather than dead as Hanoi asserts. He is a prize-winning journalist with great prestige the world over. If we can turn him around to serve our revolution, we gain valuable credibility for our struggle in the eyes of leaders of the so-called "neutral" nations.

However, if, like the leadership in Hanoi, we are to assume Brand works for intelligence agencies, isn't it better for us to take him captive at a later date and pry loose whatever secrets he possesses in order to use them against our enemies?

I have shared this strategy with Hanoi and have taken, as an indication of my trust in you, the extraordinary measure of informing you as well. To insure you are kept personally aware of my plans so that mistakes, such as the one at *Bon Sejour* are not repeated, I have assigned Madame Binh to you as my liaison officer.

This will free you to concentrate on the downfall of the Diem regime. She will be my voice in your ear and my hand on your shoulder. You must take her as a mistress, so that this closeness can be maintained without generating suspicion. This order is irrevocable.

R-3

Bao stared at the last paragraph in stunned silence. "Unacceptable," he muttered.

"Have you finished?" asked Madame Binh. "My instructions are to destroy these documents after you've read them."

"Yes, do that. And destroy my life while you're at it."

Bao banged his fist against the table. "Get away from me!" he shouted.

But the woman moved closer. "You can't order me out of my own place, you one-eyed pig!"

He started to get up, but she pushed him back down into the chair, and, in the same motion pressed her gun against his neck.

"Go ahead. Shoot me. I'd rather be dead than have you in bed," he said.

When she replied, "My pleasure," he noticed the cold, hard stare in her eyes.

"Hey, I was only joking," he said. "Lighten up, lady." But now he scrambled for time. Her dark mood permeated the room, and he felt the danger mount like mercury in a thermometer in a hothouse. If he wanted to see Madame Nhu again, he had to act fast, he told himself. But his wits had left him, and he sat frozen in fear.

At that moment, the bell over the door signaled someone had entered the shop. In a flash, Bao leapt up from the table where he was seated, slammed through the bamboo curtains and banged against the counter on the other side.

"That's pretty fast service—why Captain Bao!" Brand exclaimed.

Madame Binh moved in behind Bao and pressed the gun barrel into his ribs again. Bao adjusted his eye patch and placed his arm around the woman's shoulders.

"Mr. Brand, I'd like you to meet my fiancée, Madame Binh."

"Madame?"

"Yes, I'm a war widow," she said.

"Who insists on a five-year mourning period," Bao added. "If it were up to me, we'd wed tonight. But I'm sure you didn't come in here to offer congratulations. What can we do for you?"

"This chess set bought here a few minutes ago is missing a black bishop. I've come back to get the missing piece."

23 PRESS PARTY

While man's desires and aspirations stir, he cannot choose but error.
—Johann Wolfgang von Goethe

EXCEPT FOR THE PRESENCE of Lt. Ledger Smith, Brand found the much ballyhooed Pierre Girard press party nothing more than a reminder of everything that upset him about Western press coverage in Vietnam. He was surrounded by the "usual suspects"—his nominal boss, the *Times* bureau chief, Sheenar Tillerstein, the two wire service twins, as he called them, a gaggle of news magazine journalists, a spattering of television broadcasters and a phalanx of Vietnamese girls hired to entertain the guests.

One of the foreigners, a stringer for the U.S. media, tried to engage Brand in conversation. But the stringer's focus was on the soon-to-be-expelled Jim Robinson, a network correspondent who had run afoul of the Diem regime. Despite Brand's own threat of expulsion by Senator Kearney, but not from Diem, he blurted out, "No big deal."

Brand saw his press colleagues recoil in horror. Sheenar Tillerstein gave voice to the concerns of the others. "Surely, you realize our host, Pierre Girard, is next to be drummed out of the country, and after that, who knows?" asked Tillerstein.

"It's simple. You want to stay here?" Brand asked his listeners. "Leave politics aside and concentrate on the war we are here to cover."

Brand's *Times* bureau chief corrected him, "The corruption of the Vietnamese government, supported by U.S. dollars, is the real story, not the war."

Brand noticed Miss Lan of the Vietnamese Ministry of Information Office standing next to Tillerstein. However, Hieu's secretary showed no sign of protesting his derogatory statement about her country's government. So Brand acted on her behalf.

"How inconsiderate of you, Sheet, hurling an insult at the Vietnamese government represented by Miss Lan's employer, all the while fraternizing with her."

Brand expected a retort in kind, but Tillerstein patted the woman's arm. "Forgive him, my dear. To be so outspoken, he must be drunk."

"Not a bad idea," said Brand. He elbowed closer to the bar where Lt. Ledger Smith stood.

You haven't made many friends here tonight," the lieutenant said.

"Ledger, my boy, I'd be friends with these reporters, even if competitors, but not when they join together as a news club of consensus. I don't join any such group no matter how justified they think they are."

"A 'news club of consensus?' That's going to be a formidable group for me to deal with as an information officer."

"Be forewarned, Ledger. Like me, Tillerstein hasn't been in country long enough to size up the Diem regime in person, as insulated or isolated as he may appear. I haven't been granted an interview with President Diem yet, but I've done a lot of research before I arrived and am waiting to have my questions answered before writing about it. As far as the Diem government's viability, the jury is still out on a verdict. What bothers me is that everyone at this bash, present company excluded, seems to me to have locked arms, old hands and new. They appear to be marching to the same drummer, and I don't like it as an objective reporter."

"What can be done about it?"

"What do you say we order a drink?" Brand suggested with a wink. "Or in your case, as a young lieutenant, get drunk and grab one of those Vietnamese beauties before they're all taken. By the way, why do you suppose you've been invited with such short notice?

"I thought you'd added me to the guest list."

"Hell, it was only earlier today that I pleaded your case before General Pavler to be reassigned to the information office, too late for Girard to add you to his list. No, it appears to me you were earmarked. Someone got word of your interest in working with the press, and wanted to start you off on the right foot as a potential source in information channels—compromised as you'd be. Perhaps it was someone in the smuggling ring, who keeps tabs on persons of interest to them and has connections in this city of intrigue."

When the bartender placed the drink Brand had ordered in front of him, he looked down at it and hesitated. He remembered the last time he had ordered a drink at the Slice of Paris bar and what had happened afterward. But the memory faded with the allure of the alcoholic drink before him. He shouldn't have ordered it, he thought, but he downed the jigger of brandy anyway before he continued, "Stranger alliances have been forged in war time. Journalists learn to build our sources anywhere we can find 'em, like I could be doing with you now, Ledger," Brand said to the young officer.

"But that's different. There's a feeling of comradery between us, and we think alike."

Brand smiled and replied, "That's true, Ledger. But information is a prized commodity to the press, especially in a city like Saigon."

Brand looked down at his empty glass on the bar as he felt the "snake-bite" effect of the alcohol start to ease the tension growing in him from the encounter with his press colleagues. He ordered another drink. It wasn't long before the press party was getting into full swing, so Brand decided to press a couple hundred piasters into the hand of the bartender and send him off to select the prettiest girl at the party for his young friend.

The lieutenant drew back. "Winston, as a government source, I can't accept a bribe. Information is freely available."

Brand laughed. "No bribe intended. Look at it as compensation from a friend who's grateful for the ransom you paid to that bandit Rang to secure my release. I believe it cost you $200."

"It wasn't my money, and I would have done it for any other American."

"I know. That's what I like about you. No go on. Have a good time. Here's the barman with your hostess for the evening—a real beauty."

Ledger hesitated, but then disappeared with his new friend. For some time after that, Brand stayed at the bar. He tried not to think of his promise to Gen. Geronimo Pavler to stay off the booze, nor the consequences of his actions regarding his own expulsion at the hands of Senator Tank Kearney, Sr., who'd be only too happy to get evidence against him.

"Hell, who's to know about another drink or two?" Brand had finally convinced himself, even after the first two drinks he had shared with Ledger. "It won't matter," he thought, unless of course Alex and Geronimo had some spies at the Girard party. But that was unlikely. It might be more the case that they expected Brand to keep tabs on the press for them. But intelligence work was out of the question as far as he was concerned, and he had made that perfectly clear to both of them. In fact, that strong conviction deserved another drink.

After an hour at the bar, Brand thought of how his conduct would disappoint Maria. He called for one last drink, then staggered down the stone pathway toward the curb in search of a taxi, tumbler in hand. A pedicab driver dashed out of the line of bicycle-propelled vehicles and tilted the cab forward to admit a passenger.

"Take you chop-chop any place, cheap," the driver called, his conical hat pulled down over his face against the glare of flood lights hung from various tiers of Girard's terraced estate on Rue Espanigne.

Brand boarded the vehicle, catching his ankle holster with the Derringer inside on the foot-board, and wondered why he had worn it. "Five Oceans, and make it snappy. No long route. I'll be counting the revolutions of the wheel, and I already know how many it takes to get there," he bluffed. The operator seated above and behind him gave no indication he understood. Nevertheless, as the pedicab pulled from the curb, Brand turned his head aside and began counting the big wheel. "One, two, three...." By number 55 he dozed off.

Somewhere along the route the vehicle hit a pothole, and Brand shot upright. Through his stupor he made out a dark alley at the end of which stood a half dozen Vietnamese men armed with barrel staves. The danger cleared his head. He shouted to the driver, "It's a mugging. Turn this damn thing around chop-chop!"

"No can do, Mistuh Brand. You belong me now."

Brand turned his head around and spotted the telltale gold tooth. He quickly searched along his right ankle for the holster and grabbed the Derringer. Looking ahead, he was aware that they were less than 20 yards from the dead-end where Rang's men waited. Unexpectedly, Brand managed a speedy and surprisingly agile turn-about in his seat, reached up and shoved the Derringer solidly into Gold Tooth's throat before the bandit could react. Brand ordered, "Now pedal me out of here, or I'll shoot faster than you can grab my gun."

The pedicab turned on a dime, reversed course and with the brigands in pursuit sped from the alley. Brand, sobered by the adrenaline rush that flooded his body, kept the Derringer securely jammed into Rang's neck as he directed the bandit into the yard of a police compound on the outskirts of Cholon.

After waiting for three hours at the police station, Brand lifted his head from the small desk the police had placed in front of him where he had written his statement. He saw a familiar figure approach him as the Minister of Information, But Hieu, entered the room.

"Mr. Brand, I'm sorry to keep you waiting. General Duong Van Minh, or 'Big Minh' was supposed to be on duty for me tonight and come to your assistance. He couldn't be reached this evening after a day of perhaps playing too much tennis, or oddly enough, raising orchids, his hobby

"So I was contacted to fill in the breach, and I'm glad to come to the police station to help you. As you Americans say, tonight I'm a 'pinch hitter,' standing in for our illustrious general, who had offered to do the same for me. But I'm not the kind of 'hitter' you described in your report when you narrowly escaped a band of thugs ready to beat you when you were pedaled down an alley in a pedicab. We've talked about this danger before, and I'm surprised you took a pedicab again, especially in the evening, after being warned. We're very glad you escaped injury with your quick thinking, but I've been told you have been rather uncooperative with the local police."

Brand, still feeling hung over, bristled and answered, "Language barrier, that's all. I had asked the police to contact the American embassy, or the duty officer for General Pavler's office, for someone to come down here, sort things out and then take me back to Five Oceans. Obviously, they did neither, but bothered you instead, although they said it was protocol. Unfortunately, the gold-toothed brigand Rang chose the time for a mugging. Otherwise, we both could have been catching up on some much needed sleep."

Minister Hieu replied, "Except for the hour of the night, it is no bother to come down to the police station to secure the release of our resident American columnist for the *Times*. You were lucky, Mr. Brand, that you were able to outmaneuver the 'tiger you caught by the tail' before being bludgeoned. You may not be so fortunate if it happens again."

"I've learned my lesson. Have the police interrogated Rang yet?" Brand asked. "When last I saw him, he looked so furious that anyone who got near him would be dead by sunrise. I'm just glad it wasn't me."

"The police are aware he's no one to cross, especially by anyone who has something he wants. You've mentioned that you've come in contact with Rang before."

"Yes, and every new encounter is worse than the last one."

"Our police try to keep a close eye on his coercive activities, but so far they haven't been able to 'catch him in the act,' as you might say. Do you wish to press charges against him?"

"And sign my death warrant? Look where it got me just inadvertently being on site during a smuggling operation Gold Tooth and his gang staged. This time, without my Derringer on me, I would have been beaten to a pulp and left to die in a dark alley."

"We've talked about a smuggling ring before. Did you talk to 'Big' Minh about it as I suggested?"

"No, not since I talked with you about the incident in your office. As I said, the bandit took an instant disliking to me and the feeling was mutual. It's escalated to say the least with this second incident."

"It's difficult, Mr. Brand, for us to jail Rang. No one is willing to give us proof of his misdeeds. If you aren't willing to press charges against him, there is another sensitive matter I must bring up with you."

"Nothing could be more 'sensitive' than what I've just been through."

"This is a related but different matter, I assure you. The imminent visit of Senator Thomas Kearney, Sr., U.S. Chairman of the Senate Armed Forces Committee and his fact-finding committee, comes at a very delicate time for our government. We've assured him of heightened security for him and his team. If the Americans should learn that Vietnamese can't even protect a foreign correspondent from a 'petty thief,' we will have 'egg on our faces' when this key American personage comes to access our capabilities."

"There's nothing 'petty' about Rang in my experience with him. In delicate negotiations, embarrassment for the Vietnamese government may loom large for you, but nothing like a possible brutal physical attack does for me. Are you suggesting I forget this incident ever happened until Senator Kearney is out of the country?" remarked Brand.

"If you wish to state it like that, yes."

"The way I see it, Minister Hieu, we both have something the other wants."

"And what is it that you want, Mr. Brand?"

Brand certainly didn't want Senator Thomas Kearney to learn about his attempted mugging. The senator would be sure to inquire if there was any drinking involved on Brand's part. Brand knew he'd keep the matter under wraps, but he wanted to see if he could get something in return.

"My lips are sealed about this matter if I can get an interview with President Diem as soon as possible. As you know, I've already submitted three questions in writing to your office as is standard procedure. What I need is an influential Vietnamese authority with access to the president to speed up the process."

But Hieu smiled and said, "I see you've discerned a way to get around the long wait for an interview with our president. You have our heads 'on the chopping block' in this situation with the senator's upcoming arrival. You must know President Diem is very busy at the moment making preparations for the visit, but I will see what I can do to accommodate you. None of us want any embarrassing information leaked to the senator, now do we, Mr. Brand?"

Then the minister told Brand that General Pavler's office had provided a jeep and driver outside waiting for him.

Brand awoke at noon the next day with a bad taste in his mouth and a lingering headache. At least he didn't have to answer questions from Alex hospitalized in Nha Trang. But he couldn't avoid General Pavler, whose duty officer had arranged for him to be brought back to the BOQ from the police station long after midnight. The reporter cleaned up and made himself as presentable as he could. He took a cab to General Pavler's office to answer the general's summons awaiting him when he woke up. It was already long past the time he should have arrived at General Pavler's office. How much did the general know, he wondered? Had But Hieu been discreet in his notification to the U.S. military in the middle of the night about Brand's predicament?

"Damn! Why did he always get so upset when in the company of his press colleagues? He couldn't control the opinions of others anyway, so why did he get so critical and frustrated that he lost control of himself instead? Eleanor no doubt thought his drinking was a losing battle when she divorced him.

Brand entered Pavler's office and saw the concern on the face of the fatherly figure who had stood up for him countless times in the past. Yet the general had been stern in upholding the values displayed in the example of his own life. How Brand had hated to disappoint his mentor. Would the general continue to give him a chance to redeem himself, especially in light of Senator Kearney's pressure to expel him? Why had he sabotaged himself when he took that first drink at Pierre Girard's press party?

"Winston, I've seen you looking better. What happened last evening to land you at the police station in Cholon?" asked General Pavler. "The duty officer reported that he'd had to send a driver and jeep to the police station to pick you up long after midnight to take you back to Five Oceans."

Brand wanted to be truthful, but he hoped to avoid the issue of his drinking at the Girard party, although the general might have guessed from his appearance.

"I made the mistake of taking a pedicab back to Five Oceans after leaving the press party, General, not recognizing the driver as the bandit Gold Tooth in the dark. Instead he pedaled me into a dark alley where a gang of brigands waited waving barrel staves. Fortunately, I was wearing the holster with Derringer you authorized for me, did a quick turn-about in the pedicab seat and shoved the gun barrel solidly under his chin. I ordered him to pedal me to the police station, which he did, although furious enough to kill me if he could."

"My God, Winston, how thankful I am you escaped serious injury, or even possible death! I'm relieved you took my advice about wearing the Derringer I authorized, but dismayed you disregarded our well known warnings about using pedicabs for transportation. Why didn't you recognize Gold Tooth?"

"The brigand had his cap pulled down to shield his face and was the first to offer a ride. I should have been more careful. Had he targeted me for a mugging? Quite possible. We took an instant dislike to each other when I happened to be on site as he and his bandits pulled off a smuggling operation."

"You do find yourself enmeshed in the action as a journalist, Winston, especially when you dig deep into what's really going on. Undoubtedly, Eleanor found it hard to take."

Brand didn't want the conversation to turn to his drinking problem, so he brought the subject back to the incident with Rang, "You remember I spoke to you about the smuggling of U.S. goods, General."

"Yes, and I told you that it's being investigated. I can't discuss the situation with you, but I'm distressed that you got caught up in a situation extremely dangerous for you."

"You're telling me, General. Nothing could persuade me to get mixed up with that revengeful bandit again."

"Did you press charges against him, Winston?"

"No, it would seal my death warrant. The Vietnamese Minister of Information was summoned to the police station when they couldn't get a hold of General 'Big' Minh to help sort out the situation. He asked me the same question about pressing charges. When I declined, he let it be known that my incident with Rang would be damaging to his government's image as a 'strong dragon,' if made known, especially with Senator Kearney and his fact-finding commission soon to arrive. It would be an embarrassment, he said, if his government couldn't even protect a correspondent from a petty thief. But Rang is really a deadly threat. I plan to avoid him at all costs in the future."

"Is there anything else you want to tell me about the incident, Winston?"

The moment of truth had arrived, Winston thought. But perhaps Geronimo was giving him an out by not asking him directly about any drinking involved.

"Yes, General, in agreeing with But Hieu to disregard the attempted mugging, he promised to do what he could to secure my interview with President Diem, a mutually beneficial deal."

"Ever the probing reporter, I see, Winston. But discretion in asking sensitive questions is sometimes called for. For now, I, too, am busy preparing for the senator's visit. Perhaps the Minister of Information will be more successful than we are in persuading a stubborn president to grant you an interview."

"Thank you, General, I pledge to do my best to stay out of trouble and stick to my goal of winning a second Pulitzer Prize for excellent war correspondence in Vietnam."

"Keep that pledge, Winston, and we'll remain on the same team, giving our best to our endeavors."

"Yes, sir. As you know, my vice admiral father always demanded that I 'face the sun.' It's about time I do a better job of it."

24 WIN OR LOSE WITH DIEM

Power tends to corrupt, and absolute power corrupts absolutely. Great men are almost always bad men.

—Lord John Acton

WINSTON LOOKED UP from the appetizer plate at his usual table at Fugi's Japanese Restaurant and smiled as he saw Dr. Nick Jenicoso approaching.

"Winston, how kind of you to invite me to dinner. Believe me, it's good to see you again."

"Likewise, my friend. I wasn't sure if I would catch you off duty so you could join me, and on such short notice, too. With Alex at the hospital in Nha Trang, dinner companions are in short supply these days."

"Believe me, Winston, that's not the only shortage in Saigon. The scarcity of doctors is the reason I haven't been able to join you and Alex for dinner in quite a while. But thankfully new personnel have just arrived so I could join you this evening. By the way, I see your head injury has healed well since I removed the stitches behind your ear. But I see by the look in your eyes something else is disturbing you."

"How perceptive you are, my good doctor. I thought I had camouflaged my distress about my cancelled interview with President Diem with no alternative date in sight."

"Why did he delay his interview with you, Winston? The last I heard you were excited about a breakthrough in obtaining the chance to interview him."

"Yes, I was. I would've had to wait some time to interview President Diem, but the Minister of Information intervened on my behalf. I was scheduled for an interview with Diem yesterday, but at the last minute it was cancelled."

"Did they give you a reason, Winston?"

"Yes. It seems the President has been preoccupied with preparing for the imminent visit of Senator Thomas 'Tank' Kearney, Sr., and his fact-finding commission. President Diem hasn't had time to compose his written "on the record" answers to the three questions I submitted through the Minister of Information's office according to palace procedure."

"Were your three questions the usual, hard hitting, probing questions you are known for, Winston?"

"Yes, they were. The president does sidestep issues he doesn't want to talk about. Perhaps he didn't want to answer my questions about the rising tensions in his relationship with his U.S. ally and the lack of democratic reforms in the nine years he's been in office. But he might not be able to dodge Senator Kearney's questions on these same topics when he arrives."

"Believe me, no one enjoys talking about their weaknesses. But you've stirred my interest with your question about escalating tensions between the Diem regime and the U.S. If you wish, Winston, perhaps I can be your 'sounding board,' although I'm much better playing my own 'sounding board,' my ukulele."

"Right you are, Nick, and how you turned the trick to calm everyone on the crippled aircraft until we landed safely back at Guam! I've promised my editor, Louis Cohen, a column on my interview with Diem, but now I'll have to do a think piece instead. I have to admit I'm irritated. Without a first-hand interview, my musings lack validity and are only conjectures."

"Believe me, I'd be happy to listen to you. After all, what are good friends and doctors for but to help others? Let's call a waiter over here to order, and then we'll talk while they prepare our meals."

"I'd like that, Nick. I'll try to be more cordial with you than I was with the major-domo the last time I was here."

"What happened?"

"I was very short with him when he skipped asking me what I wanted to drink and went straight to ask for my food order."

"Maybe he had been extra busy that evening and forgot," suggested Jenicoso. "Was a simple mistake that upsetting?"

"It wasn't a simple mistake, Nick. Previously, when Alex dined with me, he told the waiter not to serve any alcoholic drinks to me because it was bad for me."

"A bit presumptuous of Alex, and not at all like him."

"I know Alex meant well, but I just don't like having others remind me not to drink. I'm sorry I took out my frustration on the major-domo and abruptly left the restaurant when he failed to ask me what I wanted to drink."

"I'm surprised to hear that, Winston. You've been much more polite since our stopover in Hawaii. I heard rumors at that time about your drinking episode in the bar."

"Don't remind me about my Hawaiian drinking drama, Nick. As a doctor you would agree with my ex-wife Eleanor, a nurse, who cautioned me against combining alcohol consumption with pain killers, such as I was taking at the time for my head injury. My bad judgment caused quite a ruckus, and I apologize for my behavior. But since then, I've made a commitment to General Pavler to refrain from drinking to avoid having my press credentials pulled."

"Believe me, I had no idea your situation had gotten so serious, Winston. Who wants to have your credentials pulled?"

"Our esteemed Senator Thomas 'Tank' Kearney, Sr., Chairman of the Armed Services Committee. He was told of my drunken behavior in Hawaii by his son Lieutenant Kearney, Jr., who was on our flight. I was cited as being a "bad example" for our troops, and even Alex was mentioned because of his association with me. Senator Kearney has been putting pressure on the *Times* hierarchy and General Pavler to have me ousted."

"I didn't know our explosives expert, Lieutenant Kearney, Jr., was the son of the senator. I can see why you haven't ordered an alcoholic beverage before dinner. Perhaps that's what's bothering you, too."

"Again, you're very perceptive, Nick. At least you haven't reminded me not to drink."

"Just remember, Winston, we are all friends looking out for each other in a foreign country at war. But here comes the waiter. Let's order our food, and you can tell me about your thoughts regarding Diem's presidency and policies."

After the two diners had placed their meal orders, Brand asked, "Where should I start?"

"Starting at the beginning always works for me. I'm especially interested whether you've figured out what's behind Diem's uncompromising attitude that so frustrates the U.S.?"

"I've wondered about that too, Nick. Even before I arrived in Vietnam, I conducted extensive research into the Vietnamese dilemma from the past to the present. But my findings remain conjecture until I'm able to speak to Diem in person to confirm my theories."

Brand continued, "I've heard the diminutive, portly Vietnamese head-of-state in his white sharkskin suit handles Americans who interview him with cool curtesy, self-possession and the impression he'd rather be attending to matters of state. When the introverted leader starts talking about his plans, he warms up, and no one can get a word in edgewise for hours."

"In that case, have you considered that Diem's 'on the record' answers to your questions may be all you'd get anyway?"

"That's what I'm worried about, Nick. Correspondents know he only tolerates a freewheeling Western press because of U.S. support to his regime. Freedom of the press is restricted by policy limitations in his own country. Diem sees interviews with the Western press as an opportunity get across what he's trying to do, rather than invite criticism."

"If the allies have the same goal, it seems to me Diem would do everything he could to strengthen the alliance."

Brand replied, "Western reporters add to the problem because of the sparsity of time they have rushing to fulfill press deadlines with stories of conflict to capture the attention of the American public. Press coverage of Diem often reflects political criticism of the regime and its ally instead of sparse war news in this early stage of guerilla insurgency. We all have our taskmasters, but the truth can be the first casualty in such situations. I'm always looking for what's actually going on under the surface of appearances in my interviews. I don't have a political agenda, as some of my press colleagues have been accused of, to lend bias to my search for the truth."

"I'm aware 'truth' is often colored by one's perspective."

"What I'm really interested in is the philosophical font of Diem's goals and policies."

"Believe me, I should have guessed as much. I know you enjoy philosophy, Winston. But in politics practical matters require compromise rather than philosophy."

"Good insight, Nick. Philosophers are criticized for having their head-in-the-clouds, but perhaps that's the problem with the Ngo brothers. Their adopted philosophical foundation of Personalism is deeply flawed as a practical remedy for their country's problems. They'd be wiser to cooperate or compromise with their ally whose support enables them to stay in power."

"Believe me, your interview may have been delayed because Diem didn't want to be "branded" in your column for his authoritarian policies," replied Jenicoso with a wink.

Brand smiled at Jenicoso's play on words. "I'm sure Vietnam's remote and stubborn leader justifies his brother Nhu's use of despotic practices as needed to keep the regime in power."

"Believe me, most of the Vietnam news reports I've read give readers negative news flashes that tell us just what a hell-on-earth this existence is. But we'd like to see something positive reported every once in a while."

"Lucky for us we have compassionate people like you, Nick, tending to the sick and wounded when we get ourselves into one mishap after another. And your positive spirit and sense of humor is refreshing!"

"Thank you, Winston. You might like to know one of my own uplifting moments was on our takeoff from Guam. Even though our aircraft encountered an engine explosion that stressed us, I was cheered by the glow that seemed to surround you and our injured Maria as you held her in your protective embrace. While I bandaged her head injury, covered her with a blanket and instructed you to continue to hold her to ward off shock, I felt the warm energy of attraction between you two that even radiated to me as our crippled aircraft struggled to recover."

"A memorable moment it was, Nick. What man wouldn't feel a glow with such a gorgeous girl in his arms? Never would I have wanted Maria to suffer, but I was happy to offer her comfort."

"The heart-warming sight of you two bundled together made me feel like getting out my ukulele and start singing."

"And you spread the warming glow to all the passengers of the damaged aircraft, calming everyone else as well."

"Believe me, how tempting it is to get off the track by discussing our lovely Maria, but I suppose I'd better get back to my task of being a 'sounding board' for your struggle to search for the truth in this tragic nation."

"Maria's certainly an intriguing subject, Doc, but much too distracting. I agree we'd better return to the situation in Vietnam before our food arrives. I haven't yet talked about Vietnam's 2,000 years of recorded history."

"Heavens, Winston! No way did I mean to encourage you to embark upon a long, complex history lesson!"

"Not to worry, my friend. I wasn't going to go into detail, just to mention that Vietnam has constantly has been invaded by foreigners—over and over again by the Chinese, then the Japanese during World War II, the French for 100 years, the communists' aggression in the north and now in the south. It's no wonder the South Vietnamese cherish their 'window of independence' in this brief reprieve in their history. Nor do they want the U.S. to become another colonial power."

"Given their long history of foreign invasions, I'm sure that's true, Winston."

"Our two cultures are vastly different. Westerners do need to learn about the history and culture of Vietnam to understand the Oriental mindset. Our young, powerful, fast-paced nation has a gap-of-understanding of a feudal/agrarian, post-colonial nation at war while struggling to nation build and modernize. Plus dealing with a rebellious population and communist aggression is quite a challenge!

"Diem has repeatedly referred to his nation's partnership with the U.S. in terms of an independent Vietnam. He stresses he's not a puppet on Washington's string, or a figurehead ruler for yet another colonial nation. Nevertheless, Diem assures the U.S. his regime is a loyal ally. In Vietnam's struggle against great odds, Diem is well aware of the need for the power of a 'strong dragon' to counter North Vietnam's aggression backed by their allies—two communist super powers, China and the Soviet Union."

"Believe me, I can understand Vietnamese sentiments."

"I fear much more serious communist aggression is to come when Ho Chi Minh has sufficiently consolidated his power in the north after the Geneva Accords in 1954 that temporarily divided the country in two at the 17th Parallel. Country-wide elections, mandated in 1956 by the Accords, were derailed by Diem, who foresaw an inevitable communist victory. But the north won't be denied. When the communists are ready, perhaps by 1965, an armed struggle will begin in earnest."

"But didn't Diem avoid such an election by pointing out that neither he nor the U.S. signed the Geneva Accords?"

"Yes, he did, Nick. But despite Diem's justification of his actions, the years that followed weren't that easy for South Vietnam. The fledgling Republic of Vietnam, begun in 1954, struggled to unite its extremely rebellious people and root out the embedded communist Viet Minh guerilla fighters in the South while grappling with needed nation building. But, it was questionable from the very start whether or not the alliance with the U.S. would hold together."

"That's the topic I'm interested in," remarked Jenicoso. Since Diem can't survive without his alliance with the U.S. and Diem is well known for his ardent anticommunism, isn't that a solid basis for our alliance with his government?"

"Diem's anticommunism is legendary from his earliest political days."

"Let's not get into an early account of Diem. I just want to know why Diem and the U.S. clash despite a common goal."

"I believe Diem's vehement nationalism, combined with his adopted philosophy of Personalism, is the culprit. His Vietnamese vision of nation building and modernization efforts is at odds with his ally's Western concepts. Only their anticommunist goal is holding together this uneasy alliance.

"Diem keeps his ally at arms' length with a lack of cooperation and compromise, which creates a mismatch of increasing frustration and distrust with his ally. What's more, the U.S. fears the Ngo brothers' grandiose Vietnamese nationalistic plans are deeply flawed leading to failure."

"That's a nutshell of information that could take a while to explain and understand, Winston. But you said Diem's fervent nationalism is at the heart of it?"

"Yes. One of the most bellicose nations on earth, Vietnam is filled with a residue of hatred for the control of others."

"Believe me, I'm reminded of the tension at the Devereau mansion dinner table when you, Monsieur Devereau and Captain Bao got into a political discussion about the French imperialism in

Vietnam. Lucette's finally stopped the heated discussion, but disagreement lingered in the air."

"Yes, I remember. Monsieur Devereau expressed the French criticism of their World War II ally for not giving them more aid in their attempt to reassert their control over their Indochina colonies after the war. Almost a decade of French fighting the Viet Minh in the First Indochina War followed. Finally, the war weary French lacked the heart and resources for the endeavor. They were defeated in the battle at Dien Bien Phu. The U.S. had half-heartedly supported their failing effort."

"Believe me, the effect of that decision remains reflected in the resentment felt by Monsieur Devereau as he runs his rubber plantation enterprise in Vietnam. He's caught between the communists and the Diem regime without French backing."

Winston replied, "Yes, in retrospect, it's as if we backed in the back door in Vietnam through aid to our World War II ally, motivated by our own subsequent communist containment policy. But the residue of exploitive French colonialism didn't leave Vietnam with a pretty legacy, and the Vietnamese know we were an ally of the hated French imperialists.

"Our waiter approaches with our food, and what a tantalizing aroma! It's time to pause our discussion."

"Yes, Nick. Let's take a break and enjoy our food."

After dinner, the two friends relaxed for a while.

"Winston, I'm scheduled soon for a trip to Nha Trang to check on Alex and then on to Quang Ngai to visit with my friend, Dr. Kalverton, who tends to the Montagnards there. Since your Diem interview is delayed, would you like to come along?"

"Thanks, Nick. I just may do that and start up-country interviews instead. In fact, General Pavler asked me to deliver a chess set requested by Alex. Besides, it wouldn't hurt to be out of town when Senator Kearny arrives."

"Believe me, I know you'd want to avoid any chance meeting with Senator Kearney.

Dr. Jenicoso glanced at his watch. "We haven't gotten into the philosophy of Personalism yet, Winston, but we have to postpone it. I have an early surgery tomorrow morning and need to return to my quarters. Perhaps in 'another time, another place' we'll have a chance to discuss with Alex how the Personalism tenets of the Ngo brothers is sabotaging the relationship between the allies.

"Forgive the reference, but Maria told me you wrote this phrase on the front of her letter. I can't help hoping you and our lovely flight attendant Maria get back together in 'another time, another place' before too long. If ever there was a chance to better one's situation, it would certainly be with such a warm-hearted companion in life as with our beauty queen."

"I know you have good intentions, Nick. I certainly share your thoughts about Maria, but I'm really not the one to better her life I'm afraid."

"How I wish we had time to look into your concerns about a relationship with our dear Maria, but I really must go."

"Thanks for being my 'sounding board,' Nick. We'll just have to wait until we can check out the rest of our discussion when we see Alex in Nha Trang."

"Don't take too long to check out a relationship with Maria, Winston. There seems to be quite an attraction between you two, but I suspect you're trying to put it on the back burner for reasons of your own. Unless my diagnostic skills have been dulled by our long discussion, it wouldn't take much for it to heat up."

"Perhaps that's why I should go up-country to do my interviews. It wouldn't hurt to avoid Senator Kearney either."

"There are always unending problems to distract us, aren't there, Winston? Take care, my friend, and hope to see you soon."

"Likewise, my good doctor. Our up-country adventures await us," replied Winston with a smile.

25 KEARNEY'S MEDDLING

Our greatest misfortunes come to us from ourselves.
—Jean-Jacques Rousseau

BRAND PACED BACK AND FORTH at Tan Son Nhut airport. If Nick Jenicoso didn't show up soon, their flight to Nha Trang to see Alex would have to be cancelled. Senator Thomas Kearney, Sr., Chairman of the Senate Armed Services Committee, and his fact-finding party, including Brand's womanizing brother-in-law, Sean O'Boyle, had just arrived. They were the last people Brand wanted to see. He had to leave immediately or risk being spotted by his family nemesis and his sister's hypocrite husband. Brand turned to depart when he saw the pigeon-toed Dr. Jenicoso approach him with a wide smile.

"Thank goodness I caught you before you gave up on me and cancelled our flight, Winston. I finished my medical duties just as soon as I could. I'm so sorry to cause a delay. Is our flight still available to take us to Nha Trang?"

Winston's anxious look gave the good doctor pause. "Whatever is wrong, Winston?"

"Senator Thomas Kearney, his fact-finding committee and my brother-in-law have just landed and are headed our way. Let's just say it's not in my best interests to be noticed by them. I've got my back turned to them, but it would be best if I could duck out of sight!"

"Is that you, Winston?" asked a tall, good looking navy captain who left the Senator's party and walked over to them.

Brand sighed, turned and said, "Sean, good to see you. I'm just about to board a flight to Nha Trang with my friend. Dr. Nick Jenicoso, meet Navy Captain Sean O'Boyle. Sean, meet Navy Lt. Commander Nick Jenicoso."

'Pleased to meet you, sir. Winston, I'm glad to catch you before you left. Your sister is most anxious for me to track you down while I'm in Vietnam and check on how you are. I didn't expect to see you right off the bat though."

"Give my love to Clemie and the children, Sean. I'm sorry I didn't stop in to see you when I came through Hawaii, but I was recovering from a head wound."

"Was your injury anything Clemie needs to know about, Winston? You know how she worries about you."

"Believe me, it has healed well. I removed Winston's stitches not too long after we arrived in Vietnam."

All three men were interrupted when Senator Kearney called Sean to rejoin his party, and he answered, "Yes, sir. I just stopped to greet my brother-in-law and his friend."

The senator bellowed, "Winston Brand? Just the obnoxious, drunken, sorry excuse for a reporter I wanted to question!"

The tall, hulking Senator approached. "Brand, you've been irritating the hell out of me with your chicken shit columns! Damn, if your arrogant, know-it-all comments, that mention me more often than not, don't ruin my breakfast each time they appear! You're as mule-headed as your old man in your opinions.

"But I put him in his place when he spouted nonsense about bailing out the French at Dien Bien Phu. You never saw a fourth star on his shoulders, now did you? And I plan to scuttle your assignment with the *Times* here, if I have anything to say about it. Why the hell do we need our troops to see a correspondent who reports on the war in between his drinking binges?"

Jenicoso saw the fury in the eyes of the two men as they stared at each other, but Winston wisely checked himself when he calmly replied, "I'm an objective reporter, Senator, and I write what I see in my free press columns. But I do apologize for my behavior in Hawaii. I've stopped drinking since I arrived here."

"We'll see if you're allowed to stay, Brand. Just don't count on protection from Operation Checkmate after I've looked into it. So be forewarned."

"I don't have any military affiliation, which would compromise my objectivity."

Jenicoso interrupted, "I haven't been introduced to you, Senator. I'm a doctor, Navy Lt. Commander Nick Jenicoso."

The senator looked askance at Jenicoso's unusual appearance and said, "Senator Tank Kearney here."

"Believe me, I'm pleased to meet you, sir, but we mustn't hold you up any longer. You undoubtedly have a full schedule in front of you today, and we have a plane to catch. So we bid you farewell with good wishes for an informative visit."

"Thank you, Doctor." The senator glanced back at Brand. "I'm not finished investigating your case, Brand," said Kearney with anger in his eyes as the group moved off.

"Believe me, Winston. You don't know how sorry I am that I was held up by duties this morning, or we'd have been off to Nha Trang long before the senator and his party arrived."

"What bad luck, Nick, but it couldn't be helped. Let's leave before the senator changes his mind and backtracks to insult me again or hurl yet another threat."

"The senator isn't an enemy I'd want to have," remarked Jenicoso as the two men walked to their waiting aircraft.

Senator Thomas Aloysius Nathaniel Kearney, Sr., and his fact-finding party settled into the Caravelle Hotel in Saigon after the confrontation with Brand at the airport and then attended an official reception. The next day their briefings began, first at the American Embassy, the CIA, and then at MAAG and the newly created MACV Headquarters. A diplomatic meeting with President Diem was scheduled for the following day.

Senator Kearney anticipated the meeting with General Pavler at MAAG/MACV Headquarters. He was determined to question him about the secretive Operation Checkmate. The senator, who loomed over the four-star general in height and girth, greeted General Pavler and said, "I know you're acquainted with the military advisor I brought along on this official visit, General. Sean O' Boyle, our trusted navy captain in intelligence from Hawaii already has been a big help to me."

"Of course, how are you, Sean, and how is one of my favorite people, your lovely wife Clemie?"

The naval officer shook General Pavler's hand enthusiastically. "She's ecstatic about my trip to Vietnam with our esteemed

Senator Kearney, sir. She wanted me to get in touch with her brother Winston, who avoided a visit with us when he came through Hawaii on his way to Vietnam. Clemie's very concerned and unhappy about it. Luckily, I ran into Winston at the airport when we arrived. He and a Doctor Jenicoso were about to catch an airplane to Nha Trang, and we had a short visit. Clemie will be glad to hear that."

"Give my love as always to dear Clemie, Sean. You caught Winston in the nick of time. He intends to do field interviews, and Dr. Jenicoso is next meeting with a missionary doctor who tends to the Montagnard people in the Central Highlands."

"Clemie will be disappointed we didn't have a longer visit, but at least I got to see her brother."

"Tell our dear girl I'll ask Winston to call her or write to her when he returns," replied the general.

Senator Kearney interrupted O' Boyle's reply, "General, as a military man, you certainly know a lot about a member of the press, notwithstanding your personal relationship with him. May I ask if Brand is cooperating with the military in any way?"

"Senator, other than a familial interest in Winston and his well-being on my part, I can't report that he has an official military connection. On the contrary, he is fiercely independent in his press role, and his motivation is to dig out the truth in the situations he encounters and report on it."

"Is he 'digging out the truth' in any situations the military is interested in too, whether in cooperation, or in a parallel investigation by chance?"

"Why do you ask, Senator?"

"First of all, I have to ask about Brand's competency for investigation into sensitive matters here in Vietnam. Reports came to me during his journey to Vietnam on a military transport plane that he engaged in drunken behavior in Hawaii, setting a bad example in front of our military troops."

"I believe your son, Lieutenant Tank, Jr., was on that flight, Senator. Is he the one who gave you that report?"

"Yes, that's right, General."

"When Winston arrived in Vietnam, I counseled him about his drinking problem. I told him that if he could stop drinking for at least a month, and hopefully after that, I wouldn't notify the *New York Times* that he was *persona non grata* in Vietnam. The Diem regime is ready to oust one journalist, with several others on their 'watch list.' As far as I know, Winston hasn't been drinking since his conversation with me. So his status is still legitimate."

"When I received Tank, Jr.'s, report, I looked into Brand's possible removal from Vietnam myself and was told he couldn't be touched because he belonged to a top secret military operation called 'Operation Checkmate.' Can you enlighten me as to whether this operation exists and what its function is?"

"With all due respect to Sean, Senator, I would have to answer any questions about the existence and function of such a top secret matter only with proper clearance. I'm sure you're familiar with these restrictions?"

"Of course, General. I will get back to you later on this matter. It grows late and Sean and I look forward to some rest and relaxation at the Caravelle Hotel after a hectic day of briefings. And I know you have yet to brief the two star general who also accompanied us on this fact-finding mission."

General Pavler responded, "In the meantime, Senator, we have arranged for your son to be transported to Saigon from the Ca Mau Peninsula to meet with you while you're here."

"Much appreciation for your thoughtfulness, General."

"Good day, then, gentlemen."

Later in the afternoon, Tank, Sr., awaited his son's arrival at the Caravelle's bar with Navy Captain Sean O' Boyle.

"Sean, my man, what did you think of all the chicken shit we were given in our briefings today?" asked the elder Kearney as he lit a cigar.

"It looks like we're on a sinking ship here in Vietnam, sir, and we'd better start looking for some lifeboats to abandon the ship with before she sinks."

"Hell, I couldn't have said it better myself! For a navy officer, Sean, you're a man after my own heart. But if we're going to extricate ourselves from this black-hole-money-pit, it's going to raise quite a stink! Damn, we'll need more than a few flimsy life boats and weak excuses to support our exodus."

"An exodus may be wishful thinking, sir. The U.S. 'support-and-training train' left the station years ago, starting with Truman, then Eisenhower, and now Kennedy, and it looks like it may escalate. If the French couldn't make it work here, and finally gave up, why does our country think it will turn out any different for us?

It's going to take someone with your leadership to turn away from disaster and reset our heading for a new course of action for our nation."

"You'd make one hell of an admiral, Sean! You have a good head on your shoulders, and I'm going to put in a good word for you in places that count."

"Thank you, sir. The competition for promotion is stiff, so your support is much appreciated."

"Well, would you look who's coming in the bar with such a burst of enthusiasm? It's my son, Tank, Jr., truly a sight for sore eyes!"

Kearney, Jr., approached the two men, hugged his father and shook hands with Sean O'Boyle. "Damn it, Dad, it's great to see you again! You pulled off a miracle of sorts for me, bringing me back to Saigon. How can I thank you enough for a much needed break from living in such a soggy hell hole in the Ca Mau Peninsula! I can't wait to bed a Saigon beauty first chance I get. You have no idea how starved I am to enjoy the favors of a beautiful woman!" He winked at Sean.

The senator ordered a drink for his son and said, "Before you go off to find a 'lady of the evening,' son, I have a private matter to discuss with you. If you'll excuse us, Sean, Tank, Jr., and I will take our drinks to my room to celebrate this reunion." The elder Kearney snuffed out his cigar in an ashtray and picked up his drink.

"Certainly, sir. I'd best be about sending home a message to my wife before dinner." He winked at Tank, Jr., who smiled mischievously back at the officer. Tank, Jr., picked up his drink and followed his father's imposing bulk out of the bar.

"That Sean O'Boyle is one helluva nice guy, Dad," said the younger Kearney as they entered the senator's room. He thinks like I do, and has an eye for beautiful women, I hear."

"Well, he'd better be more careful than you have been."

"What do you mean, Dad?"

"Damn it, son, you're in one helluva mess again!"

"You've got to be kidding! It can't be true. Ca Mau is a virtual 'desert' of available women, despite the fact that it's a watery sink hole. No 'desserts' for me in that God forsaken place. I haven't had a chance to get into any trouble yet," said Tank, Jr., who smiled at his clever metaphors.

"It's not funny, son. I've got bad news for you!"

"What is it? Has Carlotta Simone had an unexpected early delivery of her baby? I'm really sorry my slip-up has caused us so much worry and trouble. I had no intention of conceiving a baby with her. I don't want to be a father."

"No, Carlotta hasn't delivered yet, but there's a helluva Northeaster heading your way! You're a father-to-be again and your wife is due here with her parents tomorrow!"

"What!" Tank, Jr., exclaimed. "You've got to be kidding! I don't have a wife, so she couldn't be pregnant with my child!"

"The American embassy informed me today that the Province Chief at Song Be has sent a message to the American ambassador. He says you have taken his daughter as your wife, and that she is pregnant with your child. He demands you abide by your contract with him and take responsibility for your wife and your yet-to-be-born baby."

"Holy shit! I didn't sign any contract. Could her father be lying about the pregnancy to trap me? I haven't been gone that long from Song Be for him to be sure Lieu is pregnant."

"So this isn't a made-up story to extort money from us?"

"Well, I didn't think one evening bedding a beautiful 'Good Family Girl' would turn into a nightmare like this!" lamented wild-eyed Tank, Jr., downing his drink in one gulp.

Kearney, Sr., replied, "If the claim that she's your wife is legitimate, it's a very serious matter, son. Her father cited an ancient Vietnamese law, the Gia Long Code, that made his daughter your wife when you asked him to give her to you as your wife, and he granted your request. I'm afraid by Vietnamese law she is your wife. No doubt international law will surely recognize her Vietnamese father's claim as well."

"My God, how could this be happening again! I had absolutely no intention of marrying a Vietnamese woman, much less any other woman for that matter, as you well know!

"Then why did you ask her father for her hand in marriage, son?" asked his father.

"My buddies at the Five Oceans BOQ said I couldn't score with a 'Good Family Girl' unless marriage was involved. I wanted to show them how clever I was to figure out how to bed her by 'pretending a marriage.' I knew I could leave the next day, as I had a last-minute military notice of change-of-orders in my pocket. A military advisor in Ca Mau Peninsula was evacuated with dysentery, and I was re-directed to his post, because they had no one else to send at the time."

"Clever, my Irish ass! That was one buddy-challenge that burned you proper. You not only asked for the marriage under Vietnamese law, but also officially consummated the marriage, and the family has the proof of it with the pregnancy! How clever is that? Haven't I taught you how important it is to use care in indiscretions, especially after Carlotta?" asked the senior Kearney. He nervously paced back and forth.

"I guess I miscalculated, Dad. But I figured the ruse wouldn't matter with a Vietnamese woman because I'd be leaving the country when my tour is over. And she was so beautiful and so enraptured with me, I couldn't resist her and took all the pleasure I could from our so-called 'wedding night.' As a 'Good Family Girl,' she was a virgin, so I knew I wouldn't contact any disease from her. What are the chances of a pregnancy with a 'one-night-stand' anyway?" If a pregnancy had occurred by some far-out chance, I thought her family would take care of her and the baby. I'd be back home with the problem left behind me."

The senator took a cigar from his vest pocket and lit it. Smoke filled the air as he considered the sticky situation.

"Always remember, son, there is much to be gained by others who see an opportunity to take advantage of the powerful and wealthy and their kin. How often have I told you that there are always political ramifications as well as personal ones, seeing that you're the son of a U.S senator? And that's not to mention that this Vietnamese woman is the daughter of a Vietnamese province chief. You don't have the luxury of playing around without being very careful. Have you ever seen me slip up all these years? You've done so twice now, in succession no less!"

"How can I get out of this trap, Dad?"

"We need a miracle to find a loophole in this horrific mess. But, damn, I'm afraid it's too late. After all we've done to get you out of a marriage to Carlotta Simone, you had to go and get yourself married to a Vietnamese woman. I understand the whole damn village witnessed you asking her father for her hand in marriage. And the pregnancy is undeniable proof the marriage was consummated. They have this case wrapped up!

"Compensation for the woman and child won't appease the family this time, as it did with Carlotta's—for the time being that is.

Carlotta is still expecting you to marry her when you return from Vietnam. But now you're already married, with another child on the way."

"But, Dad, there was no wedding ceremony, nor vows taken in front of clergy. Just my verbal request to Lieu's father, his acceptance and delivery of his daughter to me."

"That may be true, but the ancient Gia Long Code is still viable or the province chief would have no basis for his claim. Perhaps the woman's father agreed to your request because he saw the opportunity for his daughter to have an abundant life in America. He needs to save face in his political arena, too.

"Needless to say, I'll have a hard time saving face in mine. How do you think Carlotta and her family will react to your marriage? Now Carlotta's baby will be illegitimate. And how will it affect my poll ratings with my constituents on the home front? Your one night of pleasure has gotten us into one helluva mess again, son. Bragging rights! I can't see how the hell we're going to get out of this pissing contest!"

"If we can't, think how it will screw up my life! Marriage and children were never on my radar, but you're telling me I'll have to live with it. Who in their right mind would agree to spend time in the military in Vietnam on the other side of the world from home in this hell hole if not to escape marriage? Desperate as I was to avoid marriage to Carlotta, I would never have invoked the ancient Vietnamese marriage law if I thought it would be turned against me, instead of me using it to my advantage. Damn, it just isn't fair to have no escape!"

"As I said, before we were dealing with a mayor and his daughter in the U.S. This time we've got a father in a foreign nation with Vietnamese and probably international law involved!"

"Holy shit! I'm in quick sand and sinking fast!" exclaimed Tank, Jr. Sweat began to glisten on his forehead.

"The law's got our hands tied, son. Any solution has to be legal, or we'll both be in even more trouble!"

Before the Kearneys went to dinner, Tank, Sr., asked, "By the way, son, regarding your complaint about Winston Brand being a drunkard and an unfit example for our troops on the overseas flight to Vietnam, did he do anything else to infuriate you? I'd like to kick his ass myself for mentioning me more than once with a derogatory connotation in his blasted column!

Tank, Jr., replied, "I'd like to set off a charge of TNT myself and blast him back to the United States. Not only did he become obnoxious in the bar in Hawaii when he had too much to drink, but the arrogant bastard later in Guam screwed the flight attendant from our flight to Vietnam. She's a real looker that I had my sights on during the Hawaii stopover. She had a drink with me in the bar, but left alone for her room as soon as she could.

"I couldn't believe it when later I saw her kissing Brand goodbye at the airport in Vietnam! The disembarking troops gave me a knowing look that told me they knew my advances in Hawaii had been scorned by her in favor of a middle-aged drunkard! Humiliated is a word that doesn't even touch how I felt after Maria gave me such a put-down!"

"Maria, you say. What's her last name?" asked the senator.

"Monclova. She was 'Miss Philippines' a while back."

"Maria Monclova was the flight attendant on the last leg of our flight from the Philippines to Vietnam. You're right. She's a real beauty, and none of us could keep our eyes off of her for the entire flight. I was told her father works for the diplomatic services in Manilla. What in the world could have possessed her to have a tryst with Winston Brand of all people? Didn't she witness his despicable behavior in the bar at Hawaii?" asked the senior Kearney.

"A marine major, Alex Spear, from our flight told me he had given Maria a copy of a book of Brand's poetry to read called *Fire in the Soul.* Maybe his way with words gave him a better pick-up line than I had. But she would have enjoyed herself 100 percent more in bed with me than with a washed-up, tipsy reporter. That's why I contacted you with my complaint about Brand. He's one of the most egotistical, sarcastic, son-of-a-bitches I've ever met!"

"Granted, son. Even Sean O' Boyle, his brother-in-law isn't too keen on him."

"You know, Dad, now that you mention Sean, I recall your earlier comment about a 'lady of the evening.' I have an idea about how I can slip out of my dilemma."

"I can't imagine a scenario that would work at this point."

"Well, say when Lieu and her parents arrive tomorrow at the American embassy, I meet them acting friendly. I'll mention my father is here and wishes to meet them. That will please them.

Then I'll offer to pay for them to stay at the Caravelle. After dinner, I'll ask Lieu to stay with me in my room later."

"Son, you can't continue this relationship in any way if you hope to find a way out of your obligations."

"Don't worry, Dad. As much as I'd like to spend another hot night together with Lieu, if I give her the number of Sean O' Boyle's room instead of mine, Sean might think she is a 'lady of the night' sent up to his room by the establishment to pleasure him. Sean is a very charming fellow, and most likely he wouldn't turn a blind eye to Lieu's beauty. Surely, he would invite her into his room. If she refuses, mentioning that she is looking for me, he might be bright enough to entice her to enter and wait for me, saying he's expecting me at any moment. Who's to say what might or might not transpire after that?

"Then I can claim doubt about whether Lieu is a fallen woman being passed off as a 'Good Family Girl' as she and her parents claim. I can act outraged, claim I was deceived as to her status, and refuse to recognize the marriage or pregnancy. What do you think of my idea, Dad?"

"It sound like it could explode into a public scandal, son! That's the last thing we need! Better to keep it as quiet as possible out of the press and gossip of Saigon. A stipend to parents, mother and child is our first order of business to cool their indignation. Until your tour of duty in Vietnam ends and you return to the States, I'm afraid we'll have to play this hand with quite a handicap and try to keep it under wraps."

26 REFLECTIONS

There is one art of which man should be master—the art of reflection.
—Samuel Taylor Coleridge

I DON'T KNOW ABOUT YOU, Nick, but the confrontation with Senator Kearney at the airport was not my idea of a congenial send off for our trip to Nha Trang!"

"Believe me, Winston, luck certainly wasn't with us. There was no way I could've left my medical duties any sooner than I did to meet you at the airport."

"I wouldn't have gone without you, my friend."

"I'm glad you didn't cancel our flight before I arrived. I'm really looking forward to seeing Alex again and later my friend Dr. Kalverton."

"And I as well, Nick."

"What an interesting discussion we had at dinner the other evening about your research for the postponed interview with President Diem. And here I am up in the air with you again not that long after we returned together by helicopter from Loc Ninh with the body of Capt. Eric Fletcher on board. His tragic death there at the very end of his tour of duty must be doubly difficult for his family. They prepared a celebration for his return from war, but instead had to plan for his funeral!"

Brand reflected, "Fletch was too young to be killed with so much life ahead of him with his wife Susan and their children. When I read Fletch's letter to his wife, I could tell he had the kind of home life I can only imagine by reading about it."

"Why's that, Winston?"

"My late father's biggest disappointment in life, other than not receiving his fourth star, was my failure to follow in his footsteps into an illustrious military career like his."

"Is it his view of you that gives you the conflicting issues that seem to plague you, Winston? Even if your father opposed your choice of career, isn't it really your choice whether or not to hold onto another's view of yourself? Personally, I've found looking within for our Creator's love of oneself and others, rather than without for a sense of value and approval, is what brings peace of mind."

"No wonder you're always such a pleasure to be with, Nick. No doubt what you say is true, but despite everything, don't children always want to please their parents, even if doing so goes against their own innate inclinations for their lives? To top it off, my career choice broke with a family male military tradition that even included my grandfather. But, perhaps you're right. I haven't really come to terms with my own legitimate right of freedom of choice."

"Don't take too long or the best in life may pass you by."

"Words of wisdom, I know, Nick. But the enormity of my father's vehement disapproval has stayed with me to this day. In his eyes, I never measured up. Despite the years that have passed, I can't seem to shake a feeling of guilt for making my own way. I know trying to drown that guilt in alcohol at times wasn't smart. Its temporary relief created its own helluva an after effect on myself and others.

"Now that I think of it, perhaps my haste to get the story of Fletcher's death out ahead of my competition had more to do with proving myself as a foreign correspondent on top of the action, as much as avoiding the collusion of my colleagues. But my father's disapproval is in the past. I should've shown the necessary respect for military protocol and the feelings of Fletcher's family. Instead, I wanted to beat my rival journalists with news of the first American advisor to be killed in Vietnam. My emotions got the best of me, and I must apologize. Thankfully my sister Clemie thoroughly chastised me for my attempt, and thwarted my ill-considered judgment, even though she was so happy to hear I had escaped the same fate as Captain Fletcher."

"Believe me, it does a man good to own up to his mistakes."

"I seem to be doing that quite often lately."

"Perhaps you were still in shock from the deadly Viet Cong attack on the road to the French plantation. Captain Fletcher's critical injury and death, not to mention your abduction at *Bon Sejour* soon after was quite an overload of trauma. I wasn't sure whether I would find you, Captain Fletcher and/or Lieutenant Hewlett dead or alive when I arrived at Loc Ninh."

"I wasn't sure either in my case, Nick, both on the road and later when I was abducted, until Lieutenant Hewlett and Lucette Devereau frightened off my captors at the *garçonnière*."

"Believe me, Lucette's certainly a beautiful, young French lady. Must be lonely for her so isolated at *Bon Sejour* without young people to socialize with, and no eligible man to court her. Although I thought I detected an interest developing between her and Lieutenant Hewlett."

"If Hewlett's lucky to survive, his tour of duty will be over in a year, and he'll be on his way back home to the States. Goodbyes will once again leave Lucette in isolation."

"Unless the next military advisor to be stationed here is young and unmarried," replied Jenicoso with optimism.

"I'm not so sure the military advisor stage will last that long. More American military men deployed to Vietnam are looming on the horizon as Viet Cong guerilla fighting intensifies with increased infiltration from North Vietnam."

"I don't look forward to an escalation of the war."

"We can't fool ourselves about the present 'little' guerilla war either, Nick. At night in my quarters at Loc Ninh, I felt surrounded on all sides by the Viet Cong when I saw their lights from any direction I turned. How easily those lights could turn into weapons aimed at the ARVN forces. Not only that, Major Si, the Vietnamese commander at Loch Ninh, admitted he couldn't really protect us while we were there!"

"I'm afraid the French are only safe as long as they keep paying taxes to the Viet Cong. How long will that last, and where does that leave Lucette?" asked Jenicoso.

"War time doesn't foster normal life, Doc."

"Believe me, Lucette's not the only lovely lady in limbo. We ran out of time the other evening at dinner for me to inquire further about you and our beautiful friend, Maria Monclova. When I met one of her flights at the airport, her usually sparkling blue eyes filled with tears when I mentioned you. She said she had offered you an invitation to connect with her when her flights land in Vietnam from the Philippines. She had given Alex a letter with the invitation to give to you when you returned from Loch Ninh. But when she entered the airport café, a waiter directed her to a table with her letter left there. 'Another time, another place' was written on the envelope."

Brand's reply was guarded, "Maria has only 30 minutes or so on the ground when her flights land; not much time for a relationship to develop."

"Is that the only reason, Winston? Seems to me if there's a will, there's a way."

Brand explained, "I've had quite a few attempts on my life, starting at Travis Air Force Base when I checked in for the military transport flight to Vietnam, and several since I've arrived, one of which you've mentioned at *Bon Sejour*, as well as a later failed mugging. Until I know who's trying to kill me, and the threat is removed, I can't expose Maria to any danger through a relationship with me."

"Now a mugging, too! What happened, Winston?"

"I'd really rather not get into it, but the gist of it is that I made a mistake taking a pedicab back to Five Oceans after leaving a press party, although I'd been warned not to use them. Let's just say I was able to maneuver my way out of an attempt to mug me, or worse."

"Believe me, Winston, when you said you were jinxed I had no idea how many incidents have occurred to dissuade your endeavors here. I'm grateful you've escaped life-threatening injury so far. But if you're able to resolve the threats, there's no lovelier source of comfort and care than our Maria."

"Who wouldn't be interested in our lovely Maria, Doc. I can't imagine a man who could resist such a beauty. But I wrote 'another time, another place' on the front of her envelope Alex gave me, because it sums up our options at this time. Besides, Maria's better off with someone more suited to her background and stage of life. I'm a big risk to her, or anyone, in so many ways until I sort out the considerable issues in my life."

"Be that as it may, but one can never predict nature's laws of attraction. Maria hasn't given up on you. She wrote another letter to you and left it with me when I saw her again. She said she had even written a poem for you.

"I've sensed the agitation between you two, so I've been waiting for the appropriate time to give you her second letter. You and Alex always seem to be in the middle of some kind of action going on, so it's not easy to find a time when you're not distracted. Here in flight in this closed in airplane seems to me to be the best time to give you Maria's second letter."

"Why didn't you give it to me when we had dinner together?

"Believe me, we had enough on our minds sifting through all your research information about the Diem regime. When I mentioned Maria, I got the feeling you weren't quite yet ready to receive it, so it wasn't the 'time' or the 'place' for it."

Brand laughed, "A 'got cha' response if there ever was one, Doc! Very clever play on my own words. I must confess, I took a coward's way out of answering her letter instead of meeting Maria face-to-face. Not a kind way to handle the situation. But to be truthful, you were right the other evening at dinner when you remarked about the attraction between us. I knew that with one look in her beautiful eyes, reason would disappear, and I would put her in danger through her association with me. Don't think for a minute there wasn't a monumental battle taking place within me when I let her go with that message."

"Maria's not with us now, Winston. At least you might respect Maria's effort and concern for you by reading her letter and writing a response."

Brand hesitated as Jenicoso handed Maria's letter to him. He recognized Maria's handwriting on the front of it, and the faint smell of Maria's perfume wafted up from the envelope. Brand reluctantly replied, "You're right. I'll read it later. She does deserve a written response." Brand stuck what he knew was a love letter in his pocket.

Brand flicked his finger across his nose and abruptly changed the subject as he looked out the window and said, "We're getting closer to Nha Trang. I'm looking forward our visit at the station hospital with Alex, and the opportunity to give him the travel chess set from General Pavler. Alex requested one as soon as possible, or ASAP, but such timing wasn't possible."

"Believe me, let's hope Alex is recovered by now."

"What is the treatment for his rat bite fever, and what are his chances for a quick recovery?"

"There's nothing quick about it. I was told Alex killed the rat with a gunshot and brought its head to Nha Trang for analysis. But Alex had to be treated for rabies with two weeks of vaccines after an initial dose of rabies immune globin without waiting for lab results to see if the rat had rabies or not. It's a necessary precaution against a disease that is usually fatal once established. The vaccine injections are given on days 0, 3, 7 and 14."

"What an unfortunate incident, but hopefully Alex is close to the end of his treatment if all is going well."

"Believe me, I'm a little concerned about the delay of almost a day before Alex was evacuated to the Sixth Station Hospital for treatment. When we were notified of the incident, we gave instructions to Lucette to have her staff carefully wash the site of the bite and administer iodine if possible. The bite of a large rat can be infectious in and of itself, but if the rat had rabies, that's a whole different story."

Brand looked out the airplane window as they landed. "Here we are pulling up at the air terminal, Nick."

"If Alex is well tended to, are you still interested in going with me by air to Quang Ngai tomorrow where I'm to meet my old friend, Dr. Kalverton? You mentioned your interest in field reporting, and Dr. Kalverton is one of the good guys."

"Yes, I certainly am. Thanks for the opportunity, Nick. With all the negative reporting coming out of Vietnam from Saigon, I think a positive column from the field will be a welcome relief for American newspaper readers. And if Dr. Kalverton is anything like you, I know I'll get a good story."

Dr. Nick Jenicoso and Winston Brand were greatly relieved when they walked into Alex's quarters. He looked well and was pouring over a map of Indochina at a makeshift desk. Alex looked up as the two entered and greeted them enthusiastically.

"Gentlemen, you're a sight for sore eyes. I've been cooped up here for rabies treatment, vaccines and observation for almost two weeks. The vaccine injections are certainly not pleasant, and I could've used that chess set in Winston's hands a few weeks ago to occupy my mind while delayed from my mission by medical treatment. I met a fellow patient who loved to play chess, but he's been sent back to his duty station, so now I'll have to settle for Winston as a chess partner."

"Believe me, we're very glad to see you looking so well, Alex, but I'm afraid I've talked Winston into accompanying me to Quang Ngai tomorrow to do some field reporting. I'm meeting with an old friend, Dr. Kalverton, now a missionary tending to Montagnard natives who lack adequate medical care. So, your chess game with Winston will have to wait awhile."

"I might not be here that long either," replied Alex. I'm hoping to get a clean bill of health soon and be back on the track of the radios stolen at Loc Ninh."

"Believe me, that communist ambush used as a diversionary tactic resulting in Captain Fletcher's death still bothers me, especially since Winston shared Fletcher's last letter to his wife with me on our way back to Saigon from *Bon Sejour* before turning it over to you. Perhaps we shouldn't have read such a private letter, but it really plucked the heartstrings."

"Yes, I can't imagine what such news would do to my wife Gwen and girls if she received such a letter. But before I forget, Winston, you'll be glad to know I recovered the items stolen from you at *Bon Sejour*."

"You're kidding, Alex!"

"No, I'm not kidding. When I was investigating the interior of the old barn at *Bon Sejour*, I came across a cloth bag that contained your wallet with press credentials in it, your watch, silver cigarette lighter, flask and a masculine ring with an aquamarine stone. I brought the items with me from *Bon Sejour*, and they're in the drawer of the night stand over there. In the kidnappers' haste to get away, at least one of your abductors ditched the incriminating evidence in the barn."

Brand opened the drawer. "Well, I'll be darned. It's all here just like you said, even Willie. But Willie isn't a friend any longer if I want to stay in Vietnam. Thanks, Alex. It's good to have my things back again. But I sure wouldn't have wanted you to get injured in their recovery."

"Much more intelligence was gained than the recovery of your personal items. But let's get back to you, Winston. Have you made any progress lining up an interview with President Diem?"

"Well, the Minister of Information, But Hieu, arranged for me to interview Diem. I was encouraged, but then the date set for it was delayed indefinitely, because Diem needed time to adequately prepare for the imminent fact-finding trip of Senator Kearney, Sr."

Alex replied, "I hope Senator Kearney is prepared for an hours-long briefing with President Diem. But Diem may have his hands full with the no-nonsense senator, who'll get in much more than a word or two. How did you happen to persuade But Hieu to expedite your request for an interview with the president? It usually takes quite a long time to be granted."

"Well, I was almost mugged when I took a pedicab ride back to Five Oceans from Pierre Girard's press party. Turns out the bandit Gold Tooth was my driver, but I didn't recognize him in the dark with his head held down under his cap. He drove me into a dead end alley with his gang of hoodlums waiting to mug me with barrel staves raised. Luckily, I was wearing the Derringer General Pavler authorized for me, so I quickly maneuvered around in my seat, stuck the gun securely under his chin and made him drive me to the police station. But Hieu was notified and came down to the police station hours later. I was able to talk him into helping me get an interview with Diem."

"You saved your skin that time, Winston, but I thought you were warned about taking pedicabs. Not too smart. Is there anything else we should know about the condition you were in when you took the pedicab?"

"You aren't my keeper, Alex.'"

"No, I'm not, just concerned about you, as is the general."

Brand retorted, "Well, Geronimo has two of us to worry about now that you've been taken out by a rat, and not a Five Oceans one at that."

Alex laughed and said, "You're right, Winston. But it sure wasn't funny at the time. I'm just glad I could get the medical care I needed in time."

"Believe me, I'm glad I'm not the one responsible for the two of you. Just be sure you're in the clear, Alex, before you jump back into your mission again."

"Doc, they won't let me go until they're sure I'm well and have finished my treatment. But I'm sorry to hear about Winston's aborted interview with President Diem."

"Believe me, Alex. Winston will be more than prepared when the interview actually comes about. He practiced on me at dinner the other evening."

"Alex remarked with a wink, "Don't tell me, Doc. Has Winston tried out his theory that the Ngo brothers' adopted philosophy of

Personalism has permeated their ideas of Vietnamese nation building and modernization that has set them at odds with the U.S?"

"Winston was just getting to it, Alex, but I had surgery in the morning and we had to postpone it."

Alex replied, "If I know you, Winston, postponement isn't your strong suit. How about if I relieve you and try to explain the difference between the Personalism and Western concepts?"

"Believe me, do we have enough time?" chuckled the good doctor. "Winston did tell me it's an obscure philosophy."

Alex rolled his eyes and looked at Dr. Jenicoso, "It'll have to be short and sweet, since I'm due for one of my last vaccination injections soon."

Brand laughed, "Okay, gentlemen, it's not that difficult to explain. But now you have me interested, Alex. I'm curious as to whether I got my points across in our previous discussions."

Alex took in his breath, sighed and started. "French Personalism draws on Catholic spiritualism and humanism and its concern with the ills of modern industrialization. In the 1930s, intellectuals desperately looked for a "third way," or middle way, between capitalism and communism. It's not a systemic political program, but advocates a kind of 'communitarian socialism.'"

"How in the world did the Ngo family come in contact a Western philosophical system of thought?" asked Jenicoso.

"Ngo Dinh Nhu, a self-appointed intellectual, probably encountered Personalism while studying in France in the 1930s."

"Do you have any idea why the French intellectualists called it 'Personalism,' instead of 'Individualism?"

"You've picked up on a key point, Nick. In Personalist philosophy, man as an 'individual' pursues selfish goals in a liberal society, or, he is isolated in a totalitarian state."

"What's so different about a 'person?'" asked Jenicoso.

"A 'person' possesses basic individual human rights and dignity. But here's the difference, in Personalism he also bears national responsibilities to secure the common good."

"Why is this distinction important to the Ngo brothers?"

Alex replied, "Basically, the people have to participate not only in the economic, but also the political life of the nation. Reciprocal obligations between the populace and the sovereign is the name of the game."

"Sounds like a utopian philosophy unsuited to a backward nation," remarked Jenicoso.

"Alex smiled, "But it offers the Ngos a Vietnamese way for their own resource, the populace, to do all the work of nation building and modernization at the bottom, while they sit at the top and control everything."

Brand and Jenicoso laughed, and Winston remarked, "Alex, you got to the heart of the matter in short order with a no nonsense diagnosis, just like our good doctor is known for doing in his medical practice."

"Believe me, it's essential in my profession."

Alex continued, "And how glad we all are of that, Nick. But the catch for the Ngos is that in practice such a theory doesn't work without the use of force to get the populace to lend their labor and money to rebuild their nation. The trouble is the peasants aren't even aware of their communitarian obligations."

Brand interjected, "The peasants live in a traditional way of ancestor worship centered in the family, the hamlet or village in an agrarian life style, and are often wholly ignorant of national concerns."

"But the Western idea of individual freedom goes out the window when force is used," commented Jenicoso.

"True," responded Alex. "In practice these tenets are deeply flawed. By adding the use of force, the Ngos justify it by what they deem a worthy Personalist goal."

"In other words, the 'end justifies the means,'" remarked Jenicoso. "I'm curious as to whatever tipped you off to research Personalism, Winston?" asked Jenicoso.

"I was alerted to research it because of the neon signs reportedly spread throughout the towns and cities of South Vietnam displaying Diem's so called trinity—'Personalism, Community and Collective Advancement.' It bore looking into as Diem's advertised plan to solve South Vietnam's trio of pressing problems—'Communism, Underdevelopment and Disunity.'

"In other words, Personalism gives the South Vietnamese their own 'third way' philosophical foundation for their independent nation. But its world-wide recognition is just about nil in contrast to the Marxist-Leninist tenets of the communists in the north."

Alex responded, "Nor can I imagine it has ever been used in reality as a political system, probably only existing in the contemplation of French intellectuals."

"Is there evidence of Personalist ideas used in the actual policies of the Diem government?" asked Jenicoso.

Brand explained, "Yes, I think you can see Personalist ideas infusing Diem's series of vast rural schemes in the mid to late 1950s, such as programs for land reform, land development and Agroville resettlements. These ideas have culminated in the Strategic Hamlet program begun in earnest this year."

"Believe me, the U.S. undoubtedly would support land reform and development, but why would the Ngos want to create more chaos in their country with mass resettlement programs, breaking up traditional old ways and living areas by forcing the populace to build new ones in different locations?"

Alex offered, "Perhaps it's the idea that technological backwardness needs the collective and active participation of the masses to overcome it. What better way to activate the limited and confined world of the peasants than through massive relocation and rebuilding? This idea taken to the extreme is exemplified by the country-wide collectivism of the north."

"Believe me, the result must be massive resentment in both the north and south," observed Jenicoso. "Restructuring a whole society is quite an undertaking! I doubt the Ngo brothers would trade places with the peasants in these massive movements."

"I know I surely wouldn't want to," replied Alex.

"Nor I," remarked Brand. "My correspondent status most often removes me from being a direct player in the action I'm reporting on. My father perhaps thought me a coward not to be in the middle of a military battle, instead only as a reporter on the sidelines."

"Believe me, Winston, if your father knew all the dangerous situations you've already experienced, he couldn't justify his projection on to you. Then again, we all have our separate talents that take us in different directions in life."

"You're a lot more diplomatic than my father was, Nick. But we haven't even touched on how Personalism has contributed to Diem's Personalist view of democracy."

"Believe me, it's easy to see why Diem and his philosophy are misunderstood by almost everyone!" remarked Jenicoso.

"Alex remarked, "The different views of democracy are a key sticking point between the two allies. The Ngos view democracy as a politically engaged and united population in a process of collective social improvement dependent on moral duties."

"Believe me, it doesn't leave room for individual freedom and representative government as in Western-style thinking, does it? It's authoritarianism with a collective emphasis."

Brand replied, "Your observation is right on as usual, Nick. In Personalism, humans develop 'character in society,' through moral and social responsibility, rather than through the experience of political freedoms."

"It seems to me that society and the government get the best of the deal in a Personalist democracy rather than the populace," remarked Jenicoso.

Brand replied, "Yes, Westerners look at how the government can assist the people in their own efforts. But Personalists look at what the people can do for the government."

Alex remarked, "Adopting Personalism is justification for the Ngos to mobilize the only available Vietnamese capital at their disposal, the Vietnamese labor of all classes, by force if necessary, to help them solve the problems of their nation."

"Believe me, I have to admit the number of ills Diem faces exceed more than I've heard from my patients over the years."

Alex replied, "Nevertheless, the suppression of opposition by the Diem regime is in no way consistent with the 'moral and social responsibility' in the reciprocal obligations touted in their Personalist tenets. Nor is there any sign in South Vietnam of a free press, independent judiciary or an open and competitive political system that democracy depends on."

Brand replied, "We have a political system of checks and balances, but even so, the electorate evaluates the balance of power between 'what is necessary' and 'what is too much.'"

"Believe me, is there ever enough power to satisfy any one, especially the leader of a nation? There's no chance for the populace to check it in an authoritarian government except by revolution."

Alex interjected, "Remember the quote by Lord John Acton, a British historian and moralist, which states, 'Power tends to corrupt, and absolute power corrupts absolutely. Great men are generally bad men."

Brand replied, "I guess all of us need to use the power at hand in the best way possible. If we point the index finger at others, we need to check the three fingers pointing back at us."

Alex remarked, "True, but the juxtaposition is striking of Diem's image as a religious, ascetic leader with that of his brother Nhu, whose despotic activities give Diem the nefarious means to stay in power. It's a real dilemma for the U.S."

Brand commented, "Diem has remarked that if he were deposed, whoever followed him would have to be a much more ruthless, brutal and coercive 'strong dragon' to succeed.

"But as I consider the philosophy of the 'end justifies the means,' which some associate with Machavelli, I am reminded of the lines from Shakespeare's play, *King Richard the Second*:

> …To find out right with wrong—it may not be;
> And you that do abet him in this kind
> Cherish rebellion and are rebels all…"

Alex responded, "How true that is in the long run. Even if suppression is used by a ruler for the 'just cause' of controlling a rebellious people by suppression, it makes the sovereign as much a rebel as its unruly citizens. Shakespeare warns that in the end 'it may not be.'"

"Believe me, we've had quite the interesting discussion, and we understand a lot of philosophy. But we've found nothing practical to resolve the problems of mismatched allies."

Alex smiled with a twinkle in his eye and said, "Well, at least, Nick, we're among the best informed people in Vietnam as we try to carry out our respective jobs, thanks to Winston."

Brand laughed, "I hope my readers will feel the same way."

Alex said, "Here's a practical question for you, Winston. Did Geronimo send you up here with my chess set in order to get you out of Saigon during Senator Kearney's visit?"

Brand responded, "You ought to know by now, Alex, I'm a member of the press, so I don't take orders from General Pavler. Nor can he send me wherever he wants me to go." Then Brand smiled. "However, with Senator Kearney and his military advisor, my womanizing brother-in-law, Sean O'Boyle's, arrival, I was happy to take him up on his offer. Unfortunately, we didn't leave soon enough and ran into them both at the airport today before we left.

"Believe me, it was bad luck and couldn't be avoided. The senator had some choice words for Winston, but he held his own."

"Kearney is still determined to meddle with my reporter's status in Vietnam," Brand remarked. "So, while this 'miserable excuse for a reporter,' as Kearny put it, is still allowed in the country, I think news reports from the field are in order."

"Still after you, is he, Winston? But the senator may find he can't bulldoze Geronimo," Alex commented with a smile.

"Believe me, Winston needs to give us some good stories coming out of Vietnam, like the work of my friend, Dr. Kalverton. A more dedicated missionary doctor can't be found anywhere. The Montagnards are lucky to have his medical care, especially since most Vietnamese have a deep prejudice against these primitive mountain dwellers."

Alex offered, "The U.S. Special Forces and some Vietnamese Special Forces are working with the Montagnards in the Central Highlands to train them to help in the fight against the Viet Cong and the infiltrators coming from the north down the Ho Chi Minh Trail. However, President Diem is keeping a watchful eye on the operation, fearing the natives will use their learned skills to secure their independence."

"Believe me, Alex, we'll hear all about it when we meet with Dr. Kalverton. In the meantime, take your time to recover. A rabies scare is nothing to dismiss lightly. We'll touch base with you if you're still here when we return from Quang Ngai."

"Not to worry, my friends, but we finished our discussion just in the 'nick of time,' because I see the nurse is at the door ready to give me my last vaccine injection," said Alex as he shook their hands.

Later that evening in his quarters, Brand fingered Maria's letter in his pocket, and finally decided to read what she had to say. He took it out, opened the envelope and began reading:

> Winston, this poem conveys what's in my heart:
>
> *REFLECTIONS*
> *What happened between us only God can know.*
> *An overwhelming force overcame good sense*

When an arrow struck true from Cupid's bow
And left us intertwined without recompense.
Caught in the throes of overwhelming emotion,
With its rush and flow of wave after wave,
Two souls entwined in swirls and eddies of motion,
Now caught in a fierce undertow to brave.
Trapped in rapture that will not leave,
With no solid ground in which to grow,
An unlikely pair is left to grieve,
With yearning's deep refusal to let go.
Not to be forgotten is the unforgettable,
Burning within as an ethereal light.
Can it be but the heart's cherished fable,
A dream to be, or never to take flight?
Branded with beauty of splendor on the sand,
We encountered oneness beyond time and space,
Forever captivating us o'er an unknown land,
It yearns but for another time, another place.

Brand folded the letter and exclaimed, "Maria, how you've captured our relationship in such a beautiful poem! But your lovely head is still in the clouds, and I mustn't allow myself to get swept away with our mutual passion for one another."

Winston felt Maria deserved more of an answer than he'd had time to write on the face of the envelope of her first letter. So he took out his notebook and began to write:

> Maria, good sense tells me that the "us" you write about must not have 'another time, another place,' as much as we are both drawn to each other. Although it feels as if we knew each other in a dream sometime long ago in a faraway place, we must put fantasy aside and face reality. Granted, there is an explosive chemistry that grips us when we are together. That's why we'll never be able to think rationally in each other's presence.
>
> No rhyme nor reason would pair us, unlikely as we are, with no solid ground on which to build a relationship, but only the shifting sand upon which we once took flight. Our journey to the stars will never be forgotten, but must be tucked away in a hidden place in

our hearts, only to be remembered, perhaps on a lonely night.

Go on with your life, lovely Maria, as I will with mine, trying to resolve personal issues I would never want to burden you with. Our brief encounter is one I will always cherish, but one I cannot in good conscience pursue.

Fly on, beautiful one, knowing a fire burns in my soul as well as yours, but must only light our separate ways until, if ever, there is to be another time, another place of splendor on the sand. Winston

Maria won't take no for an answer, Brand thought. The meeting of their minds and emotions before their joining had kindled a feeling of fate that had fueled their magnetic encounter. But he must stand firm for both their sakes.

Then again, he didn't want to become entangled again with another either, only to subject himself to someone else's expectations for his life. He'd been there, done that several times, first with his father and then with Eleanor.

Hell, what did his father care about what his son wanted to do with his life? Vice Admiral Willoughby Brand was blind to his son's deep desire to become a foreign correspondent. To his father he was a coward, unable to 'face the sun,' just because he didn't want to follow his illustrious father's and grandfather's footsteps into the military. The dilemma had torn him apart, with only the antidote of alcohol to give temporarily relief to his troubled soul.

He had hoped his marriage to Eleanor would relieve his torment. Once released by Hanoi after the Dien Bien Phu accident, Winston had been comforted by her tender nursing care during his injury recovery at Walter Reed Hospital in Washington, D.C. Their relationship started out with such great promise, and when he grew strong again, they were married and moved to New York where Winston was assigned to a desk job at the *Times*, instead of going back to Vietnam as a war correspondent. The marriage soon floundered as Winston slowly resumed drinking to ease his intense dislike of a desk job.

Eleanor's nursing career in New York became so successful, she didn't want to be part of such a life as Winston envisioned as a foreign correspondent. It was hard enough for her to travel to her family's home base in Maryland to visit with her mother who was ill, given the increasing demands of her career. When his drinking got out of hand again as relief from job dissatisfaction and his marriage dissolution, it certainly didn't help the situation, he admitted to himself. It was a story of two people whose careers, preferences, and/or obligations, meant more to them than their love for one another.

And now, just when he had finally secured a field assignment in Vietnam, what had he done but get entangled with lovely Maria. Undoubtedly, she had marriage in mind as well as children, especially given their passion for one another. His hopes would sink even deeper to win a second Pulitzer Prize for war reporting in such a situation. And could he survive emotionally from a possible second failure at love?

His late father's eyes were still upon him in his mind. Didn't he deserve to have a chance to prove his own worth to himself in his own way? Only then could he chance being burned once again, if he didn't live up to his own, or another's, expectations.

It was the wrong time, the wrong place. He and Maria must go their separate ways. He'd give his letter to Alex in the morning and ask him to deliver it to her at his first opportunity. Meantime, he intended to prolong his reporting up-country where he could do the job he had always intended to do, unhampered by the desires of others. Ready or not, he would make his mark on his way to winning a Pulitzer Prize.

Brand turned out the light and fell into a fitful sleep.

REBELS ALL

Mel R. Jones
Marian N. Jones

PART 3:
TWISTS AND TURNS
SOUTH VIETNAM, 1962

"General rebellions and revolts of a whole people never were encouraged, now or at any time. They are always provoked."
—Edmund Burke

27 BAO'S PLOT

Plots, true or false, are necessary things, to raise up commonwealths and ruin kings.

—John Dryden

CAPTAIN NGUYEN HUU BAO KNEW R-3 would be more than pleased that he had indeed been chosen to be the administrator of the Strategic Hamlet program under Counselor Nhu. It was exactly what R-3 had planned in his "chess match" with the Diem regime. Bao wished that he could be as enthusiastic as he knew R-3 would be with the news.

If the truth be told, Bao yearned to be back in his position as R-3's adjutant, rallying his comrades to their glorious cause. How he had reveled in their rapt attention to his every word in those rallies! R-3, unspoken and hidden away with his dark hood covering his face, had forfeited the open acclaim of the crowds in order to safeguard his identity.

But now Bao was the one set apart from his comrades. Although a double agent as before, now he must forfeit his participation in the world of his comrades, in contrast to R-3's mysterious façade that still allowed him to be part of the gathering of the faithful. There would be no accolades for Bao as R-3's adjutant anymore. Instead he was hated and reviled for deflecting to the enemy, supposedly for a higher position and rank. This perception was allowed by R-3 to convince the multitude of believers of his infidelity to the revolution. Now, too, he was tasked to deceive those in the Diem regime of his so called loyalty to them. His fate was to be a "silent hero," known only to R-3, whose authoritative restraint was the only thing standing between

Bao and the death threats from his former friends. Even though he was fulfilling a higher task for the cause, this wasn't his idea of glory.

Bao had been willing to give up his life for the revolution, but in return to have been exalted as a hero, not as now abhorred as a traitor. R-3 was almost asking too much of him. It would be R-3 who would eventually be hailed as the hero of the revolution in the South when they won the war. Bao though that if he were still alive when that happened, he would but ignominiously ride on R-3's coattails. But even so, he would always be viewed with suspicion.

Even R-3 wasn't sure of his loyalty. He had saddled Bao with the hateful Madame Binh as a dreaded watchdog, ready to kill him at any moment given the word, to make sure Bao was following orders. In some ways it was almost too much to bear.

Maybe he'd be better off dead, he lamented, but, no, then he'd no longer be comforted by the image of the lovely Madame Nhu when he happened to be in her presence. His daydreams of her were his only pleasure in his isolation from R-3 and his comrades. Her image soothed his sensibilities when forced to take the intolerable spy, Madame Binh, as his mistress.

It was a week after he had received confirmation of his new position in the Diem regime that he went to the American embassy to introduce himself to the American ambassador as administrator of the Strategic Hamlet program. Both the Americans and the Vietnamese had high hopes for this initiative.

Bao waited for his appointment time, but noticed a Vietnamese family that entered and seated themselves nearby. No doubt they also waited for an appointment with the ambassador. Bao recognized the Chief of Song Be Province, and surmised it was his wife and daughter who accompanied him. He watched the mother wring her hands and look nervously at her daughter. Bao decided to walk over and greet them, thinking it would ease their apparent tension.

"Sir, aren't you the Province Chief of Song Be and this your wife and daughter?"

"Indeed we are, and who might you be?"

"I am Captain Nguyen Huu Bao, newly appointed administrator of President Diem's Strategic Hamlet program. I'm here to introduce myself to the American ambassador. While I wait, I thought I might mention the new program to you to see if you're interested in participating in it."

"Yes, I've heard of this new plan and have not yet been informed as to how to set it up and administer it in my area."

Bao smiled and began expounding on the important new program: "Moving the peasants from their ancestral lands into a fortified hamlet to protect them from the communists needs much persuasion, or sometimes even force if necessary, but it is essential for their safety. They will build and defend the hamlets by themselves, but with training and supervision."

"Has President Diem considered resentment of the people?"

"The program is necessary, I'm afraid, as communist infiltration is increasing as we speak, and the need for protection from their subversive activities grows daily. We feel there's no time to waste to protect the population by building these fortified strategic hamlets."

"I suppose you're right," replied the province chief. "We are close to the Cambodian border in Song Be Province, and are aware of communist infiltrators from the Ho Chi Minh trail."

Both men stopped talking as the province chief's daughter moaned, became quite pale and looked like she was about to vomit. Her mother looked absolutely panicked. Bao jumped out of his chair and addressed the mother and daughter, saying he would be pleased to escort the two to the rest room. They left immediately as the daughter struggled to hold back her distress until she and her mother could get to the ladies room.

When Bao returned to speak to the province chief, he asked, "Is your daughter ill?"

The province chief looked down at his hands and hesitated. When he looked up he said, "It's really a personal, private matter, Captain, as to my daughter's distress, and why we're here to speak to the American ambassador."

'I'm sorry to intrude on your privacy. I just thought I might be able to help, as my new position with the Diem regime makes me so much more aware of the suffering of our people."

"You are kind to say that, Captain Bao, and I appreciate your concern about us. I must admit I am rather anxious about a very delicate matter."

"If you find you must discuss any such matter with President Diem, his brother Nhu or Madame Nhu, I can tell you that I see them almost daily and would be glad to inform them you need help with a private matter."

"I know President Diem very well. He appointed me as province chief himself. I intend to speak with him as well as the American ambassador."

Bao could see the father was beside himself with anxiety. He kept looking to the area of the rest rooms to see if his wife and daughter were returning. "My daughter has the most terrible, debilitating nausea. I'm very worried about her."

"Do you hope to get medical assistance from the Americans?"

"Yes, we are looking for assistance from the Americans, but it's not because we haven't already seen a Vietnamese doctor regarding my daughter's nausea."

'My goodness! It must be really serious then. I'm so sorry for your family and for your daughter."

"Thank you for your concern. I really shouldn't be speaking of private matters to you, but since you've already witnessed my daughter Lieu's distress, I should reassure you our doctor says her extreme nausea is due to pregnancy."

"Oh, what a relief to hear that news! It is a natural occurrence in the early stages of pregnancy, I'm told. I feared she was seriously ill. But surely your daughter's pregnancy has nothing to do with your seeking assistance from the Americans."

"But it is," replied the father, who slumped in his seat and put his head between his hands, concerned that his wife and daughter had not yet returned.

"I certainly respect your privacy, but I must admit it is quite a puzzle as to why the American ambassador needs to see you about problems with your daughter's nausea due to pregnancy, as distressing as it is for her and your family."

"But you're wrong, Captain Bao, her father said resuming an upright position. The father of my daughter's child is American!" the province chief blurted out.

"And where is the father?"

"That, I'm afraid, is the problem."

"Is he a military man who has rotated back to the States?"

"No, he's stationed in the Ca Mau Peninsula, and we want to see his wife and child reunited with him!"

"His wife! There shouldn't be a problem if she's his wife."

"She certainly is his wife. I delivered her to him under the Gia Long Code."

"Oh, my! Does he understand that your daughter is legally his wife despite how ancient the Gia Long Code is?"

"That's another part of the problem."

"How did this American happen to be in Song Be Province if he is stationed in the Ca Mau Peninsula?"

"He was first assigned to Song Be Province when he asked for my daughter's hand in marriage upon his arrival. She spent their wedding night with him, not knowing he had reassignment orders. He told us about it the next morning before he left, and we haven't heard from him since."

"And he hasn't made any provision for his Vietnamese wife?"

"No! And he doesn't even know that Lieu is pregnant. We are afraid he had no intention of acknowledging his marriage, nor providing for his wife. And now she is with child!"

"This is a serious problem! Are you at liberty to mention the name of this negligent husband, and now a father-to-be?"

"He comes from a prominent American family with a very famous father, Senator Thomas Kearney, Sr."

"You don't say. That does elevate the problem to a whole new level. You do need to see the American ambassador."

"We are here to insist that Lieu's American husband take the necessary measures to reunite with his wife and make provision for her and her baby."

"Would you like me to give notice to President Diem about your dilemma before you meet with him? He can get a head start on seeing how to give you and your family whatever help he can."

"That won't be necessary. We will be meeting with President Diem next, but thank you for your offer of help. We do wish to resolve this problem in a private and quiet way. Please respect our privacy with the information we have given you regarding our difficulty."

"Of course."

They both looked up as the province chief's wife and daughter returned. Just then Bao was called for his meeting with the ambassador. He told the providence chief and his family to contact him if he could be of assistance to them and bid them farewell. As he left them, he saw that Lieu didn't look much better since her trip to the rest room and appeared as if she needed to return again.

After his introduction to the American ambassador, Bao left the embassy. He couldn't stop thinking about how he would love to ingratiate himself to Madame Nhu by passing on to her the private information he had learned. It would certainly fuel her feminist crusade. Indeed, his support for her causes might make him look like a kind of hero in her eyes, fulfilling his own desires for a new kind of glory to replace his prominence as former adjutant so recently denied to him by R-3. In fact, in this city of intrigues, Bao never had dreamed such a golden opportunity would fall into his lap to enhance his status, perhaps not with R-3, but with Madame Nhu.

If I'm very careful, Bao thought, I can figure out how this information will affect each of them, what their reactions will be, and what will be the outcome. But I must be careful of R-3, who likes to control everything himself and of the she-cat, Madame Binh, whose slanted eyes see everything, and carries any "prey" she catches back to R-3 via the curio shop.

He imagined his encounter with Madame Nhu in a daydream:

> Madame Nhu would smile at him as he approached her in the giant main hall of the alternate Gia Long Palace with its high ceilings and whirling fans. Bao knew she could tell by his countenance that he was captivated by her person. Bao imagined her standing before him with her long black hair piled high on her head as her wispy bangs fell on her forehead. How his one good eye would relish the sight of her white silk *ao dai*, which hugged her well-proportioned figure. She would touch her cheek to show off her fingers with long, polished Mandarin-style nails, noticing the effect on Bao.
>
> "Come, let us sit," she would say as she led him to two big, overstuffed chairs in the middle of the hall. He could almost hear her first words to him in his mind: "It's a pleasure to see you once again, Captain Bao, but any questions you might have about the Strategic Hamlet program can be answered much better by my husband."
>
> "It's you I wish to converse with, lovely lady," Bao would answer. "I've come across information that will bring world-wide attention to your righteous cause of Vietnamese family and Morality Laws."

Bao could just imagine the rapt attention that would spring to life in her eyes.

"Please share it with me, Captain," she would say with an inviting smile upon her lips.

He would then divulge the private information he was privy to, but had promised to keep to himself: "I have met the Province Chief of Song Be, his wife and daughter at the American embassy as they waited for their appointment with the American ambassador," he would begin.

"Yes, he is an appointee of President Diem. What was he doing at the American embassy?" Madame Nhu would ask.

Although he had promised to respect the privacy of the matter, he knew he would nevertheless disregard it to promote his own agenda. He would reply, "I spoke with the province chief and learned of his family predicament regarding their daughter. You see, U.S. Senator Thomas Kearney, Sr., who is currently visiting Vietnam on a fact-finding mission, has a son who is a lieutenant in the U.S. Army stationed in the Ca Mau Peninsula."

"What is your point?" Madame Nhu would ask.

Now Bao could enlighten Madame Nhu to a matter that would touch her feminist heart. He would go on to say, "Lieutenant Kearney, Jr., first was assigned to Song Be for his tour of duty. He was so taken by the beauty of the province chief's daughter that he asked her father for her hand in marriage citing the Gia Long Code. The father complied and presented his daughter in marriage to the young man. The couple consummated the marriage that same night. But the next morning Lieutenant Kearney reveled he had re-assignment orders to Ca Mau Peninsula. He left that day, leaving behind his Vietnamese wife and her family in distress. The lieutenant's wife discovered not too long after his abrupt departure that she was pregnant with his child. Her parents are here to insist, in accordance with the Gia Long Code, that Lieutenant Kearney reunite with and make provision for his wife with child."

Bao could envision the beautiful Madame Nhu rising from her chair in indignation. "Another Vietnamese woman deprived of her rights!" she would cry out. "You must see, Captain Bao, why the family laws passed in 1958 are essential to protect Vietnamese women! They need to be enforced. But this time it's not a violation by a Vietnamese male, but one committed by the son of a prominent U.S. Senator! The Gia Long Code may be ancient, but it is Vietnamese law! And the marriage was sanctioned by her father, a province chief! It illustrates why we struggle for the decent treatment of women in Vietnam and have Morality Laws as well!" Madame Nhu would exclaim.

Captain Bao brought his mind back from his vision of Madame Nhu's animated loveliness and imagined his reply, "You will be vindicated in your crusade. And if the American press gets wind of this situation, you will have a world-wide audience to applaud your work to improve living conditions for women in Vietnam!"

The beauty of her smile would bathe him in warmth as she would reply, "How can I thank you enough, Captain Bao, for bringing this important information to me? The province chief's fatherly predicament regarding his daughter is an example of the crucial need to support Vietnamese women in a society dominated by men. I will inform President Diem and my husband of this situation immediately and ask them to send for the province chief and his family to meet with the President when they've concluded their meeting at the American embassy."

Bao could barely bring his imagined encounter with Madame Nhu to an end as he saw himself saying, "Very good, Madame. Please let me know if I can be of further assistance in any way."

But Bao would know that he had made a lasting impression upon the Vietnamese beauty he so admired. She would then say, "You've been such a help for a cause dear to my heart. Good day, Captain."

Captain Bao smiled. It would not take long for the outspoken Madame Nhu to bring attention to the information he had imparted to her in his daydream to inform very important people.

He would have pleased Madame Nhu by giving her fodder for her feminist crusade and her Morality Laws that some had previously sneered at and had outraged others.

But he must consider such an action from all angles to protect himself before he actually decided to make it a reality.

Bao believed R-3 would be pleased about further angst between Diem and the U.S. Madame Nhu would be sure to foster more hatred for the Diem regime by publicizing her unpopular cause. In this case, it would embarrass their U.S. ally with the scandal of a visiting U.S. senator and his son stationed in Vietnam, causing yet another controversy in their alliance.

In the wake of press publicity, Senator Kearney would push even more for a U.S. pullout from Vietnam when the Diem regime brings to light, through Madame Nhu, the news of a U.S. official's son trying to renege on his lawful Vietnamese marriage. The Western press would undoubtedly become involved and would assure world-wide attention to the scandal. Weakening the commitment of Diem's ally could only enhance the communist agenda and bring an enthusiastic response from R-3, he thought.

Should Bao actually take action with his scheme, he imagined it would give him a sense of pride and control of his own. Yes, he thought, even R-3 couldn't have come up with such a clever, far-reaching, complex and effective plot.

In fact, Bao thought, R-3's rival, Le Duan, in Hanoi, might look more favorably on Bao should R-3 ever fall out of favor with the North. Hadn't Bao been trained as R-3's right-hand man with extensive experience in all sectors, and was now in a position of trust in Diem's regime? Bao calculated that he was a logical choice to take over communist leadership in South Vietnam, if the need ever arose. Not an impossible occurrence, Bao thought. And in such an event, how he would rejoice to do away with the hated, tight-fisted control of Madame Binh!

But then, Bao reconsidered. R-3 might not be pleased if Bao went through with his scheme on his own. It might even result in his elimination by R-3's henchmen. R-3 demanded complete control of all activities in the south that he first coordinated with Hanoi.

But perhaps R-3's control could be circumvented in this matter, Bao thought, because of Bao's newly acquired position in the Diem regime. R-3 wouldn't want to lose the opportunity of using Bao to sabotage the Strategic Hamlet program. This fact could save him from elimination if R-3 ever discovered his part in the plot he had in mind. If he had to die, it would be with hero status, at least to someone he admired, he vowed. But when the communists took down the Diem regime, he would have no safeguard against elimination. Despite the risks, he decided to act on his scheme. How he needed the glory no longer enjoyed!

"What's up, Dad? Have Lieu and her parents arrived in Saigon yet?" asked Tank, Jr., as he sat down next to the senator at the Caravelle Hotel bar.

"Hell, if I didn't know better I'd think we've been entangled in a plot unfolding like clockwork to sabotage us!"

"What do you mean?" asked Tank, Jr.

"I was assured by the American ambassador that he would keep the problem of your pregnant Vietnamese wife a private matter until we can iron things out. But, damn, if somehow Madame Nhu hasn't gotten wind of it and is up on her soapbox championing women's rights with the American press. Your case with Lieu is in print for world-wide publication!"

"My God, I'm finished!" lamented Kearney, Jr.

"Well, there's more."

"God, no!" replied the lieutenant. "What could be worse?"

"General Pavler has re-assigned you back to Song Be, where there's no replacement for you yet, to live with your pregnant wife to remedy the situation. He attributes the predicament to original military re-assignment orders lacking timely notification of your marriage. You'll be redeemed as a shining example of respect for Vietnamese family and Morality Laws by the U.S. military," explained the irate senator.

"Holy shit! The whole hierarchy is lined up against me! How could this have happened?" bellowed the younger Kearney.

"Hold your voice down, son. Let's not give this mess any more publicity than it's gotten already. Someone is out to humiliate the Kearney name, and I won't stop until I find out who and exact our revenge!"

"Is it that drunken reporter for the *Times*, Winston Brand?"

"No, it's unlikely. I gave him a piece of my mind when we arrived, but now he's up-country doing field reporting," grunted Kearney, Sr., as he bit down on his cigar.

"Damn the luck! It would've been such a pleasure to sink his boat and send him packing back to the States," the younger Kearney said with dashed hopes.

"That's what I was planning to do while in Vietnam, son, but now it looks like we've got more than a sex-starved drunkard to deal with. I've got the feeling someone more sinister is using us to influence public opinion by taking advantage of a weakness in our family armor."

"I could kick myself for my stupidity, Dad. Your unheeded warning about being careful as a senator's son is coming home to scuttle our ship instead of Brand's."

"We're out of options for the time being, son. Madame Nhu's family laws prohibit divorce in Vietnam. So we might have to wait until your tour of duty ends here and obtain a divorce when you rotate back to the States. Meanwhile, I'll see if anyone in the CIA can find out who has targeted us."

"Are you saying I'm actually Lieu's husband, Dad?"

"Yes. For the time being, son, you'll have to obey your new orders and move back to Song Be and live with your pregnant Vietnamese wife. Meanwhile, I'll have to face the Simone family and the fallout among my constituents in Massachusetts."

"And what about me, Dad? I'm supposed to live with Lieu and remain faithful to her as she gets bigger and bigger during her pregnancy? I'll go crazy without women on the side with her family looking down my nose!"

"Son, work with me on this. Then, again, who knows what might turn up for you in Song Be? I know you want your freedom back, but Kearneys don't give up, and we always get revenge for being humiliated and used!"

R-3's aide, greatly agitated, appeared at the door during his master's evening meal. R-3 looked up. "You know I forbid being interrupted during my meals unless it's an emergency." He glanced angrily at his aide.

"Forgive me, sir. I will wait with the disturbing news I have for you until you have finished."

"What is it then? It better be an emergency!"

"Sir, the Western press has spread the news of Senator Kearney's son's reneging on his marriage to a Vietnamese woman, who is pregnant with his child."

"How did the press get the news? I was told the American embassy would keep this a private matter."

"Madame Nhu is championing the rights of Vietnamese women under the family laws with the press as her audience. She cites the American senator's son as guilty of the abuse family laws are designed to stop."

R-3 cursed! He urgently needed more time for the training of his soldiers on the stolen American radios to take place and then a quiet time so newly trained Vietnamese operators and the radios could stealthily be placed in strategic positions for the next phase of the upcoming armed struggle. But someone had acted without orders to provoke an uproar in the press sure to cause trouble between U.S. and the Diem regime. Who had stirred the pot and turned up the heat when R-3 needed it to simmer on the back burner for the time being?

There was a wild card at play, causing a major, premature disturbance in the overall plan he had coordinated with Hanoi. What's more, someone had wrested control of the situation in this matter from him! No doubt Le Duan in the north would point out the deviated plan to Ho Chi Minh and General Giap, throwing doubt on R-3's ability to control matters in the south.

No longer hungry for his meal, R-3 left the table and brought out his writing tablet. He would write to his new adjutant in the field to start an investigation into who was trying to wrest control from him. Without any connection to Hanoi, any political sense, or adequate intelligence to know his place, the rebel did not have much time to prolong his life.

R-3 placed his message in the hidden compartment of a travel chess set with instructions for it to be delivered to the adjutant through the curio shop. Another set contained special instructions for Madame Binh's watchful eye. If the investigation into the identity of the would-be-usurper turned out to be, as he suspected, Captain Bao, Madame Binh would soon discover his treachery.

But Bao would be difficult to eliminate, entrenched as he now was in the Diem regime and its Strategic Hamlet program, and especially with Madame Nhu. Perhaps the fear of death from Madame Binh would bring Bao back in line.

28 THE GOOD MEDICINE MAN

I cannot go to cure the body of my patient but I forget my profession and call unto God for his soul.
—*Sir Thomas Browne, Religio Medici*

BRAND WONDERED WHAT he had gotten himself into when he agreed to accompany Doctor Jenicoso to Quang Ngai Province. No sooner had they landed at Quang Ngai's dusty airport with its dirt runway and disembarked, than they were notified a message awaited Dr. Jenicoso that Dr. Kalverton was away on a medical emergency. What's more there was an urgent call for medical help for some wounded Americans up at Ba Tat. Dr. Jennicoso was soon off to offer his medical assistance. Brand lingered at the Quang Ngai Province Hospital, thwarted in his anticipated interview with Dr. Kalverton.

Then Brand saw a scene that captured his attention. Coming up the dusty road that led to the hospital's main entrance came a man who looked like a tired, white Gungha Din with a goat skin water bag slung across his shoulder. His thin, bony legs wobbled within the narrow confines of his walking shorts.

Brand watched as the man occasionally whirled around in the dust to give instructions to two old Montagnard men carrying something in a blanket. They followed closely on the heels of whom Brand guessed was the medical missionary. The doctor made good time despite these frequent stops. Without saying a word, the doctor shot past Brand and into the hospital. Shortly his red bandana-covered head reappeared in the doorway.

"Sir, would you happen to know if Dr. Jenicoso has arrived yet? We've got a seriously injured lad here."

"Sorry," Brand replied. "Dr. Jenicoso just left to treat some wounded up at Ba Tat."

"I was hoping for some help, but I'll have to do the surgery by myself. Please give the men a hand with the boy."

A puppy-like whimper directed Brand's attention to the blanket, held between the tribesmen hammock-style. The boy lay face-up, and Brand noticed his dark skinned features. As Brand helped support the sagging center of the blanket, he saw the massive opening in the child's lower abdomen and groin. More blood emerged to soak a temporary bandage used to stem the flow than Brand thought possible from such a frail creature. But the child only whimpered.

Inside the hospital, the old missionary hovered over two Vietnamese nurses who were arranging surgical instruments on a wooden bench. He had changed to a threadbare, white gown. On his thin frame, it hung like a woman's muu. He pointed to a spot on the bench.

"Here," he said, "put him here. Gently now, gently. The poor darling hurts all over from his wound. Thank you, sir. Now could you get an orderly in here with some whole blood? Not much time. The lad's pulse is very weak."

In one of the corridors, Brand spied a Vietnamese youth in a white jacket sneaking a puff from an American made cigarette.

"You're wanted in surgery immediately," Brand admonished the youth. "And take with you beaucoup blood."

"Okay, okay, I go." He nonchalantly snipped the fire from his cigarette and placed the butt in his jacket pocket. "But no take blood for savage boy. 'Plecious' blood not for him. I see them bring him here, very bad shape. He die soon. Old doctor clazy, all time want give 'plecious' blood to savage people."

"You go now! Take blood chop, chop, or I'll spill your 'plecious' blood in this hallway," Brand threatened, shaking his fist in the youth's direction.

The youth ran down the corridor toward the blood bank, cursing all the ugly Americans he had ever known.

This bitter exchange with the orderly left Brand disgruntled, and since the doctor would be tied up in surgery, he decided to get some fresh air. His appearance outdoors caused a soup-vendor to leave his station under a palm tree.

"Sup?" The vendor offered Brand a bowl of what appeared to be fermented fish with noodles.

"No thanks," replied Brand.

"Good chicken sup," the Vietnamese man insisted.

"You've got to be joking!" Brand looked incredulous.

"No understand, 'Melican.'"

"I'm not hungry." Brand rubbed his abdomen to indicate it bulged with food when actually he hadn't eaten since breakfast.

"Okay, okay." The soup vendor turned to leave.

"Wait. Inside hospital. Two Montagnards. Maybe hungry. You take soup; give them. I pay you now. Okay?"

"Okay, okay."

Brand paid him five piasters. The vendor left managing his two-wheeled soup cart in front of him with about as much haste as a woman pushing a baby buggy on a hot 4th of July day.

Brand knew the vendor couldn't be trusted to deliver the soup to the tribesmen. Because they were Montagnards, he'd probably pocket the money with a clear Vietnamese conscience. Damn these people anyway. The Vietnamese refused to accept the Montagnard as a member of the human race.

Brand took the soup vendor's place under the palm tree and opened his notebook. He wanted to write down notes for his column from the field. Brand began to write:

> The orderly considered the Montagnards as nothing more than savages, and there is no doubt even the dirty soup peddler regarded himself above the proud Montagnards just because he was Vietnamese. These two ethnic groups have been at each other's throats for centuries. More than one American advisor, I'm told, has reached the point of total frustration while trying to work out a reconciliation.

Brand closed his notebook in disgust and decided he would write more about this situation after his interview with Dr. Kalverton. But it wasn't until evening that both Dr. Kalverton and Dr. Jenicoso returned to the American compound in Quang Ngai City for dinner. Although both gentlemen were extremely fatigued from attending to their medical emergencies during the day, they seemed open to discussing the prejudice of the Vietnamese toward the Montagnards.

After sharing his encounters with the orderly and the soup peddler, Brand continued with his observations, "Tragically enough, the orderly and soup peddler reflect the mainstream of South Vietnamese thinking in this matter, as I remember from my time in Vietnam in 1954."

"Yes, replied Dr. Kalverton. "To the Vietnamese the Montagnard is the savage, whom they call *moi*, that roams the jungle clad only in loin cloth, shooting game with a cross bow in order to bring food and shelter to his bare-breasted wives and naked children. He is the ugly child of God to the Vietnamese, a pigmy with rotten teeth and huge feet and toes spread nearly an inch apart. He is to be ignored, ridiculed, exploited or extinguished."

"Believe me, the Vietnamese have never treated them with tenderness, or love, as you, Dr. Kalverton, treat all your patients, regardless of race, color or creed. It's easy for anyone to see that to you, my old friend, the Mongagnard is first a human being, a child of God."

"As they are. But what I really need is more help to adequately take care of their great medical need. I can only hope to get even one more doctor present to help me in my task."

"Believe me, I'd be glad to join you if I can get military orders to do so. At best, if I'm assigned here, I'd only be available part-time after treating American military wounded."

Brand broke into the conversation, "Good doctors, I'd like to know more about the Montagnards. Can you shed any more light on their plight I could use for my column in the *Times*?"

Dr. Kalverton replied, "Well, to go back to the beginning, there are several different stories of their origin, but I was told the Montagnards originally settled in the coastal areas, but were driven to the uninhabited mountains before the ninth century by invasions of the Vietnamese and Cambodians."

"Believe me, they probably came by sea at first, and that's why they settled on the coast. They seem to be of Polynesian or Indonesian extractions, because the Montagnards don't have Mongol characteristics like the Vietnamese. They are handsome people, but their habit of filing their teeth certainly doesn't enhance their looks to Westerners."

Dr. Kalverton chimed in, "And what a multitude of languages these highlanders speak, consisting of many Austroasiatic and Chamic languages! It's estimated that roughly one million of these ethnic tribe members occupy at least half of South Vietnam in its Central Highlands."

Brand exclaimed, "What a huge risk for the Diem government if it ignores that many people! Despite the apparent apathy the Vietnamese feel toward the Montagnards and their primitive practices, these same little creatures they call savages potentially hold an important key to their nation's survival."

"Believe me, I think I know what you're going to say."

Brand smiled at his friend, then continued, "It's not hard to imagine that the Viet Cong exploit the Mongagnards as simple, but reliable pawns in their intense struggle to enslave people."

"Right you are, Winston," remarked Dr. Kalverton. "Living as he does in a primitive state, scorned and mistrusted by those who rule his land, the Montagnards are an ideal target for communist propaganda and fear tactics.

"His highland village provides an inaccessible hideout for communist terrorists, and his abundant rice crops can easily be taken to feed a guerilla force. Young Montagnards are fierce fighters often persuaded, or kidnapped to fight for them."

Brand remembered Alex's captured Viet Cong document. The communist propagandist-author had written:

> In South Vietnam the U.S.-Diem clique does not bring any aid to the people...Sometimes they let hundreds of Montagnards die in epidemics. They want Montagnards to be exterminated little by little.

"Has the Diem government had any success in protecting the Montagnards within their recent Strategic Hamlet program?" asked Brand. "I've been told their nomadic custom is one of 'slash and burn' in which they clear a favorable spot in the mountains and farm it for a few years until it is no longer fertile. Then they move on to find another spot and repeat the process until they have to move on again. How would the Montagnards adapt to a single protected spot with surrounding rice fields that receive fertilizer so they don't have to keep moving?"

"We'll have to wait and see," said Dr. Kalverton.

"Are there any local stories about the Strategic Hamlet program in the Quang Ngai area that you know about?"

"Yes, although the initiative is in its infancy, the American advisor to the Quang Ngai Province Chief seems especially enthusiastic about helping the peasants.

Brand's eyes lit up. "Would you be able to introduce me to this American advisor and his province chief for an interview?"

"Why, yes. The American advisor, Maj. Jake Ireland, is sitting at a table across the room. I'll introduce him to you."

"Believe me, what an interview opportunity for you!"

Dr. Kalverton got up from the table and walked over talk to the American military advisor. He explained Winston's interest in interviewing the advisor about his plans and progress with the Strategic Hamlet program. The advisor got up from his table and accompanied Dr. Kalverton across the room. After being introduced, the advisor sat down at their table and described their successful early start.

The major explained, "Our program started with the construction of pig sties, then a follow-up with the eradication of rats which eat 85 percent of the single rice crop each year. We then introduced fertilization of the rice crops to produce two crops instead of one. I also had to obtain funding to enclose the hamlets in barbed wire to help keep out the Viet Cong, yet allow the peasants to remain in their villages close to their rice fields. Perhaps by next year these projects will have come into full fruition. All parties seem pleased and hopeful so far. If you like, Winston, you can visit the strategic hamlets-in-the-making tomorrow with me."

"Thanks, Major Ireland, that's just the kind of upbeat interview I'm looking for to report in my column."

At this point a young Vietnamese girl approached the table and bowed, wanting to get the attention of the American advisor. Brand was reminded of the peanut girl in Saigon who had thrown a grenade into the bar in order to kill him. He drew back in alarm and winced.

Ireland saw Brand's reaction and was quick to reassure him that eight-year-old Kim Chi was his ward, but wasn't supposed to enter the American dining room unescorted. He spoke to the young girl in Vietnamese, then apologized for her interruption.

"Kim Chi is most concerned that some local boys have stolen her peanuts she always sells. I told her she doesn't have to worry about making her living like that anymore because of my support, but she still persists. Her parents were killed in a Viet Cong attack, and she lost her left arm below the elbow in that assault. For the time being, she lives with a Vietnamese family while I look into the process to adopt her."

Dr. Jenicoso took an immediate interest in the child. He asked if he could look at her injury site and asked about her pain, but the young girl shied away in fear from his kindly offer to examine her and began to cry.

The advisor reassured the girl that Jenicoso was a doctor. Then he explained to Dr. Jenicoso, "The village children tease her about the raw bone left there, sticking out of her sleeve like a turkey leg, when a portion of her arm was shot away. I'm sure you can understand her upsetting reaction."

"No need to apologize, Major. But it's entirely possible that I could perform surgery to ease her pain, and when the surgical site has healed, a prosthetic arm could be ordered for her," replied Dr. Jenicoso as he smiled at the young girl. Dr. Kalverton nodded in agreement.

"What a blessing that would be for her! I will share your explanation with her and your offer of undergoing the surgery in preparation for a new arm afterwards. She'll need quite a bit of reassurance, but I'd like to schedule an appointment for you to examine her at the hospital," said the major with hopeful excitement in his voice.

"Yes, by all means do so. I plan to be here a bit longer attending the wounded from the fighting at Ba Tat."

The major looked delighted and said he would make inquiries about the procedure at the hospital. After inviting Brand to visit him for a tour of the strategic hamlets the next day, the major expressed his appreciation to Dr. Jenicoso for his offer, and he and his ward left the dining room.

"Looks like we'll all be busy tomorrow," said Dr. Jenicoso. Dr. Kalverton agreed and said he wanted to check on the Montagnard boy again, while Brand remarked he wanted to go to his quarters, take some notes and get some key questions ready for his on-site interview with the major tomorrow.

"Believe me, I think I can make quite a difference in that little Vietnamese girl's life if we can allay her fears and get through the red tape to schedule her surgery," enthused Nick Jenicoso.

"That's another good will story I'd certainly like to cover, Nick, if all goes well," remarked Brand. "There's a lot of positive work going on in Quang Ngai. It'll be a relief to the readers of my column to take a break from the bleak reports of the Saigon journalists, to know about the good being done out here in the Vietnamese countryside!"

29 OPERATION CHECKMATE

He that wrestles with us strengthens our nerves and sharpens our skill. Our antagonist is our helper.

—Edmund Burke

GEN. GEORGE PAVLER BEGAN, "This meeting of the six members of the executive committee of Operation Checkmate has been called to consider several concerns on our agenda. But before we get started, let me welcome back Major Spear, who has recovered from a rat bite and several weeks of preventative rabies treatment at Nha Trang Hospital. Welcome back, Alex."

"Thank you, General. I'm happy to report I've been given a clean bill of health and cleared to be back on our mission."

"Excellent! Perhaps you found some diversion with a purchased portable chess set delivered to you by friends."

"Yes, sir. I appreciate the thought. I had enough time on my hands to examine the set closely, and oddly enough, I came upon a securely hidden compartment in it after much probing when I discerned a thickness not accounted for by the design of the set. The hidden compartment was empty, but it occurred to me that messages could be transferred in it with no one the wiser. Where was it purchased, General?"

"I see your intelligence mind is ever at work, Major. The chess set was obtained at the Curio Shop on Tu Do Street."

"The shop bears watching for any suspicious activity."

"Good idea. I'll look into it. In the meantime, now that you're back, Major, I want to ask you if you have had any further thoughts about the situation at Loc Ninh?"

"I assume, General, you're looking for information that can't be proven at this point. I asked myself, if I were in the shoes of the unidentified communist operative, R-3, what is the purpose for the stolen American radios? The obvious answer is to interrupt our ability to communicate, but is there a much more extensive and sinister plot afoot coordinated with Hanoi?"

"We've considered several different scenarios regarding the stolen radios, too, Major. What did you come up with?"

"I wonder if there is a connection between several isolated, negative incidents but with one common element at the center of these recent disturbances. If so, it might be at the heart of our adversary's plan. Remember, R-3 moves like a master chess player would in a high stakes chess game."

Alex noted the heightened interest in the eyes of the general and his fellow committee members and continued, "Both incidents involve our communications system and the one we share with that of the South Vietnamese military. The first serious loss started with the possible abduction of two missing military transport planes that left Travis Air Force Base for South Vietnam. These two military transport planes carried mainly communications specialists."

The air force colonel interrupted, "Yes, Major, but we have no proof whatsoever of what happened to those two missing planes. They could have been sabotaged and gone down in the Pacific, accomplishing the same result of interrupting our communications operations."

"True, that's the obvious assumption the communists would want us to make. But what if there's more to it?"

"You're suggesting, Major, this mastermind chess player has a larger coordinated plan," said the senior naval officer.

"Ask yourselves, is there a possible connection between abducted American communications specialists, and now the loss of 30 stolen American radios? If we put the two together, we have a golden opportunity for the communists to have the captured American communication specialists train selected soldiers to operate the stolen American radios. What a devious plan to use against us utilizing our own people and equipment! They could create unlimited havoc in all our operations!"

The army colonel replied in alarm, "They could listen in on our communications to all our military advisors in the field and the South Vietnamese military forces they advise. Crucial intelligence about our plans would be easy to discern so they could counteract any South Vietnamese military moves."

"That's not all. There could be even more dire results."

"And that would be?" asked General Pavler.

"What if the Viet Cong use the U.S. radios with their now trained communist communication specialists to give false or confusing orders over the network to ARVN soldiers in battle, resulting in chaotic defensive, or offensive, operations? ARVN fighters would be at a severe disadvantage with false orders, sabotaged plans, and a chaotic situation in the field and could be easily defeated. The body count wouldn't be Viet Cong, but South Vietnamese with accompanying American military advisors."

"Oh, my God," responded one of the field grade officers.

General Pavler replied, "This possible scenario you've described takes our previous considerations regarding the stolen radios to a new level, Major. The two losses of communications personnel combined with the theft of 30 radios could indicate a more comprehensive plan devised by a diabolical strategist. We'll have to consider taking preventative measures."

"What are our chances of recovering our radios and possibly our communications specialists?" asked the army colonel.

General Pavler nodded to Alex to answer the question. "As of this moment, we don't know the location of either of these elements of a possible plan. But if I were to guess, the American communication specialists are in captivity in Hanoi. I think the radios are secured in South Vietnam near Loc Ninh, or possibly just across the border in Cambodia. Now R-3, in coordination with Hanoi, must bring the two together secretly. Cambodia would be the best place to do so. It is the closest place to transport the radios without detection and the most secure place to bring the American communications specialists being sent down from Hanoi on the Ho Chi Minh trail. Should any one of the American specialists escape on the way, however, this is where their plan would be the most vulnerable."

General Pavler responded, "Triple canopy jungle near Loc Ninh would make aerial observation impossible. Then, too, Head of

State, Prince Sihanouk of Cambodia, wouldn't tolerate an invasive operation across the border with no proof.

The navy captain remarked, "If your intuitions are correct, Major, we've been outsmarted by a mastermind on the chess board without any way to verify it at present."

Alex responded, "I think *Bon Sejour* is not a place of 'good stay,' as its name implies, but is actually an active player on the communist chess board. It is very possible that the plantation is a cell in the communist network. I would like to return and conduct a further investigation with the help of Lt. Rafe Hewlett, the military advisor at Loc Ninh nearby.

"It seems to me that the barn at *Bon Sejour* was burned too quickly after I emerged with the intelligence I gathered within it. There must have been something more to find, especially with the radio antenna rigged in the loft. I suspect the overseer, Mr. Ly, convinced Monsieur Devereau to order it burned so fast, ostensibly citing safety issues, to keep us from finding even more incriminating evidence."

General Pavler responded, "Well, Major, we will send you back to Loch Ninh then. Let's see if you and Lieutenant Hewlett come up with any evidence to support your conjecture. In the meantime, I'll contact the officer in charge to begin a plan to encode our communications network and that of the South Vietnamese before any more fighting occurs. However, this might entail a tremendous amount of work with much resistance based on supposition. The Vietnamese might refuse to do it without proof.

"Also, I'll notify the American and ARVN Special Forces training the Montagnards in the mountains to be on the lookout to detect any unusual movement on the Ho Chi Minh trail near the Laos and Cambodian borders."

Major Spear reiterated, "Supposition or not, we are on the defensive against the expressed and determined aggressiveness of North Vietnam toward our South Vietnamese ally. To wait for proof may be disastrous, just as my rat bite could have been fatal if I had waited for the lab report before instituting the rabies prevention protocol. It would have been too late by then if the rat had actually had rabies. The preliminary steps General Pavler has outlined will help us to be alert and prepared for a scenario I certainly hope will never play out."

"Your intuitions about the connection of these disrupting events is plausible, Major Spear, and we're glad to have a chess player with your experience in the game on our team."

"Thank you, sir. I couldn't imagine a better team leader than you, and I'm sure my fellow committee members feel the same way," replied Alex as the others nodded.

General Pavler continued the meeting by bringing up the second concern on the agenda. "As you know, Senator Thomas Kearney, Sr., is currently in country with his fact-finding commission authorized by President Kennedy. Unexpectedly, the senator has encountered quite a press storm regarding his son, Lt. Tank Kearney, Jr., who has been discovered trying to renege on his marriage to the daughter of the Vietnamese Province Chief of Song Be in violation of Vietnamese family laws.

"Despite the senator's hands being tied up with this development, he is still looking into Operation Checkmate, hoping to disband it without knowing our true purpose. We believe his motive is to get revenge on the *Times* foreign correspondent, Winston Brand, whom he believes is a member."

"What makes Senator Kearney think Winston Brand is a member of our committee, General?" asked the army colonel.

"Unbeknownst to Mr. Brand, we carry him on paper as an affiliate to protect him from the petty personal revenge of the Kearney father and son. Checkmate limits Senator Kearny's ability to put pressure on authority figures for Brand's removal from the country."

"Why are we protecting Mr. Brand, and what are the supposed allegations Senator Kearney holds against this reporter?" asked another committee member.

"We believe Brand inadvertently can aid our investigation, but Senator Kearney wants Brand sent home in disgrace, banned as a drunken example to our servicemen for a drinking episode in Hawaii during a layover of one our military transport planes."

"I've heard rumors that Brand does have a past drinking problem. Why are we endangering our operation by supporting a reporter we can't trust?" asked the air force colonel.

"Winston Brand has discussed this situation with me as a personal acquaintance of his family. He has given me his solemn promise that he'll stop drinking for at least 30 days and hopefully thereafter while in Vietnam. But when asked, he vehemently objected to being included as an affiliate of Operation Checkmate, because of his objective status as a reporter. However, we have unofficially listed him as off limits to deflect Kearney's personal vendetta. This is contingent, of course, on Brand's ability to live up to his promise. If he fails, our support of him will be withdrawn."

"Is this a personal decision of yours, General?"

"There's ample evidence Brand is dedicated to discovering the truth in his reporting. This has been a well-known trait of his reflected in his columns over the years. If he can stay sober, we believe he will be very instrumental in helping to uncover R-3 merely as Winston travels throughout South Vietnam to report on the stories he finds. Just by doing his job, he has a perfect cover to deflect suspicion of the enemy. But his findings can benefit military intelligence. However, these journalistic activities may make him a target for R-3.

"Getting back to Senator Kearney, his habitual revenge motivation is stirring even deeper waters. He has asked the CIA to investigate who learned about his son's situation and tipped off the press. He has suspicions it was done with a calculated intent to dishonor his family. We wonder if this investigation will lead us back to a communist attempt to poison the water between the Diem regime and its U.S. ally. We already know Senator Kearney's wants to get the U.S. out of South Vietnam."

"Could Winston Brand be involved in this press disclosure to get his own revenge on the Kearneys for threatening his position in Vietnam?" asked the senior naval officer.

"Brand is up-country at the moment reporting in the field and may know nothing about the Kearney ruckus. His is a lucky escape from this latest blip in the allies' relationship.

"I just wanted to alert the committee to the possibility that Senator Kearney may contact you with questions about Operation Checkmate while he is here. I assure you that Senator Kearney can't succeed in disbanding our top-secret intelligence gathering group. We are outside normal intelligence channels and exempt from Congressional oversight."

General Pavler dismissed the group of field grade officers, but he asked Major Spear to remain regarding a personal matter. Alex looked worried as he approached him. "It's nothing bad, Alex. In fact, it's going to make your day!"

"Then I can't wait to hear it, sir."

"I've received word from my wife Norma living in the Philippines that your wife Gwen and your children are staying with her, and she is helping them look for suitable quarters."

"That really does make my day, sir. I appreciate your wife's support for my family, and the anticipation of a reunion with them is overwhelming!"

"I know you can't wait to see them, Alex, but I must send you to Loc Ninh first to follow up on the stolen radios and their possible connection to the missing communications specialists in the scenario you described. We've already lost more than the two weeks of your recovery time from the rat bite since the radios were stolen."

"I can't say I'm not disappointed, General. If it were up to me, I'd take the first available flight out to the Philippines. But I'm comforted by the thought that Gwen can count on the gracious help of your wife."

"I'll be sure to give you leave to see your family when you return from Loc Ninh, Alex," promised General Pavler.

"That's something to really look forward to! I appreciate your offer more than you know. By the way, General, Winston gave me a letter for Maria Monclova to give to her when I returned to Saigon. But since her flight doesn't come in until Thursday when I'll be in Loc Ninh, I wonder if you could forward it to Maria, perhaps through your wife?" asked Alex.

"Better than in a dispatch, I'll have my aide deliver it to her when her flight from the Philippines lands on Thursday. Is there anything I should know about our lovely flight attendant and her relationship to Winston?"

"I think the two are attracted to each other, although Winston refers to them as an unlikely a couple. But he seems to want to avoid her while he has his own life issues to deal with, trying to stay sober and especially with the threats on his life. He doesn't want to put Maria in danger through a relationship with him."

"Well, Winston's love life may take another turn he's unwilling to deal with. His sister Clemie writes that she's received an inquiry about Winston from his ex-wife Eleanor. Clemie thinks Eleanor is rethinking her past marriage to Winston now that her mother has died. Her ties to the Maryland area where her parents lived have lessened considerably since they both have passed away. Eleanor still holds her nursing job in New York, but who knows if Eleanor might turn up on leave in Vietnam one of these days if Clemie's intuition is correct."

"For some strange reason, sir, Winston just can't seem to stay out of everyone's radar no matter how hard he tries."

"Searching for the truth as Winston does can get under the skin of a lot of people, but it can also attract others."

At the *New York Times* bureau desk in Saigon, Sheenar Tillerstein scowled as he wrote down the story Winston Brand dictated for his weekly *Times* column by phone from Quang Ngai. The hospital phone line Brand used was filled with static. Tillerstein often interrupted Brand, asking him to repeat sentences he couldn't hear well.

When Brand finished dictating, Tillerstein cursed, "This isn't a real news story for the *Times*, Brand! Who's going to care about an old missionary doctor caring for a dying Montagnard child? American newspaper readers want to hear about Viet Cong body counts, and whether the war is being won or lost, if they care about it at all. I'm embarrassed to relay this dribble on the Saigon telegraph to Louis Cohen for you."

"Louis told me I don't have to go through you to report my columns, but I don't have access to an international phone line in the field," Brand replied. "So we'll just have to cooperate. You're not required to edit my columns, Sheenar, so just send it, whatever your opinion may be."

"Yeah, yeah," replied the reluctant news bureau chief. "But your sentimental story about the good medicine man more than pales against the breaking news in Saigon where the press is on a hot political story that will blow the minds of American readers and blast newspaper sales into the stratosphere."

"Politics as usual in Saigon is nothing more than one intrigue after another. The intellectuals love to gossip."

"Well, Mr. Know-It-All, this time the breaking news concerns a visiting U.S. Senator."

"That's yesterday's news, Sheenar. I met Senator Kearney when he arrived before I left for up-country. But I can't tie up the hospital phone any longer, so I'll sign off."

"Before you hang up, Brand, be advised that Senator Kearney's son has tried to renege on his marriage to the daughter of the Song Be Province Chief. The press has gotten ahold of the story and has blown the scandal sky high."

"Well, you've got me there, Tillerstein. The Kearney mess is certainly breaking news! I'll be in Quang Ngai longer and will phone in a story about the Strategic Hamlet program soon."

"I just can't wait to hear about a program bound to fail."

"Keep up the good work, Sheenar. Don't let Senator Kearney and his oversexed son get away with anything!"

"Yeah, right, you'd like that, wouldn't you, Brand? And you keep sending me your scintillating stories to pass on to a very bored Louis Cohen and the *Times* readers of your now pasty column. Have you forgotten your column is called 'The Branding Iron?' Who are you going to 'brand' next with your 'goody two shoes' subjects? Where is the 'bite' of your sarcasm?"

"Not your problem, Sheenar. Give my best to Louis."

"Or we could say, 'give him your worst,' Brand, when I relay your latest column to him."

"Nice talking to you, Sheenar," said Brand as he hung up.

Tillerstein could never guess how good it felt to relay a positive story for once. Maria would like "The Good Medicine Man" column, Brand thought with a smile.

30 STRATEGIC HAMLETS

Tis not enough to help the feeble up, but to support him after.
—William Shakespeare

CAPTAIN BAO, YOU FOOL! Only an idiot would think for even one moment that he could deceive our supreme leader."

"Whatever do you mean, Madame Binh? I can't imagine what you could be ranting about."

"I can't believe you haven't been eliminated at once! Your ill-conceived plot has been reported to me by *Ayr Ba*. He alone makes decisions, coordinated with Hanoi, regarding our revolutionary activities here in the South. It's a death wish to presume to challenge his utmost authority here!"

"Forgive me, Madame Binh, but what plot are you accusing me of instigating without *Ayr Ba*'s knowledge?" Bao nervously adjusted his eye patch.

"You one-eyed usurper! You know perfectly well what I'm talking about. If *Ayr Ba* asked me to shoot you, I would!"

"Oh, how you would enjoy that, especially since you would no longer have to obey the order by *Ayr Ba* to serve as my mistress, a task repulsive to both of us."

"Do you think I don't know you pretend you are making love to Madame Nhu when you're doing your duty with me?"

"Madame Binh, do I detect a hint of jealousy? Maybe you are beginning to favor me despite your bitter protests."

"You jokester, what do you know of manly prowess such as *Ayr Ba* possesses. You are a mere adolescent in comparison."

"Yes, but I think my youthful vigor is replacing thoughts of your middle-aged lover's 'manly prowess.'"

Madame Binh heard the insolent tone in Bao's voice. "Your lack of proper respect for authority will get you killed, but for now *Ayr Ba* has decided to let you live."

"I'm not confessing to anything, but if *Ayr Ba* thinks I'm guilty of instigating a plot without his orders to do so, then why is he sparing my life?"

"It is the first time *Ayr Ba* hasn't ordered instant death to a dissident, but for the time being, you are more valuable to him as the charming Captain Bao who has ingratiated himself into the Diem regime through Madame Nhu."

"You are fixated on Madame Nhu. Remember it's Counselor Nhu whom I work for. Do you have further instructions from *Ayr Ba* as to what he wants me to do? If I'm not to be a hero in battle, what can I do as the assistant to Diem's brother?"

"As Nhu's administrative assistant, you will give adverse advice to him. Our supremely intelligent leader has set two tactics for you to pursue to ensure the failure of the program."

"What are these two tactics? Please explain to this so called 'idiot,' so that I can understand them."

"First, *Ayr Ba* wants you to encourage Nhu to build as many strategic hamlets as soon and as fast as possible, citing the increased infiltration of Viet Cong as the fear-based motive."

"Won't this tactic help the Diem regime, instead of sabotaging it?"

"Your kind of thinking justifies my use of the term 'idiot' to describe you."

"You don't need to harp on it. Just answer my question."

"The peasants will resent being forcibly removed from their ancestral lands and put into forts they are compelled to build. This rapid construction rate will increase the peasants' discontent with the Diem regime. Regardless of their custom of ancestor worship on lands passed down through generations, or their real needs, the program is only focused on locking the peasants in and locking out the Viet Cong."

"Won't the peasants be appreciative of the protection the strategic hamlets afford them?"

"That's a short-sighted question that our revered *Ayr Ba* has already surmised," replied Madame Binh with the pride of the communist revolution in her voice.

"Well, what is it?"

"Diem's government will be unable to fully support or protect so many new hamlets, and they will be easy prey for the Viet Cong to penetrate and destroy, further sowing distrust of the South Vietnamese government in the minds of the peasants," Madame Binh replied in a superior tone. "As for your role, you will become an unsung hero by urging Nhu to sow his own government's destruction while believing he's strengthening it."

"I see. We use the enemy's strength against him. But what is the attraction of being an unsung hero when there is no one to applaud one's efforts?"

"You are more a capitalist in thought than a communist, Captain Bao! In the thinking of the revolution, the state is of supreme importance, not the individual, who is expendable if not contributing to the welfare of the government. Your statement reveals your desire for individual adulation, an attribute of the capitalist. Correct your thinking or die!"

"Death, or the threat of it, is your solution to every problem of the revolution, isn't it, Madame Binh? You are a one-note bore. Nevertheless, I must put up with your chastisement of me at every turn. But what is the second tactic *Ayr-Ba* would have me oversee?"

"You are blind in more than one eye, Captain Bao, but despite you, I must carry on as *Ayr Ba* has commanded me to do. There is a debate in the Diem regime as to whether to locate the first strategic hamlets in relatively safe areas, or in Viet Cong infested areas."

"Obviously the greatest need is to start where the Viet Cong are strongest."

"That's exactly what *Ayr Ba* wants Nhu to think. But locating the first hamlets in Viet Cong controlled areas will insure their failure. You are to advise Nhu to start the hamlets in places where the Viet Cong are strong enough to insure that there are sufficient guerillas present to terrorize the peasants into fostering non-compliance."

"If that is all, you have done your duty and have passed on *Ayr Ba*'s instructions, Madame Binh. So our conversation is finished, along with your eternal criticisms."

"Just remember, Captain Bao, you are to follow your orders to the letter with no deviation whatsoever. No improvisation allowed. If you are to survive, you must abandon your 'wild card temperament' and obey orders as all loyal comrades do."

"There's no doubt in my mind that you'll be sure to pull the trigger if I don't come through, Madame Binh. But if I do succeed in the undetected sabotage of Nhu's Strategic Hamlet program, I just might earn a promotion from the Diem government for administering the program, even though I'm covertly enhancing our communist cause to subvert the effort. You could never achieve this with your lock-step approach, acting as a mere messenger for *Ayr Ba* and despised watch-dog over me!"

"We each have our part to play, and yours includes leaving U.S. Senator Kearney and his son alone from now on! Who can tell what can happen when the senator investigates the leak given to the press about his son's private situation? Senator Kearney's well known penchant for revenge might subvert your privileged position in the Diem regime if your plot is discovered and condemned by the senator. His pressure could result in your removal from office. Then consider whether you would still be valuable to R-3, you idiot!"

Bao detested the knowing look in Madame Binh's eyes as she looked directly into his one good eye.

Winston Brand entered the dining room in the American compound where he was to meet American advisor Major Jake Ireland for breakfast before the tour of the Vietnamese strategic hamlet construction site near Quang Ngai. He spotted the tall, dark-haired major sitting at a table talking to the little Vietnamese one-armed girl he hoped to adopt.

The child hung her head as the reporter approached the table. "Good morning, Mr. Brand. Don't mind Kim Chi. She is still frightened of the local boys who stole her peanuts last evening. Her foster Vietnamese family is out working in their rice fields, and she doesn't want to be alone. So she has come to me for reassurance."

"I don't mind at all. We wouldn't want a little one to remain in fear all day. It wouldn't bother me if she came with us on our tour after breakfast. Please tell Kim Chi that I'm with the press, or a *Bao Chi*, and I don't mean her any harm."

When Major Ireland relayed Brand's message to the little girl, she raised her eyes and gave him a shy smile.

"Thank you, sir. I've been trying to figure out how to care for her while being your guide. I'm obliged to you for your concern for Kim Chi."

Brand could already see another positive story shaping up about the major's planned adoption of the one-armed Vietnamese girl. He could pick up human interest details from the major and Kim Chi during the tour. Kim Chi was such a sweet-tempered young girl, and she reminded Brand of his gentle but lively sister Clemie at that age.

The strategic hamlets were some distance from Quang Ngai City. They rode on a paved road in the major's jeep through the countryside with its jade-green rice fields. Vietnamese girls in straw hats carried water from the canal to the crops.

Major Ireland began describing the mission: "Much of what we do as advisors at this early stage is to help the Vietnamese peasants with nation building projects. As I mentioned at dinner last evening, local needs begin with assisting agricultural and animal husbandry improvements. When I first arrived, the rice was yellow and looked sickly as did the peasants. The scraggly yellow rice didn't deter the rats who ate up 85 percent of the rice before harvest. Because the people were close to starving, especially in a rather barren province like Quang Ngai, we had to import rice from the Delta."

"In other words, you had a major economic problem to resolve before you could even address Viet Cong infiltration. Perhaps the Viet Cong in this area were starving as well."

"Yes. Communists who can't get rice from the peasants suffer from hunger, too. It's more severe where the Viet Cong headquarters are located in the foothills in the western part of the province. From there they stage harassing raids against the villages and towns. Many village peasants not only have seen their rice taxed, or stolen, but also their sons kidnapped and carried off at gunpoint to serve the Viet Cong."

"You are more fortunate in this area. This rice field we are passing as we drive along looks green and healthy. Is it a result of the measures you mentioned at dinner last evening that have turned things around here?"

"Yes, we started with a rat eradication program I mentioned as our first step. Then the U.S. operational mission helped us develop a fertilizer program in which we showed the peasants how to use fertilizer. The peasants can harvest another rice crop in addition to this one this year, doubling their harvest."

"You're well on your way to achieving such an essential goal." Brand felt a gentle tug on his sleeve. He turned to see Kim Chi in the back seat holding the corner of his sleeve with her good hand. She looked up from under her conical straw hat.

"Me like rice, *Bao Chi*. Me hungry when soldiers kill parents. Sell peanuts to get money for rice."

Brand smiled at Kim Chi. "Now you're not hungry?"

"'Melican' papa buy me much rice." She smiled at Ireland.

The major smiled back at the eight-year-old, but continued with the interview. "Next we built pig sties and brought in pigs which we hope to lend out for breeding in the future. The pigs bring another benefit to the people. We taught them to make compost from pig manure as a source of their own fertilizer. Next year they will be able to export pigs."

Brand felt another gentle tug on his sleeve. "Me like pigs," "Kim Chi smiled shyly. "Me play with pigs at hamlet."

"Kim Chi seems to understand much of what we are saying."

"Yes, she understands more English than she can speak at the moment, but she's picking up more words each day through her contact with the Americans. I hope to give her additional English lessons when time from my duties allows."

"Now that you're making headway with the economic situation here, has any progress been made with the strategic hamlets?"

"When I got here there was only a minimal attempt to protect the villages. The province chief could get no money to purchase barbed wire until I was able to get an allocation out of the economic aid budget. The location of the villages here is more fortunate than in other areas. The homes of the peasants here were all grouped together, so all we had to do was put barbed wire around them to make them into strategic hamlets.

"There has been much resistance in other areas where the peasants have had to be moved to a strategic hamlet. What luck that here a string of 11 hamlets form a large semicircle around low lying rice fields! In other places, peasants have been relocated some miles from their rice fields, which adds to their distress for having had to leave their ancestral lands."

"Other than the fortifications of barbed wire, what protection do the peasants have in these strategic hamlets?"

"There's more than just barbed wire at the perimeter. Outside the hamlets, deep wide trenches filled with bamboo stakes have been built, sometimes filled with water. Then comes fences wrapped in barbed wire. Then inside the fences is still another bamboo-filled trench. In some of the 11 villages these fortifications aren't completed at this time.

"In addition the peasants are backed by a village militia. And they can call on the help of regular Vietnamese army units with flares and radio appeals for help if necessary. So we've had to work toward building up a Vietnamese army division here."

"Me no like barbed wire," complained Kim Chi. "Me scratch hurt arm. Go to hospital. Get bandage."

"You remember Dr. Jenicoso, Kim Chi?" asked Brand.

The young girl giggled. "Funny hair man?"

"Yes. He knows how to help you get a new arm."

"Me 'fraid of operation. Bad soldiers hurt me. Kill mama, papa. Want no more hurt by doctor."

"Dr. Jenicoso is a kind man. He'll fix your arm while you are asleep, so it won't hurt. When you wake up, your arm will heal. Then he'll attach a new arm made just for you."

Kim Chi looked away and didn't reply.

"I've tried to explain the same thing to Kim Chi, but she has horrible memories of the Viet Cong attack. It may take a while for her to re-establish trust so she can be helped," said Ireland.

"We can only hope it will be soon. Dr. Jenicoso could be called to other duty stations at any time."

"The skilled surgeon's offer is more than generous and compassionate. We'll try our best to work it out soon. I contacted the hospital this morning."

"I sincerely hope it works out for little Kim Chi."

"No more than I do for Kim Chi's sake. But getting back to your interview, how much do you know about Quang Ngai Province?"

"I was here in the early 1950s as a foreign correspondent. I remember that Quang Ngai was known as a Red province because many of its people were sympathetic to Ho Chi Minh in the fight against French colonial rule.

Ireland explained, "After the French were defeated in 1954 at Dien Bien Phu, although many of the anti-French Viet Minh regiments had been formed of young soldiers from the area around Quang Ngai, they were called North by Hanoi after the Geneva Accords. I can guess that when Ho Chi Minh sent soldier-infiltrators into the South later, he chose soldiers who had been raised in Quang Ngai who would be familiar with the terrain and dialect.

"Not only that, but this area is of pivotal importance. The Vietnamese military fears the communists might use the province as a stepping off place to try to cut South Vietnam in half. By seizing Quang Ngai they could then try to annex the area between Quang Ngai and the 17th Parallel."

Brand remarked, "That makes your work here to improve conditions and provide protection for the peasants doubly important."

Ireland continued, "I'd like to think so. That's what makes the improvements that are taking place in Quang Ngai Province exciting and exceptional. The Strategic Hamlet program started in the Mekong Delta area, with the majority of Viet Cong there, will have much more difficulty getting established and making progress.

"The security concern of the peasant is foremost. When they feel safe, they will cooperate, but when threatened in some way by the Viet Cong, they won't hesitate to throw a grenade into a well they have just helped build to save their lives or those of their family members from Viet Cong retaliation."

Brand said, "I want to report on the situation in the Delta after I finish my interviews up-country, but in some areas the terrorism of the Viet Cong guerillas must present insurmountable odds."

"Let me advise you beforehand," warned the major, "that peasants terrorized by insurgents won't have anything whatsoever to do with Americans. If they are even seen with us, the peasant is eliminated, so they do their best to avoid us."

Brand exclaimed, "No wonder so many of my press colleagues report on the war from the Saigon bars! But the central telegraph office in Saigon is the only way for the wire services to send out copy. I have to send my columns to the *Times* by communicating with the *Times* Saigon news bureau from the field."

"Since you're reporting on the American military advisory mission here, you can use our communication network to send your report to your news desk when we return to base."

"I'd be much obliged, Major Ireland."

"Please call me Jake."

"Winston here."

They arrived at the first strategic hamlet and began their tour. Brand noticed that Kim Chi knew her way around. She visited with the children of the peasants, played with the baby pigs and looked wide-eyed at new Vietnamese babies.

"Kim Chi seems well received here."

"Yes, I'm sure the peasants not working in the fields wonder why she hasn't brought her peanuts to give them. No doubt she spread the word to her friends about the mean local boys who stole her peanuts. I'll have to buy her some more. She so enjoys giving them away now."

"Kim Chi has an endearing way about her. Her friendly, outgoing manner reminds me of that quality in a friend."

A Vietnamese soldier approached them then and spoke to the major's interpreter, who relayed his message to Ireland. The worker's construction team had run out of barbed wire. The major reassured the man that a new shipment should be arriving shortly. But then he asked the man to remain and speak to them about his experience as a defected Viet Cong infiltrator who now works for the Quang Ngai province mission as a free Vietnamese.

Brand saw the opportunity for a rare interview that the major had opened up for him, so he started asking questions through the interpreter, the first being why did he defect?

The sergeant said that he saw the north denied freedom, and the standard of living there was decreasing, bringing suffering to the people, despite propaganda to the contrary.

"I had come to South Vietnam with my comrades through Laos over a steep mountain pass. We carried Chinese, Russian and Czech weapons modified to fire ammunition made in Hanoi."

"Were captured American weapons part of your arsenal?"

"Those who were famers by day and soldiers at night, regional guerilla forces with hit and run work, used any American weapons we captured. But stocks of ammunition for these weapons were not readily available. Regular units had to rely on ammunition made in Hanoi for lengthy battles, so we used the weapons supplied to us by the north.

"Hanoi gave us some money to start with, but we were to sustain ourselves by taxing the peasantry after that. At first we had to secure our own food and water in the mountains. The Montagnards would give us some rice each day without complaint, but later we had to force them to do so. We would go into the villages at night to get food and to persuade or kidnap young men to come to the hills to fill in our ranks."

"How did you keep these young men from leaving?"

"Communists never forgive those who leave them, or try to leave them. A bullet in the back of the head is the inevitable result no matter how long it takes."

"Then it was a life and death risk for you to defect. "Why did you attempt it?"

"I thought the power of the American ally of the south was bound to win the war. Besides, I was always hungry. When I defected, I was held for rehabilitation in a camp with a re-indoctrination period lasting between six months and a year. Briefly I was able to visit with my family in Quang Ngai. The life here in the strategic hamlet is good with lots of food, protection and an important job to do."

The major received a radio message that the truck carrying the barbed wire shipment had a flat tire not far from the strategic hamlet, and the driver requested help. The Vietnamese sergeant, who had just finished his story, volunteered to take a fellow worker to locate the truck and help change the tire.

The major hesitated but then gave him permission. He warned the sergeant to be alert to the possibility that the incident could be a Viet Cong trap, even though the enemy usually struck at night. The sergeant agreed and left with another Vietnamese hamlet worker in a Vietnamese army vehicle.

It didn't take long before a radio report came back to the major from the other hamlet worker that the sergeant was dead, shot in the back of the head. The frightened worker explained that when they located the truck there was no flat tire. The driver was tied up and gagged in the driver's seat, but still alive, gesturing to them by moving his body to and fro.

Wary of sabotage, the sergeant cautiously approached the truck and quickly loosened the driver's gag. But just as quickly two men came out of the adjacent rice field and shot the sergeant in the back of the head, disappearing within seconds back into the rice field with its tall, waving stems.

"Untie the truck driver and both of you return to the hamlet in your vehicle along with the body of the sergeant as quickly as you can," instructed the major over the radio. "Leave the truck for us to check over carefully later for any additional sabotage."

The major was beside himself with this tragic turn of events. "We're always vigilant, but it's unusual for the Viet Cong to strike at midday so close to the hamlet security guard."

"Perhaps you're looking at a long delayed, but not forgotten consequence executed for a defector, such as the sergeant was just explaining to us," suggested Brand.

"But how would they have known it would be the sergeant who went out to investigate the set up incident?"

"Could someone in the hamlet be an undercover operative, who signaled the two communists waiting in the rice fields that a plan for killing the sergeant was suddenly a go?"

"You mean our supply trucks have been under surveillance for a long time, and the communists waited until the defector came out to assist a stranded vehicle? Pretty close timing with a lot of elements in play they couldn't control."

"True, but if we look at the results of the perpetrators' actions, only one goal was accomplished and that was the death of the sergeant shot in the back of the head. He just had described to us that the communists always eliminated defectors and discouraged those who might try in this way."

"My God, what patience and persistence these communists exhibit to accomplish their ends, if this is true!"

"The fear of certain death is their tool of control."

"A thorough investigation is in order in any case. We'll have to have the Vietnamese deliver the sergeant's body to his family in Quang Ngai.

"And I just hope Kim Chi is still playing with the other children in the hamlet and doesn't get wind of this tragic incident. Wouldn't you know that just when things were progressing so smoothly, the communists would disrupt it? If you don't mind, Mr. Brand, we'll have to cut short our tour of the remaining hamlets and head back to Quang Ngai City.

"Of course, Major. I'm so sorry for the unexpected death of your Vietnamese sergeant. Having seen the communist side, your sergeant seemed more than dedicated to the mission of the south where he found a better life."

"No success story is without its detractors," lamented the major, "especially here in Vietnam."

31 SPECIAL FORCES MISSION

When men are most sure and arrogant, they are commonly the most mistaken, and then have given views to passion, without that proper deliberation and suspense which can alone secure them from the greatest absurdities.

—*David Hume*

THAT EVENING at the American compound in Quang Ngai, Winston Brand once again joined doctors Jenicoso and Kalverton, along with Major Jake Ireland, in the dining room for the evening meal. The setback in morale due to the death of the rehabilitated Viet Cong defector was reflected in the military officer's demeanor.

The major lamented, "How unfortunate that today we witnessed the heavy hand of our communist aggressors, who demonstrated that no one can leave their insurgency movement and expect to survive. The slain Vietnamese sergeant had just told me, not long before he met his own death in the trap set by the enemy, about the certainty of death for defectors that keeps the Viet Cong movement intact. Sadly, the sergeant paid the price for choosing freedom and the good life he experienced living and working in the strategic hamlet."

"It's a hell of a war where the front line is nowhere and everywhere," commented Brand.

"Believe me, the communists' aggression extends down the line to civilians as well, such as Kim Chi's parents and even to little

Kim Chi who survived but with a debilitating injury. Has she shown any signs of a more positive response to surgery?"

"I was worried that word of the sergeant's death would trigger her memories of the attack she and her parents experienced. Word had spread quickly through the village of the death, and by the time I got back to Kim Chi, she had tears in her eyes. She said she felt so sad for the sergeant's family in Quang Ngai, just like she felt when her parents died, because she knew nothing could ever bring them back.

"But she stopped and thought for a minute, and then said, 'But me can get arm back. Santa Claus doctor help me!'"

The little girl's courage in overcoming her fear brought smiles to faces of the four men at the table. The sergeant's regrettable death had sparked Kim Chi's resolve, and demonstrated the desire of human spirit for new life.

"Believe me, I'll make arrangements for the surgery!"

"Our appreciation for your generous offer, Dr. Jenicoso, is boundless. Thank God there are kind, good people like you two medicine men to help patch us up."

"Believe me, I couldn't be any happier than to 'patch up' a dear little innocent like Kim Chi. What can I get for her as a gift from her 'Santa Claus doctor' for being such a brave girl?"

"The reconstruction process of her arm through surgery and, after healing, the fitting of a prosthetic arm is more than enough of a gift."

"Yes, but a child needs to look forward to life after the process with something that will represent a new way of being."

"Well, Kim Chi's quite enthralled with the beautiful *ao dais* with a high collar and long sleeves the young Vietnamese women wear."

"That's it, then. We'll order an *ao dai* made to order for her size along with her new prosthetic." The doctor's enthusiasm and the good fortune of Kim Chi enhanced the feeling of warm friendship and good will shared at the table.

"Winston, I'm sorry our tour of the strategic hamlets was cut short. Did you get enough information for your column?"

"Yes, thank you, Jake. But tomorrow I have to leave your very enjoyable company, gentlemen. I've been in contact with a Capt. Roger Hinner of the U.S. Special Forces at Ban Me Thuot and have talked our friendly pilot into giving me a lift there in the morning. As Major Spear informed me, the U.S. Special Forces in conjunction with the Vietnamese Special Forces are training the Montagnards at nearby Buon Enao to fight against the Viet Cong. Also, civic assistance is given, which includes the Village Self-Defense Program that provides for village development along with military security. I hope to write another interesting and positive column from up-country there."

"Yes," commented Dr. Kalverton, "I've heard the village of Buon Enao of 400 Rhade tribe members was contacted in late October of 1961 about instituting such a program there. Vietnamese government forces weren't able to protect the Montagnard villagers in the past, and thus many supported the Viet Cong because of fear for their lives. Then, because of Viet Cong infiltration, the government discontinued medical aid and educational programs for the mountain peoples.

"I'm sorry to say that in many ways the Montagnards live in a 'no man's land' where they are looked down upon as savages by the Vietnamese as we've discussed. They've often been displaced from their tribal lands by Vietnamese refugees, and are terrorized and used by the Viet Cong. Hopefully cooperation with Vietnam's ally to stop aggression turns out well for them."

Major Ireland added, "You'll find that detachments of 12 Green Berets train Montagnards, drawn from the dominant tribe in each area, into 'civilian irregular defense groups,' or CIDGs. The CIDGs serve as defense forces to provide a security zone around each camp. With help from Navy Seabees, Special Forces build dams, roads, bridges, schools and wells, and Special Forces medics provide rudimentary health care. And I'm happy to say that the Buon Enao expansion program will include 40 villages by the middle of next April. You should get an interesting story for your *Times* readers there, Winston. By the way, the Village Self-Defense Program instituted there is the forerunner of our Strategic Hamlet program."

"That'll certainly tie in nicely with my interview regarding your successful program here in Quang Ngai, Major."

Dr. Kalverton added, "I'm glad you're reporting on the positive endeavors being made in the field from nation building to village defense training to medical assistance. The Montagnards know little and care little what's going on in Saigon, except when the Vietnamese government is ignoring their needs and failing to give them assistance they deserve."

Brand replied, "And your humanitarian medical mission, Dr. Kalverton, I'm sure, is a spark of hope, despite your overwhelming case load here in the Central Highlands.

"On my trip to Buon Enao, I'm also looking forward to making contact again with Lt. Ledger Smith of the MAAG U.S. Information Office in Saigon. I got word he'll be in Buon Enao about the same time I'll be there. The lieutenant is also doing a story on the Special Forces mission for the newly established *Observer*, the first South East Asia publication for U.S. personnel stationed in South Vietnam. Ledger says he put together the publication at the last minute at the request of MAAG/MACV General Pavler on the occasion of the visit of Senator Thomas Kearney and his fact finding mission and then for the Secretary of Defense's visit in early May. I'm sure he'll bring me up to date on Saigon intrigues since I've been up-country."

"Believe me, there's only one intrigue worth noting as far as my interest goes."

"What's that, my good man?" asked Brand.

"Believe me, it concerns you, and whether Major Spear returned to Saigon and delivered your letter as promised."

Hoping to sidestep Jenicoso's possible injection of lovely Maria Monclova into the conversation, Brand replied, "Rest your mind, Nick. Alex always comes through whether we always want him to or not. Now I must take leave, gentlemen, to prepare for my departure early tomorrow morning.

"Jake, please give our dear little Kim Chi farewell best wishes from *Bao Chi.* Tell her I'm proud of her courage to undergo the surgery needed so she can receive her new arm. The next time I see her in her new *ao dai* with her dark pony tail swinging as she walks, I'll be pleased to see how good she feels about being normal once again with two arms."

"Believe me, her 'Santa Claus' doctor will do all he can to insure the success of the whole process."

Jake replied, "We're going in the right direction with Kim Chi's courage and the generous help of our good medicine man!"

The next morning Brand was greeted by Capt. Roger Hinner as he disembarked from the aircraft at Ban Me Thuot. "Welcome, Mr. Brand. Lt. Ledger Smith arrived a short while ago accompanied by a military photographer. We've been waiting for you so we can drive together to Buon Enao. He tells me that the two of you are already acquainted."

"Thank you, sir. I'm looking forward to learning about your mission here, and Lieutenant Smith is, too. He is a fine young man, and I'll be glad to see him again."

On the ride to Buon Enao, Ledger filled Brand in on the 'birth' of the *Observer* publication. The captain waited patiently as the young lieutenant's enthusiasm for the new endeavor monopolized the conversation. But soon Captain Hinner exercised his rank to direct their attention to the mission both were there to cover for their respective newspapers.

"Our mission here is run by the CIA, instead of MAAG control. Small groups of American Special Forces and South Vietnam's own Special Forces, the LLDB, assist in training the CIDGs as defense forces. The biggest problem facing this mission is the unrelenting tension between the Vietnamese and the Montagnards, the French name for mountain people. For decades the Montagnards, whom we've nicknamed 'Yards,' have been in an uneasy relationship with various Vietnamese central governments. These highlanders resent both the South Vietnamese government and the Viet Cong.

"The government ignores them, viewing them as savages. They suffered displacement when Diem's government settled refugees from North Vietnam in the highlands after the 1954 Geneva Accords. And Diem's regime has neglected Montagnard education and health care. Americans trying to mediate between Montagnards and Vietnamese repeatedly experience difficulties that can't always be overcome.

Brand offered, "Major Ireland in Quang Ngai has had some success with the Strategic Hamlet program there, but is still plagued with Viet Cong sabotage of their rebuilding program. I would imagine the distrust of the Montagnards for the Viet Cong relates to their exploitation, stealing food and persuading or kidnapping their sons to join them as they do in other areas."

"Fear of death is the Viet Cong tool of control for the Montagnards here, too," replied Captain Hinner. "But the Montagnards have an ally in the American Special Forces. Both of our groups are tough, versatile and accustomed to living in wild conditions. We've an affinity for each other, and find them easy to get along with. They see much humor in things."

"How did you get the Montagnards to cooperate with the Special Forces, given their history of understandable distrust with outsiders?" asked Lieutenant Smith.

"It took weeks of discussion and persuasion. The Buon Enao villagers did finally agree to build a fence around Buon Enao, to dig shelters within the village for women and children and to construct housing for a training center and dispensary. An intelligence system was needed to control movement into the village and provide early warning of an attack. A strike force maintains itself in a camp, but village defenders can return home after training and receiving arms."

"How do you weed out Viet Cong infiltrators?" asked Brand.

"First, the village chief had to certify that everyone had agreed to participate, and that everyone was loyal to the government. During training, the recruits had to vouch for one another. Five or six Viet Cong were exposed in this way in each of the 40 villages that joined in the expansion of the program."

"Are there any dissident Montagnard groups?" asked Ledger.

"In 1958 the BAJARAKA movement was organized to unite the Montagnard tribes against the Vietnamese. Also, a well-organized political and military force is known as FULRO, a French acronym for 'Forces United for the Liberation of Races Oppressed,' with the objectives of freedom, autonomy, land owner ship and an independent highland nation. We keep an eye out for members of these organizations who show any signs of revolt in our Special Forces camps," said Captain Hinner.

"Is President Diem nervous about training and arming a minority people who want independence?" asked Brand.

"The Central Highlands is a strategically important area. As the Ho Chi Minh Trail develops along the Laotian and Cambodian borders to become a major highway for North Vietnam to move men and materials south, Diem can no longer ignore the area nor the Montagnards that inhabit these forested mountains on both sides of the borders. For our part, we respect the Montagnard's loyalty and fighting prowess. They work in teams and are very good at small unit tactics, protecting each other with a family instinct. They are very brave under fire."

When they arrived at Buon Enao, Captain Hinner said, "Now we have a chance to show you the set-up first-hand."

For the rest of the day the two reporters toured all the major areas of the base camp, including inspections of village defenses, village defenders and the strike force camp. In the evening after dinner, Brand and Lieutenant Smith had free time to catch up on their recent activities. Brand noticed an uneasy look in Ledger's eyes.

"What is it, Ledger? What are you holding back?"

"I don't relish discussing it, Winston, but when Senator Kearney was in Saigon, he made intensive inquiries on the q.t. to try to dig up any dirt on you he could find, specifically if you'd been drinking. He'd heard from General Pavler about your pledge to him that you'd quit drinking. The senator wanted to find out if it was true."

"Oh, my God, Ledger! Did he discover the one time I let down my guard at Pierre Girard's press party? You were there as well as the whole Saigon press corps!" lamented Brand.

"It was quite a public place to slip up, sir, filled with news mongers who aren't well disposed toward you."

"Don't keep me in suspense. Who ratted on me?"

"Actually, no one did."

"What! I've unwisely insulted most of them. Why did they close ranks for a disliked member of the press when asked by the senator about my drinking?"

"Well, I've heard rumors it just about killed them not to indict you by snitching on your behavior at the Girard party."

"But?"

"One foreign correspondent was already ordered to leave Vietnam, but President Diem was persuaded to reconsider. However, two others are still in jeopardy with others concerned, too. I figure it was their own self-interest that kept them close-mouthed about you. It wouldn't take much to trump up reasons to send many of them home. They don't want to give the politicians any ammunition that might be used against them."

"Thank God for the human attribute of self-preservation at any cost, even to stifle their own desire to boot me out."

"Senator Kearney was not a happy man when he left Vietnam. He vowed to return to 'set things right.' I don't think that gives you much leeway regarding alcohol while in Vietnam if you want to stay. He must have a vendetta against you."

"As my editor, Louis Cohen, always tells me, I don't need to add to my list of enemies. The page is full already, and gets new entries each time I dig for the truth someone doesn't want revealed in my reporting. But thanks for the warning Senator Kearney hasn't given up on getting rid of me."

"Good luck, sir. I surely have been enjoying your *Times* columns from your interviews up-country. They're refreshingly positive in contrast to the politically-oriented reports from Saigon. For my part, I'm trying to make sure U.S. personnel in Vietnam know about the positive differences we're making, despite setbacks from the Viet Cong."

"Keep up the good work, Ledger. I knew you'd be an effective information officer."

That night Brand had a difficult time falling asleep. He realized how very close he had come to being kicked out of Vietnam. What had he been thinking, sowing his own self-destruction in public? General Pavler would've had to concede his support when confronted by Kearney with direct evidence about the Girard party incident he'd avoided asking previously.

Brand's conscience caused him true unrest. How could he have broken his promise to the family friend who had been like a father to him? He wondered when would he ever learn to 'face the sun,' his father's never ending complaint about him. Until he did, he was wise not to complicate the life of the "Miss Philippines" beauty he desired. Yet, when he finally drifted off to sleep, it was with thoughts of the ecstasy he had experienced in Maria's arms.

32 CONSPIRACY

Between the acting of a dreadful thing and the first motion, all the interim is like a phantasma, or a hideous dream; the genius and the mortal instruments are then in council; and the state of man, like to a little kingdom, suffers then the nature of an insurrection.

—William Shakespeare

THE NEXT MORNING the two men were ready to depart Ban Me Thuot. "We have to leave in different directions, Ledger. My next stop is the old imperial capital of Hue."

"What takes you to that historic mandarin city, Winston?"

"It's not Hue's palaces, tombs, parks and temples from the times of the mandarins, or the clear waters of the River of Perfumes. They're all very enticing, but I want to interview a Buddist monk at the Tu Dam Pagoda named Thich Tri Quang."

"What's the angle of your interview?"

"Major Spear informed me the Buddhists are not a majority of either the population or the army as often reported. I want to find out first-hand whether they are strictly a religious group, or if they have political intentions as well. How they view the Diem regime, and how they feel the South Vietnamese government has treated them will make an interesting column."

"Let's hope you're successful at discovering the truth without adding to your 'enemy list.' Please get word to me if there's a potential feature story for the *Observer* there. Perhaps I can persuade my boss to relieve me from my assistant's duty in dealing with the Western press for an interview in Hue."

"Will do. And I want you to know that I have a 'friend list,' too, and you're on it. I appreciate your friendship."

"As I do yours." The two men shook hands and departed.

Shortly after Brand's arrival in Hue, he went directly to the Tu Dam Pagoda, presented his credentials and asked for an interview with Thich Tri Quang. Soon the middle-aged monk dressed in gray robes approached with a younger monk, whom Brand surmised was an interpreter. Brand was struck with the extremely self-possessed demeanor of the man, who had a very pronounced forehead and an air of great intelligence. The monk introduced himself and indicated he only spoke Vietnamese which the younger monk would interpret for Brand. Thich Tri Quang noted Brand was a foreign correspondent from *The New York Times*, and asked what they could do for him.

"I'd like to interview you for my column called the 'Branding Iron,'" responded Brand.

The monk looked surprised when the interpreter mentioned the name of Brand's column, and asked if it wasn't a term used by Americans to describe a hot iron used to sear the flesh of an animal with an identifying stamp.

When Brand answered in the affirmative, he was asked how this term related to his column. Brand replied that his purpose was to discern the truth in his interviews and 'brand' what he learned as the real thing, or as lies.

The head monk gave a disarming smile. He smoothly reflected that the Buddhists had something in common with Brand in that they also are known for seeking the truth. Brand returned the smile and asked if he had time for an interview.

But Thich Tri Quang said he in the middle of an important meeting and offered his second in command, Thich Dai Tuan, to be interviewed in his place. The dominant monk offered to drop in later to speak to Brand if his meeting ended before Brand finished his interview.

Brand was disappointed, but he agreed. Thich Tri Quang departed, leaving the interpreter for Brand's interview, and shortly Thich Dai Tuan appeared to take his place.

"Please enter and make yourself comfortable, Mr. Brand," said Thich Dai Tuan.

"Thank you, I will.

When they were settled in the pagoda, Thich Dai Tuan asked, "Have you prepared questions or do you want an open discussion?"

"Yes, I have questions in mind, but first can you share with me Thich Tri Quang's early history, and how he rose to a position of such importance here at the pagoda in Hue?"

"Yes, of course. Our venerable leader is a Vietnamese Mahayana Buddhist born in 1924 in Quang Binh Province. In his early days he went to Ceylon to further his Buddhist studies. When he returned to Vietnam, he participated in anti-French activities, because he desired the independence of Vietnam."

"In other words, he joined the Viet Minh."

"Yes, he acceded to the demands of the Viet Minh to collaborate with them, as many of our patriotic countrymen did to rid our land of the hated French rule. The Viet Minh was the only force organized enough to fight for our freedom."

"Did Thich Tri Quang at any time collaborate personally with Ho Chi Minh?"

A look of suspicion flickered in Thich Dai Tuan's intense gaze. "Mr. Brand, are you asking if Thich Tri Quang still has communist leanings, or currently has contact with Ho Chi Minh?"

"If you want to answer the question, yes, I am."

"I was informed you write a *New York Times* column called the 'Branding Iron,' so I think, you wish to 'brand' our leader one way or the other. Well, his leanings are Buddhist, and his loyalty is to the well-being of our religious group, whatever the current political atmosphere in Vietnam may be, or will be. To us, 'only religions count in Vietnam,'" replied the monk.

The monk continued. "But during the French colonial period in Vietnam in the '40s, Thich Tri Quang did have dealings with Ho Chi Minh as we Vietnamese struggled to end French domination. However, since the fall of France in Indochina, and the subsequent Geneva Accords in 1954, he has fallen out with the communists and has concentrated his efforts at our Buddhist Tu Dam Pagoda until he has achieved a position of leadership here in Hue. Are you interested in our religious numbers and Buddhist influence, or our political significance in Vietnam?"

"What is the Buddhist political view of the Diem regime?"

"As Buddhists, our religious group has to be prepared to survive no matter how the political tides turn. Just as in your country, adjustments must be made with each new political administration. Vietnam has been dominated by foreign powers for much of its history. Even now the Republic of Vietnam, headed by the Diem regime, wouldn't be able to stay in power without the aid of the United States. Diem is adamant, as we all are, that the U.S. role in Vietnam remains that of an ally and not that of yet another colonial power."

"But do Catholic President Diem and the Buddhists part company in their views?" asked Brand.

"Buddhists know that President Diem comes from a very devout Catholic family. The Ngo clan long has been involved in the political and religious life of Vietnam, which can't be overlooked by the Buddhists. Diem's father, Ngo Dinh Kha was a very high-ranking mandarin, the first headmaster of the National Academy in Hue founded in 1896 and a counselor to Emperor Thanh Thai during French colonization. Kha and his second wife had nine children, six sons and three daughters. Diem's brother Ngo Dinh Can in Hue is the overseer in Central Vietnam, and Ngo Dinh Thuc has become Vietnam's highest ranking Catholic bishop. Diem has had a long political career as he has progressed from one position to higher ones, finally culminating in president of the sovereign Republic of Vietnam in 1954 to the present."

"Has Diem's devout Catholicism affected the Buddhists in Vietnam?" asked Brand.

"Diem does have eight Buddhists in his cabinet, including a vice-president and a foreign minister. But while he has tried to bring the many different groups of rebellious Vietnamese society under his control in order to stay in power and unify the country, he has become increasingly suppressive. He is supported in these activities by his brother Ngo Dinh Nhu. Nhu heads the Can Lao Party, which mobilized support for Diem's political ambitions. Nhu also heads the secret police, which keeps Diem in power through suppression of dissidents, and he enforces Diem's policies, some of which Buddhists find unnecessarily oppressive."

"Which of Diem's policies do the Buddhists resent?"

"To begin with, our limited objectives involve protocol and property. We want the government to permit Buddhist flags to be flown at public places, not just at pagodas during special religious observations. Secondly, we want Ordinance H10, adopted by former Emperor Bao Dai, to be amended to permit Buddhists to have greater opportunity to buy property. But our overall objective is for religious equality in Vietnam."

"Have there been clashes between Buddhists and Catholics?"

"Unfortunately, Diem's father Kha suffered a family tragedy caused by the Buddhists. When Kha was studying in British Malaya, an anti-Catholic riot by the Buddhists occurred. They burned a church that almost wiped out the entire Ngo Dinh clan of over 100 members who were worshipping there, including Kha's parents, brothers and sisters! Undoubtedly, such a past family disaster at the hands of the Buddhists would raise distrust of the Buddhists in Diem's mind in the present."

Brand remarked, "What a tragedy that is! I can see why Diem might be wary of the Buddhists gaining too much power. But regardless of the past, increasing civil liberties is one of the reforms the U.S. is urging Diem to make to become democratic."

"Yes, Diem's family's tragedy was then, and this is now. A new generation of monks doesn't understand the repression they experience at the hands of the Diem regime."

"Do you perceive that Diem's suppression of the Buddhists is greater than that exerted on other groups?" asked Brand.

"Whatever the degree of Diem's repression of any one group, each experiences resentment with thoughts of rebellion. Diem's greatest desire is to stay in power, so his restrictions are designed to keep any one of many various Vietnamese groups from gaining enough power to be a threat to his regime. Faced with aggression from the North as well, Diem's tries to juggle challenges to his authority at every hand, and wants to keep them all in the air under his control, perhaps impossible."

"What are your concerns regarding religious equality for Buddhists in Vietnam?" asked the reporter.

"The 'private' status of Buddhism designated by the French was never repealed by Diem. It requires us to get official permission to conduct public Buddhist activities. Furthermore, from observation, we believe that Diem funnels U.S. aid mainly to Catholic majority villages, including weapons only given to Catholics that Diem can trust. Nor do Catholics have to perform labor required of all able bodied citizens. Needless to say, Buddhists seek redress. We deserve religious equality. All suppressed groups have the potential to rebel."

"Are you suggesting that South Vietnam is a tinderbox waiting to burst into flame? That potentially the match could be struck by any of a number of rebellious groups?"

"It's a tense situation, yes, but for the time being, the communist rebels employ propaganda with hit and run guerilla warfare while building up their armed strength. However, Buddhists must watch and wait to see which side will turn out to be the 'strongest dragon,' and then we must accommodate ourselves to the situation that emerges and negotiate our concerns with the winner."

"Will continued friction between the Diem government and the Buddhists soften up the country for a communist takeover when the time comes for the larger armed struggle?"

"Who's to say? It might help the communists be victorious. But the greatest concern for the Diem regime should be whether the Americans will grow weary of supporting an authoritarian ruler reluctant to make democratic reforms."

"Are the Buddhists in contact with the north, I wonder?"

"The north won't bargain with Buddhists until Diem and his brother Nhu are out of power. The best case scenario for us, of course, would be a Buddhist theocracy in South Vietnam, but with so many factions seeking power, that is an idle dream. However, no one can predict what may or may not happen."

It was at this point when Thich Tri Quang entered the room once again. He smiled when he asked Brand if he would like to be introduced to a revered Buddhist who was visiting in Hue.

Brand agreed. He asked the name of the revered Buddhist visitor and was told it was Thich Quang Duc, and that meeting him would bring an inspired note to his column. The head monk then asked Thich Dai Tuan to go and bring the distinguished Buddhist to join them. Moments later the elderly visitor entered. After introductions, Thich Dai Tuan said, again using the interpreter, "Thich Quang Duc has done much for the faithful in his many years of service. His notable achievements include overseeing the construction of 31 new temples in Vietnam."

"I'm impressed," replied Brand.

Thich Dai Tuan then told Brand Thich Quang Duc's story, "Our revered elder monk was born in 1897 in Hoi Khanh in Khanh Hoa Province. At age seven, he joined his maternal uncle and spiritual master to study Buddhism, and his uncle raised him as a son. When he became of age, he lived the life of a hermit in the mountains for three years. Then he began to travel, spreading Buddhist teachings for the next two years, but later went back into retreat in Nha Trang to meditate and rest. After that he traveled again, this time in southern Vietnam, including two years in Cambodia to further his Buddhist studies there. His temple building phase was interspersed with these activities. After he served as Chairman of Ceremonial Rites for monks, he retired."

"That is an illustrious life of service to his faith."

The monk said, "His faith means life itself to him!"

"I am honored to meet him and hear his story"

Thich Dai Tuan added, "Perhaps, then, Mr. Brand, you might mention Thich Quang Duc's story in your column."

"Certainly, and I appreciate you taking time to talk with me." Brand then took his leave of the accommodating monks.

Brand spent the rest of the day touring the charming attractions of the city of Hue, soaking up the atmosphere of the old imperial capital. Later he sat by the River of Perfumes to compose his column for the *Times*, writing it down in his notebook. When he finished, he thought about the Buddhist situation in Vietnam. He wouldn't put his private speculations into his *Times* column, of course, but he decided he must talk to Alex Spear about his own intuitions and enlighten his awareness of the growing and potentially explosive situation developing between the Buddhists and Diem's regime.

Not that he'd compromise his objectivity as a reporter by alerting Alex, but he would act as an American citizen warning intelligence of potential danger. President Diem might regard the Buddhists as just another group to keep under control in his efforts to unify Vietnam, but with a well-known religion involved, world opinion might be easily manipulated by crafty propaganda claiming persecution. The Buddhists' cause of religious equality under a Catholic president could become a significant player in world opinion.

Despite Thich Tri Quang's reasonable and cooperative manner in the brief time he saw him, Brand's gut feeling about him came from the monk's personal intensity he sensed underlying his affable manner. Was he in league with the communists to sabotage the Diem regime for its perceived suppression of the Buddhists? Or was he just looking out for his own cause of Buddhist religious equality in a flammable political atmosphere? Whatever the case, Brand sensed Buddhist sights were set on the downfall of the Diem regime. Buddhist unrest had the potential to flare up and become a serious threat to the Ngo brothers.

Brand put his conspiracy theory aside momentarily and went to file his story with the *Times* Saigon bureau, but he didn't relish talking to Sheenar Tillerstein again. When he heard his sneering voice on the phone, Brand almost hung up.

"It's going so well for you up-country, isn't it, Brand?" said the arrogant young bureau chief. "Now you have another milk-toast column about up-country activities, this time with the Buddhists in Hue. Who cares if you have met a revered Buddhist monk who has overseen the construction of 31 Buddhist temples? What do the complaints of the Buddhists mean to your readers who have their own concerns about life? After all, Vietnam is a country that isn't on the radar of many!"

"Then you're indicting journalists here that they haven't made any impact on the public at all. Just send the story to Louis, Sheet. He needs copy to fill up my weekly column space."

"Yeah, well, if you were back in Saigon, you'd hear about real action to report on. I'm just working on a breaking story about an American military doctor who died with his patients when his medevac helicopter was shot down in Ba Tat on the way back to the hospital in Quang Ngai."

The color drained from Brand's face. He was speechless.

"Are you still there, Brand?"

"Yeah, what was the name of the doctor who died?" asked Brand, almost choked up with grief.

"A Dr. Jenicoso, a navy lieutenant commander, with a reportedly jovial manner, a crazy cowlick and a pigeon-toed manner of walking, but one hell of a surgeon, I'm told."

"And one hell of a human being!" croaked Brand.

"You knew him, then," commented Tillerstein. "It looks like up-country isn't such a place of positive activities as you depict in your reports, is it?"

"If you knew the whole story, you'd mourn his loss too."

"I'm sure you'll write about it, but I need to get this news report out, so it can be released as soon as relatives have been notified. Meantime, you need to get back to Saigon. Senator Kearney is long gone but vows to return to 'set things right.' You'd better work fast on your Pulitzer Prize before he finds a way to oust you from Vietnam."

"Yeah, thanks once again for your encouraging words. I'm going to check back in at Quang Ngai to get the whole story about the death of Dr. Jenicoso, and then I'll return to Saigon." Brand was too choked up to talk any longer. Tillerstein could never understand the tears Brand felt profusely wetting his cheeks.

Brand replaced the phone receiver and hung his head. He cupped his face with his hands as his chest heaved with his cry to heaven at the injustice of life on earth!

33 INTERLUDE II

On the attraction between man and woman society is based; but its refined is greater than its gross force, and its weight is like the gravitation of the globe.

—C.A. Bartol

NICK JENICOSO'S DEATH broke down Winston Brand's reserve. The lingering thought that he might have contributed to the doctor's death kept returning to him. Had R-3 read his column about "The Good Medicine Man?" Could the communist super spy have decided to stop Brand's positive reporting from up-country by eliminating one of the ascenders he wrote about?

Despite his reservations about seeing Maria again, he desperately needed to share his grief and explain his haunting feeling of guilt to the one person who would be experiencing the same sense of loss as he felt. He had contacted Maria about Jenicoso's death after his return to Saigon. She was as shocked and grief stricken as he was. They agreed to meet when she had a few days of layover in Bangkok.

As Winston Brand exited the plane in Thailand, his heart leapt at the sight of Maria Monclova standing in the waiting area, her eyes full of yearning as she tried to catch sight of him. Brand's thoughts raced. "My God, she's so beautiful. How in the world can I resist her?" But he knew he had to try.

When Maria spotted him walking toward her, her whole being radiated a loving warmth that reached out and enveloped him in a sea of emotions. Irresistible magnetism drew him toward her and before he knew it, they were wrapped together in each other's arms, exchanging kisses expressing the longing of their hearts.

Brand broke away. How, he never knew, but he muttered, "Maria, we must get a hold of ourselves, or the chemistry between us will overwhelm us."

They walked together out of the airport terminal hand in hand and hailed a taxi to take them to the Montien Hotel for their rendezvous. The grief they both experienced at the senseless and unjust loss of their dear friend was too fresh and too much for them to bear alone.

After they entered the taxi, Maria addressed the concern that infused their emotions, "Winston, my heart cries out in distress for our dear Nick Jenicoso. Why would the Viet Cong fire on a marked medevac helicopter? How unjust for him to have perished needlessly when he had spent his life tending to others! How can I ever forget his tender care of my injury during the near miss after takeoff from Guam? And his good cheer and ukulele playing calmed the stress of everyone on the flight—what I should have done had I not been injured."

"Never would I want to have you injured, my dear Maria, but I must say that holding you in my arms while Doc Jenicoso tended to your wound only fueled the attraction building between us. I'm sorry though that some of our earlier encounters weren't more congenial. I wish I had been more in control of myself."

Maria replied, "Even so, the magnetism between us kept drawing us together. And Nick Jenicoso was such a dear, jovial soul. He is such a treasured part of our story that I can't imagine a time when I shan't miss him."

"Maria, I have a feeling about his accident that lays heavy on my heart. As much as I miss our pigeon-toed benefactor with his unruly cow-lick and eternal optimism, I can't shake the thought that I may have played a part in his death. The guilt from this possibility has crept into my soul."

"Whatever do you mean, Winston?"

"When I reported in my *Times* column about the positive medical endeavors Dr. Kalverton has carried out with the Montagnards, and Nick's main mission of tending to the needs of our military personnel, maybe my column caught the attention of an as yet unidentified North Vietnamese operative, who is believed to have penetrated the government of South Vietnam at a very high level."

"How does Nick's death connect with your column?"

"I wonder if the positive reports I've been filing from up-country have been perceived by this secret operative as reflecting positively on the Diem regime. Did they provoke communist action to eliminate at least one of these ascenders, Nick being the first? It makes me shudder to think that if this is true, who's the next I've written reports on to suffer an untimely death? I fear for Dr. Kalverton's life as well."

"Oh, Winston, you can't carry that burden of guilt with you on a supposition. It will bury you alive!"

"I'm afraid that's why I agreed to meet you again against my better judgment. I guess I needed to grieve with you over the death of our dear friend, and ease the guilt that comes creeping into my mind and threatens to overwhelm me."

"Is that your only reason, Winston? Didn't you want to see me again as well, despite the reservations expressed in your letter?"

"Of course, Maria. I told you in my letter that there is an unexplainable deep attraction between us that we both acknowledge, as if we'd known each other before somehow. But the caution I expressed as far as my unresolved life issues remains. It's a considerable deterrent to the advisability of us building a relationship together."

"Here is our hotel, Winston. We need to grieve and comfort each other in private. Let's get checked in and settled. Then, God willing, we can share our memories and find some peace."

"That's my deepest wish, lovely Maria."

A little later, Maria left one of their separate hotel rooms Winston had insisted upon and knocked at the door to his room. Before opening the door, Winston hesitated. He felt the need for them to be together at this time of their great shock and grief. But their undeniable chemistry was surely going to get in the way and bring consequences Brand wanted to avoid or postpone for both their sakes.

Maria knocked again. Brand had intended to do his best to hold back the tide of passionate longing for each other he and Maria experienced in each other's presence. But in the back of his mind he had known before he came that he probably wouldn't be able to resist her. However, he felt there comes a time when even the most hardened reporter must seek comfort, and yes, even passion, to counterbalance life's losses.

Brand opened the door, and Maria flew into his arms. The night that followed in their Oriental paradise could barely contain the fire in their souls that found expression in their passion for each other. Finally, exhausted, they slept until late morning the next day, waking as if in a dream that was too good to be true. The euphoria that enveloped them was intoxicating, and they knew they would remember the experience always. But there was much left to be shared by kindred minds.

As they ate a brunch in Winston's room, Brand remarked, "Maria you realize, don't you, that we are really strangers to one another in many ways despite our insatiable passion?"

"Well, then, Winston, tell me about yourself, so I can know your history. Start at the beginning."

"Maria, I carry a lot of emotional baggage and the danger of outside threats to my life. I would never want to endanger you were we to become involved in a relationship."

"We're already involved in a relationship, Winston, whether we like it or not."

"Maria, you'd be safer with someone closer to your age and background without my life experiences and temperament."

"Tell me about them, dear Winston."

"You asked me to start at the beginning, so here goes: Named Winston Spencer Brand, I was born on March 21, 1926, in Norfolk, Virginia. My father, Vice Admiral Willoughby Brand II, was a career military officer, and as his only son, I was expected to follow in his footsteps.

"But to his great disappointment, I preferred to follow my mother's side of the family. They were writers and statesmen. Indeed it was my mother who named me after Winston Churchill. She even brought in the American branch of the family, named 'Spencer,' and used it for my middle name. This made me a distant cousin of the man who was destined to lead the democracies in World War II. My only sibling, an older sister named Clementine, was named in honor of Churchill's wife."

"What's your mother's name, Winston?"

"My parents have both passed, but more on that in a minute. My mother's name was Candace. None of their children's names set well with my father. He would have preferred that I be named

Willoughby Brand, III, after him and his father before him. Both had served with distinction—my grandfather in the Civil War and my father in World War II. My mother favored her distant British relatives. Why and how my mother won the argument, I do not know to this day."

"I'm sensing that there was tension in your family.

"Yes, it was to increase as the years went by. Since my late father went on to distinguish himself in the military, it's put an extra burden on my life. Those who know me seem astonished that I chose writing over a military career. Being the grandson and son of military heroes and not emulating them is something I've had to live with."

"If your parents were an unlikely match from different backgrounds, how did they get together in the first place?"

"According to my sister, my father swept my mother off her feet during a dance at Annapolis three months before he graduated at the top of his class, both academically and militarily. My mother had been bussed in from nearby Swarthmore College with a group of New England debutants from families who knew how to place their daughters in contact with suitable young men of the time. Upon my father's graduation, they were married in the Naval Academy chapel."

"There's was a very short courtship."

"My father was a very decisive and persuasive man when he put his mind to it. In the early days, the marriage seemed to be off to a good start. But soon after my sister was born, my father was posted to the Philippines, and my mother refused to take the child overseas. Her husband would be at sea for extended periods of time, and she would be alone with a new born in a strange country. And she didn't want to leave her family in Maryland, who gave her the support she needed with her first born child. So he went alone for a two year tour of duty without her and their daughter. When he returned, he rejoined his wife and child, and they moved to his next duty station at Norfolk, Virginia, where I was born."

"That's a long separation for them. Their family would have had quite an adjustment to make with many new circumstances when your father returned."

"Yes, and my birth nine months later added even more stress to the mix. But back to the conflict I experienced. Early on I felt the pull between what my mother's ambitions for me were and the course my father had set for me. Rather than give in to either side, I eventually compromised by becoming a war correspondent. This decision enabled me to combine my writing talents with the adventure and daring inherited from my father.

"So as it turned out, I became a warrior for truth, rather than a combatant in the military sense. But my own search for the truth of life led me to the study of philosophy in my college years which greatly expanded my perspective through the thoughts of history's great thinkers."

"Your study of philosophy must have pleased your mother, but your father must have considered it a waste of time when instead you could have been studying military strategy."

"You've got that right, lovely one. But my 'warrior for the truth' status pleased neither one of my parents. My mother, nor my father, saw my choice as a compromise between them. The rub was that each felt she/he had lost me to the other's world. But I was the one who lost them both to my world. I had just won the Pulitzer Prize for war reporting in Indo China in 1954 at the age of 28 when I received word that both my parents had been killed in an air crash en route to Washington, D.C."

"Oh, Winston, I'm so terribly sorry. Whatever tensions were present in your family, nothing compares to the loss of one's parents. I know this from experience when my own mother died in an air crash on her way back to the Philippines after a visit to America to see relatives. I was 12 years old. My father and I have never really gotten over her death."

"It seems we both have felt the heavy hand of the unexpected death of loved ones in air crashes. I'm sorry to hear that, Maria. You have my sympathy as well."

"Mother died when her aircraft took off from Wake Island. It experienced an engine failure that took the aircraft spiraling down into the sea, father told me. We couldn't even recover her body for burial. I have to admit, I experience a sense of terror every time I'm on an aircraft on take-off."

"But I don't understand. Your career as a flight attendant requires countless take-offs. Why did you choose such a job?"

"I knew that I had to overcome the fear of death or be consumed by it all my life. I have to admit I hid in the lavatory on our take-off from Guam. When the door flew open during the turbulence, I fell out and hit my head on the galley, which knocked me unconscious. I should have been attending and reassuring my passengers instead."

"So that's what caused your accident, and on take-off from Guam in the area of the Pacific where your mother had died!"

"I thought I had conquered my fear after all this time, but it must have been residing in my subconscious, only to be revived in similar circumstances to my mother's misfortunate accident. Thankfully we didn't suffer the same fate. I truly miss her so very much even to this day."

"Now I must admit to feeling guilty for taking advantage of your emotional state on Guam when we made love on the beach."

Maria reassured Winston, "How can we explain the waves of communication and emotion that immersed us in a yearning not to be denied? We were both part of the enchantment that engulfed us, regardless of our personal circumstances, Winston. If there is any blame, I share in it as well."

"You are too kind, my beautiful angel."

"But finish your own story, Winston."

"My parents were on their way to Washington because my father had been summoned to plead his case against a powerful group of congressmen and senators who were blocking his promotion to fourth star rank. Senator Thomas Kearney, Sr., Senate Armed Services Chairman, led those in opposition to my father's promotion, because my father advocated the use of American troops in the rescue of the French garrison at Dien Bien Phu. The old man's reasoning proved prophetic. He had earlier warned Congress, 'Either we help the French defeat communism in Southeast Asia now, or prepare to do the job on our own later.'

"So here we are in Vietnam, now trying to stem the rising tide of communist aggression years later by supporting an authoritarian Vietnamese leader quelling numerous rebellious factions in his country while fighting an invasive enemy from the north. To say that the U.S. is uncomfortable with Diem's lack of democratic reforms is putting it mildly."

"Winston, is the demolitions expert on our military transport flight from the States to Vietnam the son of this senator who opposed your father's promotion?"

"Yes, he's one who tried to seduce you in Hawaii."

"I just had one drink with him to be polite."

"The pattern of the Kearney's opposition to my family continues on, as they've now targeted me. Possibly Lieutenant Kearney's ego was pierced when you didn't comply with his plans, and maybe was further angered when he surmised we had made a romantic connection. Now the elder Kearney's sympathy for his son's supposed sense of humiliation is probably the reason he's put pressure on government and military officials to expel me from South Vietnam. He claims that I am a poor example to our troops because of my drunken behavior in Hawaii, and not qualified to report on the war.

"Granted, I was an obnoxious drunk in Hawaii. I knew better from my ex-wife Eleanor's advice that I should never mix pain killers with alcohol. But I promised General Pavler when I arrived in Vietnam, I would not drink while reporting there or I would lose his support."

"And have you kept that promise, Winston?"

"Well, I have been tempted quite a few times, fingering my flask, Willie. But I have deferred from taking a drink, except for once I don't believe General Pavler knows about, at Pierre Girard's press party. However, after the party I was almost mugged when I took a pedicab and directed the driver to take me back to Five Oceans. Instead, I ended up in an alley with thugs and only escaped when I held my Derringer under the chin of the pedicab driver and made him take me to police headquarters."

"Oh, Winston, those kind of slip-ups always lead one to self-destruction in one way or another."

"Don't I know that too well, Maria. But I've talked enough about myself. What about your story? You tell me you haven't been with a man before me, and though I realized it during our first trip to the stars, yet your responses are like those of an experienced woman."

"How can I explain it but to say that the energy between us makes us one and generates my responses to you as naturally as breathing."

"Undeniably, our combined energy has a mind of its own, and I'm not complaining. But surely you've had relationships with men before. The beauty of 'Miss Philippines' can't be missed."

"That honor is both a blessing and a curse. I'm a 'dartboard' for male egos. Take Lieutenant Kearney, for example, who obviously targeted me in Hawaii, perhaps because of my small bit of fame as

'Miss Philippines.' He was one of those who only wish to use me to inflate their egos and hope to experience temporary pleasure with me."

"And what makes you think I'm any different from them?"

"Perhaps at the beginning it was so with your poetic pick-up lines. Their eloquent words of embellished flattery are so pleasing to the feminine mind and emotions that they weaken a woman's defenses. Your way with words certainly melts my heart. But I also sense depths to your innate potential yet to be developed that is absolutely amazing and intriguing."

"You must be looking at me through rose-colored glasses."

"If so, it's a very exciting illusion. Your quest for the truth resonates with me, and I want to share what you discover."

"But maybe the truth is that I'm just a jaded drunkard who can't seem to 'face the sun' as my father always admonished me. To be frank, we must also ask ourselves if you aren't motivated to do good, being attracted to an underdog you want to restore."

"Winston, after what we have shared together physically, mentally and spiritually, can you imagine me taking the easy road and saying 'yes' to a fine young man in the Philippines? He has waited years for me to answer his proposal, but he is more a very good friend, or brother, rather than a future husband. How can I forget you, whatever the outcome of our relationship?"

"That's what I'm afraid of for both of us, Maria. If you have a tried and true young man waiting for you, I have an ex-wife who seems to have changed her mind about our divorce and has contacted my sister Clemie in Hawaii to ask about me."

"I don't blame her, Winston. Do you still love her?"

"She is more my age, Maria, just as the young man waiting for you is probably a more appropriate companion for your age, of what, 28 years, compared to my 38 tumultuous years? If nothing else, I have a history with Eleanor. Perhaps I owe it to her to put our relationship once and for all in the past before we can move forward with new relationships."

"Perhaps, Winston, but suppose the opposite happens, and you get back together again?"

"We'll just have to wait and see what happens, won't we, in both our situations?"

"If divorce has ended your relationship with your ex-wife years ago, what's past is most likely past, despite any lingering memories of a life shared together. Are you resurrecting a past love's possible renewed advances to give yourself an excuse to avoid getting too close to me, Winston?"

"Maybe, but there's one thing I haven't given up hoping for, and that's a second Pulitzer Prize awarded to a foreign correspondent each year. How does a relationship fare when one is constantly following breaking news and the other is a lovely flight attendant flying here and there? Eleanor, for her part, never wanted to put up with such unstable flexibility and separations in our relationship."

"We're quite a pair, aren't we, Winston? For all practical purposes we both should remain footloose and fancy free. So why did the fates bring us together with an attraction that really can't be denied if we are to find any peace in this life?"

Brand stroked Maria's long, black hair. "If you're finished with brunch, we can always accommodate the fates once more while we have this fleeting moment of time together."

"You're going to drive our unforgettable experiences together deeper and deeper into both our memories.'"

"Exactly what I had in mind, my lovely Venus, in more ways than one."

The next morning as Brand looked out the window of the airplane taking him back to Saigon, the world seemed a much warmer and friendlier place with Maria in it. He could still see Maria in his mind standing there in her beauty at the airport trying to gulf the distance that was beginning to separate them physically as he entered the aircraft. He had turned to wave to her, his whole being yearning for her as well, and he knew without a doubt that she would be in his thoughts a million times since that moment. Whether or not it was wise for either of them, they had formed a lasting bond together, whatever the outward expression of it in the world would turn out to be.

Just knowing of Maria's presence "somewhere out there" was part of him now, whether they were near or far apart. Perhaps Doc Jenicoso had been smiling down on them as they grieved his loss and loved each other to take away the pain. Both his friend, the irrepressible optimist who had cautioned him not to let life pass him by, and his beautiful Maria would be sorely missed in the days ahead—Doc gone forever, but Maria vibrantly alive and awaiting another time, another place, as he did, despite his misgivings.

34 HO CHI MINH TRAIL

Secrecy is the soul of all great designs. Perhaps more has been effected by concealing our own intentions than by discovering those of our enemy.

—Charles Caleb Colton

R-3 LOOKED UP from the newspaper he was reading after his evening meal when his field adjutant entered and approached him. R-3 spoke first, "The newspaper report I've been reading indicates we were successful in eliminating the American doctor who treated casualties at Ba Tat.

"The *Times* columnist, Winston Brand, has painted far too rosy a picture of the good doctor's accomplishments in Quang Ngai Province and has enhanced a perception we don't want of warm light shining around President Diem and his American ally for accomplishing such humanitarian efforts."

The adjutant replied, "I'm happy this news pleases you, Supreme Leader, but I bring a report from the field that will displease you greatly."

"What is it?"

"It concerns our secret endeavor to train our soldiers on the stolen American radios, using the captured American communications specialists to instruct them. The good news is that we've been successful in the transport of the American radios needed in Cambodia to headquarters there. As you have directed, the reserve radios have been stored in a discreet, unused building in the far reaches of the Devereau plantation."

"Good, but what about the bad news?"

"The north has transported the American communications specialists from Hanoi to our training site in Cambodia. But the trail is not so well developed in Cambodia yet, and one of the Americans escaped during a rest stop. Unfortunately, it was on our supply trail in Cambodia adjacent to Song Be Province."

R-3's countenance darkened. "Tell me the escaped American has been recaptured."

"No, Great Leader. It's rough going through the jungle overgrowth that appears faster than it can be cut down, now being soaked during the monsoon season."

R-3 turned his head, stood up and began pacing the floor. "It just won't do! If the secret operation we've planned is discovered by our enemies, not only will the Americans know their two missing transport aircraft were hijacked by us, but it won't be difficult for them to connect the communications specialists with the stolen radios and discern our most important objective at this time."

R-3's extreme displeasure made the adjutant wince. "By any chance was the American injured during the escape?"

"Yes, we believe a shot was fired that might have met its mark as the escapee disappeared into the dense jungle overgrowth. A frantic and intensive search was undertaken by a few guards, but majority of our force had to stay in place to take extreme care so no others could escape as well."

"How close was the group to the border with Vietnam when the escape occurred?"

"Very close to the compound at Song Be across the border."

"That's where an American advisor, the infamous son of American Senator Thomas Kearney, Sr. is stationed! The lieutenant has a pregnant Vietnamese wife and has just fueled the Western press with his attempted evasion of his responsibilities to her. Wouldn't he like to redeem himself with the possible rescue of an American captured by the communists! We must prevent this from happening. Double or triple the members of a search team to recapture this slippery American escapee at all costs!"

"Before you leave, tell me, "Has there been any word from Madame Binh regarding her interrogation of Captain Bao?"

"Yes, most Esteemed Leader. She firmly believes Captain Bao was the instigator of the plot against Senator Kearney and his son.

Although our comrade couldn't get him to confess, she is very suspicious of Bao's increasing fascination with Madame Nhu, which takes his mind off his very important resistance role. She recommends additional surveillance of him due to his growing sense of self-importance and arrogance due to his favoritism with the Nhus."

"Let's see to her request immediately. I also detect some jealousy evident in Madame Binh's censure of Captain Bao. Her fury could possibly hide an underlying fascination with him she doesn't yet recognize. Let's increase the surveillance of Madame Binh, too, by giving her a helper in her curio shop."

"Your command is all I need to carry out your wishes, Wise Leader. Is there anything else you wish of me before I go?"

"Yes, has there been any report on the successful elimination of the defector in the Quang Ngai strategic hamlet yet? Our stake-out has taken too long complete their mission."

"I'm glad to report another success. The sergeant no longer lives to give aid to the enemy, Distinguished Leader."

"Excellent. I wasn't happy to see yet another positive column by *Times* reporter Winston Brand extolling the success of the Strategic Hamlet program in Quang Ngai. Brand has begun to irritate me with his reports of the Diem's regime's progress in nation building, and his human interest angles to his columns catch the eye of his American readers. We'd rather see them saturated with the negative reports of the Western press.

"If Brand persists, I may have to rethink my hold on Hanoi's desire to eliminate him. Brand has an admirable spirit, dedicated to seeking the truth, but unfortunately it is not the truth of our cause. He can become dangerous to our objectives."

"Do you want us to assassinate him, Powerful Leader?"

"Not yet. I haven't made up my mind. So far we've easily countered his good reports by eliminating a personal friend of his, which may subdue his efforts.

"We don't wish to raise a commotion during this period while our communication project is in its training phase as we prepare to stand and fight for the first time at Ap Bac. We want to completely surprise the enemy with conflicting radio messages during the battle. It'll give us a victory heard around the world thanks to the press."

"Very well, we will wait for further orders about Brand."

"If Captain Bao were not so well placed in the Diem regime, I wouldn't hold off on eliminating him at once for his arrogance in acting alone without higher guidance. Creating an international incident regarding the American senator and his son is the opposite of what we planned at this point. His attempt to control matters on his own is way beyond the scope of his mission and is treasonous in our eyes. We will wait while Captain Bao is still of use to us before we eliminate him. Meanwhile, increase our surveillance of Winston Brand, Captain Bao and Madame Binh as I have ordered."

"Very good, Great Leader."

"Our first priority, however, is the all-out effort to scour the mountainous jungle area to find the escaped American communications specialist. As you leave, send in my aide with paper, pen and a portable chess set for an urgent message to Hanoi regarding the escaped specialist. We must recapture him as soon as possible!"

"'Her', Esteemed One," interjected the adjutant.

"What do you mean?"

"The escaped American is female."

Lt. Thomas Kearney, Jr., couldn't wrap his mind around the idea that his powerful father, an American senator no less, hadn't been able to help him wiggle out of his scam marriage to Lieu that had landed him back at Song Be with her and her family. Not that Ca Mau had been that great either without available women to entice into his bed in the soggy delta.

He'd heard that a Capt. Edward Markham had been sent to Ca Mau to replace him. Lots of luck to the guy in that sink hole, Kearny thought. Come to think of it though, he wondered if he had been tricked by Old Lucas McCain into believing she was a young girl by binding herself to appear as an undeveloped youngster, which would be easy for a Vietnamese female to do. Damn, he hated to be tricked or humiliated by anyone. If the "Rifleman" was really of age, he'd find out about it before he left Vietnam and make sure to taste her denied fruits.

In the meantime, he had barely tolerated the endless Vietnamese wedding customs he was obligated to observe with Lieu and her extended family. She had such a bad case of morning sickness, the rituals could barely be held with her tendency to vomit at the most inopportune times. Sharing a marital bed with her was more pain than pleasure, just the opposite of their hot wedding night together. And she was showing so early, Kearney, Jr., feared she was carrying twins. If so, it was just his rotten luck in this forsaken country that he was kicked in the butt every time he had tried to get a piece of the action.

The morning after another miserable night with Lieu, Lieutenant Kearney left the American compound on a surveillance mission in the area adjacent to the Cambodian border. The Ho Chi Minh trail passed close by in that region, and his orders were to detect any unusual movements. He accompanied a large group of ARVN troops, including some Montagnards. They were on the lookout for any possible signs or native sightings of a group of captured Americans escorted by Viet Cong coming down the Ho Chi Minh trail in nearby Cambodia.

Kearney thought General Pavler and the Vietnamese generals must be hallucinating to imagine such a scenario. He only expected to find some Montagnard villages. These native people's dialects were so strange, they'd have to communicate with sign language, unless the few Montagnards serving with the ARVN soldiers could converse with them. And how likely would their cooperation be? He already felt the underlying tension between the Vietnamese and the Montagnards in their group.

Kearney cursed the heavy backpacks with provisions and arms they had to carry through the jungle on this mission of several weeks. But it'd give him a break from Lieu and her family.

The group had taken jeeps as far as they could to approach the border area, but after several days of trekking through the highland jungle, true to Kearney's prediction, they came across a Montagnard village. The 'Yard's' reception was cool, despite the Montagnards they spotted in our group. They seemed very uneasy when the Vietnamese soldiers set up camp around their village area, cleared with their slash and burn habit.

Kearney approached the Montagnard long house with his Vietnamese counterpart and a native interpreter and questioned the village chief. Had they seen any captured Americans being escorted down the trail by the Viet Cong? They indicated no by shaking their heads, but wouldn't make eye contact, raising his suspicion. Cooperation might bring death to the tribe from the Viet Cong, Kearney knew. But then again, what if they knew something and were hiding it?

Then a little Montagnard girl came up to them and looked at Kearney's red hair in fascination. "Same, same," she said in a dialect they couldn't understand. She pointed to Kearney's red hair. Her mother immediately came for her and whisked her away. When her words were interpreted, Kearney was intrigued. No Vietnamese had red hair, but an Irish American surely might. They decided to search the long house after negotiating with the chief, but found nothing to confirm their suspicions.

However, Kearney stepped on a suspicious spot on the dirt floor of the long house. He pushed the dirt aside with his foot and discovered a round wooden cover underneath. When they opened the cover, they discovered a roughly construed ladder that gave access to a dimly perceived tunnel underneath the floor.

"What have we here?" Kearney exclaimed. "It looks like a place to hide the Montagnard women and children if this village is attacked. I think I'll take a look down there."

"Be careful," said his Vietnamese counterpart. "What if Viet Cong are hiding down there to escape our detection? The Montagnards might have concealed them because of fear of death."

"Let's smoke out anyone who might be hiding down there."

"Don't bother," said an American voice coming from the tunnel. "If that's an American with a hint of Irish brogue in his voice that I hear, I'll gladly come up."

They were astonished as they saw a head with flowing red hair appear as the tunnel occupant climbed the ladder. They witnessed a virtual Brunhilde, or female warrior type, emerge from the opening. "Boy, am I glad to see you," she said looking into Kearney's eyes.

"The feeling is more than mutual." Kearney took in her ample and curved figure beneath the black pajama clothing given to prisoners of the Viet Cong to wear. "Have you been hurt?" The Lieutenant saw a crude banana leaf bandage held on by thin plant stems on her left arm.

"Yes, but luckily a bullet just grazed my arm." She spied Keaney's rank displayed on his fatigues. "Lt. Maureen Kelly here, recently escaped from the Viet Cong. They were transporting a group of us captured American communications specialists from Hanoi to Cambodia,"

"My God! The brass wasn't hallucinating. Their scenario is a reality! Let's get you back to base and tend to your injury."

He put his arm around her waist and guided her out of the long house. Although scruffy and wounded, the spunky American officer felt so good to Kearny who was enticed by the charms of the obviously Irish American woman. Kearny should appear as a concerned officer rescuing another in need, but he could barely contain his interest in the beautiful female.

Meanwhile, from their base at Loc Ninh, southwest of Song Be, Major Alex Spear and newly promoted Capt. Rafe Hewlett were conducting a similar search with Vietnamese Major Si and a group of his ARVN troops near the Cambodian border. So far they hadn't turned up any signs of unusual Viet Cong movement when they had questioned the peasants adjacent to the Ho Chi Minh trail.

Next they proceeded to the Devereau plantation to seek permission to search any unused buildings that might serve as storage units for the stolen American radios. Monsieur Devereau reluctantly agreed to their request.

"Major Spear, I regret that you suffered a painful rat bite in our old barn, but I am happy to see you have recovered from the nasty incident with the proper medical procedure. We have numerous abandoned dwellings on our plantation where the many laborers on our rubber plantation lived during my father's time. Now that our labor force has been greatly reduced, these dwellings in areas farther out from the plantation house are no longer used and have deteriorated over the years. I am a bit reluctant to allow you to search these dilapidated buildings lest they be rat-infested and cause you, Captain Hewlett and the ARVN troops under Major Si to be bitten by rats as you were."

"We will be sure to take extra caution, perhaps just looking in the door to see if the American stolen radios could possibly be stored there by the communists unbeknownst to you and your staff," replied Major Spear.

"I want our overseer, Mr. Ly, to accompany you. He is familiar with all areas of the plantation and can facilitate your search." The Frenchman sent for the overseer.

Lucette Devereau, who had been directing the household staff appeared and greeted them warmly. "Major Spear, I'm so glad to see you recovered from your unfortunate incident at the plantation." She then glanced at the now Captain Hewlett with longing. "It's so good to see you, too, Captain. Congratulations on your promotion! We've hoped to see you more often since our last encounter."

A reciprocal longing in Hewlett's eyes reflected that in Lucette's eyes. "It's good to see you, too, Lucette. Ah'm sorry to have been so scarce, but we've been very busy both before and after Major Spear arrived back in Loc Ninh."

Major Spear interjected, "We'll check back in at the plantation after our search of the laborers' abandoned dwellings, Monsieur Devereau. Thank you for your permission."

Days later Rafe Hewlett said to Alex Spear, "Ah wouldn't be surprised if we haven't seen every square inch of this huge rubber plantation, yet we haven't turned up a thing."

"I'm beginning to think that's just what Mr. Ly wants us to find—nothing. When we go back to the plantation house, and Mr. Ly is no longer assigned to our search, we can go back later to explore an area farthest away I have my eye on. Mr. Ly said it was not on plantation property, so we couldn't continue searching there. Do you remember how it was especially secluded with trees and heavy underbrush? It could easily have hidden a dwelling we weren't meant to see."

"Ah know the area you are referring to. Ah had the same impression. But how can we revisit the area without suspicion?"

"How about this plan? We can tell the Devereaus that Major Si must return to Loc Ninh with his troops, but that we'd like to stay awhile to make up for your absence in the past month."

"Meanwhile, Major Si and his men can return undetected to search the suspicious area?" asked Hewlett.

"That's my plan. We can ask to have Mr. Ly present at dinner to express our appreciation for his help."

"It's a plan, sir." Rafe saw an opportunity opening up to give him extra time to spend with Lucette.

During dinner at the plantation, a serving girl re-entered the dining room and delivered a message to Monsieur Devereau. He looked up from reading the message and said, "Major Spear, you have a telephone call."

Alex excused himself and followed the maid to take the call. "Yes, Major Spear here."

"General Pavler on this end. Major, you're needed back at headquarters immediately. We're sending a helicopter to Loc Ninh tomorrow at daybreak to pick you up to return post haste."

"Is everything all right with my family?"

"Yes, just fine. They're settling in well in new quarters, Norma has written. I will brief you tomorrow."

"Very good, sir." Alex hung up with a puzzled look on his face. Something very important was in the works.

When Alex returned to the table, Monsieur Devereau asked, "Is everything all right?"

"Yes, but it seems I'm needed back in Saigon. Thank you, Monsieur Devereau, for your much appreciated cooperation in permitting us to search your plantation area, and of course for your gracious hospitality." He nodded at Mr. Ly and thanked him for his help as well. The overseer acknowledged the major with a hint of a smile, and left the room.

Monsieur Devereau replied, "We are glad to help. You are welcome to stay the night so you don't have to travel the road back to Loc Ninh in the dark. We don't want another ambush.

"Thank you. I'd like to leave at the break of dawn with Captain Hewlett, so I'll depart to my room as it grows late."

"Good night, sir," said Rafe. Ah'll be along soon. Ah'd like to visit a short while with Lucette before ah retire."

After Alex and Lucette's father left the dining room, Lucette led Rafe out into the moonlite terrace. Before long they were in each other's arms exchanging kisses and endearments. Lucette whispered in Rafe's ear, "Rafe, my darling, why have you stayed away so long?"

Rafe kissed her neck. "Lucette, you know ah've been advised by my superiors to cool my romance with you. The communist presence discovered in your old barn indicates that a frequent military presence here to alert them to our suspicions isn't wise. But, honestly, it's killing me to stay away from you!"

"Oh, Rafe, I feel the same way. I was afraid you'd lost interest in me. Isn't there some way we can be together without raising suspicion?"

"For now, these stolen moments are all we can count on, my beautiful Lucette. Let's not waste them."

"Rafe, spend the night with me in the *garçonnière*. We'll be sure to go back to the main house before dawn breaks. Let's give each other loving memories to keep us going during these times of separation."

"That's not a good idea, Lucette. It'll make the separations more difficult if we become intimate."

Lucette undid the straps of her sundress and the top slid to her waist. Rafe groaned. His hands explored the gift being offered to him, and then his lips met the warm flesh of Lucette's breasts. It would just be for one night, he thought. He lifted her in his arms and walked quickly to the *garçonnière.*

As dawn broke, Captain Hewlett awaited Major Spear in the jeep. No ambushes were encountered on their way back to Loc Ninh, but Alex was sure Rafe hadn't slept a wink all night.

"Captain Hewlett," said Alex breaking the silence between them. "Please remember my warning regarding the Devereaus. There is much communist activity taking place there, whether the father and daughter know about it or not. As the military advisor here in Loc Ninh, your duty is to treat the Devereaus' plantation as a military target of interest. You have a responsibility to maintain a polite but restrained relationship with the Devereaus. That includes Lucette."

"Ah'll try, sir, but it's just about killing me to suppress my feelings for Lucette. Ah may have to ask for a transfer."

"I thought as much. But for now, your best strategy is to stay away unless absolutely necessary. Please advise me at once if Major Si's troops find anything in the secret location."

Alex left by helicopter when they reached the ARVN base. He looked down from above at the base and the Devereau plantation. Both were a potential tinderbox. Captain Hewlett needed to control himself and not strike a 'match,' but rather look for the stolen radios in secrecy with Major Si and his troops. Then Alex turned his thoughts toward Saigon. Something big had happened to call him back there. He knew he would soon be in conference with the other members of Operation Checkmate.

35 A TIME TO REGROUP

The more powerful the obstacle, the more glory we have in overcoming it; and the difficulties with which we are met are the maids of honor which set off virtue.

—Jean-Baptiste Poquelin aka Molière

LIEUTENANT KEARNEY, JR., KNEW he'd never forget the journey back to base through the jungle highlands with Lt. Maureen Kelly. They had shared a tent in the evenings, but their Irish tempers had flared fiercely when Maureen had stubbornly resisted Kearney's advances.

It wasn't until the group detected the presence of a Viet Cong search party in their vicinity that Maureen broke down and sobbed in Kearney's arms. She told him she'd rather die than be recaptured, as she suspected she'd be shot anyway with the rest of her fellow American communications specialists once they'd trained the Viet Cong soldiers on the American radios. Only the hope she'd be able to save herself and the others from the prospect of death had given her enough courage for her escape attempt to get help in time. She embodied the resistance of her group to foil a communist plot using the American radios.

Kearney knew she was vulnerable with news of the threat of the Viet Cong search party in the area, but he selfishly took advantage of her anyway. He had surmised that moment would be his only opportunity to break through her reserve.

"Tom, you can't imagine what it's like to be a prisoner of the communists," Maureen sobbed. Her tears wet his shirt as he held her in his arms.

"Baby, I can't imagine the terror you've been through. But we've found you, and I promise we'll do whatever it takes to get you back to safety," replied Kearney pressing her even more closely to his eager body.

"Oh, Tom, if only we could say as much for my fellow soldiers still in captivity, whom I fear will be killed as soon as they're no longer of use to the Viet Cong. It breaks my heart that I was the only one to escape, but perhaps I can at least alert the authorities to their plight and hope with all my heart for their rescue. But what if the Viet Cong find us before we can get back to base, making my life and death escape futile?"

"Trust me. There's no way we're going to let that happen. We'll fight to the last man if they find us."

"Tom, I've tried to keep up a brave front for the sake of others until now, but I've been so very afraid inside. I just can't stop trembling with the thought of possibly going back into that hell of captivity until I'm finally shot dead when they don't need me any longer."

Kearney began soothing Maureen by gently running his hands up and down her back as he held her ever closer, and it was not long before his touch became more intimate when she clung to him as to a life saver in perilous waters. It was the breakthrough Kearney had been waiting for. He took advantage of her sudden terror to finally coax her into an intimate night together. It was a seduction he had been planning ever since he had seen her red hair appear in the tunnel opening in the Montagnard long house. But to his surprise, in the nights of lovemaking that followed, they experienced the deepest connection he had ever known before.

With great effort the group evaded their Viet Cong pursuers. Completing their mission, they arrived safely back at Song Be. The secret lovers were soon notified a helicopter would arrive to whisk Maureen off to Saigon for medical treatment and interrogation by intelligence.

Kearney told Maureen before she departed that he wanted to see her again. But she replied, with a mixture of sadness and guilt in her eyes, she was married, and it would be best for them to meet only in their dreams in the future.

As Kearney watched the helicopter swiftly remove Maureen from his life and his bed, he realized he hadn't told her how much she had come to mean to him. Nor had he told her he was also married, because he planned to divorce Lieu when he returned to the States. But Maureen had made it clear her marital status was for keeps. She had suggested they look on their stolen time together as a reprieve from death for her and a gift of her appreciation to him for her rescue.

But the memories of their intimacies with each other filled both his dreams and his waking hours. What was wrong with him, he wondered, as he usually left his conquests without another thought. Although some like Carlotta Simone and now Lieu had no intention of forgetting him. Now the tables were turned, and he couldn't seem to forget Maureen.

Did Maureen think her husband was a better lover than he was, or was she tied to him by her religion? Damn, what did it matter anyway? She's married and intends to stay that way, he thought, and decided to chalk up the experience with her as another successful seduction.

But why did he keep seeing his fingers running through her flowing red hair and exploring every inch of her lovely body? Damn, what spirit, courage and spunk she had, overcoming the awful fear she'd experienced in captivity, to try a daring escape to try to save her fellow soldiers! He'd never met anyone like her. He remembered her first resistance to his advances when she had told him, "Only in your dreams, Lieutenant!"

But now his dreams were her dwelling place, and memories of her living, breathing, voluptuous beauty and lively personality remained there to ever tempt him, and frustrate him with the futility of becoming a reality. But those dreams were a respite from the life he was forced to live, for a while at least, with his pregnant Vietnamese wife and her relentless nausea.

Maria Monclova returned to the Philippines after receiving an urgent message from her father's housekeeper, Letty, that her father had been taken to the emergency room at the hospital after a car accident. When she arrived, her father was in a hospital room with his arm in a cast.

"I'm so sorry you've been injured, Father. The nurse at the desk told me you sustained a broken arm and a few fractured ribs when someone ran a red light and hit you in the intersection."

"Did she also tell you I've been getting cranky, restless and driven to distraction with itching under my cast?" asked Pacifico Monclova of his beautiful daughter.

"Now I know I'm home, Dad, when I hear you talk like that," responded Maria.

"I hope you're here to bust me out of here, Maria. By now my administrative job with the Department of Foreign Affairs is in shambles, and I can't get this cast off for another whole month!" moaned her father.

"So when have you ever taken a vacation since mother died?" asked Maria in an effort to comfort him.

"So when have you ever taken a vacation yourself, lovely daughter?"

"It looks like we're both going to take a rest for the next month while I take care of you until your arm heals enough for the doctor to order the cast taken off your arm," answered Maria. "I've a month's leave of absence from the airlines."

"Nonsense! Our housekeeper Letty can assist me while I recover. Besides no one can cook and clean as well as our faithful Letty can since your dear mother passed. She's been through more than a broken arm and a few fractured ribs with us."

"That's just the point, Father. Letty's not getting any younger, and she's got enough responsibilities without adding nursing care for you to her list of duties. Besides, who's going to chide you to take it easy, follow the doctor's orders and entertain you during your recovery while Letty's busy with her household duties? Then there're doctor's visits to go to, possible physical therapy as you are able to tolerate it, taking work you're able to do at home to and from your office and any number of countless things I can help you with."

"You sound just like your mother, Maria."

"I know, Dad. Neither of us have really gotten over her early and unexpected death," sympathized Maria with tears seeping into her eyes.

"Dear Maria, you are heart of my heart. I'm so glad you graced our lives for 12 years before we lost your mother in her dreadful air crash. Without the recovery of her body from the Pacific Ocean, it still feels like she might return one day. But for now, we only have each other as family," reminisced the elder Monclova.

"Maybe not. I have met a man I wish I could add to our little family, but we are a most unlikely couple as he describes us. He's older than I am, divorced and has some personal problems. But, on the other hand, he is the most interesting and intriguing man I have ever met with a lively, brilliant mind, a way with words and a poetic flair. But don't worry, he's not interested in marriage and is dead set on winning a second Pulitzer Prize as a foreign correspondent in Vietnam."

"I hope he's not one of the pessimistic bunch of newspaper men in Vietnam who have been bombarding their readers with dire predictions regarding the status of the war and its leadership in that tortured country," replied Maria's father.

"Well, he's a correspondent for the *New York Times* and writes a column called the 'Branding Iron'," responded Maria.

"You don't say. I'm familiar with his column. He tries to tell the truth, but I wouldn't want to see his enemy list of people who don't want the truth to be revealed. How in the world did you become acquainted with him, much less come to the point of wanting him to join our family?" asked Maria's concerned father.

"He was a passenger on the military flight from the States through Hawaii and Guam to Vietnam on which I was the only flight attendant with the security clearance the U.S. military required. I wanted to leave the flight in Hawaii, but Major Spear couldn't find a replacement for me. My desire was to avoid Wake Island where mother perished in the aircraft accident after takeoff from there, but I couldn't abandon the flight with no replacement for me, although that was the last thing I wanted to do. But I had a premonition of trouble," explained Maria.

"Did you indeed run into trouble on the flight, Maria?" asked her father with an anxious look in his eyes.

"Yes, father, there was an explosion on takeoff from Guam. I'm sorry to say my fear got the best of me, and I hid in the lavatory, but the door burst open and I was thrown into the galley where I hit my head. As the pilot struggled to regain control of the aircraft and head back to Guam, I'm told that the marine officer directed Winston Brand to go to the galley where he picked me up. I was unconscious, and he carried me back to his seat, holding me in his arms. The doctor on board bandaged the cut on my head. When the plane landed safely, I was taken to the hospital for further medical assessment," said Maria.

"Was that your only injury, daughter, or were there others?" asked Pacifico Monclova with a worried look.

"When I was checked in at the hospital in Guam, I was told I had a slight concussion, but no lasting injury. But on the damaged aircraft, after the doctor had bandaged my head, he instructed Winston to continue to hold me with a blanket around me to prevent shock. I felt so guilty for not tending to my passengers instead of being cared for myself."

"Well, I'm grateful to Mr. Brand and the doctor on board for tending to your injury, but is that the only encounter you have had with the controversial columnist?"

Maria lowered her eyes. "I can't explain the energy that draws Winston and me together, but it's so very powerful. I have never felt anything like it before. Perhaps it is the last thing anyone would expect, and I'm sure both of us thought the same thing at first. However, when we spent time together on the beach at Guam after I was released from the hospital there, our minds seemed to find a kindred soul in each other. He shared poems with me from his book of poetry, *Fire in the Soul*, and even made up a poem for me on the spot."

"Oh, daughter, you always did have an idealistic, romantic streak in you. He must have captured your imagination and your heart with his words," responded her father. "But as your father, I can't help but advise you that you'd have a much more stable life with a man if you finally said yes to Tywan, who's been waiting patiently for your answer all these years. He loves you, has a good job at his father's bank and would be a faithful husband and an attentive father."

"I know, Dad. Winston said the same thing to me when we got together in Bangkok recently. He had tried to stay away from me to protect me and work on his life issues before becoming involved with anyone in a romantic relationship. But when the doctor who had attended me during the near miss in Guam was killed by the communists in a helicopter crash, we both needed to be together to relieve our grief over his death."

"A rendezvous in Bangkok with this Brand fellow, daughter! How serious are you getting with him, Maria?"

"He consistently advises me not to get serious, Dad. He wonders if I am looking at him with rose colored glasses. But the chemistry between us and the meeting of our minds is impossible for us to forget, whatever the outcome may be," responded Maria with frankness.

"Well, you've certainly taken my mind off of my minor injuries with your romantic revelations, Maria. Now I really have something to worry about. Perhaps the month off will help cool down your relationship dilemma with Winston Brand."

"Dad, even if nothing works out between us, my life is so much richer for having known Winston. I have to admit though, I probably won't ever forget him."

"My goodness, dear daughter. I'd begun to despair that you'd never experience the deep feelings for a man and his for you that your mother and I enjoyed with each other. But your choice seems to hold deep difficulties for you and him as well. Parents desire to smooth the way for their children, but you may have rough seas ahead of you in this relationship if it progresses, Maria."

"I realize that, Dad. Don't worry. Perhaps nothing may come of it, much to my disappointment. But let's get back to your care. We need to take it easy on Letty and enjoy our father/daughter relationship in the next month. I've needed to spend more time with you for a long time now. My life has gotten too busy lately. Let's enjoy our time together."

"Okay, Maria, It won't hurt either of us to take time to think things over as we plan for the future."

Norma Pavler received a letter from her husband, Gen. George Pavler. She knew it contained an answer to her question as to whether he would be able to join her in the Philippines to celebrate Christmas together. They had been apart much too long despite her living closer to him. He was needed in Vietnam, he had told her and had explained to her why he had extended his tour of duty there. But even a general needed time to relax with his spouse and relieve stress, especially with a foreign war and an unidentified, sinister and elusive infiltrator at work in South Vietnam whom they needed to identify and uncover.

Norma had had plenty of female activities to attend at the U.S. base at Clark Field to keep her occupied. Then, too, she had enjoyed helping Gwen Spear and her children get settled in quarters on the base. Gwen's husband Alex had also been asked to extend his tour of duty in Vietnam and had accepted. But long separations for couples, especially ones with children like Gwen and Alex were very difficult, but it wasn't only the young that felt the sacrifice.

Norma opened the letter and her face fell as she read her husband's words. He had promised Alex Spear time with his wife and children for Christmas. He would try to make it to the Philippines, too, for the holiday, depending on the state of the war at that time.

"Duty always takes priority," she said to herself. But she had accepted this when she had married a military man, especially one talented in leadership as her husband was. "Well, perhaps there's a chance he'll be able to come," she thought, and continued to read his lengthy letter:

> Our boy, Winston, is going through the ringer lately. A good friend of his, a Dr. Nick Jenicoso, was killed in a helicopter crash we believe was instigated by the communists, although it's very unusual for them to sabotage a marked medevac helicopter. Winnie feels guilty because he recently wrote a glowing story about the doctor and his friend, a medical missionary who tends the Montagnards. He hopes his column about them didn't cause the communists to target the doctor for elimination to stop his positive reports coming from up-country.
>
> I know what you're going to wonder when you read this, but Winnie didn't start drinking again because of it. So far he's kept his promise to me to stop drinking in Vietnam as far as I know, or want to know. Instead, I encouraged him to take a break and go see a flight attendant, Maria Monclova, in Bangkok. She's based in the Philippines, and you might look her up. Anyway, Winnie and Maria seem interested in each other, and I personally know he's been writing to her. When Winnie returned from Thailand, his disposition seemed much improved.
>
> You may have heard from our dear Clemie in Hawaii, as I have, that Eleanor recently lost her mother. Now both of her parents are deceased. Perhaps she's grieving and feels lonely, so she has written to both Clemie and me asking about Winston. It's only my opinion, but I don't think it would do either of them any good to see each other again. But, of course, it's beyond our control.

We're in the midst of important developments here. I'll keep in touch with you again as soon as I can. Here's hoping a Christmas together is in our future.

To the love of my life, George

Norma folded the letter and put it lovingly back in the envelope. Tomorrow is another day, she thought. We'll just have to wait and see what happens at Christmas. Meanwhile, she wanted to check up on Gwen and her children. She wondered if Gwen might know this Maria Monclova of interest to Winnie. If her airline is based in the Philippines, perhaps they could both look up Maria and become acquainted with her.

36 THE LITTLE PEANUT GIRL

Never be afraid of what is good; the good is always the road to what is true.

—Phillip Gilbert Hamerton

BACK IN SAIGON, Winston Brand waited anxiously in the airport café for Maria's flight to land. With only a 30 minute layover to see her, Winston wanted to share with her a Christmas story he had written. He had fictionalized Dr. Jenicoso's generous donation of his surgical skill to little Kim Chi of Quang Ngai to prepare her arm to heal properly. Then she could be fitted for a prosthetic arm replacement below her elbow.

It wasn't long before he glimpsed a flight attendant's cap on a figure in the doorway, but the woman who entered wasn't Maria. She looked around the room, and when she spotted Brand, she approached him and asked, "Winston Brand?"

"Yes," he answered. "Who wants to know?"

"I'm Emma Jordan, a friend and colleague of Maria Monclova. She has taken a month's leave from her airline duties to care for her father who was injured in a car accident."

"Was the accident serious?"

"Mr. Monclova suffered a broken arm and a few fractured ribs, but he needs help at home as the elderly housekeeper would be over-burdened to add nursing duties to her responsibilities. Maria told me she regrets missing the chance to see you each week, even for a short while. But she has given me a letter to deliver to you."

Brand took the envelope and removed Maria's letter. He then folded the papers on which he had written his Christmas story and put them in the envelope instead. "I've inserted the Christmas story I've written into this envelope. I was hoping to share it with her in person, but I'd be much obliged if you could give it to her when you return to the Philippines."

"Certainly, Maria's a good friend. I'd be glad to relay any further communication between you both during the month I fill in for her."

"Thanks. I'll look forward to reading her reaction to my story in her reply by the time you return next week."

"It's a pleasure meeting you, Mr. Brand. I've read your columns, and appreciate some positive news coming from Vietnam."

"Glad to hear it, Emma. Give Maria my best. I hope my story will help ease the grief we both feel at the death of our mutual friend, Dr. Jenicoso."

"I'll look forward to reading more of your columns. I like your human interest angles tied in with the story of what's really going on in Vietnam. But I must get back to my airplane. You don't need to tell me the big Connie is a target no Viet Cong could miss. See you next week, Mr. Brand."

"My pleasure. Until then, Emma." When the flight attendant left the café, Brand looked down at Maria's letter in his hand, and the faint smell of Maria's perfume drifted into his awareness. He wondered what magic kept pulling Maria and himself together, when they should both be running in the opposite direction from each other as fast as they could go. He unfolded the pages of her letter and began to read:

> Dear Winston, heart of my heart! Could I but be there to once again behold your beloved form and feel your warm embrace but for even a second, I would be filled with such happiness. The kisses we'd exchange would be too sizzling for an airport café, so we'd once again have to restrain ourselves as we did at the Bangkok airport when you arrived for our rendezvous. The longing to be in your arms again is almost unbearable. When we're entwined together, two halves of a whole, it is such a radiant, glowing, light-filled feeling of oneness, I can hardly breathe just thinking about it.

Winston put the letter down for a minute. He'd have to finish reading it back in his room at Five Oceans. The small airport café could no longer hold the emotions that blazed between Maria and himself, even at a distance on pink paper.

Damn, that woman can write, he thought. He easily could accuse her of seducing him with her words, as she had once referred to his use of poetry as "pick-up lines" designed to seduce women. The difference was she wrote from her heart, which fueled the magnetism that kept pulling him in. Maria, Maria, the "fire in our souls" for each other has little chance of ending well, he lamented to himself as he exited the café.

Nevertheless, he could hardly wait to get back to Five Oceans to read the rest of her letter.

With her father settled at home in his favorite easy chair while Letty fussed over him, Maria had taken a break and had driven across town to her small apartment near the airport to check on things there. She then drove to the airport to wait for Emma to arrive with news of her meeting with Winston.

After the Connie landed, Emma fulfilled her flight attendant duties and then left the plane. She beamed when she saw Maria waiting for her to disembark. The two women hugged in greeting, and Maria searched Emma's face to reveal the answer to her question.

"Yes, Maria, he was there waiting anxiously for you. He looked so disappointed when he saw me instead of you. I explained your change of plans because of your father's accident and gave him your letter."

Maria's face fell when she saw the letter with her handwriting on the front in Emma's hands. "Did he reject my letter?"

"No way. He opened the envelope, removed your letter and instead inserted a copy of a Christmas story he'd written about a little Vietnamese peanut girl. He asked me to deliver it to you, and said he'd be waiting for me next week in the café to receive your reaction to his story."

Maria eagerly reached for the envelope, but didn't open it immediately. She wanted to ask Emma her impression of Winston.

"Your Winston's a very intense fellow, and his penetrating brown eyes really do a number on a female. But female intuition tells me it would take an exceptionally strong woman to ride the high waves and storms of his life. Are you ready for such a voyage, Maria?"

"I'm not sure what I'm capable of, but the fates haven't given me a chance to make a choice when we're together. It's like a tsunami overtakes us, and as much as we discern we must swim against the current, we get swept away with each other."

"Just be sure you don't drown, Maria. When you feel such ecstasy, always remember the euphoria of falling in love doesn't last, as I well know. Sooner or later, the reality of the situation has to be faced. The turmoil you'd have to face with Winston could sink your ship given what you've told me about his situation and his track record. If I were you, I'd stick with your father's advice and say yes to dear, stable Tywan."

"Winston himself advised me to do the same. What is it compelling me to yearn for Winston with all my heart and soul?"

"You forgot to add 'body,' Maria. Could it just be intense physical desire? It's been known to create a rosy dream one needs to wake up from before it's too late. I have nothing personal against Winston. He was perfectly polite to me. But you must be careful that such a risk-taking, adventurous male with charismatic magnetism doesn't suck you in and swamp your good intentions. Don't kid yourself with the hope of changing him with your love. Females have tried it without success through the ages."

Maria laughed good-naturedly, and the women parted with hugs. Emma just hoped Maria's display of humor indicated she was beginning to become aware of the risks involved in her relationship with Winston. Nevertheless, Emma promised Maria she would continue to be a messenger between the two.

When Maria returned to her father's house, she opened the envelope Emma had given her. Her senses quickened when she recognized Winston's handwriting on the papers she held in her hand. She began to read his fictionalized Christmas story about Kim Chi, titled "Candle in the Dark:"

> Children all over the world waited this year for a glimpse of a man with a snow-white beard dressed in red and white, but Santa doesn't look like that anymore. If you don't believe me, ask Kim Chi, a little one-armed peanut girl who met Santa Claus face to face. She will never forget, nor will any of us who know the story.

Of course, the little Vietnamese girl didn't realize that the tall, thin man with the wide grin, who purchased a small bag of peanuts from her (paying three times the normal amount) was Santa Claus's helper. At first she thought he was just another American soldier looking for something to do on the narrow streets of Quang Ngai. But there was something different about the way he looked into her dark, brown eyes. It was if they weren't eyes at all but bright candles on a Christmas tree.

There was no echo of a "ho, ho, ho" in his voice as he inquired about the pain in her arm. Only soft sounds came from his lips like snow falling in the woods.

When he gently raised her sleeve, exposing the raw bone left there after a portion of her arm had been shot away, she didn't cry the way she usually did when the village children teased her. His touch was soft as swan's feathers, his fingers soothing.

"Yes, I know something can be done about that," he said in a language she had heard the Americans use, "but first we'll have to consult your parents." Then in perfect Vietnamese, he explained he wanted to talk to Mother.

"Impossible," she told him. "Mother is with the angels."

"Your father?" he asked.

"Him gone, too. Viet Cong shoot. Same time shoot me. Do this," she told the kind man, pointing to the empty place below her elbow, but smiling proudly because she had spoken his language.

When he took her good hand in his, she followed him to the jeep parked by the curbside, not the least bit surprised that Santa's helper didn't use Santa's sleigh pulled by eight tiny reindeer. Besides, she had heard the other children in the village say that sometimes Santa used a helicopter to get around on Christmas Eve.

Later in the hospital she actually met Santa Claus himself, but he was dressed in a white cap and gown, instead of red and white, as he gave instructions to his helpers, some Vietnamese, some American, but all dressed in white and paying more attention to her than anyone else in the world ever had.

When she awoke the next evening, he was gone. Gone, too, was the pain in her left arm. There was no horrible bone sticking out of her sleeve like a turkey leg. In its place was a clean white bandage. And on the table beside her bed was a small Christmas tree with a note pinned to it. She knew it was from Santa even before the nurse started reading:

Dear Kim Chi,

You certainly slept a long time for an eight-year-old girl, right through Christmas Eve when all the other children here in the hospital were receiving their presents. It's a wonder their happy laughter didn't awaken you.

I wanted to give you your present personally, but there are some wounded up at Ba Tat, and they need my help. I'm sure you understand.

Before next Christmas, Kim Chi, you will have a new arm. We've ordered one from America especially for you. You'll be able to comb your long, dark hair by yourself, and even wear a pony tail when walking in the woods, so that the branches will not catch your hair.

With your new arm, you'll be a normal little girl with two arms like the other children, so we've made arrangements for you to attend school in Quang Ngai. Never again will you have to sell peanuts on the corner in the rain.

The nurse has a beautiful new *ao-dai* for you to wear. It has a high collar, and is as stylish as any you could find in Saigon. Oh, yes, it has long sleeves with pretty flowers painted on them.

You'll be a beautiful girl—and when I get back I want to be the first to promenade with you down the boulevard. I know my helper will want to come along, too. 'Til then, Merry Christmas to you, Kim Chi.

Love, Nick

But why was the Vietnamese nurse crying, Kim Chi wondered? Surely, Santa's letter was filled with joy, not sorrow. Soon she realized that Santa's letter made everyone cry at the hospital, so she put it under her pillow where they couldn't see it.

One night she overheard two Vietnamese orderlies talking about the doctor who had died of burns in a helicopter crash at Ba Tat on Christmas Day. They said the doctor was brave; he wouldn't accept any water for himself until all the other burn casualties had been treated, but by then it was too late for the doctor.

"Was it Santa Claus?" she cried.

"No, silly little girl," said one of the orderlies. "It was an American doctor. Santa will be back next year—don't you worry."

Happily Kim Chi fell asleep, clutching the letter under her pillow.

As Maria finished reading "Candle in the Dark," she felt tears cascading down her cheeks from reading the sentimental story that so reminded her of the loss of their dear friend, Dr. Jenicoso and the plight of the little peanut girl who had needed his help. The human tragedy juxtaposed against the goodness of the human heart described tore at her heart strings. Winston had written an inspired gem of a story!

As Maria wiped away her tears, her father entered the room with Letty at his side. He was taken aback by the sight of Maria's tears and asked, "What's wrong, Maria?"

It took Maria a minute to answer. "I'm just back from my short visit to my apartment and the airport to greet Emma. She met Winston Brand on her Saigon stopover, and he gave her a letter to give to me with a Christmas story in it he had written and wanted to share with me. I just finished it, and it is so touching, I couldn't contain my tears. That's all, Dad."

Her father then asked if he could read it as well, and Maria nodded. When he looked up after reading it, Maria could tell he was touched as well.

"I can see how difficult it is for you to resist Winston, Maria, but as attractive as he is to you, my advice still stands regarding your future. The roller coaster emotions of a great romance are not a stable foundation to build a life on with a mate. Don't sell Tywan short. You'd be wise to take a closer look at him and the fulfilling life he could offer you."

"There are no guarantees in life, Father. We have both learned that from mother's early death. Would you have given up the soul-satisfying years you did spend with her if you knew you would have so many years after her death to live without her?"

Maria saw a tear roll down her father's cheek, and she knew what his answer was. He would never have given up his time with her mother, no matter how short it was.

Winston Brand had shared his Christmas story with his sister Clemie, as well as Maria, and both women had responded to it enthusiastically. They encouraged him to share with others his story of human goodness expressed by the doctor for the little Vietnamese girl. The women said it pulled at one's heart strings, too, that the doctor continued caring for patients in his crashed medevac helicopter before his own needs despite his own injuries that caused his death. It was such an inexplicable tragedy of life. Clemie indicated that if a hard-nosed reporter like he was could reveal a soft spot in his heart for a little Vietnamese girl by writing her story, it would help others understand the war experience for civilians.

Brand hesitated to send it to his editor, Louis Cohn, to hold for his Christmas column and decided to try it out on a cynical male like Sheenar Tillerstein first.

After Tillerstein read the story, he exclaimed, "Oh, my goodness, Brand. This takes the cake. Now I'm really convinced you need to change the name of your column from 'The Branding Iron' to 'The Soap Opera Sweepstakes.' I can't believe you'd write such a sentimental 'tear-jerker' for a newspaper column under your tag line."

"Don't forget, Sheenar, the *Times* has female readers as well as male ones. In this world of opposites, who says I can't 'brand' stories as 'good' as well as 'bad'?"

"Suit yourself, Brand. But you can put me to sleep reading your columns any time when I don't have a deadline to meet."

"Thanks, Sheet, you're a good sounding board," said Brand as he headed out the door.

"It's 'Sheenar,' Brand, not 'Sheet,'" called Tilllestein.

Brand thought, "Darned if he wasn't starting to like Tillerstein." He'd noticed his sour bureau chief had blinked his eyes more times than usual as he'd read Brand's Christmas story.

37 EXPEDIENT ENCOUNTERS

The experience of others adds to our knowledge, but not to our wisdom: that is dearer-bought.

—*Hosea Ballou*

WHEN MAJOR ALEX SPEAR RETURNED to Saigon from Loc Ninh and checked in at military headquarters, he was immediately ushered in to meet with General Pavler.

"Welcome back, Alex," greeted the general. I've great news to share with you I couldn't reveal over the phone at the Devereau plantation. Our supposed communist scenario connecting the stolen radios with the missing American communication specialists is a reality. We've recovered an American escapee from the Viet Cong near Song Be, and low and behold, she is one of the missing radio specialists!

"Lt. Maureen Kelly was on one of the hijacked military transport planes that disappeared from Travis Air Force Base en route to Vietnam. Held captive in Hanoi, she and her fellow soldiers were being transported from Hanoi to Cambodia to train the Viet Cong on our stolen radios."

Alex exclaimed, "What a breakthrough!"

"The rescue of Lieutenant Kelly was made by Senator Kearney's son!"

"Lieutenant Kearney, Jr.? Sir, I hope the woman was able to fend off Kearney's advances on top of all the other trauma she's been through!"

"Traumatized is right! Lieutenant Kelly believes her fellow Americans most likely will be shot when no longer of use to them, or continue to be held as prisoners of war. It's what motivated her to take the terrible risk of trying to escape to bring help to the Americans still in captivity and notify the American authorities of the communists' activities."

"Will I be able to interview her, sir?"

"We've already done so and asked her about the stolen radios. She said she can only guess that those radios needed for the training must be in the Cambodian headquarters already. We can't rule out that some are stored in a separate location awaiting the new trainees."

"Sir, we've searched the likely Devereau plantation area thoroughly, checking the abandoned buildings out to its far reaches, but found absolutely nothing! However, both Captain Hewlett and I had a gut feeling about one suspicious area the Devereau overseer, Mr. Ly, didn't want us to search. We planned to have Major Si and his troops go back to search this area while we had dinner at the plantation including Mr. Ly."

"We've heard from Captain Hewlett already, Alex, that Major Si and his troops did indeed find a renovated building in the suspicious area you mentioned."

"I knew it! Were there any American radios stored there?"

"No, but they did find a U.S. shipping label caught in a crack in a far corner inside the building. The grass around the dwelling had been recently trampled, too. We figure some radios were stored there, but were hastily removed after you stopped searching the plantation," surmised General Pavler.

"Where would they relocate the radios, sir?"

"Major Si and his men are again searching the abandoned dwellings his team already investigated to see if any of the radios were quickly transferred to them to avoid detection. We are awaiting word on any discoveries they might make."

"It seems Mr. Ly knows more about communist activities than he lets on," commented Alex. "I'm sure the Devereaus are upset about these subsequent searches."

"Yes, of course, but they don't want to object too much, lest they be labeled communist sympathizers. The Devereaus and their rubber plantation are a remnant of French colonial days. Now they are caught between Diem's South Vietnamese government and the

Viet Cong. Perhaps they can still operate only by paying taxes to the communists. But it won't go well for the Devereaus if their plantation is discovered to be a hotbed of communist activities, with or without the Devereau's knowledge."

"I'll be anxious to learn what, if anything, the third search at the Devereau plantation turns up, General. Meanwhile, when Lieutenant Kelly is up to it, will I still be able to conduct a second interview with her?"

"Let's wait until tomorrow, Alex. Our medical people are giving her aid for a slight arm injury and checking her emotional state now that the adrenaline rush during her escape, rescue and first interview calms down. As an escaped POW, she needs to be evaluated."

"Right, sir. Her rescue is fantastic luck! It's a setback for R-3, but the question remains for the allies to decide what to do about a still viable plot to snarl our communications."

"I've called an Operation Checkmate meeting for this afternoon, and I have invited the CIA head here in Vietnam to join us. The CIA is already operating in Laos and Cambodia as well as Vietnam and will be crucial in the effort to try to free the other American captives."

"I'll be there, General, but first I need to check in at Five Oceans. Is Winston back from up-country yet? I heard about the tragic death of Doc Jenicoso, and I'm sure it has grieved Winston, as it has me."

"Yes, Winston was greatly disturbed by the injustice of a medevac helicopter being shot down and was very upset about the loss of his friend. Winston is worried that his newspaper column about the humanitarian activities of the two doctors in Quang Ngai Province was noticed by R-3. He wonders if R-3 eliminated the good doctor to stop his positive reports."

"I just hope it hasn't caused Winston to start drinking."

"No. He can't afford to do that. As I wrote to Norma, I encouraged him to take a break and to go see Maria Monclova in Bangkok. I thought Winston and Maria might console each other about Dr. Jenicoso's death. Winston resisted the idea at first, but then he conceded and flew to Thailand to see Maria for a few days. When he returned, he looked much better."

"That's good to hear, General. If Brand's in his room, I'll catch up on his news and return for our meeting."

When Alex arrived at Five Oceans, he found Winston in the room adjacent to his, smoking a pipe with maple scented tobacco, and typing out some interview questions on his portable.

Alex greeted his friend, "Winston, it's really good to see our *New York Times* positive columnist again, refreshing us all with glimpses of nation building and humanitarian efforts going on in Vietnam, but what's with the pipe smoking? It smells like maple scented tobacco you're using. Is it mine?"

"Alex, good to see you again. Yes, I hope you don't mind. I decided to follow your example. Pipe smoking seems to be more helpful than cigarettes when doing contemplative, creative work. But I have to wonder if my positive reporting hasn't affected those who are trying to do something good in this nation of rebellious people. I sorely miss our friend, Doc Jenicoso, and still can't believe he's gone long before his time. He was such a good friend and part of our travel group to 'Nam.'"

"You've got that right, Winston. A stranger sight you might never see. Who can forget his unruly cowlicks and pigeon-toed walk, but a kinder more compassionate heart than his would be impossible to find."

"He sure did care about people, didn't he, Alex? And a finer surgeon you couldn't come across. I really miss him."

"I do, too, Winston! General Pavler just told me you spent a few days in Bangkok with Maria Monclova. I'm sure our lovely flight attendant's grief for Nick's death was heartfelt, too."

"Maria was devastated over the loss of our dear friend. She reminisced about how he stepped in for her when she was injured and got everyone singing with his ukulele on our struggling aircraft."

"A good soul for sure. How did your visit with Maria go? The last I heard you were determined to stay away from her."

"Doc's death was a little more than we could bear alone. It did us both good to grieve together. But now it's much harder to stay away from her. But that may be overcome by circumstances. Just today I got word that Maria's father was in a car accident, and she's taking a month off from her airline job to take care of him."

"Was the accident serious?"

"A broken arm and a few fractured ribs."

"I'm sorry to hear that. I wish I could take a break. General Pavler promised me a week's leave to spend with Gwen and the kids after returning from Loc Ninh, but now new developments have delayed my leave until Christmas. By the way, how'd you like to spend Christmas in the Philippines as well? General Pavler is hoping to spend it with his wife Norma there, and I with Gwen and the kids. Maria might like to see you again."

"Don't tempt me. I'm already fighting an inward battle regarding a relationship with Maria that's pulling me in opposite directions and threatening to tear me apart."

"Why is that, Winston?"

"I have no business forming a relationship with any woman right now while I'm working on my own personal issues, not to mention the threats on my life. I'm here primarily to report on the war effort, hopeful to win a second Pulitzer Prize for my efforts. I've just been here since February, and I already have two women to contend with, distracting me from my reporting."

"Some men would be happy to be in such a position, Winston. But who's the second woman besides Maria?"

"It's my ex-wife, Eleanor. I've been told by General Pavler that Eleanor has been writing to my sister Clemie and him asking about me. Her mother died recently, and they both think Eleanor may contact me soon asking for a reconciliation."

"How do you feel about that?"

"That's a good question. I won't know unless it actually happens. I certainly care about Eleanor's well-being and always have, but our marital relationship was anything but smooth. We both had other priorities that were more important to us than our marriage. Whether that has changed remains to be seen."

"How will this affect your relationship with Maria?"

"Another good question. To be honest, I've often thought Maria would be so much better off with a young man in the Philippines who's asked her to marry him and has been waiting for her answer for a long time. I'm ten years older than Maria, nor do I want to burden her with my personal baggage. But, damn, the chemistry between us has a mind of its own!"

"That bad, huh?"

"That good, you mean, and that's the problem."

"Well, good luck with your love triangle, Winston. But my concern is whether your life has been threatened again?"

"I've had a reprieve since I arrived, but lately, after I returned to Saigon from up-country, I've had the feeling that someone has been following me, sort of in a surveillance mode."

"Really! We'll have to look into that. Thanks for alerting me, Winston. What's next on your travel itinerary?"

"I'd like to look into the Strategic Hamlet program in the Delta. The effort is going well in Quang Ngai, but I hear it's having serious problems in the south. I have an interview this afternoon at the Gia Long Palace with Colonel Bao, who heads the program for President Diem's brother Nhu."

"'Colonel' Bao? I thought he was a 'captain!'"

"Yes, he was, Alex, but his important job as administrator of the Strategic Hamlet program required more rank. So he was temporarily promoted to colonel by the Ngo's, despite the protests of the ARVN generals. He's a favorite of Madame Nhu."

"Well, try not to get mauled by the 'outspoken tigress,' if she happens to be there, Winston, or be taken in by her charming colonel friend."

"What do you mean, Alex?"

"Don't expect to leave the palace without not-too-subtle pressure to write about Madame Nhu's family laws and Morality Laws, as well as her women's paramilitary organization, all the while Colonel Bao smiles, but calculates how he can use you."

Brand replied, "I've met Colonel Bao before at the Devereaus and later at the curio shop where I purchased your travel chess set. My intuition also tells me he wants to rise to the top whatever the cost, or whomever he uses. But there's a whimsical, almost sentimental quality to him, too, that may be the downfall to his ambitions."

"So you met Colonel Bao at the curio shop where you purchased my chess set. That's interesting. After you left Nha Trang, I discovered a hidden compartment in the bottom of that chess set. When I went to exchange it, the proprietor said it was a place for a chess instruction sheet, but she didn't have any available. All the other sets had the same hidden compartment, so my pretext for being there was to exchange my set, but I had to order one without it instead."

"Yes, at the time, Colonel Bao introduced me to his fiancée, Madame Binh, the proprietor of the curio shop."

"Just so you know, Winston, we have the curio shop under surveillance. I hope your meeting with Colonel Bao goes well, but always remember to be on your toes, Winston, whether at the palace or anywhere else, in this city of subversive intrigues and plots."

"How can I forget, Alex, when every time I go past your wall map of incidents there are more red flags stuck in it? But given my record of close calls, another reminder certainly doesn't hurt. By the way, Alex, I've written a Christmas story about Kim Chi, the little Vietnamese peanut girl of Quang Ngai. Maria and my sister Clemie both love it, but my bureau chief, Sheenar Tillerstein, isn't a fan. There's a copy of it here on my desk. You're welcome to read it. I'd like to hear your comments."

"Will do. I'll bet Gwen would like to read it, too."

"I'm submitting it to my editor, Louis Cohen, to hold for my Christmas column. We'll see whether Louis runs it or not. "But it's time for my interview. Great to have you back, Alex!"

After Winston left for his interview with Colonel Bao, Alex read Winston's Christmas story. It certainly tugged at one's heartstrings, Alex thought. The women in Brand's life were apt to think so, too. The sentimental story was likely to sink him deeper into his relationships with them. However, Brand's trip to the Delta would remove him from any womanly wiles. What was it with Winston Brand? A cloud of contention swirls around him wherever he goes, and it never seems to dissipate. But that must be a reporter's life when he dives deep for the truth.

As Brand entered the Gia Long Palace he ran into the Vietnamese Minister of Information, But Hieu, who said he was there for an appointment with President Diem.

"'Top of the day' to you, Mr. Brand, as you Americans like to say," greeted Minister Hieu. "What brings you here?"

"Greetings to you, too, Minister Hieu. I wish it were for my long-awaited interview with President Diem, but I'm here to interview Colonel Bao about the Strategic Hamlet program."

"No doubt another fine column is in the mix to be added to your remarkable lineup of reports from up-country, Mr. Brand. I'm sorry your interview with the president was postponed. Senator Kearney's imminent visit was the cause. I was told further delay occurred because you left for up-country. President Diem is extremely pleased with your reporting in contrast to that of the rest of your press colleagues."

"I'm only interested in getting to the truth, Minister Hieu. I always strive to be an objective reporter. If what's going on turns out to be negative, I'll report that, as well as the good nation building and humanitarian efforts that are going on during President Diem's watch."

"President Diem's 'watch.' I'll have to remember that American idiom. The Vietnamese never think of such clever ways of expressing themselves as you Americans do."

"A free society fosters creativity, Minister Hieu. Aren't we all interested in freedom for an independent South Vietnam?"

"Yes, of course, but it's 'easier said than done.'"

"Another American expression in your collection. Soon you'll have more idioms than your American allies."

"An interesting thought, but I must take this opportunity to express our sympathy for the death of the American doctor in a medevac helicopter crash. I'm told he was your friend."

"More than a friend. He was an example for all of us of human compassion and kindness for his fellow human beings. I've written a Christmas story about his endearing support to others. He performed surgery for a little one-armed Vietnamese peanut girl before the communists sabotaged the helicopter which crashed with him aboard."

"Such an unfortunate tragedy!" said Minister Hieu. "I wasn't informed that the helicopter was sabotaged. But you say you have written an inspiring story about the doctor and the little Vietnamese girl? We'd like to mention it as a news item in our Vietnamese newspaper to inspire our own people."

"Of course, I wrote it to inspire others."

"I want you to know, Mr. Brand, you are still in line for an interview with President Diem, as busy as he and his brother are with their grand scheme, the Strategic Hamlet program."

"Thank you, Minister Hieu, but quite frankly, I'm not going to hold my breath waiting for an interview with the president."

But Hieu smiled. "'Hold your breath waiting.' I haven't heard that American idiom yet. I'll have to remember that one! But I will do my best to see your interview request granted, Mr. Brand, in light of your cooperation with us."

"When I do get to interview the president, I'm more than anxious to ask him face-to-face about the regime's adoption of the Personalist philosophy, and how it affects Diem's policies that seem to be at odds with American ideas."

"Yes, our president and his brother seem quite obsessed, even rather 'intoxicated,' as you Americans might say, with the tenets of Personalism and how it can be implemented in our policies. But you'll be able to learn more about it in your interview with Colonel Bao."

"I'm looking forward to it, Minister Hieu. And I'm glad to hear you confirm my conjectures about the importance of Personalist ideas to the Diem regime."

"Always glad to be of help to our American friends."

But Hieu was called into President Diem's office, but turned before he left and said, "Please send a copy of your inspiring Christmas story to my office, if you would, Mr. Brand. I've certainly enjoyed talking with you."

"Likewise," said Brand.

Shortly, one-eyed Colonel Bao appeared and smiled warmly at Brand. "Greetings, Mr. Brand. Welcome to the Gia Long Palace."

"Well, I've certainly received a warm welcome here already. I just met the Minister Hieu, and we had an amusing conversation about American idioms before his meeting with President Diem."

"We try to be good allies, Mr. Brand."

"Congratulations on your promotion, Colonel Bao. You're quite the right-hand man of Diem's brother Nhu now."

"Thank you, Mr. Brand. It's a pleasure to see you again after our dinner together at the Devereau plantation and our brief encounter at the curio shop when I introduced you to my fiancée. I'm told you've asked to interview me about our very important program. Let's go to my office to talk where we'll be more comfortable."

When they were seated Brand said, "I visited a successful strategic hamlet in Quang Ngai. The government strengthened its ties with the rural peasants through this program there. In other areas it has encountered significant problems."

"You're correct, Mr. Brand. We are trying to increase peasant loyalty by providing protection and economic support. However, any new endeavor has its difficulties to overcome. In the long run, we believe the Strategic Hamlet program is the tool to accomplish all our national goals—military, social, political and economic in one overall program."

"That's quite a lot to hope for from one program. Is the philosophy behind it the regime's adoption of Personalism?"

"Yes, Counselor Nhu, who's quite the intellectual, understands Personalist tenets and how to apply them in helping to solve our nation's many pressing problems. The Ngo brothers want to rebuild South Vietnam from the bottom up with the labor of the peasants at the hamlet and village levels. They want to instill in the people a sense of connection and responsibility to the nation for the good of all, in addition to their own family interests in their separate hamlets."

"It's a Personalist idea, and I'd like to discuss with you how its tenets have been reflected in past projects. I've researched the regime's three major projects in the mid to late 1950s: the Land Reform, Land Development and Agroville programs."

"When I was accepted for my position, I was briefed on the Land development Program, which was a compulsory large-scale resettlement program for inhabitants of the overcrowded central lowlands, and for refugees from the north after the Accords of 1954. They were moved into new centers on uncultivated lands in the highlands. However, the native Montagnards in these areas were displaced and forced to move into permanent settlements, too. Its purpose was to develop the sparsely populated Central Highlands while nurturing a socially coherent, civic-minded population—a Personalist idea, I believe."

"Yes, it is. Weren't there different types of centers organized at that time?"

"Yes, previous to 1960, the South Vietnamese government had developed two different types of centers for resettlement, or agglomeration. One was for Viet Cong families, people with relatives in North Vietnam, or people who had been associated with the Viet Minh, who had fought with the communists against French colonial rule. Such a center was called 'qui khu.'

"The other type of center was called 'qui ap' and was for people loyal to the South Vietnamese government, but out of reach for government protection, so they suffered from Viet Cong attacks. Thousands of people lived in 23 of these centers by 1960, but this mass resettlement caused resistance to such collectivity, and many had to be forced to move."

"The use of force isn't a Personalist tenet, Colonel Bao."

"True, but unfortunately Viet Cong attacks had increased by 1959, so the use of force was often necessary. Our regime successfully suppressed communists in the south in the mid to late 1950s. But then Hanoi, previously reluctant to enter into armed action in the south, seemed to change its mind and greatly increased infiltration of troops and supplies into south. It's a cause for great concern to this day, Mr. Brand."

"The Agroville program in the Mekong Delta begun in 1959 was also a reaction to increased communist activity in the south, wasn't it?"

"Yes, the Agroville program was aimed at reasserting government authority in that watery area. Villages there are strung out for miles along canals and waterways. Agrovilles were designed to improve security and raise the standard of living for the populace there. The peasants relied on their own resources to build the agrovilles, or mini towns."

"I take it the project was like the 'New Villages' of Malaya, formed during the British resettlement there."

"My, Mr. Brand, you are certainly up on your research! But the Agroville program was more than a copy of the Malaya 'New Villages.' Agrovilles embodied the Ngos' vision of a Personalist revolution built from the bottom up."

Brand retorted, "And I might add, a revolution that sidestepped American ideas and intervention. But Americans have been concerned with the large-scale coercion of the masses, creating populace resentment and the opportunity for corruption in such large settlements. It doesn't bode well for a sustained popular base of support."

"Very insightful of you, Mr. Brand. The Agroville program has stalled for some of these reasons to be replaced by the Strategic Hamlet project, planned for already settled areas."

"So, how does the Strategic Hamlet program add anything different to its predecessor programs?"

"The Strategic Hamlet program is our chance to forge an independent Vietnamese nation in our own way so that our nation can eventually stand on its own two feet. We certainly appreciate American support in our nation rebuilding and modernization projects. But we can't continually depend upon American aid. Who knows if it could lead to a de facto takeover by America?"

Brand replied, "The U.S. global strategic interest is in stopping the spread of communism rather than a goal of imperialism. But America's dubious about Diem's 'go-it-alone' direction and the weaknesses of such nationalist and Personalist thinking in his deeply flawed policies."

"We realize we can't proceed alone without U.S. support at this point, given the demands of our ambitious Strategic Hamlet program in our nation at war. But unfortunately President Diem won't compromise with the Americans when your Western ideas of nation building clash with his Vietnamese vision. He is a fervent Vietnamese nationalist, and he believes strategic hamlets reflect Vietnamese goals and methods in nation building and modernizing through a grassroots mobilization of the people, whether or not Americans favor his policies."

"The trouble is Diem forgot to get the crucial support of the populace and his ally on board first."

"That does give one pause for reflection, Mr. Brand. But I am not a policy maker, just an administrator, so you'd best take up those concerns with President Diem in an interview."

"I've tried, but to no avail. Meanwhile, go ahead, Colonel Bao, with your input on the Strategic Hamlet program."

"Our first concern is security. There are about 10,000 communist insurgents throughout South Vietnam now in 1962. They formed the National Liberation Front, or NFL, and it has achieved control over large sections of the South Vietnamese countryside, especially in the Mekong Delta. We want to concentrate the peasants in these fortified hamlets to give the populace more security so they aren't victims of the terror tactics of the Viet Cong, forcing their support. We hoped large-scale resettlement wouldn't be required, however, thousands of families in the Mekong Delta had to be moved."

Brand commented, "The burden falls on the peasants to provide the labor, money and materials for the construction of these fortified hamlets, and provide for their self-defense."

"And why shouldn't they, since the populace is the beneficiary? What's more, their common personal struggle binds the inhabitants of the hamlet together. We encourage each strategic hamlet to organize a self-defense group of up to 100 armed men, who can enforce curfews, check identity cards, and expose any hard-core communists who might have infiltrated it."

"Where did you start these new hamlets?"

"We began in Binh Duong province bordering Saigon on the north in March."

"But that's a Viet Cong stronghold!"

"What better place to start than where it's needed most?"

"I would think a more secure area would be a better choice for the initial phase of the program to ensure success. Placing a strategic hamlet in a communist-dominated area would enclose many communist sympathizers within the hamlets, who then would be given identification cards," commented Brand.

"Nevertheless, we face more and more infiltrators coming from the north each day, and we need strategic centers to be built to work from. We can iron out the details later. I have advised Nhu that it's imperative to build as many hamlets as possible as fast as possible!"

"And does Nhu agree with you, Colonel Bao?"

"Yes, he already favored speed in construction and my advice reinforced his own inclination. As of this September, 4.3 million peasants have been housed in 3,225 completed hamlets, and 2,000 more are still being constructed."

"That's quite a lot in a short time!" Brand had an incredulous look in his eyes. "What about having enough time to choose wise locations for these new hamlets? The resistance of the peasants to being moved from ancestral lands and sometimes far from their rice fields surely isn't going to garner their support, but their hatred instead."

"My, Mr. Brand, so many negative questions. You are quite the pessimist! I'm surprised, since you have recently shown such a positive side to yourself with your inspiring reports in your columns from up-country. These positive reforms the South Vietnamese government is making do take time and effort. But we must get started before the communists overrun not only the hamlets, but our whole country!"

"But, good grief, Colonel, the Diem regime is depending on a popular base of support that doesn't exist. They are displaced people, who have no idea they have communal and national responsibilities, but are expected to bear the burdens anyway. Are they going to be willing to die to support these endeavors of the nation?"

"We shall see, won't we, Mr. Brand. In the meantime, I hope I've answered your interview questions to the best of my knowledge. But before we adjourn our interview, I promised Madame Nhu I'd briefly inform you how she has contributed to better the new Vietnamese society. Our lovely and charming 'First Lady' of Vietnam" is just as fervent in improving the lot of women in Vietnam as her husband, Counselor Nhu, and her brother-in-law, President Diem, with their nationalism."

Brand remembered Alex's prediction that his interview with Colonel Bao would also include Madame Nhu's feminist causes. The slick move by Bao, even without her actual presence, irritated Brand, but he tried to be polite.

"You can inform me about Madame Nhu's projects, Colonel Bao, but I can't promise they will appear in my column. I haven't met Madame Nhu, but I did see her at a rally."

"Yes, I remember seeing you there with Major Spear. Today, when I mentioned my interview with you to Madame Nhu, she also remembered seeing you at the rally. I offered to share her concerns about women's rights with you, and was rewarded by her lovely smile. But let me ask you, Mr. Brand, if you are a married man?"

Brand was surprised by the question, but reluctantly answered, "I was married for four years, but divorced for the last two years." He was hardly prepared for Bao's reply.

"Forgive me, Mr. Brand, for asking such a personal question, but I wanted to illustrate Vietnamese family laws to you. In Vietnamese eyes, you are still married to your wife, because divorce is not an option in Vietnam. And the family laws of 1958 make adultery an offense that can result in a prison sentence. Polygamy and having concubines are unlawful, and divorce can be obtained only by presidential dispensation."

One blunt question deserved another, Brand thought, so he asked, "Are Madame Nhu's countrymen happy with such strict laws and harsh punishment?"

Colonel Bao smiled, "Perhaps you make that judgment because you aren't aware of the cruel and inhuman treatment of Vietnamese women by men prior to the family laws. Women had no legal rights and could be discarded at will.

"Forgive me again, Mr. Brand, if my illustration is too personal, but if you have had any liaisons since your divorce, even if you have been strongly in love with another, in Vietnam, society must still defend the legality of the legitimate family, despite whatever 'wild-couples-in-love' experience."

Brand remarked, "This must also hold true if the wife is the one to ask for a divorce from her husband."

"A wife must abide by family laws as a man does. Madame Nhu also has sponsored morality bills banning prostitution, contraceptives, abortion, animal fights and taxi dancing."

"Dancing? What's wrong with dancing?"

Bao gave a surprising answer. "Madame Nhu meant to ban taxi girls, not dancing, but Vietnamese men are very jealous and don't want Vietnamese women to dance with American men, so they included dancing in the bill. She's vehement Vietnamese women's rights have to be addressed, and she's the one to do it!"

Brand thought Madame Nhu's husband and President Diem had their hands full dealing with her. He asked Bao, "Regardless of Madame Nhu's genuine feminist zeal, doesn't its effects rub off on Diem and create hatreds for his regime? Saigon's cynical elite and the Western press refer to her as the 'Dragon Lady.'"

If Brand thought he had made a telling point, swiftly he was put in his place. Colonel Bao asked, "What time will ever be right to address centuries-old customs and abuses regarding women? It hasn't happened so far. Madame Nhu believes that while the Nguyen family is in power, they have to do what they can to stop the abuse of women and punish those who won't respect the family laws and Morality Laws!"

Brand thought about the other side of the coin. How would the Ngo brothers fare in a court trial regarding charges against them for their immoral, brutal suppression of political opponents? But he held his comment, and hoped to end the interview. Bao, however, interjected a new topic of great interest to Madame Nhu, the Paramilitary Women of Vietnam.

"Madame Nhu believes women have the best chance to obtain their rights if they have their own army in order to win the descent treatment of women from the many reluctant, devious and hypocritical men of Vietnam."

Brand replied, "Of course, I assume this description of Vietnamese men doesn't include the President, her husband, or yourself Colonel Bao."

"No, I am fortunate to receive praise for waiting five years for my fiancée, Madame Binh, to get over her grief for her deceased husband before she finally agreed to be engaged to me."

"Very praiseworthy indeed, Colonel Bao."

Bao quickly changed the subject. "Unfortunately, Madame Nhu's family relationship with her parents isn't a happy one. Perhaps that motivates her reforming spirit regarding the family. Her mother, Madame Tran Van Chuong is a very strong-willed woman whose forthrightness on political subjects is unusual for a Vietnamese woman. Madame Nhu's own frankness is reminiscent of her mother's."

Brand added, "Madame Nhu's father is an ambassador in Washington, I believe, and her mother is an observer at the United Nations."

"Yes, most of the Ngo/Chuong family members hold one position or another. Although many admire Madame Nhu's parents, she and her mother are very hostile to each other. Her father infuriates her. Although her wealthy family had 20 servants waiting on her, she received little attention from her mother."

"You're very privy to Madame Nhu's private feelings."

"On the contrary, Mr. Brand, Madame Nhu's feelings about her parents are very well known, and it doesn't take long to learn how religious beliefs in the family differ either. While her father believes in Confucianism, her mother is a Buddhist, as Madame Nhu had been before she converted to her husband's Catholicism when they were married."

"That's quite a mixture of religious thought!"

"Yes, Madame Nhu's marriage to her husband, who was then chief archivist at the Indochina Library, relieved her from the situation with her parents. She and her husband's happiest time together were from 1946-1954 in Dalat where they had defied the French, the communists and had prepared support for Nhu's brother when he returned from exile."

"Our conversation about Madame Nhu has been quite interesting, but I can't speak directly for her causes."

"I understand that, Mr. Brand, but who knows when your background information about Madame Nhu might become relevant in your reporting of future events."

"Thank you for your time, Colonel Bao."

"It's been a pleasure, Mr. Brand."

Brand returned to Five Oceans after his interview with Colonel Bao. Alex's prediction had indeed come true. Brand smiled when he remembered Bao's description of "wild-couple-in-love" romances when one of the partners was a divorcé. Madame Nhu certainly wouldn't smile about his "wild-couple-in-love" romance with Maria as he did. But was he mistaken though to be so quick to treat it lightly? When he and Maria were entwined in love's embrace, it was impossible for them to even begin to think clearly about its implications.

Alex met Winston for dinner, and the look on the reporter's face told Alex the outcome of the palace interview without his even asking. "So my prediction before you left for your interview, Winston, turned out to be accurate."

"So much so, that when the interview on the Strategic Hamlet program concluded, Colonel Bao slipped seamlessly into a discussion of Madame Nhu's fervently held causes."

"You're seldom outmaneuvered like that, Winston, but one must be polite with our Vietnamese hosts. You won't advocate her causes in your column, I'm sure."

"No, but I don't think we've heard the last from her."

"That's what concerns many. But you might like to know my meeting this afternoon turned out extremely well. We've at least checked R-3 halfway."

"That's excellent news! Can you tell me about it?"

"Yes, since you and Rafe Hewlett experienced the diversionary tactic in Loch Ninh, but it's not for publication. Major Si and his troops discovered 15 of the stolen American radios in the previously searched buildings of the French rubber plantation. However, they encountered fierce resistance by communist guerilla fighters. A prolonged battle broke out, but the ARVN troops won the day."

"Recovering those stolen radios has been on your mind for quite some time, Alex. I'm just sorry that their theft occurred at the expense of the life of Capt. Erik Fletcher. Rafe Hewlett and I still struggle with our failure to save him, even though it was hopeless."

A waiter came to the table and gave a written message to Alex. A look of horror appeared on his face as he read it.

"My God, what is it, Alex?" implored Winston.

"Major Si reports a giant smoke cloud in the area of the Devereau mansion. He thinks *Bon Sejour* is going up in flames!"

38 END OF AN ERA

Oh! That a dream so sweet, so long enjoy'd should be so sadly, cruelly destroy'd.

—Thomas Moore

MY GOD, THE PLANTATION HOUSE must be in flames!" exclaimed Capt. Rafe Hewlet. He had spotted billows of smoke in the evening sky in the direction of the rubber plantation.

Hewlett was helping Major Si and his troops to secure the 15 reclaimed radios at the ARVN base at Loc Ninh when he realized his worst nightmare was taking place.

"The Devereaus are in danger! We have to go rescue them," Rafe told Major Si. Rafe desperately feared for Lucette and her father's lives.

"Wait!" warned the ARVN major. "Remember last time we try rescue? No help. Instead, very bad ambush. Many soldiers die, much equipment lost. Viet Cong steal unguarded radios.

"I warn you—Viet Cong try to repeat ploy. Want to steal radios back again. We won the day, but communists rule the night. Consider, it may not be Devereau mansion on fire."

"If you and your troops won't assist me in rescuing the Devereaus, ah'll just have to go by myself," shouted Rafe. He started to leave the room.

"*Trung-try* Hewlett, we can't authorize your mission or vouch for your safety! You risk ambush like *Trung-try* Fletcher!"

"Ah couldn't save Eric, but maybe ah can rescue Lucette and her father," said Rafe. He left to go to his jeep.

"We can't authorize driver for you!" Major Si called after him.

Rafe could feel he was being watched as he drove to the plantation as dusk turned into darkness. There were no lights gleaming in the countryside as there were every night to remind the ARVN troops that the Viet Cong could strike at any time given the order to do so. That he hadn't been ambushed yet led Hewlett to believe the Viet Cong were waiting to see if a larger rescue force was behind him, lured away from the base.

Rafe made it to the Devereau plantation mansion in record time. His heart fell when he saw it was indeed the plantation house that was on fire and already was engulfed in flames. Rafe scanned the area in the light of the fire for Lucette and her father. Not seeing them, he left the jeep a safe distance away and hurried to enter the fiery inferno calling their names. He found Lucette collapsed by the statue of Aphrodite just inside the burning entrance. He picked her up and carried her outside and administered CPR to her. When she finally revived, Rafe asked her, "Where's your father?"

Lucette weakly answered, "I looked all over for him after I heard an explosion. Then our wooden mansion started to burn. I couldn't find him anywhere, and finally the smoke got so bad I could hardly breathe. I tried to get out the entrance, but I must have collapsed. Thank God you came and found me, Rafe, but I've got to go look for my father."

Just then they heard voices. Rafe reached for his weapon.

"Wait, Rafe, it might be father."

"Or it might be the Viet Cong ah assume started this fire."

"Lucette, is that your voice I hear? Who is with you?"

"It's Captain Hewlett, Father. He saved me."

"Thank God, daughter. I'm so relieved to see that you're all right! I've been frantic trying to return to the mansion to find you when I saw it burning. Mr. Ly had asked for my help to put out a fire in one of the out buildings resulting from the fighting that took place there today. But then he disappeared, and I turned and saw the mansion in flames. Some of my workers have come along to help me search for you."

"Captain Hewlett found me unconscious at the entrance, carried me out and revived me."

"And not a minute too soon," said Monsieur Devereau. They saw a section of the second story crash through to the first floor with flames and sparks shooting in all directions.

"Oh, Father, our dreams have burned up. The fire we have always feared for our wooden mansion has happened!" sobbed Lucette in her father's arms.

Rafe said, "And not without human help, ah'm afraid. It may be that the Viet Cong wanted to lure Major Si and his troops here to rescue you from the fire in order to once again recapture the unguarded radios we recovered this afternoon. They could have started the fire with a thrown grenade."

Suddenly Lucette asked, "Where are the household staff, Father? Did Mr. Ly take them, too, to help put out the outbuilding fire?"

"No, Lucette, they have disappeared with Mr. Ly."

"Monsieur Devereau," said Rafe, "we must seek what protection we can. We are not out of danger from the Viet Cong. What about the *garçonnière*? Is it still intact?"

"Yes, we passed it on our way back to the house. I think it's far enough away from the mansion not to catch any sparks from the flaming structure."

"Ah need to take Lucette there in my jeep. Please come with us and ask your workers to follow us on foot to the *garçonnière*, where they can stand guard for us."

"Good idea. Let's go immediately."

When they were settled in the *garçonnière* and the immediate danger had dissipated, the enormity of what had happened came over the Devereaus. Lucette fell into her father's arms and began weeping, "Father, all your work for so many, many years is being reduced to smoldering ashes before our eyes as our beloved *Bon Sejour* burns to the ground. What will become of us? When news of the fire reaches mother in Paris, she will be devastated this happened when she was away visiting our relatives. Wouldn't she want us to save what was ours?"

"And we did, Lucette, for all these many years. Let's be thankful we are still alive. The rubber trees are still viable. I want to stay and see if I can manage the plantation with our other overseers and the loyal workers I have left. Without the plantation mansion, I don't need a household staff, and I can always make do with the *garçonnière* as living quarters before deciding whether or not to rebuild a modified *Bon Sejour*.

"But what about mother? She will want to return to you. Surely, her return would be too dangerous for her. Won't you go back to France to live with mother and me and our relatives?"

"If I can't salvage the plantation, I will join your mother and you, and we will try to rebuild our lives," replied Monsieur Devereau. His shoulders sagged with concern.

"Father, please come back to France with me now as we join mother. We couldn't possibly be happy without you. How lonely it would be for all of us if we are separated."

"Dear Lucette, you've stayed with us much longer in Vietnam than you should have. You need to build your own life with your mother and family in France. *Bon Sejour* is no longer a 'good stay' for you or your mother. Only the *garçonnières* are left."

"Nor for you, Father."

"My dear daughter, remember that the rubber plantation supplies our livelihood. I need to see if it still can be sustained before I would consider leaving. But be rest assured, if the plantation can't be saved and operated efficiently enough, I'll see if I can sell it and join you and your mother in France. But for now, when daylight returns, you must go back to the ARVN base with Captain Hewlett. Major Si and Captain Hewlett will assist you in contacting the French embassy in Saigon. They'll make arrangements to take you back to Saigon and connect you with a flight back to France, so you can join your mother and her relatives."

"Oh, Father, how could it have come to this? I'm not ready to leave you here alone without mother and me."

"We have no choice, dear Lucette. Now try to get some sleep. You and Captain Hewlett must be alert to detect any signs of danger on the drive back to the Loc Ninh base at dawn."

Rafe could hear Lucette sniffling through the night as she tried to quiet her fits of weeping, while Rafe and her father kept watch inside the *garçonnière*. A few plantation workers guarded the outside of the building. At times, Rafe could see the Frenchman holding his head between his hands as he, too, faced the fate finally meted out to him by the Viet Cong.

Rafe was so glad he had dared to drive to the plantation to rescue Lucette. No doubt if he hadn't found her in time and carried her out of their smoke-filled, burning home, she would have perished. For that, he would be eternally grateful. If the Viet Cong had been waiting for Major Si and his troops to follow him to the plantation, they would be greatly disappointed, Rafe thought. Major Si wasn't going to be humiliated twice by possibly losing the radios again.

At the break of dawn, Rafe and Lucette quietly and swiftly made their way back to base at Loc Ninh in the jeep after a tearful goodbye between Lucette and her father. Rafe was counting on Major Si's premise that the Viet Cong weren't interested in a single jeep with two passengers, when they had expected a large rescue group to ambush. It was an anxious ride back to base, but they made the journey without incident.

Rafe perceived that Lucette was in shock, so he took her to the medical clinic on base to be checked. Major Si had notified headquarters in Saigon of the probable fire at *Bon Sejour* the prior evening. While Lucette received care at the medical clinic, Rafe contacted the French embassy to make arrangements for Lucette to be flown to Saigon by helicopter from Loc Ninh. Her flight to France was scheduled in the next few days. Rafe's heart ached at the thought of Lucette's departure. No doubt she would be safer in France, and safer away from him.

R-3 cursed the setbacks he'd been informed of, one after another. It was bad enough one of the escaped American communications specialists had been rescued, returned and interrogated, but the enemy had been able to recapture 15 of their stolen radios.

What's more, General Chien had taken matters into his own hands by setting fire to the *Bon Sejour* mansion. The fool tried to use the same diversionary tactic used before to try to deceive the ARVN at Loc Ninh with the hope of stealing unguarded radios once again. R-3 wasn't surprised it hadn't worked.

His minions were getting out of hand, making their own decisions without checking with him first. If he'd been consulted, he'd never have ordered such an action. It had resulted in devastating consequences for their cause. General Chien had destroyed one of their key pawns on the chessboard of rebellion, and severely weakened their position in Loc Ninh.

R-3 knew he'd have to get General Chien in line again as he had done with Bao. At least one-eyed Colonel Bao was now following instructions again, advising Nhu to use speed to construct as many strategic hamlets as possible as quickly as they could in communist stronghold areas. Diem's government would never be able to support and protect them all adequately. These fortified hamlets could be infiltrated easily. This, added to the resentment of the peasants for being relocated, constituted a masterplan for failure of the initiative.

Colonel Bao had redeemed himself, but R-3 knew he must still be watched. His more than obvious fascination with Madame Nhu could compromise his loyalty to their revolutionary cause. And General Chien must be relocated rather than eliminated, R-3 decided. He would be needed when the armed struggle began in earnest. But for now he had to be replaced with a more clever and loyal general, who could rebuild the cell at Loch Ninh. Once ARVN had recaptured the radios stored at *Bon Sejour*, General Chien should have realized it was a lost cause to try to get them back again. R-3's anger grew every time he thought of the enormous cost of losing their organized cell at *Bon Sejour*.

Mr. Ly's escape to Cambodia couldn't be helped, as he'd been compromised when his communist leanings were revealed. Keeping the ARVN search party away from the building where half of the stolen radios were stored was a dead giveaway as to his loyalties once its location had been detected and searched.

But in retrospect, R-3 thought, they still had enough radios to train their soldiers on in Cambodia. Hanoi had wanted to move their training location to a nearby organized area to avoid detection by the American CIA. But R-3 had convinced R-1 and R-2 in Hanoi it would be another setback to their timetable for the use of the radios in causing confusion of the enemy in the planned battle at Ap Bac after the American New Year.

There would also be the danger of other prisoners escaping in another move. R-3 was confident they could complete the training required in Cambodia before the CIA could locate their hidden headquarters there.

Yes, R-3 reassured himself, they'd had setbacks, but their plan was still viable. They'd have less radios to place in strategic locations in South Vietnam in the future, but they could make the extra effort to transport the radios to specific locations as needed.

R-3 calculated that the American advisors to ARVN commanders hadn't figured out what the Viet Cong planned to do with the stolen radios. Even if they had, they wouldn't have time to make defensive adjustments to their communications systems before the beginning of January. The masterplan could still work and work very well. 1963 would begin as planned with a Viet Cong victory over ARVN at Ap Bac. The Western press would lament the defeat in news reports for some time to come.

R-3 then summoned his adjutant and gave him instructions for the relocation and replacement of General Chien.

39 A BEVY OF SPIRITED LADIES

Ladies, like variegated tulips show; 'tis to their changes half their charms we owe.

—Alexander Pope

IN HAWAII, WINSTON BRAND'S SISTER Clementine prepared for Thanksgiving dinner to be shared this year with Eleanor Brand, her former sister-in-law. Eleanor had written to her and asked if she could visit with Clemie, Sean and their three children during a stopover on her way to Vietnam to see Winston.

"I'm sorry to intrude on you at Thanksgiving time, Clemie, but I need to reconnect with my family since mother died."

"You know you're always welcome, Eleanor. We're more than happy to have you visit. You're a lot more thoughtful than my brother was when he stopped over in Hawaii in February on his way to Vietnam. He completely ignored us. I've made several attempts to stay in touch with my wayward brother by letter, and once he called me by phone and has written to me twice, but he has been less than enthusiastic about actually visiting."

"Winnie is the reasons I wanted to come and talk to you, Clemie. You made such an effort to talk Winnie and me out of a divorce years ago. I know you're Catholic, and divorce isn't a word in your vocabulary, but I wish I'd listened to you then. I regret my decision. Our story together isn't finished."

"What a turn of your intentions! But a reconciliation attempt could be a hard road to travel, Eleanor. After all, Winston did put your marriage ahead of his career when he agreed to work those four years on the *Times* desk job, just so he could stay in one place to be with you. Unfortunately, it's when his drinking got out of hand."

"Winnie's drinking frightened me, Clemie. Maybe I panicked with career, parental care demands and Winnie's desire to be out in the field eating away at him. I just couldn't handle it all and didn't see any way out other than divorce. I was so foolish, Clemie. I wish I had made Winnie my priority when he was so miserable on his desk job. We should have had children together that my ailing parents could have enjoyed, too, while they were still with us."

"But Winston still seems set on winning a second Pulitzer Prize as a foreign war correspondent, Eleanor. Evidently his career remains his deepest desire."

"Winnie and I have been getting older in these past two years since our divorce. When mother passed away, I realized that all the important people in my life were gone, and I was alone in the world. I'd like to make it up to Winnie for putting my career and my parents' concerns ahead of him."

"What do you have in mind now, Eleanor? Are you thinking of remarriage? What about your career?"

Clemie, Winnie's still in my blood. I want to reconcile and have children with him while I'm still able. Winnie has to consider this, too, if he wants heirs to carry on the Brand name while he's young enough to be a real father to them. My career is no longer my first priority."

"Children, too, Eleanor? My goodness! I've never really heard Winston talk about children until recently. He wrote a very touching Christmas story about a little one-armed Vietnamese girl who was befriended by an American surgeon before he was tragically killed in a helicopter crash."

"Oh, Clemie, please let me read it."

"Of course, Eleanor. Winston said he has submitted it to his editor at the *Times* to hold for his Christmas column, so the whole world will be able to read it soon. But listen. Is that a car door I hear slamming? It must be Sean and the children home from the beach. They'll be so excited to see you again, Eleanor, especially Billy, who's sure to remember you."

"And I'll be so glad to see them again, too," said Eleanor with a wistful look in her eyes.

Clemie's children burst into the house in wet bathing suits, trailing sand in that spread across the floor. They immediately spotted the two women sitting at the kitchen table.

"Wow! It's Aunt Eleanor," said Clemie's oldest son Billy. He gave her a damp hug, and she reciprocated.

"Billy, you're getting Aunt Eleanor all wet!" exclaimed Clemie. "And look, you've got quite a sunburn."

"I'm not as sunburned as all those ladies at the beach in their skimpy bikinis Dad kept worrying about," Billy said. "He sent Timmy over to ask one lady to join us under our beach umbrella, because he said she was getting a bad sunburn."

"How thoughtful of him," said Clemie. "Did you all have a good time at the beach?"

The three children chimed together in agreement. "Yes, and the sunburned lady even bought us ice cream cones," said Billy.

"Wasn't that nice," Clemie said, looking askance at Sean.

"Hey, she was all alone. Tourists never know when to get out of the Hawaiian sun," Sean countered. "How are you, Eleanor? You're really looking great! But I'm so sorry to hear about your mother passing away."

"Thank you for your sympathy, Sean. I have to admit I've lost some weight while taking care of my mother before she left me all alone in the world."

"You know you're always welcome to visit us, Eleanor. You and Clemie have always been good friends."

"Yes, we are," said Clemie. "Eleanor is on her way to Vietnam to try to reconcile with Winston."

"Good luck with that attempt, Eleanor. I was in Vietnam not too long ago and met Winston at the airport. I was with Senator Kearney's party, and we had just arrived. Winston was at the airport, too, ready to board a flight to go up-country to do interviews for his column. I happened to see him and was able to speak with him briefly. However, Senator Kearney, who headed our fact finding group, came over and had some unpleasant things to say to him. The senator has it in for Winston."

"How well I remember Winnie stirring up the pot for others with his reporting. The truth he'd dig up wasn't always what they wanted to see in print for all the world to see. Still, we need the press to keep a check on government," said Eleanor.

"Father could never understand that Winston preferred to fight his battles on paper rather than on a military battlefield," remarked Clemie. He always chided Winnie for not 'facing the sun.'"

"Winston made the right choice for himself. We certainly 'faced the sun' today at the beach. Clemie, the children are wet and need to change. I'll chat with Eleanor while you help little Susie change clothes, and make sure the boys do, too."

"Will do," said Clemie. She left the kitchen.

Sean sat down with Eleanor at the kitchen table and whispered, "I trust you have kept your silence about the time you found me in bed with Clemie's best friend," said Sean.

"I would never hurt Clemie by telling her about that incident. But I'm sure Clemie knows deep down, even if she's in denial, what an unfaithful man she's married to. I'm sure she keeps up the illusion of your marriage for the sake of the children, and because of her religious convictions."

"Thanks for the vote of confidence, Eleanor. I'll have you know I would never leave Clemie. She's a wonderful wife and mother, and I'm glad to support my family in any way I can."

"Except with fidelity."

"Hey, I'm a healthy male. I'm very careful in whatever I do. Besides, what Clemie doesn't know won't hurt her."

"Don't kid yourself, Sean. You're too smart to get caught, except for that one time, but you're chipping away at the foundation of your marriage every time your wandering eye spots a likely target."

"Clemie knows I like to flirt. What's the big deal?"

"It's when you carry it through to a liaison or an affair that you violate your marriage vows and inevitably create an underlying layer of distrust that silently permeates and eats away at your relationship with Clemie."

"You should talk, Eleanor, there are other ways to undermine a marriage. You didn't give Winston your all either, did you? Your career, your parents and your attachment to your home base did a number on your commitment to Winston. So I wouldn't point a finger at any one else if I were you, Eleanor."

"You're right, of course, Sean. We're quite the self-centered individuals, aren't we? But I intend to change my ways and see if Winnie and I can reconcile. I'd like to have a child with him before my child-bearing days dwindle down."

"The ticking clock syndrome, I see. Well, you'd better not wait too long, Eleanor. I heard a rumor when I was in Vietnam that Winston and a lovely Filipina flight attendant were spotted together after a near miss upon takeoff at Guam. Later, they were kissing at the airport and enjoying it a little too much.

"Senator Kearney had a lot to say to me on our way to Vietnam about Winston's drunken behavior in Hawaii and his apparent seduction of the lovely lady in Guam, a woman that his son had his eye on. I saw her on the last leg of our flight from the Philippines to Saigon. She was our flight attendant and is quite the looker who could melt any man's defenses."

"That's not good to hear," said Eleanor. "Any word on whether it was a brief liaison, or something more involved between Winnie and this woman?"

"You'll have to ask Winston when you see him. That's all the information I have. I can only forewarn you to a potential complication to your reconciliation plans," said Sean.

Clemie re-entered the kitchen and heard the trail end of Sean's comment. "What complication are you talking about, Sean? Do you mean Eleanor's plan to try to reconcile with Winston?"

Eleanor answered, "Sean told me about a rumor that Winnie is romantically involved with a Filipina flight attendant."

"Oh, he must mean Maria Monclova. Aunt Norma has written to me that she's looking forward to meeting Maria and her father. Gwen Spear and her children are living in the Philippines, too, and both women are planning to meet Maria soon. I believe Maria has taken off a month from her job with the airlines to care for her father injured in a car accident."

"There you go, Eleanor. You've got a month to try to win Winston away from his interest in Maria Monclova."

"Or his Pulitzer Prize," commented Eleanor.

Maria Monclova and their devoted housekeeper Letty carefully laid out the settings for tea, cucumber finger sandwiches and assorted sweets. They had just finished when the doorbell rang. Letty turned to answer it, but Maria said she would do it herself. As she opened the door, Maria saw two immaculately dressed women with warm smiles who greeted her.

"I'm Norma Pavler," said the older of the two, and this is Gwen Spear. She tells me you've met her husband when you were a flight attendant on the military transport aircraft to Vietnam."

"Yes, I did. I'm so pleased to meet you both. Won't you please come in and have some refreshments while we visit?"

"We'd love to," Gwen Spear replied.

Maria introduced the women to her father, and Letty began to serve tea.

"Mr. Monclova, we're sorry to hear about your car accident and hope your recovery is progressing well," said Norma Pavler.

"Thank you. Maria is taking good care of me, and Letty's cooking and cleaning is top-notch as usual."

"How fortunate for you. But I must extend our sympathy to you, Maria, for the tragic death of your friend, Dr. Jenicoso. My husband wrote to me that you and Winston Brand, who's been like a son to us since he was little, had a very close relationship with the good doctor," continued Norma.

"Yes, we went through a near miss together on that same military flight on takeoff from Guam. When the plane suddenly lurched, I fell and hit my head in the galley which knocked me unconscious for a while. Major Spear sent Winston back to check on me while the doctor was attending others. Winston picked me up and took me back to his seat and held me in his arms. He noticed the cut on my head and helped stop the bleeding until Dr. Jenicoso came to tend to me. When I came to, the doctor was using butterfly stitches on my wound, and then he bandaged my head with gauze from his medicine bag.

"I wanted to get up to tend to my passengers' needs as the plane had stabilized by then and was heading back to Guam. But the doctor was worried about shock. He placed a blanket over me as I lay in Winston's arms and told us both to stay as we were until we returned to Guam. Then the doctor got out his ukulele and soon everyone on the crippled aircraft was singing. Dr. Jenicoso was doing what I should have been doing, relieving everyone's stress."

"That's quite a story, my dear," said Norma Pavler. "I'm so glad the plane made it back to Guam safely. And I'm sure Winston wasn't too upset at all to have a beautiful woman in his arms to tend to on the way back."

Maria blushed. "Winston was kind to care for me."

Gwen Spear said, "Alex was very concerned to get the military flight safely to Vietnam, but you had only signed up as flight attendant as far as Hawaii. When he couldn't find a replacement with the proper security clearance, he was so relieved, although you hesitated, when you graciously agreed to stay with the flight all the way to Vietnam."

Maria's father then spoke. "My daughter is reluctant to fly in and out of Guam. Her mother died in a plane crash over the ocean after takeoff from Wake Island on her way back from the States to visit relatives when Maria was only 12. I don't think either of us has gotten over her loss in all these years. The Pacific Ocean became her final resting place."

Both women expressed their sympathy over such a tragic loss. Norma Pavler said, "Then the airplane takeoff from Guam with an engine explosion soon after was twice as traumatic for you, Maria, since it could've been a repeat experience."

Maria's father interjected, "Thank God that she didn't suffer the same fate as her mother! I don't know if I could have survived another loss like that. Maria and I are all that's left of our family."

Maria chimed in, "But let's get on to a more cheerful note. Tell us, Gwen, how you and your children are doing with your adjustment to life in the Philippines."

"The children and I are quartered on an American base with a school located there. It's quite similar to what they're used to back home, except the people and the climate are quite different for us Bostonians. Little Alex was quite upset to leave his friends behind when we moved recently, but Alesha was quite happy she was going to see her daddy again. I could say ditto to that! It's been a longer separation than usual this time, and my heart just aches to see my husband again, even though we write letters to each other each day when we're able."

Maria's father offered his observation then, "I've advised Maria to accept the marriage proposal of a fine young, local man, who's waited a long time for her to make up her mind and answer him about his proposal. Her life would be so much more stable with him than what you two ladies must endure with separations from your husbands for long periods of time.

"Maria's had enough time to travel here and there, so I've been urging her to settle down with Tywan and have children with him. Of course, I wouldn't mind having Maria back in the Philippines permanently, living near me and giving me grandchildren to enjoy. The month she's taken off to help care for me as I recover from my car accident has brought back many memories and made me realize just how much I've missed her when she's on the job. Although she has a small apartment near the airport here, she still hadn't had that much spare time to spend with me previous to my accident."

"Understandable, Mr. Monclova," said Norma Pavler. "Who's to say we wouldn't also enjoy a stable life, but unfortunately we can't always predict whom we will fall in love with, or what kind of life a partnership with a loved one will involve."

"That's what I've been discussing with Maria since she told me about her recent rendezvous with Winston Brand in Bangkok. There's quite an age difference between them, and as much as they gave comfort to one another as they grieved their good friend's tragic death, it's time for her to put their short relationship behind her and say 'yes' to Tywan, who's so much in love with her."

"Father, you presume too much. Winston has brought up the same points to me. I haven't committed myself to anyone," said Maria trying to cover her embarrassment.

Norma Pavler smiled at Maria with compassion in her eyes. "Don't worry, Maria. Fathers are always protective of their daughters. I understand your father's concern, especially with such a beauty as you are."

"Thank you Mrs. Pavler. You project quite a motherly warmth that I've missed since my own mother's death."

Maria's father spoke up once again, "I'm so sorry Maria's mother couldn't have been with us to see Maria crowned 'Miss Philippine' a few years back."

Both women congratulated Maria on her honor.

Maria responded, "It's been a much appreciated honor, but it's made me very wary in dealing with men, who often aren't interested in anything in a woman like me other than my celebrity status, not that I'm that famous."

"Maria's handled her celebrity status very well," said her father. In fact, she's almost shied away from men too much, including Tywan. But I worry about the look in her eyes when she mentions Winston Brand. They've made a connection that's going to make it difficult for them to forget each other."

Norma Pavler said, "Maybe Maria has read Winston's book of poetry, *Fire in the Soul* that so touches women's hearts, except for that of his ex-wife Eleanor, whose passion has been for her nursing career. And Eleanor certainly excels at that, since she's head of nursing at her hospital in New York.

"Maria, if you're fascinated with Winston, it may pass as it has for other women since his divorce when they realize Winston hasn't given up his desire for a second Pulitzer Prize. His passion to reach that goal is still as intense as Eleanor's was for nursing."

"You said 'was,' Mrs. Pavler. Do you mean that has changed?' asked Maria.

"Please call me 'Norma,' dear. Yes, both my husband and I have heard from Eleanor recently since her mother died, asking about Winston. We are both worried she might contact him about a reconciliation. Their marriage was anything but smooth, and it didn't have a good effect on Winston."

"You see, Maria," said her father. "A good marriage needs a solid foundation of love and commitment like your mother and I had. It's what you could build with Tywan without previous complications."

"I'm sure things will work out as they should," said Norma. "We've certainly enjoyed getting to know you both and taste Letty's delicious treats. Gwen has a new babysitter for her children, so we regret to have to take our leave so soon."

"It was so kind of you both to think of us and grace us with a visit. When my father recovers more, he won't have so much time to focus on my love life, what little there actually is of it," said Maria with a friendly smile. "Please come back and see us anytime."

"We'd love to," said Gwen. I'm so happy to make a new friend while waiting for my overworked husband to take a break from duty, honor and country."

"Don't I know all about that!" exclaimed Norma Pavler. "But somehow we manage, don't we, dear? We'll keep in touch, Maria. Stay well, Mr. Monclova. Best wishes for your recovery."

Maria and her father thanked the two women for their visit.

After the two women left, Norma exclaimed, "My goodness, Gwen. Winston is really in trouble now! That young woman is an absolute beauty, both inside and out, and there's no doubt she's very much in love with Winston, whether she admits it to herself, or others, or not. And if Eleanor is interested in a reconciliation with Winston, nothing in heaven or on earth can stop her!"

"Oh, my," said Gwen. I'm so glad my Alex is such a 'Straight Arrow!' Otherwise, these separations and their complications would be intolerable."

"It'll be quite a drama for Winston to contend with. I just hope this love triangle forming doesn't cause him to break his promise to George to refrain from drinking, at least while in Vietnam," said Norma.

Gwen replied, "Alex has mentioned his friendship with Winston. Perhaps he'll be a good influence on him and help him keep on the straight and narrow.

"Let's hope so, Gwen. Let's hope so."

Major Alex Spear returned to Five Oceans the next day at noon where he found Winston in his adjacent room distractedly trying to write his column about the Strategic Hamlet program. Maple smoke permeated the room as Winston fiddled with his unwieldly pipe. Winston looked up anxiously when Alex entered, worried about the Devereaus, but Alex's calmness reassured him.

"Alex, I hope your unruffled demeanor means you've received word that Monsieur Devereau and his daughter Lucette have survived the *Bon Sejour* fire."

"Yes, I'm extremely thankful to say that we were informed by Capt. Rafe Hewlett that father and daughter have survived without injury. But the mansion is a total loss."

"Thank God, the Devereaus are safe!"

"Yes, I am relieved as well!"

Alex went on to describe the details of the incident and then indicated Lucette was flying back to France the next day.

"Can I speak to Lucette before she leaves?"

"You'll have to inquire at the French embassy, Winston. They are handling her care and arrangements. I have seen her already and talked to her about her recollections of events. I wished her well with her mother and relatives in France."

Brand remarked, "I guess it's too much to ask of the fates for the good news to last. Not when the Viet Cong interfere in any way they possibly can. Their sinister leader, R-3, is an unrelenting master chess player in this power struggle."

"And remember that for yourself, Winston. Just because you haven't experienced direct threats to your life recently doesn't mean R-3, or Hanoi, might not change their minds about you."

"A good reminder, Alex. By the way, did you have a chance yesterday to read my Christmas story before your afternoon meeting? I forgot to ask you about it at dinner last evening."

"It's very touching, Winston and I must admit the memories of our dear friend, Nick, and his compassion for others gave me a lump in my throat with the thought of his passing. But what good he left behind, especially for an innocent young victim of the Viet Cong. I'm sure Gwen and our children will enjoy your touching story, too. Well done, my friend."

"Thanks so much, Alex. I think I'll head over to the French embassy and see if I can visit with Lucette before she leaves tomorrow. Maybe I'll take a copy of my Christmas story to give her and bring her some hope."

"Give our lovely, gracious French girl the best wishes of all of us as she and her family cope with their unexpected new circumstances," said Alex as Brand headed out the door.

Lucette Devereau looked up from her travel itinerary when she sensed someone approaching her.

"Winston, how very nice to see you again before I have to leave. What a comfort to see a familiar, friendly face."

"Lucette, I'm so very sorry for what you've been through. You're probably still in shock. But how glad I am you escaped the fire at *Bon Sejour* with your life."

"Thank you, Winston. You know how it feels to encounter the unexpected when you were kidnapped at *Bon Sejour*, but thankfully rescued in time."

"Yes, you and Rafe were key in foiling my abductors."

"Rafe was key to my safety, too, when he found me unconscious and carried me out of the smoke and flames at *Bon Sejour*. I'm so relieved father is all right. I confess my heart hurts terribly to have to leave him after all these years together at the plantation."

"Will Monsieur Devereau be able to salvage his operation there, do you think, Lucette?"

"That's a question none of us can answer yet, but I wish father would come back with me now. I fear for him. Our fire tragedy revealed those we thought were trustworthy weren't at all. Father will have to see if he can find the loyal support he needs. Another overseer is taking over Mr. Ly's chief position. Thankfully our rubber trees weren't affected by the fire, but the mansion is a total loss."

"Now your father won't need a household staff though."

"No. He plans to live simply in the *garçonnière* where you were held captive temporarily, Winston, but he'll need someone to cook and do light housekeeping. My household staff escaped injury because they disappeared before the fire started. I'm grateful for that, but it disturbs me to realize that they'd probably been given prior notice. Their loyalties weren't with our family either."

"Major Spear told me that Mr. Ly has disappeared."

"Yes, although he led father away from the mansion before the fire started, so perhaps he had some loyalty to him. How father will fare with his newly promoted overseer is a worry."

"What about you, Lucette? You've now been uprooted from the only life you've ever known," sympathized Brand.

"I was very lonely there, Winston, except for my parents, of course. So, it was probably inevitable to be attracted to a young, single man such as Captain Hewlett. Rafe was attracted to me, too."

"Not hard to imagine, Lucette. You're a lovely woman."

"Thank you, Winston. But Major Spear advised Rafe not to pursue a relationship with me, due to suspicious Viet Cong activity the major discovered in our old barn."

"I'm sure Alex did so in order to protect everyone's interests. An overly conspicuous military presence at *Bon Sejour* would foil any covert surveillance," surmised Brand.

"Yes, I know Major Spear was protecting all concerned, but the longing for each other Rafe and I experienced was almost too much to bear with the forced separation. When Rafe and Major Spear did come back to *Bon Sejour* on a mission, I must confess I took advantage of Rafe by seducing him. Rafe valiantly attempted to resist me, but I used my womanly charms to overcome his defenses. We spent the night together in the *garçonnière* undetected, although I think Major Spear suspected as much."

"What will come of your relationship with Rafe now that you must return to France?"

"Of course, we couldn't have foreseen what would happen so quickly, cutting off time for our relationship to grow. Rafe told me to move on with my life. Worried whether he'd survive his tour of duty at Loc Ninh, he couldn't make any promises."

"I'm sorry to hear that, Lucette. It's yet another difficult circumstance for you to endure."

"Winston, I want to speak to you of a private matter. After the romantic night Rafe and I spent together, I can't be sure I haven't become pregnant because of it. It's quite early yet, but if it's true, I wouldn't want to trap Rafe into a marriage because of it."

"Don't you think Rafe deserves to know if you discover he's a father-to-be?"

"I don't want any possible pregnancy to be the reason he comes looking for me. Instead, because he sees a future with me in marriage. Then I'll tell him, if it's true. Meanwhile, I'll write to him to keep up our contact. I would appreciate it if you would encourage Rafe whenever you happen to see him to come see me after he completes his tour of duty."

"I'll certainly keep your confidences, and encourage Rafe to come to see you. I sincerely hope things turn out well for the two of you. I brought along a Christmas story I wrote to give to you if you're interested that gives us all hope in difficult circumstances.

"How thoughtful you are, Winston. I shall share it with mother and my relatives when I see them."

"Best wishes, Lucette, in the new chapter in your life, and that goes for your father, too, as he tries to salvage his operation."

"Thank you, Winston. I've so enjoyed getting acquainted with you. I wish you well, too," said Lucette. She hugged Brand goodbye, and he felt her tremble with apprehension. She got her courage up though and smiled as he departed.

40 CONFRONTATION

All's fair in love and war.
—Francis Edward Smedley and Frank Farlegh

"IT JUST WASN'T WORKING," Brand lamented to himself. "Lucette and Rafe were right about the agony of separation, just as it was true of Maria and himself. The more he tried to put Maria out of his mind, the more she made her home there. He'd decided not to meet Maria's friend Emma at the airport every Thursday to receive Maria's letters and poems written for him. He knew she wrote to him every day, and he had done his share of writing to her, too.

But no matter what he was doing, he would always be there to receive Maria's correspondence from Emma and give her his to take back to Maria. Even more disturbing, he found himself working harder on his reciprocal letters and poems to Maria than he did on his columns for the *Times.*

It was insidious, he thought. In fact, it was downright addictive. How paradoxical that he should be able to stop drinking, only to turn around and become addicted to Maria. The muse of poetry had inspired him to turn eloquent and prolific enough to fill a second book of poetry.

Perhaps it was the only way he and Maria could find during separation to release the insistent longing for each other that had pervaded their lives, unasked for but unavoidable, since the fates had brought them together. And the physical desire for Maria had reached the point of no return.

Before he traveled to the Mekong Delta area to report on the preparedness of ARVN troops and on the effectiveness of the strategic hamlets there, he decided to surprise Maria with a short visit to Manilla.

Emma had told him Maria was always there on her return flight to the Philippines to receive his letters, so he booked a seat on her return flight the third week of Maria's time off. Emma was delighted for Maria, and said she couldn't wait to see Maria's face when she returned, not with letters, but the man himself. Brand couldn't wait either.

The plane's arrival in Manila didn't come too soon for Winston. The minute Winston saw Maria as he debarked, their radiant energy pulled them together so joyfully that no restraint could stop them. Emma watched the distance between them rapidly dissolve until they were so wrapped in each other's arms she could hardly distinguish one from the other.

"How is anyone ever going to keep them apart?" Emma thought. If Maria's father could see what she had just seen, he would know it would take an earthquake to separate them. But even if Mr. Monclova managed it, she knew Winston and Maria would always remain halves of a whole. She prayed that each of them would be strong enough to handle what their different worlds would throw at them to separate them. No doubt Maria would take Winston to her small apartment near the airport, and nothing would separate them in the next few hours at least.

General Pavler looked up from the report on his desk when his Chief of Staff entered his office.

"Sir, there's an Eleanor Brand waiting to speak to you. She says you're acquainted with her. She appears to be very determined. Is she related to the *Times* reporter?"

The general lifted his eyebrows and let out a sigh. "Yes, she's his ex-wife. Please show her in."

"General Pavler stood up and greeted Eleanor when she walked into his office. She came around his desk and hugged him. "It's so good to see you again, our dear general." She smiled warmly at him.

"Good to see you as well, Eleanor, but I'm very sorry to hear about your mother's passing."

"Thank you, General. My parents blessed my life, but it was difficult dealing with their health problems in the end. When first my father and then my mother passed, I became aware of a hole in my life. And when mother finally died, I felt like an 'orphan,' all alone in the world with no family left."

"That's true for others, too, Eleanor. We often don't realize what a significant part of our lives parents are, for better or worse, until they're gone."

"I'm an only child, so the feeling of loneliness is acute."

"You've written to me asking about Winston. Is he the reason you're here in Vietnam?"

"Yes, I want to contact Winnie and possibly reconcile with him. I stopped in Hawaii to see Clemie on my way here and told her about my plans. So, I've volunteered my nursing skills at the Red Cross here for the next six months to give Winnie and myself time to connect and heal our relationship."

"Does Winston know you are coming to Vietnam to see him?"

"No, he'd probably tell me not to come."

"My goodness, Eleanor, you must really be serious if you've come all this way, and into a war zone on top of it, just to have a chance to talk to Winston."

"I really couldn't follow Winnie all over the world as his job as a foreign correspondent would require with my mother fighting cancer alone after my father passed. I know Winnie was miserable on his desk job, but I had a very responsible position in my head nursing job as well. When Winnie's drinking got out of hand, I was frightened. What could I do? Something had to give with demands on all sides and me in the middle. So I asked him for a divorce."

"What about your head-of-nursing job in New York, Eleanor?"

"I've taken a leave of absence, so I can iron out my relationship with Winnie once and for all. Although we're divorced, I strongly believe our story together remains unfinished. Circumstances had forced us apart, but the feelings for each other remain, at least on my part, and I need to resolve them before I can move forward."

"But the divorce was ultimately your choice, Eleanor."

"Yes, and I regret making the decision I did. Was I angry because Winnie so desperately wanted to go back into the field? Possibly. Could I have waited at home for him to return to see me in between assignments? Probably. But his drinking clouded the mix, and didn't portend well for the future. I regret not having children early on with Winnie. I realize that now I'm alone in the world."

"Haven't you met anyone of interest since your divorce?"

"I've met eligible men, but the funny thing is, despite Winnie's obvious flaws, he's still in my blood."

"Well, I'm happy to report that Winston stopped drinking since he's been in Vietnam, but I'm afraid he's been developing a relationship with a Filipina flight attendant. He's mentioned he has mixed feelings about becoming involved with any woman until he resolves his personal issues."

"When I visited Clemie and Sean and their dear, little children, Sean told me he'd heard a rumor to that effect when he was in Vietnam with Senator Kearney. But he said that if it's true, it was probably in its very early stages."

"I believe that's the case, Eleanor. There's ten years difference between Winston and Maria Monclova, and Winston seems to want to concentrate on winning a second Pulitzer Prize at the moment. But even so, he and Maria seem drawn to each other.

"He's taken a break for a few days to fly to the Philippines to see her while she's on leave to take care of her father, who was in a car accident. So, I'm afraid Winston isn't in Saigon at the moment."

"Be all that as it may, General, but I believe Winnie and I still need to address our unfinished relationship before either one of us can move forward. I care enough to try to set things right as I said, one way or the other, although I'd surely like to reconcile with Winnie. And now that he's stopped drinking, I'd even like to persuade him to have a child with me before we both grow too old to be good parents to a youngster."

"You surprise me, Eleanor! Winston's mixed feelings about your offer of reconciliation going to be compounded by the shock of your proposal to have a child with him!"

"Maybe so, but he recently wrote a touching Christmas story about a little, one-armed Vietnamese girl befriended by a doctor. Clemie has a copy and let me read it. Perhaps he's softened his attitude about having children after meeting the young girl and writing her story."

"Yes, I've read the story, too. But I don't think I'd spring that plan on him right away, Eleanor. He'll need to get over the surprise of seeing you in Vietnam first, and then with your reconciliation plan."

"Of course, but Winnie and I have always had good chemistry between us, so we'll see where it leads."

"I just hope that Winston doesn't start drinking again in the middle of all these developments," cautioned the general.

"I certainly hope to avoid a relapse, too, but it's time for us to conclude our story, as I said, one way or another." Please let Winnie know I'm here to see him when he returns from the Philippines, General."

General Pavler sighed again as Eleanor left his office. Eleanor looked great, he'd give her that, and she'd pleaded her case well, but he had a gut feeling this development wouldn't go well for Winston and Maria.

"Winston," said Maria, our surprise rendezvous is even more delightful than our last, if that's even possible. I'd like to stay here in my small apartment with you for the next two days. But it approaches dinner time, and I must at least check in with my father. He will be worried about me that I've been gone all afternoon and haven't returned yet."

"Yes, go ahead and call him to ease his mind, Maria." Winston couldn't take his eyes off Maria's naked beauty as she left his arms to call her father. He felt desire for her so intensely, he just couldn't get enough of her. So Winston followed her to the phone.

Maria tried to sound normal as she talked to her father, but it was difficult with Winston intimately caressing her as she spoke. When she hung up, and Maria turned to him, Winston couldn't restrain himself and once again joined with her in a passion of lovemaking that couldn't be denied, or delayed. After their joining found its fulfillment, Winston noticed Maria's tears.

"What's wrong, my lovely goddess? Why are there tears in your eyes?"

"They're tears of utter joy, my devastating prince. I never knew an experience of such total bliss could exist."

"Nor have I ever experienced anything so intensely blissful either, Maria. Can we spend the night together here? What did your father say?"

"He wishes to meet you and wants us to come for dinner."

"The inquisition awaits me, I see. I don't know what to tell your father, Maria. I can't even explain myself to me where you're concerned. I know what reason tells me to be true about our unlikely relationship, but it becomes totally swamped with emotion and desire when we're together. I keep chiding myself that your young man, who has proposed to you, doesn't deserve this interference from me, and it greatly disturbs my conscience. But it, too, disappears in a cloud of euphoria at the mere thought of you.

"I really don't feel worthy enough to propose to you at this point, and I ask myself why I continue to taste the ripe fruit of your passion that's also an insatiable hunger in me. What in the world can I say to your father, who I'm sure wants to protect you, as I should be doing?"

"Oh, Winston, talking about protection, we were too carried away just now by the phone to use protection!" Maria exclaimed.

"You're right, my beautiful mate. We didn't even notice. Possibly we just picked the joker from the deck of cards of life. We can't play the joker, but it could play us, and it could be the decisive card in our passion for each other, Maria. We'll just have to see what happens.

"For now, I'd better tell your father we plan to get to know each other better as we consider an engagement. If a pregnancy should come to pass because of our slip-up just now, you'd be getting the poorer end of the bargain with me as a husband, Maria."

"Don't say that, Winston. We each seem to be so much more together than we are as individuals. We power the light within ourselves in each other's presence, and become a bright, shining oneness."

"Maria, I hope you never take off your rose-colored glasses when you look at me. I surely need sun glasses whenever I look at your beauty and the soul-fire within you."

"I must warn you, dear Winston, my father senses the warm glow that unbidden lights my eyes where you're concerned, and he fears for me. Now he will see the magnetism between us in person when we come to have dinner with him. As much as I love my father, my life choices as an adult must be mine to make. In a normal situation, I will live many years without him."

"But apply this logic to me, too, Maria. With ten years between us, if our lives are joined in marriage, you will most likely have many years without me as well."

Maria laughed and her eyes sparkled. "But maybe not so with your child, or children, Winston," Maria teased.

"Vixen," said Brand. And their passion overtook them again before they got ready to meet Maria's father.

"Maria, you're late!" growled her father as she and Winston opened the door and entered. "Letty has had to keep dinner warm in the oven for the longest time."

"I'm sorry. But, Father, I'm pleased to introduce Winston Brand to you."

"Brand," replied Pacifico Monclova.

"Winston, meet my father."

"Glad to meet you, Mr. Monclova." Brand's stretched out his hand, but Maria's father looked away and ignored the invitation to shake hands.

Maria was disturbed by her father's slight of Winston, but said, "Well, Father, we're here now, so let's make the best of it. Shall we sit down to eat?"

"Yes, if our food isn't all dried out for staying in the oven for so long!"

"Don't worry, Father. We'll manage just fine."

During dinner Maria's father just pushed his food around his plate and ate very little. His stony silence cast a gloomy aura around the table that Maria struggled to lighten.

"Today I met Emma's flight at the airport expecting her to bring me a much anticipated letter from Winston, but instead I was almost overcome by the wonderful surprise of seeing Winston in person. Now he even has the chance to meet my family."

The elder Monclova looked up from his still full plate and scowled as he saw Maria and Winston smiling at each other. They looked intently into each other's eyes, and he saw their desire for each other.

What an unexpected intrusion into your schedule indeed, my dear daughter, but you still needed to be respectful of your obligations to others."

"I did call, Father."

"Yes, but way past dinner time."

Winston interjected, "I'm sorry I wasn't able to give Maria more notice beforehand, sir, but I was able to get a flight at the last minute and had no way to notify her beforehand."

"When Maria didn't return from the airport as expected, I became quite worried. She and I are all that's left of our family after her mother perished in an aircraft accident on her way back to the Philippines after a visit to the States."

"Yes, Maria has told me about the devastating loss of her mother. I, too, lost my parents in an air crash but much later in life than at Maria's tender age."

"And yet Maria persists in her airline job despite my protests, flying here and there, worrying me to death," complained her irate father.

"Father, we've been over this countless times. It's not healthy to live life controlled by fear."

"Confronting your fear by facing so many take offs and landings safely may give you confidence, Maria, but I'm the one back home never knowing when the phone next rings whether or not I'll be told of another plane crash in which you've perished."

"Father, please. Let's not dwell on the negative, but please enjoy Winston's visit with me instead. You've hardly touched your food."

"I've lost my appetite, but I see Brand has finished. I'd like to speak to you privately, Brand."

Maria looked stunned. "That's uncalled for, Father. This is the first time you've met Winston!"

"But it isn't your first time, is it, Maria? It's time for me to make myself perfectly clear about where I stand."

"It's not necessary at this early stage in our friendship."

"Friendship, my eye!"

Winston stepped into the escalating confrontation and said, "It's okay, Maria. This is your father's home, and you are his dear daughter. Understandably, he wants to protect you, and I'll listen to what he has to say and answer any questions he'd like to ask me in private."

Winston followed Maria's father into his study. Mr. Monclova shut the door and indicated Winston should sit in the chair facing his desk. He seated himself in the chair behind his large desk.

"Maria tells me there is quite an age difference between you, and that you've been married before and divorced. What's more, you're a controversial columnist for the *Times* and a war correspondent subject to following conflicts around the globe."

"Yes, that's true."

"As Maria's father, I consider that lineup a serious detriment to your relationship with Maria."

"I've mentioned these considerations to Maria myself, but she's willing for us to get to know each other better anyway."

Winston saw a thundercloud forming in Monclova's countenance and his face drew into a deep frown. He was silent for a moment and then looked straight at Brand with a determined look in his eyes. "I want to be honest with you, Brand. I'm going to do everything in my power to dissuade Maria from having anything to do with you, much less pursue a romantic relationship with you. I can see disaster ahead for her with your contentious career that will take you far and wide and with the considerable baggage you carry with you of a failed marriage, a drinking proclivity and dangerous assignments in war zones. Your prospects as a possible future husband and father to her children add up to zero in my view!"

"I see Maria has filled you in on my challenges. But I'm sorry you feel a relationship between Maria and me has no potential. We both feel otherwise, even though I've previously mentioned the points you've raised to her. I've tried to stay away from her several times because of them, but the pull of attraction between us doesn't bend to reason."

Maria's father's face took on a reddish flush matching the fury in his eyes. "Where is your conscience, Brand, taking advantage of a naïve, idealistic young woman, who romantically looks at you like a knight in shining armor, overlooking your weaknesses that keep you from living a stable, upstanding life?"

"I think you've said enough," said Brand with growing anger at the disrespect in Maria's father's voice.

Just then the doorbell rang, and Winston heard voices come through the closed door. Maria's father said, "Our discussion isn't quite finished. I've invited a visitor who's just arrived. Tywan is a longtime friend of our family. He has proposed to Maria quite a while ago, but she has hesitated to give him an affirmative answer. They have known each other since childhood. I can't think of a finer young man, more Maria's age, who would be a loving, stable husband and father to Maria's children as he is. He is my heartfelt choice for Maria, and he has my blessing if Maria should choose to accept him. I intend to do everything I can to encourage her to do so!"

"You certainly say what you think, Mr. Monclova, even though I hear you work for the diplomatic service."

"I don't pull any punches when my daughter's welfare is at stake, Brand. It's my right to protect my daughter as her father should."

Mr. Monclova got up, walked over to the door and opened it. He turned to Winston and said, "I want you to meet Tywan and see for yourself that your harmful interference in Maria's life is unwelcome and detrimental to Maria's well-being. Her life with Tywan can be so much better for her than with you."

Winston got up and followed Maria's father into the living room. He could hardly believe warm, loving and gracious Maria could have a father so disrespectful he would humiliate a guest. But as Winston entered the room, Tywan moved over to where Maria was anxiously pacing and put his arm around Maria in a shower of her father's approving smile. Winston felt ready to punch out this so-called fine young man, even though Maria shied away from him very upset.

Winston said to Maria, "Please show me to your phone." He called for a taxi to take him to a hotel in Manila, and made a second call to rebook his return flight to Saigon in the morning. Maria was beside herself in extreme distress.

Brand's tolerance had ended, and he had to leave before his temper got the best of him. The blatant and total rejection of Brand by Maria's father, emphasized by his pointed acceptance of Tywan, ended the possibility of any kind of relationship with Maria's father. Winston had spent his whole life rejected by his own father, and he wasn't about to repeat the experience with Maria's father.

Heartbroken, Maria pleaded, "Please, Winston, please don't leave. I apologize for my father. I'm totally in shock he would treat you so disrespectfully. Please, my darling, consider our deep, heartfelt feelings for each other. Please, my love!"

"Your family is part of your life that you can't turn your back on, precious Maria. Never would I want to take anything so dear away from you. And I know I won't be able to tolerate my life rejected by yet another father. I truly won't ever fit in here, and I love you enough to let you go for your own sake."

"I love you, too, Winston, with all my heart. Please don't leave me, my darling. You are the love of my life! It'll be such a lonely life without you!"

"Mine, too, Maria, mine, too." The taxi had arrived and was waiting. Greatly disturbed, Winston kissed a tearful Maria goodbye and left.

As the taxi pulled him away from the woman he realized he did indeed love, he couldn't bear to look back and see the tears cascading down Maria's cheeks. He had to wipe away the wetness that began to seep from his own eyes. Their afternoon of bliss would have to last him a lifetime, one without Maria, now the other half of himself. It truly would be such a lonely life without her.

The joker indeed had the last laugh on them all, Brand thought. Nothing would ever be the same for any of them after such a demeaning confrontation.

REBELS ALL

Mel R. Jones
Marian N. Jones

PART 4:
COMPLICATIONS
SOUTH VIETNAM, 1962–1963

"Every war involves a greatest or less relapse into barbarism. War indeed, in its details, is the essence of inhumanity. It dehumanizes. It may save the state, but it destroys the citizens."
—Christian Nestell Bovee

41 TOUCHING BASE

We have been born to associate with our fellow-men, and to join in company with the human race.

—Cicero

ALEX WAS THE FIRST PERSON Brand ran into after returning to Vietnam from the Philippines, where he had experienced both the ecstasy and the agony of knowing Maria. He had surprised Maria with his visit, and their togetherness in her small apartment had been a love nest of pure ecstasy. But the dinner invitation her father had insisted on had turned out to be pure agony. Her father's rejection of Winston had even outdone his own father's disapproval, for despite Willoughby's intense disappointment, Brand knew his father did care for him. Mr. Monclova's rejection was total.

"You're back early from your visit with Maria, Winston. Does that mean things didn't go as you had expected?"

"You can say that again!" exclaimed Brand.

"I have a little time left on my lunch break, so I've returned to Five Oceans to retrieve a letter to Gwen I wanted to post today. I had forgotten to take it with me this morning. While I'm here, is there anything you'd care to share with me?" asked Alex. "Perhaps it would help to talk things over."

"Don't I wish I could share some good news with you, Alex, although when I first arrived in Manila, Maria and I shared an absolutely unforgettable time together at her small apartment near the airport. I've never had such a deep connection to another than that I've experienced with Maria."

"That sounds like good news to me," remarked Alex. "So what didn't turn out as you expected, Winston?"

"My anticipation was to spend the few days with Maria alone. But my surprise visit delayed her expected return home. She needed to check in with her father so he wouldn't worry when she hadn't returned. He invited us both to dinner, and there was no way we could get out of it without offense to him.

"Well, we were reluctant to leave, and so we were late getting there. Things went downhill from the moment we arrived. The warmed over meal was served by their cook Letty, and any attempt at civil conversation at the dinner table was very strained. Maria's father barely touched his food. When we finished the meal, Mr. Monclova asked to speak to me alone. Although Maria objected, I deemed it only polite to agree. That was the single polite gesture that followed."

"That does sound ominous."

"Ominous doesn't even begin to describe what followed. Maria's father unleashed a tirade on me, citing all the reasons he believed my relationship with Maria would be detrimental to her. I'm sure Maria could hear his raised voice."

"I imagine you were shocked at his bluntness and hostility toward you after just meeting you for the first time."

"I'm sure he meant for it to be the first and last time he'd ever see me again. He was dead serious about running me out of his daughter's life. But the points he brought up were nothing different from what I'd already brought up with Maria."

"No relationship is without some complication." The separations between spouses in the military are serious complications to married couples needing infinite adjustments."

"Mr. Monclova went way beyond complications. It was an all-out attack. He invited the young fellow, Tywan, who had proposed to Maria, over after dinner. Her father made it clear in word and deed that the young man had his approval as a husband for Maria. This encouraged Tywan, who smiled at Maria and tried to put his arm around her, although she shied away."

"A diabolical intent to make you feel very unwelcome, I see. What was left to you but to leave?"

"I called for a taxi, stayed overnight in a hotel in Manila and took a morning flight back to Vietnam, and here I am."

"How did Maria react? Knowing her gentle, hospitable warmth, I'm sure she was as shocked as you were at such humiliating and disrespectful treatment of you by her father."

"Maria was beside herself, and begged me not to leave. It just about killed us both, but I had to break it off with her for her sake and for mine. I could never cause her to lose her family she loves, and I don't think I've come to terms with my own late father's disapproval of me even yet. I'm certain I couldn't handle her father's total rejection of me, too."

"Winston, I'm so sorry to hear your story. Is your breakup final with Maria?"

"It has to be. We really can't stay away from each other when we're together. The insurmountable consequences involved of continuing our relationship could only destroy each of us."

"How are you going to handle this, Winston?"

"I'm not going to start drinking again, if that's what you're asking. Just knowing Maria is 'somewhere out there' gives me reason to go on as she would want me to do. I'm going to return to what I came here for, and that's being the best foreign war correspondent I can be."

"Glad to hear it, Winston. By the way, I spoke to General Pavler this morning. He asked me to give you a message when you returned from the Philippines."

"Is it anything urgent? Is my sister Clemie okay?"

"Nothing like that. He just said to ask you to stop in to see him at your convenience."

"Thank goodness it's not another crisis. I'm feeling too numb and in shock to handle anything more at the moment. Do you know what he wants to talk to me about?"

"I'll leave that to him." Glad to have you back, Winston. I'd best be getting back to work. See you later, my friend."

"Before you go, Alex, do you know if Lt. Ledger Smith is on office duty today? I'd like to check in with him."

"I believe so." "He's doing a fine job with our first publication for the armed services in Southeast Asia. The *Observer* is what was needed to help tie our military community together here in Vietnam. And it was just the thing to impress Senator Kearney during his visit in May while you were up-country. I'll tell Lieutenant Smith you'll see him soon."

After Alex left, Brand was tempted to open his desk drawer where he kept Maria's letters and poems to read them once again. But then he realized it would just bring him more agony than he could stand at the moment. He decided to throw himself back into his work as the best way to carry on, although there was no doubt he had left his heart behind with the beauty that had filled the gnawing emptiness within him. Despite their separation, he knew they were ever joined somehow.

"Why, Winston, it's good to see you again," said Lt. Ledger Smith as Winston stepped into his office.

"Likewise, Ledger. I wonder if you have a few minutes to update me with your news? I'm interested in how your publication, the *Observer,* has been doing. And did your article on the training of the Montagnards at Buon Enao go over well?"

"Very well regarding both your questions," said Ledger. "General Pavler wants me to be sure units from all the services share equally in the articles published. I think the newspaper is helping to promote a sense of cohesiveness between the services and the two commands."

"Yes, I suppose there have been a lot of adjustments to be made since the creation of the MACV command in February."

Ledger replied, "MACV is the overall command, but MAAG still supervises the military advisors. It's going to take some time for the missions and roles of each command to be sorted out and organized properly. However, some bitter rivalries between services have developed when the use of helicopters that arrived not too long ago has been designated to be under army control, rather than that of the air force. Of course, that information is 'off the record.'"

"Don't worry about that, Ledger. I really came over to see how you're getting along."

"You may be surprised to know I have been teaching English to a group of Vietnamese college students, five females and four males, in my spare time. We meet weekly in the evening in the home of a Vietnamese businessman."

"That must relieve some stress from dealing with the insistent inquiries of our press corps."

"I'll say, and the students are very eager to learn. They have even been teaching me some of the customs of the Vietnamese.

One I've had to be very cognizant of when I'm invited to their parents' homes for dinner."

"What's that?"

"Westerners who allow a Vietnamese host to see the soles of their shoes indicates that the foreigner thinks he's better than the person to whom he's just offered the bottom (sole) of his existence. I've had to keep my feet flat on the floor."

"That would make a great human interest article for the *Observer*," remarked Brand. "Are there any other customs you could add to such an article?"

"Well, I know Southeast Asians like quiet Americans who don't use their voices as bludgeons in order to get their point across. The Vietnamese are a soft-spoken people who shun loud arguments. They consider the Chinese to be the world leaders in 'vocal variety.'"

"Diplomatically put."

"Another custom is baffling to Americans. Some who offer candy to Vietnamese children don't understand why they run away when the Americans motion them to come closer. To the Vietnamese, waving the hands in a 'come here' fashion means 'get lost' to them."

"I'll have to remember that one when I'm out in the field."

"Now that you mention it, Winston, I think it would make a good article for the *Observer*. I remember my Vietnamese students have given me a list of twelve dos and don'ts for American soldiers. I have it here in my desk."

"I'd like to hear it."

Ledger began:

1. Try to speak a few words in the Vietnamese language, even if it's a mere "*Chao co, manh gioi?*" ("Hello, miss, how are you?")
2. Make a big fuss over how good that glassful of tinted water tastes, even though to you it looks like a watered down Coke. It's the national beverage—tea—and if you serve it yourself, be sure it's never warmer than room temperature.
3. Remember to take your camera when you visit Vietnamese friends. They love to have their pictures taken, and they appreciate your interest.

4. Remember that the Vietnamese are your allies and your hosts. You are the foreigner, but they want you to feel at home.
5. Never touch a Vietnamese woman in public unless she offers you her hand. In some communities, a woman who allows herself to be touched by a foreigner may be ostracized. Few are willing to take that risk.
6. Don't pat a child on the head or the back of the neck. These spots are considered the sacred temple of the spirit.
7. Never ridicule a local religious group however strange or even queer their habits may appear. Be especially cautious with the religious sect called Cau Dai. They have many unusual divinities in the temple in Tay Ninh, including a bust of Victor Hugo.
8. Don't belt down drinks one after another. The Vietnamese drink very moderately and appreciate those who do the same.
9. Never discuss politics with local merchants, taxi drivers or bar girls. It will only bore them.
10. Don't be seen carrying a local souvenir from any village even if you have paid for it. The person who sold you the crossbow or ornamental rice bowl may know you paid for it, but you can bet the communists will make sure everyone else in the village will think you stole it.
11. Don't try to make like St. George if you're suddenly confronted by Vietnamese dressed as dragons. On festive occasions these generally friendly "dragons" are out to impress the people with a display of their prowess and represent a mythological power Westerners don't have to worry about. What is important is that you be regarded by the people as one of the strongest "dragons."
12. Don't forget when you practice a local custom, you do it because you want to. The Viet Cong do it because he has to, and the Vietnamese people know the difference.

"That's a colorful list of customs, Ledger. Fans of the *Observer* should enjoy reading about them. But I'll have to say, I should've been cognizant of one of those 'don'ts' the night of the Pierre Girard press party. I certainly 'belted down' more drinks than I should have, if any, that evening. But I've 'gone on the wagon' since then."

"So you told me when we met in Buon Enao. That was some party," said Ledger. "But I have a confession of my own to make. I appreciate your paying for a Vietnamese comfort woman for me to enjoy that evening with. But although I was tempted to take advantage of your offer, I had to pass up on the opportunity. You see, I'm married."

"I'm sorry, Ledger, I didn't know you were married."

"I should have told you then and there, Winston, but I was tempted until I though it over and knew better. After you left and the Vietnamese woman went off to try to interest another man, I went back to the bar and had more to drink than I should have, too. The loneliness can get to a man over here. I got talking to a lovely Vietnamese serving woman, who could speak English, and we've struck up a friendship. She told me where she works during the week, and against my better judgment I've been going there many evenings to see her. It's gotten to the point where I'm afraid I might violate my marriage vows with her, which I'd promised myself I'd never do."

"I can see where you're going with this, Ledger. It's very hard for married men and women to be separated from their spouses for an extended period of time—a year for your tour of duty in Vietnam."

"My wife and I hadn't been married that long before I came to Vietnam, and I have to consider that if I'm unfaithful to her, my wife could do the same to me while I'm gone when she's lonely as well. It's a worry all the way around."

"I'm afraid I can't advise you, Ledger. I don't have a good track record with women, but I can wish you the best."

"Thanks, Winston. It's helpful to get my concern off my chest and out in the open, so I can look at it more clearly. As always, I appreciate your friendship."

"If you publish your Vietnamese manners article in the *Observer*, I'd be willing to reprint it with your permission in my *Times* column. It's an interesting twist on war reporting. That reminds me to tell you that I wrote a Christmas story about a one armed peanut girl befriended by an American surgeon that I'm hoping my editor will agree to print as my holiday column."

"Is that the surgeon who was recently killed in a tragic medevac helicopter crash?"

"Yes, and he was a good friend. All who knew him deeply grieve his loss."

"I'm sorry for your loss, Winston. But please ask your editor if we can print your Christmas story in the *Observer* for the holidays, an even exchange if you will."

"Sounds like a plan. Let's see if we can make it happen."

"Where are you off to for your next column interview?"

"I'd like to go down to the Mekong Delta area and report on the progress of the Strategic Hamlet program there, and also ARVN troop training and engagements with the Viet Cong. But first I have to stop in to see General Pavler. He sent a message for me to stop in to talk to him at my convenience. I hope he's in his office this afternoon."

"I believe he is. Good luck down in the Delta, Winston. I hear things are not going as well there as in Quang Ngai."

When Brand checked in at General Pavler's office, he was ushered in after a short delay. Right away the general noticed Brand's lack of enthusiasm, previously so evident upon his return from Thailand. "You're back early from your visit to the Philippines, Winston. Alex said he'd seen you at the lunch hour at Five Oceans, but he didn't say why you came back so soon."

"Don't ask. It'll just depress me more to repeat the story I told Alex earlier."

"I take it things didn't go well there."

"Let's just say that Maria's father is dead set against any relationship whatsoever between Maria and me. He's got her future all planned out for her with a local young man who's already proposed to her. Apparently, it's the only way he thinks he can keep Maria in his life in Manila. His total rejection of me in any kind of relationship between Maria and me was blatant and humiliating, to say the least!"

"That bad, huh! I'm sorry to hear how disrespectfully you were treated, Winnie. I'm sure Maria had no idea what her father had in mind to do."

"No. But I had to break it off with Maria. I can't take her family she loves away from her if she would pursue a relationship with me, and there's no question I have any chance whatsoever of fitting in with hers."

"It sounds like a repetition of the difficulties you've had with Willoughby, but one without the least bit of regard for you. Perhaps I should hold off on what I wanted to say to you."

"Well, you'd better tell me now, because I need to get back to work as soon as I can. I'm headed south to the Mekong Delta next, and I may not be back for a while."

"As you wish, but it's not the best time to impart what I've been asked to tell you."

"Is it trouble between Clemie and her husband?"

"No, rather it's about you and your ex-wife Eleanor."

"I've heard that she's been asking about me, but as you can see, I'm not in any kind of place to worry about that now."

"Eleanor's a very determined woman as we all know. She's here in Saigon hoping to reconcile with you. Your ex-wife has signed up as a volunteer with the Red Cross here for the next six months in order to see if she can persuade you to iron out your past relationship difficulties with her and move on into the future together."

Winston put his hands over his face and lowered his head. He finally looked up and said, "There's no way I'm in any shape to talk to Eleanor right now, General. Please tell her you've alerted me to her plans, but I need some time before I can see her. I'll see if I'm up to it when I return from the Delta. Convey my sympathy to her for the passing of her mother."

"That's just it, Winston. She says she's all alone in the world now that both her parents are gone, and it's made her re-evaluate her thinking about her past priorities. I should forewarn you that it's not only a reconciliation with you she's got in mind, but also having a child with you before you both get too old to be parents."

"The whole package to fill her loneliness, I see. She just forgets too often about the feelings of the other person involved in her plans. Well, if she's changed, I've changed as well, and I can't say I'm looking forward to talking with her. But I need to be civil to her, and respect her request to speak with me. I know how it feels to be rejected without a qualm or second thought. Just not now."

"I'll tell her the next time I see her. But about your trip to the Delta, I hope you won't be disappointed with what you experience. There are some problems with the strategic hamlets, and ARVN troop reports are concerning. With the biggest concentration of Viet Cong guerillas in South Vietnam in the Delta, I have to caution you to be on alert for your own safety there, and interviews may be more difficult."

"I should check in with my bureau chief, Sheenar Tillerstein to get briefed on the press angle there before I leave. My Tho is close enough to Saigon that my press colleagues have probably ventured out of the Saigon bars to make a few trips to the region."

"Take care, Winston. By the way, Eleanor left a letter from your sister Clemie with me to give to you when you returned. I have it in my desk. He located the letter and gave it to Winston.

"Then Eleanor has made all the rounds already. Give me a break from women!" said Winston as he left the general's office with Clemie's letter in his hand.

General Pavler thought, "Good luck, Winston. Clemie is sure to throw her opinions into the mix, too." But Winnie seemed too numb to the general to be shocked by any of it. He had probably gone beyond shock though his experience with Maria's father and his breakup with Maria. The general decided to write to Norma about Winnie's situation. She was like a second mother to Winston, and would have an intuition what, if anything, could be done to help him recover.

"Well, Brand, long time no see. You're one of the last people I expected to see today, even if I am your bureau chief boss," said Sheenar Tillerstein ensconced in his tiny office.

"Remember, you're my boss only for straight news, Sheenar. Louis's my boss for my columns that go straight to his desk."

"Oh, yes, you're too senior to be bothered with daily wire-news deadlines like I am. Why I haven't even had much time to see Lan these days."

"How is our secretary at the Vietnamese Minister of Information's office?"

"She and her boss, But Hieu, are just fine, helping the press get their stories on how well the Diem regime is doing with nation building and military accomplishments against the Viet Cong. There's only one problem. None of us believe it."

"So I noticed in your press reports, Sheet."

"I keep telling you, Brand, It's Sheenar, not Sheet."

"Oh, yes, thanks for reminding me," smirked Brand.

"So, what do you want?"

"I'm about to travel to the Delta to do some interviews there. I thought I'd check in to see what you know about war in Vietnam's rice bowl."

"You've got to be kidding," replied Sheenar.

"Why?

"All you'll find there is rice, water and Viet Cong guerillas. The ARVN troops there are a joke. All that seems to be important to them is not to suffer any casualties. So most of the time nothing is happening there on the ARVN side of the war. But plenty of Viet Cong guerilla fighters are having a hay day with hit-and-run attacks and ambushes in the Delta."

"What about the Seventh ARVN Infantry Division at My Tho? Don't they have an energetic military advisor there helping to get the ARVN troops into shape?"

"You've been up-country too long, Brand, or in Bankok or Manila, as rumor would have it. But the Seventh is mainly in reserve as coup protection for Diem. The military advisor there can't get Arvin moving, and everything shuts down at sunset when Charlie comes into his own."

"Is this first-hand knowledge, or is it just hearsay?"

"Go down there and see nothing going on with ARVN troops for yourself. I've got deadlines to meet."

"If nothing's going on, what do you have to report?"

"Only the false VC body count reports they keep sending up to headquarters," said Tillerstein.

"What about the strategic hamlets being constructed there?"

"It's a Vietnamese circus. Who can tell the difference between a peasant and a Viet Cong infiltrator? Or who can predict which peasant is a farmer by day and a guerilla fighter by night? The Viet Cong concentration in the Delta is so much heavier there that the strategic hamlets just enclose the communists along with the peasants. Sabotage, infiltration, intimidation, you name it, and it is going on in the strategic hamlets there. Diem may even have to order some of his own hamlets bombed that have become communist strongholds."

"I haven't heard such a bleak report since I returned to Saigon, Sheet. You've been cramped up in this tiny office with your typewriter too long for your own good. Maybe you need to spend more time with Lan at the Vietnamese Information Office to hear the other side of the story."

"You don't have a daily deadline to meet, do you, Brand?"

"Thanks for the briefing, Sheenar. I'm off to make arrangements to leave for the Delta tomorrow to see what's going on there for myself," said Brand on his way out the door.

"Just don't take any side trips to Thailand or Manila on the way," sneered Tittlestein as he turned back to his work.

"Never gave it a thought," said Brand as he felt like a knife had wedged in his heart as he spoke the lie.

42 AFTERMATH

We shape ourselves the joy or fear of which the coming life is made,
and fill our future's atmosphere with sunshine or with shade.
—John Greenleaf Whittier

MARIA MONCLOVA AWAKENED with eyes almost swollen shut from the crying fits she had experienced in the night. The new day seemed surreal to her, as if nothing in her life was in its right place anymore. It was as if an almost finished puzzle had been broken into its many disconnected pieces once again and couldn't ever be put together in the same way as before.

She had been stunned into disbelief that her beloved father, the grieving but gentle parent who had comforted her through all the days of horror after her mother's sudden tragic death years ago, could suddenly show such a dark side of parental love.

The only thing Maria could think of to have caused his outrageous behavior was perhaps awareness of his age and vulnerability since his accident. Did it make him even more intolerant of the thought of losing her to Winston, who might very well take her away from the Philippines? Granted, her acceptance of Tywan's proposal would assure her father of a much more pleasant life in his old age with her nearby and future grandchildren to enjoy.

Had she misjudged the depth of her father's loneliness that he would sacrifice her happiness to fulfill his own needs? But then he could say the same thing about her. She and her father had long consoled each other since her mother died. Apparently, her father really meant it when he said he couldn't bear it to lose Maria, too. Whatever had caused her father's unacceptable behavior toward Winston, it had shocked her to her very core.

But even that paled with the shock she felt when it caused the sudden, unexpected ripping of Winston out of her life. The wound left behind defied recovery.

How could she ever, ever forget the joy she had experienced when she saw Winston step out of the plane in Manila? It could never be measured. He had come to see her despite his deep reservations about the obstacles in their relationship. She knew it meant he had moved past them enough to continue building his relationship with her. Her heart had rejoiced that he finally had opened the door to his own guarded heart to her.

Not only that, but at her small apartment their joining had obliterated his reluctance so much she could feel his heart and soul joining with hers in an ecstasy beyond imagination. They truly were halves of a whole now, no matter how their lives would play out.

To say that neither of them could have expected the violence of her father's resistance against that joining was an ultimate understatement. Her father undoubtedly sensed their connection when he saw them together at dinner surrounded by the euphoria of their recent lovemaking. She still couldn't believe the savagery of her father's blatant rejection of Winston had really happened, wasn't just a bad dream. And what's more, he had humiliated Winston further by inviting Tywan to visit after dinner to put his stamp of approval on him, while branding Winston as rejected with no recourse. Unbelievable!

Maria didn't blame Winston for leaving. Her father had given him no alternative. Winston's last words to her were to declare his love for her, words she had longed to hear, but it would be the only time she would ever hear them again. She had told him she loved him, too, and begged him not to leave her. But Winston had replied he couldn't stand between her and her family she loved, nor could he withstand the rejection of her father added to his late father's disapproval. It would truly be a lonely life for both of them without each other!

What to do? Maria was caught between two people she loved and ended up with neither of them. Winston was gone from her life and nothing would ever be the same again with her father. Though she still loved him dearly, his disrespectful behavior with

Winston had placed a barrier between them that wasn't there before. Their family connection had a deep flaw in it now, and the hole it left in her heart was gaping wide open.

How ironic, she thought, that before that fateful dinner meeting, Winston had even mentioned their getting to know each other better prior to a possible engagement to marry. That they had slipped up using protection that one time may have caused Winston to look that far ahead in their relationship. But it indicated the fire in their souls for each other was going in a mutually satisfying direction in his mind.

Winston had become so filled with desire for her that he couldn't refrain himself from a lovemaking frenzy with her even while she was on the phone to her father indicated to her how far along with her he had come, as she had with him.

Perhaps her voice over the phone hadn't sounded as normal to her father as she had tried to make it, when Winston was so close to total joining with her while kissing and fondling her as if he'd absolutely die unless he could have her as close to him as he could possibly get her. She had ended the phone conversation abruptly, as she had turned to Winston and was soon bathed within by the seeds of love in their heavenly embrace. What magic had possessed them to cling to each other in yet another sea of love before they were able to get themselves together to leave the apartment?

In retrospect, she realized she hadn't fooled her father on the phone. He had easily surmised the passionate extent of their connection to each other, and it had fueled his fear of losing her to Winston and the decimation of his plans for Maria's future with Tywan in the Philippines.

But reality brought Maria up short in her thoughts. Suddenly the memories of her afternoon of glory with Winston swept over Maria, and she knew they wouldn't be repeated. She cried out with huge sobs that made her chest heave, "How can I live without you, Winston?" Maria cried out. Hot tears cascaded again down her cheeks, as her heart yearned for the one who had been lost to her as her chosen partner in life.

Winston had tried valiantly to distract himself with stops to check in with friendly faces before he was to leave for the Delta the next morning. But his heart had resounded in tune with Maria's heart as he had left the Philippines. Winston had barely contained the sorrow within himself as his flight had winged its way out of

Manila on its way to Vietnam. In his room at Five Oceans at the end of the day, he finally gave in to the need to re-read Maria's letters and poems he had denied himself that morning.

As he opened his desk drawer, he saw Maria's latest poem to him on top of the pile. It was entitled *Fork in the Road.* His connection with Maria when he had received the poem had come to the point of his choice whether to pursue it or not. At the time, he had bombarded himself with all the reasons why he should not for both their sakes, but when it came right down to it, he had to admit to himself that he just couldn't let go of his kindred soul who had brought such light and love into his life. Yes, love, he knew in his heart. They did love each other. So, at the "fork in the road," he had chosen the road that lead to Maria and their love for each other.

And it was all that he'd ever hoped for in the warmth of her embrace, only to be snatched away from both of them, as the road was turned into a dead end by her father. What a cruel turn of events the fates had allowed for a love that blazed so brightly and beautifully. But, despite the torment of their parting, the love remained, bringing peace to his soul. For now he knew he and Maria had somehow "come home" to each other in their remaining time on earth. They would live within each other's hearts, enabling them to carry on as the other would want them to do. With that thought, Winston fell into a restless sleep with Maria's poem clutched to his heart. Clemie's letter was left unopened on his desk, filled he knew with enthusiasm for his reconciliation with Eleanor.

R-3 heard the voice of the soup lady in the lane outside his window. It wasn't long before he met Madame Binh in his quarters after she took off her disguise at the back entrance of his residence as dusk turned to darkness.

R-3 addressed her, "Madame Binh, I thought you were instructed to no longer come to my residence now that you are the mistress of Bao. It wouldn't serve our cause for you to be accidently discovered here. Why have you come?"

"My Revered Leader, I have a matter of great importance to inform you about. My curio shop has been compromised as a message center for our revolution."

"What happened?"

"An American military officer I've never seen before came to my shop with a travel set he said had been purchased for him by a friend. He had noticed the slight extra thickness at the bottom of the set and discovered the thin space with a bottom compartment after much trial and error to try to open it."

"Was it one of ours with a message in it?"

"No, my Supreme Leader. I'm very careful to safeguard our messages, but the officer complained about the hidden compartment and asked to exchange it for one without it. He could see identical travel chess sets on the shelf. Without asking he proceeded to examine each one. I couldn't refuse him without raising suspicion."

"Did the officer discover the hidden compartments in the other sets?"

"In every single one," Madame Binh answered. "I told him it was a space where the instructions for the game could be stored. But he said he already knew how to play, and wondered why I didn't have copies of the instructions for anyone who asked for them to store in the compartment. You know, *Ayr-Ba*, I must have merchandise to fill my shelves to appear as a normal shopkeeper, but I have no other kind of chess set to display in the shop except those with the hidden compartments."

"Our oversight. Did you offer to order him a set without the compartment?"

"Yes, and he said he'd stop back in later on to exchange it with the one he had in hand."

"Was the officer American or Vietnamese?"

"He was an American, a major I think."

"Ah, Major Spear has tracked us down once again. He's relentless and so very observant, a friend of reporter Winston Brand, too," commented R-3. "Those two truth-seekers are becoming quite the irritants to me and our noble cause. Let me think how we can remedy this concern now that the curio shop has been compromised as a crucial message center."

"If I may be so bold as to relate Colonel Bao's solution to salvaging our message center, I would, if you would give me permission, Great Leader," offered Madame Binh.

"And what does our colonel suggest?"

"Colonel Bao believes we should add other products to our curio shop that will attract Vietnamese women shoppers as a front to cover the real function of the shop. He's confident Madame Nhu would participate by recommending feminine products, such as perfume like the scent she uses, different colors of nail polish and remover in bottles, hair ornaments she likes to wear, and, later on, even shoes with high French heels, beautiful *ao dais* and *non la* conical hats."

"Has Colonel Bao considered that our male messengers might look out of place in such a shop with a gaggle of women vying to buy the latest fad for ladies?"

"I hadn't thought of that, *Ayr-Ba*."

"Perhaps you were too dazzled by these feminine products for seduction of men to notice. Do you contemplate that they might turn Bao's head away from looking with adoration at Madame Nhu to gazing at you?"

"No, of course not! I'm only focused on our glorious cause and the wish to salvage the function of our message center as a crucial link in our worthy endeavor," replied Madame Binh.

"If that's so, Madame Binh, let us relieve our stress over this concern by enjoying each other once again as in the past."

"As you wish, *Ayr-Ba*, but shouldn't I get back before I am discovered visiting you, which might call into question my role as Bao's mistress?"

"That's why you were instructed not to contact me again directly. But while you are here, we will reaffirm our commitment to our cause together," commanded R-3.

Later, Madame Binh put her disguise back on as the old soup vendor lady and departed from R-3's residence with instructions to go ahead with disguising the curio shop with a new line of products that appealed to women. She was cheered that she had saved her curio shop, but she'd had to pay a price for it.

Earlier she had felt privileged to be R-3's mistress, but things had changed now that she was Bao's mistress instead. She realized that Bao was right when he said a younger, vibrant male, such as he was, made a better lover than R-3. Madame Binh found that her awe of R-3 and his powerful position was being eroded day by day as she served as Bao's mistress, even if she had to admit she knew Bao pretended she was Madame Nhu whenever he made love to his lowly shopkeeper fiancée.

R-3 wasn't fooled by Madame Binh. He could see a problem developing with Bao, his fascination with Madame Nhu and Madame Binh's growing attraction to the younger Bao. Better to remove Bao from the Gia Long Palace for a while and from Madame Binh's growing enjoyment as Bao's mistress, he surmised.

Bao, having found favor with the Nhus, had secured his safety on all fronts. His position as assistant to Nhu in the regime's Strategic Hamlet program was key to its downfall. Bao knew it, and so did R-3 who had planned it. But Bao could be seduced by his growing sense of power into making decisions on his own. Bao's focus on women, evidenced by his growing admiration of Madame Nhu, could tempt his loyalty away from the revolution over to the enemy's cause.

Then again, despite Bao's professed dislike of Madame Binh, he was satisfying his mistress as revealed by Madame Binh's lukewarm response to sharing his bed. R-3 knew his performance was not lacking this time.

Yes, Bao could be controlled more effectively if removed from Saigon to spend more time in the fertile field of propaganda in the Delta. This would suit R-3's plans to increase negative reporting by the Western press of the lackadaisical ARVIN troop performance and the sickly strategic hamlets there, so easily infiltrated.

Not wanting to disturb Bao's cover in any way, R-3 would allow Madame Binh to dally with adding feminine products to her curio shop, while he moved his message center discreetly to a new Saigon shop selling health pills of all kinds, even Chinese aphrodisiacs of powdered rhinoceros horn, an easy cover to explain men's traffic in the shop. Messages could be concealed in pill bottles and powder packets. R-3 doubted Madame Binh would even notice the reduced number of curio shop messages in her excitement of trying out all the feminine wiles she seemed so eager to order and sell in her shop.

How R-3 would have liked to eliminate both Bao and Madame Binh on the spot! Madame Binh was almost useless to the cause now. And Bao's ideas and plots formed without R-3s instructions would have marked his death long ago had he not secured his safe refuge with the Diem regime for the time being.

The next morning Brand was waiting at Five Oceans for a taxi to take him the 30 miles south to My Tho in the Mekong Delta. When he spotted a thatch of red hair as an officer entered the lobby, he knew immediately it was Senator Kearney's son, Tank, Jr.

The lieutenant spoke first when he saw Brand. "Well, if it isn't our favorite *Times* reporter, who's been known to drink too much at times."

"How's life been treating you, Lieutenant?"

"You know it's interesting you should ask me that question, Brand, but I should ask it of you. I heard a rumor yesterday that your looker of a flight attendant has finally seen the light and dumped you. Of course, she should have done that right off the bat and taken up with me instead.

"You must've been talking to Sheenar Tillerstein."

"So what if I have? He's got his finger on the pulse of what's happening in this sorry country. He said you came back to Vietnam less than 24 hours since you left for Manila. That's why I really don't have to ask you how life is treating you lately, because I already know," retorted Kearney. "It's too bad, Brand, but when chicks get over looking for a father figure, they find out that young blood carries the day."

"Well," replied Brand, "I hear your 'young blood' has carried you right into matrimony and fatherhood. But here I am footloose and fancy free, while you have a wife and a flock of children on the way to put a damper on your 'young blood.'"

'Don't you believe it, old man! Life hasn't left me without diversions, except when I was stationed in Ca Mau Peninsula, that soggy sinkhole with no available women to bed. There was only that sassy 'Old Lucas McCain, the Rifleman,' whom I'm convinced tried to trick me into thinking she was a child by binding her chest. But I may yet unmask, or unbind, her deception before I leave Vietnam."

"Forgive me, Lieutenant, but what do you mean calling a female 'Old Lucas McCain, the Rifleman,' a male character played by Chuck Connor on the popular TV show?"

"If you ever had met her, you'd know what I mean. The crazy chick couldn't get enough of American flicks, and she picked up sayings that she'd shoot at you like the 'Rifleman.' Now Capt. Edward Markham has taken my place there, receiving all her zingers instead of me."

"That's a colorful story. I'm on my way to the Delta today to spend some time gathering material for my columns. I'll have to look up Captain Markham and Old Lucas McCain."

"Yeah, but watch your step there so you don't sink into the watery muck of the Delta, or step on any 'mine traps.'"

"Thanks for the tip, Kearney. What brings you back to Saigon from Song Be?"

"Lieu is about to deliver twins and is under a doctor's care at the hospital. It's going slowly, and they're hoping the first baby will get into the proper position so a C-section won't be necessary. Meanwhile, I'm staying at Five Oceans with a buddy. Now I'm on my way back to the hospital, although, to be truthful, I'd rather be out looking for some action with a beautiful woman in an *ao dai* and a *non la.* It's been pretty boring in Song Be, except for once that turned out to be unforgettable, but not repeatable."

"Yeah, well, join the club, Kearney. Even a 'young blood' can strike out every now and then. Things don't always turn out the way we want them to in the long run."

"You know, Brand, you seem much more affable than the last time I saw you in Hawaii. I don't feel so hostile to you anymore since Maria dumped you. I know how it feels when she turns her back on you. She only had a drink with me in Hawaii just to be polite and couldn't wait to leave me."

"I've stopped drinking, so maybe that's improved my disposition. But when you figure out women, let me know."

"Sorry about that, Brand, but it's always 'young blood,' so I'm afraid you're in for more disappointment."

"Maybe, but you keep up the good work, Kearney," said Brand, with an undetected hint of sarcasm in his voice.

"You bet I will. And if you come across Old Lucas McCain in Ca Mau Peninsula, tell her I've figured out her deception and plan to see her again before my departure from Vietnam."

"Will do," replied Brand. "I'm sure she'll be glad to see you again." Brand's taxi arrived, and he said, "Good luck to you and your father."

"The same to you," replied Kearney, scratching his head at the change he'd witnessed in Brand. Was Brand's amiable manner a new cover up, or was it his drinking that had been the fuel for his obnoxious behavior in the past? But Kearney had other pressing matters on his mind rather than linger any longer on an assessment of the dumped Brand's behavior. Kearney smiled to himself at the thought of Brand's rejection by Maria.

That evening Lt. Thomas Kearney, Jr., sat at the bar of the Caravelle Hotel to take a break from attending Lieu with her parents at the hospital. She wasn't having an easy time of it. He thought he'd had enough to drink when his vision seemed to blur and was filled with the sight of a female approaching with hair as red as his, surrounding a beautiful face that was beginning to look very familiar.

"Maureen?" Kearney asked as the woman and her friends were about to pass him. Intense green eyes focused on him and then broke into the light of recognition. She asked, "Tom Kearney?"

Kearney answered, "The very one, rescuer of beautiful damsels in distress, here in person. Can fate have brought the girl of my dreams back to my side?"

"Yes, it's the very one rescued by you."

"Won't you come have a drink with me and catch up?"

Maureen hesitated, and then waved her friends on, saying she needed to repay Kearney for a past favor with a drink. As soon as she sat down next to Kearney at the bar, memories of their time together flooded her mind. She silently debated whether she should've accepted his invitation to join him.

"I've been up-country in Song Be since you were whisked away in a helicopter, Maureen. I'm surprised you're still in Vietnam, in Saigon no less."

"Tom, I'm afraid I should have been more explicit when I told you I was married. My husband is, or was, one of the American communications specialists with orders as I had on that hijacked military transport plane. One of the reasons I took such a risk to escape was to try to save him and my fellow soldiers from our captors."

"Did it work? Have they recovered the Americans held captive in Cambodia?"

"Not yet. That's why I'm still here in Vietnam waiting to see if the CIA can recover him and my team."

"It's been several months since I rescued you, Maureen. Do they still have hope of a rescue?"

Maureen's face fell. "Each day that passes, there's less and less reason to hope. But in the meantime, I've been assigned to a communications unit here in Saigon."

"I'm so sorry, Maureen. I wish your valiant effort had been rewarded with the rescue of your husband and team."

"You don't know how much I pray for that every day. Why are you here in Saigon, Tom?"

"My Vietnamese wife is in labor at the hospital with twin births due. One baby's in the wrong position though."

"Oh, my goodness! I didn't know you were married, and with a Vietnamese wife in labor with twins! What are you doing here in the bar?"

"Trying to relieve the stress of waiting for a complicated birth. Lieu is being monitored very carefully by the doctor and her parents are with her. So I thought I could take a break."

"You told me previously your tour of duty will be up in late February. I assume you'll be taking your wife and babies back to the States with you."

"To tell the truth, Maureen, I'm reaping the consequences of being too arrogant to consider the results of my actions on others. My marriage to Lieu was only a trick to get a 'Good Family Girl' in Song Be into bed with me, all the while I had unexpected reassignment orders to Ca Mau Peninsula in my pocket and would leave the next morning. To fool her father, I used an ancient Gia Long code to ask him for her hand in marriage, thinking it no longer applied, but it turned out the code is still enforceable. To complicate matters, Lieu got pregnant from our one night encounter."

"What happened then, Tom?"

"To make a long story short, I was caught in my own stupidity, and the military transferred me back to Song Be and my pregnant Vietnamese wife. What's more, divorce is illegal in Vietnam due to its family laws. Although if it was, and I could've obtained a divorce, I would've supported Lieu and the twins. But I don't love Lieu, so I plan to seek a divorce when I return to the States with her and the twins."

"Oh, Tom, what a very sad situation for everyone involved."

"My own fault. But what about your situation, Maureen?"

"I don't know if my husband is dead or alive. He could be in a prisoner of war camp, but I'm afraid he and our friends could've been shot once they were no longer of use to the communists." Maureen's eyes watered and a few tears rolled down her cheek.

"I'm sorry. You must be in a sort of limbo then."

"Yes, it's a miserable place to be, Tom, and sometimes I'm so lonely and discouraged I want to go home to the States and wait for word there to see he is alive and rescued."

"Do you have any children, Maureen?"

"No, unlike you with two on the way."

"Well, I must be truthful with you. I also have a daughter born not too long ago who's illegitimate, because I have a Vietnamese wife now. It's causing quite an uproar back home in Boston in my father's senatorial district. I'm not proud to tell you that I don't love her mother either, and never planned to marry her. I'm afraid I've made a mess of my life, and I'm ashamed to admit it didn't even bother me until I met you."

"Why did I make a difference to you, Tom?"

"You'll probably think this is a pick-up line, but in truth you're the first woman I could ever have said 'I do' with. I admire your courage, and your beauty constantly beguiles me in my dreams since I've met you. But you and I are both married, even though we spent unforgettable nights together."

"I haven't been able to forget you either, Tom, but I hoped I wouldn't run into you again. I have felt so guilty that you are in my dreams as well, even though I'm well aware your confessions are those of a classic womanizer burdened with all its unexpected and unwanted consequences."

"Could we steal one more night together, Maureen, to see us through all the lonely nights ahead of us?"

"Tom, your wife is in labor. You're incorrigible!"

"I'll call the hospitable and check on Lieu first."

Kearney proceeded to call the hospital and learned there wasn't much progress. He left a number to reach him at the Caravelle Hotel, and then he propositioned Maureen once again.

"We've been drinking, and in the morning we'll regret our stolen moments, Tom."

"It's on both our minds, Maureen. Just one more beautiful memory," said Kearney. His hands slipped up her side to her breasts as he kissed her.

It was early the next morning when the phone rang in the room they had engaged at the Caravelle Hotel. Kearney reached across Maureen's naked beauty as he answered it. The panicked voices of Lieu's parents were in the background as the nurse said that an emergency C-section would take place shortly, and that Tom should come to the hospital immediately.

Maureen had awakened when the phone rang and saw the anxious look on Tom's face. When he hung up, she asked, "What's wrong, Tom?"

"I'm so sorry to say that I have to leave you and go to the hospital as soon as possible. Lieu is about to undergo an emergency C-section.

"Of course, you must go."

"Please stay in touch, Maureen. If nothing else, just having known you a short while eases my soul."

"But, Tom."

"Please, Maureen, I just can't let you go."

"You have to, Tom, and so do I."

"Please remember me. I really must leave for now." Kearney blew Maureen a kiss and left the room.

Not much later, Lt. Thomas Kearney, Jr., watched in awe as he became a father for the second and then the third time. A baby boy and a girl had just joined the Kearney clan.

43 FORAY INTO THE DELTA

The head learns new things, but the heart forevermore practices old experiences. Therefore our life is but a new form of the way men have lived from the beginning.

—*Henry Ward Beecher*

BRAND ENTERED THE OFFICE of U.S. Army Lt. Col. Jeremiah Galloway, military advisor, and sensed his intense energy.

"Colonel Galloway, Winston Brand here, columnist for the *New York Times*.

"Good to meet you, Mr. Brand. I've read your column, the 'Branding Iron.' I admire your style, Brand. You dig out the truth and tell it like it is. But, I'll be damned if you're going to find anything around here to report on though. I can't seem to get Arvin moving no matter how much advising and encouraging I do."

"What seems to be the difficulty, sir?"

"I don't even know where to start listing the problems. I could be talking to a blank wall for all the response I get for my advice. I don't even need to be here for all of the major purposes outlined in my job description.

"But it wasn't this way at first. When the previous colonel was in charge of the Seventh Division, we had some military successes. Along with the paramilitary, Civil Guard and Self Defense Corps, we killed more than 2,000 Viet Cong. Thousands of others were cut off from supplies."

"Why did it change?" asked Brand.

"We've suffered some South Vietnamese casualties, and the colonel was called to Saigon and reprimanded by President Diem. Apparently, Diem wants the military, especially the Seventh Division which saved him from a coup by paratroopers in 1960, to protect his regime rather than to take on the Viet Cong.

"When the colonel returned, action dwindled in our area. Suddenly self-preservation became first and foremost. He was reluctant to suffer troop casualties. But the colonel wanted to look good on paper, so sometimes he plans raids in areas with no known Viet Cong there. Or sometimes ARVN troops don't go at all but report it as an actual mission. And I've heard some troops with a Buddhist upbringing let the enemy go after capture, so they can save face in the Oriental tradition."

"That sounds like a plan to accomplish nothing!"

"You can say that again. And at sunset everything here shuts down, and the night is given over to the Viet Cong."

Brand affirmed, "I've heard about that myself in other areas of South Vietnam. But, I'm sure the Vietnamese military needs to be trained to use all the modern warfare equipment we're supplying them with."

"Oh, we train them, but whether they're willing to use it in battle is only the first difficulty. ARVN is filled with Catholic political friends and allies of Diem that often have little military ability, but who are loyal to Diem and will stop any attempted coup. And the Delta area presents other challenges for us.

"I've read your reports from up-country, Brand. I wish we could realize some of the gains here in the Mekong Delta that have been made in less populated areas like the Central Highlands. Most of the Vietnamese live in the Delta, so the concentration of the Viet Cong is highest here. Yet it's such a crucial area. The Mekong Delta is South Vietnam's rice bowl. It's about ten feet above sea level, crisscrossed by 1,5000 miles of canals and 300 miles of river."

Brand replied, "Yes, I'm aware of those figures, and I've been told the Delta is 26,000 square miles of the most agriculturally rich area of South Vietnam."

"Yes," said Colonel Galloway. "Hell, the Mekong River is one of Asia's great rivers, which, as you know, starts in the high plateau in Tibet and travels 2,800 miles to the South China Sea into which it empties through five water ways that lace the Mekong Delta, a really soggy place that's difficult to defend."

"How many Viet Cong do you estimate now live in the Delta?"

Colonel Galloway looked Brand in the eye and said, "I'm guessing between 30,000 to 40,000 regular hard-core Viet Cong soldiers, and between 80,000 to 100,000 irregulars—farmers by day who have been intimidated into being guerillas by night.

"Can you believe it? I've even heard rumors of American-Vietnamese plans to sweep the Viet Cong out of the highlands and coastal plains deeper into the boot of the Mekong Delta to isolate them from their outside sources of supply that come through Laos and Cambodia on the Ho Chi Minh trail. Just what we need here, more Viet Cong, who might just as easily be supplied by sea instead. 'Military idiocy,' if you ask me. But that's just the tip of the iceberg."

"What's below the tip of the iceberg?" asked Brand.

"The priority of the Diem regime is to stay in power, and the U.S. is paying him $1,000,000 a day to accomplish it. Why? Because the priority of the U.S. is to stop the spread of communism in former French Indochina, and avoid the so-called 'Domino Theory.' If Vietnam falls to the communists, the U.S. fears other countries of former French Indochina will follow suit and fall like an upright line of dominos off balance. We are allies of the South Vietnamese government only because of the shared goal of anti-communism."

"What's wrong with that?" asked Brand.

"Well, Diem can't fight communist aggression unless he's in power. And to stay in power, he has to use some very undemocratic measures, in fact by running an authoritarian government, often by the brutal suppression of its people."

Brand replied, "Yes, I've discussed this concern with others. The 'end justifies the means' theory is a common practice of autocratic rulers. Diem sidesteps the kind of Western style democratic reforms the U.S. constantly urges him to adopt."

Galloway remarked, "I see our common goal, but I believe the motivations of Diem and the U.S for fighting communism are at opposite ends of the scale. The more we urge democratic reforms, the more autocratic Diem becomes in order to stay in power. And he continues to alienate group after group of its citizens with his confusing policies. To me, it looks like an inevitable dissolution of partnership over time, and it's a damn shame. It could be avoided."

"You certainly tell it like you see it, Colonel."

"You're right, Brand. It's my opinion that fighting the Viet Cong is the furthest thing from the minds of the Seventh."

Brand replied, "But certainly the time will come, as the Viet Cong strengthens, when ARVN troops will have to fight."

"I'm doing everything I can as senior advisor to push the ARVN commanders to take the fight to the Viet Cong. We need to find the Viet Cong and destroy them! I know you probably peg me as someone itchin' for a fight, but we need a decisive victory to boost morale and competence."

"But you have limited authority being just a military advisor to the ARVN commanders,"

"You've got me there, Brand," replied Colonel Galloway. We advisors have to work through the South Vietnamese commanders, and can't intervene on our own and order troops into battle. As a U.S. advisor, though, when the Vietnamese commanders do order their troops to fight, I can call in U.S. H-21 helicopters for troop airlift with UH-1B helicopter gunships to protect them. I can also call in U.S. Air Force Air Commandos in reserve."

"What resources can the Vietnamese call into the mix to support ARVN, or back it up if it should falter in an attack?"

"'Off the record,' of course, the commander of the Seventh infantry battalion can call in:

* Two Civil Guard battalions from his regional forces.
* A company of M-113 personnel carriers from the Seventh.
* Two infantry companies at Tan Hiep Airfield.
* A parachute battalion.

But I'm sure the Viet Cong are already aware of our resources."

"They haven't been called up in force yet, have they?"

So far, my planner only has to concentrate on either killing or capturing the Viet Cong before these slippery, guerilla fighters disappear into the countryside. The Viet Cong have yet to stand and fight. We've encountered mostly skirmishes with the Viet Cong guerillas. We believe we have good intelligence, and are trying to improve it even further on both the U.S. and Vietnamese sides, so that we won't be surprised in any way. This intelligence can alert us to larger troop numbers if detected. I see the problem as whether or not our forces will adequately stand and fight in a battle despite our numbers and modernized war equipment."

"What about the Strategic Hamlet program in the Delta?"

"It's not going as well in the Delta as you witnessed in Quang Ngai, Brand. Settlements are much more strung out in the Delta than in the Central Highlands. Establishing these hamlets in heavily occupied Viet Cong areas is often counterproductive, and sometimes it almost accomplishes the opposite of its mission. The alienation of the peasants, dislocated from their ancestral lands, ends up destroying any loyalty they might have had to the central government.

"Or, the hamlets can become so infiltrated by Viet Cong, they almost become VC fortifications in some cases as I see it. The Viet Cong can force peasant cooperation through fear of death for themselves and/or their families."

"I was advised that this was the case before I arrived."

"Another problem occurs when the hamlets are placed quite a distance from the peasants' rice fields. These negative aspects, plus the peasants' forced labor to build their own hamlets, don't add up to a positive plan. Not only that, but the government can't support and adequately protect the large number of hamlets being built so swiftly," explained Galloway.

Col. Nguyen Huu Bao knocked lightly at the open door, smiled at the two men and said, "I couldn't help hearing your less than optimistic comments about our Strategic Hamlet program here in the Delta, Colonel Galloway."

"Come in, Colonel Bao," said Galloway as he returned Bao's smile. "Our friend, Winston Brand of the *Times* just asked me about your program here, and I had to tell it like it is."

"Just like you always do, Colonel. Mr. Brand, it's a pleasure to see you again. I enjoyed our interview at the Gia Long Palace about this very initiative not too long ago."

"Our charming Colonel Bao is in fine form today. But I can't sugar-coat what's happening in the Delta."

Colonel Bao replied, "But you must remember, Colonel, to have patience with the Vietnamese. After all, the Strategic Hamlet program just started in March. We've made rapid progress since then, but it'll take a while to get things up to speed, just like everything else in its early phases."

"True, but the Viet Cong work faster on sabotaging and/or infiltrating the hamlets than the peasants can build them," remarked Galloway. "That doesn't make for sound progress."

"Life is full of obstacles, but we must keep persevering as you do as senior military advisor to the Seventh Infantry Division here in My Tho. We all do the best we can with what we have to work with. But it's not as bad as you think, Colonel Galloway, and patience will win the day in the end."

"Ever the optimist, aren't you Bao? Would you be free to escort Mr. Brand to see some of your strategic hamlets?"

"Yes, I'd be glad to if Mr. Brand has time to accompany me on my rounds today to some of the local hamlets."

Brand replied, "A tour would give me and my *Times* column readers a chance to see a first-hand report on the program in action in the Delta. I'll have to say I'm impressed, Colonel Bao, that you go out in the field to obtain your own perspective on how things are going as administrator of Nhu's program."

"As I do my field work, I always remind myself there are two ways to look at anything, Mr. Brand, not only what yet needs to be done, but also what already has been accomplished and is helping. Although some of our hamlets do suffer from Viet Cong infiltration, nevertheless, others are more successful and make it that much harder for the Viet Cong to harass them. Something is always better than nothing," Bao remarked with an ingratiating smile.

Colonel Galloway interrupted, "Damned, if you don't have a smooth manner, Bao. I guess I could use more of that approach as a military advisor. But the gap between where the Seventh's preparedness should be and its present state is wide enough to drive a tank company through. We need to make more progress, and the sooner the better."

"Come now, Colonel, it's not really that bad. Keep on doing your excellent job of encouraging us Vietnamese. It's human nature to copy what others do, and you set a fine example of the direction in which we should proceed."

Brand spoke up, "I'll be off then with Colonel Bao to see for myself if the glass is 'half empty' or 'half full.' Thank you Colonel Galloway for a most interesting interview. When I return to base later, I'd like to make arrangements to travel tomorrow to the Ca Mau Peninsula to interview Capt. Edward Markham stationed there as a military advisor."

"We'd be happy to assist you, Mr. Brand. In the meantime, be sure Colonel Bao doesn't fill you with too much optimism."

"Don't worry, sir. I always try to be objective."

Brand noticed their Vietnamese driver drove very slowly along the dirt road to the first hamlet Brand and Bao went to visit. Bao explained, "We have to proceed carefully to be sure we don't run over any mines in the road, Mr. Brand. I don't want to alarm you, but Colonel Galloway told me a mine exploded the other day near here and injured some of our troops. However, he told me this road has been cleared of mines just this morning, so we should be all right."

"I'm in if you are," replied Brand. "By the way, how do you respond to Colonel Galloway's criticism that the Strategic Hamlet program is overextended without adequate protection? He says that hamlet defenders are not trained and disciplined well enough to withstand a significant Viet Cong attack. So he worries that the regular army will have to reinforce too many vulnerable hamlets if called upon when the army is already spread too thin. So it significantly drains the regular Vietnamese army when it has to react to hamlet calls for help in addition to regular duties. Has the Diem government considered this flaw in its countryside protection plan?"

"Who has not suffered from time to time with too few resources at hand to meet additional demands? What can I say, Mr. Brand, except that we are doing the best we can. I'm here in the Delta to do an assessment of the progress of our Strategic Hamlet program. My job is to locate the areas where weaknesses occur and find ways to address these needs."

"A challenging job, Colonel. Will you be visiting as many hamlets as possible in the Delta?"

"Yes, as far as our manpower will reach in the time allowed me to make my report to my boss."

"You may be here for some time then," observed Brand.

"Don't I know it! My fiancée, Madame Binh, will have completed refurbishing the curio shop by the time I return."

"What kind of refurbishing is she engaged in?"

"She wants to add a line of women's products to the curios sold there to boost sales, which have lagged for some time. Madame Nhu has graciously agreed to inform Madame Binh about what items to stock and where to order them. Such a gracious gesture of such a lovely lady, who has much more weighty concerns to attend to, such as her family laws, Morality Laws and her paramilitary women's group, in addition to her family responsibilities, as we discussed during our interview. "

Brand replied, "Yes, I remember you informed me Madame Nhu is intensely dedicated to Vietnamese women's fair treatment. But it comes on centuries of women's abuse of one kind or another. It's as difficult for her society to accept, as it is for President Diem to agree to institute democratic reforms urged by his ally."

"Change isn't always easy to accept, is it, Mr. Brand?"

After touring strategic hamlets in varying stages of construction for most of the day, Colonel Bao turned to Brand as they arrived at the last hamlet on his itinerary. "It's been a long day for you, Mr. Brand. I will be some time at this last stop. I see there's an ARVN truck parked at this hamlet. Would you like me to check if they're ready to return to headquarters and could take you along?"

"Do you know if there are any new issues at this hamlet that we haven't covered in the previous hamlets?"

"No, Mr. Brand, I believe it's just a lot more routine matters as we've witnessed this day."

"Well, I do plan to leave early in the morning on my trip to the Ca Mau Peninsula, so I suppose I should take you up on your offer. However, I know the Viet Cong have had time to place new land mines on the road back to base."

"It's always a risk traveling around the Delta."

"I don't speak Vietnamese, however, so I'm concerned should we run into trouble."

"Yes, I see how that would be a concern for you, but perhaps a soldier who speaks English is at the hamlet. I'll check if he's here and see if he and the troops can take you back to base."

When Colonel Bao returned, a handful of ARVN soldiers accompanied him, and Bao told Brand one of them could speak English. They would take him back to base in their truck. Brand thanked Colonel Bao for the tour of the hamlets and boarded the troop truck.

The ARVN truck got underway, but Brand couldn't dismiss a sixth sense that told him he'd be better off traveling with Colonel Bao. He asked the English-speaking soldier to tell the driver to stop and take him back to the hamlet so he could retrieve something important he had left in the jeep.

The troop truck turned back and stopped at the hamlet while Brand searched the jeep. He took a while, so the troops got out of the truck and lit cigarettes Brand had given them as they waited. Suddenly Brand heard an ear-piercing boom, and he and the soldiers were flung to the ground. He turned back and saw the truck had blown up with a huge pillar of flame that shot up into the sky with billows of smoke all around.

Suddenly Colonel Bao and the inhabitants of the hamlet appeared, reacting to the shock wave from the blast. Brand could hear Colonel Bao searching for him among the troops. Bao found Brand next to the jeep and breathed a sigh of relief that Brand was uninjured. Bao uttered a torrent of apologies for the near miss.

Colonel Bao exclaimed, "What a disaster! I'm so glad no one was hurt! I didn't expect you back at the hamlet, Mr. Brand. But how fortunate you and the soldiers weren't in the truck when it just blew up!

"I can only surmise a timed explosive device was placed in the truck at some time. I discovered an attack occurred here the previous evening, and the soldiers were here to interrogate the peasants about it. But when we arrived, they had finished their mission and were ready to return to base. It's possible they were a target for elimination. But thank goodness our only loss is the truck which is still burning."

"I didn't see any suspicious activity around the truck while I waited," offered Brand. "But once underway, I realized I had left my notebook in the jeep and asked to go back to the hamlet to retrieve it. I couldn't get started writing my column without it."

"I thought I saw you put it in your pocket earlier where I see it resides now. But you must have found it before the blast. We'll have to return to headquarters immediately in the jeep to report this sabotage incident and send another truck back for the troops. Again I apologize for not securing better protection for a member of the press."

Brand replied, "I was duly warned about the dangers in the countryside in the Delta before I decided to accompany you. I'm just glad I survived to see another day."

Odd, Brand thought, as they traveled back to headquarters. If he hadn't asked to return to the hamlet, the truck would have been far enough away from it so the blame for the explosion would have been laid on communists up the road, rather than back on Colonel

Bao's doorstep. He recalled that the then Captain Bao had also been present when he had been kidnapped at *Bon Sejour*. Was it a coincidence that these two life-threatening incidents happened while Brand was in Bao's vicinity? He vowed to keep his distance from the colonel in the future, whether or not there was any connection between Bao and these incidents. Perhaps he was just jinxed by the colonel's presence.

Colonel Galloway met them when they returned to headquarters. He was livid when informed of the bombed truck and the near miss of Winston and the ARVN soldiers, but extremely relieved no one was injured. Colonel Bao expressed his deep concern as well. Bao went on to see to other duties, and Galloway asked Brand what he thought had really happened.

Brand raised his eyebrows and said, "Wouldn't we both like to know! I suspect the bomb was hidden on the truck all along. Someone had to order the timer set before we left the hamlet. Who did it and how it went down can only be supposition. But the fact that the hamlet had been attacked the night before and the soldiers were there to interrogate the peasants looks to me like the incident was set up beforehand.

"I don't think I initially was the prime target of the bombing, but when I happened on the scene with Colonel Bao, it would be a tempting scenario to make it look like I was a random participant at the last minute when I decided to return to the base early at Colonel Bao's suggestion. If someone wanted to get rid of me and escape suspicion for planning my demise, the opportunity fell into his lap out of the blue."

"So you think you might have been a last minute target presented by circumstances and acted on by impulse?"

"Who's to say? I just know I've had more than my share of near misses since I arrived in Vietnam, and I've been warned repeatedly to question anything the least bit suspicious."

"Of course there'll be an investigation into the incident, but I'm afraid it will turn up nothing as usual. The best I can do is advise ARVN transportation to have the vehicles checked before they leave the base, but again it will be like talking to myself," remarked Colonel Galloway.

The two Americans went on to discuss what Brand had discovered in his visits to the hamlets during the day.

Brand related his observations. "Most of the peasants were working in their rice fields, but the elderly and the children remained in the hamlets. They were reluctant to speak to us, but one elderly peasant told us he didn't like the Viet Cong because they taxed his son two hundred piasters a year and a bag of rice he couldn't afford, but had to pay.

"But he said the Vietnamese district chief had helped his family get some pigs and a bag of fertilizer. Government troops patrol the road during the day while the Viet Cong remained in the rice paddies, he added, but at night the Viet Cong came to the villages to try to steal their food and kidnap their young men. When attacked, the hamlet officials would call My Tho for help, but no one would come after dark."

Colonel Galloway remarked, "The old man might not live to see another day if the Viet Cong find out he spoke to an American. Often we can't answer a hamlet's call for help if we're off helping another hamlet, and it's difficult to get the Vietnamese to do anything after dark."

"It seems the glass is half empty from your perspective, but Colonel Bao always seems to see it half full."

"True. But, regarding your request, we've made arrangements to get you to the Ca Mau Peninsula in the morning to meet with our military advisor at Phuoc Xuyen, Mr. Brand. But let me advise you again to watch your step here in the Delta to be aware of possible hidden mines."

"I appreciate your assistance and your warning, Colonel Galloway, and as Colonel Bao would say, it's been a pleasure to meet you," said Brand.

Brand was driven by jeep past emerald green rice fields tended by peasants with their conical hats in the brutal heat of the next day. Rivers and canals lent their humidity to the stifling air making the journey quite unpleasant. When he reached Phuoc Xuyen, he was already exhausted. The mosquitos at night in this place must be ferocious, he thought. No wonder Kearney had told him it was like a world away from the environment at Song Be in the Central Highlands. But considering the warning from Colonel Galloway about land mines, Kearney's expertise in explosives would have been put to good use in the far reaches of the Delta here in the Ca Mau Peninsula. Brand wondered if he would meet Kearney's Rifleman, Old Lucas McCain, while visiting.

Capt. Edward Markham greeted Brand as he arrived at a small *beau geste*-type fort in the middle of a jungle. The military advisor said he was one of 12 soldiers based there in the gnat-sized Military Assistance Advisor Group (MAAG) compound next to a Vietnamese village. There was only a football field sized rice paddy between them

"What brings you here to this far-flung outpost, Mr. Brand?" asked Captain Markham.

"I've been briefly acquainted with Lt. Thomas Kearney, Jr., who was stationed here temporarily when the former military advisor was medically evacuated with a severe case of dysentery. He told me a colorful story about a Vietnamese girl the soldiers called 'Old Lucas McCain, the Rifleman.' I thought I'd look into her human interest story for my column for the *New York Times*."

"And quite a story it is. Won't you come into our headquarters tent where I can tell you her story, Mr. Brand?"

When they were seated inside the tent, Markham began by explaining that their MAAG mission was to advise a Vietnamese battalion charged with protecting all the villages in the area from the communist terrorists. But the peasants in the village across the rice paddy didn't want anything to do with the Americans for fear of reprisals from the Viet Cong. That is, until the night the village had been set on fire by the communists. This happened before either Kearney or Markham were posted here.

"Colonel Galloway at My Tho warned me that the Viet Cong would kill any peasant seen talking to an American, and I still fear for an old man who spoke to me at one of the strategic hamlets I visited in the area," said Brand.

"Rightly so, Mr. Brand. Dieu Minh, or Old Lucas McCain, was paid to do domestic chores for the Americans, despite threats by the Viet Cong to anyone who worked for the Americans. The first thing I heard from Old Lucas McCain, was about Kearney's insistence she find women from her village to share his bed right from the get-go. Nguyen, his Vietnamese interpreter, had warned her of this, so she had bound her chest to appear to be an adolescent before she met him for the first time. She apparently fooled him, and he was very unhappy she couldn't find any women willing to risk their lives to satisfy his needs due to Viet Cong retaliation. However, he was recalled to his original post before long. I was his replacement. She said this to warn me if I had similar ideas.

Brand interjected, "I see. Fortunately, she was well advised by the Vietnamese interpreter to take precautions regarding Kearney's predatory eye looking for women to bed. But go on with your story."

"From what I understand, Old Lucas McCain's acquaintance with the Americans came the night of the fire in her village. The standoffish peasants were at the gate of the MAAG compound asking for help in putting out the fire. Somewhere in the crowd stood Old Lucas McCain. She wasn't old, and her real name wasn't Lucas McCain, then or now. But when her ability to shoot anybody down with a single word, phrase or sentence faster than Chuck Connors did the bad guys on TV, someone named her after the Rifleman, and it stuck.

"Anyway, Old Lucas McCain burst from the group at the gate and shouted a stream of Vietnamese words at the sentry at 3:00 a.m. Nguyen, the interpreter, said she wanted the 'Melican soldiers to come help her village and pointed to the row of houses along the road where men, women and children scampered across the roadway with salvaged items from their homes and dropped them into the wet rice paddy, then dashed back for more.

"It was strict MAAG policy never to venture from a compound at night unless on an authorized patrol, but the Americans decided to help the villagers. The fire was under control by four o'clock the next afternoon, but half of the residents were left homeless."

"That's a devastating loss for the villagers. What happened next?"

"The military advisor called headquarters in Saigon, and two days after the fire, four transport planes from Saigon arrived at the nearest airport with food rations, building materials, engineers and civic action officers to handle community rehabilitation projects. They rebuilt the village and when it was finished, they took all the credit.

"All the MAAG compound got was Old Lucas McCain, but she turned out to be the best deal of all. She adopted the Americans, and the compound gate was always open to her as she would come and go. She picked up quite a bit of English slang without knowing its true meaning and was like a camp mascot. When a soldier did get out of line, she would call him a number ten G.I. son-of-a-bitch. This would put the would-be Romeo in what the rest of the soldiers agreed to be his proper place among the camp's ten enlisted men."

"Is that the extent of her story?"

"No," replied Markham. "Often she was the butt of jokes. By the time I arrived after Lieutenant Kearney was transferred, Old Lucas McCain had been working for the Americans since after the fire. One of her jobs was to make the beds of the officers each morning. I heard my sergeant named Friedman chastising Old Lucas McCain in his tent my first morning here. I went to check on the reason for his outbursts. When he saw me enter the tent, he decided to change tactics and gently said to her, 'Did you make my bed this morning?' She nodded. 'Good girl,' he said. 'For making my bed, I'm going to give you a nice English lesson.' Her face lit up with happiness. 'Now repeat after me,' he said. 'My name is Old Lucas McCain. I'm a no good son-of-a-bitch who can't make a bed worth a damn.' She recited it verbatim, and all day long she stopped everyone she met and repeated the phrase until they grew tired of it."

Brand smiled and then asked, "Besides the English slang she heard in the camp, where did she get the phrases she shot at the soldiers when she thought they needed it?"

Captain Markham replied, "We had movies every night. Old Lucas McCain never missed a feature. If it wasn't a western, she would rotate among the men so that every soldier could claim her as his date. But on western nights, you couldn't get near her. Every kid in the village was her honored guest. She herded them in and out of the compound so expertly that not even a pack of cigarettes was stolen."

"What interesting anecdotes! But did anything more serious than the village fire occur that she got involved in?"

"Yes, the Viet Cong hit our compound one Sunday after chapel services not long ago with a mortar barrage that was designed to keep us pinned down while they terrorized the villagers. With deadly accuracy they hit one tent after another, but most of us had taken up positions in our foxholes on the perimeter of the compound.

"Someone slipped into my foxhole during the excitement. It was Old Lucas McCain, who pulled the reluctant Nguyen behind her. I asked them what they were doing there, and Nguyen said

Old Lucas McCain was crazy, because she wanted me to shoot a boy on a white buffalo in the rice paddy that didn't look more than six years old. When I turned to chew her out for such a cruel suggestion, she was lowering my automatic carbine from her shoulder. Out in the rice paddy the little buffalo boy lay doubled up on the ground along with the huge white beast whose hide was dotted with red splotches. I yelled at her and grabbed the rifle. That's when I noticed that the only sound I heard was my own voice. The shelling had suddenly stopped.

"Sergeant Friedman called me over to the headquarters tent which had been hit, and we found Sergeants Benson and Smith, our radio operators, who lay bloody and lifeless near the radio console where they had tried to summon help. Apparently they had gotten through before the mortar hit their tent, as the South Vietnamese battalion later moved into position around the compound for security. No more attacks came during the night."

"So sorry to hear about the deaths of your radio operators, Captain. But I have to ask what happened to Old Lucas McCain?"

"Sergeant Friedman is assigned to intelligence for the detachment, and he interviewed the villagers. They had never seen a white water buffalo around here before. It seems that little kid on the freakish white buffalo was pinpointing targets for those damned communist mortars. Old Lucas McCain had saved her village and protected the compound by taking out that kid and his buffalo."

"My God," said Brand. "What kind of war is this?"

Captain Markham continued his story. "A week passed before anyone saw Old Lucas McCain. Then she came into camp carrying a small Buddhist altar. Without a word to anyone, she set up the altar where we had replaced the headquarters tent, lit three joss sticks and began to pray. When she finished her meditations, I asked her where she had been for the last week. She said she had gone to the temple to say a prayer for Benson, Smith and the little buffalo boy. She also said a prayer that I wouldn't hate her. When I told her I didn't hate her, she said, 'Oh, happy! If *Dai Uy* hate me, I surely die.' This was close to a line from a Liz Taylor movie she had seen."

"This couldn't be the end of her story."

"Not at all, replied Ed Markham. "Later, Sergeant Friedman, Corporal Andrews and I went to Saigon on official business, and we asked Old Lucas McCain if she would like to go along with us. I had Nguyen explain to her that while there we planned to have her tested for an interpreter position with the detachment. Nguyen didn't like the idea of another interpreter, but she was delighted at the prospect of obtaining more income and legal status with the detachment. But first she had to pass the interpreter's test. Corporal Andrews, our personnel specialist, thought up a scheme to help her pass the oral examination despite her broken English."

But you've indicated her English comprehension increased from watching your nightly movies, and she was becoming easier to talk to, but was it good enough to pass an exam?"

"Andrews' scheme was to have her clam up when the exam started, so we could pass her off as a timid Einstein. The idea was for us to tell the young lieutenant in Saigon who gives the exam that he'd scared the hell out of her and tell him there'd be no more questions. He figured the second lieutenant would then pass her to get us off his back. I was very dubious of the Andrews' Plan, but whatever the outcome, Old Lucas McCain would see Saigon. We bought her an *ao-dai* and a French parasol to twirl over one shoulder as we walked along. It pleased us to witness her immense joy over this experience.

"When we arrived at the examination office and the exam started, the second lieutenant took a fountain pen from his shirt pocket and held it up to Old Lucas McCain. 'Name this in English,' he demanded. She said nothing. Friedman burst in and accused the lieutenant of scaring her. The sergeant then said, 'Why don't you start by asking her name?' The interpreters' interview and the Andrews' Plan ended abruptly when she said, 'Friedman know. My name's Old Lucas McCain, and I'm a no good son-of-a-bitch who can't make a bed worth a damn.'"

"Well, that's a surprise ending to her exam I could use in my column," commented Brand with a smile.

"It isn't the end of her story though," said Markham. "She told me she was sorry she could not be my interpreter like Nguyen and appeared downcast after her exam failure. I told her she could still come and go in the compound as before, but she was still edgy. I was tempted to console her that night in Saigon, having had more to drink than I should. I'll have to admit I was very attracted to her, but I knew better than to try to compromise her, such as Lieutenant Kearney might have done. Nevertheless, I did touch her inappropriately at the hotel. Her reaction was unexpected. She removed her *ao-dai* from her body, and I momentarily glimpsed her agonizingly beautiful, naked body, but only long enough for her to slip into her old pajama-style street clothes.

"Where are you going?" I asked with indignation.

"'Melican girl maybe show body to man, but never sleep with man who no speak, 'I love you.'"

"Those damn movies have ruined you," I growled, knowing my actions were out of line.

"I know 'Melican way now. No speak love, no sleep!"

She was gone before I could say another word. That might have been the end of our little altercation, but Old Lucas McCain returned later with two teen-age Chinese prostitutes. They couldn't have been more than 13, because when she ordered them to strip in front of me, I could see their breasts were no larger than crab apples. I refused to sleep with them, but she couldn't understand and kept saying, "They sleep with *Dai Uy*. No need *Dai Uy* speak love."

After I gave the prostitutes money without partaking of their services, I ordered her to take the girls back to where she found them. She obeyed but left with tears in her eyes, believing she had displeased me yet again. She was so distraught, I decided to follow her and apologize for my inappropriate actions toward her earlier. It was a good thing I did, because shortly afterward my hotel room got the brunt of a communist plastic bomb aimed at taking out the reported Americans staying at the hotel. Luckily, Friedman and Andrews were out on the town and escaped as well, and our group returned to the base camp the next day."

"Can I meet this unusual and unique Vietnamese sprite?" asked Brand. "Would she allow a photo to be taken? I could send it in to the *Times* to accompany my column."

"Don't we all wish you could, but I'm sorry to tell you that Old Lucas McCain is dead!"

"What? She's dead! What happened?"

"The Viet Cong bastards caught up with her two weeks ago. They held a mock trial in the village charging her with collaboration with Yankee imperialists and sentenced her to death. They shot Old Lucas McCain quickly because the villagers attempted to come to her aid. Though they were too late to save her, the villagers were able to run the communists off. Her funeral was the biggest in the history of her village. All the villagers agreed to mourn her for free. They remembered her part during the village fire. In the aftermath of Old Lucas McCain's death, the villagers keep the Viet Cong away now without government help, and they caught and hanged six VC after Old Lucas McCain was buried. They got the ones who killed her. For us who mourn her death, on all the Buddhist holidays, we burn those silly little candle sticks for her."

Brand had his column, but he couldn't help feeling the loss of Old Lucas McCain along with Captain Markham, his fellow soldiers and the villagers across the rice paddy. No matter that his bureau boss would scoff at another sentimental story, this time from the Delta.

44 MESSAGE FROM MARIA

There is nothing in the world that remains unchanged. All things are in perpetual flux, and every shadow is seen to move.

—*Ovid*

WHEN BRAND RETURNED from the Delta, there was a letter on his desk from Maria next to the unopened one from Clemie. Who put Maria's letter there, Winston wondered? He didn't have to wait long to find out as Alex appeared after work.

"Winston, glad to see you! How did it go in the Delta?"

"It was sure a reality check in comparison to my earlier forays up-country," replied Brand.

"And how did you get along with our outspoken Colonel Galloway at My Tho?" asked Alex.

"I got a huge dose of the truth, as the good colonel sees it. But Colonel Bao was there assessing the strategic hamlets, and he took me on a tour of the area. I could see first-hand that there's certainly a kernel of the truth in what Colonel Galloway contends. The situation is a lot more critical in his area than in Quang Ngai because of the denser population and larger numbers of Viet Cong. But as predictable, Colonel Bao was more optimistic."

"Yes, I can imagine," replied Alex. "But the press corps is quite enthralled with the colorful, energetic Colonel Galloway, who can't wait to get things moving, and they often echo his opinions in their wire-service reports. Diem, of course, only puts up with our 'free-wheeling' reporters because of our country's aid. Such freedom of the press is folly to his Oriental way of thinking."

"But for me personally," said Brand, "you need to know that I was involved in another near miss situation in the Delta."

"How did it happen, Winston?"

"Colonel Bao was in the Delta assessing the strategic hamlets there, and happened in on my conversation with Colonel Galloway. He asked Bao if I could accompany him on his rounds that day to get first-hand information on the program in the Delta, and Bao pleasantly agreed. All went well until the end of the day at the last hamlet on the list. It was getting late and Colonel Bao asked if I wanted to return to base before he was finished. An ARVN truck was parked at the hamlet, and Bao arranged for me to ride back with the soldiers. I had an appointment the next day in the Ca Mau Peninsula."

"Did the truck run into a land mine on the way back to base, Winston?"

"No, much worse. I had an uneasy feeling as we got underway, so I told a soldier who spoke English that I needed to return to the hamlet to retrieve my notebook I supposedly had forgotten in the jeep. When we returned, I took my time looking for the notebook, and the troops got out of the truck to smoke cigarettes I had given them. Suddenly the truck exploded and we were flung to the ground but were far enough away that no one was hurt. A huge fireball shot up into the sky, and billows of smoke surrounded us.

"Thank God you weren't hurt, Winston! That would have been the end of you and the troops, too! It must have been a time bomb set to go off en route back to base. Did you see any suspicious activity around the truck before you left?"

"No, and I had remained outside the hamlet while Colonel Bao went inside to talk to the ARVN troops about me accompanying them back to base."

"Then, either the timer was set before you arrived and was meant to take out the returning ARVN troops in their truck, or someone undetected placed it on the truck, or set the timer of one already embedded once you boarded the vehicle, but before it started out."

"My sixth sense tells me it might have been a last minute impulsive setup to take me out, but that could be my suspicious nature given the number of near misses I've experienced since I arrived in country. At any rate, I seem to have been jinxed several times Colonel Bao has been in my vicinity, as ingratiating as he tries to be to me. Perhaps I should steer clear of him in the future just to be safe."

"The Delta is not the safest place to visit, Winston. I'm just thankful your intuition kicked in to help you avoid a fatal mishap. I'll make it a point to check out what turns up in the investigation Colonel Galloway is sure to order."

"I appreciate your help, Alex, but Colonel Galloway wasn't too hopeful anything would turn up. But, getting around to what's called a 'pink elephant' in my room, how did the letter from Maria get on my desk?"

"Why, I put it there, of course."

"And how did you get it?"

"It came by a rather circuitous route. First, my dear wife Gwen and Norma Pavler went to visit Maria to console her when they heard of your disastrous meeting with her father and the subsequent breakup between the two of you. They had met her and her father previously on a far more pleasant visit."

"And?" asked Brand.

"They found a very distressed young lady, whose father has continued to pressure her to accept the proposal of a local young man. Distraught because her father kept inviting this Tywan to dinner each night, Maria told Mr. Monclova she'd have to move to her small apartment near the airport, as soon as the month she promised to care for him was up, and he was well enough to return to work.

"They asked Maria if there was any way they could help her, and she said their visit was a breath of fresh air to her. Before they left, however, Maria slipped the letter to you into Gwen's pocket without a word when her father wasn't looking."

"And, of course, Gwen forwarded it to you to give to me."

"True. By the way, I see that you didn't open your sister Clemie's letter before you left for the Delta."

"Since General Pavler said Clemie was okay, I wasn't up to any more female intrigue at the time. Clemie is sure to have championed Eleanor's case in her letter. And I don't know if I'm in any better shape even now to read about her opinions."

"Well, at least you've had a little more time and space and a change of scenery to help you settle your emotions."

"I'm afraid my emotions will never be settled where Maria's concerned."

"I'll leave you to make your own decisions about the letters, Winston. I'm going to have dinner with your friend, Ledger Smith. By chance, would you like to join us?"

"Thanks, but I'll have to pass on that. But please give Ledger my best regards."

After Alex left, Brand looked at the letters on his desk, but didn't open them. Instead, he lay down on his bed to rest and to consider matters he had tried to put aside while regaining his equilibrium. But knew he had to address them sooner or later. Without intending to, he fell asleep, his dreams filled with Maria.

Winston awoke in the middle of the night. He must have been exhausted from the frantic pace he had set since leaving Maria in the Philippines. As he turned on the light in his room, he looked at the desk with Maria's letter lying unopened on the top. He had the feeling that should he open it, his life would be changed forever.

It was a love letter, of course, the kind she always wrote to him. As he picked up the letter, the scent of Maria's perfume awakened his senses as it always did. He opened it and glanced at the first words, then closed his eyes as the image of her in all her natural beauty took shape in his mind. If this was infatuation, he knew it would grow and mature into a love that would last a lifetime, because it was planted in their hearts. He started reading:

> Dear Winston, heart of my heart, half of our whole,
>
> Where are you out there, my love? Please come to me, my darling. Let's no longer live in our past lives before we met. We've moved on, and it's impossible to go back, nor do we really want to.
>
> I can't live grieving my mother's death like I did in the past, locked into a time that had passed so long ago. Nor would she want me to. Or my father either, if he'd stop to think about it. Life is meant to be lived, and I want to live it with you, no matter if you're off to faraway places demanded by your career. I will wait for you no matter how long it takes, no matter the complications. I love you, you know.
>
> I send you all my love from your "someone-out-there," your other half, who wishes she was right there snuggled in your warm embrace, exalting in the warm, wet kisses of ecstasy we'd exchange in every way possible

as over and over again bliss fills the essence of our joined souls.

Your Maria in love

Oh, Maria, Winston thought as the seducing warmth of her loving and sensual thoughts seeped through his body, mind and soul. How ripe for the plucking she was and so ready for her mate, her partner in life. How could a mortal man resist her? But would a damaged and threatened man such as he was ever live up to her expectations, or be able to keep her safe? God knew he had made many mistakes in his life, but even so he felt this was a step of love that destiny had prepared for him at his birth. His heart told him that, come what may, the love between Maria and himself couldn't be denied.

It was time to go to Maria with an engagement ring to begin the courtship dance of life, no matter the formidable obstacles that faced them. They really couldn't live without each other anymore, and their commitment to each other would make the best Christmas gift ever. He would purchase the ring in the morning and make arrangements for a Christmas visit with her, this time solely at her apartment, a love nest where they could journey to the stars together again and again!

Eleanor Brand stopped in to see General Pavler on her morning off from her nursing duties. She asked if he had notified Winston she was in Vietnam and wanted to see him. He replied in the affirmative, but said Winston had been in the Delta doing interviews.

"Is Winnie back from the Delta yet?"

"I believe he returned last evening," replied the general.

"I've been thinking of how I could arrange a meeting with Winnie. If Norma comes to Vietnam to see you for Christmas, would it be convenient if you both somehow arranged for us to meet?"

"I'll be spending some time with Norma, of course, but it will be a long-deserved time together in the Philippines for the holiday. And we're looking forward to having Christmas dinner with Maj. Alex Spear and his family. His wife and children are also quartered in the Philippines."

"Then I'd like to give Winnie an invitation. Perhaps when you're gone, both Winnie and I will be alone, and I could persuade him to have Christmas dinner here with me in Saigon," posited Eleanor.

"That's up to you and Winston to decide, Eleanor. But I will pass along your invitation when next I see him."

"Thank you general. I'd be so grateful. I've written down my address so you could give it to Winnie. I'm there most evenings. I know you're a busy man, so I'll take my leave and hope for the best concerning Winnie."

General Pavler was beginning to feel a little awkward about his middleman status between Eleanor and Winston, and he hoped Winston would relieve him of his duties in this regard soon.

The next morning Winston had acted on his nighttime decision and had purchased an engagement ring for Maria. He marveled he had actually done it, and fingered the small box that held it in his pocket. He was at the curbside after his purchase, hailing a taxi when suddenly he was surrounded by a passel of pedicabs and roughly pushed into one by several ruffians.

"Rang give you 'nother ride, Mr. Brand," said a voice behind him. "No yell or jump out. Gun in back of head."

"Goldtooth!" exclaimed Brand. "I should've pressed charges against you. Then you'd be in jail instead of abducting me."

"Too late," replied Goldtooth. "This time you belong me!"

Winston slowly regained consciousness when he heard voices around him, and felt intense pain as he was being lifted onto a stretcher. Blood trickled down his face from his forehead. Terribly bruised and lacerated, his body looked like it almost had been beaten to a pulp.

"What your name?" asked a uniformed Vietnamese orderly.

"Brand, Winston Brand," he said through swollen lips.

"You in pretty bad fight. Left on doorway to Red Cross. We find. Take you inside. Need plenty help."

Winston lost consciousness again. When he next awoke, his head and body were wrapped in bandages. He was in severe pain and sore all over.

"My God, Winnie. Who did this to you?" said a familiar female voice.

He could barely open his swollen eyes, but when he did, he saw Eleanor tending to his wounds.

"What am I doing back at Walter Reed Hospital, Eleanor?"

"You aren't in the States, dear Winnie. This is Vietnam, and you've been very badly beaten up."

"Why do you want a divorce, Eleanor? I can still go out in the field if you're willing to wait for me at home. You can take care of your mother while I'm away. I promise I'll come back to you," said Winston, seemingly in a daze as he lapsed back into unconsciousness.

Eleanor was still shaken after seeing Winston in such bad shape. She had returned from her morning off duty to thankfully find him still alive after whoever beaten him almost to death. Thank God whoever it was had not left him to die in an alley somewhere, but had brought him to the entrance of the Red Cross. He'd had no identification on him and nothing in the pockets of his torn and bloody clothes.

But now when he had momentarily regained consciousness, he seemed to be hallucinating about the past, as if he were in a time warp. She'd have to let the doctor know about that. This wasn't the way she had envisioned seeing Winston again, but she was intent on staying with him and nursing him back to health like she had done before so many years ago.

The days passed quietly for Winston and Eleanor. She was constantly at his side in the hospital as he struggled to recover from his widespread injuries. She had notified General Pavler of Winston's almost fatal mishap, the extensive extent of his injuries and of his hazy memory. General Pavler came to see Winston. Others Eleanor met for the first time—Major Alex Spear, Lieutenant Ledger Smith and finally Sheenar Tillerstein of the *Times*. All were shocked that they could hardly recognize Winston as battered, swollen and bruised as he was.

The *Times* had given Brand a leave of absence to recover from his injuries. But when it came time for his release from the hospital, it was apparent he couldn't live on his own, still barely able to move around in a wheel chair. Eleanor stepped in and asked him to come live with her at the apartment she had rented, and he was very grateful. She had asked to be relieved of her duties at the Red Cross until she could nurse Winston back to health.

Winston was so familiar with Eleanor from their days of marriage that she was a constant comfort and support to him as she had been after he had been injured at Dien Bien Phu and released by the communists who had captured him there. This time, however, Winston's injuries were much more extensive. Eleanor was a lifesaver for Winston, not only because of her excellent nursing care, but also because Winston had sustained a severe psychological trauma.

At first Winston used a wheel chair when he was awake and up for a while, but suffered a great deal of pain, especially piercing with any need that required him to move. Eleanor carefully monitored his pain medications. Psychologically Winston remained almost numb, shut down and still in shock for quite some time as his body slowly began to heal from so many severe injuries and lacerations. But sometimes the pain was so grievous, Winston begged Eleanor to let him die.

But she did her best to alleviate his pain and was with him constantly. They slept together at night so Winston wouldn't inadvertently reinjure himself in the dark, waking up from nightmares that plagued him. It comforted him to feel Eleanor close by soothing him after these episodes.

When Christmas arrived, Eleanor served a delicious Christmas dinner to Winston using her kitchen that was well stocked with food supplied by both her nursing friends and Winston's friends. But now General Pavler and Maj. Alex Spear had left for their Christmas holiday with their families in the Philippines. Winston and Eleanor celebrated the holiday together in her apartment.

The Christmas Day with Winston Eleanor had envisioned when she arrived seemed like a world away from the actual critical circumstances that had brought them together following Winston's beating. She knew that Winston desperately needed her during his recovery. It was doubtful if he would have survived without her help. She was very glad for both their sakes she had decided to come to Vietnam to try to reconcile with him. Their story indeed was not finished, although Eleanor never would have wanted her Winnie to have experienced such trauma and suffering.

Norma Pavler had been shocked when she heard the news of the brutal assault on Winston. Her late dear friend, Candace Brand would have been beside herself at the reported condition of her son had she still been living. Winston had been like Norma's own son. Their friendship with the Brands had lasted through the years ever since Winston and Clemie were little.

But she thanked God that Winston was still alive and that Eleanor was there to nurse him through a very long recovery.

From what her husband George had told her, Winston had been beaten within an inch of his life, as if the supposed Vietnamese mugger had vented his anger on him for all the years of foreign control over the Vietnamese through the centuries.

She and Gwen had gone over to see Maria at her father's house and given her the news about Winston's assault. Maria was in deep despair and anxious about his vicious beating. She wanted to drop everything, despite her father's objections, and fly to Vietnam to see him. But Norma dissuaded her, trying not to frighten her, by indicating the extent of his injuries, both physical and psychological.

When Maria heard that he was living at his ex-wife Eleanor's apartment in Saigon after being released from the hospital, she said she was grateful to Eleanor for the care she was giving Winston, without which she was informed his recovery was extremely questionable. Maria would have gladly nursed Winston back to health herself, but knew she didn't have the medical nursing skills Eleanor possessed. Maria also realized her presence would upset a delicate recovery. Their passionate relationship needed 'another time, another place.' She hoped Winston could recover enough to work his way back to her 'someday, sometime, somewhere.'

But she did ask if Winston had received and read her letter. Gwen said her husband Alex had told her he found Maria's letter opened and the pages inside spread out on his desk when he had gathered up Winston's things to take to Eleanor's apartment. Alex was safeguarding Maria's communications with Winston until he recovered. Maria seemed relieved to hear that news, and said she was soon to go back to her flight attendant job, but reluctantly would not try to see Winston at this point.

Norma had dealt with Winston's sister Clemie as well. Clemie was completely panicked when she was informed of Winston's mishap, and wanted to fly to Vietnam immediately to see him. Norma had dissuaded Clemie's travel plans as gently as she could, but had to get firm with her in the end, promising to keep her informed of Winston's condition as often as possible. Clemie was so glad Eleanor was there to help her brother get through his ordeal and hoped it might set the foundation for their reconciliation as he recovered. She asked Norma to relay her deep appreciation to Eleanor.

Norma had prepared for the holidays with extra care to cheer her husband and Alex's family as much as she could to counter-balance the underlying fear for Winston's life on everyone's mind. The Christmas dinner with the Spears had been delightful because of the Spear's children, whose joy at an American Christmas in a new land for them was infectious. It made life seem normal for that brief period of time.

But it hadn't lasted. It wasn't Winston's condition that caused the abrupt change in plans this time, but news from military headquarters in Vietnam that Viet Cong radio signals were detected by intelligence in Ap Tan Thoi near My Tho. Her husband George and Alex Spear had departed immediately on their way back to Vietnam by military aircraft from Clark Field. Norma sensed but yet another crucial incident was developing. What could she and Gwen do, but pray for the safety of their loved ones?

R-3's field commander in the Delta, Colonel Nguyen Van Phong, had arrived in Saigon and entered his residence by the secret passage most often used by his field adjutant. He asked Colonel Phong if he was sure the Americans had intercepted their radio transmission in Ap Tan Thoi, near the Seventh ARVN Infantry Division, as he had intended for them to do.

"Yes, Noble Leader, the stages of your master plan are unfolding just as you have directed. The American radio transmitter, first captured at Loch Ninh, has been transported successfully from Cambodia to Ap Tan Thoi, and two Vietnamese soldiers, newly trained by the captured American communications specialists in Cambodia, are on site in the Delta.

"We have detected American aircraft in the area suspected of employing intelligence listening devices, and we have sent out radio transmissions easily picked up by them. Using the radio transmitter we have intercepted news of ARVN's planned attack plan underway to capture this very instrument. Fortunately for us, ARVN's radio communications are not encoded. ARVN has been fed information that we have 120 Viet Cong soldiers in Ap Tan Thoi to protect the radio transmitter."

R-3 smiled. "ARVN and the Americans have taken the bait as we have predicted! Are your troops all in place in Ap Tan Thoi as planned? We will surprise the allies, who try to subvert our supreme cause, when we stand and fight for the first time!"

"Yes, most Exalted Leader. We know from their radio transmissions that their plan is to attack Ap Tan Thoi from three different directions, north, south and southwest."

"Are preparations to meet their attack completed?"

"Yes, Supreme Leader, we have 320 regular soldiers positioned at two locations, Ap Tan Thoi and Ap Bac, separated by a mile-long canal between them. Our troops have dug a series of deep foxholes in front of this irrigation ditch behind trees, grass and shrubs with an unobstructed field of fire in the surrounding rice fields. These foxholes are deep enough for one man to stand up and can accommodate a two-man machine gun crew. The ditch behind the foxholes will allow our units to communicate with each other. We also have troops along a tree-lined creek in the southeast. Our positions cannot be easily detected from the air or the ground."

"Excellent, all is in readiness then. Have you made good use of the information from our well-connected journalist and undercover Viet Cong agents in Saigon in implementing anti-helicopter and anti-M-113 training?"

"Yes, our Noble Leader, we received the information, and we have studied U.S. weaponry and ARVN's plans and manuals diligently," replied Colonel Phong.

"R-3 replied, "These well carried out preparations will give us a great advantage. I expect you to use the radio transmitter to listen in to the enemy's radio transmissions they foolishly left without being encoded. At crucial times during the battle to come, we'll use the transmitter to issue confusing orders to ARVN and the Americans as planned."

"I will oversee this important task myself," replied Colonel Phong. "Despite ARVN's larger troop force and help from the Americans and their war machines, we shall realize our first major military victory against them!"

"Good," replied R-3. "Let us remember that of all the peoples of the world, the Americans are the most arrogant and ignorant. They are like the serpent, who, when confronted by the mongoose, can only see a meal such as he has devoured many times before. Bolstered by each success, the snake is blind to the speed and alacrity at which the mongoose moves. Therefore, the snake will not always succeed. Once the serpent has barred its venomous fangs, it has already lost the struggle. Its ignorance and arrogance have poisoned the creature's ability to win the confrontation. A wily prey, aware of the predator's weaknesses, can use them to become the victor instead of the intended victim. So comrade, in this struggle with the Americans, we must view every encounter with the awareness that they are coming from the two fangs of arrogance and ignorance we'll use to defeat them and gain our own advantage."

Colonel Phong replied, "As always, Revered Leader, your strategy is one step ahead of the hated enemy who aids the Diem regime. They don't understand our land, its people, its culture and our intense desire to unite as one nation under Ho Chi Minh, free at last from foreign devils, who think they know better and wish to exploit us!"

R-3 smiled, "Well said, general. Let's show the Americans at Ap Bac how very ignorant they are, even of their own ally! And the Western press will enhance our victory boosting our morale and our perceived strength and resolve in world opinion."

After Colonel Phong left, R-3 sent for his Saigon operative. When he arrived, R-3 said, "I've been considering how we can effectively reign in our local bandit, Rang, or Goldtooth. He far exceeded my orders for mere surveillance of the *Times* columnist, Winston Brand. Some minor harassment I could have tolerated, but I've received a report that he and his gang of ruffians mugged and almost beat the reporter to death without my authorization. This was definitely not my plan, at least at this point."

"Have you decided how to handle Goldtooth, Noble Leader?" asked the operative.

"He grew up with one of the ruffians in his gang, and they have always worked closely together in Goldtooth's many subversive operations. I think it's time to teach Goldtooth a lesson as to who directs his activities. Eliminate Rang's lifetime friend and chief of his operations immediately. And let Rang know that if he disobeys my orders again, he is next on the list to be eliminated. His friend's position as chief of Goldtooth's operations is to be filled with a comrade of our choice, whom Rang will accept and who will be his replacement, if necessary."

"It's as good as done," Supreme Leader."

45 DEBACLE AT AP BAC

Then with the losers let it sympathize, for nothing can seem foul to those that win.

—William Shakespeare

ELEANOR BRAND HEARD a knock on the door, and when she opened it, she saw Major Alex Spear standing there with a sack of Christmas packages in his arms.

"Major Spear, how nice to see you! Won't you come in?"

"Please call me 'Alex.' Although I'm not dressed like Santa Claus, I come bearing gifts from family and friends to cheer you and Winston and to wish you both a Happy New Year."

Eleanor smiled, "How very thoughtful, Alex! Winnie can use some friendly stimulation to help motivate the return of his interest in life again. Here, let me take the sack of packages and put it under our Christmas tree to open later."

Alex entered the main room of the apartment and said, "What a nice job you've done decorating for Christmas, Eleanor. Your place looks so cheerful and cozy. I'm not only the one in the spirit of the holiday."

"Thank you, Alex. A cheerful environment does wonders to encourage a positive attitude."

Alex saw Winston sitting in a chair with a book opened on the table next to him, as if Eleanor had just stopped reading to him to answer the door. "Winston, I'm glad to see you again. Eleanor has been taking good care of you, I see."

"Alex, you're a sight for sore eyes, and I mean sore. I thank God every day for Eleanor's loving care."

"'Aunt' Norma also cares for you, Winston. She has gone all out and prepared a bundle of Christmas cheer for you and Eleanor. Along with a Santa Claus sack of gifts, she's baked a big batch of Christmas cookies she said you couldn't eat enough of when you and your sister Clemie were little."

Eleanor remarked, "Norma didn't stop making her famous Christmas cookies when the Brand children grew up either. I remember her delicious assortment of goodies of all sizes and shapes decorated with various toppings she shared with us every Christmas. How kind of her to think of us once again. I'll go in the kitchen and make some tea, so we can enjoy a taste, if you have time, Alex."

"I'll make time, Eleanor, and while you're in the kitchen, I'll bring Winston up to date on news as we wait."

When Eleanor left the room, Alex took Eleanor's chair next to Winston and showed him a copy of the *Times* featuring his column's Christmas story. "Winston, you've gotten quite an overwhelming, positive response to the gem of a story you've written. There've been countless 'Letters to the Editor' about it, and even some asking about possible adoption of the little one-armed peanut girl."

"Major Ireland has beaten them to it, I presume."

"You're right. Major Ireland sent word that he loved the story, and so did little Kim Chi when he had it translated for her. He said she cried at the part where the kind doctor was killed in a helicopter crash. Kim Chi is healing well from her surgery, and his adoption process for her is progressing well."

"Good to hear," said Winston. "Kim Chi is a darling a little girl. How fortunate she got up her courage to have the surgery just before we lost our good doctor, Nick Jenicoso."

Eleanor returned with a steaming teapot, cups and saucers and a tempting array of Norma Pavler's Christmas cookies on a tray. She set it down on the table next to Winston, and he seemed comforted by the sight of the familiar Christmas cookies that were a custom from his childhood. Anticipation sparkled in Brand's eyes for the cookies he knew were baked with love.

"While I was in the kitchen, I overheard your conversation with Winnie, Alex. I'm thrilled to hear the *Times* published his Christmas story, and that readers enjoyed it as much as I did when I first read it while visiting Clemie and her family in Hawaii. I'll have to admit there were tears in my eyes as well as in Kim Chi's when I finished reading such a touching story. I'm so sorry about the tragic death of Dr. Jenicoso, a friend to all if there ever was one, I hear."

"I certainly enjoyed reading Winston's Christmas story, too, when he first showed it to me. We all mourn the death of our unforgettable friend, Dr. Nick Jenicoso."

"I never had the privilege of meeting the good doctor, but after reading Winnie's story, I feel like I knew him, too, and also mourn his death."

"Dr. Nick Jenicoso was one of a kind," said Winston.

"I'm sure people all over the world who've read your column featuring the story, Winston, share our sentiments as well. Even my children, Alex and Alesha, not to mention my dear wife Gwen and 'Aunt' Norma, had tears in their eyes, too, by the end of the story."

Winston smiled, but Alex could see that the effort stretched the healing skin on his face.

Eleanor noticed it, too, and said, "I've been addressing Winston's scarring and subsequent tightening of his skin by applying liquid vitamin E on Winston's scars after they healed enough, so they will eventually loosen and fade."

"Eleanor's the best nurse a man could have, and now she's helping me to heal a second time as she did after my first injury at Dien Bien Phu."

Alex replied, "It appears that not only military men get injured in war, but journalists too close to the action are in the same danger."

"There are all kinds of war," said Winston. "This time somehow I got involved in a bandit war directed at me for some reason. Goldtooth and his ruffians almost beat me to death."

"Have you got any idea of why they attacked you?"

"It started when he tied me up while his gang stole U.S. goods as I was interviewing Lt. Ledger Smith regarding the U.S. supply system. I've told you about the attempted mugging after the press party. Each incident gets more virulent than the previous one. The gangster apparently holds deep grudges, although I really haven't done anything against him, except resist his attacks on me. Was his motive simple mugging, or was he afraid of exposure of his smuggling ring by me in the press? I don't know, except you can see before you the cost of my encounters with him."

Eleanor expressed her sympathy and concern for Winston as did Alex. He could see that Eleanor still loved Winston dearly. But he realized that as time went on in Winston's recovery, the journalist's relationship with Maria Monclova would come back to him and cause quite a love triangle. But Winston appeared to be finding comfort in his familiar past with Eleanor for the time being, and his healing was paramount now. He didn't need to figure out complex relationships at this point.

So Alex decided to keep Maria's letter, given to him by Norma Pavler at Christmas in the Philippines, in his pocket to give to Winston later in his healing process. For the time being, Eleanor's care and comfort was what Winston needed, and Alex didn't want to upset their routine in any way. He would ask Gwen in a letter to notify Maria of his decision, and the reasons for his delay in delivering her letter to Winston. Knowing Maria, he believed Winston's recovery would be a priority in her thinking, too. But he would give her letter to Winston when the time seemed right.

"I hope you'll enjoy Norma's gifts as well as her mouth-watering cookies," said Alex. "She went to so much effort to make a merry Christmas for all of us during our leave in the Philippines." Alex noticed a flicker in Winston's eyes at the mention of the Philippines, but Alex continued on with his description of his children's Christmas joy that had cheered all of them at Christmas dinner at the Pavler's.

"How are your wife and children doing with their move?" asked Eleanor.

"Young Alex was upset leaving his friends in Boston, but he is slowly making new friends at the elementary school on the base. Little Alesha was so glad to see me, she clung to me every chance she got. And, of course, seeing Gwen again was long overdue and an absolute joy for us both."

"Eleanor remarked, "Winston's father was gone a lot being in the Navy as well, but 'Aunt' Norma was always there for everyone, I was told, even for Winston's mother Candace, during the absence of their husbands."

"Speaking of military duties, I have to get back to the office. We have a situation I'll call 'a live one, ready to explode' any minute in the Delta," said Alex, who saw a spark of interest in Winston's eyes, as did Eleanor.

"We won't hold you up, then, Alex. How we appreciate your visit of Christmas cheer. Come back to visit us any time."

"Thank you, gracious lady, and keep up the good work in your recovery, Winston."

"Good to see you again, Alex," replied Winston.

On his way back to military headquarters Alex felt shocked once more at the extent of injuries Winston had sustained. He was making progress and was starting to heal thanks to Eleanor's excellent nursing care, but he had a long way to go yet. The quiet life with Eleanor was just what Winston needed if he was to recover fully, both physically and psychologically and eventually re-enter an active life again. How strange, and yet how fortunate, that Eleanor should turn up in Winston's life just when he so desperately needed her. Alex was glad he had taken the time to visit with them and deliver Norma's gifts to cheer them, but the developing confrontation at Ap Tan Thoi and Ap Bac needed all his attention now.

After Alex left, Winston said to Eleanor, "Alex was really worried about something, despite his holiday cheer. Something big is going down. I just know it."

"Whatever it is, Winnie, it seems to have sparked your interest. It was so thoughtful of him to bring Norma's sack of good cheer to us in the middle of his concerns."

"It's just like Alex. At first he irritated me to no end, but he has turned out to be one of the best friends anyone could ever want. Like you are as well, Eleanor."

"As you mentioned to Alex, I nursed you back to health after your injury at Dien Bien Phu, and I'm determined to do it once again, Winnie."

"My face is aching from all this talking, Eleanor. The scars are tightening my skin."

"Then it's time for your daily liquid vitamin E face and body massage to help soften up your scars and skin."

"Thanks, Eleanor. You ease my suffering in so many ways."

"Let's get your dear six-foot body stretched out on the bed so I can administer the healing oil over all your scars and massage out the stress you feel."

The relief and relaxation Winston felt from Eleanor's oil massage were so welcomed and enjoyed by him, that for the first time since his terrible beating, he felt the stirrings of his manhood. With effort he reached out for Eleanor to embrace her in profound gratitude for her loving care, and she carefully responded in kind.

"Eleanor, come lie with me. It comforts me so."

"It's only early afternoon, Winnie, hours until bedtime."

"There's always been chemistry between us, Eleanor, and I'm afraid it's starting to kick in for me again. If I am able, would you like to celebrate New Year's Eve, not many hours away, with me as we used to do?"

Eleanor remembered the happy days of their marriage, and the chemistry between them that had brought them together years ago. She responded to Winston's request. As carefully as they could manage to allow for Winston's injuries, they joined together in celebration of the arrival of the year to come.

R-3 was jubilant upon hearing the news Colonel Phong reported to him on the battle of Ap Bac that had taken place on January 2, 1963.

"Wise Leader, everything turned out better than we could have hoped for!" exclaimed Colonel Phong. "You are truly a genius to have master-minded such a well-planned trap! We did indeed lure the enemy into a battle designed to spotlight their weaknesses. We have stood and fought Diem's military, supported by his powerful U.S. ally, even though they outnumbered us four to one. We achieved our first major victory and the psychological boost we so needed for the morale of our troops. Our strength and resolve is clear to the peasant base and world opinion, too!

"Indulge me then, Colonel. Give me an overview of the events as they unfolded in the battle," encouraged R-3.

Colonel Phong began: "The allies' battle plan leaked to us was much too complex for even a seasoned military force to execute. It needed pinpoint precision, but the will of the Vietnamese military was not behind it to enable it to work even in a mediocre way. President Diem's orders to limit casualties to the Seventh Infantry Division and their local resources as his ant-coup protection ultimately caused their defeat."

R-3 replied, "We provoked the Allies to plan to attack us anyway when they detected our radio transmissions and our false information of 120 troops to guard it. But go on, tell me how things worked out."

"The enemy's triple attack plan to encircle us from the north, south and west got off to a bad start. They requested 30 helicopters to airlift a battalion to the northern landing zone. Unfortunately for them, they only received ten helicopters."

R-3 smiled. "Yes, we planned diversionary actions in other areas so the enemy had to split up their resources."

"With only ten helicopters, three trips were needed, but only the first company of the battalion of troops actually arrived at the planned time. Luck was with us. Fog rolled in and stayed for about two and a half hours, so the first company had to dig in and wait."

R-3 asked, "In the meantime, what happened in the south?"

"The Civil Guards marched up from the south in two columns. The first column approached the southern tree line of Ap Bac and halted at a paddy dike about 150 yards away from our well-fortified troops hidden by the outcropping of trees, shrubs and high grasses on the dike fronting the hamlet. Part of one company proceeded into the open rice field to reconnoiter. Our unseen troops opened fire from their foxholes, and the enemy troops retreated to the paddy dike, suffering eight dead."

R-3 smiled and asked, "Were the Civil Guards able to dislodge our guerillas in the foxholes with flanking maneuvers?"

"No, Supreme Leader. They unsuccessfully tried for the next two hours, but the province chief failed to send the second Civil Guard column to support or rescue the first, so our troops had them effectively pinned down in the south."

R-3 commented, "How predictable. The province chief and Diem loyalist wanted to save the Civil Guards as anti-coup insurance for Diem, who sabotaged his own government troops' effectiveness! What happened in the north once the fog lifted?"

"To make a long story short, Revered Leader, the three ARVN companies in the north fared no better than the Civil Guards in the south. Once all companies were in place, they marched south in three separate columns. During the next five hours, they made three major assaults against our well concealed troops, but they couldn't break our line of defense."

"Excellent," said R-3, who couldn't seem to stop smiling. "So both the ground attacks in the north and south were bogged down. What happened in the west?"

The reserve companies from Tan Hiep airstrip were called up. The American Colonel Galloway reconnoitered possible landing zones in an army spotter plane and flew over the western tree line, but our troops were hidden from his view. Although suspicious, he instructed the ten CH-21 helicopters with the first reserve company to be inserted 350 yards out in the middle of the rice paddies west of Ap Bac. At that distance, they would be out of range of small weapons fire from the dike."

R-3 observed, "Obviously, our troops in the western tree line held their fire so as not to mark their position."

"That's correct," said Colonel Phong. Luck was with us again. To our great advantage, the American command helicopter pilot decided not to follow Colonel Galloway's instructions and landed the helicopters 150 yards out in the paddies, instead of the requested 350 yards. The reserve troops disembarked under our fire, and the helicopters were hit multiple times.

"One Ch-21 was too severely damaged to get off the ground, so a second Ch-21 helicopter was sent in to rescue the helicopter crew, but it also was immobilized. Then one of the Huey gunships was sent in to pick up the crews of the two downed CH-21s, but it was hit and flipped over and crashed. At the same time a third CH-21 was heavily damaged and was forced to land in the rice fields a short distance away."

A jubilant R-3 exclaimed, "Unbelievable! Four helicopters down, including a new Huey gunship! Our people's fear and awe of helicopters ended that day when they saw the helicopters are vulnerable and can be taken down. We couldn't have planned a better scenario. It's the psychological victory we needed!"

"But it gets even better, Noble Leader. A fourth CH-21 returned to Ap Bac to try to rescue the downed helicopter crews. It was heavily damaged by ground fire and it, too, had to land on the muddy rice paddy."

"Five helicopters total downed? Incredible!" replied R-3.

"The Americans suffered three dead, as well as eight wounded. The story, however, gets even more dismal for the allies. The disembarked reserve company and the downed helicopter crews still needed to be rescued, so they turned to the armored personnel carriers, the M-113s for rescue support."

R-3's smile disappeared. He remarked, "In the past, our fighters had fled when these awesome 'green dragons' appeared."

Colonel Phong replied, "But no longer, Great Leader. The commander of the M-113s wouldn't take orders from the Americans, only from the reluctant province chief."

R-3 commented, "The province chief didn't want the troops to fight in a battle that Diem really didn't want to take place. Colonel Galloway will rue the day he finally got his way when we set the trap to force the reluctant Vietnamese to fight us. Did the M-113s ever move, Colonel Phong?"

"The virtually indestructible ten-ton mini-tanks were finally ordered to move forward. The heavy M-113s can cross the shallow streams and rivers of the Mekong Delta, but they bogged down in a deeper canal. The M-113 crews and infantry men aboard had to cut down brush and trees to fill the canal to allow the M-113s to cross. The farther muddy bank of the canal was especially difficult for the M-113s to climb. When one tank got across, it often had to pull the next tank up and so on."

"Delays, delays and more delays, all to our advantage, a good thing, because we don't have anti-tank weapons," said R-3.

"The M-113s finally approached our hidden troops in the west and stopped cold just short of the dike. Our Viet Cong troops rose from the trenches firing machine guns and charged the M-113s. Shocked and with their leader knocked unconscious, the tank drivers turned and retreated."

R-3 exclaimed, "Another fearsome American war machine defeated! Our people must have felt emboldened."

"Yes, sir. In reality the fight was over. Dusk began to descend. Our troops, having won their huge psychological victory, began moving out of Ap Bac into the swampy plains to the east. Colonel Galloway in his spotter plane saw what they were doing and requested that the parachute battalion be dropped into the eastern Viet Cong path to seal off their escape route."

"So the stubborn American colonel didn't want to give up!"

"No, but again, instructions were not followed. The Vietnamese colonel instead ordered the paratroops to be dropped west of the village, instead of east, where they would have suffered heavy casualties. But even this cautious move turned bad when the paratroopers were dropped into the rice paddies in the west within small arms range. Again, our rear guard kept them pinned down, but let them go when darkness fell."

"I couldn't have predicted a better result, Colonel Phong," said R-3. "I'm sure the outspoken Colonel Galloway will express his extreme frustration and rage by openly accusing the South Vietnamese soldiers of being incompetent and cowardly, even though he knows the influence of President Diem on their leaders."

Colonel Phong said, "Our Viet Cong troops killed 80 South Vietnamese government troops with well over 100 wounded."

"And our side?" asked R-3.

"We suffered 18 killed and 39 wounded."

"What a victory! It was worth the risk we took to achieve it," said R-3. "Our guerillas stood their ground and fought against a modern army four times their number. The enemy had armor, artillery, helicopters and fighter-bombers, but their commanders and soldiers for the most part were unwilling to fight and suffer casualties, thanks to President Diem. Well done, Colonel Phong!

"Now we can sit back and let the Western press do the rest of the job for us. They finally have some action to report on to justify their earlier negative reporting."

46 TWO LOVES

It is the most momentous question a woman is ever called upon to decide, whether the faults of the man she loves are beyond remedy and will drag her down, or whether she is content to be his earthly redeemer and lift him to her own level.

—Oliver Wendell Holmes, Sr.

ELEANOR'S CONSTANT NURSING CARE and her daily oil massages to facilitate Winston's healing led to the gradual resumption of sexual relations between them after their first joining.

As much as Eleanor wished to have a child with Winston, she wanted the choice to be mutual. So, Eleanor decided to ask Winston how he felt about conceiving a child with her.

"Isn't it a little late to be having this discussion, Eleanor?" asked Winston. "For all we know, a child could be growing in your womb as we speak."

"Why haven't you been concerned before to take care, Winnie, when we've long enjoyed the intimacy of our previous marital state? Becoming pregnant with your child would be a joy to me, but I didn't want to take advantage of your vulnerable state to achieve my desire."

"Eleanor, I've recovered enough to realize the potential of a pregnancy in our relationship. Earlier, General Pavler told me of your deep desire to have a child with me. At the time, it was out of the question, but now we both know that without your loving care, there probably would be no me to go on to meet whatever life experiences await me."

"Are you saying, Winnie, that a child coming from our union is a reward for me in helping to give you your life back?"

"There's no question I wouldn't have survived without you, Eleanor. We're both aware I'd been beaten to within an inch of my life. The psychological damage was just as bad. You know there were times I didn't want to survive with the unbearable pain I had to endure, even with the help of pain pills. It's taken all the strength and determination I have to be able to get this far in my recovery with your loving support.

"A child of ours would be an expression of that part of our lives we have shared together, and our concerted effort to bring me back to life. There's no doubt that a child between us would be conceived in love."

"But that's only the beginning, Winnie. A child needs both parents together to provide the nurturing, protection and role models to develop properly in an environment of love. Would you be there to share a life with me and our child?"

"In some way, I certainly would be, Eleanor, but I'm not exactly sure how at this point. I can't say what our legal status will be until I am fully recovered and can discern what course the life you have helped me restore will take. We might still be at odds with the future renewal of my career as a war correspondent and the kind of life that entails. It doesn't lend itself to a husband and father at home, although I would certainly do my best to offer financial support as I am able."

"Oh, Winnie, why is it that our paths in life meet in a blaze of light together, only to go off in separate directions?"

"Don't despair, Eleanor, a part of me will always be with you, even more so if we should conceive a child together. You have helped me to feel like a man again after a totally weakened, almost lifeless state. How could I not but share in the life of a child with you, should I still be able to? A reward for you, Eleanor? No better was ever deserved, but it's more an expression of a caring life being restored and a new one possibly beginning.

"But knowing my condition and status, if you want us to use protection, we can certainly do that. But let's not deprive ourselves of our intimacy, Eleanor, if you continue to be willing to share it with me. For my part, I don't want to let go of the comfort we find in each other's arms. It invigorates not only my body, but also my soul as well. Perhaps that's selfish of me, but we certainly have a connection, and always have had since we first met."

"I appreciate your being honest with me, Winnie. Reward or not, I certainly came to Vietnam with the intention of reconciling and the hope of persuading you to have a child with me. I really wouldn't want anyone else to be the father of my child if it should happen. I feel it was meant to be a part of our story that really wasn't finished yet. But I realize now that it would but start a new beginning between us that you're not able or ready to commit to yet."

"I wish I could assure you about the status of our relationship, Eleanor, but I must also be honest with you regarding my relationship with another woman that was drastically interrupted by my horrific beating."

"Whatever the outcome of our time together here, Winnie, I will always treasure this time with you and hope you will see your way to remarriage with me one day. But until then, your recovery still has a long way to go, and it's our priority now."

"Eleanor, you deserve to know that I have been active sexually with this other woman. We were very careful to use protection, but we did slip up once. It's unlikely a pregnancy would result in a single encounter, but you should be aware of this before you continue to be intimate with me."

"Do you love this woman, Winnie?"

"Yes, I do, but from the beginning great obstacles have plagued our budding relationship, especially with ten years between us for starters, not to mention the total rejection of me by her father. Despite these setbacks, I finally had decided to turn a blind eye to the complications and actually bought an engagement ring the morning I was almost beaten to death."

"Was it a middle-aged affair that turned serious, Winnie?"

"Perhaps it started that way, but for some unknown reason we are powerfully drawn to each other, despite all kinds of complications. It's as if it is fated, that there's some life lesson or experience that needs to be lived out with her. Of course, that possibility would have been mute, except for your loving care, Eleanor. I'm certain I wouldn't have made a recovery on my own.

"To be completely honest about my relationship with Maria, I know she would be much better off accepting the proposal of a local young man in the Philippines, who has been waiting for her answer for a long time. Her father certainly favors him and would be glad to never see me again. I've said this to her several times, and I believe her father reminds her of it daily, but Maria claims that Tywan is only a friend to her."

"Well, a woman with two proposals at once, though without knowledge of the intended second proposal from you, Winnie, must be quite a woman. I must admit, I'm rather speechless."

"I'm sorry you have such a fellow as me in your life, Eleanor. I can't even figure myself out, much less how I manage to get in such controversial situations, or dilemmas, one right after another. I'm probably not the answer to your dreams, but to your nightmares instead."

"You're the one with nightmares, Winnie. Let's put matters to rest that can't be resolved right now and not worry about the future. I'm content to be with you now, the only place any of us can live, one moment at a time."

"I don't really deserve you, Eleanor, nor Maria for that matter. You'd both be better off without me."

"And live a boring life without the 'fire in our souls' you manage to kindle, despite the cloud of complications that always seem to surround you like a whirlwind?

"You've been honest with me, Winnie, and I want to be the same with you. I know how miserable you were all those years on the *Times* desk job just so you could accommodate our marriage and my concerns. I'm sorry the priorities I set for myself at that time in my life didn't put you first on my list, as you had tried to do for me. I truly regret my mistake."

"With your father gone at the time, and your mother ill with cancer, you couldn't let her down, Eleanor."

"No, but I could have cut back on my career obligations and spent more time with you. How often I regret my decision to divorce you, but I became afraid when your drinking got out of hand. I knew you desperately longed to be back out in the field where I couldn't go with you, caught as I was in the middle of everything".

"But you're here now, Eleanor, and there's no doubt I desperately need you if I'm to recover my life again."

"At least you're never boring, Winnie."

"Well, boring is my name right now, and I'm thankful you can put up with me."

"I can do more than put up with you, dear Winnie. I think it's time for your daily oil massage. Would you like to continue this discussion in our bedroom?" asked Eleanor with a glint in her eye.

God forgive him, Winston thought, and Maria as well, but he needed the care, comfort and healing touch of Eleanor to help him return to life, "to face the sun" again, as his father would always remind him.

"Maria, you haven't heard one word I've said to you!"

"Father, you've said it so often, it's emblazoned on my mind."

"We can't ignore your pregnancy. The morning sickness you've suffered through already indicates that you don't have much more time to make a decision about it. Did the doctor say how far along you are?"

"It seems I conceived the day you humiliated Winston at dinner that sent him away. I'm due the latter part of August."

"Have you considered an abortion, Maria? It's not too late, but it will be before too long."

"How can you suggest that, Father? You're speaking about the life of your grandchild! I remind you that you've often lamented about how small our family is now, and here you are talking about the death of a blessing of new life coming to us."

"How can I welcome such a new life when it isn't Tywan's, but that of an American who'll take you both out of my life?"

"Father, you married an American, and you worked out a solution. Mother married you and lived in the Philippines."

"And look where that got her, an early death coming home to us from a visit to the U.S. to see her family, when her plane crashed out of Wake Island and destined her to a grave in the waters of the Pacific Ocean and us to a life without her! Combining two different worlds isn't easy, Maria, and if I could, I'd spare you that fate."

"But you loved mother more than life itself. You've said you'd never give up the time you had with her, despite the years you've had to be alone. That's the way I feel about Winston."

"You've told me that before, Maria, but the fates you claim brought you and Winston together have departed. Now your journalist clings to life under the care of his ex-wife, who must still care for him if she's willing to see him through such a long recovery. You can't be so blind, Maria, that you don't see a reconciliation between the two developing even as we speak. Your relationship with Winston only lasted a matter of months, while his ex-wife probably has had years with him."

"But those few months were unforgettable, Father, and the result of the love we shared is developing here within me as our child that will ever connect us."

"Tywan is still willing to marry you, Maria, even though you're carrying another man's child. He loves you so, and will look after you and give you other children as well. Please be reasonable, daughter!"

"But it's not Tywan's child, Father," protested Maria.

"What can a father do? I see the road ahead of you, Maria. Who will support you and your child? You do not even know if Winston will survive his terrible beating. And already you've had to ask for more time off from the airlines. As your pregnancy progresses, very soon you'll have to quit your job. Thank goodness I've been able to go back to work to support you, but it's only a short-term solution. A child needs a young father to support and protect both you and your love child. Tywan would be such an excellent role model for a child, and could give you children for your child to grow up with."

"What you say is true. Without a doubt Tywan is a fine young man, but I just don't love him. He's only a dear friend to me. My happiness is also a prime factor in any successful marriage and family to follow."

"Nevertheless, he loves you even though you have already put him through much, and you may grow to love him as well. He'll be a safe haven for you and your child, which you desperately need right now, especially as a single pregnant woman with the father of your child having been brutally injured and living with his ex-wife as he recovers."

"Nevertheless, the fates are not yet done having their way in this situation. I can only be thankful for the care Winston is receiving in his recovery, but when he is well, then we can find a resolution agreed to by all parties. Let's not act before all the facts are in for all concerned."

"Maria, you are a hopeless romantic with illusions that may very well fail you."

"Regardless, Father, I must not act hastily in a direction I feel is not right for me, Winston, our child and Tywan. I can't go against my inner guidance. Perhaps I can go to work in a department store as I did before until the baby is due in order to make ends meet."

"No, dear, you need family support at a time like this. You're welcome to live at home with my financial support, Letty's cooking for us, and perhaps Tywan's help if needed for doctor's appointments when I'm at work."

"Father, remember that Tywan has to work, too, at his father's bank. I can drive myself to my doctor appointments."

"Not if you're as sick as you were this morning, Maria. You've yet to eat anything substantial."

"Father, you'll have to let up on your pressure on me to marry Tywan for both our sakes. I don't want to lead him on."

"We'll see how things develop, Maria, but I'll try my best not to make you uncomfortable. But please don't fault me if I slip up now and again."

"Father, you're incorrigible!"

"It's only because I love you so, daughter!"

"I know, Father, but I have my destiny to live, and we will just have to see how it works out."

47 TURNING POINT

We do not know either unalloyed happiness or unmitigated misfortune. Everything in this world is a tangled yarn; we taste nothing in its purity; we do not remain two moments in the same state. Our affections as well as our bodies, are in a perpetual flux.

—*Jean-Jacques Rousseau*

BRAND, YOU'RE LOOKING BETTER than the last time I saw you, although you still appear pretty rough around the edges," remarked Sheenar Tillerstein.

"Thanks a lot, Sheet."

"It's Sheenar, Brand. I keep telling you."

"You're a sight for sore eyes, Sheenar. What brings you here to see me?"

"Can't your boss just stop by to say hello and see how you're doing?"

"Louis Cohen sent you, didn't he, Sheenar, to find out when I'm able to get back to work?"

"Well, our editor might have said something like that. It was fortunate you filed those columns from your interviews in the Delta when you got back before you were beaten. And Louis had your Christmas story already in the hamper. But a couple of months have gone by since Christmas and readers are asking about your columns."

"I'm flattered, Sheet, I mean Sheenar, that I've been missed. Do you mean to tell me that the two sentimental stories I've filed have gone over well with readers?"

"Even better than your usual hard-hitting columns, Brand. "Who'd have thought?"

"Certainly not you, Tillerstein. I hear you and your press friends have been hitting hard against Diem and the South Vietnamese and American militaries after the debacle at Ap Bac."

"As well we should, Brand. Even Colonel Galloway, military advisor to the Seventh Infantry Division, called the operation a 'damned incompetent mess.'"

"Reported in the good colonel's colorful language, I see."

"He shoots straight from the hip, Brand. You should be the first one to applaud his telling the truth, just like you."

"You mean the truth as Galloway sees it."

"Colonel Galloway was there at Ap Bac, Brand. You weren't. Do you know something the whole world doesn't know by now?"

"Don't get me wrong, I like Colonel Galloway. Let's just say that all the facts may not be in yet on Ap Bac."

"How would you know when you were laid up and out of action when the skirmish took place just after New Year's Eve?"

"Well, I wasn't totally out of action, Sheenar, but I'm talking about the underlying currents of motivation behind the South Vietnamese military's lack of compliance with what I understand was a very complex military plan. Then there's the strategy of the enemy to consider, too."

"So what does that mean? The action speaks for itself. Talk about ARVN's incompetence! Even after the battle the next day, some press and government troops got shot at by friendly fire when the troops were sent to retrieve bodies. It appears the South Vietnamese were trying to 'save face' by pretending the Viet Cong were still there, and the commander had troops fire on an imaginary enemy."

"Perhaps he views the press as an enemy."

"Very funny, Brand."

"Seriously, I'm glad no one was hurt, but it just points up the underlying motivation of the South Vietnamese military. You even noted before I ventured into the Delta that it's obvious they want to avoid casualties. Are you aware of the attempt by the paratroopers in 1960 to assassinate Diem and take over the South Vietnamese government in a coup? It was the Seventh Infantry Division, only 30 miles from Saigon, which rushed to Diem's defense and stopped the coup. You even remarked when I spoke to you that it's in Diem's best interest to keep the Seventh in reserve as his anti-coup protection."

"So what?"

"President Diem has authority over the military. His commanders knew he didn't want his backup to sustain heavy casualties."

"You can say that again. Their token resistance at Ap Bac didn't amount to a 'hill of beans' in the battle. They appeased the Americans, who were 'hot to trot' to capture the Viet Cong radio transmitter, by going into battle, but the result of their effort only infuriated and frustrated their ally even more."

"If Louis needs another column from me, I could write a think piece comparing the battle of Dien Bien Phu, where the French tried to execute a plan against the communists destined to fail, with that attempted by the allies at Ap Bac."

"That would make Louis happy, a state very rare for him."

"I knew Louis was behind your visit. I'll dictate my column to Eleanor, and when it's ready, I'll let you know."

"How is your lovely ex-wife, Brand? I hear she's gone above and beyond to help you recover from your beating."

"A better nurse you could never find."

"Is that all she is, Brand? What about that beautiful Filipina flight attendant, a former Miss Philippines?"

"I know you have your finger on the pulse of gossip in Saigon, Sheet, but please leave my affairs out of the eye of public scrutiny."

"It's Sheenar, Brand. You obviously make that mistake just to irritate me."

"I'll try to do better, Tillerstein. But let me ask how things are going between you and Lan, But Hieu's secretary, in the Vietnamese Minister of Information's office these days?"

"Can you think of a better way to tap into what's going on in Saigon than by dating the secretary through which all information passes to and from the Minister of Information?"

"'You've got me there,' Sheenar. It's a saying used by Colonel Galloway when I brought up the fact that he was a military advisor only, with no authority over the South Vietnamese military."

"Well, the fiasco at Ap Bac has put the war in South Vietnam on the map and the front pages of the world's newspapers. Too bad you weren't even there to add your two cents worth, Brand."

"I'm sure you and your press colleagues more than made up for my absence, Sheenar."

"That we did, and I wouldn't even be here now, except that news has finally dwindled about Madame Nhu berating the Americans for getting the South Vietnamese troops into an unnecessary battle where Vietnamese soldiers were killed. Likewise, news leaked about President Diem's demand that Colonel Galloway be fired has ceased since Diem has reneged under U.S. pressure to defer it for the time being. And even General Pavler's attempt to put a good face on things by reminding reporters that the Viet Cong have been driven out of Ap Bac has lost steam."

"So, you're here because there's been a lull in news since Ap Bac has already been analyzed to death?"

"We need to keep Louis happy, if that's possible."

"So what does Louis have in mind when he sent you to check on when I can get back to work?"

"Well, there've been rumblings of Buddhist unrest in Hue. Louis remembered your interviews with key Buddhists awhile back. The Buddhists will be celebrating Buddha's birthday on May eighth, and Louis wondered if you'd be well enough by then to go back to Hue to cover the celebration and see if you can uncover the cause of the unrest there and write a column about it."

"Sounds like an interesting assignment. I'll have a couple more months of recovery time until early May, so I just might be able to accommodate old Louis. Tell him I'll make it one way or another. I can use my contacts from my former interview there to get a closer look at what's going on."

It was then that Eleanor came back from an outing, and Brand warmly greeted her. "Eleanor, come in and greet my *Times* bureau chief, Sheenar Tillerstein, whose enlightening visit I've just been enjoying."

Tillerstein acknowledged Eleanor's greeting and added, "Eleanor, you've been working too hard helping Winston recover. You look a little under the weather. I hope Winston hasn't been too demanding a patient for you."

"Not at all Mr. Tillerstein. I remember meeting you when Winston was first hospitalized after his beating, and you came to see him."

"Please call me Sheenar, Eleanor. I've brought Winston news from our boss, who wants to know if he is able to travel to Hue in early May on Buddha's birthday to do a story on Buddhist unrest there."

"Oh, my, that's a long trip for Winston. I'm sure he'd love to do it, but we'll have to step up his physical therapy so he's able to make a trip like that."

"He's looking better, thanks to your care, Eleanor, but you may be getting the short-end of the bargain. You seem tired."

"I'll see she gets more rest," interjected Winston.

"Take care of yourselves, you two. And let me know when you finish the column you mentioned, Brand. I'll come back myself to pick it up."

"Nice to see you, Sheenar. Give Louis my best regards."

"Will do."

After Tillerstein left, Eleanor sat down in the chair next to Winston. "Eleanor, you do look tired. How did your doctor's visit go? Do you have a touch of the flu as you feared?"

"No, Winston, it's not the flu."

"Could it be that you're pregnant then?"

"Yes, Winnie, for better or worse, we are going to be parents. It seems our New Year's Eve celebration together has indeed turned into a new beginning with a new life developing, despite our unsettled situation. I'm due in late September."

"Don't be afraid, Eleanor. A child is what you hoped for when you ventured to Vietnam to reconcile with me. You've not only saved my life, but now you're nurturing a new life as well. Your loving efforts have resulted in a blessing for all of us, and gratitude is our response. But for you, the Brand name would be lost, and Willoughby and Candace and your parents as well would be grateful that you won't be alone anymore."

"But what about you, Winnie? Will you be with us?"

"I'm glad, Eleanor, to give you and our child a part of me that had all but disappeared from this world. My beating brought home to me my mortality. Coming back from the 'shadow of death' has made me think of more than just myself and my needs. Now I feel the desire to pass on whatever of my essence is good to the next generation while I still can."

"But I know you well, Winnie. When you're strong enough, you'll be back out in the field stirring things up with your probing interview questions. Hue will be your first stop."

"Will you be all right if I go?"

"Who's taking care of whom here, Winnie? But I appreciate your thinking of me. So far the doctor said everything is progressing normally with the pregnancy. Morning sickness is typical, and the physician gave me some pills to help. I stopped to load up on saltine crackers on the way home. But my morning sickness should abate a month before early May."

"When I've recovered more, and your pregnancy progresses, we'll have to think of your return to the States if the situation deteriorates here in Vietnam, Eleanor. Let's assess our options at the beginning of July when you will be six months pregnant. Did you keep your parents' home in Maryland?"

"Yes, and, Winston, my inheritance from my parents is more than adequate to meet our needs."

"I'll certainly take leave and accompany you back to the States if we decide on this course of action. And I'll see you settled there with as much hired help as you need."

"But you'll have to return to Vietnam and your *Times* job here, won't you, Winnie?"

"Yes, for the time being, at least. Do you still have friends there you can socialize with, and who can look in on you, especially as your pregnancy gets closer to your due date?"

"Yes, I do. But I would miss you terribly, Winnie. This time together has been a gift of heaven for me!"

"And for me, Eleanor. But our time together isn't over yet. Let's continue to enjoy each other while we can."

"I know it's that 'fire in your soul,' sparking to life again that will bring a parting in our story once again."

"But, thanks to you, it also has kindled the spark of a new life to bless us and to ever connect us. We must be grateful for that, and the chance to spend some treasured time together in this uncertain world. You must take care now for the life of our child and of your own health. I promise to work more diligently on my physical therapy to regain my strength again."

"You have an inner strength you have yet to fully discover, my dear Winnie. It will see you through the trials and tribulations of your life."

"As do you, dear Eleanor."

When Eleanor went to lie down and rest, Winston had the intuition he should open the letter from Maria that Alex had given him recently when he had come to visit. Now with Eleanor actually pregnant, the time had come when he'd have to face the complex relationships he had before him with Eleanor and Maria.

Winston opened the book into which he had placed Maria's letter, unopened, to read at a later time. But the time had arrived. Again he sensed the faint scent of Maria's perfume from her letter. "Dear God," he muttered as he opened the letter. Lieutenant Kearney had called him an "old man" when it came to attracting women. But her perfumed letter left him helpless to avoid being turned on by the memories of Maria wrapped up in his arms in a frenzy of lovemaking.

Winston put the letter down for a moment and wondered if he shouldn't wait to read it. He was about to put the letter back into the book when suddenly he was gripped by the intense desire to read it and see what she had to say, no matter how it would complicate his life, and now the life of others. As always, Maria's letter was a love letter, and he could see that it ended with a beautiful love poem. He began reading:

> Darling Winston, my so-badly-injured love,
>
> What has happened to the fates, who had allowed us to walk on the mountaintop together, only to separate us with your horrible beating, just as I had hoped we could reach out to our future together?
>
> Oh, Winston, I am in the depths of despair to hear of your pain and suffering experienced when you almost left us. My dearest, could you feel my spirit of love calling you back from the darkness into the light of love waiting patiently for your return?
>
> I've been told your ex-wife has appeared like an angel of healing to lovingly give form to the love strengthening your desire to return, when such pain and discomfort threatened to drown you. Don't let go, precious one, heart of my heart, love of my life! It would be such a lonely world without you. How could we bear it not to be together? It's unimaginable, my love!
>
> If you could but fathom the depth of my love for you, you will return to me one day on the tides of a passion for each other that will never die. I'll wait for you, my one-and-only-love, as long as it takes. My spirit

is with you in each second of your recovery. I'll love you forever, my darling. Let me say it to you in a poem:

You are the only love for me.
No other will ever, ever do.
Could but my prayers be heard by thee,
You'd feel the power of our passion anew.
A rip-tide would pull us out into love's sea,
Where you and I alone in bliss could float,
And where no one else could ever imagine to be,
So embraced in passion as we in our own love boat.
And we'll never, ever want to come back
Once we set sail for a life of deepest love,
A soul-mate's journey of life with no map,
Granted but once in a lifetime from above.

I love you, Winston, with my whole heart, and I am ever thine! Come back to me, my darling, when you are well once again! Remember that my love is ever calling to you.

Your Maria in love

Winston folded the letter, put it back in the scented envelope and slipped it in between the pages of the book once again. He held his head in his hands as memories shook him to the core and filled his mind with images of the wildest lovemaking with Maria he had ever experienced. It was as if they frantically tried to become one and couldn't rest until united in the most heavenly warmth either had ever known. Winston was so deeply touched by Maria's letter, but overcome with conflicting emotions. He lay back in his reclining chair and fell instantly into a deep sleep.

Eleanor came in later after her rest and found Winston fast asleep in his chair. She picked up the book in his lap and was about to put it on the side table when she saw the edge of an envelope sticking out the side. She removed the envelope and saw it was addressed to Winston. Immediately she sensed the faint smell of perfume, and her heart jumped with anxiety. She guessed it was from Maria. She put the letter back in the book and decided to ask Winston about it when he awoke.

Winston must have sensed Eleanor's presence and awakened as she placed the book on the table. He noticed her anxious look and asked her if anything was wrong.

"It's none of my business, Winnie, but when I came in I saw you sleeping in your chair with a book in your lap, I picked it up to put it on the table and saw the edge of an envelope sticking out the side. I took it out and saw your name written on the front and smelled a scent of perfume coming from it."

"Did you open it and read it?"

"No, Winnie, but I thought I'd ask you about it when you awoke. Is it a letter from Maria?"

"Yes, it is. Alex has had it for a while, but decided not to give it to me until I was recovered enough to deal with it. He didn't want to disturb my recovery when I was too weak. He said he relayed his decision to Maria through his wife Gwen. Maria sent word back to Alex that she understood the reason for his decision, and that my recovery was the priority for her."

"As it is with me. I can only hope that if you have read it, you are at a point where it won't set you back with life's complications."

"I have to say that you and Maria are too good for me. The fates have surely brought us all together in a situation that seems unresolvable. I can't see any answer at this point but to remain true to my responsibility to you and our child.

"I had thought when I regained my equilibrium that Maria would certainly want to let me go, a disfigured and battered older man that a younger woman with her whole life ahead of her would be wise to put in her past."

"Your condition is only temporary, Winnie. As your press colleague remarked when he left, you're already looking better, and it's only a matter of time until you regain your strength."

"You're too kind, Eleanor. Maria must feel the same way as you do. I have finally read her letter, and she writes that she is patiently waiting for my recovery and awaits my return."

Winston saw the look on Eleanor's face that her heart had sunk at the news. "I want to continue the honesty between us, Eleanor. Go ahead and read Maria's letter, and you'll see that Alex's decision to delay giving it to me in my severely weakened condition was wise."

When Eleanor finished reading Maria's letter, she said, "My goodness, Winnie, this young woman seems to be deeply in love with you. And she's another poet like you. I can see what a temptation she must be for you. The passions of youth are so much more intense than those of middle age."

"Don't get me wrong, Eleanor. I am very sincere in our intimacy together, both in our marriage and now in our reconciliation. But it isn't just passion with Maria. It's as though there's something more powerful than each of us that draws us together. To resist that power because of multiple complications in such a relationship, I tried to stay away from her for the longest time. But Dr. Nick Jenicoso's tragic and untimely death brought us back together in our grief over the loss of such a dear, kindly friend.

"Again, after a rendezvous with her in Thailand, I stayed away for a time, but finally gave in and went to the Philippines to surprise her while she was on a leave of absence from her work, caring for her father. He had been injured in a car accident. Her father asked Maria and me to join him for dinner, but he hardly touched his food. He kept his peace while we ate, and when we finished, he asked to talk to me alone, despite protests from Maria. He minced no words to tell me I wasn't welcome in his family, that he favored the young man who had proposed to Maria. Then he had the gall to invite Tywan over after dinner to show his favor for Tywan instead of me."

"That was a rough experience, Winnie."

"You're telling me it was rough! It was humiliating and downright cruel and disrespectful. So, again I stayed away from Maria, for her sake as much as mine, this time thinking it was for good. But then Maria sent me a letter. I received it after I got back from my Delta interviews, a letter like the one you just read. And that's when I put blinders on and bought her an engagement ring, only to be immediately kidnapped, mugged and almost beaten to death."

"And that's when I entered the picture."

"As a blessing to help save my life. But I can't put the blinders of passion on again, Eleanor. You know first-hand where that got me last time. I must focus on regaining my strength so I can go back to work while we await the birth of our child."

"I can only pray your plan works out that way, dear Winnie," said Eleanor with a sigh.

48 LEDGER'S LAMENTS

Thou will lament hereafter, when the evil shall be done and shall admit no cure.

—*Homer*

LEDGER, WHAT AN UNEXPECTED surprise! It's good to see you again. What brings you here to see me?" asked Brand.

"I wanted to see how you're doing, Winston, and to bring you issues of the *Observer* you might be interested in reading."

"Yes, I'd really like to see the results of your creative endeavors with the military newspaper, and to catch up on the news in the military community here in Vietnam. You might like to know the readers of my column enjoyed reading about the Vietnamese customs Americans need to be aware of to mind their manners while in Vietnam. There were some interesting 'Letters to the Editor' about it. Thanks again for sharing the information with me."

"You're very welcome, Winston. I'm glad the piece got an appreciative reception, as did the enthusiastic response of your Christmas story in the *Observer.*"

"I'm glad to hear it. Will I be reading about the American military response to the battle at Ap Bac in these issues of the *Observer*, Ledger?"

"Such as they are."

"What do you mean?" asked Brand.

"Our information office has been caught between a rock and a hard place in dealing with the press, Winston."

"What's the problem?"

Ledger hesitated for a minute and then said, "Can I confide in you 'off the record,' friend to friend, Winston?"

"Of course. I'll most certainly respect your confidences, Ledger, as I always do."

"First let me say I really appreciate your going to bat for me when you brought my information background to the attention of the military. I'm certainly better off in the public affairs office that I was in supply at the mercy of the black marketers, Goldtooth and his gang."

"I can certainly appreciate that sentiment. My own encounters with Rang keep getting more and more violent until he and his ruffians almost beat me to death!" exclaimed Brand.

"I'm sorry, Winston. I should have asked how you are before starting to air my own complaints."

"It's been a slow recovery, but I've had excellent nursing care to help bring me back to life."

"Where is Eleanor?"

"She's resting. I've insisted she take care of herself so I don't exhaust her taking care of my needs."

"She's certainly a lovely woman, and she deserves accolades for helping you come this far in your recovery. I hope my visit won't disturb her."

"I'm sure it won't, but continue with your concerns."

"Sometimes I think the mess between the military and the press is comparable to black market corruption."

"In what way, Ledger?"

"Well, I think it starts at the top with President Kennedy and the situation in French Indochina we inherited from the French as their ally in World War II, and which Kennedy inherited from Eisenhower, who had to deal with the demise of France's colonial empire.

"Hold on, Ledger, let's get back to the present. We can't do anything about the past."

"If only we could learn from it though," moaned Ledger. "Looking back, press-wise, World War II was an era where the press was almost an ally of the government as we fought along with our allies against world menaces threatening almost everyone in some way or another."

"Granted, but in Korea there was a gradual change when the press became more adversarial to the government."

"That's just it, Winston. Now we have a handful of young wire-service correspondents reporting on a war with mostly spotty action so far, until Ap Bac, that is. So what do they do to fill their daily quota of news stories to keep their jobs? They turn a critical eye to the governments of both of the allies and the military of each to stir up some conflict they can report on to create reader interest."

Brand replied, "Unfortunately, the increasing alienation between the allies and the deep flaws of Diem's policies are concerning."

"Even so, Winston, I prefer your endeavors to go around South Vietnam and report on conditions in different areas. Many complain about the Western press reporting from a Saigon bar."

"Thanks, Ledger, but to be fair to my press colleagues, I have the luxury of being a weekly columnist, but they must meet daily deadlines sent by telegraph in Saigon. I've had my own difficulties filing field columns due to poor communications."

"Well, the press has gotten out of Saigon occasionally, mostly to the Delta. My Tho is only 30 miles from Saigon. The military has security restrictions about what we can and cannot share with the press, but the attitude of the young reporters shows more and more disrespect for our responsibilities. They think it's their God-given right to know absolutely everything that's going on with the war effort," lamented Ledger.

"It's quite a tightrope you have to walk between the military and the press as an information officer."

"That's true whenever we come in contact with each other, but it's happening less and less often. When it's my turn to give the daily 5:00 p.m. press information sessions, fewer and fewer reporters attend, and those that do hardly pay attention. I'm limited in what I'm allowed to say, and often have to say, 'No comment.'

"The reporters think the military is lying to them. But it is an appropriate answer when they ask questions that would affect security, or reveal classified information. More and more they're turning to outside sources to get their information, and in many cases it's unreliable in this city of plots, subplots, gossip, criticism and double agents."

"Does the press have any valid criticisms?" asked Brand.

"Well, some of our problems come from President Kennedy, who is trying to 'beef up' our commitment to South Vietnam, but wants to keep it from being revealed to world notice. When the reporters can see a transport ship bringing helicopters in on the Saigon River, and they receive a 'no comment' to their questions about it from us, our credibility suffers."

Brand commented, "Kennedy must be thinking of the press as they acted in World War II, that they'll support the war effort without question. But the loyalty of the press without criticism is hardly the case in Vietnam. And there you are, Ledger, on the frontlines with the contentious press. So, your 'tightrope' ends up between a rock and a hard place."

"Yes!" exclaimed Ledger. And it doesn't help that military thinking also reflects the past where in battle there were frontlines, ground gained or lost, victory or defeat. The adjustment in thinking in a guerilla war doesn't always happen. Unreliable communist body counts often plague the military."

"Western thinking in the Orient isn't a good match," observed Brand.

"To add to the difficulty, Winston, the press often interview Colonel Galloway, the adviser of the Seventh Infantry Division at My Tho. They look up to him as some kind of hero who tells it as it is, despite what it might do to his career or military priorities."

"I've met the charismatic, Colonel," responded Brand. "The South Vietnamese government is greatly bothered by the colonel and the press. I was told the colonel was in Diem's crosshairs after Ap Bac. President Diem already has tried to oust one member of the press, but later backed down in both instances. He has threatened to do the same to another."

Ledger replied, "The stories the press files from here are having a really negative impact on public opinion. After the debacle at Ap Bac, it's solidifying the reporter's contentions."

"That puts a lot of stress on you in your job, but in the long run, the time is limited when print journalists hold sway over news reports. The advent of TV coverage will bring the war into the world's living room, despite the cumbersome equipment the TV men have to lug around, but no doubt technological innovations will improve that burden. Mine and my colleagues' careers are due for quite a change," observed Brand.

"But meanwhile, Winston, the press situation here is about as bad as anywhere in the world, and getting more toxic as time passes. To make matters worse, in-service rivalry between the services and uncoordinated lines of authority, which haven't had time to be sorted out yet, make for a confusing and anxious workplace of internal wars. The *Observer* is my solace until the unstable work environment is worked out."

"I'm sorry to hear of your difficulties, Ledger, but I'm looking forward to reading the issues of the *Observer* you brought. Your 'quagmire' in trying to do your job reflects our country's in the sorry state of affairs in Vietnam."

"Talking about affairs, Winston. My personal life is in a quagmire of sorts as well. As hard as I've tried to resist the Vietnamese woman I told you about before, I finally gave in. Was it the constant stress I'm under in my job that needed some sort of relief, or was it just an excuse to justify my descent into lust? I know it's so wrong, but I just can't seem to turn away from her. Every time I try, I fail.

"I do love my wife back home, and I know she doesn't deserve this kind of behavior from me. I can only pray that an illegitimate pregnancy doesn't occur by accident, although I'm always very careful. And then I wonder if my wife isn't doing the same thing at home because of her loneliness. Here I am being comforted by a Vietnamese beauty, when I don't want my wife to ease her own loneliness with someone else. What kind of selfish and adulterous man am I?" asked Ledger.

"Your wife probably isn't under the same kind of pressure as you are in a war zone, but I can't offer advice in the female department, Ledger. It's tough trying to figure out matters of the heart, not to mention disciplining a male's natural attraction to the opposite sex, so difficult in situations of prolonged spousal separation. My best wishes go with you upon your return to your wife in the States without the crisis of leaving a Vietnamese woman with an unwanted pregnancy behind. A great number of mixed heritage children will be abandoned in Vietnam if this war drags on and more troops arrive."

"In my case, I'd be responsible if so, but we're very careful. It's my problem to work out, but it relieves me to tell a trusted friend. Thanks for letting me vent. I'd hoped to bring you cheer, not to burden you with my problems, but soon my tour of duty ends and my *Observer* runs to you will end."

"I didn't realize you're about to leave Vietnam."

"I rotate back to the States in early March. I'll let you know when I get the actual date. A successful adjustment to my marital situation when I return is quite a concern. And I worry about the Vietnamese woman I've been so intimate with. Now I must face the consequences of lingering guilt over my unfaithfulness, affecting both women and myself."

Brand replied, "Guilt is a heavy burden we all carry in some way, and emotions don't always bend to reason or conscience. But I'll be sorry to see you leave, Ledger. True friends give life richness, too. Your personal confessions will go no further. Thanks for bringing me the *Observers.* They keep me up to date while I'm isolated in my recovery. However, I want to regain enough strength by early May to go to Hue for Buddha's birthday to write about Buddhist unrest there."

"That's good news, Winston, and a testament to Eleanor's incredible nursing care. Please give your lovely lady my best wishes for her own health as well."

"I will do that. Glad you stopped by, Ledger."

"Thanks, Winston, for being a much needed friend in this rebellious country."

"Likewise, Ledger. Take care."

R-3 looked thoughtful for a moment as he gave instructions to his adjutant. "We want to be careful not to interfere with Hanoi's plans and interests regarding the Buddhist unrest in Hue. But my resistance cohorts in Hanoi have indicated our next big effort to discredit the Diem regime after Ap Bac is in Hue."

"What are Hanoi's connections in Hue, Noble Leader?"

"Let me just say this, the Hue Buddhist leader Thich Tri Quang's brother works for Ho Chi Minh in Communist Vietnam's Ministry of the Interior, and his brother's duties include direction of the subversion in South Vietnam. Thich Tri Quang is also a disciple of Thich Tri Do of Hanoi, who is the head of the Buddhist front organization there, which operates only by favor of and for the purposes of our communist regime.

"Thich Tri Quang has publicly stated that Buddhism and communism are compatible in his opinion. No one can say for sure if he is allied with us, or if he merely cooperates when it serves his purposes. Perhaps the welfare of Buddhism in Vietnam is his main agenda, regardless of the political situation. What we have in common is the fall of Diem's regime."

"Revered Leader, I've heard the Diem regime has powerful family connections in Hue."

"Yes, Hue is Diem's family home. His brother, Ngo Dinh Can serves Diem as an overlord of Central Vietnam. And Diem's brother Ngo Dinh Thuc is the Catholic Archbishop of Hue. Can you think of a better place than Hue to foment Buddhist unrest than in a Catholic stronghold?"

"What do you want me to do, Supreme Leader?"

"First, send this message, disguised in a pill bottle, to our field adjutant in Hue. Use our message center in Saigon."

"Won't we use the curio shop for this purpose anymore?"

"No, only for inconsequential messages. Madame Binh has turned the compromised shop into a gathering place for a gaggle of Vietnamese women wanting to buy female products," replied R-3 with a look of disgust. "She is no longer of use to us, except as Colonel Bao's fiancée in the eyes of the Diem regime.

"My orders are for our comrades at Hue to step up their infiltration of the Tu Dam Pagoda there, and I trust you to see to even more subversion of the Xa Loi Pagoda in Saigon. Our people need only shave their heads and put on a saffron robe to be admitted as a monk."

"Easily accomplished, *Ayr Ba*."

"Oversee these infiltrations and keep me informed."

"I understand, Noble Leader."

"Good. The Diem regime will find no rest trying to counter our plans until it is too late!"

49 A MULTITUDE OF DILEMMAS

There are two ways to be fooled. One is to believe what isn't true; the other is to refuse to believe what is true.

—Søren Kierkegaard

I'VE BEEN THINKING, Eleanor," said Brand.

"What is it, Winnie?"

"I've been in Vietnam a year now. Without your loving nursing care I wouldn't be here to get back into field reporting in Hue in a couple of months."

"You're ever the adventurer, Winnie."

"My restless nature gets the best of me, and was partly to blame for the dissolution of our marriage. But I've been blessed by your restorative care once again to allow me to venture out to search for the truth."

"A bit like Socrates, aren't you, Winnie, questioning others in your search?"

"Yes, but often I find little truth known by others outside their area of expertise. Perhaps I'll never find the truth in anyone else unless I learn to 'know thyself' first."

"Socrates knew that he didn't know the truth, and that nobody else did either. But he was accused and sentenced to death by those who became offended when their ignorance was exposed by him. I don't want that to be your end, Winnie!"

"Nor do I. My own ignorance should be my first concern. What do I see if I stand back to look at myself except my goal to win a second Pulitzer Prize to establish my worth as a foreign war correspondent? Why do I still feel the need to validate my choice of career? No matter how much I try, my late father's disappointment is still in my head insisting I 'face the sun.' I hope I learn to 'know myself' and get squared away before our child is born, and we attempt to guide another soul in this crazy life."

"Do you remember the quote by Winston Churchill your mother Candace used to comfort you with?"

"Yes, she'd repeat it to me whenever she could see I was becoming overwhelmed by father's disapproval. She'd say:

> *When you're 20, you care what everybody thinks.*
> *When you're 40, you stop caring what everybody thinks.*
> *When you're 60, you realize no one was ever thinking of you in the first place.*
>
> *—Winston Churchill'*

"Perhaps we need a lifetime of learning our lessons through experiences as we seek peace within ourselves. Don't be impatient, Winnie," responded Eleanor.

"You know how much I enjoy philosophical thought, Eleanor. Plato's famous 'Allegory of the Cave' in the *Republic*, comes to mind in my quest for the truth."

"Yes, Winnie, you've talked about it often in the past. But what makes you bring it up now?"

"This lengthy recovery period has given me a chance to slow down and reflect on my reporting."

"How is the 'Allegory of the Cave' related to your work?"

"I look at the survival of Vietnamese culture over centuries, incorporating changes adopted from foreign invaders. But it fundamentally stays the same despite different adopted images. It reminds me of the chained prisoners in a cave in Plato's allegory who are shackled by the legs and neck, facing the cave wall since childhood."

"I know you're going somewhere with this, Winnie, but you're taking the long way around."

"And for a reason. Be patient with me Eleanor. Do you remember the structure of Plato's cave?"

"How could I forget your vivid description, Winnie? The shackled prisoners could only look at the wall of the cave in front of them and only see the shadows cast there by people walking in front of a fire behind them carrying different objects, which cast the shadows."

"Good memory, Eleanor! But only the objects made the shadows and not the people carrying them because of a low wall that concealed the people walking past the fire behind the prisoners with the objects. When the people carrying the objects talked to one another, wouldn't the chained prisoners think the shadows on the wall made the sounds and were real?"

"Very likely. It's coming back to me now. Certain honors and commendations were established for those who most clearly remembered things, such as the order of the objects brought by, and it would bring esteem and power to the recipients."

"How I appreciate you, Eleanor. You have always indulged my philosophical discussions. Regarding my war reporting, I question whether I'm working among the prisoners in their 'cave of culture,' such as in Plato's allegory."

"Are you saying that the condition of the prisoners never changes, only the different illusory shadows on the wall?"

"You would have done well in my philosophy classes, Eleanor. Plato's allegory tells us there's more to it than chained prisoners and an unreal puppet show in the cave."

"Yes, a freed prisoner is dragged up the cave's steep ascent and out into the bright sunlight, causing him pain, rage and temporary blindness," remembered Eleanor.

"Plato shows us how much more awaits not only the prisoners, but also the one forced up into the light. At first such a liberated one desperately needs a period of acclimatization. But eventually he can view things directly, including the light of the moon and stars."

"This allegory must relate to your great passion to search for the truth, Winnie."

"How right you are, my dear. The freed prisoner sees things themselves. It's not the same as 'knowing' images on the wall, which passes as the norm in the cave. If, in compassion, the liberated one returns to the cave to free the remaining shackled prisoners, he would be severely challenged despite his good intentions. At first he would be blinded by the darkness he encountered in re-entering the cave, and the chained prisoners would ridicule the transformed one, saying he had gone up the ascent only to come back down with his eyes ruined."

"The allegory has a dark ending as I remember."

"When the freed prisoner's eyes finally adjusted to the darkness of the cave, he persisted to try to free the prisoners from their chains to lead them into the light."

"Oh, Winnie, if they could, they would kill him, motivated by their own fear of another way of looking at life that would make their old way of thinking disappear! For them to keep familiar illusions from disintegrating into the nothingness of a dream, no measure would be too drastic for them to take!

"It reminds me of your experience in searching for the truth. If you 'upset the apple cart' too many times, such a death could become your fate!"

"Indeed, my editor and others have warned me about my need to reduce the number of people on my enemy list. Since the beginning of my Vietnam assignment, I've had too many close calls. But what's really disturbing me, Eleanor, is that even when I do positive reporting, the darkness in human nature is still threatened by the light revealed by good works."

"I can still feel your sense of guilt for possibly contributing to Nick Jenicoso's unjust demise, Winnie."

"An uneasy, relentless feeling in my gut about the incident keeps haunting me. But I have another disturbing concern related to the allegory, too."

"What is that, Winnie?"

"As much as my passion is to find the truth, I wonder if I am nothing but a 'freed prisoner,' who hasn't ascended into the light, but is still in the 'cave' telling everyone about conditions in the darkness. As I report what is and is not going on in the 'cave,' I find none of the shackled prisoners want to hear it anyway. What have I really accomplished? What if I'm just reporting about an unreal world where the light of truth is not to be found? Or maybe I'm just finding fault with those in the cave who don't live up to my standards or expectations as my father has always done with me."

"Is truth only found up the steep ascent in the sunlight?"

Winston replied, "According to Plato, there's even more to it than that. All things come from the Good. Even objects seen in the sunlight outside the cave, Plato asserts, don't represent the truth. Instead, he sees the 'ideas' behind objects as the truth of what is real."

"These are deep thoughts, Winnie, but it seems to me Plato's philosophy still leaves us hanging in the wind. Why does Plato's 'Good' find it necessary to create these 'ideas?' There must be more to it. We can get lost in philosophical thought, but what are the practical answers we need to help us make sense of a crazy, ever changing world of opposites?"

Winston replied, "It's true that relying on reason for answers can only take us so far with no resolution. Perhaps, in the end it requires a 'leap of faith.' The play between darkness and light in all of us is certainly a puzzle, isn't it, Eleanor? Is it a process of choice over time that depends on our willingness to bring the darkness in us to the light that will reveal the truth? Or is it a 'Catch-22' situation with no escape on our own?

"I know my own rebellious nature is a hindrance to me, and I dare say most of us are 'rebels all.' But your care and concern for others, like Nick Jenicoso displayed, certainly puts you on the cave's ascending pathway I should be on as well."

"It's one step at a time in this life on earth, Winnie. I've made my share of missteps, as we all have. Let's just be thankful you're recovering from your near-death beating and can live to try again for another day."

"Thanks to you, Eleanor."

"Oh, Winnie, I should've given you more love and care in our marriage."

"Likewise for me, Eleanor. But enough of these deep, philosophical thoughts for the time being. We seek truth, but somehow we never seem to find it."

"It surely keeps us ever searching though, doesn't it?"

"Yes, it does, my dear Eleanor. But what do you say if we focus on the present instead? I've received word from Ledger Smith that he is leaving Vietnam tomorrow as his year-long tour of duty has ended. I would like to go to the airport to bid him farewell with my best wishes for his future."

"Do you want me to go with you, Winnie? You haven't been out much since your beating."

Winston laughed good-naturedly. "You mean I need a pregnant woman of two months to protect me from Goldtooth?"

"Laugh if you must, Winnie, but you still need some looking after. We have several months of healing to get through before you're off to Hue the beginning of May."

"And who's going to look after you, Eleanor, if you have morning sickness tomorrow?"

"What a pair we are, Winnie. But let's give it a try. I know you and Ledger have become good friends, and I'd like to bid him farewell, too."

"Only if you're up to it Eleanor. I'll have to warn you though that tomorrow's Thursday, the day that Maria used to fly into Saigon from the Philippines on flight attendant duty. I have no idea if she continues to fly that schedule, or not. In any case, there is only a 30 minute layover."

Eleanor replied, "If so, then perhaps it's time we met. We'll just have to see what happens."

The next day Winston and Eleanor went to the airport to see Ledger off, but they weren't the only ones there to bid him farewell. They saw Ledger in the waiting area with a beautiful Vietnamese woman in his arms, trying to soothe her as she clung to him crying. Ledger looked upset, too. Winston and Eleanor wondered whether their presence would only complicate Ledger's situation, but just then Ledger spotted them and brought the woman with him to greet them.

"Thanks for coming to see me off, Winston and Eleanor. I really appreciate it. This is my friend Mai, who is sad to see me leave Vietnam. I'm thankful for her friendship that has helped me stay sane during this tour of duty, and I'm reluctant to leave her as well. But the time has come to say goodbye."

Brand replied, "It's nice to meet you, Mai. I'll miss Ledger, too, as will Eleanor. Ledger, I want you to know life seldom brings along a true friend, and I'm happy to say that somehow we've trusted each other from the outset. Eleanor and I wish you the best. We'd like to keep in touch."

"Thank you both. I certainly would like to continue our friendship even if by long distance. By the way, someone is waving to you over there, a man with red hair. It looks like Lieutenant Kearney with a baby in his arms. And his Vietnamese wife is with him also carrying a twin baby. I think it's her parents who are there, too, to see them off and to help with the babies before they board the aircraft."

"Yes, you're right. If you'll excuse us, Ledger, we should return Lieutenant Kearney's greeting. We're glad to meet you, Mai, and best of luck to you, my friend."

"Thanks, Winston, I'll need it. Nice to see you again, Eleanor. Best wishes to you both."

Winston and Eleanor went over to greet Lieutenant Kearney, his wife and her parents. Winston addressed the younger man, "Your tour of duty in Vietnam ends, Kearney, just like Lieutenant Smith over there, whom we just bid farewell to."

"Yes, that's right, but, my God, Winston, you look like you've gone through a meat grinder. I heard about your mugging, but the scars from your beating are shocking!"

"Thanks a lot for the encouragement, Kearney. I'd like you to meet Eleanor, a lovely lady I was privileged to be married to until I became an obnoxious drunk."

"Pleased to meet you, gracious lady," said Kearney. "I pity you if you went through that stage with him. I saw the obnoxious side of Winston in Hawaii, and it, among other things, got us off on the wrong foot. But he's more affable now that he's stopped drinking, and we're getting along better."

"Eleanor is an invaluable nurse, and she's supporting me in my recovery, hopefully helping me to restore a decent appearance over time," remarked Brand.

"That may be hard to do, given you never did have much to work with in the first place." Kearney winked at Eleanor.

"Thanks a lot. I thought we had buried the hatchet."

"Just kidding, old man," said Kearney.

"I see you're rotating back to the States with your family. Quite a testament to 'young blood,' I'd say, with a wife and twins to boot in just a year here."

"You'd better believe it, Brand. Seems I can't turn around without one of my women getting pregnant, given the vigor of 'young blood,' of course. Sorry you're 'over the hill' for such experiences, Brand."

"Yes, I remember you telling me earlier that there was another pregnant woman in your life." said Brand.

"Well, yes, but she's no longer pregnant. She has given birth to a baby girl back in Boston, stirring up quite a controversy in my father's senatorial district. Don't think I haven't heard about it from my old man."

"You're building quite a Kearney clan with the arrival of three children in such a short period of time!" exclaimed Brand.

"Sorry I can't say the same for you, old man. Eleanor has a task in front of her just trying to help you look decent."

Kearney turned to Eleanor and winked again. "Brand and I have had our differences, but we've settled down, although I can't resist baiting him, nonetheless."

Eleanor replied, "Lieutenant Kearney, in all seriousness, I'm glad I arrived in Vietnam with the desire to reconcile with Winston just when the violent bandit beating occurred in mid-December. What a fortunate turn of fate that I was here just when Winston needed my nursing care."

"I'll have to say, Eleanor, you're a whole lot better to look at than Winston at the moment, and I know he appreciates that as well as your nursing capabilities," said Kearney.

"Don't let us keep you, Kearney. Your baby might need attention before you board the plane, if my nose is any indication. You'd best call your wife over to attend to changing chores."

Lieutenant Kearney introduced his wife and her parents to Winston and Eleanor as he handed the twin he was holding to the mother, and said, "It's been a pleasure meeting you, Eleanor, and I'm sure we'll hear more from you, Winston, now that you've started writing your column again. My father undoubtedly has read your recent commentary on the similarities between the French failure at the battle of Dien Bien Phu, and that of the Diem regime and its American ally at Ap Bac."

"The next column will be from Hue in early May," Brand replied. "But in the meantime, we both wish you and your family the best of luck."

"Thanks, Brand, you'll need good luck, too, if you stay in this sinking ship of a nation too much longer as the situation deteriorates. Positive reporting may become more and more difficult, if not impossible. But you're a lucky man, Brand to have such a lovely lady help you recover."

"Don't I know it! Best regards to your father, too," said Brand as Kearney and his family moved toward the gate area.

It was then that Brand saw a striking female with red hair standing at the edge of the crowd of onlookers. He saw Kearney turn and look at her with intense longing in his eyes, and he could sense the sensual energy palpitating between them. The yearning between the two redheads reminded Winston of Maria's beautiful face and her eyes filled with the magnetic pull of love drawing kindred souls to become one, once reflected in his own eyes. As Kearney moved away from the crowd with his family, Brand saw the sadness in the woman's face as tears began to seep from her eyes, and Kearney's eyes reflected the same sad emotion before he turned away.

Brand thought he'd never have believed it if he hadn't seen it first-hand with his own eyes! Kearney, the womanizer, had finally fallen in love, and it looked like he had an armful of complications to go along with it. "Join the club, Kearney," Brand said to himself.

Eleanor broke into Brand's thoughts as she touched his arm and said, "There's a young woman, a flight attendant, coming toward you in a very excited state."

Brand's heart jumped as he turned, expecting to see Maria, but instead he saw her good friend Emma waving to him. When Emma saw Eleanor standing next to him, she slowed down and approached hesitantly. Emma seemed to make up her mind about talking to him and said when she reached him, "Winston, how wonderful to see you up and about! You look like your injuries are healing well."

"Hello, Emma. Thanks for your friendly greeting. Please meet Eleanor, who's responsible for helping my injuries to heal and my scarring to gradually fade.

"I'm pleased to meet you, Eleanor. All of us who have known Winston are grateful for your excellent nursing care to bring him back to his old self."

"Please, Emma. No more references to 'old.' I'm having enough trouble looking at myself in the mirror these days. But to be truthful, Eleanor is the reason I'm here talking to you today. I can't say life was all that appealing after my horrific beating when I was wracked with unending pain, despite the pain pills."

"It's a wonder you survived, Winston, but we're all so very glad you did." Emma looked at Eleanor and then back to Winston when she said, "I bring you warm greetings and prayers for your complete recovery from the Philippines."

Winston replied, "I assume you're referring to Maria's good wishes, but don't worry, I've told Eleanor about my relationship with Maria. I do intend to see Maria and talk things out between us, but I need more time to heal before I feel capable of sorting things out in my relationships."

Emma fingered Maria's letter to Winston in her pocket. She shivered when she thought of all the lives at stake, and realized a go-between wasn't the one to make decisions for others. She decided not to give Winston Maria's letter.

Winston saw Emma's discomfort and broke the silence. He asked, "Is Maria well? I thought Thursdays were her scheduled times to be the flight attendant on the Philippines to Vietnam and back run."

"Maria doesn't work for the airlines anymore."

"Has she married Tywan, then?"

"No, she hasn't, but her father keeps pressuring her to. She has decided to work for a department store like she did before she went to work for the airlines," replied Emma.

Emma turned to Eleanor and said, "Maria is very happy for your care of Winston. She knows how seriously Winston was beaten."

"Thank you for telling me, Emma. I want to be honest about my relationship with Winston if you're wondering. We have been divorced for two years, but I came to realize that I didn't feel our story was finished. So I came to Vietnam, not knowing about Winston's experiences here, with the hope of reconciling with him and perhaps even to persuade him to have a child with me. Little did I dream he would be beaten almost to death! I was so glad I could use my nursing skills to help him heal in order to reclaim his life."

Brand appreciated Eleanor's honesty spoken in a kindly manner, but he saw Emma's face fall, her face turn pale and her balance appeared unsteady. "Are you all right, Emma? You look so pale all of a sudden, and I fear you might faint."

"I'm sorry Winston, Eleanor, I just have to cease being a go-between and make decisions that aren't mine to make. All I can say is that you really need to talk to Maria, Winston, before you make major decisions for your life. There's much more at stake than you know. I'm sorry but I must get back to my duties now," said Emma as she hurried off.

Brand said, "Well, this farewell visit to the airport has been much more than I expected, Eleanor."

"Yes, Winnie, it has. The encounter with Emma certainly raises some red flags. I think you're wise to work things out with Maria before you make any decisions about our relationship, besides, of course, our mutual decision to have a child together which is already *fait accompli*. You will have to find out what Emma meant when she said that 'there is more at stake than you know regarding Maria.'"

"I know you understand my position, Eleanor. I'm just not ready to cope with any more drama at this point when I'm just starting to get a hold of myself again with your help. Setbacks could be very costly for me, whether physical or psychological. Right now we need to continue as we are, you protecting yourself and your pregnancy and me continuing to heal so that I can go back to work in the field in a couple of months. I can't promise anything to anyone until I get back on my feet again."

"Perhaps this outing was too much for us, Winnie. I think we've had enough excitement for one day. It's not too late to tend to your oil and massage treatment when we get home."

"Sounds like a good idea, Eleanor. I'll have to admit I'm more tired than I thought I'd be."

"Let's go home, then. Your friends are soon to be safely in the air en route to new experiences in their lives, and we wish them well."

"That we do," replied Brand.

It was a few days since Emma had talked to Winston and Eleanor at the airport in Saigon that she sat talking with Maria in her small apartment near the Manilla airport.

"You actually saw Winston in person at the airport, Emma! What I would give just for a glimpse of him again! How did he look?"

"He still looks pretty rough, Maria. He's healing and his scars are beginning to fade a bit. But one look at him, and you know he's lucky to be alive."

"Oh, my dear Winston! I can hardly bear to think how badly injured he was!"

"Maria, his ex-wife was with him at the airport. It must have been one of his first outings. When I spotted Winston, it looked like he was saying farewell to a friend, a lieutenant in the military, I believe. The soldier had red hair and was accompanied by a Vietnamese woman, her parents and two babies, one of which the lieutenant was holding, possibly a twin."

"If that was Lieutenant Kearney, Jr., as far as I know, he wasn't exactly a friend of Winston's. To think that Kearney was accompanied by a Vietnamese woman and twin babies no less is hard to believe. Not like the Lieutenant Kearney I was acquainted with. But more to the point, tell me about Eleanor."

"You would like her, I think. You've told me before she is a nurse, and I could tell that from her kindly interest in others. She's more mature, probably closer to Winston's age, and lovely in her own way. She and Winston seem very comfortable with one another. You are right to be grateful to her, because she's undoubtedly the main reason why Winston has survived. Oh, Maria, I hate to say this to you, but Winston certainly needs Eleanor, if but for a while longer," said Emma.

"Do you think Winston loves her?" asked Maria.

"No doubt. But his relationship with her doesn't seem to be the passionate, magnetic attraction to each other you and Winston share. As I said, it seems more like a comfort and caring connection, with Eleanor's nursing skills a big part."

"Even so, do you think there's any hope for me?" asked Maria with an anxious look.

"Once Winston regains his strength, I'm sure of it, Maria. I saw his eyes light up when he turned to see if it was you when I waved at him. Once he saw it was me instead, the light dimmed, but he was still interested in talking to me to find out how you're doing. He also asked whether you had married Tywan after I told him you had left your job with the airlines for the department store job. But I assured him you had not."

"Do you think he wants to see me?"

"Right now he's reluctant to do so. He said he will come to see you when he's healed enough to be competent to sort things out with you. I sincerely believe he's not up to dealing with any complex situation at this time. Peace and quiet are needed for him to heal both physically and psychologically, I think. You would think the same thing had you been there."

"Oh, dear. I did so want to share with Winston the news of my pregnancy. Did you give him my letter, Emma?"

"To tell the truth, I panicked when Winston said he wasn't up to dealing with his relationships just yet. Giving him your letter wasn't the right thing to do at this time. Forgive me, Maria, but I feel it isn't my place to be in the middle when so many lives are at stake that don't pertain to me personally. I panicked at the thought and didn't give your letter to him."

"I guess I'll have to live with that if Winston's wants more time to recover before he can deal with our situation. However, he doesn't know how much more is at stake."

"I did imply that to him, but I could see he wasn't ready for that information," replied Emma.

"Did anything else happen?"

Emma's face fell. "I don't know if you're ready to hear what Eleanor said to me."

"Oh, no! What else? I guess I'd better face whatever it is. What did she say?"

"She just explained to me why she had come to Vietnam."

"Can you tell me?"

"Yes, but it could upset you. I don't believe she meant any harm, but she said she wanted to be honest. She came to Vietnam to reconcile with Winston and possibly even try to persuade him to have a child with her."

"Oh God, no! Here I am already three months pregnant, and who knows if Eleanor isn't pregnant as well!"

"She didn't say she was, Maria."

"No matter. Her intent is there. What a complicated situation this is! No wonder Winston isn't up to coping with it yet. I was hoping to be able to tell father I had notified Winston about my pregnancy, but I'll just have to be patient until Winston recovers more. But thank you for trying to deliver my letter. I know you've carried it for weeks hoping to find someone at the airport who could convey it to Winston."

"I don't think Winston has forgotten his love for you, Maria. He does intend to see you when he is well enough."

"There is comfort in that. But in the meantime I have to deal with father who won't stop trying to pressure me into marriage with Tywan. But at least I have a part of Winston with me as our child grows within me," said Maria.

"If Winston is as much in love with you as you are with him, it will work out someday regardless of the complications."

"I'm counting on it, Emma," said Maria.

50 HUE

The king-becoming graces, as justice, verity, temperance, stableness, bounty, perseverance, lowliness, mercy, devotion, patience, courage, fortitude, I have no relish of them.

—*William Shakespeare*

WHEN WINSTON BRAND ARRIVED at Tan Son Nhut airport near Saigon in early May, he saw Alex Spear walking toward him in civilian clothes. "Fancy meeting you here today, my friend. You wouldn't have been sent by General Pavler to check on me on my first *Times* assignment since my beating, now, would you?"

"That would certainly be a side benefit as I accompany you on your flight to Hue, Winston, but I'm very seldom off duty, despite what you think seeing me in civvies," replied Alex.

"You want to blend in with the crowd of onlookers at Tu Dam Pagoda during the celebration of Buddha's birthday I take it."

"As do you."

On the flight to Hue, Alex briefed Winston 'off the record' on his mission to the old imperial capital. "We believe R-3 is upping the ante in his next attempt to discredit the Diem regime with the Buddhist unrest in Hue. He got the best of us in the propaganda battle at Ap Bac. He demonstrated to the Vietnamese peasants and the world that Viet Cong will stand and fight to win the day against the South Vietnamese military's attack, even backed by their U.S. ally and its military war machines."

"Did ARVN's efforts in recovering some of the stolen American radios pay any dividends in the battle outcome?"

"Let's just say, if there were any, ARVN's reluctance to encode their radio transmissions, despite our attempts to have them do so, cancelled out any advantage we might have had with the recovery of some of the stolen radios," replied Alex. "But we're still trying to convince ARVN to use encoding for use in radio transmissions in any possible upcoming battles."

"Change in any Oriental culture with an ancient history is an uphill battle, I'm sure," replied Brand.

"Which brings us to the Buddhist unrest, which is ripe for what we surmise is R-3's next subversive move," said Alex. "Unfortunately, President Diem inadvertently has played into R-3's hands and poured fuel on the fires of Buddhist unrest when, on May sixth, he revived a Vietnamese government regulation and had it printed on a circular against giving any flag precedence over the national flag in public places or in public view. This was just two days before Buddha's birthday celebration today. The city of Hue, I'm told, has already been bedecked with Buddhist flags."

"Why would Diem take such a divisive action that only can add to the unrest in Hue, especially right before Buddha's birthday?" asked Brand.

"Word has reached me that Diem was irritated a few days earlier when in Da Nang an excessive number of Vatican flags were flown by Catholics there, whereas the national Vietnamese flags were few in number and some were tattered and torn. Notwithstanding Diem's Catholic background, he wants to emphasize the Vietnamese flag in his struggle for nationalism to be the primary mindset of the Vietnamese people, regardless of separate religions," replied Alex.

"A Personalist tenet, I see, but his circular to that effect couldn't be more ill-timed. It's a wonder Diem couldn't see that, given he already has a problem with Buddhist unrest in Hue, and you say the Buddhist flags have already appeared in profusion there. It's a heavy-handed move sure to cause resentment at a sensitive time, if not a scenario for violence."

"It's a perfect setup for R-3 and Hanoi. The Buddhists will be sure to see Diem's action as once again attempting to curtail their freedoms, and deny them religious equality no matter that it also pertains to Catholics and all other faiths. That's why I'm on my way to Hue," explained Alex.

"In my earlier interview with Buddhist leaders and my subsequent column, I explained their grievances and how they feel Diem's policies and actions reveal his favoritism for the Catholics in a myriad of ways, even though Diem has Buddhists in his cabinet," remarked Brand.

Alex replied, "We were informed by the Diem regime that the Vietnamese Minister of the Interior arrived in Hue yesterday and realized the potential for a volatile situation to break out. He received authorization to inform the administration in Hue not to apply the circular in this one instance."

"Can you imagine the animosity that would be created if Vietnamese officials placed national flags alongside the Buddhist flags already on display?" asked Brand.

"It would be quite a confrontation," said Alex. "That's why the Interior Minister also took the precaution to visit the Buddhist leaders at the Tu Dam Pagoda to explain the flag regulations and assure them that they would not be enforced on this particular occasion."

"Have you heard whether the concerns of the Buddhist leaders were assuaged by the Interior Minister's intervention?"

"Yes, they were very pleased, according to the Interior Minister. Even Thich Tri Quang joined in expressing his satisfaction with the arrangements," said Alex. "But we don't believe it for a moment. R-3 would never let a situation like this pass in order to bring the failures of the Diem regime into the limelight, whether the Buddhist leaders are in league with him or not, but they'd both like to see the regime fall."

"Has something happened already?" asked Brand.

"Early reports indicate some Hue police took down a number of Buddhist flags before they got word from the province chief that changed their orders," said Alex.

"Communications in Vietnam are slow to say the least. But what an opportunity for communist mischief to strike!"

"Yes. As far as we can tell, despite the meeting of the Interior Minister with the Buddhist leaders at the Tu Dam Pagoda to de-escalate the situation, apparently just the opposite happened. Some monks from the pagoda went around Hue to tell people to take down the Buddhist flags, saying it was because of Diem's orders to 'ban the Buddhist flag.'"

Brand replied, "I had an uneasy feeling about Thich Tri Quang when I briefly met him before he turned me over to another monk for the interview. Now it appears that his strong anti-Diem sentiments have incited him to take action, seeing Diem has handed him the perfect opportunity to discredit his regime."

"In any case, Hue is a hotbed of potential conflict during this celebration," said Alex. "We'll just have to see what happens when we land."

When Alex and Winston arrived at Tu Dam Pagoda, they saw blatant evidence of their suspicions as they viewed big banners with anti-government slogans.

"These anti-government political slogans at a religious ceremony are unprecedented," said Alex. "Any slogans, speeches or objectives of a large meeting under the rules of a government at war have to be approved in advance."

"Then, the Buddhist unrest situation here has just turned into an active conflict with the display of these anti-government slogans," said Brand.

"Just what we anticipated would happen. You'll get more drama for your column than you thought, I'm afraid."

The religious ceremony at the pagoda began as approved. But as the ceremony progressed to its midpoint, Thich Tri Quang suddenly grabbed the microphone and read anti-Diem slogans into it. Then he gave a hate-filled anti-government speech about Diem's supposed 'ban on Buddhist flags,' although such a ban hadn't been decreed by the Diem regime. His speech created great upset and excitement in the crowd.

"This isn't good, Winston. Not only is the alleged ban on Buddhist flags not true per se, but also it has been recorded on tape. The religious ceremonies of Buddha's birthday are always broadcast the same evening by the radio station.

"So, it's obvious the earlier conciliatory attitude of Thich Tri Quang has been abandoned. His illegal actions regarding the anti-government slogans and now his speech at a religious ceremony have revealed his true and deliberate intentions to incite the crowd against Diem. Some real trouble could break out this evening at the radio station!"

It was early evening when the crowds at the Tu Dam Pagoda were encouraged to go to the radio station. Alex strongly requested that Brand remain behind in quarters while he went there with the crowd. He assured Winston a full report of the actions taken there. As usual, Brand put up an intense argument, claiming he didn't work for Alex, was an objective reporter and needed to get a first-hand report.

Nevertheless, Alex reminded Winston of his promise to Eleanor that he would take it easy on his first foray into the field after his beating. Besides, Alex could see that Winston was tiring after a long day at the pagoda, and he was finally able to convince the stubborn reporter to acquiesce.

About 8:00 p.m., Alex stood in the crowd gathered at the radio station. Suddenly Thich Tri Quang arrived with the tape recording in his hands that contained his anti-Diem outbursts at the earlier religious ceremony. He demanded the radio station director play his tape containing the illegal anti-government propaganda. As Alex had surmised, he was refused. The Buddhist leader then turned to speak to the crowd in the grassy courtyard of the radio station. In an inflammatory speech, he directed them to shout at the director for his refusal to play the tape.

When the mob began to press forward onto the cement veranda, the radio station director locked himself inside the station and phoned the province chief and the military authorities. The province chief, a Buddhist, arrived and tried to dissuade the Buddhist leader from his objective, but was refused. So the province chief ordered armored cars to come and disperse the mob.

Then Alex saw the head Buddhist signal some faithful followers to break windows, force doors and enter the radio station. The frenzied crowd threw stones at policemen and firemen who were aiming giant hoses at those trying to enter the radio station. Alex saw the province chief appeal to the firemen to turn off the water, and he took Thich Tri Quang inside the station. Two extremely loud explosions then sounded on the veranda of the radio station.

Earlier, the assistant province chief, who commanded the armored cars, had arrived in the dark and couldn't get close to the station because of the crowd. When he heard the explosions, he feared a Viet Cong attack, so he fired three shots in the air to signal his troops to throw concussion grenades. The melee Alex had feared began.

When those in the radio station came out onto the veranda, they saw blood pooling there and quickly ascertained that there were seven adults dead and one child dying on the concrete.

Alex did not remain at the scene, but returned to quarters as the crowd fled. Alex knocked at Brand's door and entered. He was bruised with torn and soaked clothes. Shocked, Brand asked, "Have you been mugged, Alex?"

Alex sat down in a chair and tried to compose himself. "It was a mob scene at the radio station, Winston. Police and firemen with fire hoses tried to disperse the excited crowd, but people were killed by two explosions on the station veranda. Armored cars showed up, shots were fired and grenades were thrown. The crowd broke up, and I almost got run down by people all around me retreating in a mob panic."

"I'm damn glad you weren't one of the casualties, Alex!" As our dear friend, Nick Jenicoso once said, you and I always seem to end up in the center of the action."

"A grenade exploded pretty close to me, but I'm more roughed up than anything. I thought violence might erupt, but I didn't think deaths would result. I think the two explosions that killed people on the veranda were caused by VC plastic bombs, rather than grenades. Whether the communists just took advantage of the chaos, or were part of a preconceived plan is the question."

Brand asked, "Do you think the Viet Cong, known for using plastic bombs, were ordered by R-3 to cause the deaths on the veranda? Did he want to cast the blame on the Diem regime?"

"I wouldn't be surprised," replied Alex.

Brand remarked, "If I know the press, they'll run with this incident without an investigation and put the blame on Diem's Vietnamese troops, their leaders and the local authorities."

Alex surmised, "If R-3 was involved, the chess master's strategy pays off once again. This current situation is going to reflect badly on the Diem regime. Supposed religion persecution certainly will be cited."

"I agree with you. This isn't going to go away, and it looks like it's only the beginning of the trouble Diem is going to have with the Buddhists. I'm going to talk to Eleanor about returning to the States before long in her condition."

"Is Eleanor ill, Winston?"

Brand hesitated and realized he had inadvertently revealed personal information. "Not exactly. We haven't actually told anyone yet, but Eleanor is four months pregnant."

Brand saw the astonished look on Alex's face before his friend replied, "I don't know exactly what to say, Winston. Congratulations to you both, of course, but I'm afraid I can't help being surprised. I've delivered a letter from Maria Monclova to you not too long ago. You've obviously made a decision regarding the two women with Eleanor's pregnancy."

"Eleanor's pregnancy isn't an accident, Alex. She came to Vietnam to reconcile with me and desired to have a child with me. When Eleanor first arrived, it would have been impossible, because I had made up my mind to be engaged to Maria, despite the obstacles. I had even purchased an engagement ring for her.

"But fate intervened when I was almost beaten to death. I truly might not have survived without Eleanor. We did reconcile through the healing ordeal we've shared, and the child was conceived in love on both our parts."

"You must intend to remarry Eleanor then. Will you let Maria know about your decision and Eleanor's pregnancy?"

"Here's where it gets tricky for me, Alex. I intend to be honest with both Maria and Eleanor. I have already told Eleanor about my prior relationship with Maria. I even mentioned the passionate nature of my relationship with her."

"Hearing that couldn't have been easy for Eleanor. Can she live with that knowledge?"

"Eleanor pulled me back from the brink of death helping restore what life I have left. She deserves what I could give her in return. We do have a past together, and we are very comfortable with one another. Nor did I feel it'd be fair to youthful Maria to be saddled with a beaten up old man.

"However, when I was finally well enough to deal with my complex relationships, you gave Maria's letter to me. I didn't open it at first, but when I finally read it, the depth of my feelings for her came flooding back into my mind and almost overwhelmed me. I shared Maria's letter with Eleanor so she'd understand the situation I must come to terms with. I told Eleanor I'd have to work out my relationship obligations to Maria before I could make a decision about remarriage to her. So many doubts enter my mind, not only regarding my feelings for Maria in light of Eleanor's pregnancy and desires, but also because of the requirements of my career which became such an obstacle with Eleanor before. That kind of life is difficult to share with a wife and child."

"Neither is my career, Winston. Somehow couples make it work, although it's certainly not ideal. But I have a feeling you love both women, perhaps in different ways. Eventually, though, you'll have to choose one or the other."

"I just hope I can keep my head when I go to see Maria and explain myself and my situation. There's such a powerful attraction between us, I can't guarantee I'll be able to resist her. It'll only complicate matters further.

"For now I still need to be with Eleanor. I want to escort her back to the States as things become even more unsettled in Vietnam, perhaps returning there in late July by the time she is six to seven months along in her pregnancy. I want to see her safely settled in her parents' home she inherited with plenty of hired help and the support of her friends before I have to return to my job in Vietnam."

"I can't help being astonished by your news!"

"Please keep Eleanor's pregnancy to yourself, Alex. I wouldn't want word getting back to Maria before I get Eleanor back to the States and settled. When I return to Vietnam, I'll have to go see Maria and settle things with her. I'm sure her father and Tywan never want to see me again, but Maria deserves an explanation from me in person just as Eleanor has had."

Brand saw the look of concern in Alex's eyes, and then said, "I could end up with neither of these beautiful, loving women, and it would serve me right. I really don't deserve either of them. I don't know what they see in me."

"Don't sell yourself short, Winston. I think you're right in talking Eleanor into returning to the States before too long. The Buddhist situation has turned violent with more violence to come. I'm sure R-3 will direct the communists to infiltrate the Buddhists to help take down the Diem government."

"That's exactly my thinking, Alex. Vietnam is no place for a pregnant American woman close to giving birth. Claimed religious persecution in the mix won't yield to Nhu's police brutality in world opinion. How R-3 takes advantage of every weakness in the Diem government! If Diem keeps up his record of ill-conceived crackdowns, he'll have a full scale war with the Buddhists on his hands. The ending won't be pretty for Diem, the South Vietnamese or us."

R-3 viewed the report from his field adjutant in Hue as confirmation of a chess move even better than R-3 himself had hoped for. It was going to be easy to pin the eight deaths at the Hue radio station on government troops and province officials. Public opinion against the Diem government would be swayed long before the investigation reports could be concluded and reported. It was now time to bring the Buddhist unrest to Saigon.

51 THE FINAL DECISION

In truth there is no such thing in man's nature as full and settled resolve either for good or evil, except at the very moment of execution.
—Nathaniel Hawthorn

DAMN, BRAND, YOU'VE MADE quite a comeback since you've gotten back on your feet!" said Sheenar Tillerstein. "I'll have to admit your column on the Buddhist incident in Hue was top notch. The press corps here may not agree with all the points you made, but you got into the fray and told exactly what you saw. Field reporting in action is quite exciting!"

"Thanks, Sheenar, but the action's moved from Hue to Saigon now, so there's plenty to report on here, too."

"Much as it pains me to say it, your first-hand reporting here in Saigon shows a lot of insight. It's right up there. I'll have to hand it to you, Brand, you've got guts. How you were able to get into Xa Loi Pagoda in Saigon and get an interview with Thich Tri Quang took some doing. But the top monk may regret granting you an interview. You reported he was using the pagoda as a propaganda and subversive base to topple the Diem regime. Watch your back when you're out and about, Brand! And if it's true the communists have infiltrated the movement, they might not like the public exposure either. You just might attract a plastic bomb rather than a Pulitzer Prize."

"You might have something there, Sheenar. I've already been mugged, ambushed, escaped several bombings, kidnapped and almost beaten to death. Meanwhile, you and your colleagues most likely have cornered the Pulitzer Prize for this year, given my long absence due to my beating. Nevertheless, digging out the truth is my only path to objective reporting despite the risks.

"But as to the Buddhist situation, it's unclear whether the communists are using the Buddhist movement to further their own ends, or are in league with them. But I do know the head monk deliberately provoked the crisis in Hue, however, to foster disorder with his trickery in a careful, clever plan. It's probable the deaths in Hue at the radio station were caused by plastic bombs typically used by the Viet Cong. But the deaths weren't caused by the ARVN-thrown concussion grenades used to disperse the crowd."

Tillerstein replied, "But the Hue press has reported that ARVN troops were responsible for the deaths. The Buddhists insist Diem's government officials are to blame."

"It's true that Diem has compensated the families of the victims, but he has refused to admit responsibility demanded by the Buddhists. An international investigation into the incident is underway, but Buddhists have already achieved the propaganda victory they desire. They definitely seek the downfall of the Diem regime as evidenced by the continuing flare ups of Buddhist issues in Saigon, Hue and around the countryside," said Brand.

"Well, your analysis seems to be true, Brand. Since Hue, the Buddhists in Saigon have participated in numerous hunger strikes and a first-time demonstration by 500 monks in front of the National Assembly on May 30th."

Brand replied, "Nor did Diem calm matters when ARVN and the police poured chemicals on the heads of Buddhist protestors in Hue on June third, sending 67 to the hospital."

"Yes, the Buddhist protest rebellion is in full swing and getting uglier every day," commented Tillerstein.

Brand continued, "Diem knows the Buddhists are out to topple him, but he's got his hands tied by the U.S., advising him to be conciliatory to the Buddhists. Any attempt of his to restore order can be blown up as harassment of the Buddhists, who protest for religious equality. I'm afraid it's a no-win situation for Diem."

"As I said, Brand, if you continue to expose these controversial claims in your columns, you're undoubtedly in the crosshairs of both sides in the crisis."

"What can I say, Sheenar? The truth is the real news no matter who gets upset."

"It may be safer to do that in a country like the U.S., but in a country at war, you might want to think twice, Brand."

"You have a good point, Sheenar. In fact I'm planning a short leave of absence to escort Eleanor, my ex-wife, back to the States because the situation is deteriorating quickly here."

"Don't let me hold you up, Brand. The sooner you return to the States, the better for both of you."

Just three days later on June 11, 1963, the Buddhist monk, Thich Quang Duc, whom Brand had met in Hue last year, burned himself to death at a Saigon intersection to protest what the Buddhists saw as Diem's repression of the Buddhists. The photographs of the self-immolation shocked the world and blackened both Diem's image and that of his ally. The U.S. privately threatened to remove aid to Diem's regime if he didn't placate the Buddhists.

Then, on July 7th, a group of journalists were attacked by Nhu's secret police as they covered Buddhist protests on the anniversary of Diem's rise to power. Winston and Eleanor decided to make arrangements to leave for the States in late July when Eleanor would be more than six months pregnant. In the midst of increasing turmoil in Saigon, they cleared Eleanor's Saigon apartment and checked into the Caravelle Hotel in preparation for their departure. They planned a stopover in Hawaii to visit Brand's sister Clemie on the way.

General Pavler stopped in to bid them farewell before their departure, as did Alex. Brand had informed the general earlier that Eleanor was pregnant, but General Pavler was still astonished that Eleanor's wish for a child with Winston had actually come true. He wished them well and thought it was wise for Brand to take Eleanor back to the States. The situation in Vietnam was getting more volatile each day.

Winston and Eleanor looked forward to a day of rest when their flight reached Hawaii. Brand reassured Eleanor he wouldn't upset her with his dislike of his brother-in-law when they visited with Clemie, Sean and their children. Clemie had planned a special dinner for them. The children had been fed earlier after playing games with their uncle and aunt, and they prepared for bed time.

After the children's bedtime rituals, Clemie served a late dinner. They chatted over Clemie's elaborately prepared feast. Clemie said to Eleanor, "We're so thrilled your pregnancy is going so well! I had almost given up hope Winston would give me a niece or nephew to enjoy."

"Yes, I'm thankful I received a good report on my checkup before I left Vietnam," replied Eleanor.

Clemie turned to Sean with a smile and said, "I can hardly wait for the baby to arrive. Little did we dream when Eleanor left us last fall she would arrive in Vietnam just when she was so desperately needed to help bring Winnie back to health after such a terrible beating."

"And that's not all she did," quipped Sean.

"Sean," exclaimed Clemie. "Please mind your manners. Perhaps you've had a little too much wine already."

"What?" asked Sean. "It's just my way of congratulating them on Eleanor's pregnancy. I've got new respect for Winston's masculinity. Not only is he going to be the father of Eleanor's baby, but also the father of twins by his Filipina lover, all within a month of each other!"

Utter silence ensued around the table for several minutes. Then a shocked Clemie said, "Sean, this is no time to joke about such a sensitive subject!"

"Oh, it's no joke, Clemie. 'Aunt' Norma called just a little while ago when you were getting the children ready for bed. She was so shocked when I told her Eleanor was pregnant, she blurted out the news that Maria Monclova was expecting Winnie's twins at the end of August!"

"Oh, my God!" exclaimed Winston and buried his head in his hands. Eleanor asked if she could be excused from the table and went to the guest room with tears seeping from her eyes and running down her cheeks. Clemie sat in shock.

Sean said, "Sorry, old man, I thought you and Eleanor knew about the pregnancy with the birth of Maria's twins so close at hand. I can't imagine why you weren't told."

Dazed, Winston got up from the table and said, "I need to go comfort Eleanor."

Clemie confronted Sean, "Why didn't you talk to me before you blurted out such unexpected, sensitive information?"

"Sorry, Clemie, I thought they knew. Someone should have told them long ago."

"Maybe Winnie wasn't well enough to deal with it," said Clemie. "It's incredible how my brother always gets himself in the center of one difficulty after another."

"I know how," said Sean, winking at Clemie.

"Sean, be serious. Winnie looked like he's just received the shock of his life, and Eleanor looked devastated!"

"Hey, we have three children, and we've survived. I'm sure Winston will, too. And Eleanor got just what she wished for when she went to Vietnam to reconcile with Winston and have a child with him."

"But you have one wife, and bigamy isn't an option for Winston. What in the world is he going to do?" What a dilemma! That question must have startled 'Aunt' Norma into blurting out Maria's news. If father were living, the look on his face at such news would be unforgettable!"

"But it's Winston's life and his decisions, not that of your late father's, Clemie."

"Yes, I know. But what a profound revelation for Winnie and Eleanor to deal with!"

"Winston should have been more careful," said Sean. Clemie looked askance at Sean.

The next day Winston and Eleanor continued their journey on to the U.S. mainland. Once they arrived, it took almost a month for Eleanor to give notice of termination of her nursing job to her hospital in New York and to relocate to Maryland. Winston made sure she was settled in with every arrangement to keep her comfortable and secure in her parents lovely home, now her own.

When it was time for Winston to return to his job in Vietnam, Eleanor said, "Winnie, no matter what happens after you speak to Maria, I'll always treasure the time we had together while you healed. I'm so glad I was there for you. It's a great comfort to me that part of you will always be with me in our child."

"How grateful I am, Eleanor, for your help in the restoration of my life. Whatever the outcome of this complex relationship situation, please know that I'll be a part of your life and our child's in whatever way I can. Our baby was conceived in love, and we'll try to nurture her or him with as much love as possible. I feel so much better that you're safely back in the States."

"I am, too. Thank you, Winnie, for helping me to get settled with such generous help as I await the birth of our baby. But I must admit, our time together was so precious to me, and I'll miss you terribly! Take care, my dear Winnie."

"And you as well, my lovely Eleanor."

As soon as Winston left, Eleanor broke into tears, but then she told herself she had to take courage for the sake of their child. She wasn't alone anymore.

Winston had notified Emma of his arrival information in the Philippines. She was there to meet him when his plane landed.

"Emma, you didn't tell me Maria was pregnant with twins the last time we met!"

"Remember, Winston, you said you needed more time to heal before you could deal with your relationship situation. I had Maria's letter in my pocket, but when you made your wishes known, I decided not to give it to you. But there's no time to waste. Maria's already at the hospital in labor, and Norma Pavler is with her."

"Good grief! I arrived in the nick of time. And are her father and Tywan with her?"

"They're there, too, pressuring Maria to marry Tywan before the twins are born, so they can have his name. They've requested a priest to be on standby in case Maria agrees."

"We'll see about that!"

"They're serious, Winston."

"Do you think Maria will agree?"

"No way. Norma Pavler has told Maria you're on your way to see her, and that you know about the twins. She even told Maria that your ex-wife is pregnant with your child."

"God Almighty, what in the world must Maria think?"

"Maria asked Mrs. Pavler if you had remarried Eleanor, and she told her you needed to see Maria before any decisions were made. Maria said she hoped you'd get here in time before the twins were born."

"How far along is she?"

"She's been in labor for quite a while, but she's not ready for the delivery room quite yet. It won't be long though."

When they reached the hospital, Winston went right to Maria's room. Fortune smiled on him. Maria's father and Tywan had left to get something to eat shortly before he arrived. Norma Pavler was with Maria when Winston entered the room. Maria's eyes danced with delight as she saw Winston approach. Norma gave Winston a big hug and quickly left the room. She told them she'd stand guard outside the door.

"I didn't know about your pregnancy, Maria, or I'd have come as soon as I found out."

"You're here now, Winston, my darling, and that's all that matters to me."

"Well, my beautiful Maria, look what we've done together," said Winston as he gently touched her extended abdomen.

"It's a miracle, Winston, and I cherish these gifts of life about to join us, as I cherish you, my love. You are the 'fire in my soul' whatever happens. There is no one else for me but you. I love you so!"

"And I love you, despite all the complications. Emma says Norma has told you that Eleanor is also pregnant."

"Yes, Norma told me about a month ago. You and Eleanor were on your way to the States."

"That's when I first found out about you and our twins. I must admit, it was quite a shock. It took a while to get Eleanor resettled in the States. But I want you to know that without Eleanor's loving care, I wouldn't be here now with you. How can I explain her pregnancy other than she had wanted to reconcile and desired to have a child with me? She gave us a gift of my restored life, and she received a gift of a child in return. I can only hope that you understand."

"Well, maybe all three of your children will grace each other's lives," said Maria smiling.

Brand was blessed, and he knew it. He bent over Maria's bed and kissed her soundly. The magic between the two of them weaved its way into their hearts as they knew it always would.

Just then there was a knock at the door. Norma came in with the hospital chaplain. He introduced himself and explained that Maria's father had asked for a priest to be in attendance in case of a marriage before the birth of twins. But he was sorry to relate that the priest couldn't make it. He was called at the last minute to administer the last rites to a patient.

"Are you certified to conduct a marriage ceremony, Chaplin?" asked Brand.

"Why, of course, I just volunteer here at the hospital part time as the priest does. I have my own congregation."

"Could you marry this beautiful, pregnant lady and myself before she's about to give birth to our twins?"

Well, it's highly unusual, but the priest did give me a marriage license application. The names haven't been filled in yet. We'd have to have two witnesses."

Maria moaned as a strong labor pain suddenly shook her whole body. She cried out and when the contraction subsided, she said, "I don't have much time left before delivery."

Brand asked, "Will you marry me, Maria?"

"With all my heart, I will," Maria answered.

The chaplain asked Norma if there was another witness. She quickly called Emma into the room, but Maria's friend was followed by her father and Tywan, who had just returned from lunch, and demanded to know what was going on. Mr. Monclova looked at the chaplain and asked where the priest was.

Maria answered, "Father the priest couldn't come because he's administering the last rites to a member of his congregation. But there's no need for a priest. Winston has returned and has asked me to marry him, and I have agreed. The chaplain is prepared to perform a brief ceremony to marry us."

I most violently object," bellowed Maria's father. "I have raised you as a Catholic, Maria, and I forbid you to marry a divorced man, whose ex-wife is carrying his child! Winston Brand is most unsuitable to be married to a Catholic woman!

The chaplain interjected, "We've been interrupted before I could ask you necessary questions, Mr. Brand. Have you certified proof of a lawful divorce?"

"Yes, I do," responded Winston. "I brought an authorized copy back with me from the States."

He handed the document to the chaplain, who read it, and said, "I see no legal reason I can't marry two consenting adults who request my services to join them in matrimony," said the chaplain. "If there is a child of a first marriage, the courts rule on the matter of custody and visitation, but it is not an impediment to a second marriage for a legally divorced adult."

Maria's father's face reddened in fury. "I absolutely won't have it! I will challenge my daughter's marriage to this man in any way I can find!

Maria groaned and cried out with a strong labor pain.

"Mr. Brand, we must proceed with this ceremony before it's time for the delivery room," emphasized the chaplain.

Winston said, "I agree, Chaplain. As soon as this labor contraction relaxes, let us proceed with the marriage ceremony."

Tywan then spoke up, "Maria, I have always loved you and I always will. Even though these babies you carry are fathered by Mr. Brand, I am the one who always will be here for you. If you marry Mr. Brand, the twins will suffer from having an absent father when he is off covering foreign wars, and you are left alone trying to cope with raising twins. But if you marry me, I would accept them as my own, if you agree. Please, please consider my proposal of marriage before you marry out of our religion to an older man who has an ex-wife and a child with her on the way. He will bring you untold complications."

Maria's father burst in and said, "Maria, I, too, see nothing ahead for you with this man but disaster. He is the last man on earth I'd ever want to see married to my daughter!"

Brand spoke up for himself, "Mr. Monclova, I spent my whole life trying to accommodate the expectations of others and often had to suppress my real purpose in life. I was in a state of guilt on both counts. I chose a journalistic career instead of the family male traditional military career my father and grandfather before him deemed worthy. You remind me of my own father's disapproval of my career choice and later that of my ex-wife. Maria has accepted me as her marriage partner and what I have to offer her, come what may. May I respectfully remind you that it is our choice to marry and not yours to make. I'm not about to let you dictate a choice that's not yours."

"Let me remind you, Mr. Brand, that you haven't known Maria for even a year and only then in very few encounters or through correspondence during that time. I have been looking out for Maria's welfare since she was born. For you to indicate that I have no stake in her life now is very offensive to me!"

"Father, I appreciate and love you, and I'm grateful for your care, support and concern over the years. But I'm a grown woman now with my own life ahead of me with Winston and our twins soon to be born. It is my time, and I have chosen the man I want to marry and partner with in love for the rest of my life. Whatever the consequences of my decision, I shall bear as does any woman who makes her marriage vow. Tywan has been a dear friend since childhood, but my heart belongs to Winston. Now do you wish to remain for our marriage ceremony or not?"

"I shall remain, Maria, but I'll do everything in my power to see if I can get the marriage annulled."

"And you, Tywan. Do you wish to remain?"

"Yes, but I'll always look out for you, Maria, as I am allowed. I do love you," said Tywan choking back his emotions as tears made his eyes glisten.

Brand said, "Let us begin the ceremony, Chaplain, but we don't have much time left. We must wait for Maria's labor pain to subside she's suffering through just now."

As soon the intense contraction ran its course, Maria and Winston made their vows to each other and the chaplain pronounced them man and wife. Brand kissed Maria none too soon before she pressed the call button because of another intense labor pain. They all had to leave the room as the nurse arrived to check on Maria. After her exam, the nurse called for Maria to be taken immediately to the delivery room. Winston followed, allowed to go with her now that he was her husband.

In the waiting room, Maria's father's face went completely white. He turned to Tywan and said, "My God! I called for a priest to be present in case Maria agreed to marry you at the last minute, Tywan. But the fates turned against us and a chaplain turned up instead who was able to marry a divorced man to Maria. The priest couldn't have married them!"

Tywan was speechless! He seemed paralyzed and a feeling of desperation was reflected in his eyes! The love of his life was lost to him!

Norma Pavler, who also sat in the waiting room with Emma, took pity on the pair's extreme distress and approached Mr. Monclova and Tywan.

"We've met before, Mr. Monclova. I'm Norma Pavler. I can explain what happened while you and Tywan were at lunch."

"Did you bring Brand here to confuse Maria when all was set up for her to marry Tywan?"

"No, Winston came of his own volition and asked Maria to marry him, and she agreed."

Norma noticed Tywan's eyes began to tear up. She turned and said to Tywan, "Maria's told me you care deeply for her and had proposed long ago. I'm sorry you're so distressed, but her heart belongs to another."

Tywan turned away and walked over to a chair in the corner. He sat down to hold his head in his hands while tears streamed down his cheeks.

Maria's father's eyes blazed. "We'll see just how legal their marriage is. There must be a way to annul it under these unusual circumstances!"

Norma replied, "The twins are Winston's after all, Mr. Monclova. It's only right their father should marry their mother and claim them."

All went well in the delivery room. Maria delivered first a boy and then a baby girl. She wished to name them Brendon and Brenda. Winston was too awed by the successful births of such darling little bundles of life to do anything but agree. In fact, Winston was in future shock as he looked down at the twins' innocent, adorable faces. He had gotten married and become the father of twins in little more than an hour! He couldn't be happier as he gazed with wonder at two perfect babies. Maria looked like a Madonna with two precious little ones snuggled against her breasts.

Winston had a lump in his throat, but when he found his voice, he said, "Well, Mrs. Winston Brand, I don't think anyone could top the domestic drama of this day. I'm thankful beyond words that I could get here in time for Brendon and Brenda's births. Getting married to their beautiful mother in the nick of time before they arrived is a dream come true!"

Maria replied, "Babies have a mind of their own. They must have known somehow that you'd make their debut, claim their mother as your wife and make them legitimate in the process," said Maria with love shining in her eyes.

"Our happy news will undoubtedly be bittersweet for Eleanor, but I think she knows the fates have destined a time for you and me to be together, just as there was time for me and Eleanor. Although, I can't help but wonder if you both would be better off without me complicating your lives."

"Never, Winston, as far as I'm concerned. For me there is no other who lights the 'fire in my soul.' I could never have felt really alive in my life without our love," said Maria.

"I love you, my beautiful wife. I can only pray that you can put up with me and my career. It took its toll on Eleanor."

"But she came back for more, Winston, didn't she? That says something about your being unforgettable," said Maria with a twinkle in her eyes.

"Whether that's good or bad remains to be seen," said Winston. "But for now my happiness is almost too much for a mortal man to contain! How I love you, Maria!"

"I love you with all my heart, Winston! You make my dreams come true," replied a very contented and happy Maria as she looked at the man she loved and their precious babies held safe and loved in her arms.

Later when Maria's father and Tywan were allowed to visit, Winston could see in Tywan's eyes that he felt about Maria the way she felt about Winston. He had a premonition that Tywan would be there for Maria and the twins when he couldn't be. Maria's father, on the other hand was livid, complaining and contemplating all the possible ways an annulment might apply to invalidate Maria's marriage to him. But it was much too late.

"No way," Brand thought. "If Maria's father found any loopholes, they'd just get married again."

Winston knew he'd have to return to his job in Vietnam soon, but for now he had been informed that there was a ban on commercial flights into Vietnam. On the day of his marriage to Maria and their twins' birth, President Diem had authorized martial law be set in place because of the mass demonstrations by the Buddhists, which he feared would lead them to Gia Long Palace in Saigon to topple his government. He also cracked down on the Buddhists throughout South Vietnam with the Vietnamese Special Forces trained by U.S. advisors.

The miracle man of the 1950s hoped to pull off another miracle in the Buddhist crisis in the summer of 1963, but his misalliance with the U.S. was in deep trouble.

Until martial law in South Vietnam was lifted, Brand had time to enjoy Maria and the twins. He had called Eleanor to explain his actions and to reassure her that he would return to the States for the birth of their child in a month. Eleanor's disappointment about his marriage to Maria was extremely keen, but, gracious lady that she was, she wished them well. Brand repeated Maria's wish to her that all three children would grace each other's lives as time passed. Winston knew his decision was a far from a perfect solution to his complex relationships, but it was the best he could do to follow his own heart. He felt it was right that he and Maria be given a time together to experience their love for each other, as he had had with Eleanor, and that the twins be given his name and have his support.

Clemie's reaction to his marriage to Maria was a different story all together. Her religious beliefs influenced her wish that Winston and Eleanor remarry. However, it was his life to live, Winston thought, not Clemie's. He hoped in time Clemie would come to enjoy a relationship with Maria and the twins as she had had with Eleanor. Then again, he felt he needed to be more understanding of Clemie's situation with a philandering husband. It couldn't be easy for her.

It was hardly a perfect world, but for now it was enough to have a beautiful wife, twins and another child soon to be born to a loving mother. One step at a time, he told himself. What would his late father say if he knew his son loved two women, one passionately and the other with loving care, concern and deep gratitude? Winston thought that in this complex situation he had done the best he could to "face the sun." It was only the beginning of a new chapter in all their lives.

52 TRANSITIONS

The evil which one suffers patiently as inevitable seems insupportable as soon as he conceives the idea of escaping from it.
—Alexis de Tocqueville

BRAND REMAINED IN MANILLA staying at Maria's small apartment while Maria was in the hospital. He visited with Maria and their babies each day until it was time for Maria to come home. Winston had also been busy arranging for help for Maria, as he had done for Eleanor. He set up a bank account with funds to care for the needs of his new family while he was back on the job in Vietnam. Money from his invested family inheritance would provide for both Maria and for Eleanor, who had her own family inheritance as well. Once Maria and the babies settled in with a live-in nurse and cook to help her, Maria knew Winston would have to return to work soon.

Winston had read press reports that at midnight on August 21st, the day he and Maria were married and their twins born, Diem's brother Nhu had ordered ARVN's Special Forces to begin a synchronized attack on Buddhist pagodas in South Vietnam, and ARVN troops occupied strategic points in Saigon. Buddhists at the Xa Loi Pagoda in Saigon were surprised when ARVN troops vandalized the pagoda altars and stole the charred heart of self-immolated Thich Quang Duc, although a few monks escaped with his ashes.

The very next day, August 22, a new U.S. Ambassador to South Vietnam had arrived in Saigon. Four days later, the ambassador met with President Diem and asked him to remove his brother Nhu from power, because the attacks ordered by Nhu against the Buddhists had been carried out by American-trained Special Forces personnel funded by the CIA. Diem hadn't consulted with his ally.

The U.S. also had warned President Diem to silence Madame Nhu who had continually ranted against the Buddhists as communist collaborators. She had complained that the U.S. had taken South Vietnam as its satellite. And then she had shocked the world when she had mocked Thich Quang Duc's self-immolation as a "barbeque." Other Buddhist self-immolations followed, and subsequently the press had reported that Madame Nhu had said, "Let them burn and we shall clap our hands," as she offered to provide more fuel and matches. After the ARVN raids on the pagodas on August 21, reports followed that Madame Nhu had described the attacks as "the happiest day of my life since we crushed the Binh Xuyen in 1955." No one, it seemed, could restrain her vitriolic outbursts, and many thought Madame Nhu had put the finishing touches on the fall of the Diem regime.

President Diem ignored the U.S. warnings and kept his brother Nhu in power. He replied to the critics of Madame Nhu that she was obliged to expose "extremists" to the public.

Brand's last day in the Philippines with Maria arrived before he had to return to Vietnam. "Right or wrong, Maria," Brand said, "Diem's refusal to remove his brother and sister-in-law from his regime just puts another nail in his coffin. Obviously, he can't afford to remove the support of his family when his country is at war on so many fronts, both interior and exterior. But the Buddhist propaganda will do him in. The U.S. wants Diem to be conciliatory with the Buddhists, but he has no intention of doing so."

Despite Brand's dire political predictions, Maria smiled as she saw Winston hold his son Brendon against his chest while he patted the baby's back to retrieve an elusive burp after his feeding. Maria had just finished nursing Brenda and was trying to burp her as well. She said, "Oh, Winston, this is my dream come true, being here with you as your wife and together caring for our twins. I love you so, my darling!"

"So do I love you, my absolutely beautiful wife and mother of our adorable twins. But my heart aches with the thought that my editor has called me back to work since my month of leave was over days ago, and the ban on commercial flights into Vietnam long has been lifted. Louis Cohen has been more that patient with my personal concerns, quite astonished to say the least, but news is breaking every day in Saigon, and he needs me to get back to start interviewing and writing my columns again."

"Well, your loving wife will be here patiently waiting for you whenever you get a chance to slip away."

"How I wish I could at my first chance, but instead I must soon depart for the States again when Eleanor gives birth. How distraught I feel for having put you and Eleanor in such a complex situation."

"You're more than worth it, Winston, love of my life. Whatever it takes to make our marriage and parenting work, I'm willing to give," said Maria.

"How you could love me so much is heaven's gift to me, Maria. And our babies are so beautiful and handsome. What little miracles of life they are! I'm so blessed that I didn't die from my brutal beating, or give up in pain afterward, or I would've missed our blessed marriage, the birth of our two darling testaments to our love and giving my name to them.

"But leaving you and our dear little tykes is going to be the hardest thing I've ever done. I'm only beginning to realize how very deeply I've missed you, Maria. You know, I had purchased an engagement ring for you the morning I was kidnapped and beaten. I'm sure Goldtooth stole your ring as well. I'll replace it as soon as I can and add a wedding ring, too."

"Until you just told me, Winston, I would never have known you had purchased an engagement ring for me. That symbol of your intentions meant you were opening your heart to me without reservations, ready to commit to our lives in love together. And I shall pick out a wedding ring for you as well, my love. I wish I could thank Eleanor for her gift of care for you, although it would be insensitive to do so at this time. I so appreciate a time and place we can be together, which the fates promised us when they brought us together."

"Eleanor has my deepest gratitude as well. And it's my sincere hope that my children will come to know and love each other as the years pass."

"As do I, Winston."

"With you in the Philippines, I'll be able to spend more time with you and the twins, but I hope to get to know my child in the

States as well. A tricky situation, I know, and far from ideal, But it is what it is, and I can only be thankful that you and Eleanor are loving, caring people. If you ever get a chance to meet her, I'm certain you will like each other."

"Just be careful in your adventurous interviews, Winston. You're important to all of us."

"As is my family to me, my love."

"Winston, Brendon is asleep in your arms, and Brenda is fading fast. Let's put them in their crib under nanny's watchful eye and enjoy our last night together before you return to Vietnam tomorrow."

"What a splendid suggestion! Let's snuggle together as best we can while you're healing and love the night away."

Maria laughed and said, "You mean until the next feeding!"

"I bet Brendon will be the first to wake up with a huge appetite," said Winston as he took Maria in his arms. "The twins aren't the only ones who get hungry, as I can hardly wait to experience all the ways love can be expressed!"

When Brand returned to Saigon, he once again stayed in the room next to Alex's at Five Oceans. When Alex saw Winston, he said, "Is that the father of twins I see now sporting a mustache? If you're trying to keep up with Lieutenant Kearney with his two women and three babies, you're certainly on your way with Eleanor soon to give birth!"

Winston laughed. You're right, Alex. I hadn't made the comparison, but when Eleanor delivers very soon, this 'old man' will have caught up with Kearney's 'young blood' record. But it's not easy keeping up with it all, I'll tell you. And I have my editor demanding more columns from me since there's so much going on in Saigon right now."

"Yes, indeed," said Alex. I'm sorry to say the U.S. and President Diem are unfortunately on a collision course, both having fallen into trap after trap, orchestrated, or taken advantage of, by R-3. He's a chess player par excellence. Unfortunately, no one seems to be looking at the big picture to see how they're being played. Our own country seems blinded by the desire to avoid world-wide censure for supporting Diem, who's now seen as a petty dictator who persecutes religious groups and brutally oppresses his own people to stay in power. The communists, and now the Buddhists, have become masters of propaganda to orchestrate Diem's downfall."

"What you have just said reminds me of the plan laid out in the captured communist document you showed me on the way to Vietnam," remarked Brand.

Alex replied, "And it's working. I'm afraid a coup by Diem's generals is in the works. But we think the generals are waiting for the assurance from the U.S. that aid will continue should Diem be deposed in a military junta takeover. Diem's refusal to fire his brother and to somehow gag Madame Nhu hasn't gone over well in Washington. President Kennedy doesn't like to have his face blackened in world opinion as a supporter of an ally accused of religious oppression."

"So all R-3 has to do now is sit back and watch his victims self-destruct like the master chess player he is."

"I'm afraid so," said Alex.

Before Brand had to return to the States in late September as Eleanor's due date approached, he filed as many columns as he was able to manage. When he arrived in the States, Eleanor was heavy with child. She greeted him warmly, but with a hint of sadness in her eyes. Winston knew she wished him well, but she had had to let go of her hope that they'd remarry once Winston had notified her that he had married Maria.

Eleanor asked if he had brought along a photo of his twins. Her motherly, nurturing qualities kicked in when she saw the photo and exclaimed, "What beautiful, healthy babies they are, Winston! Just think, our child will come into the world already having a brother and sister. I was an only child, so having siblings will be so special for her."

"Does the doctor think it's a girl?"

"He doesn't know for sure, but from the baby's size, he's guessing it's a girl. Come, Winnie, see how I've decorated her room in anticipation of her arrival. My friends and I have had such fun shopping for a crib and all the unbelievable number of items that are now available for babies."

"First tell me, Eleanor, how's your pregnancy progressing, and how're you feeling?"

"It's going just fine, as I've written to you in my letters. But it's getting more and more difficult getting out of a chair. I'll be glad to get my old figure back soon. But come see the baby's room, Winnie."

Winston walked into the room and exclaimed, "This is the cutest baby's room I could've ever imagined, all decked out and supplied to the hilt! The thought, care and love you've put into it reminds me of the way you decorated your apartment in Saigon to cheer me while I was recovering from my beating. And now you're passing on that cheerfulness to our baby."

"I'd like to pass on your name to our child, too, Winnie. Although we're divorced, I still have your last name, and I'll list your name as father on her birth certificate even though we didn't remarry."

"I wouldn't have it any other way, Eleanor. I'm her father, and she should have my name and all the support I can give her in my unusual situation."

"Does Maria understand our connection, Winnie?"

"Yes, she does. She knows I wouldn't be here for any of my children but for your loving care, Eleanor. So we all have much to be thankful for. But, let's think about the love instead of the complications. As I told Maria, I think both of you would like each other."

"Thanks for telling me, Winnie. But I imagine you must feel at times that there's just not enough of you to go around."

"But I never ever forget that what there's still left of me, you helped salvage, Eleanor. We mustn't think of what we don't have, but enjoy the blessings we do have."

Eleanor smiled, but then suddenly she grimaced as she felt her first strong labor pain. She called her doctor who asked her if her water had broken yet. She answered in the negative, but he asked her to come to the hospital to be checked anyway as an older-mother-to-be. Eleanor remained in the hospital when her water broke there, and she had a long first-birth labor. But she successfully delivered the sweetest-tempered baby girl they could have ever wished for!

Winston exclaimed, "Oh, Eleanor, she's so beautiful, and she's already curling her hand around my finger! She's absolutely enchanting!"

Eleanor beamed and said, "Looking at it in the opposite way, Winnie, she's already wrapping you around her finger."

"That she has, Eleanor. I'll bet she'll become a very talented nurse like you. What name do you have in mind for this little darling?"

"Well, I thought about naming her 'Candace' after your mother, Winnie. Our baby girl was with us as we worked together to restore your health, just like your mother would have done if she had been alive."

Eleanor saw how touched Winston was and even saw his eyes glisten with a few tears. "How thoughtful of you, Eleanor. You never cease to amaze me with your loving ways. Candace it is, then, with my wholehearted approval!" exclaimed Winston as he gently placed Candace in Eleanor's arms. "I'm sure mother is looking down on this scene. She would have tears of joy running down her cheeks if she were here."

"And we can only hope little Candace and the twins will have the opportunity to share in the feeling of family somehow that would have made your mother three times as happy."

"I can just hear the twins calling their sister 'Candi.'"

When Eleanor and Candace came home from the hospital, Winston made sure they were settled in with a nanny in addition to Eleanor's housekeeper/cook before he had to leave once again.

"You know, Eleanor, it serves me right for getting into such a complex situation, especially with such a demanding career, but I'm afraid I'll be spending more time on my job than I will with any of my children. In the meantime, although I can't be your husband, I'm here in spirit with you as you nurture our daughter who combines the best of both of us in her tiny, sweet self."

"It means the world to me, Winnie. I'll always have a part of you with me in Candace. I wish we could have remarried, but I know your twins deserve to have your name. Although I wish you could be with me, Maria will now have her time with you as I have enjoyed. But I shall miss you terribly."

"Thank you, Eleanor." Brand winked at her and said, "You know, our reconciliation was a lot more pleasant than the last few years of our marriage when I was an obnoxious drunk at times. I'm so glad we had that time of reconciliation together, and I've matured at least enough to know what's important in life. I have stood up as best I can to 'face the sun' as father would say."

"Don't you think we should amend that statement now, Winnie, to as 'grandfather' Willoughby Brand would say?"

Winston smiled and kissed Eleanor on the cheek and then the dear, little baby girl in her arms. Then he reluctantly headed to the door.

"Winnie," Eleanor said as he turned, "don't be too hard on Clemie and her opinions. She doesn't have an easy life, and she loves you just like I do."

"I love you, too, Eleanor. God forgive me for loving two women!"

"Take care, Winnie."

"And you and baby Candace, too, Eleanor."

After Winston's departure, Eleanor's brave demeanor collapsed, and she broke down into sobs that wakened Candace, who suddenly remembered she was hungry. She found nourishment and comfort at Eleanor's breast, as did Eleanor with her precious bundle of life in her arms.

Winston stopped in to see Maria and the twins in the Philippines on his way back to Vietnam. Maria wanted to hear about the birth of the twins' baby sister and was delighted to hear that she was named Candace after Winston's mother.

"The twins will love calling their sister Candi, and I'm glad Eleanor is recovering well."

Winston took a photo of Candace out of his wallet and said Eleanor wanted Maria and the twins to have it.

"Oh, Winston, what a darling, little baby girl! I'll have to say you make beautiful children!"

"I know it's far from an ideal situation, Maria, but I do hope the children will look on each other as family while growing up. As Eleanor reminded me, the twins already have a new baby sister, and they're just over a month old."

"Believe me, you're always in the middle of the action!"

"Maria your words remind us of the expressions of our dear, late friend, Dr. Nick Jenicoso. "Nick would be throwing up his hands in wonderment at how things worked out, but he'd be glad I wasn't letting life pass me by anymore."

"And then he'd bring out his ukulele and get us all singing as he strutted about," replied Maria, smiling in joy.

"We must treasure every moment we have in life that's filled with love, Maria. Let's not waste even a moment."

"Winston, my love, shall we put your words into action before you have to leave once again?"

"All you needed to do, Maria, is say the word. I never could resist you. I don't know why in the world I ever tried."

"The season of our love has arrived, Winston, and you never have to worry about trying to resist me again."

"A dream come true for a mere mortal man!"

"You mean a man with 'fire in his soul,' that I love with all my heart."

"Yes, 'fire in my soul,' in my heart and in other places as well." Let me show you how much I love you, my beautiful Maria."

53 MUSINGS

Though reading and conversation may furnish us with many ideas of men and things, yet it is our own meditation must form our judgment.
—*Dr. L. Watts*

IT WAS NOT A REASSURING SCENE in Saigon when Brand arrived. The bustling everyday essence of Saigon life seemed to him to have been sucked out and replaced with the thick, dank, sinister air of a plot, or plots, forming. Brand just knew the makings of a major coup were in the works, and he guessed the U.S. didn't object, or maybe was even a co-conspirator of it.

He wondered if the U.S. State Department, the U.S. embassy and the CIA along with Diem's generals were collaborating in the downfall of Diem. Brand's intuition told him the U.S. had run out of patience with Diem's continuing resistance to democratic reforms and conciliation efforts with the Buddhists. Diem's Personalist ideas for his vision of an independent Vietnam had already resulted in quite a misalliance with his ally. Brand guessed it wouldn't be long until the U.S. might let the Vietnamese generals do the work of taking down the Diem regime, while it remained behind the scenes. A military junta was in line to take Diem's place.

When Brand returned to his room at Five Oceans, he found a message from But Hieu asking him to come to his office. Brand was puzzled but took a cab into Saigon to meet with him. When he arrived, Hieu's secretary looked at her appointment book and told Brand no appointment with him was scheduled. Brand showed Lan the note from the Minister of Information that awaited him when he arrived back at Five Oceans after being on leave.

"Oh, Mr. Brand, I'm sorry, but that note must have been left for you some time ago while you were gone. Please wait while I check with Minister Hieu about this matter."

Shortly Lan returned and said Minister Hieu would see him. Brand entered the office and saw Hieu sitting behind his piano desk. Hieu got up to greet Brand and shake hands with him. "Mr. Brand, I wondered why we didn't hear back from you, but Lan said you had been on leave."

"Yes, and for quite some time, I'm afraid."

"Nothing serious, I hope."

"No, quite the opposite, I'm glad to say. But why did you send me a message to meet with you?"

"As you American say, it's 'better late than never,' but President Diem finally had granted your interview. Your absence caused you to miss your appointment to see him in person, but I have his written 'on the record' answers to the questions you submitted quite a long time ago. Our apologies, of course, for the very, very long delay in his response to you, but perhaps his written response still can be of use to you."

"Thank you, I'm glad to have it. I certainly need to catch up on my column writing after being on leave. I hope President Diem might have included some current information on the Buddhist crisis for his regime."

"I'm sorry, Mr. Brand, but I believe he limited his response to those earlier questions you submitted. Perhaps he would've commented on more current events if you'd been available for the personal interview."

"It couldn't have been helped, but at least I hope Diem has answered my conjectures about his fervent nationalism buttressed by his adopted philosophy of Personalism as the font of his vision of nation building and modernization."

"That may be "water under the bridge' now, Mr. Brand. President Diem is struggling for his political life, insisting on no compromise with the Buddhists contrary to U.S. advice."

"I've heard rumors of a coup. What are your plans, Minister Hieu, if a coup is indeed successful?"

"A successor to Diem will need a Minister of Information, so I hope to remain in my position whatever may happen. But life can be like a chess game, Mr. Brand, and one must plan ahead to counter unexpected moves. I assume I'll still be working with you and your press colleagues, however regrettable it'll be if President Diem is deposed. But we'll just have to see what happens."

Brand remarked, "Yes, I've been told you like to play chess, Minister Hieu, as do I. I was even able to beat Ho Chi Minh once when I was a captive of the communists in 1954 and recovering from an injury in Hanoi at that time."

"How interesting, Mr. Brand. I've heard that very few have ever been able to beat the communist leader at chess. So you must be an exceptional player. We should take the time to have a chess game of our own sometime."

"Yes, indeed. But in the meantime, thank you again for holding on to President Diem's answers to my questions for me."

Just then there was a commotion at the door to Minister Hieu's office, and the official turned to the side to see what had happened. His secretary had tripped and fallen to the floor, and he hurried over to help her up.

But Brand stood stock still and looked as if he'd been struck by lightning. He had seen the side view of But Hieu's face and an old memory came crashing into his mind. When Brand had played chess with Ho Chi Minh after his capture at Dien Bien Phu, he had seen that same profile reflected momentarily in a mirror on the wall behind the communist leader before Ho got up, excused himself and left. Brand had been afraid it signaled his reprieve from any ill treatment while he played chess with the communist leader was over.

But Hieu turned back to Brand, "Whatever is the matter, Mr. Brand? You look like you've seen a ghost! But never fear, Miss Lan is all right. She tripped when she entered to tell me my next appointment had arrived. I'm sorry to have to end our pleasant encounter."

"It's not just Miss Lan's fall, Minister. When you turned to the side to check on the disturbance, your profile reminded me of one I briefly glimpsed in a mirror many years ago."

"Why would that be shocking to you, Mr. Brand? You've certainly seen me enough times before to have seen my profile. Besides, don't we Vietnamese look quite similar in profile to American eyes?"

"Yes, yes, of course. It's just that I had such a deep, profound emotional reaction just now for some reason."

Brand saw the silent calculation in the minister's eyes. Then But Hieu said, "Could you possibly be thinking of our conversation and be imagining the horror the South Vietnamese people would experience should a communist takeover ever take place after the rumored imminent fall of the Diem regime?"

"Perhaps that's it, Minister Hieu. And if ultimately a communist takeover does occur, it makes me wonder what you would do then?"

"Let's not think the worst, Mr. Brand. Your mind is way ahead of actual events."

"That's so, but now that I think of it, your office is the perfect place not only to feed propaganda to an adversary, but also to keep up to date on all the goings on in a current regime."

"Why Mr. Brand. You are the bold one to make such a suggestion. Have we not served President Diem and you and your press colleagues well in our duties to the South Vietnamese government and people?"

"Yes, of course. It just occurred to me what a chance for mischief is inherent in the office of information."

"As is also true of all journalists, is it not, Mr. Brand?"

"*Touché*, Minister Hieu. I'm reminded of my interviews with Buddhist leaders when I asked them the question of how they would react to a possible change in government. They replied that they would have to accommodate the victors, such as Americans do with a change of political party after an election. How would you handle such an occurrence, sir, should ever a communist takeover occur?"

"You're always the inquisitive interviewer, I see, Mr. Brand. But which of us can say what we shall do under adverse circumstances? Doesn't that remain to be seen? Who actually knows who is a friend or an enemy? One can be friends under certain circumstances and find oneself as an enemy in other situations."

"In other words, sir, you're indicating that the advantage or disadvantage to oneself, or cause, can determine whether the other is seen as a friend or an enemy?"

"In practice, it is often so, Mr. Brand. So we must count our blessings when others see us as friends, or to their advantage, when tomorrow's circumstances could change the other into an enemy.

But as interesting as this philosophical discussion is, I have another person waiting to see me. I will keep trying to get you the interview with President Diem you desire, depending upon possible events that might develop. So sorry you missed the interview when you were on leave."

"Of course, thank you for your time, Minister Hieu."

The intense calculation reflected in the minister's eyes upon Brand's departure gave the reporter a chill down his spine that denied the official's affable parting words. Brand realized he shouldn't have been so outspoken.

After Brand left, his head was spinning with possibilities. It couldn't be, could it? Many Orientals looked similar in profile, but looking at a frontal view could be totally different. Why had Hieu's profile suddenly caused such a vivid memory to flash into his mind and jar him to the core? He hailed a taxi and arrived back at Five Oceans in a daze. Alex was just leaving, but when he saw Winston looking rather disoriented, he walked with him back to his room.

"Winston, I've never seen you look so stunned. What's the matter? Are Maria, Eleanor and the babies all right?"

"Yes, but you'll never believe what just happened to me. I can't even believe it myself. It can't be true!" Brand sat down and put his face between his hands.

"My God, Winston, what is it?"

"It's almost too incredible to be true! I was at But Hieu's office just now and saw his face in profile when a brief memory from 1954 when I was in captivity in Hanoi suddenly struck me like lightning and violently shook me."

"Are you talking about the innocuous collector of American idioms, But Hieu, Winston? Are you saying you saw But Hieu in Hanoi?"

"No, never in person, but once when I was playing chess with Ho Chi Minh, I saw the reflection of a profile in the mirror on the wall behind him. Ho must have been signaled by this person, because he got up, excused himself and left. I remember I had feared my deferment from ill treatment so I could play chess with Ho was at an end. When that didn't happen, I never gave it another thought until today when Hieu's profile must've triggered something in my subconscious mind. It was such a fleeting image, but I just can't seem to shake it. It must seem inconsequential to you, Alex, as it would to me but for my involuntary reaction. It's made me wonder if Hanoi has been worried that I could identify Hieu as being in the communist camp? Is that the reason for all my mishaps?"

"We can't overlook any clue in trying to identify R-3, but a memory of a fleeting profile image from 1954 doesn't give us much to go on. The strength of your intuitive reaction, though, gives us cause to move him up on our suspect list. R-3 won't go away if the Diem regime falls. No doubt he'll be with us for the duration of the war, whenever that will be. I'll mention your jarring memory flash to General Pavler when I go back to work, but for the time being, we must be content heightening Hieu's surveillance."

"Thanks, Alex. I know the sudden memory of a fleeting profile image isn't much proof, but why in the world did I get such an unexpected shocking reaction or intuition?"

"Why did you go to see Hieu?"

"He had left a message to come to his office, but it was about a long past appointment to interview President Diem. I was on leave at the time and missed it. At least I received the written answers to my questions I had submitted long ago."

"I hope those answers give you enough material for your columns. We'll talk about the implications of your intuition later at dinner, Winston. For now, I must get back to work."

When Alex left, Brand could hardly focus his mind on writing his next column. He had the answers President Diem wrote to his questions in front of him, but they almost blurred before his eyes while his thoughts ran wild with suppositions. When he finally settled down, he saw that Diem's answers to his early questions were predictable with no new insights.

But Brand was haunted by the seriousness of the situation of American/Vietnamese relations that could very shortly end with a coup. He asked himself if he and other Americans had given enough consideration to Diem's concerns by failing to imagine what it was like to be in his shoes. Were good Americans, well intentioned, but idealistically naïve with perfectionist expectations, actually arrogant and ignorant in their missionary zeal to impose Western democratic values on an Oriental nation? Had they taken the time to learn Vietnamese culture, history, politics, psychology and values, perhaps distracted by other pressing concerns? Democratic reforms Diem continued to ignore and the Americans kept trying to impose were a real sticking point between the two allies. And Diem's authoritarianism was a thorn in the side of his ally.

Brand remembered Plato's definition of democracy as "a charming form of government, full of variety and disorder, and dispensing a sort of equality to equals and unequals alike." Hadn't Diem been reported to say that to make democracy work even remotely, the inequality between his people must lessen? There was no viable middle class in Vietnam as in America to give a solid foundation to democracy. Eighty-five percent of the population in South Vietnam were peasants who continued to live in a feudal type society grounded in ancestral lands, ancestor worship and Confucianism. Diem believed even the beginnings of democracy would have to come much later after much development of his people.

But then the Ngos had a different idea of democracy permeated with Personalist tenets. In fact it was more of a communitarian socialism, a 'third way' between capitalism and communism for the Vietnamese to use in nation building and modernizing. The brothers' fervent nationalism had kept their ally at a distance until the chasm between them was about to crack wide open. Diem's refusal to compromise and cooperate with U.S. demands regarding the Buddhist crisis and to severe relations with Nhu for his brutality and suppressive measures as well as with Madame Nhu for her blatant, shocking expressions in the press had propelled the crisis over the top.

Brand made some more notes for his column but his thoughts were still scattered, so he decided to put them aside when it was time to meet Alex for dinner.

Alex greeted Winston and asked, "With all the distraction regarding your meeting with But Hieu, I forgot to inquire if everything is okay with Eleanor and the birth of your child?"

"Couldn't be better, Alex. Eleanor has named our darling baby girl Candace, which was my mother's name. Candi is the sweetest, most even tempered little baby anyone could ever hope for. I'm afraid she's wrapped me around her little finger already. And Eleanor is doing well with much support to help her, as does Maria have with the twins."

"That's wonderful news, Winston. Did you stop to see Maria and your twins on the way back to Vietnam?"

"Yes, and I couldn't be more blessed that both Eleanor and Maria seem positively inclined to view their babies as siblings that can grace each other's lives in the future. Both women wanted to see photos of each other's babies. It's such a complex, incredible situation, I still can't believe it, but we're all trying to do our best with such a crazy scenario."

"That's really great news, Winston. Did you get started writing your column after I left this afternoon?"

"Yes. After calming down from the upset over my meeting with But Hieu, I began to reflect about our situation in Vietnam for my column. The looming threat of a major coup in the air is so ominous, I thought about all that has occurred since we arrived in Vietnam in February 1962 when the Presidential Palace was bombed."

"What an unwelcoming incident that was, Winston, when we weren't sure at first whether or not we were the target of the attacks. Diem escaped assassination in that attempt by a few of his own air force officers. But here we are a little over a year and a half later, coming up on the last few months before the close of 1963, and Diem's own people are plotting against him again!"

Brand grimaced, "It should give one pause, when the greatest threat comes from the citizens, rather than avowed enemies. Perhaps Diem and I should both cultivate more friends before it's too late."

"It may be too late for the Ngos with their ally. Impatient, disgruntled, can-do Americans in key positions want to see more action and progress in winning the 'little war' here, in instituting democratic reforms and in conciliatory overtures to the Buddhists. Our negative world image in supporting a perceived, uncooperative despot seems to have cemented the intent of the coup conspirators.

"I did speak to General Pavler about your intuition regarding But Hieu, and he was very interested in following up by increasing his surveillance. But General Pavler is very concerned about these signs of a developing coup. He hasn't been asked for his input by the State Department, the American Embassy or the CIA."

"How unusual, Alex, not to include the evaluations of the military on site in such a far reaching decision. The avoidance of his input doesn't bode well. A coup must be imminent!"

"So it seems. Kennedy's attitude has fluctuated greatly. His several fact-finding mission reports have given him conflicting views. But he's more swayed lately by the ambassador, who's here on the scene and is inclined to encourage the generals' coup."

"I can just imagine R-3s jubilation if his strategies succeed in the fall of Diem's government, only ironically to be sanctioned by Diem's ally. It appears that the 'enemy is us!'"

"If a coup succeeds, many will remark that they can scarcely believe the Americans could depose an ally in the middle of a war situation. But Diem's paranoid worry about a coup is not without cause. It has been fueled by many plots against him since 1954, such as the shelling attack on the palace by the national police in 1955, a serious assassination attempt in 1957, and a paratrooper's coup in 1960 that almost succeeded and the latest when ARVN officers bombed the palace. But even given Diem's continued refusals to cooperate with the U.S., it's questionable whether U.S. support for a coup is wisest at this point."

Brand remarked, "I remember the quote of Vice President Lyndon Johnson, who visited Vietnam in May 1961 and met Diem. The press reported that he called Diem the 'Winston Churchill of Asia.' When Johnson was accused of exaggeration, he replied, 'Diem's the only boy we got out there.'"

Brand continued, "What an incredibly weak fallback position the U.S. has with generals who don't have political experience nor public support! If the U.S. gets rid of Diem, the responsibility for the escalating war with the North is bound to fall upon us! I can't believe how catastrophic and short-sighted it is for the U.S. not to have a viable 'Plan B' when we ditch 'Plan A' with a sovereign ally in the midst of a war!"

"That's what worries General Pavler and the rest of us. I'm reminded of a quote by French President Charles De Gaulle spoken to U.S. President Kennedy in May 1961 regarding Vietnam. He said, "I predict to you that you will, step by step, be sucked into a bottomless military and political quagmire."

Brand remarked, "I've experienced firsthand in the Delta Vietnam's soft, watery area that gives way underfoot,' not to mention the threat of landmines there, and so I can relate to the quagmire we've sunk into. But I'm afraid we're about to go in deeper with much more of the Vietnamese story to go."

"Does the *Times* want you to stay and continue to write your column from Vietnam, Winston, whether there's a coup or not?"

"Yes. You know I lost five months recovery time after my beating, so my hope for a second Pulitzer Prize for international reporting in Vietnam won't be realized for 1963 when the award is given next May. But if the war doesn't end, there's always another chance in the future."

"By remaining in Vietnam, Winston, your time with your wife and children won't be as frequent as you might wish, as is my situation with my dear Gwen and Alex and Alesha."

"I can only try to be there for them as much as I'm able, Alex, but thankfully Maria's location in the Philippines isn't too far away. It'll be more difficult to see Candace and Eleanor in the States though. But although I don't have a chance for Pulitzer Prize for this year, I've really received the greatest prize a man could hope for. Not only did I escape death many times so that I could be blessed beyond measure with a loving wife, three babies and a reconciled past with Eleanor, but also, all was accomplished by God-given strength to remain sober. My gratitude is overflowing as I've 'faced the sun' as my father never thought I would."

Alex responded, "I wonder if your father was thinking more of himself than you when he would say that to you, Winston?"

"Whatever do you mean, Alex?"

"Well, because of your rejection of a 'traditional Brand male military career,' perhaps even subconsciously, your father took it to mean his and his father's chosen careers didn't 'measure up' as worthwhile pursuing in his son's eyes even when he had devoted his adult life to it, earning many military honors. Maybe it was more about his self-esteem than yours."

"I would have never turned it around and looked at it that way, Alex, if you hadn't mentioned it. Perhaps there's something to that idea. And here I've spent my life feeling guilty for not 'measuring up' to his expectations."

"Most of all, Winston, I think we need to 'know thyself,' as you philosophers like to quote Socrates, to realize our worth. And it may take all we've got to give to walk the road ahead of us in Vietnam.

"If Diem's Minister of Information, But Hieu, is indeed our long sought after super patriot communist leader and infiltrator, he's not going to go away when the military junta takes over from

Diem. With all the change, it's going to be even easier for him to make his chess moves to work toward a communist victory in the south. And the military junta will be all the more unwilling to shake things up even more by investigating Hieu when they are busy trying to consolidate their own power while dealing with increased aggression."

"But now we have our first big clue to R-3's identity, Alex, and we can be much more alert with increased surveillance of his activities."

"Yes, Winston, but turn that thought around and realize that your encounter with him also has given him his first big clue that we may be on to him!"

"You're right, Alex. The stakes have escalated for both sides as we head into the future. You know, my philosophical mind inclines me to ask if it isn't human nature itself that causes conflicts that on the national level can lead to war?"

Alex remarked, "Looking back on history, mankind has made little progress toward peaceful coexistence. Since the dawn of time, wars, murders, waste and destruction have continued without cease. But don't we all still desire peace?"

"It's a paradox, Alex. When we look at man's 'behavior,' we see both good and evil, and all degrees in between, in the actions of man in relation not only to others, but to himself as well. We are neither always good nor always bad. The appearance of evil, bigotry, rape, theft, murder, pillage, destruction, greed, lust, coercive manipulation, war, etc. must be juxtaposed against acts of charity and love as evidence of human goodness."

"As you've reported in your many fine columns, Winston. But we've yet to find a solution to such a dilemma."

"Well," replied Brand, "optimists envision education, or the eradication of poverty, or the abolishment of inequality reflected in the class system to free the masses, as a cure for the ills of mankind."

Alex observed, "To strive for the betterment of mankind is a worthy goal, Winston, but aren't these economic, sociological, and educational utopian ideals actually impossible to accomplish? We've seen first-hand how the Ngo brothers' Personalist ideal couldn't work without the use of force, and even so failed."

"Believe me, that's the 'fly in the ointment' as our dear, departed friend Nick might say. Pessimists see human reason and will as defective, reality as flawed with little if any possibility of redemption on our own accord as John Milton has expressed. Here, I have his words in my notebook:

> *For though it were granted by us divine indulgence to be exempt from all that would harm us from without, yet the pervasiveness of our folly is so bent, that we should never cease hammering out of our own hearts, as it were out of a flint, the seeds and sparks of new misery to ourselves, till all were in a blaze again.*

This pessimistic view of human nature is reinforced by the Biblical view of sinful man after the fall, with salvation only through belief in Christ, in contrast to the opposite description of man's creation in the image of God."

Alex remarked, "And that brings us back to the beginning of our discussion, Winston. How do we account for that which is good in our natures, especially in view of some of the worst as seen in war experiences? Is goodness a potential only to be developed, or is it innate, awaiting awakening?"

Winston replied, "Even the most advanced of us haven't completely conquered the rebellion in our hearts which impedes our progress in our search for the truth. I'm well aware, Alex, of those rebellious parts of my own nature that conflict with my desire for peace."

"And here we are, Winston, in one of the most bellicose nations on earth, with rebellion everywhere we look, whether without or within. Is there any peace to be found?"

"Perhaps that depends upon every one of us, Alex, individually and collectively, whether we choose peace or war, union or rebellion."

"You know, Winston, I have a feeling that before this Asian war is concluded, free citizens the world over could be plunged into rebellion in this battle for hearts and minds, leaving few neutrals anywhere in the free world. By taking one side or the other, we continually enter into conflict with one another."

"I'm reminded, Alex, of what our good doctor, Nick Jenicoso, once suggested to me. He said that perhaps real, lasting peace is only found within by one's own choice. Maybe Nick's choice for peace was what made him such a joy to be around.

"It occurs to me that it may be impossible to find peace without in a world of change where the pendulum of time, wound up by mankind's desires, swings back and forth between oppositions. But let's hope more often than not in our search for the truth, we remember Shakespeare's admonition that 'to find out right with wrong, it may not be,' that if we try to do so, we 'cherish rebellion and are rebels all.'"

REBELS ALL

Mel R. Jones
Marian N. Jones

EPILOGUE
SOUTH VIETNAM, 1963

"...To find out right with wrong—it may not be;
And you that do abet him in this kind
Cherish rebellion and are rebels all."
—William Shakespeare

EPILOGUE

The hearts of all his people shall revolt from him.
And kiss the lips of unacquainted change.
—*William Shakespeare*

IN LATE OCTOBER, President Diem and his brother caught wind of the planned coup and organized their own "false coup" to counter it. They thought the false coup would look to the U.S. like a "neutralist coup," which would demand a U.S. withdrawal from South Vietnam in favor of a neutralist government. The U.S. would oppose this. The Ngos began to activate the false coup. Their supposedly faithful general, who had ruled Saigon as its military governor since the crackdown on the Buddhists, was given authority to direct troop movements in and around Saigon and to occupy the main streets and public buildings. The Ngos then would appear to have crushed a neutralist plot, and their faithful general would be revered as a national hero to demonstrate the strength of the Diem government. But this false coup had the opposite effect of further alarming President Kennedy.

Subsequently, the wily generals told Diem's military governor that as a "national hero" he should ask Diem to reward him by giving him the title of Minister of the Interior. But Diem refused. He had already given the general a large cash reward. But the disgruntled general turned traitor to the Ngo brothers, and provided the key to the military junta for a successful coup.

The coup took place on November 1, 1963, starting at 1:30 p.m. when a battalion of marines stormed the National Police Headquarters. With troops already in Saigon to defend against the false coup, within three hours Tan Son Nhut airport and all of the city of Saigon were held by coup forces except the Gia Long Palace and the Presidential Guards Barracks. The coup Diem had always feared was in progress.

By this time, the Ngos realized their trusted general was a traitor. Diem's other loyal supporter, head of the Special Forces, couldn't help, because he had been tricked into a lunch meeting with the generals at the Joint General Staff (JGS) Headquarters and was shot. Diem's nearby go-to supporter and commander of IV Corps in the Delta was blocked from coming to Diem's rescue by forces in charge of Saigon. Saigon's military governor had also placed a colonel sympathetic to the coup in charge of the Delta's Seventh Infantry Division in My Tho.

President Diem phoned the U.S. Ambassador and asked what the U.S. attitude toward the rebellion was. The ambassador told Diem the generals had offered Diem and Nhu safe conduct out of the country if he resigned. Diem's only answer was that he was a chief of state and that he was trying to restore order. He said he had tried to do his duty.

The Presidential Guard Barracks was overrun by midnight and the palace fell at dawn the next day, but Diem wasn't there. He and his brother had secretly fled at night to hide in the house of a Chinese businessman in Cholon, a suburb south of Saigon. Diem called Gen. 'Big' Minh in the morning when the brothers finally realized that commander of the IV Corps in the Delta couldn't get through to rescue them. He said he would meet Minh at the palace to surrender and resign. But Diem failed to appear, angering and humiliating Gen. 'Big' Minh, who had made elaborate preparations for the event.

Later the Ngo brothers were found at a church where they had gone to hear mass. They were seized and put into an armored personnel carrier with their hands bound behind them. With Gen. 'Big' Minh's nod, his aide shot both of them in the back. Nhu's corpse was stabbed repeatedly. The initial claim that the brothers had committed suicide was proven false when photos taken of the bodies showed their hands tied behind their backs.

Brand shook his head in disbelief when he heard the sordid tale. The coup had occurred and the Ngo brothers were dead. He wondered how the U.S. could justify covertly supporting it. The president had to have given the green light for the coup. Was it the inexperience of a first term U.S. president with no credible insight into the realities in Vietnam that led him to do so? Or had he been persuaded by those in his administration who thought they knew better? The American ambassador was the liaison with the generals and had notified them there would be no interference from the U.S. to the ill-advised coup, which already was too far in motion to backtrack.

The Diem regime was no more. Had the Ngo brothers finally reaped what they had sown? Not only had Diem lost power and whatever control he had over his rebellious people for the past nine years, but he and his brother had lost their lives as others had lost theirs under the Ngos' rule.

Brand knew that Madame Nhu was in America on tour in the U.S. with her oldest daughter when the coup took place. He was glad her other three children were allowed to leave the country safely to reside in Rome with their uncle, the Archbishop of Hue, until their mother arrived there.

The so-called crazy Ngo family would no longer appear to grab the attention of the world and receive the barbs of judgment against them. There was only emptiness left in the besieged and looted palace where the Ngos had recently held sway. Shakespeare's famous quote from Macbeth upon learning of the queen's death came to Brand's mind as it described the emptiness on the stage:

> *Life's but a walking shadow, a poor player*
> *That struts and frets his hour upon the stage,*
> *And then is heard no more. It is a tale*
> *Told by an idiot, full of sound and fury,*
> *Signifying nothing.*

The populace expressed an initial feeling of joyful freedom with the death of the Ngos, but it was soon replaced by a feeling of depression. Would this same scenario be played out again and again with the same dismal ending—the fall of successive South Vietnamese governments? Would the communists finally take over Vietnam? Brand determined to report it all. Would But Hieu indeed turn out to be the communist mastermind chess player in the south, R-3?

R-3 grasped the king from his chess set, raised it above his head in victory and said to his adjutant, "The king is deposed and dead at last, and our enemies have done the job for us! What a victory in our chess match with the Diem regime!"

"Yes, Noble Leader," said his field adjutant. "I have a message for you from Hanoi."

R-3 opened it quickly and exclaimed, "R-1 and R-2 are jubilant! They can't believe the Americans are so stupid as to support a coup of an ally in the middle of a war! And who's to replace Diem? I believe we'll see a moving circus carousel of new leaders as the members of the military junta ride up and down as it goes around and around, grasping for the brass ring. Yet which one of them has adequate political experience and/or popular backing to hold on to such power? The Americans undoubtedly will have to prop up one leader after another as their own level of participation escalates."

"Yes, Esteemed Leader. The foreign 'strong dragon' will be tested again and again, but will not succeed. We'll fight to our death to win our great revolution!"

"Many more chess matches are ahead in this grand chess tournament to win a unified Vietnam for the communist revolution. But win we will!

"But for now, pass the word to our comrades in the field to intensify our struggle during this time of transition. We shall see how Colonel Bao fares with a new administration. Later, I will give you more specific instructions, but I must leave now. I've been summoned to give my input to a meeting of the fledgling military junta. It seems I'm needed by both sides in the next chess match challenge, but I'm ever loyal only to one."

Maj. Gen. Duong Van Minh ('Big Minh') took over the presidency of the Republic of South Vietnam, totally dependent on the continuation of the promised U.S. aid, but he lasted in office only three months before being toppled by Brig. Gen. Nguyen Khanh…

It was only three weeks after the Ngo brothers' assassinations that on November 20, 1963, President John Fitzgerald Kennedy was assassinated in Dallas, Texas. The Vietnam War's early phase ended in 1963. American involvement would continue to escalate as the war saga unfolded year after year until 1975.

ABOUT THE AUTHORS

Mel R. Jones's diverse military career included serving several years as an enlisted soldier in the U.S. Army. Later he became an artillery officer and a public information specialist attaining the rank of Lieutenant Colonel. His public affairs duties included serving as press aide and speech writer for the Secretary of the Army.

Jones's other notable assignments included two tours of duty in Vietnam, the first of which in 1962-1963, he created and edited the *MAAG/MACV* (Military Assistance Advisory Group / Military Assistance Command, Vietnam) *Observer*, the first official U.S. Armed Forces Publication in Southeast Asia.

A second Vietnam tour in 1969-1970 as public affairs officer for the 1st Air Calvary Division, required Jones to accompany his unit into Cambodia, where he established a press center in a hostile area of operation and provided support to international media as spokesperson for the spearhead division.

As the first public affairs officer for all recruiters during the startup for the Volunteer Army, Jones authored the U.S. Army Recruiting Command's *Public Affairs Handbook for Commanders and PAOs*. He was inducted into the U.S. Army Public Affairs Hall of Fame in 2001. During his Army career he earned the Air Medal, Bronze Star and Legion of Merit among other awards.

After his Army career, Jones worked as public relations director for several firms including the Experimental Aircraft Association. Later he established his own public relations firm. He graduated from Florida Southern College with a B.A. degree in international relations and a minor in journalism and later earned two masters degrees, the first in international relations at Boston University and the second in mass communications at Marquette University in Milwaukee, Wisconsin.

Jones's published works include a book of poetry, two non-fiction books, and a WW II mystery novel as well as numerous magazine and newspaper articles. The late Mel R. Jones is survived by his wife, Marian, his children Beth, Grace, Mark and Matthew, seven grandchildren and seven great grandchildren.

A writer's daughter, **Marian Nelson Jones**, encouraged her husband, Mel R. Jones, to develop his interesting novel ideas. The characters, plots and settings expanded and grew in their discussions together, and Marian wrote down the stories from Mel's dictation.

Marian, a former teacher, with a previously published article in *U.S. Lady,* titled "A Rendezvous With Rome," completed her late husband's unfinished novel, *Rebels All*, after his passing. Her English and history majors at Carroll University in Waukesha, Wisconsin, and the depth of experience in her creative partnership with her gifted storyteller husband combined to assist her in bringing to light the vision of *Rebels All.*

OTHER TITLES BY MEL R. JONES

Other titles written by Mel R. Jones include a book of poetry entitled, *In the Eye of the Storm*, 1965, a non-fiction book *Above and Beyond: Eight Great American Aerobatic Champions*, Tab Books, Inc., 1984, co-author of *A Silent Siren Song, the Aitken Brothers Hollywood Odyssey 1905–1926* with father-in-law Al P. Nelson, Cooper Square Press (an imprint of Rowman Littlefield Publishing Group), New York, 2000 and novel *Pursued: Ten Knights on the Barroom Floor.* The co-authors of *A Silent Siren Song* won a Distinguished Service to History Award of Merit from the Wisconsin Historical Society in June 2001. An inspirational article, "Candle in the Dark", based on Jones' first tour of duty in Vietnam, was published in *This Week* magazine in December 26, 1965.

Jones also wrote numerous magazine and newspaper articles, including magazines such as *Proceedings, Amphibious Warfare Review, Sea Power, Army, Guardsman, Infantry, Armor, Aviation Week & Space Technology, Family (Army, Navy, Air Force Times), TWA Ambassador, The Flying A, Catholic Digest, Wisconsin Trails* and others. In addition, he wrote a museum guide, *Putting Wings on Dreams,* for the Experimental Aircraft Association.

IMAGE ATTRIBUTION

Front Cover:
Bell UH-1 Iroquis (Huey), SDASM Archives, No Known Copyright Restrictions

Stock Photo 39537370—Map of Vietnam by Robert Biedermann under 123RF Comprehensive Extended License

Stock Photo 24370721—Handsome writer with pipe focused on his letter texture background by captblack76 under 123RF Comprehensive Extended License

Stock Photo 53759165—Asian beauty woman relaxing on beach during summer vacation travel. Face closeup of Chinese Caucasian mixed race fashion model posing with bracelets and sun care makeup for skincare concept by maridav under 123RF Comprehensive Extended License

Back Cover:
1960s Morning at the Market, Saigon, Vietnam Postcard—Góc Hàm Nghi-Võ Di Nguy, manhhai, CC BY 2.0

Author Photo of Mel R. Jones and Marian N. Jones by Joseph Szebeni, True Image Photography, used with permission

Interior:
Map of SOUTH VIET-NAM, manhhai, CC BY 2.0

Palace Bombing, February 26, 1962, manhhai, CC BY 2.0

Saigon 1961—Le Loi Avenue, manhhai, CC BY 2.0

July 01, 1963—President Diem reviews honor troops in Saigon, manhhai, CC BY 2.0

Vietnam War Buddhist demonstration, 1963, manhhai, CC BY 2.0

Angelic Oversight, Walt Stoneburner, CC BY 2.0

Author Photo of Mel R. Jones by Joseph Szebeni, True Image Photography, used with permission

Author Photo of Marian N. Jones by Lifetouch, used with permission

Cover Design by Timothy Flatt, Timothy Flatt Studio, used with permission

Mel & Mare Publications, LLC logo by Timothy Flatt, Timothy Flatt Studio, used with permission

ALSO BY MEL R. JONES

A suspenseful and adventurous escape to an exotic land awaits you in PURSUED: TEN KNIGHTS ON THE BARROOM FLOOR!

Do you dare to leave the commonplace behind and venture into the realm of a "land that time forgot?"

Are you willing to be swept up into a past-time through a present-day crime investigation?

Could your curiosity compel you to find out what happened 30 years ago in a captivating "story-within-a-story" in which piece by piece an intricate puzzle takes shape?

Will you join this dangerous pursuit as a deadly mystery unfolds to ensnare the investigative team in a web of international intrigue?

Who are the pursuers, and who are the pursued? Why is their very survival at stake?

Find out today in Mel R. Jones's novel, *Pursued: Ten Knights on the Barroom Floor!*

Enjoy a visit to our website, Mel & Mare Publications, LLC, at m-mpublications.com for informative blogs, an embedded video author biography and other titles.